THE DREAM OF THE RED CHAMBER

Hung Lou Meng

THE DREAM
OF THE RED
CHAMBER

A Chinese Novel of
the Early Ching Period

PANTHEON BOOKS

The English translation,
by FLORENCE and ISABEL McHUGH,
is based on the German version,
Der Traum der Roten Kammer,
Insel Verlag, Wiesbaden,
which Dr. Franz Kuhn has translated
and adapted from the Chinese.

The woodcuts illustrating this volume
are reproduced from the *Hung Lou Meng T'u Yung*
(illustrations and poems to accompany
The Dream of the Red Chamber),
a block book produced in 1884,
after older models.

CONTENTS

ix

INTRODUCTION

INTRODUCTION

Author: The authorship of the *Hung Lou Meng*, which first appeared in 1791, was for a long time unknown. As late as 1921 Dr. Hu Shih's exhaustive research made it possible to ascribe the first eighty chapters of the original, which has one hundred twenty chapters, to Tsao Hsueh Chin, and the remaining forty chapters to Kao Ngoh, one of the two editors of the first printed edition published in 1791. This dual authorship seems to indicate that Tsao Hsueh Chin probably left more than eighty chapters and that Kao Ngoh edited, expanded, and correlated the remaining forty chapters.

The versions on which the present text is based are an edition of 1832 published by the Tsui Wen Company, and a modern annotated version with commentary published by Commercial Press, Shanghai.

Title: Chinese architecture provides for the mass of the population low, one-story buildings. A mansion with a second story is called *lou*— and *Hung Lou* stands for "Red Two-Story Building." According to Buddhist usage, it is also a metaphor for such concepts as worldly glory, luxury, wealth, and honors—similar to the Buddhist interpretation of "red dust" as "worldly strivings," "the material world."

Period: The text does not mention any particular date. However, there are implicit indications that the action takes place during the Ching Dynasty (1644-1912). Official titles and ranks correspond to those of the last dynasty, and Manchuria could be referred to as a province only since the Ching Dynasty. According to the findings of Dr. Hu Shih, the author Tsao Hsueh Chin wrote about contemporary events and his own experiences. Internal evidence indicates that the main narrative covers the period between 1729 and 1737.

Place: The text speaks alternately of the capital and Chin ling. The capital under the Ching Dynasty was Peking. Chin ling, which means "golden tombs," is probably an allusion to the well-known imperial burial places in the vicinity of Peking. The mountains outside the city gates, where the Prince Hermit lives in seclusion, suggest the famous western mountains near Peking, with their splendid temples.

The *Hung Lou Meng* has been described to the Westerner as a forbidding literary monument with hundreds of characters. Only one

European before myself, Bancroft Joly, an English consul in China, has dared to approach the task of translation. However, he did not even reach the halfway point of the original. His two-volume translation, *Dream of the Red Chamber*, was published by Kelly and Walsh in Hong Kong in 1892-93.

Another more recent attempt to make the *Hung Lou Meng* accessible to the Western mind came from the Chinese side, Chi Chen Wang's translation and adaptation, *Dream of the Red Chamber* (George Routledge & Sons Ltd., London, no date). But Mr. Wang's work covers barely one-fourth of my version and, particularly in its later part, is more in the nature of an abstract than a translation. He eliminates a great many details of compelling interest to the Western reader, and also a number of incidents essential to the logical development of the story, for instance, the entire magnificent dream vision toward the end of the book (Chapter 49 in the present version), which is one of the literary peaks of the novel and quite indispensable to it.

My translation into the German, on which the present English translation is based, presents about five-sixths of the original. It is intended not so much for a restricted scholarly audience as for the general reader interested in Chinese literature. Though my translation is not a complete one, I may still claim to be the first Westerner to have made accessible the monumental structure of the *Hung Lou Meng*. My version gives a full rendering of the main narrative, which is organized around the three figures of Pao Yu, Black Jade, and Precious Clasp. I have treated the secondary plots more or less comprehensively according to their importance, always with a view to avoiding gaps in the story development. There can be no doubt that sociologically this novel is of the greatest interest. But it can claim our attention equally on purely literary grounds: the narrative is compelling, the characters are most vividly individualized, the background is impressively and realistically drawn.

In China the *Hung Lou Meng* is considered the outstanding classic novel of the Ching Dynasty. A considerable body of critical literature has grown up around it. The general assumption is that the author drew on his own experiences and that his hero, Pao Yu, is a self-portrait. Tsao Hsueh Chin was the pampered son of a rich and highly cultivated Mandarin family in which the lucrative office of Inspector of the Imperial Silk Factories in Kiangsu had been hereditary for generations. In spite of his great intellectual gifts, he failed at the Literary Examinations and was barred from office. He took refuge in the spheres of philosophy and letters.

Chinese literary criticism has offered other solutions to the puzzle, however. A not improbable theory identifies Pao Yu with the youthful

Emperor Chien Ling (r. 1736-1796), of whom it is said that, like Pao Yu, he had the habit of licking the rouge off the lips of the young ladies of his entourage. According to this theory, Pao Yu's father, the stern Chia Cheng, represents Emperor Yung Cheng (r. 1723-1735), Chien Ling's predecessor. This theory has much to commend it. Among the host of characters in the novel, Chia Cheng is the pure type of the stern Confucian. History preserves the memory of Emperor Yung Cheng as that of the great Confucian on China's throne, the ruler of common sense and social consciousness.

*Though at first sight the *Hung Lou Meng* appears to be an inexplicable chaos of innumerable characters and events, on closer scrutiny the novel reveals itself to be a harmonious structure, well ordered, logical, consistent. The main characters—Black Jade, of a nearly saintly chastity; the Princess Ancestress, earthy and motherly; Precious Clasp, womanly, warm, sensible; Bright Cloud and Mandarin Duck, touchingly loyal and devoted; Chia Cheng, stern and dutiful—are admirably drawn. But the many secondary figures also fill their positions solidly and have their definite functions within a carefully calculated plan. To give one example among many, the seemingly gratuitous appearance of the old servant and grumbler at the opening of the novel becomes meaningful when he reappears at the end of the story and the reader realizes that the old warrior functions as the unwanted and unheeded prophet.

The two mysterious monks that keep reappearing add an element of the supernatural; they are messengers from the beyond. They represent the recurring motif of the fundamental themes of the work, which is undeniably Taoist. The action begins with a prologue in the Phantom Realm of the Great Void, the Taoist heaven; it ends with an epilogue in the Blessed Regions of Purified Semblance, which is another name for the same sphere. Four times we see characters pass through the gates of the Great Void, which, in Taoist language, means to renounce the world: Shih Ying, the Cold Knight, Grief of Spring, and finally Pao Yu, the hero himself.

A second motif of the novel seems to me the matriarchy, eloquently represented by the Ancestress, who, always optimistic and ready to celebrate, admonishing and pacifying, holds the family together. The Confucian philosophy of life, of course, could not be absent from a Chinese novel. It appears in the person of Pao Yu's father, Chia Cheng.

What, briefly summarized, is the core of the novel?

From the Confucian point of view, it might be the story of the wealth and honor of a great and noble house and its self-destruction. The house is rehabilitated in the end through the intellectual and moral achievement of a son hitherto considered degenerate—since Pao Yu dutifully conforms to the wishes of his parents and submits to the ordeal of the examinations.

From the Buddhist and Taoist points of view the answer might be: It is a story of the gradual awakening, purification, and final transcendence of a soul originally sunk in the slime of temporal and material strivings.

From the Western point of view the answer might be this: It is the case history of a highly gifted but degenerate young aristocrat, a psychopath and a weakling, asocial, effeminate, plagued by inferiority complexes and manic depressions, who, though capable of a temporary rallying of energies, founders among the demands of reality and slinks cravenly away from human society.

The last stage of Pao Yu's development, his change into a spirit, goes beyond the comprehension of the Western mind. For Taoism is not only a theory but, above all, practical experience.

And finally, the often-mentioned spirit stone probably symbolizes the innate disposition, the spiritual nature, of a man, which he may not betray without risking the loss of his essential self.

The goddess Nu Kua and the 36,501 stones for the repair of the pillars of heaven, with which the novel starts, are mythological metaphors of rather prosaic significance. Countless as stones, men inhabit the earth; among them Providence picks a certain number and assigns them to administer the State as members of the hierarchy of officials and to preserve the mass of the people from the threat of anarchy. Pao Yu was rejected as unfit for this service, but he had been touched by the hand of the goddess and ennobled by her touch. Laziness makes him wish to be an ordinary stone among stones, but a higher destiny frees him and he becomes conscious of his quality as "Precious Stone." For this reason our novel has a second title in China, *Shi tou chi*, "The Story of the Stone."

FRANZ KUHN

THE CHIA FAMILY

Princess Ancestress, née Shih, widow of Chia Tai Shan, second Prince of Yungkuo. Ruler of the eastern and western palaces

Chia Ching (Prince Hermit), son of Chia Tai Hua, the second Prince of Ningkuo. Retired to a Taoist temple

THE SENIORS

Chia Chen (Prince Chen), son of Chia Ching; in his place master of the Ningkuo palace

Chia Shieh (Prince Shieh), elder son of the Princess Ancestress; master of the Yungkuo palace

Chia Cheng, younger son of the Princess Ancestress

Princess Chen, née Yu, wife of Prince Chen

Princess Shieh, née Hsin, wife of Prince Shieh

Madame Cheng, née Wang, wife of Chia Cheng

THE JUNIORS

Chia Yung, son of Prince Chen

Chia Lien, son of Prince Shieh

Chia Pao Yu, son of Chia Cheng by his wife, Madame Cheng

Chia Huan, son of Chia Cheng by his secondary wife Chao; half brother of Pao Yu

Chia Lan, son of Chia Chu, the deceased son of Chia Cheng

Mistress Yung, wife of Chia Yung, also known by her childhood name, Ko Ching

Madame Phoenix, wife of Chia Lien

Widow Chu, mother of Chia Lan

Beginning of Spring, daughter of Chia Cheng and his wife, née Wang; sister of Pao Yu; Imperial secondary wife

Taste of Spring, daughter of Chia Cheng by his secondary wife Chao; half sister of Pao Yu

Grief of Spring, daughter of Chia Ching, the Prince Hermit

Greeting of Spring, daughter of Prince Shieh by a secondary wife

RELATIONS OF THE CHIA FAMILY

living within the confines of the Ningkuo and Yungkuo estates

Black Jade (Miss Ling), daughter of Ling Ju Hai, granddaughter of the Princess Ancestress

Aunt Hsueh, née Wang, sister of Madame Cheng
Precious Clasp (Pao Chai), daughter of Aunt Hsueh
Hsueh Pan, son of Aunt Hsueh
Mother Yu, stepsister of Princess Chen
Second Sister Yu, elder daughter of Mother Yu; later Chia Lien's secondary wife
Third Sister Yu, younger daughter of Mother Yu

PRINCIPAL WAITING MAIDS

ANCESTRESS

    Mandarin Duck

    Amber

    Numskull

MADAME CHENG

    Gold Ring

    Nephrite Buckle

PHOENIX

    Little Ping

    Little Fong

    Siao Hung

PAO YU

    Pearl

    Musk

    Bright Cloud

    Autumn Wave

PRECIOUS CLASP

    Oriole

    Apricot

BLACK JADE

    Cuckoo

    Snowgoose

GREETING OF SPRING

    Orange

    Chess Maid

GRIEF OF SPRING

    Painting Maid

TRANSLATORS' NOTE

To avoid confusion, male names have been transliterated, while nearly all female names have been freely rendered in an approximation of their literal meaning.

Forms of address used throughout the book:
  Tai tai (literally "great-great"), for the master's wife.
  Old *Tai tai*, for the master's mother.
  Nai nai, for the wife of the master's son.
  Mei mei (literally "younger sister, younger sister"), for younger sisters and young female cousins.

The term "secondary wife" is used in preference to concubine, since the Western connotation of concubine does not apply to the moral and legal status of concubines in China, who are formally taken into the family.

THE DREAM OF THE RED CHAMBER

CHAPTER 1

Shih Ying is carried away in a dream and receives a revelation. Amidst the toil and welter of daily life Yu Tsun finds the maiden of his heart.

OUR STORY BEGINS IN SUCHOW, THE STRONG CITY SITUATED IN THE southeastern edge of the great plain of China. Beyond the Emperor's Gate, which leads into the quarter of the rich and aristocratic, the region of comfortable living and "red dust," stretched the "Ten Mile Street." In a narrow bottleneck of that street, close by an old temple familiarly known as the "Temple of the Gourd," lived the respected citizen Shih Ying with his good and virtuous wife, née Feng.

Shih Ying was one of the most respected, if not the most aristocratic, people in his suburb. Being the fortunate possessor of a nice country estate, he was able to live a life of leisure. He was not a lover of honors or riches and was quite happy just tending his flowers, cultivating bamboo, or reciting poetry over a glass of good wine. In short, he lived an idyllic and unworldly life. Only one thing was lacking to his complete happiness: he was already past fifty and had no little son to rock on his knee. Fate had granted him only a little daughter, now three years old, named Lotus.

On one of those seemingly endless summer days he was poring over his books in the library. Overcome with the heat, his head had sunk down and his forehead lay against the edge of the table. As he dropped off to sleep he seemed to be wandering through an unknown dreamland. While he was walking two priests joined him on his way and went along beside him. One of them was a Taoist, the other a servant of Buddha. He heard the first saying to the second: "Why did you take the stone with you?"

The bonze replied: "In order to intervene in a love drama which by the will of fate is about to be enacted in the earthly world. The hero of the drama has not yet experienced his earthly reincarnation. I wish to take the opportunity of sending the stone into the world to enable the hero to play his role in that drama."

"And where does the drama begin?"

"That is a strange story. In the distant west, on the shores of the River of the Spirits, where stands the boundary stone of the three existences, the plant Purple Pearl once grew. At that time our stone was still living a restless, wandering life. The goddess Nu Kua, whose task it was to repair the damaged posts of the gate of heaven, had finally rejected it as unfit, because of its composition, out of the 36,501 stones

3

which she had set aside for her purpose. By contact with her divine hand it had become possessed of a soul, hence it could change its location whenever it pleased, and make itself larger or smaller. It felt painfully conscious day and night of the humiliation which it had suffered in being rejected by the goddess as unsuitable.

"In the course of its wanderings it came one day to the palace of the Fairy of Fearful Awakening. The fairy, who knew its higher destiny, took it into her household staff and gave it the title of 'Guardian of the Radiance of the Stone of the Gods' in the Palace of the Red Clouds. But it simply could not settle down and give up its wandering life.

"It used to steal away frequently from its duties in the palace and go off to the shores of the River of the Spirits. There, one day, it discovered the plant, Purple Pearl. It became very fond of Purple Pearl and to show its affection used to sprinkle it daily with fragrant dew. Thus it saved the delicate plant from fading away too soon. Thanks to the beneficent refreshment with fragrant dew, through which it drank in the finest powers of the mutual relations between heaven and earth, it was enabled later to drop its earthly form of plant and take human shape. The delicate plant turned into a young girl.

"An invincible longing often drove this young girl beyond the calm 'Sphere of Banished Suffering.' When she was hungry she loved to eat of the 'Tree of Secret Love Fruits.' When she was thirsty she loved best to sip from the 'Source of Drenching Grief.' Again and again she remembered how in the past, when she was a frail plant, someone used to water her with sweet dew, and her longing to requite that kindly deed never left her. I cannot repay him by doing the same for him, she used often to think to herself. But if it should be granted me, in my next existence, to meet him as a fellow being on earth, then I hope I shall thank him with as many tears as I can shed in a whole long life.

"That, then, is the prehistory of the love drama which by the will of Providence is now about to be enacted upon earth. Those taking part, among them the plant Purple Pearl, are already preparing to step down upon the earthly stage. Therefore let us hasten to take back our stone to its mistress, the Fairy of Fearful Awakening, so that she can enter it in the list of those taking part in that drama, and send it to join the other players."

"Very strange indeed," remarked the Taoist. "To repay a debt of gratitude with tears is definitely something new. The story seems to me to be sufficiently worthwhile to induce us too to step down into the dust of the earth. Perhaps we may succeed thereby in effecting the redemption of some erring souls. This would indeed be a meritorious work."

"That is certainly my opinion too. I therefore propose that we first of all deliver our foundling, the stone, to the Fairy of Fearful Awakening, and later descend ourselves also, when all the actors in this drama of misfortune are already met together down below. Up to the present only half of them are gathered there."

"Good. Let us be off, then, to the Palace of the Red Clouds."

The sleeper Shih Ying had followed every word of their conversation. He now stepped ahead of the two, who were walking beside him, saluted them with a bow, and addressed them as follows: "Reverend Masters, this simple fellow was an accidental listener to your strange conversation. He did not understand its full meaning. If you would favor him with a more detailed explanation of it, he would listen most devoutly and respectfully. He would very much like to profit in some small measure from your wisdom, and so not sink into the vortex of foolishness."

"It is not permitted to us to speak in advance of matters concerning destiny," was the reply. "When the time comes, think of us. If you do so you will escape the fiery pit of perdition."

"May I not at least see the object of your conversation?"

"That is permitted to you, by the will of Providence," said the bonze, passing him the desired object. Shih Ying took it in his hand and looked at it. It was a lovely jade stone with a fresh, pale radiance. On the upper surface were engraved the four ideographs *tung ling pao-yu*, "Stone of penetrating spiritual power." The bottom surface too showed a series of small written characters. Shih Ying was about to decipher them when the bonze took the stone out of his hand again, saying: "We have arrived at the Realm of Illusion," and strode on ahead with the Taoist. Shih Ying saw them walking in through a high stone archway, over which stood the words in big letters: "Phantom Realm of the Great Void." On the two pillars of the arch he read the couplet:

When seeming is taken for being, being becomes seeming,
Where nothing is taken for something, something becomes nothing.

He was about to hurry after the two men when a frightful clap of thunder resounded in his ears. It seemed as if the earth were about to collapse. With a loud cry he woke up. He opened his eyes and blinked at the glowing orb of the evening sun, which was blazing slantwise through the banana leaves. Already he had half forgotten his vision.

The nurse appeared on the threshold with little Lotus in her arms. Shih Ying took the child from her, pressed it tenderly as a jewel to his bosom, and dandled it and played with it for a while. Then he took it with him outside the hall door, and stood there looking at the noisy throng in the street. He was just about to go back into the house when two men in priestly attire passed by—one a servant of Buddha, the other a disciple of Lao Tzu. The bonze was barefooted. His shorn head was full of scurf and scratches. The Taoist was lame in one foot; the hair of his bare head hung about in an uncombed tangle. Along they came gesticulating wildly and laughing like a pair of madmen. They stopped in front of Shih Ying's threshold and remained a moment staring at him and the child. Then the bonze suddenly began to sigh loudly, and he said to Shih Ying: "Sir, what ill-fated creature is that you hold in your arms? It will bring nothing but sorrow to its parents!"

Shih Ying thought the man was mad, so he took no notice of his talk. But the bonze continued to address him with great emphasis. "Give it to me! Give it to me!" he urged, pointing to the child in his arms.

This was too much for Shih Ying. He pressed the baby more firmly to his breast, and was already turning to go away, when the bonze broke into a shrill peal of laughter and called out after him:

> "A fool dotes;
> Tender blossoms
> Are cut by the frost.
> Take care
> at New Year,
> Fire and flame."

Shih Ying hung back. He would have very much liked to have the mysterious rhyme explained to him. But he heard the Taoist priest say to the bonze: "From now on our paths divide. We shall work apart. After three aeons I shall await you in the well-known cemetery on the Pei Mang Hill near Lo yang. We shall then go back together to the Phantom Realm of the Great Void and have the affair of the stone obliterated from the register."

"Good," Shih Ying heard the bonze reply, whereupon the two suddenly disappeared. Shih Ying was still in a dazed and stupefied state, thinking over the strange incident, when he saw his good friend and neighbor Chia Yu Tsun coming towards the house. Yu Tsun was a poor young student who lodged near by in the Temple of the Gourd. He was the son of an official in Huchow, who had died early, leaving his family in poor circumstances. A year ago he had set out to make his way to the capital, intending to enter for the great public examinations and win fame and success. He had only got as far as Suchow, however, when his money ran out. So he had found temporary refuge and lodging in a monk's cell in the Temple of the Gourd. Here he continued his studies industriously, at the same time earning his board and keep by writing for the unlettered. In this way he had made the acquaintance of Shih Ying, and was soon on terms of friendship with him. For Shih Ying had a great regard for the art of letters, and he took a keen delight in the profound and genuine culture of the brilliant young scholar.

Yu Tsun now approached with a polite bow saying: "I see that you are leaning against the doorpost and craning your neck. No doubt you are looking out for any novel happenings in the town?"

"That is not it," replied Shih Ying, "but the child was restless, and I tried to distract her a bit by taking her to the door with me. My worthy brother has come just at the right time. Let us go in and shorten the endless day with pleasant conversation."

He gave the child to the nurse and showed his visitor into the library. They had barely had time to drink a bowl of tea and exchange four or five sentences when the host was called away to another visitor in the outer room. Shih Ying asked his friend to remain but to excuse him for a few minutes. So Yu Tsun stayed and passed the time of waiting rummaging and searching out old books from among the volumes in the library. While he was thus engaged he suddenly heard, through the window, the clear tones of a feminine voice. He laid the old books aside, slipped over to the window, and leaned out. Not far from the window he saw a young girl bent down between the flower beds. She was picking flowers and humming a song as she did so. She was not exactly ten-tenths beautiful, nevertheless she was quite uncommonly charming. At any rate, Yu Tsun remained at the window, staring steadily out at her. Then, chancing to look up, she also caught sight of him.

He is poorly clothed, it is true, but stately in form and appearance, she thought to herself as she turned away hastily. What handsome features he's got, and what expressive eyes! He must surely be the scholar Yu Tsun, the friend of whom my master speaks so much, and whom he is so anxious to help whenever he has a chance. Yes, it must be he, because all the other people who frequent our house are of the well-to-do classes. But one has only to see him to understand why our master always believes that he will not have to go about much longer in such old and torn clothes. She could not resist looking back once more at the window. Then she disappeared farther into the garden.

Yu Tsun was immensely pleased at having obviously made an impression on her despite his shabby appearance. That girl is both wise and observant, he said to himself, and she can perceive the higher value of a person like myself despite unfavorable circumstances.

Moved by these thoughts, he strode meditatively through the garden and out into a street by a side door. For the guest was remaining to dinner, as a servant had informed him, and so it would be too long for him to wait. He could not forget the little incident of the pretty girl in the garden who had turned round twice to look at him.

On the evening of the Mid-Autumn Festival, after the usual family meal was over, his patron went round to invite him to drink a friendly glass of wine alone with him in his library. Yu Tsun was sitting by himself in his monastery cell in a melancholy mood. Contemplation of the harvest moon had inspired him to write a poem of eight lines in which he had described in cryptic words his recent experience and revealed the secret wishes which it had awakened. The thought that an unkind fate would deny him the fulfillment of his desires made him sigh deeply, look up full of sorrow at the moon, and bring forth the following additional lines:

> In darkness languishes the precious stone.
> When will its excellence enchant the world?
> The precious clasp hidden away
> Longs for wings to fly to the bride.

While he was repeating these lines over to himself in came Shih Ying.

"It seems to me that my worthy brother makes high demands of life and considers himself much above the common herd," he remarked with a smile.

"Oh, I was not referring to myself," replied Yu Tsun, embarrassed. "That's an old poem. It just occurred to me by chance. You flatter me in thinking it mine."

Shih Ying gave his invitation and took Yu Tsun back with him to his library. He drank his health gaily and encouraged him to help himself from the many dishes of dainties which he kept on tirelessly ordering for him. Thus it happened that Yu Tsun, accustomed as he was to the spare diet of a monk, fell more and more into that mood of exhilaration in which the mouth expresses the things which move the heart. The pleasant sound of strings and flutes and merry songs drifted in from the street and from the neighboring houses. Up in the heavens hung the shining white orb of the full moon. In a trice Yu Tsun had improvised a quatrain in praise of the harvest moon.

"Magnificent! Divine!" cried his host, enthusiastically. "Once more my worthy brother has given a proof of his poetic ability. I have always said that you would not wade for long in the slough of dejection. Soon you will be floating upon the clouds. I congratulate you in advance. Do me the honor to drink!"

And he reached him another beaker of wine filled with his own hand.

Yu Tsun emptied the beaker. Then he took a deep breath and said: "Pray do not think that it is the wine which has inspired your humble younger brother with daring words. I am confident that I shall be able to pass the examination and have my name written in the list of the chosen. But of what avail is all my ability if my travelling trunk is empty? The road to Peking is a long one. If some good souls do not help me, I fear I shall not make it with the little I earn as a scrivener."

"Why has my worthy brother not spoken of this sooner?" his host interrupted quickly. "I have been thinking of this matter for some time past, but I did not trust myself to broach it. Now, however, I can make up for lost time. True, I am not a highly educated man; nevertheless I know what is seemly between friends. Next spring, after an interval of three years, a State examination is to be held again. My worthy brother must on no account miss this opportunity and he must therefore set out for the capital as soon as possible in order there to prove his abilities. I shall bear the cost of the journey and of everything else that is necessary. My worthy brother shall at least not have squandered his friendship in vain upon an unworthy person."

He whispered an order to one of his servants. The man disappeared and came back straight away to lay before his master's protégé a moneybag containing fifty shining ounce pieces, and two beautiful quilted winter coats. Meantime the master of the house had been looking through the calendar.

"The nineteenth is a favorable day for setting out on a journey," he continued. "My worthy brother should take timely steps to secure a hired boat for that day. And perhaps, when the year is over, I shall once more have the honor of basking in the radiance of your presence, after the wings of your talents have carried you up to giddy heights. That would indeed be a day of high festival for me."

Yu Tsun was so exhilarated by the wine that he only mumbled a few banal words of thanks before settling down once more to easy and loquacious chatting and drinking. Not until far into the night, about the time of the third drum roll, did the friends take leave of each other.

The next morning Shih Ying remembered that he had also intended to give his protégé letters of introduction to two civil servants whom he knew in the capital. He therefore sent a servant over to the Temple of the Gourd to ask Yu Tsun to come over once more to receive these letters of recommendation. But on returning, the servant reported that Yu Tsun had set out very early that morning. He had left with one of the temple bonzes a farewell greeting for his patron and a further message to the effect that people of education like himself were in the habit of considering only the matter in hand and were not influenced by superstitious directions in the calendar. And that was that, whether Shih Ying liked it or not.

Light and shadow change swiftly. The first full moon of the New Year, the time of the Lantern Festival, had come around again unperceived. In the evening Shih Ying had sent a servant to take his little daughter outside the hall door so that she might enjoy the sight of the gay lanterns and the merry fireworks—the "spirit fires." The servant had gone right into the throng of the Ten Mile Street. He found so many fascinating sights and sounds there that he was completely spellbound and could not tear himself away. But needing a moment's privacy, he thoughtlessly left the child in his charge sitting on a stone parapet in front of a strange house while he disappeared round the nearest corner. When he came back the little girl was gone. He searched the streets and lanes for her all night, but in vain. The next morning, being too much afraid of punishment to return to his master's house, he fled from the town and ran back to his native village.

Shih Ying, in desperation, sent his whole household out to search for the lost child, but without success. Then, mourning fell upon the house which had formerly been such a happy one. Both parents were already past fifty, and could scarcely hope to have more children. Their sighs and lamentations did not cease, either by day or by night, and soon physicians and soothsayers became daily guests in the house. But the loss of their child was not to be their only misfortune.

On the fifteenth day of the third month, namely, on All Souls' Day, a fire broke out in the Temple of the Gourd. The Brother, who was cooking the sacrificial foods, had carelessly allowed the flames of the fire to shoot out over the pan and set alight the parchment panes and wooden frame of the kitchen window. All the buildings round about had bamboo fences and wooden walls, so the flames spread rapidly from the Temple of the Gourd to the neighboring house, and thence farther and farther from house to house. Soon all the streets around the temple were one single mass of flames, against which the inhabitants and the town fire brigade strove in vain. The fire raged for a whole night before burning itself out. Shih Ying's house too had gone down in ruins and ashes. The inmates had barely been able to escape with their lives. So what could poor Shih Ying do but bow his knees and utter short sighs and long ones?

At first he and his wife went to live on their country estate. But they found life hardly tolerable there, for owing to drought and famine the whole countryside was overrun with robber bands, which fell upon the villages like swarms of bees. Soldiers came to drive away the robbers, but they in their turn became a scourge which made country life highly unpleasant. On account of all this the sorely tried Shih Ying decided to sell his land. He then went with his wife and two maids to live with his father-in-law, old Feng, in the safe town of Ta yu chow. Old Feng, who was likewise a former landowner, was fairly comfortably off. All the same he was not exactly overjoyed at seeing his son-in-law coming to seek refuge with him in such a wretched state of want. Happily, Shih Ying did not come empty-handed; he brought some cash with him—the proceeds of his landed property. This he handed over to his father-in-law, asking him to buy a little house and a piece of land for him on the outskirts of the town. Old Feng did this most willingly, though it must be admitted that half the money disappeared into his own pocket. With the other half he bought a very rickety old cottage and a piece of worthless land. Now Shih Ying was somewhat spoiled by his previous life of pleasant leisure; he much preferred lingering over books to occupying himself with practical things such as tillage and harvest work. It was small wonder, then, that such tasks, carried out so much against his grain, were not blessed with success, and at the end of two years he was completely destitute. His father-in-law was thoroughly dissatisfied with him and blamed him for being lazy and soft. True, he did not say these things to his face, but he complained of him behind his back to others. Shih Ying, who got to hear of this indirectly, felt grieved and depressed. The disappointments and vicissitudes of the past few years had worn him down visibly. He had become an old man who had nothing more left to hope for.

One day he was taking a leisurely stroll along the street leaning wearily on his stick, like an old man. Suddenly a wandering Taoist monk of very odd appearance, dressed in a ragged smock and wearing bast sandals, came limping along beside him. He could hear the monk murmuring:

> "Sweet world-forsaking! Precious solitude!
> Honor and fame: how little worth are these!
> The great ones of the world, when all is done,
> Are but a mound of earth, with grass thereon.
>
> "Sweet world-forsaking! Precious solitude!
> Riches and gold—who would be fain of these?
> Our clutching hands seize them, and cannot hold:
> One day we must leave all—yes, wealth and gold.
>
> "Sweet world-forsaking! Precious solitude!
> Do lovely women, then, ensnare your hearts?
> These swear to love one man till death doth part:
> He dieth—soon another claims that love.
>
> "Sweet world-forsaking! Precious solitude!
> Are children, and their children, your desire?
> Loving parental hearts wear out in vain:
> The only thanks which children give is—pain."

"Your words touch my soul to its very depths, honored Master," said Shih Ying with a sigh to his travelling companion. "Will you allow me to supplement your verses with a few sentences expressing the experience gained in the course of my own wretched life?"

"Proceed!" cried the disciple of Lao Tzu with friendly encourage-

11

ment. Thereupon in well-chosen and skillfully disposed words Shih Ying improvised a melancholy homily on the splendor of his past life, the misery of his present situation, and the transitory nature of all earthly things.

"Splendid! You have put it all in deeply impressive words," said the monk admiringly, when Shih Ying's outpouring had ended.

"I should like to go along with you," said Shih Ying simply. He took the heavy knapsack from the monk's shoulders, and buckled it onto his own. Then, without even going back to his house, he joined the strange holy man in his casual wandering.

His disappearance formed the subject of conversation for some time in his quarter of the town. His wife almost died of shock and grief, it was said. When all inquiries for his whereabouts proved in vain and the missing man failed to return, she went back to the house of her parents with her two maids, and from that time on, working day and night with her needle, she strove to keep up the household for herself and her aged father.

One day the elder of her maids was standing at the street door buying yarn from a hawker. Suddenly she heard the yamen outriders as they came nearer and nearer down the street shouting: "Make way! Make way!" The new district Mandarin was taking up his office today, the people told her. Leaning back in the doorway, she watched the procession pass. It was a stately cortege. In front were postillions on horseback, then came police and yamen officials in two lines carrying banners and the insignia of office. In between the lines was the great official sedan chair with the Mandarin in his scarlet State robe seated in it. Behind walked more flunkies. The maid gave a start. It seemed to her that she had seen the handsome face of the man in the scarlet robe sometime somewhere before.

When the procession had passed by she went into the house again and had soon forgotten the trifling incident.

Late in the evening of that same day, just as everyone was going to bed, there was a sudden loud and peremptory knocking at the door of the Fengs' house. A troop of yamen servants were outside demanding to be let in.

"The old Governor has sent us," they said in a chorus. "We have a load to deliver."

Old Feng was as frightened as if a tiger stood in his path. What new trouble was this, in the name of heaven? If you want to know you must read what the next chapter has to report.

CHAPTER 2

In Yangchow a high-born lady joins the company of the Blessed. In the tavern Yu Tsun learns more about his noble relatives.

As soon as old Feng had recovered somewhat from his shock, he went to the door and asked the people from the yamen what they wanted. "A certain Shih Ying is said to live here, and we have orders to take him to the old Governor," came the answer.

"My name is Feng, but my son-in-law's name is Shih Ying. He no longer lives in this town, however; he joined the wandering monks and hermits two years ago."

"Then you must come with us instead of him," they said. And they took old Feng along with them and brought him to the yamen of the new Mandarin.

It was late at night when old Feng returned home to his family, who were awaiting him anxiously. His report at once banished all their fears and turned their sadness into joy.

"The new Mandarin's name is Chia, with the surname of Yu Tsun. He is a native of Huchow, and in former days when he lived for a time in Suchow he was a good friend and neighbor of my son-in-law, Shih Ying," recounted old Feng. "As he was passing by our house yesterday in the ceremonial procession, he espied our maid Apricot standing in the doorway. He remembered her and concluded that her former master, Shih Ying, must live here. He wanted to renew the old friendship, so he sent his men along. He was very much distressed when I told him of the sad fate of his former benefactor. He also inquired for my granddaughter, and deeply regretted her disappearance. He promised me that he would have an official search made for her whereabouts. When I was taking leave, he gave me a present, moreover, of two ounces of silver."

"Our new Mandarin is a friendly, affable gentleman!" was the unanimous verdict of the family.

Early the next day messengers again arrived from the yamen. They brought two ingots of silver and four pieces of satin for Shih Ying's wife. The Mandarin sent them—so the message ran—as a small return for the kindness he had enjoyed in her husband's house. The messengers handed old Feng a personal note as well. In it the Mandarin asked if he might take home the maid Apricot to be mistress of his side-chamber. Old Feng, who was very happy at being thus honored, naturally gave his consent to this. In gratitude the Mandarin sent him a hundred ounces of gold, and many more gifts for Shih Ying's wife, and the same evening he had the maid Apricot fetched in a gay little red sedan chair.

Lucky Apricot! Who would have thought that the two hurried glances which she had once bestowed upon the poor student Yu Tsun while plucking flowers in the garden should one day decide her fate? But merely being accepted into the side-chamber of the highly respected Mandarin Yu Tsun was by no means the end of her good luck. A year afterwards she bore him a little son, and when the mistress of the principal chamber fell ill and died soon afterwards, Apricot was raised to the rank of principal wife. It could well be said of her:

In the chance look of an eye—lifelong happiness.

Here we must mention that as soon as his patron had given him means for the journey, Yu Tsun had gone straight off to the capital, without waiting for the lucky day which had been looked up for him in the calendar. There he passed his examination brilliantly and gained the third highest doctorate, *chin shih,* which procured him acceptance into the "hall of silk-blossoming talent" and entrance to public office. He was assigned to provincial government and appointed District Mandarin of Ta yu chow. Unfortunately, he prejudiced his career by certain faults of character. Consciousness of his unusual ability led him to show a lamentable lack of respect towards his colleagues and superiors and of consideration towards the common people. He thus made himself equally unpopular with both his superiors and his subordinates. After scarcely two years in office, he found himself denounced at Court. He was accused of having arbitrarily abolished old traditional rites and national customs; of hiding, under the mask of correctness, a wolfish and tigerish disposition; of fomenting disorder in his area of jurisdiction and making life unbearable for the population. Thus ran the letter of censure which his Provincial Governor submitted at Court.

The dragon face of the Son of Heaven darkened, and the Imperial hand wrote on the margin of the letter of complaint an angry decree relieving the accused official of his post, to the joy of his jealous colleagues.

Yu Tsun bore the blow with philosophic resignation. In the past two years he had saved enough from his salary to enable him to live a care-free private life for some time. Having duly handed over office to his successor, he gave up his house, sent his wife and servants, well provided with money, back to their families for the time being, and set out on a great roaming tour of the country. Free of all responsibility and care, with no other hindrance than "the wind on his shoulders, the moonlight in his sleeves," he wished to be free for once and to travel about for a time just wherever he wanted to, learning to know the country and the people.

In the course of his travels he came one day to the capital of the important salt-mining district of Yangchow. He learned that a certain Ling Ju Hai was the newly appointed Royal Treasurer of the salt mines there. The family of this Ling had basked in the Imperial favor from ancient times and had been raised five generations ago to the second class of nobility. According to the letters patent the title was to have descended only to the third generation, but by special Imperial favor it had been extended to the present Lings, father and son, thus carrying it down to the fifth generation. Besides their exterior nobility the family Ling were also endowed with the ancient inherited fragrance of a highly developed culture and education, and our Ling too was not only the son of his fathers but, by his own attainments and a brilliant career, had proved himself worthy of them.

He was in his fifties and was the last of his line, for apart from a little son of three who had died recently, fate had not granted him any male descendant despite the many concubines who filled his side-chambers. Only a little daughter, the delicate, precocious Tai Yu, Black Jade, had been presented to him by his principal wife, née Chia. Black Jade, as an only child, was tended with exaggerated love and care, and being intelligent and quick-witted, was educated with the utmost care, just as if she were to replace the son who was unfortunately lacking.

Precisely at the time when Yu Tsun came to Yangchow Mr. Ling was looking for a clever tutor for his little daughter. After all his wanderings, Yu Tsun, on his side, felt a wish to follow for a change a regular occupation which would enable him, moreover, to replenish his exhausted funds. He found the suitable sponsors in two former fellow students whom he met by chance in his lodgings and who were well acquainted with the treasurer of the salt mines, and thanks to their recommendations he received the post of tutor in the Ling household.

His position was not particularly arduous and left him plenty of free time, for his pupil was a tender creature who, owing to frequent indispositions, could study only very irregularly. Two young waiting maids always kept her company during her lessons.

He had thus passed two years in his quiet and pleasant post when the mother of his pupil fell ill and died. The good child had dedicated herself with such touching devotion to nursing her sick mother, and after the mother's death had fulfilled the many elaborate mourning conventions so exactly, that her already delicate health suffered seriously and the lessons had to be stopped for a long time. During this period Yu Tsun was left to himself a great deal, and when the weather was fine he availed of his leisure to make frequent excursions into the surrounding countryside.

On one of these excursions he had visited an old temple hidden in a copse outside the town, and then had found a village inn near by where he went to refresh himself with a glass of wine. In the tavern he unexpectedly met an old acquaintance from the capital. He was the curio and antique dealer Leng, with whom he had become friendly when he had stayed in Chinling for the State examination. He esteemed Leng as a practical businessman, and Leng esteemed him as a man of knowledge and culture. Leng was on his way back from his native place, where he had celebrated the New Year, and had broken the journey at Yangchow, where he was staying with a business friend for a few days. Just by chance he too had made a trip into the country that day. After the unexpected meeting had been duly celebrated with drinks, a mutual exchange of news started.

"Any news from the capital?" asked Yu Tsun.

"Nothing of importance to you except perhaps that the circumstances of your noble relations are beginning to change."

"I do not know what noble relations you mean."

"I mean two princely houses who, like you, bear the family name of Chia and therefore are of your clan; and I do not think you need deny this relationship."

"Ah, you must mean the two houses of Ningkuo and Yungkuo?"

"Yes, exactly."

"You are right. We are in the same genealogical table. But since the Han dynasty the Chia clan has spread all over the provinces and so one can no longer identify all the branches of the family. Besides, such a great social difference separates the illustrious houses of Ningkuo and Yungkuo from my humble person that it would be most impertinent on my part to claim their relationship."

"I am not so sure of that. Recently the two families of Ningkuo and Yungkuo have been going down seriously; the former splendor is beginning to diminish."

"I can scarcely credit that. Last year, when I was travelling through Chinling, and passed along the street of which one entire side is occupied to the east by the Ningkuo palace and to the west by the Yungkuo palace, I got an impression of the utmost splendor and greatness. Certainly, there was not much going and coming at the gates, but inside those great halls and single-story pavilions everything was still in perfect condition and undiminished splendor. And behind them that magnificent park, with its cliffs and crags and fishponds and exotic plants —no, that did not look in the least like decay and decline."

"Now, Doctor Know-All, how can one judge just by the outside? The centipede goes on wriggling when he's already dead. Naturally, in spite of everything, the two houses are still more splendid and imposing today than the average aristocratic home. But the difficulty of feeding so many mouths and of maintaining such a large and expensive household in a manner becoming its rank is continually increasing. Such an establishment needs to be wisely financed, and that is what has gone wrong in recent times. But still more serious is the fact that the former ability of the family is diminishing in the younger generation."

"What? Is the education of the younger generation proving at fault in that house of ancient hereditary culture? I can hardly believe it. But I must confess that I am not well informed about all the circumstances. Perhaps you will have the kindness to enlighten me?"

"With pleasure. It is now five generations since the family of Chia was raised to princely rank. It was two blood brothers who first bore the princely title as a reward for their splendid services to the Throne, the elder as Ningkuo Kung, Prince of the Honor of the Throne, the younger as Yungkuo Kung, Prince of the Peace of the Throne. The decline of the family had already begun with the grandson of the former. He fell a victim to the folly of the Taoist heresy, devoted himself to alchemy, and thought of nothing else but brewing elixirs of life and baking vermilion pills. He lives as a hermit in the mountains in front of the capital and allows his son Chen to hold the title in his place. This Prince Chen, who has got a sixteen-year-old son, is therefore the present ruler of the Ningkuo palace. But unfortunately he does not rule worthily, for through his father's fault he was deprived of a sensible upbringing. He lives for his humors and pleasures, and unhappily there is no one who dares to tell him the truth. In short, everything is going to rack and ruin in the palace of Ningkuo.

"In the palace of Yungkuo matters are somewhat better. There the Princess Ancestress, widow of the second Prince of Yungkuo, is the ruler. She belongs to the noble family of Shih, from the Chinling neighborhood. The elder of her two sons, Shieh by name, the present holder of the princely title, is a friendly, somewhat phlegmatic gentleman, who likes a quiet life and does not trouble too much about the management of the estate.

"The younger son, Cheng, on the other hand, possesses outstanding gifts of mind and character. He is really worthy of his illustrious progenitor and had always been his favorite. At the wish of his grandfather and also following his own bent, he received a sound and thorough training for the civil service. Through special Imperial favor he was exempted from the third State examination and is now an assistant in one of the ministries.

"There are two strange incidents worthy of mention regarding the family of this Chia Cheng. The first of his four daughters, namely a child of his principal wife, one of the Wang family, was, strange to say, born on the first day of the first month. But here is something still more curious: A year later Madame Cheng gave birth to a son, who came into the world with an opalescent, crystal-bright jade stone in his mouth! And this stone, moreover, showed distinct traces of an inscription! The son was therefore named Pao Yu or 'Precious Stone.' Have you ever heard of anything more extraordinary?"

"I must confess I never have. Presumably this phenomenon points to a remarkable future."

"That is the general opinion, and the boy is in fact the avowed favorite of the Princess Ancestress. But just listen! According to ancient custom they placed a whole lot of toys near the child on his first birthday, in order to ascertain his gifts and his future aptitudes from the choice which he would make. And what do you think the child clutched at? Not at any boy's toy, mind you. Instead, he reached for the cosmetics and powder boxes, bangles and hair ornaments! His father was not exactly pleased with this choice and expressed the opinion that the boy was unlikely to grow up manly and would probably be a weakling and a dandy, and since then he has not been able to stand him. Of course, because of this his grandmother spoils him all the more. Now, at twelve years of age, he is a very wayward but intelligent and precocious boy. Many astonishing utterances have already come from his childish mouth. He said once, for instance, that it seemed to him that females were made of water while males were made of clay; for in feminine society he always felt revived and refreshed, whereas in male society he felt dull and depressed. Now, what do you think of this extraordinary pronouncement? Wouldn't you say he is possessed by the demon of lustfulness?"

"I do not know; perhaps he is misjudged," said Yu Tsun thoughtfully. "It may be an inherited disposition, and if so, how can the boy help it? I have come across a similar case myself. During my two years' wandering around I happened to be tutor for some time to the son of a Nanking family. When he had his lessons alone he was a difficult and insufferably inattentive pupil, with whom one could do absolutely nothing. He always declared that in order to be able to learn and to concentrate, he needed girls near him; and, in fact, in the presence of his young cousins, who lived in the same house, he was quite a different person. He would then be the best-mannered, gentlest, most well-behaved boy one could imagine. The mere word 'girl' seemed to excite an almost holy reverence in him. 'Before you utter the word "girl" with your filthy mouth, kindly rinse it out with pure water and perfumed tea, or else I will break your teeth and poke out your eyes!' he used to warn his household servants and valets. When his father thrashed him he used to cry out: 'Chieh chieh!' and 'Mei mei!'— 'Sister! Little sister!' When his cousins laughed at him because he was not ashamed to cry like a girl when he suffered pain, he explained to them that the mere words *chieh chieh* and *mei mei* were a magic formula to him which made him forget the most terrible pain. What do you think of this strange case?"

"It is very similar to what I have told you about our Pao Yu. In the palace of Yungkuo too there is no lack of the indispensable *chieh chieh* and *mei mei*. Pao Yu has no less than three 'sisters' around him. The fourth and eldest, who was given the name of Beginning of Spring because, as I already mentioned, she was born on the first day of the first month, no longer lives at home. As she is remarkably beautiful and gifted, she was deemed worthy of being accepted into the Imperial Palace for attendance on the Empress. The next in age is a daughter of Prince Shieh and is called Greeting of Spring. The third sister, again, is a child of Cheng by another wife. She is called Taste of Spring. The fourth in age is a sister of Prince Chen of the Ningkuo palace and is called Grief of Spring. The Princess Ancestress loves to have these three grandchildren around her. They are usually together, learn their lessons together, and are in every way virtuous and well-behaved young girls."

"How, exactly, was the late wife of my present employer, Mr. Ling, related to the families of Ningkuo and Yungkuo?"

"She was a sister of the brothers Shieh and Cheng of the Yungkuo branch of the family."

"It is a pity she died; she was a most noble lady. And her daughter, my pupil, is in no way inferior to her. The poor child has taken the early death of her mother terribly to heart. Has Prince Shieh also got sons?"

"He has two, and the younger of them, twenty-year-old Lien, is deserving of mention. True, he has bought the rank of a subprefect, but he avoids books and any official activity as much as possible, and has more of a head for business matters. He has been married for the past two years to the beautiful and clever niece of Chia Cheng's wife, one of the Wang family, and he helps his uncle Cheng to manage the Yungkuo estate. But as a matter of fact his energetic wife, who enjoys the greatest respect and admiration, takes a far greater part in the management than he."

"Thank you for all this friendly information. I am now adequately enlightened on the subject of my noble relatives. It seems to me that many influences, both good and bad, are combined in the family."

"Whether good or bad, what does it matter to us outsiders? Let us have another drink!"

A few more glasses were emptied, and then they set off for home. Dusk was falling and they had to hurry to be in time before the city gates shut. On the way a man came running after them, beckoning and shouting from quite a distance: "Congratulations, brother Yu Tsun! Congratulations! I have been running after you half the day to bring you good news."

If you want to know who this person was and what good news he had to bring, you must listen to the next chapter.

CHAPTER 3

Mr. Ling gives his guest from the West an introduction to the Yungkuo palace. The Princess Ancestress takes a motherless child lovingly into her home.

YU TSUN STOOD AND LOOKED BEHIND. THE PERSON WHO HAD BECKONED and called out to him from far off was a former fellow student who, like himself, had been dismissed from a government post some time ago and since then had been living in his native town, Yangchow.

"There's good news for you and for me!" he said to Yu Tsun, beaming with joy. "An Imperial edict has just been issued graciously permitting us to resume office. Now it is a matter of stirring ourselves and looking around for patronage."

After mutual congratulations the two friends parted, each making for his own dwelling.

"He is right; you must look around for patronage," said Leng to Yu Tsun. "What about asking Mr. Ling to use his influence for you at the Yungkuo palace?"

Yu Tsun acted on his advice. But first of all he procured the latest edition of the State newspaper, and in fact he found in it the edict announcing his rehabilitation.

The next day he presented himself before Mr. Ling and put his request to him.

"What a strange and favorable coincidence!" cried Mr. Ling. "Just by chance, and before you made this request of me, I had already written a letter of introduction for you to my brother-in-law Cheng, of the Yungkuo palace. It happens that my mother-in-law, the Princess Ancestress, wishes to take my motherless child into her home. She has already sent two boats with attendants to fetch the girl, but the departure has been delayed on account of her indisposition. Now, however, she is sufficiently recovered to make the journey. I was availing of this opportunity to give her a letter of introduction for you to my brother-in-law Cheng, as I wished in this way to repay you in some measure for the good services which you have rendered my house.

Would it not be doubly advantageous, since you are going to the capital in any case, if you accompanied my daughter and introduced yourself personally to my brother-in-law?"

Yu Tsun bowed politely and with many earnest words of thanks assured Mr. Ling that he would carry out the commission with pleasure.

"May I ask what is the rank of your brother-in-law?" he added. "I fear that it might appear presumptuous if a man of my rough manners were to venture into such an illustrious presence."

"Now, now, no exaggerated modesty, please!" said the Count, smiling. "After all, you belong to the same clan. Actually, I have two brothers-in-law in the Yungkuo palace. The elder one, Prince Shieh, holds the title of a marshal of the first rank. The younger, Cheng, is an assistant in the Ministry of Public Works. He is a man of simplicity and generosity, and possesses a great deal of the 'breath' and stature of his great ancestor. There is no haughtiness or aristocratic pride in him. You can approach him without hesitation and with absolute confidence. As regards the expenses necessary for your advancement, I have arranged for these too in the letter. Moreover, I have fixed the date of departure as the second day of next month."

Accordingly, on that day Black Jade embarked on one boat with the female servants while Yu Tsun followed her in the other with the male staff. There had been some tears and some fatherly admonitions before the little one would consent to going.

"I am already past fifty and do not intend to marry again," the Count had said to his young daughter. "Here at home you are deprived of the advice and guidance of a mother and the merry company of sisters. You will find both in the home of your grandmother. I am doing this for your good."

After several days' travelling they arrived in the capital. Yu Tsun put on his best coat, made his way to the Yungkuo palace, and handed in his visiting card. Chia Cheng was already expecting his visit, because the letter of introduction had been sent on in advance, and he received Yu Tsun at once. He found his visitor to be a man of stately and prepossessing appearance and extremely well spoken—just the type of man of culture and knowledge, as well as refined bearing, whom he greatly esteemed. And as he, following the tradition of his illustrious forefather, liked to assist the weak and oppressed, he did not hesitate to appeal to the Sovereign in Yu Tsun's favor, with the result that within two months the latter had the good fortune to be appointed Prefect of the district of Ying tien fu, close to the capital.

But let us return to Black Jade. When her boat was moored and she stepped on to the river-bank, she found awaiting her a sedan chair and a whole crowd of servants and luggage trucks. At home she had often heard her mother speak of the wealth and grandeur in which the relatives in the capital lived. This display of attendance on the journey and upon arrival was a foretaste of what was in store. There on the spot were three kinds of servants, each lot dressed differently. And how well equipped they were, and how well fed and well cared for they looked!

Black Jade resolved to act with the utmost prudence and circumspection in her new home and never to say a word too much. Otherwise she might possibly be laughed at as being provincial and unsophisticated. On the way she could not refrain from peeping out right and left through the silk gauze curtains of the sedan chair, and she could not get over her astonishment at the crowds of people and the great bustle in the streets and squares which surrounded them once they had passed in through the city gates. She had never known anything like that in Yangchow.

After a long march the procession passed, on the right, by a great triple-arched gateway, flanked by two massive cowering marble lions. Each of its three doors had a knocker in the form of an animal's head. About a dozen servants in splendid, brightly colored livery were squatting in front of the doors. Through the side doors, which were open, a lively stream of people were passing in and out. Above the middle door, which was closed, Black Jade read the inscription written on a tablet in five large characters: "Ningkuo palace, built at the Imperial command."

A little farther west her sedan chair was carried through a gateway of similar style and size, and on the same side of the street. This was the entrance to the Yungkuo palace. At first they went straight ahead about the length of an arrow-shot. Then, at a turning, the sedan chair was put down, and four young fellows in smart livery came and took the places of the former bearers. At the same time the female attendants got out of their sedan chairs and from this point followed Black Jade's chair on foot. The procession halted once more, this time at a gate covered with flowering creepers. The bearers stepped back while the female attendants hurried forward, opened the door, and helped Black Jade descend. Supported on either side by a sturdy serving matron, she stepped through the Gate of Flowers. From the Gate of Flowers two covered passages led to an open entrance hall, in the middle of which stood a stone slab, beautifully decorated with strange, landscape-like cross-hatching and supported on a red sandalwood pedestal. This was the spirit screen. Behind the entrance hall the way led through three small pavilions into the great inner courtyard which lay in front of the five-room dwelling of the Princess Ancestress. The building was resplendent in brilliant colors, and the pillars and roof beams were richly carved. Covered verandas, leading here and there through overhanging

黛玉

rocks, extended along the sides of the building which overlooked the courtyard. They were alive with the twittering and screeching of brilliantly colored parakeets and parrots, whose cages were swinging everywhere from the walls and pillars.

Several ladies' maids dressed in red and green were sitting on the steps of the stairway which led to the central apartment of the building. As Black Jade approached they rose and came towards her smiling and curtsying, led her up the steps, and, calling out "Miss Ling is here," drew the glistening curtain cords. Black Jade walked in and found herself facing a group of women; one of them, a silver-haired matron, came forward supported by two servants, one on her right and one on her left.

That must be my grandmother, thought Black Jade to herself, and was about to kneel down to make her kowtow right away. But the Princess Ancestress came up to her and with outstretched arms clasped her to her breast.

"My heart! My liver! Flesh and blood of my child!" she cried in a voice so stifled with emotion that the room became filled with the sounds of sobbing and sniffling, and Black Jade too could not keep back her tears. They all pressed around her speaking loving and comforting words. At last she pulled herself together somewhat and dutifully made her kowtow before the Princess Ancestress. Then the introductions began. "This is your eldest aunt; this is your younger aunt; this is your sister-in-law Chu, the widow of your late cousin, Chia Chu." This went on for quite a while, Black Jade taking a step towards each person and bowing in salutation.

"The three young ladies may come!" said the Princess Ancestress, turning towards the company. "In honor of our guest's arrival they are being excused from their lessons today."

After some time the three girls, Greeting of Spring, Taste of Spring, and Grief of Spring, appeared escorted by three worthy matrons and six young waiting maids. The first was of medium height, plump, with ice-fresh cheeks and a little flat nose which looked as if molded in goose-fat—a charming sight. The second was slender, slim-waisted, with somewhat sloping shoulders, a face oval as a duck's egg, and, beneath perfectly arched brows, two soulful eyes with a most fascinating glance —an arresting sight. The third, as yet too childish in face and form to make a verdict possible. All three were dressed in the same simple way and wore similar agraffes and bangles.

After the introductions were finished the company sat down and drank tea, and then began to overwhelm Black Jade with sympathetic questions. What had her mother's malady been? What medicines had she been given? How did the mourning ceremonies pass off? And so on.

The Ancestress could not get over the fact that her favorite daughter should have gone to her rest before her. Then the attention of all was directed on the new member of the household herself. They found her strikingly grave and mature for her twelve years of age. Her form was so delicate that she seemed scarcely strong enough to bear the trifling weight of her clothing. And yet there was in her transparent, pale face a curious shimmer of voluptuousness and love of life. Anemic, they all thought to themselves.

"You look ailing. Do you do nothing for your malady?" she was asked.

"I have been sickly from my earliest childhood, and ever since I have been old enough to use chopsticks I have been swallowing medicine also. I do not know how many doctors have treated me, but none could help me. I remember when I was three years of age an unkempt, ugly wandering monk wanted to take me away from home and put me into a convent. My parents would not hear of it. Then he told them that in the bosom of my family I would never become a healthy person, because the inevitable daily annoyances and troubles of home life would harm me. I should see no other relatives except my father and mother if I were to be well. Naturally, no one took the talk of the dirty, crazy monk seriously. Since then I have been treating my illness with the health-giving ginseng root and blood-strengthening pills."

"That is sensible," said the grandmother. "Those are also our trusted home remedies, and I shall see that you get your accustomed daily ration of them here too."

She had not finished speaking when the sound of laughter and chatter sounded from the park, and Black Jade heard a woman's clear voice saying: "Oh, I'm terribly late in coming to greet our distinguished guest."

While Black Jade was still wondering who this might be who ventured to burst so gaily and boisterously into the solemn and formal atmosphere surrounding the revered First Lady of the family, she saw a smartly dressed young woman enter, surrounded by a crowd of ladies-in-waiting and maids. She was glittering with jewels and beautiful as a fairy, and her vermilion lips were parted in a sparkling smile. Black Jade had hurriedly risen from her seat.

"You do not know her yet," said the Princess Ancestress to Black Jade with a smile. "This is our famous merry household fairy, without whom we should all be dull and bored. Just call her Phoenix!"

"But I do not even know her real name yet," said Black Jade embarrassed.

"She is your sister-in-law, Lien. Her maiden name is Phoenix," several voices explained to her. Now she could place her. Her mother had often told her about this sister-in-law. She was the beautiful and clever niece of Uncle Cheng's wife, née Wang, and wife of Chia Lien, Prince Shieh's second son. After the formal greetings had been exchanged, Madame Phoenix took the young girl familiarly by the hand and coolly inspected her for several minutes from head to foot. Then she brought her back to her seat by the side of the old Princess and sat down beside her.

"To think that any human form in the world could be so tender and delicate!" she exclaimed, turning to the old lady. "I would not have believed it possible if I had not been convinced of it with my own eyes. The poor little *mei mei!* How sad that she should lose her mother so young!"

She dabbed her eyes with her handkerchief to rub away some tears.

"Do you want to reduce us to tears again? Our eyes are only just dried," said the Princess Ancestress jocosely. "Our guest is tired from the long journey, and besides she has delicate nerves. Better not open the old wound, but let the past rest."

Madame Phoenix obediently resumed her usual merry manner at once. "Grandmother is right and the careless child deserves a slapping," she said, holding out her little lily-white hands with a comic gesture, like a school child who expects to be caned. Once more she took Black Jade by the hand and plied her with every possible question about her age, health, education, favorite dishes, and favorite games. She hoped she would be happy here and not suffer from homesickness, and if she lacked or needed anything, would she please not ask the simple chamberwomen or maids but come straight to her sister-in-law, Phoenix.

"Has Miss Ling's luggage been brought up?" she asked, turning to her attendants. "And are the rooms prepared for the servants whom she has brought with her from Yangchow?"

She attentively handed her guest tea and cake, and then began to discuss with Aunt Cheng practical matters such as household expenses and clothing. Black Jade got the immediate impression that this sister-in-law was the soul of the whole great household.

This first reception was followed by a visit of introduction to Uncle Shieh and Uncle Cheng. At the Gate of Flowers Black Jade, escorted by Aunt Shieh, got into a big, dark blue, lacquered wheel sedan with a light blue silk awning, which was drawn at first by bearers and later by mules which had been specially trained to go at a very gentle pace. For it was a long distance to the residences of the two uncles, and there were many courtyards and gateways to be passed through. At last the sedan chair was set down and Aunt Shieh took Black Jade by the hand

and led her into a reception hall. It seemed to Black Jade that this part of the gigantic homestead must have once been part of the park, so romantically did the various buildings, each highly ornate and of the most superb architectural style, lie nestling among groups of trees and rocks.

Aunt Shieh sent a messenger to the library for her husband, but the Prince excused himself on the plea that he was not feeling well. His niece must make herself quite at home here and not be homesick. Her cousins were in themselves silly and simple little creatures, but when they all got together it would be very pleasant. And if she was ever in any trouble she must not hesitate to open her mouth.

Black Jade remained standing while she listened to this message from her princely uncle. After a short time she took her leave and was then taken in the wheel sedan drawn by mules along the endless paths which led to Uncle Cheng's residence. First she was brought into the central reception hall. She looked around her in astonishment. What splendor and what marvels met her gaze! Raised high on a stand formed of nine intertwined golden dragons stood a tall tablet, on the azure background of which three large ideographs in gold announced that this was the "Hall of Glory and Beatitude." On the wall behind it was an inscription of the date on which the Son of Heaven had honored the first Prince of Yungkuo with this tablet. Wherever she looked she saw works of art with the Imperial sign-manual engraved upon them. Here, on a red sandalwood table with snake-pattern carving, stood an ancient three-foot-high tripod kettle covered with verdigris. There, there glittered magnificent goblets of embossed gold. Here, again, sparkled transparent bowls of crystal. Along the walls stood sixteen carved seats of precious cedarwood. But Black Jade had not nearly enough time to admire all the valuable objects assembled here, for they soon moved on, out of the reception hall, into a tastefully and comfortably furnished living room situated to the east of it. Here there was no lack of snug divan seats in the corners, with cushions and upholstered back-rests, soft armchairs and carpets, and lacquered tea tables all set ready for tea; footstools, incense bowls from which rose bluish wreaths of smoke, as elaborate in formation as beautiful signatures, filling the room with aromatic vapors which vied with the perfume of the fresh flowers that adorned a beautiful porcelain vase fashioned in the form of a woman.

Not far from the window stood a great internally heated couch covered with an exotic scarlet plush overlay. It was divided in two by a low couch table which stood in the center of it covered with books and tea things. To the right and left of this table comfortable back-rests with soft red cushions embroidered with scaly gold dragons held out an invitation to recline.

Aunt Cheng was already reclining at the right side. With a friendly wave of the hand she invited her niece, as she entered, to recline comfortably on the left. But Black Jade said to herself that no doubt the master of the house was accustomed to rest on these cushions and hence it would be unseemly of her to take that place. She therefore modestly sat down on a simply covered chair near the couch, and not until she had been asked three times to do so did she change over to her aunt's side.

"Your uncle is in the temple today, fasting and attending services," said the aunt, "but he will soon come home and greet you. Meantime he has asked me to say a few words to you from him. Your three cousins are all intelligent, well-brought-up girls. You will all learn your lessons nicely together, do needlework and have pleasant games, and I think you will also get on well together. But there is one thing which makes us parents uneasy: we have a truly incorrigible young son who is a real torment and a mischievous imp in the house. He also is in the temple today fulfilling a vow, but he will be back towards evening and then you will get to know him personally. I want you to know the facts in advance. It will be best if you treat him as your cousins do, that is, take as little notice of him as possible and leave him alone."

Black Jade remembered that her mother had often spoken of a nephew who had been born with a jade stone in his mouth and was a somewhat strange, freakish boy who, instead of keeping to his books, loved roaming about the women's quarters playing all sorts of silly pranks, and in spite of this was very much favored and spoiled by his grandmother, with the result that no one dared to be severe with him.

"Ah, Aunt means no doubt the cousin who was born with the jade stone in his mouth?" she asked, smiling. "Mother often spoke of him. He is Pao Yu and is a year older than I, is he not? Mother thought he was just inclined to be easygoing and playful but that otherwise he was very polite and nice to his sisters. Now, I shall be in the company of my girl cousins most of the time, and I shall not have much opportunity of meeting this cousin and provoking him to tricks. The house is so very roomy."

"Oh, do not say that!" replied Aunt Cheng, laughing. "The confounded boy cannot do without the company of girls and will be able to find you even if you do not look for him. As long as the girls do not take notice of him he behaves tolerably, but one word too much from them is enough to make him do the maddest things just through sheer high spirits. So you must remember this and not let yourself be either charmed by his honey-sweet words or frightened by his foolish rages."

A servant entered and said that the old *Tai tai* bade them come to supper. Aunt Cheng took her niece by the hand and led her out through

28

a back exit and across by many zigzag paths. On the way she stopped once and pointed to a dainty house built in three tiers with a veranda running all along the south side.

"Your sister-in-law Phoenix lives here," she said, smiling. "No doubt you will be going in and out here often. Whenever you want anything you have just to go to her."

At last, after much winding in and out, they passed through a covered corridor and found themselves in the garden behind the residence of the Princess Ancestress. The old lady was already awaiting them in the dining room. Despite her modest protests, Black Jade was obliged, as guest, to take the place of honor at her left side. Three chairs to the right and left of the Princess Ancestress remained unoccupied. Actually, they were meant for Aunt Cheng and the two sisters-in-law, Phoenix and Chu. But today these three were in attendance on the Ancestress. Sister-in-law Phoenix placed fresh chopsticks before her for each course, Aunt Cheng served her soup, and sister-in-law Chu served the other dishes to her. Later Aunt Cheng had to sit at her right-hand side. The three "Spring" girls ate at a separate table. The meal was eaten silently and ceremoniously. From the swarm of serving women and girls, of whom some noiselessly carried the dishes in and out while others stood ready in the anteroom with washbasins, dusters, and hand towels, not the slightest cough or clearing of the throat was audible. Black Jade had to be very attentive in order to adapt herself to the many forms of table etiquette which were new to her. For instance, perfumed tea was served immediately after the meal. She was about to drink it reluctantly, for at home she had always been taught that it was harmful to drink tea straight after a meal, but the example of the others soon made it clear to her that this tea was only meant for rinsing out the mouth. With the words "You others may go; I wish to talk to our guest for a little while alone," the Ancestress rose from the table.

"How far have you gone in your reading?" she inquired of her grandchild.

"I have just finished studying the Six Classical Books," replied Black Jade. "And what are my cousins reading?"

"Ah, they can barely understand a few words."

There was a crunching on the gravel outside, and immediately afterwards a servant announced: "Pao Yu is coming."

Black Jade looked towards the entrance in eager expectation. Thereupon he walked in. She was most pleasantly surprised. He wore on his head a purple cap interwoven with gold and trimmed with brightly colored jewels. A golden band in the form of two dragons snapping at a pearl encircled his forehead. His close-fitting dark red jerkin, embroidered with golden butterflies and bright flowers, was fastened with a colored belt woven in a design of flower stems and ears of corn. Over the jerkin he wore a slate-blue satin Japanese cloak, embroidered with eight bunches of flowers, and fringed at the edges. His feet were enveloped in blue satin shoes. His face was as bright as the mid-autumn moon, his color fresh as spring flowers in the morning dew; his hair was as sharply outlined above his temples as if it had been cut with a knife, his eyebrows seemed as if painted on with India ink, the fine outline of his nose betokened boldness of character, his eyes glistened with the wet shine of autumn waves, his mouth seemed to smile even in ill-humor, and his glance radiated warmth and feeling even in anger. A golden chain in the form of a snake encircled his neck, and also a silken cord of five colors from which hung a beautiful stone.

Black Jade was taken completely by surprise at his appearance. It is strange how familiar his features seem to me, just as if I had met him before, she thought to herself.

As soon as the Princess had returned his salutation, she bade him go and say good day to his mother, whereupon he immediately disappeared. When he returned after a little while he was no longer wearing his cap. His front hair was dressed around his head in single short pigtails interwoven with red braid, which were drawn up and joined on the top of his head to form a crown. He wore his back hair in a long jet-black shining pigtail which was wound around a braid decorated with four big pearls and eight golden pendants representing the various emblems of the eight Taoist saints—the Sword, the Flute, the Lotus Flower, and so on. Instead of the blue cloak he now wore a satin coat of a flowered silver and red pattern, below which showed fir-tree-green flowered silk brocade trousers. Dark red thick-soled satin slippers covered his black-stockinged feet. His countenance was, if possible, more radiant than before. The natural color of his cheeks triumphed over the artificial effect of powder and paint, his glance was soulful, his speech was a smile. But his character expressed itself most eloquently in the highly expressive play of his brows. All the hundred human feelings seemed to find place in a corner of his eye.

"Will you not greet your cousin at last?" the Princess Ancestress smilingly asked her favorite, who had sat down politely at her side, apparently overlooking the new cousin completely. But of course he had seen her. He now stood up, went over to the young girl, and with his hands raised to his breast made a slight bow to her. Then he returned to his place and gazed at her for a while fixedly and attentively. He found her different from the other girls. How full of contradictions was the expression of her features! Her eyebrows, like two finely outlined threads of smoke, were close together and seemed to express sor-

寶玉

row, even when she was quite merry. Her soulful eyes looked serious even when she was laughing gaily. She was beautiful, but her beauty was clothed with the cloak of suffering. Her eyes were always glistening as if full of tears. And how faint and soft was her breathing. In repose she was like the dewy reflection of a flower in water. In motion she was like a willow branch trembling in the wind.

"I must have met her before," murmured Pao Yu to himself, lost in thought.

"What ridiculous nonsense you are talking again! How could you have met her already?" His grandmother's voice recalled him to reality.

"But her face—it seems so familiar to me—just as if we had met again after a long, long separation," he murmured.

"All the better, for then you will get on well with her," remarked the old Princess with a smile.

Pao Yu stood up, then sat down right beside his cousin and regarded her once more with attention.

"Have you gone far in your reading of literature, *Mei mei?*" he asked her.

"Not very far. I have had barely two years' education and am still at the beginning," replied Black Jade.

"Were you also born with a jewel in your mouth?"

"No. Such a silly thing as that scarcely happens twice."

Her harmless remark caused him to break into a real rage. He tore the cord with the stone on it from his neck and flung it scornfully on the ground.

"Nasty thing! What do I care about you?" he cried abusively to the stone. "Are you a bit of me, a being endowed with reason, that people make so much fuss about you? Away with you! I am sick of you!"

The ladies-in-waiting stood around the enraged boy, terrified. One of them picked up the cord with the stone and handed it to the old Princess. The Princess hurriedly clasped her grandchild in her arms.

"Control yourself, child!" she said reproachfully. "Be angry with people if you want to. But what harm has this innocent stone, this bit of yourself, done to you, that you treat it so roughly?"

"None of my brothers and sisters has a horrible stone like this attached to them, not even this new angelic cousin," he sobbed. "So it must be a useless, bad thing. I don't like it!"

"Your new cousin also came into the world with a stone like that," lied the grandmother to quiet him. "Out of filial devotion she buried it with her mother, to whom she was greatly attached, so that even in death a bit of herself would be close to her mother. It is through shyness that she has not spoken of it to you. And now be sensible. What would your mother say if she heard of your behavior?"

He became thoughtfully silent and allowed his grandmother to fasten the cord with the stone round his neck with her own hands. A chamber-maid entered and asked where the young lady was to sleep in future.

"We shall change Pao Yu over to my apartments, and Miss Ling can move for the time being into the green pavilion in his place. Later on, when the winter is over, we will arrange another place for her."

"Ah, dear, good Grandmother," begged Pao Yu, "let me stay in the green pavilion! I can sleep quite well in a side-chamber. I am so noisy, I would destroy your peace."

"Very well, you may," the grandmother decided, after a moment's consideration.

Accordingly, from that time the two cousins shared the green pavilion which was part of the premises of the old Princess. Each of the two children had their own personal domestic staff in attendance on them day and night. Black Jade had brought with her from Yangchow her own serving matron, Mother Wang, and a little ten-year-old waiting maid called Snowgoose. The Princess Ancestress found little Snow-goose too young and Mother Wang too old for service, so she gave her granddaughter, in addition to her own household staff, the waiting maid Cuckoo. Besides these she got as her staff half a dozen maids for the light and heavy work, just like her cousins. Pao Yu had an elderly serving matron, Mother Li, and a smart young trustworthy waiting maid. This maid, who enjoyed the special confidence of the Princess Ances-tress, was called Pearl. That night, a long time after it had become quiet in the side-chamber where Pao Yu slept, the maid Pearl noticed that there was still light in the inner bedroom, and that people were talking there. Being curious, she slipped in in her nightdress. She found Black Jade sitting on the edge of her bed talking to the maid Cuckoo.

"Why is the young lady still up?" she asked, astonished.

"Sit down, sister," Black Jade invited her amiably. Pearl also sat down on the edge of the bed. Then Cuckoo made her report. The young lady had been weeping in a heart-rending way this first evening, she said. Her eyes had filled with tears again and again as soon as she wiped them dry. She was disconsolate over having provoked the son of the house to a fit of rage at their very first meeting, and she felt she was a bringer of misfortune.

"Dear young lady, you should not take a thing like that so tragi-cally," said Pearl, smiling at Black Jade. "I fear you will experience much more crazy and extraordinary behavior from him in the future. If you take everything to heart like that, I fear you will become quite ill with heart trouble. You must not be so sensitive!"

"Thank you, sister! I will think of what you say," said Black Jade, somewhat calmed, and soon afterwards she was able to get to sleep at last.

When Black Jade went next morning with her cousins to wish Aunt Cheng good morning as usual, they found the aunt and Phoenix in lively conversation over a letter from a relative, which two messengers had just brought from the town. Black Jade only half understood what the lively discussion was about. Her cousins enlightened her. The letter was from Uncle Wang, an elder brother of Aunt Cheng, and concerned a distressing affair in which their nephew Hsueh Pan was involved. Young Hsueh Pan, a son of Aunt Cheng's sister, presuming on the power of the family to protect him, had killed a rival in a quarrel, and was now to answer for it before the Prefect of Ying tien fu. You will learn from the next chapter the ramifications of this painful affair, and how it is connected with our story.

CHAPTER 4

An unfortunate girl finds an unfortunate suitor. A little bonze from the Temple of the Gourd acts as judge.

As already mentioned, after his reinstatement Yu Tsun got the position of Prefect of Ying tien fu thanks to the patronage he received through the influence of Lin Ju Hai and his brother-in-law Cheng. Immediately after he took up office the case of a murder committed in his district less than a month previously came before him for hearing. In a quarrel over the ownership of a pretty slave girl one buyer had had his rival beaten to death. The plaintiff was the servant of the murdered man. In his evidence he declared:

"The murdered man was my master. My master had bought the slave fairly from her owner, a child-thief, and had also paid the purchase price, but it was arranged that he was only to bring the slave to his house three days later, because that day was stated in the calendar to be a lucky day. Now the rogue of a child-thief had used this interval to secretly sell the slave a second time, namely, to a man named Hsueh Pan. My master heard in time of this deal and set off to fetch the girl from the slave dealer, but the servants of that brutal fellow Hsueh Pan, who, relying on the power of his family, has contempt for law and justice, stopped him by force and beat him to death with sticks. The culprits then made off with the slave girl, and there has been no trace of them since. It is already a month since I made a charge, but your predecessor in office did not take up the case. I beg of you to have the murderers traced and to give them the punishment they deserve, that justice may be done and innocence may triumph over wickedness."

When Yu Tsun had listened to the end, he angrily hit the judge's table with his fist.

"What! A murderer is let go scot-free! How is that possible?" he cried indignantly. "I shall immediately write out warrants for arrest, and send detectives to the relatives of the murderer. And if they do not disclose the whereabouts of the murderer voluntarily, they will be tortured!"

He was just about to take up his writing brush when he noticed that one of the yamen secretaries who were standing around the judge's table winked at him quite visibly. He realized that the secretary obviously wished to communicate something of importance to him, so he laid down his brush, interrupted the sitting, and withdrew to his private office. There he spoke privately to the official concerned.

"The old Governor has probably completely forgotten my humble self since he came into his high administrative office?" began the man with a cunning smile. "But of course it is already eight or nine years since we met."

"As a matter of fact, your face is very familiar to me, but I cannot really recall at the moment . . ."

"Yes, indeed, when fortune smiles on them, great gentlemen do not like to look back upon their early struggles. But you surely still remember the Temple of the Gourd?"

Now Yu Tsun knew who he was.

"Why, of course, you were the young brother who used to clean the incense vessels and had the cell next to mine in the Temple of the Gourd in those days. Tell me, how have you been getting on since then?" he said laughing, and amiably invited the other to take a seat.

But the man who was now a yamen secretary remained politely standing and recounted briefly how he was homeless after the burning of the Temple of the Gourd, but soon decided to let his hair grow again and, having long since tired of the cold and dreary convent life, became a yamen servant.

"But now sit down!" said Yu Tsun, giving him a friendly push onto a chair; but the other only ventured to sit shyly on the edge of it. "Old friendships made in times of poverty and want should not be forgotten. Moreover, we are now in my private office and not in a public court. So why this ceremony? But now explain why you winked at me just now as I was about to write out the order for arrest."

"Has no Protection List been placed before you since you have been in office here?"

"What do you mean by Protection List?"

35

"It is customary nowadays for government officials in the provinces to keep a secret list of the names of all the specially prominent, well-off, and influential citizens domiciled in their district, above all the 'Wearers of the Belt,' or former high officials who have important connections with government circles at the Court. A prudent provincial magistrate will take great care not to come into conflict with these important people, otherwise he endangers his position or in certain circumstances even his life. That is why it is called the Protection List. Now, that man Hsueh Pan is one of the prominent people of the district whom one dare not annoy. That is why your predecessor in office did not take any steps in the murder case, although Hsueh Pan's guilt is quite obvious."

While he was speaking he took from his pocket a folded paper which he handed to Yu Tsun. It was the Protection List which he kept for his personal use. Yu Tsun found it full of the names of the leading families in the district, and beside the individual names, written in the common tongue, were marginal notes of what people said about the families in question. Among others he read the four names Chia, Shih, Wang, and Hsueh.

"These four powerful families," the secretary explained to him, "are all blood relations or connected by marriage, and are bound together for good or ill. The punishment you mete out to one family hits all four; the honor you show to one family is shared by the others. Besides this powerful family bloc at his back, the murderer Hsueh Pan also has an influential connection at the Court and in the provinces. If you now issue a warrant for the arrest of his supporters, how many people will you actually have to lock up?"

"Hm. I had not thought of that. But what line am I to take in this matter, then? Evidently the murderer's whereabouts are well known to you?"

The secretary gave a cunning smile.

"If I may speak frankly, old Governor, I may say that I know not only the whereabouts of the murderer but also a good deal about the other persons implicated, the murdered man, the slave dealer, and the slave girl. If you will be so kind as to listen to me patiently, I will tell you the whole story absolutely correctly.

"The murdered man was named Feng. He came from a modest family of civil servants, and since his parents died, having no brothers or sisters to share the heritage, he was able to live modestly on what his father left him. The twenty-year-old was by nature averse to women, and preferred the companionship of men. Probably Providence intended to make him atone for some crime committed in a previous existence when to his misfortune it led him to that child-thief who had the slave girl. At all events, quite contrary to his usual habits, he became infatuated with the slave girl at first sight, decided to make her his concubine, and renounced all intercourse with men for the future. The fool took the matter so seriously that he even looked up a lucky day in the calendar for taking home the girl, and that was the third day after he had made the bargain and paid the purchase price.

"The cunning slave dealer now took it into his head to avail of the interval to sell the girl again for cash, this time to Hsueh Pan. But before he could clear off with the double proceeds, he fell into the hands of the two rivals, neither of whom wanted his money back, but both of whom wanted possession of the girl. So he was nearly beaten dead by the two of them. Then the two rivals fell upon each other. Thanks to his large suite of servants, Hsueh Pan had the advantage. Those fellows beat the unfortunate Feng until he was so weak that he could not stir any more. He died three days later. But his rival then went off to the capital with his booty and his suite of servants, not as a fugitive, but quite coolly, openly, and at his ease, like any innocent traveller, just as if nothing at all had happened. But now comes the most remarkable part of the story. Who do you think that slave girl was?"

"How should I know that?"

"Little Lotus, the daughter of your great friend and patron, Shih Ying, of your Temple of the Gourd days!"

"What on earth are you saying? But she was hardly three years old when she was stolen that time on the evening of the Lantern Festival. And you say the thief was only selling her now, eight years later?"

"It is the custom of child-thieves to keep the little girls they steal and bring them up until they are twelve or thirteen years of age and then put them on the market in another part of the country. So the man who stole our little Lotus kept her hidden in his lair near Suchow for eight years, and then he brought her here to Ying tien fu to sell her. I am not mistaken; I definitely recognized her again. For during his stay here the thief actually lodged in the same house where I do, with the little girl.

"We monks of the Temple of the Gourd were on the most friendly and neighborly terms with little Lotus. The trustful child used to come over to the temple every day and we used to play with her and have all sorts of fun. That is why her face remained impressed upon my memory. Her features have developed and gained in their beautiful proportions in the course of the years, but they have remained essentially the same. Besides, I recognized her by her birthmark, a freckle the size of a grain of rice between her eyebrows above the bridge of her nose.

"Once when the slave dealer was out and she was alone in the house, I went to her and questioned her urgently, but she was unwilling to speak out. She must not speak or she would be beaten, she said, quite scared, and she insisted that the thief was her father, who had to sell her to pay his debts. When I continued to press her with questions she began to weep and said she could not remember her early childhood. But later on she betrayed herself. The day that young Feng bought her I listened at the door and spied into the room through a crack. The slave dealer had celebrated the deal with young Feng and had got thoroughly tipsy. Believing herself unobserved, Lotus let a deep sigh of relief escape her. 'Today my debt from a former existence has at last been paid off!' she cried. But when she heard that she would be fetched by her suitor only three days later, her cheerfulness changed to sadness.

"I watched out for the next time that she was alone, and sent my wife to her room to speak words of comfort to her. My wife said to her that the fact that young Feng was waiting for a lucky day to take her home showed that he had honorable and serious intentions towards her, and looked on her as a wife and not as a slave; since this man, who had always been known as a woman-hater, had paid a heap of money for her, he must be very much in love with her indeed. She should wait patiently for the three days, then her lucky hour would come, and she would find a pleasant life and a good home. At this she became more tranquil.

"Who would have thought it would all turn out quite differently? The following day the rogue of a slave dealer sold the poor thing again, this time to that fellow Hsueh Pan. If it had been anyone else at all it would not have been so bad. But that this brutal libertine and spendthrift, who is known among the people as 'the Mad Robber Count,' should become her master—that was the last straw! Showering blows on her as thick as autumn leaves, he dragged the poor thing away with him, more dead than alive. One can really feel sorry for her hapless suitor, young Feng. His joy came to nought, and he sacrificed his life and his money in vain."

Yu Tsun sighed deeply.

"The poor things! Who knows what crimes they may have committed in a former existence, since they have to atone so much now. For the girl is also to be pitied. True, her first suitor could not offer her anything like the comfort and the luxury which she now enjoys in the house of the second, but on the other hand she must share with many other women the favor of a spoiled, bad-tempered pleasure-seeker, whereas in the house of the other she would have been the only wife and mistress. But what's the good of philosophizing afterwards? For me, the important thing just now is to make a wise decision."

"Esteemed sir, long ago in the Temple of the Gourd you used to be a very shrewd, clearheaded man. Therefore, after so many years' professional experience, it really should not be difficult for you to come to a decision. After all, you owe your present position to the patronage of these same families Chia and Wang, who belong to the set of that Hsueh Pan. Do you want to fight against the stream and annoy your protectors? I advise you to drop the matter gracefully, so that you may be able to look your patrons in the face without embarrassment in the future!"

"Hm, that sounds reasonable. Nevertheless, it's a matter of a human life. How could I dare to repay, by acting with partiality and defeating the ends of justice, the trust which the Son of Heaven has placed in me!"

"You may be right in theory. But in practice, unfortunately, one cannot always heed such moral considerations nowadays. 'The wise man adapts himself to circumstances,' says the old maxim. 'The wise man strives for a friendly settlement and avoids wicked conflict,' runs another trustworthy rule. If you were to act strictly according to theory, you would very soon lose your position and consequently no longer be able to justify the confidence of the Son of Heaven; indeed, you would actually risk losing your head."

Yu Tsun was thoughtful for a moment.

"Good. What, then, in your opinion, should be done?"

"I have a splendid plan. When you continue with the case again to-morrow, play the severe, pitiless judge, shout and rage and issue a warrant for the arrest of the murderer Hsueh Pan. Do not put it into force, however, but, instead, just to appease the other side, have some unimportant members of his household here arrested, and examine them! I will visit these people in their prison cell behind your back and let them know that the matter is not to be taken so seriously, and that they should say at their examination that their master, the murderer Hsueh Pan, has meantime died of a sudden illness. Moreover, I will see to it that a death certificate made out by the chief members of the Hsueh clan, and the officials of the Ward concerned, is produced.

"In the further course of the hearing, in order to stifle any possible discontent on the part of the people, you will play a little at calling up spirits and stage a public performance with an altar of sacrifice and magic wands, and cause the spirits of the dead to announce that they had been enemies in a former existence and, meeting on a narrow pathway, had killed one another; that the murderer Hsueh Pan had been afflicted with a malignant disease by the avenging spirit of the murdered Feng, and had also died. Therefore, the murder was already atoned for, and apart from punishing the fraudulent slave dealer, there was no necessity for the authorities to pursue the matter further.

"If you wish to do something more, you can sentence the Hsueh family to compensate the relatives of the murdered man for the costs of his burial. The Hsueh family are rich. They will not mind paying five hundred or a thousand ounces. The dead man's relatives are insignificant, humble people. They will be glad to get a nice sum of money into their hands and to shut their mouths. What do you think of this little plan?"

"Impossible!" said Yu Tsun with an evasive laugh. "But I'll think the matter over again."

He did not need to consider for long before deciding on the plan. And then he carried it out, point for point, just as his adviser had whispered to him, with the result that there was no murmuring among the people, and both parties were satisfied. Finally he wrote two letters, to Chia Cheng and Marshal Wang Tzu Teng, the influential uncles of the criminal, informing them that the proceedings against their worthy nephew had been satisfactorily settled and that they need not be the least troubled about it any more. And thus, thanks to the cunning idea of a former little monk from the Temple of the Gourd, law and justice were set aside and a painful lawcase was liquidated in an ingenious way.

But after this Yu Tsun found the proximity of the unpleasing sharer of his secret disturbing and uncomfortable. It pained him to think that the former temple bonze might tell tales or by careless gossip disclose to the people the obscure, miserable past of the present highly respected magistrate. Therefore on the excuse that the secretary had acted in a blameworthy manner in the execution of his duties, he took the first available opportunity to pack him off to a distant position in his district. But this is enough about Yu Tsun for the present. Let us now talk about Hsueh Pan.

Although descended from a good family redolent from generation to generation of the highest culture, Hsueh Pan, as the only son of an early-widowed mother, had been spoiled and pampered from childhood, and deprived of any serious discipline or guidance, and had only had a very superficial education. Thanks to old and good connections, which he owed to his forefathers, and to having inherited a fortune of some millions of taels, he had procured the lucrative position of a privileged buyer for the Imperial Wardrobe; but apart from the fact that his name stood in the register of contractors of the Ministry of Finance and that he regularly drew his emoluments, he left the actual execution of his official duties to his agents and trusted employees, as he understood nothing about business. He himself lived completely for his passions, and passed his time in cockfighting, horse racing, and riotous living. He was a spendthrift and a voluptuary, a licentious, brutal fellow of rough manners and arrogant speech.

His mother, a sister of Marshal Wang Tzu Teng of the capital and of the wife of Chia Cheng of the Yungkuo palace, was now forty years of age, and besides this son she also had a daughter about thirteen years of age, named Pao Chai, "Precious Clasp." In her soft, rounded beauty, Precious Clasp resembled a smoothly polished, glistening agate. But her perfect polish was not only physical. Thanks to her great zeal for learning and to the care her late father had bestowed upon her education from earliest childhood, she was ten times better educated than her brother, Hsueh Pan, who was her senior. But when she realized that her widowed mother could expect no real help from her ill-behaved elder child, she had laid aside her books for the past few years in order to relieve her mother of the household worries, like a good, conscientious daughter.

On account of her outstanding virtues and qualities, she had recently been placed on the list of the young women annually chosen from among the respected families of the nobility and mandarin class throughout the Empire, to be presented at Court and retained there, some as concubines of the Emperor, others as ladies of the Court and chaperons to the Princesses. For the present Son of Heaven valued the exalted teachings and philosophical writings of Master Confucius, and desired that the Princesses at the Court should be favorably influenced and encouraged to exemplary behavior by the companionship of girls educated in the classics.

Now, when Hsueh Pan decided to escort his sister to the Court, he did so for three reasons. First of all, he wished to take the opportunity of visiting his relatives in the capital; secondly, he wished to present himself to his employers, the Ministry of Finance, and to settle some official business matters; but the third and most potent reason of all was that he wanted to enjoy himself. For it had always been his desire to know the capital with its splendor and gay life, of which he had heard so much praise.

All preparations for the journey had already been made, the numerous trunks as well as the presents intended for the friends and relatives had been packed, and a favorable day for departure looked up in the calendar, when the previously mentioned incident with the slave dealer happened, in the course of which the unfortunate Feng lost his life and little Lotus fell into the hands of Hsueh Pan. Leaving the household in the care of some of the older trusted servants, Hsueh Pan had set out for the capital with his mother, sister, concubines, baggage, and servants, on the prearranged day. The affair of the murder did not trouble him in the least; to him it was just a trifle which could be disposed of with a handful of dirty coins.

Actually, Madame Hsueh had intended to stay with her brother Marshal Wang in the capital. But shortly before they reached the walls of the Imperial City news reached them that Marshal Wang had just been appointed Imperial Marshal of the Nine Provinces and had received orders to proceed without delay on a tour of inspection of the frontiers. This news was a secret relief to Hsueh Pan. Now, he said to himself, he would be free of the irksome authority and supervision of his uncle and have absolute freedom for his pleasures, and he thanked heaven for having disposed matters according to his wishes. The altered circumstances now rendered a family council necessary.

"We should send some of our servants on in advance to fix up one of our own houses which has been unused for years," the son suggested. The mother was against this.

"Why all this fuss? What have we got relatives for? We can stay either with my brother Wang or my brother-in-law Cheng. There is plenty of room in the Yungkuo palace. We can still move into one of our own houses later on."

"Uncle Wang is in the midst of preparations for his journey to the frontier; his house is in confusion. It would really be somewhat tactless of us to invade him like a swarm of hornets," said the son, doubtfully.

"You are right. Well, then we shall go to the Yungkuo palace. My sister has invited me again and again to visit her, so she will be happy to have us as her guests. But I quite understand that you want to be free and unhampered, so you may go and look for quarters of your choice wherever you like. But I shall go and stay in the Yungkuo palace with Precious Clasp."

Naturally, Hsueh Pan could not go off and leave his family right at the beginning; that would have made a bad impression on the relatives. So, suppressing his displeasure, he submitted to his mother's wish and sent off messengers to announce their arrival at the Yungkuo palace. There the travellers were received with the greatest cordiality, and both the Princess Ancestress and Aunt Cheng urged them to stay on. Uncle Cheng had a suite of ten unused rooms prepared for the guests in the southeastern tip of his domain—the so-called Pear Garden.

The Pear Garden was a delightful pleasure house set in enchanting surroundings in the park, the favorite dwelling of the first Prince of Yungkuo in his old age. With its grounds it formed a separate, walled-off area within the estate. To the inside it was connected with the dwelling of Aunt Cheng by a little gate and a narrow path, and to the outside it had its own exit to the street. This latter fact was specially pleasing to Hsueh Pan, for it enabled him to go in and out unimpeded and without the annoyance of his movements' being checked at the gate. Altogether, the displeasure he had felt when moving in diminished more and more. His fear that his uncles would supervise him at every step proved unfounded. Uncle Cheng had his ministerial work, and Prince Shieh, who as elder had first authority in the place, was far too easygoing to bother himself about the goings-on of the many different inmates of the house. He preferred to meditate in his library and over a chessboard and only wanted to be left undisturbed. Hsueh Pan on his part found among the various male cousins in the two palaces just the companions he needed. Most of these cousins wore "silk trousers" and "airy coats"—jovial, merry young people, from whom even he could learn much in the art of *savoir-vivre*. If he had a wish for a little game of cards, a drinking bout, a stroll through the town, or an amorous adventure, there was always suitable company to be found for it. In short, Hsueh Pan had no cause to complain of boredom, and made himself so much at home in his new surroundings that in the course of one month all thought of changing his quarters had vanished. How the main story goes, after this digression, will be seen from the next chapter.

CHAPTER 5

The spirit of Pao Yu wanders about in the Phantom Realm of the Great Void. The Fairy of Fearful Awakening vainly interprets for him in songs the Dream of the Red Chamber.

VERY SOON BLACK JADE HAD BECOME THE AVOWED FAVORITE OF THE Princess Ancestress, and was put before the other grandchildren in every respect, just like Pao Yu. These two had become as closely attached to each other as glue and lacquer and were now an inseparable pair. In the daytime they sat side by side and went about hand in hand; in the evening they stood taking a long and affectionate leave of one another and slept wall to wall.

Now this new cousin had suddenly come to the house. Although not much older than the other cousins, Precious Clasp was so polished in her manners and of such charming appearance that according to the general verdict even Black Jade was not her equal. Besides, she knew how to win the hearts of all, even the servants, by her friendly, compassionate ways, whereas Black Jade was a solitary individual and went around with her head in the air. With secret annoyance in her heart, Black Jade felt herself displaced in the general popularity by her new cousin, and her annoyance turned to resentment when she perceived that even Pao Yu was not untouched by her charm.

Pao Yu was still too immature to discriminate tactfully between an old privileged friendship and a new acquaintance; for him one cousin was the same as another. In short, Black Jade felt offended whenever he said a friendly word too much to Precious Clasp, and this led to many scenes of jealousy in the course of which she would rush weeping to her room, and in the end forgive the faithless one again and again when he would come running after her with bowed head and apologize to her with youthful impetuosity.

One day at the time of the plum blossoms Prince and Princess Chen had invited the near-by relatives to visit them in the Ningkuo palace. After the company had walked about for a while in the Garden of Assembled Perfumes, which was shimmering in the full splendor of blossomtime, they all sat down at one great table to the usual family feast, about which there is nothing special to say.

At the end of the meal Pao Yu felt sleepy and expressed the wish to lie down for a while. Mistress Yung, the beautiful young daughter-in-law of Prince Chen, undertook to conduct him herself to a room which she thought seemed suitable for a midday nap. It was a small, beautifully and comfortably furnished guestroom, but two mottoes which decorated one of the walls caused the boy obvious discomfort. For when he read:

> For knowledge of nature and the world
> Do not neglect the sciences.
> For knowledge of the human heart
> Devote yourself to the study of history

he turned petulantly back and said: "Let us get out quickly!" His beautiful companion thereupon laughingly offered to give him her own bedroom.

"But, Mistress, the uncle cannot well sleep in the niece's bed; that would be contrary to all good form," objected a chamberwoman, who was in attendance.

"Ah, why be so prudish? The uncle is after all still a boy," replied the young woman, laughing, and leading Pao Yu, who in kinship was in fact her uncle but in age could well be her nephew, into her bedroom. As he entered he was met by a wave of delightful perfume which intoxicated his senses and melted his bones.

"Oh, it smells nice here!" he remarked with pleasure, and his pleasure increased when he saw a painting by Master T'ang Pei Hu representing someone sleeping beneath begonia branches in early spring, and read the following words written to the right and left of it:

> Gentle coolness surrounds the dreamer—early spring!
> The breezes which caress him—fragrant as wine!

In silent admiration Pao Yu let his eyes wander round the splendid furnishings of the room. Here on the dressing table was a bronze mirror which would have done honor to the mirror palace of the Empress Wu of the T'ang dynasty. There was a magnificent flat golden dish on which the celebrated dancer "Flying Swallow" might once have danced before her Imperial lord. That splendid jewel-studded couch on a raised dais would have been worthy to adorn the bedroom of Princess Shou Yang in the Han Chang palace. The strings of pearls which hung around the couch might have been fastened there by the hand of Princess Tung Chang.

"What a beautiful room!" cried Pao Yu, enraptured.

"Yes, isn't it? Even spirits and genii could feel happy here," remarked his niece, smiling.

Saying this, she threw off the blossom-white bedcover with her own hand, and arranged the soft pillow embroidered with mandarin ducks, which the "Red Maiden" might once have clasped to her bosom as she yearned for her lover. The swarm of waiting maids and chamberwomen helped Pao Yu to undress and put him to bed on the couch; and then they all withdrew noiselessly. Pearl and three other chambermaids had to keep watch outside the bedroom door.

"Take good care that the cats do not start fighting under the window and disturb your master's rest!" Mistress Yung impressed upon them thoughtfully.

Hardly had Pao Yu shut his eyes than he felt himself carried away into a land of dreams. His beautiful niece seemed to hover in front of him and lead him to a fairy palace with walls of jasper and pillars and balustrades of ruby, surrounded by the rustling of treetops and the murmur of silver brooks.

"It's good to be here," he sighed happily in his dream. "I much prefer being here to being at home, where I am always watched and always expecting blame and scoldings from Father and Mother." His guide had disappeared in the meantime. He listened. From somewhere or other beautiful celestial singing like a woman's voice resounded in his ears. Immediately afterwards he saw a most lovely fairy appearing from behind a hill and gently floating towards him. Pao Yu raised his hands to his breast in greeting and said to her, bowing: "Sister fairy, I have lost my way. Would you be so kind as to direct me, and tell me who you are?"

The fairy replied: "I am the Fairy of Fearful Awakening. I live not far from here, in the Phantom Realm of the Great Void, in the Sphere of Banished Suffering, behind the Drenching Sea of Trouble, on the Heights of Liberated Spring, in the Grottoes of Everlasting Perfumes. I judge the Play of Wind and Clouds between human beings and settle the unbalanced debts of love between unhappy maidens and languishing youths. It is not chance but destiny which leads me to you today. I shall lead you to my kingdom and entertain you in my palace with a bowl of celestial tea plucked by myself and a goblet of magic wine which I have brewed. My maids shall entertain you with their magic dances and sing to you the twelve new spirit songs from 'The Dream of the Red Chamber.' Will you follow me?"

"I will," agreed Pao Yu joyfully and followed the fairy. It was not long until the fairy led him through a high stone arch, over which he read the inscription: Phantom Realm of the Great Void. On the pillars to the right and left was written:

> When seeming is taken for being, being becomes seeming,
> Where nothing is taken for something, something becomes nothing.

Very shortly they passed through a palace gateway, over which was written in big letters: Sea of Lover's Grief and Heaven of the Passions, while to right and left stood written:

> Passions without end, old and new,
> Swell broad as the earth, wide as the sky.
> Too late, amorous youth, languishing maid, is your repentance,
> Ah, to atone for the guilt of wind- and moon-play costs pain!

That's true, thought Pao Yu to himself, in his innocence. If only I knew what is meant by "passions old and new" and by "to atone for the guilt of wind- and moon-play." I must certainly find out through personal experience.

In making this resolution he had unconsciously invited the wicked demons of sensual agitation to come into his body and take up their abode between his heart and his diaphragm.

After passing through another gateway, they came to a row of apartments, on the closed doors of which he read strange inscriptions such as Department of Love's Folly, Department of Jealousy, Department of Morning Tears, Department of Night Sighs, Department of Spring Grief, Department of Autumn Suffering.

Pao Yu asked if he might view the different chambers. The fairy shook her head. In the apartments, she said, there were registers of the memorable destinies of numerous women and girls, of whom some had already lived and others were yet to live. To a human being like himself, with his profane eyes and his body of dust, it was not to be granted to glance into the future. "Follow me," she said. "I have something far more beautiful to show you than these tiresome registers."

Pao Yu followed the fairy farther into the interior of the palace, until they came to a glittering hall. His eyes were quite dazzled by the splendors which appeared before him here: walls of jasper, floors of gold mosaic, glistening panes of glass, purple curtains in front of red doors, luminous colored pillars, artistically carved roof beams, and all around gardens full of spirit plants, and marvellous flowers, and rare

警幻

perfumes. While Pao Yu was still sunk in amazed contemplation, he heard the fairy call in to the hall: "Come out and greet your worthy guest!" Immediately four elves appeared at the entrance. They wore light feather garments, lotus leaves hung from their shoulders as sleeves, their stride was a dance, their walk was a glide, a gentle radiance like autumn moonlight enveloped them. When they noticed Pao Yu, a look of disappointment crossed their flower faces, and they said reproachfully to the fairy: "We thought you were bringing Purple Pearl, for whom we have waited so long, to visit us. Why do you bring this dirty creature here instead, and allow him to soil and profane by his presence this dwelling of pure maidens?"

Pao Yu heard this with shame, and he would have liked to run away at once. He was well aware of the fact that they were right, and that in the presence of these pure beings he really seemed an insufferably dirty person. But the fairy took him kindly by the hand and said to the elves with a smile: "You do not know the why and the wherefore of my action. I really wanted to go to the Yungkuo palace today, as I had promised you, to fetch your sister, Purple Pearl. But as I was passing by the Ningkuo palace on my way there, I met the ghosts of the two ancestors of the Yungkuo and Ningkuo palaces. They implored me to take charge of their descendant Pao Yu. After a hundred years of fame and splendor their families are threatened with ruin, and among their many great-grandchildren Pao Yu is the only one who is capable of perpetuating the race in honor. It is true that he is of a somewhat peculiar and frivolous disposition, but his intellect and talents justify the greatest hopes. All he lacks is the right guidance. Therefore, they earnestly asked me to warn him of the dangers of foolishly trifling with love and following the instincts without restraint, to guard him against pitfalls and allurements and direct him on the right path. They would be grateful to me forever if I do this.

"Moved with pity, I have brought him here in order to have him learn and realize the folly of earthly sensual indulgence. Perhaps it will be possible to awaken him, so that he will take my warnings to heart for his future life, and so become proof against dangers."

When she had finished speaking she led Pao Yu into the hall. Inside, a wave of indescribably sweet perfume, such as he had never smelled before, assailed his nostrils. When he asked what the perfume came from, the fairy informed him, smiling: "In your world of dust this aromatic mixture is quite unknown. It is distilled from the manifold juices of precious young plants and rare trees which grow on holy mountains. It is called the Marrow of Gathered Perfumes."

They sat down at the table and drank a most wonderful tea, such as Pao Yu had never before tasted.

"What is the name of this kind of tea?" he asked.

"A thousand red drops in one mouthful," replied the fairy. "The shrub grows near the Grottoes of Everlasting Perfumes on the Heights of Liberated Spring, and its leaves are boiled in the morning dew of magic flowers and plants."

"It is a wonderful tea!" said Pao Yu approvingly, nodding his head. He looked around the room once more. His glance fell on jewel-studded lutes, precious tripods, incense vessels, old paintings, new mottoes on the walls. Nothing required for the equipment of a comfortable living room was lacking. There were even velvet dusters hanging under the windows to wipe away the dust from time to time. Then he asked the names of the elves. The fairy introduced them: Elf of Amorous Dreams, Great Mistress of Passion, Golden Maiden of Sorrowful Longing, Bodhisattva of Avenged Lovers' Rancor.

Meantime young maidservants had laid the table. They now carried in a sumptuous meal and filled amber goblets with a choice golden wine from crystal jugs.

"What is this wonderful wine?" asked Pao Yu.

"It is prepared from the pollen of a hundred flowers, the juices of a thousand plants, the marrow of unicorns, and the milk of the phoenix, and it is called A Thousand Delights in One Goblet."

Pao Yu did not weary of drinking the wine freely and praising it fervently. Meantime twelve dancing maidens had appeared and taken up positions in front of the table.

"To what text shall we dance?" they asked the fairy.

"To the twelve new spirit songs from 'The Dream of the Red Chamber'!" the fairy ordered.

The dancers bowed obediently and began to sing and dance to the gentle music of their twelve-stringed silver lutes and the measure of their sandalwood castanets. In order that he might understand it better, the fairy ordered a servant to hand her guest the written text of the twelve songs, and now he sat and tried to understand the meaning of the performance, listening to the music while his eyes followed the text. Yet his efforts were in vain. True, he could not escape the effect of the music, but what the text, with its many cryptic sayings and hidden allusions, might mean remained a complete mystery to him. But the melody was so exquisite and charming and so superbly performed as to bewitch the mind and intoxicate the senses, and he asked no troublesome questions in the intervals, but only listened to the music while just reading the text mechanically.

At last the girls had finished the long performance of the twelve songs. Actually, they were about to continue with a last refrain, but the fairy, who had noticed the sleepy indifference of her guest, signed to them to go away.

"It was all in vain," she sighed. "The fool has remained un-awakened."

Pao Yu was glad that the fairy stopped the performance, and he him-self hurriedly called out to the girls not to sing any more. He felt ex-hausted and sleepy from the meal and the abundance of wine, and asked if he might lie down for a while.

The fairy gave orders to clear away, and had Pao Yu led into one of the women's chambers. He thought he had never in his life seen such luxurious furnishings as he saw here. But a still greater surprise awaited him. He found in the room a young girl who resembled his cousin Precious Clasp in form and beauty but in expression and demeanor was the image of his cousin Black Jade. While he was still feeling quite dazed, he heard the fairy say: "Ah, how many green-windowed inner chambers in the houses of the rich and aristocratic of this world of dust are misused by frivolous youth for sinful amorous play! The reason that I take such a kindly interest in you is that you are the most in-veterate amorous profligate of all time."

Pao Yu stammered, abashed: "Sister fairy, you are mistaken. It may be that I am lazy at lessons and have brought on myself deserved parental rebuke. But I am not aware that I am an amorous profligate. After all, I am still too young and I do not know what it is to be profligate in love."

"There are two kinds of amorous profligates, the carnal and the intellectual ones. The first strives only for physical possession; he is in-satiable in his sensual desires, and regrets he cannot have all the beau-tiful women and girls under heaven as prey for his lusts. You do not be-long to that category, but to the second. Your dissolute desire seeks the intellectual company of girls, therefore you would have been quite a suitable mate for the women's apartments of our spirit kingdom; whereas in the world of dust you will not be understood; there you will become an object of mockery and contempt. Touched by the pleadings of your two ancestors, I have led you into my kingdom, welcomed you with magic tea and fairy wine, and tried to awaken you with spirit songs. Now I present to you my younger sister, Ko Ching, so that she may share your couch tonight. The hour for your union is favorable. The joys of this bridal couch in our Phantom Realm will enable you to form an estimate of the delights of the bridal chamber in your world of dust. From today on wake up and change your former ways! Direct your mind to the wise teachings of the Masters Confucius and Mencius and resolutely tread the path of common sense."

When she had finished speaking she confided to him some further intimate information regarding the practice of the "Play of Cloud and Rain." Then she shut him into the chamber. Still quite confused and stupefied, Pao Yu followed her instructions and carried out with Ko Ching that time-honored practice of which an exhaustive description would no doubt be superfluous.

The two found so much delight in each other and had so many caressing and affectionate words to say to one another that they did not want to part the next morning. Hand in hand, they walked out of the palace and got lost wandering about. They were so engrossed in each other that they did not notice the road at all. Suddenly they found themselves in a wilderness of thorn bushes and thick brushwood and saw that wolves and tigers were their travelling companions. Then the road suddenly came to an end. They were standing on the bank of a dark rushing stream, over which no bridge led. While they were still hesitating as to where they should flee from the wild beasts which were pursuing them, they heard the warning voice of the fairy behind them, crying: "Stop! Do not go farther! Turn back!"

"Where are we?" asked Pao Yu.

"At the Witches' River," cried the fairy. "It is a thousand fathoms deep and runs a thousand li in zigzag windings. No boat and no boatman can find the way through this labyrinthine stream. Only the old ferryman Mu Ku Chi would be able to take you across in his raft. But he does not do this for gold or silver; he does it only if Destiny commands him. If he does not help you, then you are lost, and all my trouble will have been in vain. . . ." She had not finished speaking when a sound like a peal of thunder came from the Witches' River, and a swarm of night demons and river devils rose up from the river with a roaring sound and came fluttering up to Pao Yu shrieking terribly, to seize him and drag him into the depths of the river. Cold sweat dripped from his body like rain, and in his terror he cried out: "Ko Ching, save me!"

Thereupon he woke up from his dream. The maid Pearl was sitting on the bed with the three other maids, and she clasped him tenderly to her with comforting words: "Do not be afraid, Pao Yu! We are here!"

Pao Yu had cried out so loudly in his dream that his cry was heard outside by his niece, the beautiful Mistress Yung. "No one in the whole house knows my childhood name," she said to herself surprised. "How is it that he called me by my childhood name in his dream?"

She was not able to explain it, but she did not dare to ask the dreamer.

CHAPTER 6

Pao Yu tries for the first time the "Play of Cloud and Rain." In the Ningkuo palace he becomes acquainted with his nephew Chin Chung.

Pao Yu lay on the bed for a while longer, quite exhausted and giddy from the experience of his dream. He felt as if he had lost something. Having strengthened himself with a few sips of cinnamon soup, he got up and the maid Pearl helped him to dress. As she was about to fasten his garter her finger chanced to touch his bare thigh and she felt something like cold, sticky sweat. She drew her hand back in alarm.

"What has happened to you?" she whispered. His blush and a light pressure of the hand was the answer. Now, Pearl was quite an intelligent girl and besides she was two years older than he and already knew the facts of life. She understood at once, blushed herself, and did not ask anything more.

When she was helping him to undress again that same night before he went to bed, she happened to be in the room with him alone for a while.

"Look here, dear sister, you will keep it to yourself, won't you?" he begged her, blushing again.

"What did you actually dream, that this happened to you?" she replied, with an understanding smile.

"I cannot tell it all to you in one word." And he began to describe his dream adventure in detail. When he came to the part of his story where the fairy instructed him in the practice of the "Play of Cloud and Rain," Pearl coyly covered her face with her hands and doubled up with laughter. Pao Yu had always been very familiar with Pearl. He liked the friendly, pretty little thing better than all the other maids and servants. Pearl on her part was aware of the special position of confidence with which the Princess Ancestress had honored her. Because of this she permitted herself some liberties in her association with her charge.

In short, she did not hesitate to try out at once with him the "Play of Cloud and Rain," whereby they faithfully followed the instructions imparted to him. Luckily, they were left undisturbed while thus occupied. From that hour he no longer treated her as a servant but as an intimate friend, and she rewarded his confidence with still more ardent devotion.

One day Madame Phoenix was over in the Ningkuo palace visiting Princess Chen and her daughter-in-law Mistress Yung. At his own request she had taken Pao Yu with her. While the three ladies were conversing as usual about household matters the time seemed very long to him. Mistress Yung, who noticed that he was restlessly fidgeting about this way and that way on his seat, said to him:

"My younger brother, for whom you recently asked, happens to be here today. He is probably in the library now. If you like, go and welcome him!"

Pao Yu quickly slid down from the heated divan.

"Why do you not have him come here? I should also like to make his acquaintance," suggested Madame Phoenix. "Or perhaps I should not ask to?"

Mistress Yung tried to dissuade her from her request. The boy was so shy and simple, quite different from the cheeky, lively boys of the Chia clan. She would be disappointed and would only be inclined to laugh at him. But Madame Phoenix stuck to her request, and so to please her Chin Chung, for so the boy was called, was brought in. Madame Phoenix was most agreeably surprised. The boy, who bowed to her and politely inquired about her health, compared very well with Pao Yu, who was the same age. He was somewhat slimmer than the latter, but in beauty of face and form, in liveliness of expression, in his whole deportment and his charm of manner, he almost surpassed him, except that he was a little shy and awkward, almost like a girl. Madame Phoenix took him by the hand, drew him down to her side, and began questioning him energetically about his name, age, lessons, and everything possible. Meantime she had hurriedly sent some servants of her retinue back to the Yungkuo palace belatedly to fetch some gifts such as are usually presented by the elder to the younger upon first meeting. Bearing in mind the close friendship between Madame Phoenix and Mistress Yung, they chose some specially valuable presents, namely, a piece of silk for a new coat, and two gold medallions inscribed with the wish that the owner would win first place at examinations. Madame Phoenix considered these gifts too insignificant, so great was her sympathy for her new nephew.

While the ladies then settled down to a game of chess, Pao Yu took the opportunity of leaving the table with his nephew and going to chat with him undisturbed in a side room. The boy had made a deep impression on him. When he first saw him, he thought to himself, quite abashed: Compared to such a person I am no better than a dirty pig or a mangy dog! Who knows, if I, like him, had grown up in the cold poverty of a simple, honorable, middle-class family, I might have made his valuable acquaintance long ago and not dawdled away my time uselessly as I have done up to now. What is the good of riches and rank? This silk finery which I wear only hides the hollow, rotten core of an inferior being. These luxurious meals, on which I feed every day, only conceal the dirty refuse-pit of a corrupt character. The two conceptions, riches and rank, mean nothing but dirt and poison!

The painful reflection of Chin Chung upon seeing Pao Yu for the first time, in all his finery and with his large retinue, was exactly the opposite. Oh, what misfortune, he mused, to come from a poor, even though honorable, civil service family! That is indeed the curse of poverty, that it sets up an insurmountable barrier between people like him and people like me. If it were not for that I should probably long ago have enjoyed the advantage of his company.

Thus, both one and the other of them was moved by confused, foolish reflections. After a few opening questions about books and studies, they became friendly. Pao Yu was so eager to get to know the inner family circumstances of his new companion that he quite forgot about the dainty morsels and fruits which had been sent over to them from the table. He learned that at the moment Chin was without schooling, as his previous tutor had had leave of absence for months past. His father was old, sickly, and overburdened with official duties, and therefore unable to bother much about his education. All he could do at present was to go through his old lessons over and over again, but unfortunately he lacked the company of a good comrade, for one could learn much better in company than alone.

"That is what I think too!" interrupted Pao Yu eagerly. "You know we have a free family school here for those members of the clan who cannot have their own tutor or do not want to keep one. At my father's wish I myself am soon going to attend this school for a time; for my former tutor has also got several months' leave, and my father does not want to have me sitting around idle meantime, forgetting what I have learned. I would have been attending the school long ago if I had not been ill. Besides, Grandmother was against it up to now, because she thinks that in a class with a lot of pupils there would be nothing but disturbance and mad pranks. But my father now insists that there must be an end to my idling. Would you not like to come to our school too? Then we could learn together and help one another. Won't you speak to your father about it?"

"With pleasure! Only recently my father greatly praised the institution of your family school. In fact, he has been intending to apply to my sister's father-in-law, Prince Chen, to accept me. But he has put off doing so again and again because he did not like to bother his illustrious relatives about such a trifle, and did not wish to seem obtrusive. But if my uncle thinks that his nephew would be of any use to him in the school, maybe to stir the India ink or to clean his writing implements, perhaps he would see about the matter himself and put in a word of recommendation? How grand it would be if we could study

54

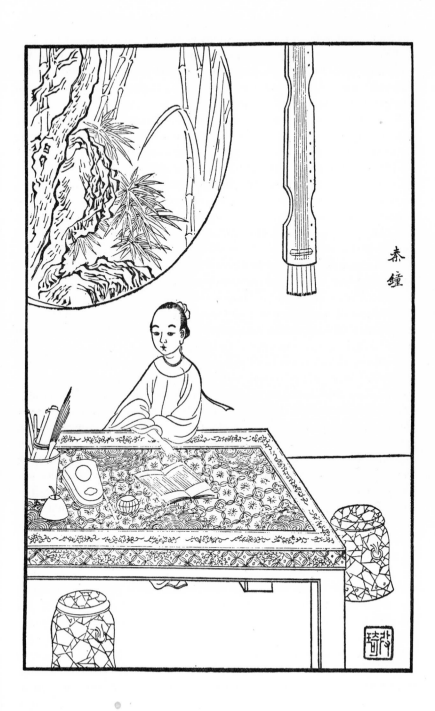

秦鐘

together! Besides, we could become real friends and give our parents less to worry about. There would be many advantages in it."

"Do not worry! I will speak about it to my grandmother at once. We will also tell your sister Yung and my sister-in-law Feng of our wishes, and you yourself must talk to your father. Then we shall see if the thing can be managed."

Meantime darkness had fallen and the time had come to get their lanterns. The two finished their earnest consultation, joined the company at the table again, and watched the ladies playing chess for a while. Princess Chen and Mistress Yung lost the game to Madame Phoenix and pledged themselves to pay their gambling debt by standing a banquet and theater the evening after next. Then they sat down again for an evening snack, after which the guests started to depart.

"Who is going to take Chin Chung home?" Princess Chen asked her women attendants.

"The majordomo has ordered Chiao Ta to do so," they said. "He is tipsy again and in his usual abusive humor."

"It is just too stupid to choose that old boor as an escort," exclaimed both Princess Chen and Mistress Yung at the same time, with annoyance. "But to cancel the order now would only irritate the old man."

"Is the carriage ready?" asked Madame Phoenix, turning to her attendants.

"It is waiting in front of the great hall," they replied. Madame Phoenix said good-by, took Pao Yu by the hand, and walked through the brightly illuminated hall between a solemn double row of silent servants to the carriage. Among the servants was old Chiao Ta, who was so drunk that he could not be prevented, even before the visitors, from disturbing the stately farewell ceremony by kicking up a horrible row and uttering filthy abuse. His rancor was directed against the majordomo Lai Sheng: "Is that the thing to do, to chase out an old man like me on a cold winter's night?" he howled at him. "When there's an unpleasant job to be done, I'm good enough for it, but for a nice job there are others. Is that justice? And to think that such a clumsy, blind tortoise should be majordomo! But beware that old Chiao Ta does not raise his foot and crush you, you miserable worm!"

During this volley of abuse Chia Yung walked through the hall by the side of Madame Phoenix and escorted her to her carriage. When the old man would not stop reviling, in spite of appeals from the other servants, Chia Yung rebuked him angrily:

"Will you shut up at last? If not, I will have you tied and locked up until you are sober again! And we shall see if you get out this time safe and sound!"

But the angry old man refused to be intimidated. He walked up to him menacingly, shouting: "Little friend, don't play the great gentleman before old Chiao Ta! If your forefathers did not dare to reprimand old Chiao Ta, how dare you, little cock, start cackling! Where would all your greatness be today without old Chiao Ta? Nine times I snatched your grandfather from the jaws of death! It was he who piled up all your riches. Is this treatment the thanks I get for my good services? Instead of rewarding me properly, you blow yourself up like a frog and play the great gentleman! The least I can expect is that you keep your mouth shut. Otherwise, just take care that my sword does not go into your body white and come out red!"

"Why have you not got rid of that dangerous old bandit long ago?" whispered Madame Phoenix to her nephew from the carriage window, disgusted at the painful scene. "He is endangering the reputation of the whole family and making you a laughingstock before the people."

"You are right," agreed her nephew, nodding; and he ordered the servants to fetter the old man and lock him up in an empty shed near the stable. While they were dragging him away by force, Chiao Ta continued to shout and rage. "I will go to the Temple of the Ancestors and complain to the great old master! He shall learn what a clean-living brood he has left behind! Whoring like rutting dogs and fowls; cousins and brothers-in-law carrying on together 'scratching in the ashes'— that's all the accursed brood is good for! . . ."

In the face of this horrible, grossly obscene speech, which caused the sun to disappear behind the clouds in shame, and made the souls of the listeners almost leave their bodies in horror, the servants who were dragging him away could do nothing but stop his mouth with mud and horse manure.

Madame Phoenix and her nephew Yung, who understood every word of his abusive speech, behaved nevertheless as if they had heard nothing. But Pao Yu, in his innocence, could not refrain from asking Madame Phoenix during the journey in the carriage: "Sister, what did he mean by the expression 'scratching in the ashes'?"

Violently angry, which was quite unusual for her, she rebuked him: "Do not ask stupid questions! You not only listen to the foolish chatter of a drunkard, but have to ask questions about it! Just wait until I tell your grandmother! You will pay for this with a thrashing!"

"Ah, dear big sister, please do not tell on me! I certainly will not ask such a stupid question again," pleaded the frightened Pao Yu. Indeed, he would not have asked if he had known that the expression 'to scratch in the ashes' referred to illicit association between a father-in-law and a daughter-in-law.

"Very well, dear child," said Madame Phoenix, quickly appeased.

"And when we are home I shall speak to Grandmother and ask her for your sake to help to have your nephew Chin Chung admitted to your school."

CHAPTER 7

Pao Yu is shown the gold amulet of his girl cousin. The girl cousin is shown Pao Yu's stone.

Two DAYS LATER THERE WAS A GREAT BANQUET AND THEATRICAL PERformance given in the Ningkuo palace in honor of the relatives in the Yungkuo palace. Pao Yu missed his cousin Precious Clasp in the crowd. He had not seen her for days. He was told that she was not quite well and was keeping to her room. He so longed to see her again that, early that afternoon, while the rest of the family was still together, he accompanied the Princess Ancestress back to the Yungkuo palace, and was able then to steal off to the Pear Garden by unfrequented side paths, untroubled by tedious attendants and undesired watchers. He first politely greeted Aunt Hsueh who was sitting over some sewing with her maids. She embraced him warmly.

"How touchingly thoughtful of you to come over to see your aunt in this cold weather! But get up here quickly on the warm kang! And then strengthen yourself with a bowl of hot tea!"

"Is Cousin Hsueh Pan at home?" asked Pao Yu.

"Ah, I have great trouble with this playboy," sighed Aunt Hsueh. "He is like a horse without a bridle or halter. Not a single day does he spend at home."

"Is Precious Clasp well again?"

"Yes, thank you, she is. It was very kind of you to send someone over lately to ask how she was. She is in her room now. You can go in and visit her. It is warmer there than here. I will follow later on; I want to clear up my work here first."

Pao Yu accepted her suggestion only too willingly. He slid down quickly from the kang and rushed off to the room with the red brocade curtain before the door. Lifting the curtain, he stepped inside. There he found Precious Clasp sitting on the heated divan, likewise busy with her needle and thread. Her hair was tied in a loose knot on top of her head. It was black as lacquer and shone like oil. She wore a honeycolored padded coat, a pink waistcoat trimmed with two-colored gold and silver squirrel fur, and a short onion-colored slit tunic. Her lips needed no rouge, her blue-black brows no brush; her face was smooth as a silver dish, and her eyes were like almonds swimming in water. The fact that she was so sparing of her words and so prudent in her speech was interpreted by many as pose and affection. "I am on the guard against foolishness," she was wont to say, explaining her cautious way.

"Are you well and cheerful again, sister?" asked Pao Yu.

"I am very much better," she replied, and, smiling, invited him to sit down beside her on the warmed divan. The maid Oriole came and poured out tea. There were some conventional inquiries for Grandmother, aunts, and cousins, and at last the conversation became personal. Now her eyes were fixed on the five-colored cord from which dangled the precious stone.

"I have heard so much about your stone, may I look at it closely just once?" she asked. As she spoke she came nearer to him. He also sidled up a little closer to her, took the cord with the stone from his neck, and laid it in her hand. Precious Clasp looked attentively at the shining thing in the palm of her hand. It was about the size of a sparrow's egg and shone with a subdued pinkish hue like light morning clouds, and it felt as smooth to the touch as clotted cream. It was contained in a fine protective net.

On the front of the stone was written in minute script: "Stone of penetrating spiritual power." Under this were two lines, each consisting of four symbols:

> Never lose me, never forget me!
> Glorious life—lasting prosperity!

On the back were three lines, each of four engraved characters.

> First: I drive away wicked spirits.
> Second: I cure you of trouble of mind.
> Third: I announce happiness and misfortune.

Precious Clasp hummed twice in a low voice:

> Never lose me, never forget me!
> Glorious life—lasting prosperity!

Then she looked at the maid, Oriole, who was standing beside her. "Why do you stand there gaping instead of making haste and pouring the tea?" she asked.

Oriole answered with a giggle: "The two lines which you have just repeated are quite familiar to me. They are very much like the lines on the gold medallion around your neck."

"Is it possible?" interrupted Pao Yu quickly. "You wear a medallion with eight similar ideographs? Do let me see it!"

"Nonsense! Do not listen to her chatter!" objected Precious Clasp, laughing.

But Pao Yu insisted.

"I have shown my amulet, so do me the same favor, dear sister, please!" he begged.

Precious Clasp could resist no longer.

"Well, it is true. I also wear an amulet. If it were not for the lucky inscription I would not drag around the heavy, awkward thing with me every day."

With these words she loosened the clasp of her chain and showed the piece of jewelry which had been hidden under the seam of her dress. It was a massive golden medallion, studded with pearls and jewels. Pao Yu took it out of her hand and held it eagerly before his eyes. Right enough, there on the front and the back were eight characters likewise engraved in minute script. They read:

> Never leave me, never reject me!
> Precious youth—lasting bloom!

Pao Yu read the two lines twice aloud.

"They complement the lines of my stone exactly; together they form a four-line stanza!" he cried, joyfully surprised.

"A mangy-headed bonze once gave her the lines, and advised her to have them engraved on a gold medallion," Oriole threw in importantly.

"That's enough. Stir yourself and pour out our tea!" said Precious Clasp, cutting short her chatter.

"Where have you come from?" she said, turning to her visitor and changing the delicate conversation. But Pao Yu did not hear her question; his attention was fixed on the strange fragrance which emanated from her. For when viewing the amulet they had drawn close to each other.

"What perfume have you used, sister?" he wanted to know. "I have never smelled it before."

"Perfume?" she said slowly. "I am not in the habit of spoiling my good clothes with perfume." Then, after a moment's reflection, she continued quickly: "You're right, it must be the smell of the medicine which I took this morning."

"What is the name of your medicine?"

"Pills of cold balsam."

"Oh, let me also taste those fragrant pills!" he begged.

"You silly thing!" she burst out, laughing. "How can one swallow any medicine at random!"

They stopped short in their conversation. The voice of a servant announced from outside:

"Miss Ling is here!"

And immediately Black Jade entered.

"Oh, am I disturbing you?" she asked, smiling, with a hurried glance at the pair. Pao Yu had risen and politely offered her his place on the warmed divan.

"And why should you disturb us?" said Precious Clasp casually.

"I just thought . . . naturally, I would not have come if I knew that he was here."

"I don't see what you mean," replied Precious Clasp coolly.

"I mean that it would be far nicer for you if you did not have all of us visiting you at the same time, and then have no visitors at all. Better have him today and me tomorrow. That would give more variety and better distribution of our visits. You would not feel either too neglected or too much besieged. Is that so difficult to understand?"

"Is it snowing outside?" asked Pao Yu, to change the conversation, pointing to Black Jade's red cloak.

"It has been for a long time," the voice of his nurse, Mother Li, who had accompanied Black Jade, replied from outside.

"Bring me over my raincoat," Pao Yu called out to her.

"Ah, when I come, he must go, of course," remarked Black Jade pointedly.

"Who said that I wanted to go now? I only wanted my coat to be here for later on when we're going," he said, trying to pacify the over-sensitive cousin.

Pao Yu and his two cousins passed in to the living room, where Aunt Hsueh had meantime set a table with all kinds of sweet dishes and dainties. Pao Yu had recently praised a dish of geesefeet and ducks' tongues which he had eaten at Princess Chen's for the first time. To please him Aunt Hsueh had had this dish prepared for him today.

"But it tastes even better with some wine," the spoiled Pao Yu remarked. Aunt Hsueh thereupon sent for the very best wine which she had in the house.

"No wine, please!" his old nurse, Mother Li, objected.

"Just one goblet!" he begged.

"No!" insisted Mother Li severely. "If your mother or grandmother were present you could drink a whole jugful for all I would care. But I am responsible for you now, and I do not want to get into trouble as I did lately when some fool gave you wine the moment I turned my back. I had to bear reproaches for days on end over that. You do not know, *Tai tai*, what a rascal he is, and what he can do when he has even one drop of wine," she said, turning to Aunt Hsueh.

"All right, do not excite yourself so much, old nurse!" said Aunt Hsueh, laughing, to calm her. "You shall have a goblet yourself too. In this weather wine is good for one, to protect one against colds. I shall take care that he does not drink too much, and I shall be responsible for him to his grandmother."

Mother Li yielded, and was taken into the servants' room by a maid, to share a cup of wine with the others.

"But, please, cold wine! I do not care for it warm," Pao Yu was heard again.

"I can only allow you to have it warmed," objected Aunt Hsueh. "Cold wine makes one's hand shake when writing."

"At home you have the opportunity every day of increasing your knowledge, and you do not yet know anything about the nature of wine?" Precious Clasp added somewhat sarcastically and precociously. "Wine makes one hot and rises to the head. But one can do away with this effect if one takes the wine warm. Cold wine, on the other hand, runs through the body and spreads its harmful influences through all the five intestines."

What was said by such a beautiful mouth must of course be right and sensible, so he had the warm wine served to him.

But it was not a matter of just one goblet. As soon as that strict watcher, Mother Li, had withdrawn, he could drink to his heart's content, encouraged by Aunt Hsueh. At last, towards evening, he was slightly tipsy and so tired from all the drinking that he would have liked to accept Aunt Hsueh's invitation to spend the night in her house. But Black Jade who did not like his intimacy with the Hsueh family, was able to prevent it.

"Are you not thinking of going home at last?" she asked him.

His dull eyes blinked at her. "When you go, I will go with you," he replied.

Whereupon Black Jade immediately rose and bade farewell. He followed her example politely, and asked for his wraps. When the maid, Snowgoose, put the broad-rimmed, reddish-brown, monkey-fur winter hat somewhat awkwardly on his bent head, he pulled it off again and rebuked her angrily.

"Let me do it!" said Black Jade hurriedly running over to him. He willingly submitted. How gently and carefully her delicate fingers manipulated his coiffure! So skillfully did she fix his hat on his head that his hair remained unruffled; the inner hatband fitted against his forehead exactly, and the red velvet tassel the size of a walnut dangled down to just below the rim.

At home, on account of his tipsiness he was not taken in to the evening meal but sent straight to bed. The maid, Bright Cloud, was awaiting him in his room.

"Well, you're a nice one!" she greeted him, laughing, pointing to the writing table where the writing implements were still lying just as she had left them for him in the morning. "You got me to prepare a whole lot of India ink for you this morning, and you wrote only three characters. Then off you went. I waited for you here all day in vain. But now, set to work quickly and write until the supply of India ink is exhausted!"

"Where are the three characters you spoke of?" he wanted to know.

"Indeed, you must be tipsy! When you left this morning you told me to fasten the characters outside on top of the door. I went up on the ladder myself and did the job for you. My fingers were quite stiff with cold."

"Ah, I remember now. Give me your hand. I'll warm it in mine!"

He took her by the hand and drew her with him outside the door to look at the characters on the door. Just then Black Jade came along.

"Dear sister, please say quite honestly which of the three characters, in your opinion, have I done best?" he asked anxiously.

Black Jade looked up. There, resplendently drawn in three large characters, stood the proud inscription: Purple Chamber of the Fragrance of Culture.

"I find all three characters simply masterly," she approved, with a smile. "What about painting a beautiful inscription like that for my room?"

"Ah, go on. You are just making fun of me. But where is Pearl?"

Bright Cloud curled her lips and pointed to the bed. Pearl had made herself comfortable there. She lay in her clothes, apparently sound asleep.

"Very early to go to sleep," he remarked, laughing. Then he reflected for a moment.

"Where are the curd balls, which I had sent here from the midday meal? I asked sister-in-law Chen to send some over, as I wanted to eat them in the evening. They were meant for you, as you like them so much."

"I thought at once they were meant for me and was looking forward to eating them in the evening. But then Mother Li came along and took them. You had already eaten quite enough, and she would prefer to give them to her grandchild, she said."

Another maid brought him tea.

"A bowl for Cousin Ling as well," he ordered.

"She has gone long ago," they laughingly told him.

He drank just one mouthful, then stopped.

"But I had maple tea made for me this morning, and I said distinctly that it was to be infused and drawn off three or four times, for only then does it taste good. Why do you give me this other tea?"

"I had prepared a pot of maple tea for you," replied the maid, "but Mother Li drank it."

In a rage Pao Yu flung the full china bowl to the ground, so that it crashed in fragments and the contents splashed the maid's skirt.

"Mother Li! It's always Mother Li! Who is she, anyway, that everyone must submit to her and die of awe before her? She nursed me for a bit when I was a child, that's all! That does not give her the right to put on airs here as if she were the Princess Ancestress herself. She must be chased from the house, then it will be better for all of us." And he would have gone straight off to his grandmother to complain of her if the maid Pearl had not intervened. Pearl had only been pretending to be asleep. She wanted to allure him when he returned and found her there before him on the bed, so that he would flirt with her and make love to her. She had not bothered to listen to the preceding discussion about the three written characters and the curd balls, but the crash of the smashed teacup made her jump up nimbly to try to calm him. At the same moment a servant sent by the Princess Ancestress came to ask the reason of the noise.

"It is nothing, really," countered Pearl, before he had time to speak. "I was pouring out tea and I slipped because there was snow on my shoes; so the cup fell out of my hand and got broken."

And when the servant had gone she continued, turning to Pao Yu: "If you want to drive Mother Li away we others shall go too. No doubt you will find it easy to get better than us."

He remained silent and allowed himself to be undressed and put to bed. Very soon his tired eyes closed. Pearl did not forget to take the stone amulet from his neck and put it carefully wrapped in a handkerchief under his pillow, so that it would be nicely warm next morning and not harm him by making his bare neck cold.

Early the next day the nephew Yung from the Ningkuo palace arrived accompanied by his brother-in-law Chin Chung, to present the latter to the Princess Ancestress. The old lady was just as charmed by the young boy as were the other ladies of the house. He was kept for the midday meal and loaded with gifts on leaving. The Princess Ancestress gave him a purse and a golden statuette of the divinity of letters. She considered him a suitable companion and schoolfellow for Pao Yu and gladly agreed that he should be accepted into the family school.

"You live far away from here," she said to him, "and in very hot or in frosty weather you will find the journey too much. At such times you can remain here for as long as you like and stay with your uncle Pao Yu. It is better for two to study here at home than to associate with a pack of lazy young rascals."

Chin Chung's father was highly pleased with the good reception which his offspring had been given by his aristocratic relatives and was very glad that the question of the boy's education had now been solved without the humiliating necessity of a visit of petition. He saw that his son would be in the best hands in a school of which the Principal was the worthy old Chia Tai Ju, a splendid scholar and Confucian. Of course he could not avoid paying a formal visit to the latter and giving him the customary gift of money. He did not wish to be too much behind the better-placed parents of other boys in this matter. Thus, this little insignificant governor's secretary had to pinch and scrape and calculate in every way in order to get together the entrance gift of twenty-five silver pieces proper for a person of his station. After the father and son had paid their respects and presented their gift to the Principal, the uncle and nephew set out for the school on a lucky day which Pao Yu had chosen in the calendar. The next chapter will tell of the riotous incidents which were to take place in the school soon afterwards.

CHAPTER 8

Chia Cheng reprimands his delinquent offspring. Ill-behaved boys create a disturbance in the school.

THE DAY PICKED OUT IN THE CALENDAR FOR THE FIRST ATTENDANCE at the school had arrived. The maid Pearl had risen early and got ready the writing materials and books for her master, and now she sat sadly waiting on the edge of his bed for him to wake up. As she helped him to dress he noticed her dejected look.

"Dear sister, why do you look so unhappy?" he asked her. "I hope you do not feel cast aside and unwanted now, because I am going to school?"

"It is not that," she replied, smiling. "One has to be educated, otherwise one gets nowhere in life. But just now I have been thinking one should not overdo even learning. Study is like food: too much doesn't agree with you. You must consider your health and enjoy a little leisure sometimes. During study keep your attention only on your books, but in your hours of leisure think of the people at home who are near to you. And one thing more: do not get involved in any trouble or fights with your fellow students. You know that your father won't stand for any nonsense. It has been on my mind to remind you of that before you go."

Pao Yu promised to take her advice to heart.

"You will probably be freezing in the schoolroom," she continued. "Anyway, I have packed up a fur coat for you; I have also given your servants a hand-warmer for you. But you must ask for these things when you are cold. The lazy rascals will not stir a hand for you on their own. Do think of your health!"

"Thank you, I will certainly take care of myself. But you need not sit here all the time in my room while I am away, getting bored to death. Go over to Cousin Black Jade and talk to her."

On Pearl's advice he also took leave of his grandmother and his parents before going off. The last person he went to see was his stern father, Chia Cheng. Today it happened that the latter was back early from his office and entertaining some visitors in the library. In the midst of the conversation his son entered and, falling on his knees, offered his greeting—*tsing an*—and announced that he was going to school. Mr. Cheng regarded him with a contemptuous smile. "Do not disgrace me before these worthy gentlemen with your jabbering about 'going to school,'" he said mockingly. "For all I care you may go on with your childish tricks, but kindly leave me in peace! Your presence soils this respectable place."

"Do not be so stern, worthy old friend!" his visitors, who had risen from their seats, urged him benignly. "Let our young nephew go to his school happy. He will certainly get over his boyish ways soon and make a glorious name for himself in two or three years. And you, esteemed nephew, should not dally here, but say farewell, for it is almost dinner-time."

And two of the worthy gentlemen took Pao Yu between them and led him out of the room.

"Who is accompanying him?" asked Mr. Cheng of the retinue of servants who were waiting for his son outside the door. Four strong fellows came forward, bowed their knee, and offered their *tsing an*. Mr. Cheng turned to the biggest of them, who was called Li Kwei and was a son of the nurse Mother Li. "You, fellow, are responsible to me for him!" he said. "What has he learned up to now? Nothing but empty words and jumbled phrases. His belly is full of cunning wickedness. But just wait! As soon as I have leisure I will have you stripped naked and then we shall settle our accounts over this useless rascal!" In utter consternation Li Kwei pulled off his cap and touched his head to the ground.

"Old Governor," he stammered, "this miserable fellow would not dare to lie to you. But the young Governor already really knows by heart three parts of the holy book of *Shih Ching*, the *Book of Songs*. He has come to the part which tells of the stag crying in the distance and the lotus leaf drifting on the waves."

These particulars caused the worthy gentlemen to laugh aloud, and even Mr. Cheng could not keep up his stern expression but had to smile.

"And even if he knows thirty chapters of the *Shih Ching* by heart, that is still just as much vain noise and illusion as if a person who steals a bell were to stop up his ears and pretend to be dumb," he said. "Give my kind regards to the old schoolmaster and tell him not to waste his time teaching the *Shih Ching* and such antiquated useless rubbish; he should rather make them study the Four Classical Books so thoroughly that his pupils will know the text by heart from beginning to end. That is the most important thing."

"*Shih*, yes," murmured Li Kwei eagerly, and as the old Governor said nothing more he withdrew quickly with his companions to where Pao Yu was waiting outside, alone and neglected. "Did you hear, little brother?" said Li Kwei to him on the way. "He'll have us stripped naked and thrashed. In other places a little honor and glory comes to the servants from the master. We, on the other hand, spend ourselves in vain in your service and only get rewarded with scoldings and beatings. We would be happier if we were treated with a little more consideration in the future."

"Do not take it badly, good elder brother!" urged Pao Yu kindly. "As soon as I can I will show my gratitude for your good services and invite you to be my guest."

"That would be too great an honor, little ancestor! It will be enough if you would listen to me if I have something to say to you."

They were back at the residence of the Princess Ancestress. She was talking to Chin Chung, who had come to fetch Pao Yu. After another farewell the uncle and nephew set off together for the school. But it suddenly occurred to Pao Yu that he should also bid farewell to Black Jade. He therefore turned back again to the green pavilion. There he found his cousin at the window in front of a mirror, busy doing her hair. When she heard that he was on the way to school, she said with a slightly ironical smile: "To school? Splendid! You will certainly become a great man and pluck cinnamon flowers in the Palace of the Moon. It is a pity I cannot go with you."

"Dear *Mei mei*, you will wait with the supper until I come back from school, won't you?" he begged. "And I would like to help you to make up your face as usual. Please postpone doing it until I come home again!"

"Will you not say good-by to Cousin Precious Clasp too?" she called after him as he was leaving. He only smiled and at last went off to school with his nephew. The school had been founded by the first Prince of Yungkuo, and according to the founder's intention it was primarily meant for the gifted sons of the poorer families of the clan, who could not afford the luxury of their own private tutors. The school was supported by the contributions of those members of the families who had attained lucrative positions. These contributions provided the pupils not only with free education but also free food. According to the deed of foundation, the Principal was to be an old and worthy scholar, proved in the virtues of the Confucian philosophy.

From this first day of attendance at school together, Pao Yu and Chin Chung became inseparable comrades. They went to school together and came home together, they sat together at their lessons and stood together during recreation. The Princess Ancestress treated Chin Chung as if he were a grandchild or great-nephew by blood. She often kept him as her guest for three or five days on end, and she also helped him generously with clothing and other necessities. After two months Chin Chung was as intimate with everyone in the Yungkuo palace as if he belonged to the family.

When it came to satisfying a mood or humor, Pao Yu was apt to be neither particularly sensible nor logical. Thus, he suggested that good-fellowship should be the keynote of relations with his nephew. "We are the same age and studying side by side. Why should we keep up the ceremonial distinction between uncle and nephew? Let us in the future call each other friend and brother!" He kept dinning this into the other's ears so continually that at last Chin Chung overcame his initial shyness and accepted the suggestion.

The many pupils at the family school almost all belonged, it is true, to the same clan and were all more or less interrelated by blood or marriage, but as the proverb so aptly says, even among dragons there are nine varieties, and each variety is different from the other. In short, it is easy to realize that there were snakes and vipers creeping around among the dragons of the family school, and that high and low were mixed together.

It was inevitable that the two handsome, blossom-fresh young newcomers should very soon attract general attention among their fellow pupils, Chin Chung on account of his gentle, mild ways and his bashful, shy nature, which made him blush like a girl when spoken to; Pao Yu, on account of his wealth and his self-assured bearing, his masterful behavior, his ease and skill with words. Their close friendship was much remarked upon and discussed behind their backs. Envy and jealousy did their worst. In short, it was not long before the relationship of the two was whispered about and secretly discussed everywhere both inside and outside the schoolrooms.

Friend Hsueh Pan too was attending the family school, but less through zeal for learning than for certain private ends. When he heard for the first time of the existence of this school, in which there was such a choice selection of charming young boys, this news at once awakened base desires in him. Pretending that he wished to improve and enrich his knowledge, he had procured his admission from old Tai Ju by a substantial gift of money. In reality, he wanted to be like the fisherman who fishes for three days, and idles about for the next two days while his nets are drying. He had less interest in learning than in forming friendships with boys. He did in fact find among the pupils some who let themselves be enticed by gifts of money and other favors to be accommodating to his purposes, which it is not necessary to discuss in more detail. Chief among these were two elegant boys, who on account of their smart and attractive appearance were nicknamed Hsiang Lien, "Fragrant Attachment," and Yu Ai, "Precious Favorite." In the school they were on a whole admired, but only in secret, for through fear of Hsueh Pan none of the other boys ventured to make friends with them.

Pao Yu and Chin Chung were also attracted to these two soon after coming to the school, but through fear of Hsueh Pan did not dare to show their liking, and confined themselves to admiring glances from a distance. And Hsiang Lien and Yu Ai reciprocated in kind. Day after day the same secret game went on in the class during instruction: from four different seats four pairs of eyes met and spoke together the silent language of love. In conversation during recreation they expressed their hidden sentiments and feelings by means of gentle allusions and ambiguous phrases.

But carefully though they carried on this secret game, it could not remain hidden from the sharp eyes of certain sly boys. Consequently, there was much winking, and suggestive clearing of the throat, and coughing behind the backs of the four.

The Principal, Chia Tai Ju, happened to be absent from school one day owing to a domestic celebration. To keep his pupils busy he had given them one half of a stanza. They were to compose a complementary second half. That was their assignment. He had entrusted the care of the school during his absence to his assistant and grandson, Chia Jui.

Just by chance Hsueh Pan was absent from the school that day. Chin Chung and Hsiang Lien availed of his absence to signal each other by glances more open than usual, and finally, on the pretext of attending to the wants of nature, they stole away to the farthest corner of the school courtyard for an undisturbed conversation.

"Would your father object if we were friends openly?" Chin Chung had just asked the other, when they heard someone clearing his throat behind their backs. Greatly startled, they turned around to find a fellow pupil, one King Yung, standing before them laughing maliciously. He had sneaked along secretly behind them. Unlike the gentle Chin Chung, Hsiang Lien was inclined to be hot-tempered.

"What does this silly coughing mean? Are we not allowed to speak together?" he said to the mischief-maker, embarrassed and annoyed at the same time.

"Don't let me disturb you!" the other replied mockingly. "But if you claim the right to speak, may I on my part be allowed to cough? Though if you have something to say to each other, why do you not do so openly? One just wonders what secret doings you're up to here. Let's not pretend; I know all about it! And now you can have your choice: either you let me in on your game and I'll keep my mouth shut, or the whole school will hear about it."

"What is there to hear?" asked Chin Chung and Hsiang Lien both together, blushing to the roots of their hair.

"The truth!" replied the other, laughing. Then he clapped his hands and called out loudly across the school yard: "Hi, come here! Freshly baked pancakes for sale!"

The two friends rushed raging into the school and complained to Chia Jui, who was in charge, of their schoolfellow's gratuitous insults. Now, this Chia Jui put profit above conscience; he used his position as teacher in the school to fleece thoroughly the pupils entrusted to his care. Hence he did not try to check Hsueh Pan in his disgraceful doings but he actually aided and abetted him to win the favor of the rich libertine and thus obtain money and good meals.

If Chin Chung and Hsiang Lien believed they would be protected by Chia Jui, they were very much mistaken. Chia Jui bore a grudge against Hsiang Lien, because while the latter was going with Hsueh Pan —this drifting water plant had meantime dropped him for new friends —he had never procured the least favor for him from his rich patron. When the two, therefore, came with their complaint, he showed himself very offhand and promptly took the side of their enemy, King Yung. Moreover, at the time King Yung was in high favor with Hsueh Pan, and that was all that mattered to him. True, he did not dare censure Chin Chung, in consideration of his influential friend Pao Yu, with whom he did not wish to quarrel. But all the less did he restrain his displeasure towards Hsiang Lien; he blamed him before the whole class and pointed him out as a quarrelsome disturber of the peace.

Annoyed and hurt by the undeserved blame, Hsiang Lien went back to his seat in the class, whence he signalled his displeasure by glances, growling, and whispered abuse to his friends. King Yung, on his part, felt obliged as victor to make himself important and conspicuous by significant nods, grimaces, and self-complacent mutterings directed to this side and that.

"I've just caught them in the darkest corner of the courtyard," the whispering went to right and left. "I saw them quite distinctly kissing and caressing, and I heard them talking about wanting to belong to each other. And they were so much engrossed in their important conversation that they never even noticed me!"

Among the listeners on the near-by seats was one who was much annoyed by such talk. He was sixteen-year-old Chia Chiang, who belonged to the Ningkuo branch of the clan. Prince Chia Chen had taken him in as an orphan child and brought him up as his own son. But his extraordinarily close friendship with Chia Yung, the Prince's son, had caused suspicious whispering and comment among the servants which had finally come to the ears of the Prince. In order to save his house from disrepute the Prince had recently decided to have his foster son live outside the Ningkuo palace. Thus Chia Chiang was more or less personally stung by King Yung's nasty talk and as intimate friend of Chia Yung, felt impelled to stand by the latter's brother-in-law, Chin Chung. To be sure, he did not want to get personally involved, as he was afraid of a quarrel with Hsueh Pan if he should openly take sides against the latter's protégé, King Yung. Being clever, he chose a good way of attaining his end without taking any personal risk, but remaining comfortably in the background.

On the favorite pretext of having to relieve himself, he suddenly disappeared from the class. Outside in the school courtyard he went up to Pao Yu's attendants, took aside Ming Yen, who was known as a turbulent, daredevil fellow, and thoroughly incited him against King Yung. He insisted that by insulting Chin Chung, King Yung had also insulted his master Pao Yu, and if the shameless fellow was not made to shut up very soon he would take still greater liberties in the future. Having performed the work of incitement, he returned to the class, calmly put on his outdoor clothes, and asked permission of Chia Jui to leave the school a little earlier today, as he had an urgent errand to do. He wished to be out of the way of the approaching storm, which he himself had provoked. He was just in time, for already Ming Yen, who had been stirred up by him, came rushing into the classroom, his face blazing red, and without using the title of "young gentleman," which was fitting for him as a servant to use, he called out roughly and without respect:

"Which of you here is King Yung?"

When the boy he was looking for was pointed out to him, he seized him boldly and firmly by the shoulder, and shouted at him: "Whatever we do with our behinds is no damn business of yours, you chicken-arse! Be glad if we leave your old man in peace! But I advise you, King Yung, to kindly leave my young master alone!"

There was general pandemonium in the class. Chia Jui exhorted the intruder to behave somewhat less wildly. But King Yung, whose face was yellow with rage, cried: "Rebellion! Anarchy! A slave dare not take liberties like that! But just wait, I'll have a word with your master!"

He freed himself from Ming Yen's grasp, and was about to fall on Pao Yu. At that moment Chin Chung heard a whizzing noise close to him. By a lucky chance he moved aside, so that the missile which was slung by an unknown hand—it was a square India ink stone—whizzed by within a hair's breadth of the back of his head, and clattered down on a bench farther up in front, between the places of Chia Lan and Chia Chun. At the same time a china pot full of India ink was broken into fragments, and the books which lay about were splashed all over with ink. In reply a heavy book box was hurled from this bench to the back, but it fell short and landed on the bench of Pao Yu and Chin Chung, where it knocked down the books and writing materials and shattered Pao Yu's tea bowl too. Meantime little hot-tempered Chia Chun had jumped up to fight whoever had thrown the India ink stone. In a trice a tangle of fighters had formed round King Yung, who had suddenly got hold of a feather duster, the long bamboo handle of which he brandished wildly and hit out with. Ming Yen also got a blow from it. This, in turn, gave Ming Yen a reason to call in his three colleagues who were waiting outside, the servants Sao Hung, Chu Yo, and Mo Yu, to support him. The three rushed in like a swarm of hornets, shouting wildly: "You bastard brood dare to raise your weapons against us!" Mo Yu was armed with a wooden door bar, while Sao Hung and Chu Yo brandished horsewhips in their hands. In the wild confusion which now followed, the despairing deputy schoolmaster tried in vain to make his warning and imploring voice heard. They were all utterly beyond control; discipline and order were at an end. Some joined in heartily just for the fun of it, hitting out in all directions; others stood on the benches and tables and egged on the fighters by clapping their hands and shouting: "Stand firm, stand firm! Flay them! Flay them!" Only a few of the more timid boys kept shyly away from the general tumult. The whole class was like a boiling caldron. The intervention of some of the older, more sensible servants such as Li Kwei at last brought the uproar to an end. To the question regarding the cause, the answers were varied, everyone attributing the blame to someone else. Li Kwei saw to it first of all that the warlike Ming Yen and his three companions were got away from the scene of battle. Then there was quietness. Pao Yu was just wiping with the lapel of his coat a bleeding wound which his friend Chin Chung had received on the forehead from the handle of King Yung's feather duster, when along came Li Kwei.

"Have my books put together and send my horse!" he ordered Li Kwei. "I shall ride straight off to old Tai Ju and complain of his deputy. He not only failed to give us protection against those who insulted us, but even encouraged the offenders to do us violence; and this led to the general attack. Ming Yen was quite right to come to my aid. They hit him and Chin Chung until they bled. Naturally, I cannot remain longer in this school." Li Kwei pacified him and tried his best to dissuade him from his purpose. It would not be very nice or becoming to worry the worthy old gentleman about such a trifle, he said.

"And you are to blame for it all," he continued, turning to Chia Jui. "As deputy schoolmaster and brain of the class you should have intervened justly and not let things go so far. Instead, you looked on idly and let the mischief develop."

"I warned often enough and called for order, but they did not listen to me," protested Chia Jui.

"Take it badly or not when I speak so openly, sir, but it is your own fault that you are not respected in the school," Li Kwei continued his censure unflinchingly. "If you had always behaved in a blameless manner, you would be respected. The matter may still be very unpleasant indeed for you if it comes to the ears of the worthy old Master Tai Ju. You must strive to unravel the tangled net as quickly as possible, sir."

"What do you mean by unravelling?" interjected Pao Yu indignantly. "I am going to make a complaint."

"Either King Yung leaves the school or I do not come any more," added Chin Chung.

"It would be a fine thing indeed if we were to yield the ground before that insolent fellow!" said Pao Yu, flaring up in anger. "I shall see that *he* gets out. Anyway, how is this King Yung related to us?"

"He is a nephew of Mrs. Chia Huang of the Ningkuo branch," the voice of the servant Ming Yen was heard to say from outside the window. "Mrs. Huang is his aunt on the father's side. She is always on her knees to our second mistress, Madame Phoenix, to make this or that request or petition. It is impudent enough for such a wretched lickspittle even to rub shoulders with us. How can we be expected to respect such 'masters'?"

"Be silent, son of a bitch!" muttered Li Kwei aside to him. "What are the flybites of other people to you?"

"Then he is a nephew of sister-in-law Huang," remarked Pao Yu contemptuously. "Good, I will go to her and give her a piece of my mind about her scamp of a nephew."

"Why take all that trouble yourself?" the turbulent Ming Yen interjected again. "Let me go! I shall tell her that the old Princess Ancestress wishes to speak to her. And I'll take her over straight away in a hired coach. In your grandmother's presence one can make a statement much better."

"Be off!" Li Kwei rebuked him. "Or do you want to get a thrashing?

I have only just managed to quench the fire, and you want to poke it up again! If you don't stop trying to stir up your master I will have you punished."

While Li Kwei was trying with all his might to make peace in the school dispute, the deputy schoolmaster Chia Jui, who was thoroughly frightened, was begging and beseeching first Chin Chung, then Pao Yu, to spare him and let the matter be hushed up. After holding out for a long time Pao Yu at last declared that he would be prepared to refrain from complaining if King Yung would make a full and formal apology. King Yung was now pressed hard from every side. He reluctantly consented to make a slight bow in token of apology to his chief opponent, Chin Chung, whom he had so grievously offended. But Pao Yu did not consider this reparation sufficient. He insisted upon a full ceremonial kowtow. Chia Jui implored King Yung to give in. "Be wise," he urged, "and remember the proverb:

> Banish the moment's anger,
> And spare yourself many days' anguish."

Coerced and urged on all sides, King Yung at last submitted and consented to perform the required kowtow. And with this the school brawl ended.

CHAPTER 9

The Prince Hermit's birthday is celebrated in the Ningkuo palace. The sight of Phoenix awakens carnal desires in the heart of Chia Jui.

KING YUNG HAD INDEED PERFORMED HIS KOWTOW OF APOLOGY, BUT he was still devoured with resentment. Having come home, he said to his mother, née Hu: "This Chin Chung is just as distantly related to the house of Chia as I am; he is only connected by marriage and has no better claim to a place in the family school than I have. But on the strength of his close friendship with Pao Yu he thinks he can put on airs and look down on the like of us. If he at least behaved blamelessly one could excuse him, but he must think we are all blind, he carries on so openly, now with this, now with that one. The quarrel was due to the fact that I caught him at it today. And must I lie down before him after that?"

"Do not be so headstrong, and keep out of other people's affairs!" his mother advised him. "Thanks to my intercession with Aunt Huang, and to her ceaseless petitions to Madame Phoenix, you have been lucky enough to procure a scholarship in the family school. Do you want, through your defiance, to throw away the benefits of this free education? What should we do then? We cannot afford the luxury of a private tutor. Besides, you get free meals in the school, and how could I manage to clothe you properly except for this saving in food? And you think a lot of being well and neatly dressed. Besides, you have to thank the school for the valuable friendship of that elegant young gentleman, Hsueh Pan. In the one year you have been friendly with him, he has given you up to seventy or eighty taels. Where else would you have so many advantages combined if by your obstinate folly you forfeit the chance of staying on at the school? You might as well try to climb up to heaven. Therefore be sensible and swallow your resentment!"

To this King Yung had nothing to reply, so he just had to swallow his anger. The mother had succeeded in silencing her son, but she herself could not refrain from telling Aunt Huang, who visited her the next day, the whole story of the incident in the school, from beginning to end. Aunt Huang was a sister of King Yung's deceased father and the lawful wife of one Chia Huang, who was a poor collateral relation of the Ningkuo branch of the family. He had only a very small private income and was notorious in both the eastern and the western palaces for the frequent begging visits which he paid, together with his wife, now to Princess Chen, now to Madame Phoenix.

When Aunt Huang heard of the humiliations which had befallen her nephew in the school, she felt that her family pride was hurt. So she got into her carriage again as quickly as she could and drove straight off to the Ningkuo palace. She wished to pay her respects to Princess Chen and then to complain to the latter's daughter-in-law, Mistress Yung, of the behavior of her brother Chin Chung. But she did not succeed in carrying out her intention. When, after a few preliminary words about the weather, she asked the Princess why her daughter-in-law was not to be seen, she learned that young Mistress Yung had been seriously ill for the last two months and was unable to receive visitors. The whole household was worried and troubled about her, and tomorrow a new doctor, a young man, was expected, the skill of all the other doctors who had been consulted having proved in vain. Moreover, everyone in the Ningkuo palace was fully occupied preparing for the celebrations which were to take place in two days' time in honor of the birthday of the head of the family, the Prince Hermit Chia Ching. Under these circumstances the visitor rightly thought it would be tactless to bring forward a complaint about a mere trifle. Besides, the kindly way Prince Chen personally invited her to stay to a meal helped to change her initial ill-humor into a feeling of satisfaction, and so she took her leave in the end without having touched on the school incident by a single word.

"What on earth did she want?" the Prince asked his wife when the visitor had departed. He suspected that it was some new request.

"Nothing special. In the beginning something seemed to be on her mind, but in the course of the conversation, when I told her about the illness of our daughter-in-law, her face became more tranquil. She was actually considerate enough not to accept your invitation to a meal. This time she did not ask for anything."

The Prince nodded thoughtfully. A visit from sister-in-law Huang without a request seemed to him decidedly odd.

"I visited our Elder today in his hermitage out in the mountains and invited him to come here the day after tomorrow to receive birthday congratulations from the whole family," he reported. "The old gentleman declined with thanks, however. 'I do not wish to be disturbed in my contemplative peace,' he said, 'and I have no desire to return to your world of conflicting opinions and to take part in a useless, noisy feast. If you wish to give me pleasure, see that my recently completed treatise on "The Blessedness of Work in Solitude" is neatly and perfectly copied out and engraved upon wood for the purpose of making copies of it. I would prefer that a hundred times to any outward display of festivity. As far as I am concerned, the family may feast to their hearts' content at home with you for the two days. But spare me from gifts and visits! Even you may spare yourself the trouble of a visit, but if you insist upon making me a kowtow of congratulation, well, you are at liberty to make it now in advance. But kindly leave me in peace the day after tomorrow!' In these circumstances, then, there is nothing for us to do but celebrate without the old gentleman. Give your orders to the majordomo Lai Sheng in good time to arrange the two days' banqueting."

The Princess accordingly sent the necessary instructions to the majordomo by her son Chia Yung. Then Chia Yung had to go to the western palace and personally invite the "old *Tai tai*" and the "big *Tai tai*" and the "second *Tai tai*" and sister-in-law Phoenix to the birthday festival.

On the morning of the birthday Prince Chen sent his son to the "Great Elder" at his hermitage. A troop of servants had to drag with them sixteen large gift boxes filled with select dishes and chosen fruits.

"Tell the Elder," he said to his son, "that your father has complied with his orders and is refraining from paying a visit. At home, before the assembled members of the family, he will dutifully show his reverence by performing a kowtow before the Elder's throne of honor. And do note whether this form of respect meets with his approval."

The first visitors to appear were Chia Lien from the Yungkuo palace and Prince Chen's foster son, Chia Chiang. They viewed the arrangements of the tables with curiosity, for they wanted to know what entertainment would be offered. They were informed that a company of actors and a troupe of musicians had been engaged and were just now getting ready to appear on the garden stage. The chief guests, who were received by the Prince and Princess Chen at the entrance to the reception hall and accompanied up the steps, gradually arrived. They were Princess Shieh, Madame Cheng, and Madame Phoenix, with Pao Yu and the others. Only the Princess Ancestress had remained at home.

"The old *Tai tai* is the oldest of all the kinfolk, our Elder is only her nephew, and no doubt it was presumptuous of us to expect her to take the trouble to come over for a nephew's birthday," remarked Prince Chen, hiding under a smile his unpleasant surprise at the absence of the Ancestress. "But we invited her all the same because of the beautiful autumn weather and as the chrysanthemums are just in full bloom with us. We thought it would give her pleasure and entertainment to take part in the general family gathering and to see all the children and grandchildren together. It is a pity that we are deprived of the pleasure of her presence."

"Only yesterday she still intended to come," Madame Phoenix replied quickly, instead of Madame Cheng, who really should have answered. "But last night she upset her stomach with a fresh peach and this morning she felt too weak to go out. She wishes to be excused, and asks if there is anything special on the table to send her over a morsel to taste, but nothing rich, only invalid food."

The Prince was satisfied.

"I thought at once there must be some special reason for her not coming. Usually she loves these family parties so much."

The conversation turned to the illness of Mistress Yung and to medical matters. Then Chia Yung appeared and reported on his visit to the Prince Hermit. The old gentleman had shown himself visibly pleased at the attentions planned for him, and asked his son, Prince Chen, to give the best possible hospitality and entertainment to the whole family. Moreover, he again expressed the wish that his treatise on "The Blessedness of Work in Solitude" should be quickly printed. It would be the greatest birthday pleasure possible for him to see his work printed in an edition of ten thousand copies and circulated.

After the sumptuous banquet, served to the male and female guests separately, had been successfully consumed, and the company had rinsed their mouths and washed their hands, Chia Yung appeared again and invited the ladies to come to the theatrical performance in the garden. The gentlemen had already taken their seats. Four Imperial princes, six princes, and eight counts had sent their congratulations together with presents, he said. He had had all the gifts registered in the Estate Office and given the various messengers their receipts, and the messengers had been decently served with food and drink.

Princess Chen accepted her son's report with satisfaction, and then rose from the table with the other ladies in order to see the theatrical performance in the garden. Madame Phoenix left the company. She was longing to pay a visit to the patient, Mistress Yung, of whom she was very fond. Pao Yu expressed the wish to go with her.

"But do not stay too long in the sickroom! Remember, the patient is your niece!" his mother impressed upon him.

Soon afterwards, at his cousin Phoenix's side, he entered the familiar room which awakened in him a secret memory of that strange dream in which he was carried off to the Phantom Realm of the Great Void. How terribly his poor lovely niece had changed! She wanted to get up from her bed when her visitors entered, but Cousin Phoenix anxiously pressed her down on the pillow again.

"Do stay quietly on your back, good *Nai nai!* Otherwise you might get dizzy," she said, sitting on the edge of the bed and taking the patient's hand. "Oh, how thin you have got, you poor thing, since I saw you last!"

"Yes, unfortunately I have lost weight!" sighed the patient, forcing herself to smile. "It is my misfortune not to be very well. What love and kindness I have enjoyed from all sides! My parents-in-law treat me as if I were their own child. My husband, although he is so young, esteems me as I esteem him; our marriage is a most happy one. And also from the other relations, both old and young, I receive nothing but kindness and sympathy. And now this silly illness comes along and prevents me from repaying all this. And to you, dear Aunt, I should like to make some acknowledgment for all your touching love and attention, but unfortunately I lack the strength to do so. I feel as if my end were near. Who knows if I shall live to see the New Year?"

While they were talking Pao Yu was looking steadily at the painting on the wall, which represented a person sleeping beneath begonia branches, to the right and left of which was written:

Gentle coolness surrounds the dreamer—early spring!
The breezes which caress him—fragrant as wine.

The remembrance of his own spring dream, which he had experienced in this same room and with this same beautiful Ko Ching whom he now heard uttering gloomy presentiments of death, gripped him powerfully and touched him to the very core. He felt his heart pierced by a thousand arrows, and his eyes filled with tears. This did not escape Cousin Phoenix, who herself was deeply moved. But she remembered that the purpose of her visit was to cheer and comfort the patient, and not to make her still more sad by wearing a sad face.

"Pao Yu, do not behave like an old woman!" she cried, rousing her

可卿

cousin out of his soft mood. "Your niece is still young and will be able to overcome this little illness. She makes out that she is much worse than she really is.

"You should not give in to such gloomy thoughts! That does not help to make your condition better," she admonished the patient gently.

"Above all, she must get back her appetite, then I shall not be worried about her any more," interjected the young husband, Chia Yung, reassuringly.

"That is my opinion too," agreed Phoenix. "And now be so good as to take Pao Yu back to his mother. She told him emphatically not to stay here too long. I should like to stay alone with our patient for a little while."

The uncle and nephew then left Phoenix alone with the patient and went to the theatrical performance in the Garden of Assembled Perfumes.

Phoenix stayed on for a long time by the sickbed, and they had to send for her three times before she came away. After she had quietly and thoroughly discussed all kinds of confidential matters with the sick woman and tried to cheer her up, she at last stood up to go.

"Well, I wish you a speedy recovery, and I will come again soon," she said on departing. "Meantime, do not be downhearted! The new doctor will certainly cure you."

"Perhaps he will be able to give me some relief, but he will not be able to alter my fate even if he were gifted with supernatural powers," replied the patient with a weak smile. "I know perfectly well that I am only dragging on from day to day."

"Do not give in to such ideas! Your fears are quite groundless. You are having the best possible care now, and luckily you belong to a family where there is no lack of every available remedy, even the best and dearest ginseng. But now excuse me, I must go back to the others."

"You must excuse me for not seeing you out, and do please visit me soon again when you have time!"

"You may rely on me!"

Sunk in thought, Phoenix, after traversing many winding paths, came through a side door into the Garden of Assembled Perfumes. The charm of the scenery which surrounded her here made her slacken her pace and stroll along thoughtfully.

The ground at her feet shimmered yellow with chrysanthemums, from the hills and slopes aspen trees and silver poplars nodded. Ornamental bridges stretched over murmuring brooks, narrow zigzag pathways crossed wide roads which led to moon terraces. From cliffs shining springs trickled down. Exquisite perfumes came borne on the breeze from fruit trellises. From time to time a light gust of wind from the west made the reddish tops of the trees, which stood here and there in artistic groups, tremble and shake. The song of the golden oriole and the chirp of the grasshopper could still be heard in the warm sunshine. Up above, the watchtower beckoned from a steep height; down below, the water pavilion with its triple arched roof was reflected in the lake. In the distance the playing of flutes and the beating of drums could be heard.

Phoenix was walking along quietly completely absorbed in the beauty of the scenery, when she suddenly heard herself called by someone who emerged unexpectedly from behind an artificial stone cliff and now stood before her.

"*Tsing an,* Sister-in-law!" he greeted her, bowing politely.

Phoenix stepped back startled.

"Is that you, Chia Jui?" she asked a little uncertainly.

"How is that? Don't you recognize me, Sister-in-law?"

"Yes, I do; only I was rather confused by your sudden appearance."

"It must indeed be Providence which has caused us to meet here," Chia Jui remarked with an oily smile. "I stole away from the table just now to take a little walk after the meal in this quiet secluded spot. And here I meet you! Really, it must be the work of Providence."

While he was speaking his little eyes, bright with wine, blinked fixedly and brazenly at the beautiful woman opposite him. Phoenix had sufficient knowledge of human nature to enable her to size up the situation by nine-tenths.

"I have always heard much that is good and praiseworthy of you," she flattered him, with assumed friendliness. "And now hearing you speak I know that people have not exaggerated when they praised you as a man of intellect and great worth. Unfortunately, at this moment I must deny myself the privilege of a long conversation with you, as I am expected to join the ladies over there. But perhaps we shall meet again another time."

"It has long been my intention to pay my respects to you. But through consideration for your tender youth, I did not venture to do so up to now," interjected Chia Jui eagerly.

"Oh, among near relations age and years are not so important," she said, seeming to encourage him and putting on a charming smile.

Chia Jui could hardly contain himself for secret triumph. I would never have dreamt that I would succeed so easily with her! he thought to himself, while his mien betrayed his lustful desires so distinctly and disgustingly that Madame Phoenix thought it advisable to get rid of him as quickly as possible.

"Hurry back to your companions, otherwise you will have to pay a fine of a drink," she urged him cunningly, and in fact she succeeded in making him move hesitantly away, though he could not refrain from turning round again and again to look at her. She let him go on a good way, and then she herself followed slowly. On the way she thought to herself: A man like that has a human face, but behind it there's only a beast. My word, he will get to know me yet if he dares try any liberties.

At a bend in the road behind a projection of rock three serving women came breathlessly towards her. Princess Chen had sent them to look for her, being quite worried because she had stayed away so long.

"After all, I am not a spirit that can fly," remarked Phoenix dryly, continuing at her easygoing pace, not in the least disconcerted.

"How many acts have already been performed, then?"

"Eight or nine."

Talking and chatting away, they arrived at the spectators' entrance to the garden theater. In front of the entrance Phoenix caught sight of her cousin Pao Yu engaged in a visibly lively and exuberant conversation with a crowd of young waiting maids and actresses.

"Mind, no silly tricks, Cousin Pao Yu!" she called over to him in mocking threat.

"This is the stairway to the upper platform," said a maid, leading the way. "The other ladies are all up there already."

Phoenix tucked up her skirt and followed the maid up the steps to the upper platform. Princess Chen was waiting for her at the top of the stairs.

"You have been gone a long time," she said with gentle reproach. "Since you find it so difficult to tear yourself away from your beloved niece, it will be better if you move over to us at once and go to live with her. But now take your seat. Here is a program. Read it through and see if there is a piece which you would like to have performed."

"Why am I to have that honor? That is a matter for the others who have precedence of me in rank and age," protested Phoenix modestly.

"Oh, please choose; we others have chosen already," said Princess Shieh and Madame Cheng.

Phoenix read the program attentively and indicated two items, the sketch "Ghostly Apparition" and a song accompanied by lute music.

"Where are the gentlemen gone to?" she asked, bending down to look over the balustrade.

"To the Pavilion of Crystal Brilliance to continue their drinking; and they have taken the band with them," she was told.

"Aha, they want to be to themselves; who knows what mischief they will be up to behind our backs!"

"You cannot expect everyone to be as good and virtuous as you are," said Princess Chen jocularly.

When the theatrical program had come to an end the company sat down to another abundant meal. After this the female guests took their leave. Pao Yu went with them, trotting on horseback behind his mother's carriage. The other male members of the clan remained on for a long time drinking merrily together, and continued their revels the next day.

After that meeting with Phoenix, Chia Jui had no more peace of mind. He wanted to see the beautiful sister-in-law again without fail, and as the foolish fellow had almost convinced himself that she had made advances to him in the Garden of Assembled Perfumes, he was brazen enough to call repeatedly at the Yungkuo palace to pay his respects to her. But it always happened that Phoenix was not at home. At last he was lucky enough to meet her.

It was at the beginning of the twelfth month. Phoenix had just returned from one of her frequent visits to the eastern palace and had changed her visiting frock for a nice comfortable house gown which the maid Little Ping had carefully warmed at the stove.

"Did anything special happen in the house while I was away?" she asked the maid.

"Nothing special. Mrs. Wang sent the interest she owed you on the three hundred taels. And Chia Jui inquired again whether you were at home. He wished to pay his respects to you."

Phoenix shuddered with horror.

"Is the fellow bent on ruining himself? Well, I shall just let him visit me!"

"Why does he want to visit you?" asked the maid. Phoenix told her of that fatal meeting two months previously in the gardens of the Ningkuo palace.

"What? Does the mangy toad lust after tender swan's flesh?" cried the maid indignantly. "How can a man disregard all the rules of the basic human relationships like that? Such presumption deserves to be punished with death!"

"Let him come! He will experience something more than he bargains for!" declared Phoenix, smiling.

What Chia Jui was to experience will be revealed in the next chapter.

CHAPTER 10

Phoenix maliciously incites an unrequited passion. In spite of warnings, Chia Jui looks into the forbidden side of the Wind and Moon Mirror.

PHOENIX HAD HARDLY FINISHED THE SENTENCE WHEN A VOICE FROM outside announced: "Chia Jui is here."

"Let him come in," ordered Phoenix.

Beaming with joy all over his face, the visitor entered, bowing and scraping and rubbing his hands, and burst out with a rush of questions about the "esteemed" well-being and the "precious" and "nephrite" health of his hostess. She welcomed him with hypocritical friendliness, invited him to take a seat, and served him tea.

The fact that he was permitted to see her in her negligee attire made him soft as cheese, and his amorous gaze dripped honey as he asked, suddenly resolved to come straight to the point:

"Why is Cousin Lien not here?"

"How can I know where he may be?" she replied with an air of in-difference.

"Perhaps his foot became entangled in some gentle snare on his way home?"

"Possibly. Men are like that; they fall in love at first sight with the first woman they meet."

"Oh, Sister-in-law, I am certainly not one of that inconstant kind."

"Then you must be a praiseworthy exception. One could hardly find one man in ten of your sort," she flattered him. And he found her flat-tery so pleasing that he almost felt as if she were fondling his ear and stroking his cheek.

"You must suffer great boredom in your solitude, day in, day out," he bravely continued.

"Indeed, yes. And my only comfort is when someone comes to visit me now and then and breaks the monotony."

"How would it be if I were to take over this role of your comforter in loneliness? I have plenty of free time and would be at your disposal every day with the greatest pleasure."

"Surely you are joking! Would you really take as much trouble as that?"

"May I be struck by lightning and split in two halves if my intentions towards you are not sincere! Up to now I did not really trust myself to show my feelings, you were always said to be so terribly strict and cor-rect. But having convinced myself of how entertaining and charming and delightful you are, I shall no longer refrain, but shall hasten to come to you, and I will give my life willingly if only I may enjoy your company!"

"What a high and noble nature your words betray!" she said, assuming an enraptured tone. "How absolutely different you are from your simple cousins Chia Yung and Chin Chung, whose attractions are merely superficial and who do not possess a scrap of understanding or delicacy of feeling."

This praise tickled his very vitals and encouraged him to edge closer and closer to her side and to fondle her with his eyes more and more brazenly. His glance rested boldly in the region of her lotus-shaped girdle pocket. He was in a fever to touch her.

"May I have a close look at your ring?" he asked her, boldly trying to grasp her hand.

"Not so vehement, please!" she rebuffed him gently. "What if someone should catch us unawares?"

He quickly moved away from her again as obediently as if it were a matter of an Imperial edict or a command of Buddha.

"Now you must go!" she said, smiling.

"Do not be so cruel, but let me stay a little longer!" he begged.

"Impossible!" she breathed. "There are too many people about here during the day. It would be too risky. But tonight at the time of the first night watch wait for me outside in the park by the western covered passage."

Chia Jui received this with a feeling of keen delight, as if a precious jewel had fallen into his hands.

"You are not joking, are you, Sister-in-law? And are we safe from eavesdroppers there?" he asked excitedly.

"Do not worry! I will give leave of absence to the servants who are due for watch there tonight; and once the gates above and below are locked, no one can come through," she reassured him.

He hurried off in blissful anticipation of what was to come. As dusk was falling he slipped once more into the Yungkuo palace precincts, and shortly before the gates were locked took up his position in the passage indicated. Soon the surrounding park lay in complete darkness and silence. Not a human sound was to be heard. Half the night through he waited and listened in vain. She had made the appointment with him for the first night watch. The second night watch had passed meantime, and she had not arrived. Then it became clear to him that he had been hoaxed and he decided to get away. But he tried the east gate and the west gate in vain. They were securely locked and bolted from the outside. He now tried to climb the wall; but it was too high and there was no ledge or foothold anywhere by which he could heave himself up. For good or ill, he had to pass the whole night in the inhospitable, empty passage. That was far from pleasant at that wintry season. An icy wind blew right in around the edges of the door and window and cut him pitilessly to the very bone. His limbs were stiff with cold when morning dawned at last and an old gatekeeper came and first opened the eastern gate and then began rattling at the western one. As soon as she turned her back, he slipped swiftly from his hiding place and flew like smoke out through the eastern gate. Luckily, everyone was still asleep at this early hour, so that he was able to escape unseen from the estate by a postern gate at the back. Then he ran home to his grandfather's house. For Chia Jui, who was orphaned young, lived with old Tai Ju, who maintained him.

The old gentleman kept the grandson under strict control and supervision and watched him conscientiously to prevent him from loafing about and neglecting his studies. The fact that the rascal had remained out the whole night naturally merited the severest reproof from his grandfather. He suspected that wine and women had kept him out, and when he arrived home at last in the early hours of the morning he met with anything but a friendly reception. The grandfather could certainly never have guessed that the matter was actually far worse than it seemed, and that the scoundrel was well on the way to creating a serious family scandal.

Mopping the cold sweat from his brow, the night reveller appeared before the enraged old gentleman and tried to lie himself out of his predicament as well as he could. Yesterday, when visiting a relative he had stayed too late and had been kept for the night. But Tai Ju read the lie on his face.

"You should not go out without my permission!" he said severely. "And for deceiving me as well, you deserve all the greater punishment."

And he made him kneel down and gave him thirty or forty strokes with a cane. Besides this, he left him without food for the whole day and gave him as additional punishment an appropriate lesson to learn kneeling out in the yard. After having been frozen through all night, the poor devil had to atone still more for his folly with a thrashing, hunger, still more cold, and some strenuous brainwork.

But all these sufferings failed to cure his depravity. Scarcely two days had passed when he slipped across again during a free hour to the Yungkuo palace. He was once more received by Phoenix. She had decided to cure him even more thoroughly this time. At first she acted as if she were offended and reproached him for having failed to keep his word recently. With secret, malicious pleasure she listened to his protestations to the contrary and let him tell her all he had endured and suffered on her account. Then she suggested a new meeting for that same evening, but in a different place. She indicated a little unused garden house, close behind her dwelling. He was to wait for her there.

"But you really mean it?" he asked diffidently.

"If you do not trust me, you need not come," she informed him coolly and abruptly.

"I shall come even if I have to suffer a hundred deaths!" he declared passionately.

Whereupon she graciously dismissed him. While she was holding her council of war and preparing all the measures to entice him more thoroughly than the first time into the trap, he, waiting at home, could scarcely contain his patience. For he had not the slightest doubt that this time he would attain his end. But first he had to wait until relations who by chance had come that day to visit had left the house. And then he had to be patient a little longer until his grandfather retired to rest after the evening meal. At last he was able to venture forth. It was high time. Darkness was already falling and the people were carrying lanterns in their hands in the streets. Shortly before the gates were closed he successfully slipped into the Yungkuo palace grounds and stole into the empty garden house close behind the dwelling of the beloved one. There he sat and waited, and in his excitement and impatience he was like the proverbial boiling kettle on the hearth. But to the left no human form showed itself, and to the right no human sound was to be heard.

Already anxious doubts were rising in his bosom. Would she leave him another whole night waiting and freezing in vain? But then he suddenly heard soft footsteps. He stepped to the door and saw a ghost-like shadow emerge out of the darkness and come straight towards him. He had not the least doubt that it was Phoenix, and without thinking long or waiting to distinguish black from white, he rushed at the approaching form like a hungry tiger at its prey, seized it in his arms, and carried it to the couch inside the little house.

"Beloved, I had almost died of longing!" he groaned, while his lips sought those of his supposed sweetheart and his hand excitedly fumbled for her garter. What easy game he had! The beloved let him have his way completely, and did not stir. He had now gleefully opened his own clothing and was just getting down to work when a gleam of light from outside made him stop short.

"What's going on here?" asked someone who had slipped in unnoticed, carrying a lighted candle. It was Nephew Chia Chiang.

"Uncle Jui had gentle impulses," came the laughing reply from the couch. The voice betrayed to the horrified Chia Jui that he had taken his nephew Chia Yung for the beloved. Overcome with shame, he tried to run away, but Chia Chiang blocked his path.

"Stop! Stay here! Aunt Phoenix has already told everything to the old *Tai tai*. In order to escape your attentions she has played a little trick on you. The old *Tai tai* is enraged at your behavior and has ordered us two to take you to her at once. Come along!"

"Dear nephew, let me get away and do not betray me!" begged Chia Jui, utterly dismayed. "I promise you a fat reward."

"I could let you run off," replied Chia Chiang, "but first I must know exactly how much you are willing to pay. And a verbal promise is not enough for me; you will have to sign a promissory note. For the sake of decency, the amount in question can be put down on the note as a gambling debt."

"Agreed. But where can we get paper and ink here?"

"They will be brought to you immediately. Wait one moment!"

Chia Chiang disappeared and at once returned with writing materials. After lengthy bargaining Chia Jui had to agree to write out a promissory note for fifty taels. Chia Chiang put the note in his pocket and took Chia Yung by the hand to depart. But suddenly Chia Yung became refractory and declared defiantly that he would tell the story to all the clan in the morning. This threat gave Chia Jui a new fright, and even induced him to humiliate himself by making a kowtow to his torturer. But the latter would not let him go until he too had a promissory note for fifty taels in his pocket.

"Well, for today we will let you go free on our own responsibility," said Chia Chiang magnanimously. "But now you must get off, it is only a question of which way. You cannot go through the domain of the old *Tai tai,* for all the gates are locked. And you dare not venture near the residence of Great-Uncle Cheng. He is still sitting up over his official documents. Woe betide you if he were to catch you! But you cannot stay here any longer, either; at any moment one of the servants may come over, for there is a storeroom near by. The only exit possible for you is the back park gate; but we must first go out and see if the coast is clear, for if you were caught, it would be bad for us too. I know a certain place where you can wait for us in the meantime. Come with us!"

He blew out his wax candle, seized Chia Jui by the hand, and dragged him out. He carefully groped his way in the darkness until they got into a farmyard where they stopped beneath a stairway. "You are safe here for the present," he whispered. "Squat down on the ground and keep very quiet until we come back and call you!"

He went away with the other youth. Chia Jui squatted obediently on the ground at the edge of the stairs, hardly daring to breathe. While he was crouching there thinking over his strange position, he suddenly heard above him a gurgling, splashing noise and immediately a thick, disgusting fluid—human excrements—was poured over him. A suppressed cry escaped him, but immediately remembering that he had been ordered to keep silent, he pressed his hand to his mouth. The evil-smelling liquid dripped down his forehead and cheeks, drenched his clothing through from top to bottom, and made him shiver with cold

and discomfort. How long must he endure this miserable state? He was immensely relieved when at last he heard the two return and call out: "Quick, get away, get away!" He got up quickly from his crouching position and ran in great bounds to the back garden gate. Completely exhausted and out of breath, he arrived about midnight in front of his home. The houseboy who opened the door shrank back startled at sight of him.

"What has happened to you?" he asked, holding his nose.

"I fell into a cesspool in the dark," lied Chia Jui; and he rushed to his room, where he threw off his odorous clothes and washed himself thoroughly. Although he was dead-tired, he could not sleep a wink that night, his mind was so agitated by the adventure he had gone through. Indeed, he could not but feel a grudge against the beloved one who had played him such a vile trick, but her lovely image, which persistently flitted across his mind, again dispelled the grief and rancor and only left place for one craving—to be permitted to fold her in his arms in spite of everything. To be sure, his desire for further visits at the Yungkuo palace had vanished completely after this last experience.

A period of real suffering now began for him. The persistent dunning by his two creditors for payment of the promissory notes which they had extorted from him, the constant fear of being found out by his strict grandfather, the consuming, unfulfilled desire for the beloved woman which reduced the unmarried twenty-year-old to frequent nerve-shattering finger play; added to this the burden of the debts which he felt heavier day by day, and finally, the cold which he had caught as a result of his two nocturnal adventures—all these things had the cumulative effect of making him a sick man in a short time. He lost his appetite, his digestion failed, he felt heavy and giddy as if his legs were made not of bones and sinews and muscles but of cotton-wool; his eyes became dull, as if vinegar had been sprayed into them, he spat blood when he coughed, fever and sleeplessness tortured him by night, by day he suffered drowsy exhaustion. When he did go to sleep he fell into restless dreams and stammered in delirium. Such were the manifold infirmities which came upon him by degrees in the course of a year.

His anxious grandfather tried all possible doctors, and made him swallow pounds of medicine, but it was all in vain. Only a good dose of ginseng could save him, said the doctors. But where could a poor scholar get the means to acquire this unusual and expensive drug?

The old Tai Ju turned to his rich relations in the Yungkuo palace. Madame Cheng, to whom he made his request, passed it on to Madame Phoenix, the mistress of the kitchens and stores. She asked her to weigh out two ounces of ginseng for him. But Madame Phoenix had no intention whatever of helping the invalid, whom she preferred to see die. She replied that she had recently given her last supply to the sick wife of Marshal Yang, at the request of the Princess Ancestress. Let her try to get some from her mother-in-law, Princess Shieh, or from Princess Chen, for, after all, it was a matter of a human life, urged Madame Cheng. But Madame Phoenix sent neither to the house of Chen nor to the house of Shieh but scraped together a small remnant of waste roots from her own supply, scarcely one-tenth of an ounce, and sent the rubbish to the home of the invalid. The *Tai tai* Cheng sent it but would be unable to send any more, she gave word. She deceitfully told her aunt, however, that in accordance with her instructions she had borrowed two ounces of the best ginseng for the sick man. Naturally, the miserable refuse which she really sent him did not have the least effect.

One day a lame wandering Taoist monk knocked at old Tai Ju's door, begging for alms. He offered in return to cure anyone of any illness of mind or soul. Chia Jui, who from his sickbed could hear the stranger commending his power of spiritual healing, became intensely excited and loudly implored those around him to bring the master to his bedside so that he might save his life. They complied with his wish and brought the lame priest into the sickroom.

"Save me, Master!" the sick man implored again and again, kowtowing in his bed to the visitor.

The priest, lost in thought, observed him for a while and then he said: "Your illness cannot be cured by medicine. But I have a precious object here with me, which I will give you. You need only to look at it every day, and you will get well again."

With these words he rummaged in his knapsack and drew out a veiled mirror. The back of the mirror, in which one could also see one's reflection, had the inscription engraved on it: Magic Mirror of the Moon and the Wind.

"This mirror comes from the airy phantom castle of the Fairy of Fearful Awakening in the Phantom Realm of the Great Void," the priest explained. "Its power consists in purifying corrupted souls and freeing them from impure thoughts and desires. The fairy has entrusted it to me in order that I may save highly educated and high-minded young people like you, and so preserve them from destruction. But you may look only in the reverse side of it. A thousand times, ten thousand times, beware of looking in the front side! Remember that! Remember that! I shall return in three days and take back the mirror. In the meantime it will have cured you."

He had hardly finished speaking when, to the astonishment of the bystanders who tried in vain to hold him back, he vanished into thin air.

The invalid asked the company to leave him alone. Why should he not try out the mirror? The strange priest had diagnosed his condition remarkably correctly; this the others could not know, of course. So he took the mirror in his hand and looked, as the priest had told him to, into the reverse side. He recoiled in horror. A skeleton grinned at him from the mirror!

"Did the accursed fellow only want to frighten me?" he cried angrily. "Now I will just look into the forbidden side."

And he turned the mirror and looked into the other side. O marvel! The lovely image of Phoenix met his gaze! She was smiling at him and beckoning him to her with her hand. Blissfully happy, he felt himself drawn, he knew not how, into the mirror by some magic force, and enjoyed with the beloved one the passionate Play of Wind and Cloud. When this was over she led him gently out of the mirror again. He found himself once more lying in his bed, still groaning and moaning from the aftereffects of the delightful experience.

Now he turned to the mirror again and looked once more at the other side. Again the horrible skeleton grinned at him, bringing a cold sweat out of his pores. Though still exhausted from the first enjoyment of love, he could not resist the temptation of looking into the forbidden side of the mirror a second time, and again Phoenix beckoned him and smiled at him alluringly and drew him with magic power into the mirror, once more to perform the Play of Wind and Cloud. The experience was repeated four times. When she led him out for the fourth time he suddenly felt himself being seized by two men, who put him in iron chains.

"I will follow you! But let me take the mirror with me!" he cried aloud.

These were his last words. Those outside had heard his cry. They opened the door of the sickroom and peeped inside and could just see him staring at the mirror with wide-open eyes, when it slid to the ground as his grip loosened. They all pressed around the bed, but the sick man did not breathe again. They found the sheets wet with traces of human emissions. The servants washed and dressed the dead man and laid him on a bier in accordance with custom. Then they informed his grandparents that he had passed away.

The relatives raised a loud dirge and did not fail to abuse the lame priest and his magic mirror.

"The magic mirror must be destroyed; otherwise it will do still more harm," cried old Tai Ju angrily; and he ordered them to throw it into the fire. But before they had time to carry out his order a voice was heard in the air saying: "Why do you want to burn my mirror? It is innocent. The dead man himself is to blame. Who told him to ignore my prohibition and look into the wrong side?"

At the same time the mirror rose from the ground of itself and floated out through the window. Old Tai Ju rushed out the door after it and tried to catch it, when he saw the same lame priest standing there.

"Who dares to seize my mirror?" he heard him crying in a threatening voice, and then he saw him stretch out his hand and catch the floating mirror. The next moment both priest and mirror had vanished into nothingness.

CHAPTER 11

Ko Ching dies and receives the posthumous title of wife of a mandarin of the fifth rank. Phoenix takes over the household management in the Ningkuo palace.

TOWARDS THE END OF THE YEAR THE NEWS CAME FROM YANGCHOW that Black Jade's father, Ling Ju Hai, was very ill and urgently desired to see his daughter once more. The Princess Ancestress thought it right that the father's wish should be granted, and so she sent her granddaughter home under the escort of her cousin, Chia Lien. Pao Yu was naturally very sad at being deprived of the company of his favorite cousin for a considerable time. Phoenix, too, found it hard to bear the long separation from her husband. Added to this was her anxiety for the seriously sick friend in the eastern palace. She passed the lonely evenings until bedtime as best she could chatting and gossiping merrily with the maid Little Ping.

One night, though tired from talking and working late, her restless thoughts kept her lying awake long after her maid Ping was fast asleep. By patiently counting on her fingers she had at last managed to lull herself into an uncertain doze. Outside, the third beat of the drum had just announced midnight when it seemed to her that her niece Ko Ching was standing beside her bed.

"Well may you sleep, dear," Ko Ching said to her, smiling, "but I, of course, have to set out on the return journey today. Would you not like to accompany me part of the way? We have always been so fond of each other and understand each other so well that I did not wish to go without saying good-by to you. Besides, I have many things to say to you which I would never confide to anyone else. For you are not an average woman, and in the matter of intellect and energy you are the equal of any man or any high official."

She now explained in a long discourse that she was concerned for the future of the house of Chia. True, the Chia clan had endured, strong and powerful, for hundreds of years already, but blossoming is likely to be followed by decay, and the day might come when the mighty tree would fall, and the crowd of monkeys which it had sheltered in its branches and crown up till now would be scattered in every direction. This meant that in good times provision should be made for bad times. Two things were on her mind: the consolidation of the family school and insurance of the perpetuity of the quarterly sacrifices to the ancestors. She entertained a fear lest lean times should come when there would be no funds available for these two objects. She would therefore like to recommend the Elders of the clan to take advantage of the present favorable circumstances and buy up as much land and property as possible in the neighborhood of the family vaults, thereby forming a lasting and inalienable family foundation. The purpose of this foundation must be to maintain the family school and assure the perpetuity of the ancestors' sacrifices from the proceeds of the communal lands. A fortune dedicated to such cultural purposes would, even if the worst came to the worst, be safe from seizures by the State in the event of the offices and dignities of the heads of individual families being forfeited and their private fortunes confiscated, in consequence of Imperial disfavor or the like. In such an emergency the members of the family concerned would, moreover, find a place of refuge in the lands of the family foundation, where they could continue to support themselves by farming. The family school would then give the sons and grandsons the possibility of rising in the world once more. Farming and education—these were the two solid pillars upon which a great aristocratic family like the Chia clan must rely if the inevitable vicissitudes of fortune were to be outlived and if the clan was to be proof against downfall. The speaker ended with the quotation:

Spring passes, fragrance fades,
Be watchful of the position acquired.

Phoenix had followed this intelligent discourse with profound attention. She was just about to ask some questions when, through the stillness of the night, she heard the Cloud Gong booming at the second gateway. Its heavy thud resounded four times. That was the signal that somebody in the house had died. Phoenix started up, alarmed, out of her light sleep, and immediately a messenger appeared with the announcement that Mistress Yung of the eastern palace had just passed away. Phoenix dressed quickly and hurried over to her aunt, Madame Cheng. Needless to say, the sad news of the early death of the young and beautiful lady, who was so universally beloved, caused sobbing and lamenting everywhere, in the eastern as well as in the western palace.

Pao Yu also got news of the death during the night while he was in

94

bed. It made him start up violently and jump out of bed. As he did so he felt a stab through his heart like the stab of a dagger and at the same moment he spat up a mouthful of blood. The maids ran to him in consternation and asked what was the matter with him and whether they should send for a doctor, but he would not have it.

"It is of no importance," he said. "It is a little heart attack caused by the sudden shock. Some blood has gone out of its course."

He dressed and went to the Princess Ancestress to ask permission to go over while it was still night to visit the bier. The Princess Ancestress pointed out in vain that one should avoid the unclean proximity of a fresh corpse, that his health might suffer if he were to go out in the middle of a winter's night, and that it would be wiser to wait until the morning. He would not be dissuaded. At last the anxious Ancestress allowed him to go in a closed carriage and in the care of a numerous retinue.

Despite the late hour, he found the entrance gateway to the Ningkuo palace wide open and brightly lit up, and there was an excited coming and going of people with torches and lanterns in their hands. From the inner rooms he could hear loud cries of lamentation which made the hills tremble and the mountains shake. Pao Yu also gave free vent to his sorrow with many tears and loud laments by the side of the bier. Then he greeted the relatives, who had come in a dense crowd.

A time of strenuous commotion and excitement now followed in the Ningkuo palace; for Prince Chen made it his business to carry out the customary mourning ceremonies in honor of the beloved departed with all possible pomp. No less a person than the Court Necromancer of the Imperial Observatory was given the order to fix the days and times of the various ceremonies. He directed that the burial should take place in seven weeks' time; that during those seven weeks the body was to remain on a bier in the house of mourning; that on the third day after the death the seven weeks' mourning ceremonies were to be opened by the issue of the death notices; that a hundred and eight bonzes were to recite their Buddhist requiems in the great hall while ninety-nine Taoist priests were to offer sacrifice and pray according to the Taoist rite for the salvation of the departed before an altar to be erected by themselves in the Tower of Heavenly Balm. That, besides this, fifteen bonzes and fifteen Taoist priests of high rank were to hold pious devotions in front of the spirit tablet of the departed lady in the Hall of Glorification in the Garden of Assembled Perfumes.

The only one of the whole clan whom the sad event left untouched was the Elder of the house, the Prince Hermit Chia Ching. He himself would ascend sooner or later into the heavenly spheres, so his message ran. Why should he emerge now from his holy solitude and soil himself again with the red dust of this world, after he had happily attained to some degree of purification and perfection? Accordingly, he took no further notice of the event, but remained in his hermitage, and left the entire execution of the mourning program in the hands of his son, Prince Chen.

Right at the beginning of the mourning period an episode occurred which attracted much notice and called forth great praise. A maid of the deceased lady, one Jui Chu, in an effort to give visible expression to her sincere sorrow at the death of her mistress, had hit her head so hard against a wooden post that she had died of the effects. The whole clan praised the behavior of this maid as an extraordinary and memorable example of self-sacrificing fidelity and devotion, and Prince Chen ordered that, as a reward, the brave girl should be buried with the ceremony due to a granddaughter by blood and that her spirit tablet also should be set up in the Hall of Glorification in the Garden of Assembled Perfumes.

Yet another episode indicating praiseworthy piety and devotion was announced. Another servant, one Pao Chu, nobly offered to allow herself to be adopted posthumously as a daughter of the deceased woman who was childless, in order that she might carry out during the mourning period and at the funeral the difficult and onerous role incumbent on a surviving child, which demanded among other things that she should walk by the coffin swaying from side to side during the whole course of the funeral procession. Prince Chen accepted her offer with grateful emotion and rewarded her by directing that henceforward she should be called "Miss" and respected as a daughter of the house. And Pao Chu undertook her duty as a daughter in such a conscientious way and exaggerated to such an extent the prescribed lamenting and wailing beside the coffin that she almost lost her life by it.

In his efforts to carry out the funeral with as much outward magnificence as possible, Prince Chen saw himself hindered, to his annoyance, by one circumstance. "My son possesses neither rank nor office," he reflected. "The only thing he has to be proud of is a title of doctor of the first and lowest degree acquired by purchase. The inscription on the banners of honor of his late wife will look paltry and mean indeed. The deceased will, moreover, be deprived of any official mourners. This is a painful deficiency."

Then it happened very appropriately that on the fourth day of the first week of mourning, Tai Kuan, the influential chief Imperial eunuch and superintendent of the Imperial Palace, came to pay a visit. Messengers went ahead bringing gifts for his sacrifice to the departed spirit. Then he himself appeared in the big State sedan chair, his arrival being ceremonially proclaimed by heralds and gong beaters. Prince

Chen invited him into the Pavilion of the Resting Bees, where they were able to chat undisturbed, and in the course of the conversation he put forward his request regarding promotion for his son. The chief eunuch understood at once what he was driving at with his guarded hints.

"If I understand you aright, you would like to give a greater air of brilliance and importance to the funeral," he remarked, smiling.

"Your assumption is right, old Chancellor of the Interior," Prince Chen hastened to confirm.

"Hm, your request comes just at the right time. I know by chance of a nice, suitable vacancy for your son. Of the three hundred officers' posts of command in the Imperial Palace Guard, there are two vacant at the moment. True, one post I have already given away elsewhere— namely, to Count Hsiang Yang's son. Since the Count has requested me repeatedly and urgently, and moreover had sent one thousand five hundred silver taels to my house, I could not very well turn a deaf ear to his request, especially as we are very old friends. Someone else has applied for the remaining vacancy, it is true—the fat Provincial Treasurer Yung Hsing, who wants it for his son, but I have not answered his request yet. You are therefore free to hand in a statement of your son's curriculum."

The Prince did not have to be told twice; he ordered his secretaries to write out the requested curriculum on nice red paper. The chief eunuch read the paper on the spot, then he handed it to a young man of his retinue with the words: "Take this paper to my old friend Chao, the Minister of Finance. Give him my kind regards, and ask him to prepare a document of investiture for an appointment of officer in the palace guards with letters patent for a button of the fifth rank. Say that I shall fetch the document myself tomorrow and bring with me the appropriate amount of duly weighed silver."

The young attendant nodded and left. A little later the chief eunuch himself stood up to go. Prince Chen politely accompanied him to the outer gate.

"Shall I send the money to the Ministry or to your house?" he asked, as his visitor got into the sedan chair.

"It might prejudice you with them if you sent it to the Ministry. Better send me the round sum of a thousand taels to my house, then you will have no further bother," was his answer. Prince Chen thanked him exuberantly.

"When the mourning period is over I shall not fail to go personally to your noble threshold and take my unworthy dog of a son with me, so that he may dutifully make his kowtow of thanks to you," he assured him.

As early as the following day Chia Yung received from the Ministry his document of investiture and his letters patent of rank, and from that day the spirit tablet of the deceased lady bore the inscription "Spirit tablet of the Lady Ching, by marriage of the house of Chia, by Imperial patent wife of a Mandarin of the fifth rank."

In front of the wide-open outer gates of the Garden of Assembled Perfumes there shone from high posts two bright red notices, visible from a distance, which announced in large gold letters that the obsequies of "Lady Ching, by letters patent wife of an officer of the Imperial Palace Guard in the inner precincts of the Red Forbidden City" were being held here.

Prince Chen was very happy and relieved that his request had been granted so quickly. But there was still another dilemma which greatly disquieted him.

His wife was ill and confined to bed, and just in these days when there was a rush of visits and receptions, and there were so many arrangements to be made, the mistress of the house, who could deputize for him with dignity and keep the servants in control, was sadly missed. Her absence was a calamity. How easily could transgressions against custom occur, which would leave him open to the mockery of his noble and illustrious guests. As it was, the servants were used to easy discipline and now, without direction and supervision, they would if possible be even more careless. The Prince was in a sweat of anxiety, and confided the matter to his cousin Pao Yu. The advice which Pao Yu whispered in his ear made his troubled face brighten up, and he resolved to follow it at once.

He left his male guests alone and appeared shortly afterwards accompanied by Pao Yu in the ladies' sitting room. As luck had it, there were present only Princess Shieh, Madame Cheng, Madame Phoenix, and a few other ladies, all close relations. Prince Chen himself did not feel very well today and was exhausted from the rushing around and night watching of the last few days. He had twinges of pain in his limbs, and limped into the room, supported on a stick, groaning and with difficulty. The ladies rose from their seats when he appeared, and Princess Shieh asked anxiously: "Do you not feel well? You look exhausted, you should rest and take care of yourself."

The Prince, clutching his stick, got down on his knees with difficulty to salute the ladies with his *tsing an*. The ladies signed to Pao Yu to help him up, and asked him to take a seat. But the Prince modestly insisted on making his request standing.

"The unworthy nephew has come here to ask a favor of the two worthy aunts and the esteemed cousin," he began, forcing himself to smile. And then he told of the embarrassment he was in owing to the lady of the house being laid up just now, and he asked if Madame

王熙鳳

Phoenix would be willing to help out by taking over the role of mistress of the house during the weeks of mourning.

"That all depends on whether Aunt Cheng can do without her," remarked Princess Shieh laughing.

"She is still young and inexperienced, and will scarcely be able to undertake such a difficult task. What if she were to make some mistake? It would be better if you would ask someone else," said Aunt Cheng, dubiously.

But Phoenix did not consider the matter for long. She was confident of her ability for the difficult task, and as the princely cousin begged and implored so pathetically, she gave her consent. The Prince thanked her with a low bow and straight away gave her full authority in writing. He warmly impressed upon her that she should manage the servants and the palace housekeeping funds quite freely and absolutely at her discretion just as if they were her own servants and her own funds. Further, he suggested that she should move over to the Ningkuo palace for the period of her management in order to spare herself the frequent journeys back and forth. But Phoenix said, smiling, that she thought she could not be done without in the Yungkuo palace either, so she would prefer to come over every day.

That same day Phoenix took up the management. The first thing she did was to make a list of the names of all the staff. And then, every morning at half-past six punctually, she held the roll call. With this list in her hand and the wife of the majordomo Lai Sheng by her side, she had each manservant and maidservant—more than a hundred, in all—come to her one after another, and she herself set them their tasks for the day. And even when she had had only a few hours' sleep, she never missed this hour of the roll call. She demanded the same punctuality from the servants. Her own servants all had watches and were trained to be punctual to the minute, she told the staff. There must also be watches in the Ningkuo palace. Among other things, she introduced a daily consultation hour from ten until half-past eleven, when all requests and needs were to be submitted to her. Every evening at seven o'clock she made the round of the entire premises. She took stern measures against any dawdling or negligence. Once when a servant was missing from the roll call she punished him with twenty strokes and the deduction of a full month's wages. This had its effect. The slovenliness which hitherto had reigned in the Ningkuo palace was replaced by stern discipline, and the long weeks of mourning ceremony passed off to the great satisfaction of Prince Chen and, thanks to the energy and discretion of Phoenix, without the least violation of form or custom which would have given cause for mockery or laughter.

CHAPTER 12

Pao Yu meets the Prince of the Northern Quietness on the road. Chin Chung enjoys himself in the nunnery.

THE PRINCIPAL DAY OF THE WEEKS-LONG OBSEQUIES, NAMELY, THE day of the funeral procession, had come. After the company had spent the whole night long feasting in the brilliantly illuminated halls and being entertained by the performances of two troupes of players and one troupe of acrobats, the gigantic funeral procession set out early in the morning for the Temple of the Iron Railings, where the ancestral vaults of the two princely families were. The cortege, which followed the coffin with its sixty-four bearers, all dressed in dark green, stretched for well over four miles. The adopted daughter, Pao Chu, who tottered along beside the coffin in an attitude of complete dejection, sobbing incessantly, led the procession. The male relatives, friends, and funeral guests—among them princes, counts, and high officials—followed on foot; then came the female members of the families and female funeral guests in more than a hundred carriages and sedan chairs, and finally the numerous servants and the bearers of the customary banners, symbols, and funeral gifts.

At regular intervals along the route the procession passed brightly colored sacrificial tents, erected by prominent individual mourners for the purpose of presenting a wayside offering of sorrowful music to the dead lady as she passed. The owners of the first four of these tents were the Princes of Tung Ping, Nan An, Hsi Ning, and Peh Ching. As their respective titles, "Prince of the Eastern Covenant," "Prince of the Southern Peace," "Prince of the Western Tranquillity," and "Prince of the Northern Quietness," betrayed, their bearers were descendants of meritorious men of Imperial blood, who had helped the founder of the dynasty in his conquest of the Empire. Of these four, again, the bearers of the title Peh Ching Wang, Prince of the Northern Quietness, were the most famous and the most respected, because their ancestor had taken an exceedingly prominent part in the foundation of the ruling dynasty. The present holder of the title, Prince Chi Yung, an exceptionally handsome young man not yet twenty, was, moreover, loved and respected by all for his charming modesty and friendliness. In consideration of the warm, brotherly friendship which had existed between his ancestor and the first Prince of Ningkuo, he would not be denied the privilege of appearing today personally in his sacrificial tent, in order to render the last honors to the dead lady when her coffin passed by.

Immediately after the audience which had brought him to the Imperial Palace at five o'clock this morning like every other morning, he changed his Court dress for a white mourning garment, and had himself taken to his mourning tent in his State litter, preceded by men beating gongs, and followed by his ceremonial umbrella and a great retinue. There he had waited patiently, sitting in his litter, until the funeral cortege came by from the Ningkuo palace. Around him, also waiting in silence, crowded his troop of servants, and a respectful silence likewise reigned among the masses who stood ranged on either side of the processional route in the neighborhood of the princely tent. At long last, winding its way from the north, and looking all white like a silver stream, came the endless funeral procession.

Runners and ushers, who had hastened out far ahead of the actual procession to clear the route, had meantime sent back word that His Excellency the Prince of the Northern Quietness was present in person in his funeral tent. Prince Chen halted the procession and, accompanied by Prince Shieh and Chia Cheng, went aside to greet the distinguished guest in his sacrificial tent. All three fell on their knees before the Prince and paid homage to him with a ceremonial state kowtow, as befitted his rank. Smiling courteously and quite naturally, without any affectation, as if he were among good old friends, the Prince, sitting in his litter, returned the salutation with a slight bow.

Prince Chen expressed thanks for the unmerited honor which the Prince had shown him by appearing in person. The Prince, in reply, referred to the old hereditary terms of friendship which existed between the two houses, in view of which his coming was only to be expected. Then he made a sign to his master of ceremonies to offer the sacrifice in honor of the dead. When the ceremony was at an end he turned courteously to Pao Yu's father and asked: "Where is the young gentleman who came into the world with a jewel in his mouth? It has long been my wish to enjoy the pleasure of his acquaintance. Will you please ask him to come over here?"

Chia Cheng hurried back to the funeral procession, to return immediately afterwards with Pao Yu. Pao Yu too had long cherished the wish to meet that Prince of whom people always said with such enthusiasm that he united outward beauty with nobility of soul and the first and highest degree of unaffected and kindly tact. But the complete lack of freedom of movement which his strict father imposed upon him had made this impossible hitherto. Therefore he was all the happier when his ardent wish so unexpectedly found fulfillment today by the wayside. As he entered the tent, full of eager expectation, he looked up at the Prince who sat enthroned before him on his litter, august and full of dignity. He was wearing on his head the silver-winged cap with white tassels worn by princes. His white, knife-pleated mourning garment was embroidered in a design of five-clawed dragons, and he wore

北靜王

a red leather belt studded with emeralds. His face was like a jewel, his eyes were lustrous stars, beauty radiated from his whole form. Pao Yu eyed him with secret admiration, and it was with no less satisfaction that the Prince's eyes rested upon his visitor. Pao Yu was wearing a silver cap, and round his forehead was the usual gold band in the form of two dragons snapping at a pearl. His white mourning garment, which was embroidered with a snake design, was fastened by a silver belt set with pearls. His face glowed with the freshness of a spring flower, his eyes shone like lacquer.

When he had paid his homage to the Prince, the latter opened his arms wide and drew the boy to him.

"Truly, it is not in vain that you bear your name," he said, smiling. "You really look like a 'Precious Stone.' But where, actually, is the stone with which you came into the world?"

Pao Yu promptly took out the stone, which he wore on a five-colored cord hidden under his coat, and handed it to the Prince. The Prince examined the amulet and its inscription carefully.

"Has the stone already shown its magic power?" he asked.

"Up to the present it has had no chance of doing so," replied Chia Cheng for his son.

While the Prince went on speaking in terms of the utmost astonishment about the strange birth phenomenon, he fastened the cord with the amulet back on Pao Yu's neck with his own hands. Then he drew him into a more intimate conversation about his age and his studies and other personal things. Enchanted by Pao Yu's clear, distinct speech and the pleasing tone of his voice, the Prince remarked to Mr. Cheng: "Your little lord seems to be a real young phoenix. Far be it from the unworthy Prince to utter flatteries to his honored old friend, but who knows, perhaps the fame of this young phoenix may one day outshine that of the old one."

"Oh, my loathsome young cur is falsely misleading you into such golden eulogies," replied Mr. Cheng with a smile. "But if, thanks to your inexhaustible princely favor, your prophecy should be fulfilled, it would be a source of the greatest joy to me and to my house."

"I would only point out one thing to you," continued the Prince thoughtfully. "Because of his many perfections, your little lord is doubtless surrounded with very special love and tenderness at home by his revered grandmother and the whole family. But such love can easily lead to pampering, and in this lies the danger for young people like ourselves that an otherwise good education might be utterly nullified. I know this from my own experience, and I think that the same may be the case with your little lord. If, as I believe, your little lord is hindered at home in the full development of his abilities, there is nothing to prevent him from visiting me frequently in my cold home. True, I myself am worthless and without merit, but I enjoy the advantage of being acquainted with many of the most distinguished men of the Empire, and when one of them comes to the capital, he seldom fails to grant me the honor of a favorable glance from his blue-black eyes. Thus it happens that many high and noble spirits meet in my cold dwelling, and your small princeling would find in my house many opportunities for advantageous and beneficial exchange of thought."

Chia Cheng accepted the gracious invitation without hesitation and with many polite bows and thanks. The Prince now unfastened a prayer chaplet from his wrist and handed it to Pao Yu.

"Because of the unexpectedness of this, our first meeting, I have no worthy gift at hand with which to honor you," he added. "But for the present please accept these prayer beads of carved yunnan root as a small sign of my regard. They were a gift from the Son of Heaven."

Pao Yu passed the chaplet on to his father, and both expressed their thanks. Chia Cheng and Prince Shieh then besought the Prince not to allow himself to be detained any longer by the funeral procession, but the Prince gently insisted upon remaining until the corpse had passed.

"The departed lady has joined the blessed," he said. "She is now a higher being than we ordinary mortals who are still toiling in the red dust of this earthly world. Although by the favor of the Son of Heaven I have been permitted, unworthy though I am, to inherit the rank of Prince, it would be an impertinence on my part if I were to take precedence over a blessed spirit."

And so Prince Shieh and Mr. Cheng and Pao Yu could not do otherwise than take leave of the Prince and let the procession proceed once more. But they ordered that the funeral music should cease as a mark of respect for as long as the Prince remained in his tent. The Prince waited for the whole procession to pass by; only then did he continue on his way.

After the procession had passed through the city gates into the open countryside, Prince Chen decided that the time had come to invite the male mourners, who up till now had been following the coffin on foot, to continue the remaining stretch of the route, to the Temple of the Iron Railings, in a more comfortable manner. Accordingly, the older gentlemen took their places in their carriages and litters while the younger ones mounted their horses. Pao Yu wanted to mount his horse too, but Madame Phoenix, fearing that he would take advantage of the greater freedom of movement and lack of supervision, once outside the town, to indulge in all sorts of wild pranks, asked him to get into her carriage.

"Come, dear cousin, get in," she invited him with a smile. "I know you always like feminine society. Therefore you will surely feel much more comfortable in my carriage and by my side than in the company of those apes on horseback."

Pao Yu dismounted obediently from his horse and slipped into her carriage, and the two continued their way chatting merrily.

After a while two servants on horseback came galloping up and announced to Madame Phoenix that the procession was just approaching a resting point. Would not the *Nai nai* wish to rest for a time and change her garments? Madame Phoenix agreed to this and ordered her carriage to follow the two guides, who turned aside from the highway into the open countryside. At Pao Yu's wish, his friend Chin Chung joined the party on horseback.

After going a short stretch they arrived in front of a farmhouse. It was a modest little dwelling of a few rooms in which the numerous family lived crowded together. When the simple folk saw the magnificent carriage with its elegantly attired occupants and its formidable train of servants, of course they stood and gaped in astonishment as if it were a heavenly apparition.

Madame Phoenix got out and disappeared into the straw-thatched cottage. She had previously told Pao Yu that he could look around the farm for a bit with his friend and follow her in a little later. Pao Yu understood the hint and set out with Chin Chung on a tour of inspection of the farm.

He had never seen the various farming implements before. He did not even know their names, and had to ask the servants who were accompanying him to explain their use and purpose. When told, he could not get over his astonishment at the number of new things he was learning there.

"Only now do I understand the meaning of the old proverb about the rice in the dish, of which every grain is the result of endless trouble and exertion," he remarked thoughtfully.

In the course of his tour he came to a room in which he saw, lying on the kang, a strange implement which seemed to him even more curious than the others. That, he was told, was a spinning wheel with which was made the yarn that was later woven into cloth. Full of high spirits, Pao Yu jumped up on the kang and began turning the spinning wheel. A peasant girl about seventeen years of age came up and stopped him.

"That is not for playing with!" she said. "You will put it out of order!"

Pao Yu promptly desisted. "This is the first time that I have seen a spinning wheel," he excused himself, with some embarrassment, "and I wanted to try it, just for fun."

"You don't understand how to work it, but if you would like I shall show you," said the girl, amiably.

"This is getting really interesting," whispered Chin Chung into Pao Yu's ear, at the same time plucking his sleeve.

"Stop chattering or we shall come to blows," retorted Pao Yu jocularly, giving the other a cuff. He too was all eyes for the pretty girl, who had meantime set the spinning wheel in motion and was reeling off the finished yarn with skillful fingers. Pao Yu thought he had not seen such a charming sight for many a day, and he could not tear his eyes away from the graceful spinster.

But alas, their pleasure was prematurely interrupted by an old woman, who called over from the other side of the farmyard. In a trice the pretty girl had jumped down from the spinning wheel and run out of the room. Pao Yu gazed after her disappointed, then went back to the farmhouse with the servant whom Phoenix had sent to find him, to share the frugal breakfast which the friendly peasants had prepared for their guests. In return for the meal Phoenix had little packages of broken silver distributed among them by the servant Wang, after which the party went back to the carriage and set off to rejoin the funeral procession.

At their departure their carriage was surrounded by the farm folk, big and small, but Pao Yu looked in vain among the crowd for the pretty girl of the spinning wheel. Yet when the carriage had gone a short way he was to see her again. Surrounded by some village children, she came towards them from the opposite direction chattering and laughing, and carrying in her arms a small boy, apparently a little brother. Pao Yu gazed at her with tenderness. Unfortunately, the carriage had already gained a lively pace and, like a cloud chased by the wind, went all too quickly past the group. When Pao Yu looked back once more the girl was already lost to view.

Towards noon the procession reached the goal of its journey, the Temple of the Iron Railings. The bonzes, who had taken up their positions in front of the temple in two rows on either side of the road, welcomed the procession with drums, cymbals, banners, and pennants. In the temple yet another Buddhist requiem for the dead was held, sacrifice was offered and incense was burned, after which the coffin was placed in the side chamber of an inner hall. The deceased's adopted daughter, Pao Chu, also withdrew into this same chamber together with her bed equipment, there to spend the next three nights until the burial.

In the course of the afternoon most of the funeral guests took their leave and went back to the town. Only a few of the nearer relatives remained, and took up their quarters in the temple for the three days until the burial. Princess Shieh and Madame Cheng also returned home that day. They intended to take Pao Yu with them, but Pao Yu was so pleased with the unaccustomed change of this stay in the country that he contrived to be allowed to remain there in the company of Phoenix until the end of the solemnities.

The Temple of the Iron Railings had been erected long ago by the two ancestors of the Ningkuo and Yungkuo dynasties, and destined as a hereditary burial place for all those members of both families who should die in the capital. It was maintained from the proceeds of an estate which had been bequeathed to the temple in addition to the temple lands proper. Thanks to the rich revenues yielded by this convent farmland, the temple was maintained in the best possible style, and on occasions such as the present one neither ample board nor suitable accommodation was lacking for the funeral guests.

Phoenix preferred, however, to spend the three nights until the burial in a nunnery situated not far from the Temple of the Iron Railings. Accordingly, after the temple bonzes had carried out their priestly duties and the majority of the funeral guests had bidden farewell, she repaired together with Pao Yu and Chin Chung to the Convent of the Watery Moon, as it was called. This nunnery was also known as the "Bread Convent" among the country folk around, because it had a bakery which produced excellent bread. The Abbess, with two younger nuns, received the guests at the convent gate and accompanied them to their guest cells. Then, while Phoenix and the Abbess sat down for a good long chat over a bowl of tea, Pao Yu and Chin Chung passed the time strolling through the courtyards and halls and examining the interior of the convent. "There goes Chi Neng," remarked Pao Yu suddenly, nudging his companion. Chi Neng was one of the two young nuns who had received them shortly before.

"Yes, but what about her?" answered Chin Chung with affected indifference.

"Do not be such a humbug!" said Pao Yu, laughing. "Who was it who embraced her so tenderly in Grandmother's room one time when no one was looking, eh?"

"It would never occur to me to do such a thing!" retorted Chin Chung, embarrassed.

"Well, I will not interfere. But will you please speak to her and ask her to bring us some tea?"

Chin Chung did as he was bidden. "Little Neng," he called out, "please be so good as to bring us some tea." From her childhood little Chi Neng had been frequently in and out of the Yungkuo palace on messages from the convent. Everyone in the palace knew her, and Pao Yu and Chin Chung had already exchanged many a glance and many a

joke with her. Now she had grown into a mature young woman and had gradually awakened to an awareness of the Play of Wind and Moon. The handsome, lively Chin Chung had won her heart, and he on his part had become very fond of the charming creature. True, they had not yet had an opportunity of indulging in intimacy, but in their secret hearts they had long been united.

So Chi Neng ran into the kitchen, and after a while, with a pot of tea in one hand and a plate of cakes in the other, came along to the guest cell occupied by the two young boys. The two held out their tea bowls to her at the same time.

"Me first, please!" begged Chin Chung.

"No, me first!" pleaded Pao Yu.

"What contention for a bowl of tea!" she said, her lips curling in a pert smile. "You are really behaving as if it were honey to be licked off my hand." In the end Pao Yu succeeded in having his bowl filled first. While seeming to sip the drink, he tried to engage Chi Neng in conversation, but unfortunately another nun came along and called her away. Strangely enough, as soon as she was gone the two boys suddenly found they had no more appetite for tea and cakes, and leaving both almost untouched, they went out again in search of new discoveries.

When Phoenix retired in the evening to her "Cell of Immaculate Chastity," the Abbess who accompanied her, seeing that only a few trusted chambermaids were near, broached the subject of a personal request.

"I have something on my mind," she said, "which I should like to discuss one of these days with your aunt, the *Tai tai* Cheng, but I should like to have your good advice first," she began.

"Please speak out and tell me what it is," replied Phoenix.

"Holy Amida Buddha! I have to begin rather far back," groaned the Abbess. Then she went on:

"You will recall that before I took over the rule of this convent, I was Abbess of the Convent of Good Works in the Chang an district. A rich patron of that convent, one Mr. Chang, used to stay in the convent every year with his family in order to offer sacrifices and burn incense with pious devotion. He has got a daughter named King Kuo. During one of these visits it happened that a young Mr. Li, a brother-in-law of the Prefect of Chang an, was staying with us too, and he saw the young lady King Kuo. He fell in love with her at first sight and insisted that he wanted to marry her, but when he sent his intermediaries to Mr. Chang's house he heard to his grief that King Kuo was already formally engaged to the son of the City Commandant of Chang an. Therefore Mr. Chang could not do otherwise than refuse the suit of young Mr. Li.

"But young Li would not take no for an answer, and insisted upon

110

pursuing his suit. Mr. Chang, who did not at all like getting into bad terms with the family of the mighty prefect, was extremely embarrassed and felt inclined to give way to his wishes. Unfortunately, the City Commandant, hearing of young Li's designs, came rushing along angrily to Mr. Chang and made a terrible scene. It was a nice state of affairs if a young lady could contract several engagements at the same time, he stormed. He had no intention whatsoever of renouncing the first engagement and giving up the girl, and he would go to law. He did in fact bring an action against Mr. Chang for the fulfillment of the promise of marriage. Mr. Chang, who definitely wished to get out of the first engagement, turned in his dilemma to me with the request that I should find some influential advocate for him in the capital, he did not mind at what cost. Now, as I was Abbess there at the time, I feel that I am primarily responsible for the fact that young Li and Miss King Kuo met in the convent, and I also feel indebted to Mr. Chang for old times' sake. Therefore, I was unable to refuse his request and I promised him that I would do my best for him.

"For this purpose my intention was to avail of the kind support of your aunt. As far as I know, Marshal Yun Kwang of Chang an is a good friend of your family, and if your aunt would move her husband to write requesting the Marshal to intervene, I have no doubt but that the City Commandant would give way to pressure from his commanding officer, the Marshal. If your aunt should be disposed to take up the matter, Mr. Chang would be ready to make any monetary sacrifice, even if it were to make him bankrupt."

Phoenix had listened attentively.

"The matter in itself offers no difficulties," she remarked with a smile, "but of late my aunt has not concerned herself with requests and acts of mediation of that kind."

"Oh, but could not you yourself take up the matter, esteemed *Nai nai?*"

"I am not interested in money, and moreover I do not concern myself with such transactions," said Phoenix, discouragingly.

But the Abbess would not let the personal advantage which the business offered her escape her so easily. She searched strenuously for another argument to win Phoenix. At last she found it. With a sigh she continued: "Mr. Chang already knows that I intended to seek influence for him in your palace. What will he think, then, if my efforts are in vain? It will simply not occur to him that you refrain from such transactions as a matter of principle and that you scorn monetary gain. He will think, on the contrary, that your family is so lacking in power and influence that it cannot carry through even such a trifling matter as that."

This argument worked. Phoenix felt her family honor attacked, and she saw in this a convenient excuse for giving up her attitude of aloofness. In actual fact she by no means despised a little financial gain.

"Oho, you have known me for quite a long time," she said vehemently, "and you should surely know that I do not fear even the devil himself and his court, when it is a question of getting my way. So, let Mr. Chang produce three thousand ounces of silver and I will have the matter put right for him."

"Splendid, if that's all you want!" cried the Abbess, delighted.

"But let him not imagine for a moment that it is for his money I will help him," continued Phoenix. "To pull strange, stubborn oxen by the halter for money! That is something which I prefer to leave to other people. I need those three thousand ounces of silver merely for the expenses of my emissaries, so that they shall have a little tip for their trouble and their running hither and thither. I do not ask a single copper coin for myself. At the moment I have ten times as much—some thirty thousand silver ounces—over and to spare, so I am in no need of money."

"Yes, of course. And may one trust that the gracious *Nai nai* will lose no time, but will get to work straight away tomorrow to fulfill her kindly promise?"

"You see for yourself, I am sure, how extremely busy I am, and how everyone turns to me. But since I have given my word, you may count upon my fulfilling it promptly."

"Good. My mind is at rest now. And since I know that the matter is now in your hands, I have no doubt as to its successful outcome," flattered the Abbess. "A clever, energetic woman like you succeeds so easily. She has only to give one little wink."

Praise such as this pleased Phoenix, and though she was tired, she remained quite a while longer talking earnestly with the Abbess.

Meanwhile Pao Yu and Chin Chung had availed of their free time to examine the convent thoroughly and observe its various apartments in detail. Therefore, when the evening grew darker, Chin Chung had little difficulty in finding his way unseen to Sister Chi Neng's cell. And he was lucky, too. She was alone, busily washing up tea things by the light of a lamp. Without any more ado he took her in his arms and hugged and kissed her as hard as he could. At first the little creature resisted fiercely and stamped and kicked, in an effort to free herself.

"What do you mean?" she cried. "I'll scream out!" But she did not scream.

"Darling, I am dying of longing for you!" he pleaded. "And if you don't listen to me I shall die here on the spot."

"What are you thinking of? Here in this narrow convent cell, where we may be surprised at any moment? It won't do here! Have patience until I am out of this and free," she whispered.

"That is cold comfort for my burning need. Fire such as mine must be quenched at once," he groaned. And already he had blown out the lamp, leaving the room in pitch darkness. Now she no longer put up much resistance, but let him lift her up and carry her over to her kang. True, she struggled a bit and bent and swayed, but she did not cry out, and she let him have his way. He was in full swing, and the cloud was about to discharge its rain, when the couple suddenly felt themselves grasped by a strange hand and torn apart. Whoever it was had crept in silent and unobserved. The hearts of the lovers almost stood still with fright. The intruder now betrayed his identity by a suppressed giggle. It was Pao Yu. Chin Chung leaped to his feet.

"What do you mean by this?" he cried, enraged.

"Let me in on your bit of fun, too. If you do not, I will raise the alarm," threatened Pao Yu, laughing.

But the frightened Chi Neng had already fled from her cell under cover of the darkness. Pao Yu drew his friend out of the room with him.

"Now, which of the two of us is the stronger?" he asked jokingly.

"Very well, you may come in on our game as much as you like in the future," replied the other, speedily mollified.

The next morning Madame Cheng sent for Pao Yu, asking him to come home at once. But Pao Yu had so enjoyed his brief stay in the Convent of the Watery Moon that he contrived to get permission through Phoenix to remain on there one more night with his friend. Then, on the third day, they returned together to the town, after Chin Chung and the nun Chi Neng had exchanged numerous kisses and come to many secret agreements.

In fulfillment of her word to the Abbess, Phoenix had already, the previous day, confided the aforementioned matter to one of her confidential servants, Lai Wang, and sent him back to the Yungkuo palace with instructions to get a letter written to Marshal Yun Kwang of Chang an, ostensibly on behalf of her absent husband, Chia Lien, by the latter's secretary. He rushed off to Chang an with this letter the same day. The Marshal, who was indebted to the Yungkuo palace for previous good services, could not do otherwise than accede willingly to a request coming from thence. He accordingly exercised the desired pressure on his subordinate, the City Commandant, to such good effect that the latter relinquished his resistance and cancelled the engagement between his son and the daughter of the rich citizen Chang.

It had taken barely two days to carry through the whole transaction, for the distance between Chang an and the capital was only a hundred li. There was naturally no question of heavy outlay in tips and the like. Phoenix kept the tidy little sum of three thousand taels all for herself, and nobody in the Yungkuo palace except the trusted servant Lai Wang and her husband's secretary heard a word about the whole matter. This success strengthened Phoenix's self-confidence and encouraged her to undertake numerous similar shady transactions later on, on her own initiative, undeterred by any qualms of conscience.

CHAPTER 13

Beginning of Spring is exalted by Imperial favor and chosen to be Mistress of the Phoenix Palace. Chin Chung sets out prematurely on his journey to the Yellow Springs.

ONE DAY, WHEN THE BIRTHDAY OF CHIA CHENG WAS BEING CELEBRATED in the Yungkuo palace by a great family banquet, a doorkeeper appeared suddenly in the midst of the feasting and announced excitedly: "The chief Imperial eunuch, Hsia, superintendent of the six royal harems, is outside. He bears an Imperial message."

The announcement naturally put the whole company into a state of commotion. The banquet and the theatrical performance were abandoned at once. The male heads of the families hastened to the great reception hall, where they gathered around an incense table which was specially reserved for receiving Imperial messages; an order was given to open the center panels of all the doors for the Imperial ambassador, and the company, kneeling in devout silence, awaited the arrival of the chief eunuch. He was already approaching on horseback, accompanied by a large retinue of under-eunuchs. He dismounted in front of the entrance to the great hall and, with a smile on his face, mounted the steps leading to the south front of the hall. There he remained standing, and did not, as expected, produce a written decree, but simply announced: "At the command of the Most High One, Master Chia Cheng shall proceed at once to the Hall of Respectful Approach for an audience."

Having pronounced this brief message, he left forthwith without even taking a sip of tea. Everyone was puzzled. Was the mysterious message to be interpreted favorably or unfavorably? But Mr. Cheng had no time to consider the matter at length. He changed quickly into Court attire, got in his carriage, and hastened to the palace.

Tortured with uncertainty, the Princess Ancestress sent one mounted messenger after another at short intervals after him. Nevertheless, she had to wait two double hours before any news arrived. At last four breathless, gasping servants reached, all at the same time, the inner gate which led to the apartments of the Princess Ancestress.

"Good news!" they cried from a distance. "Our master asks the old *Tai tai* to go at once to the Imperial Palace together with the other ladies of the house, to render thanks for Imperial favor."

The Princess Ancestress, who happened at the time to be pacing up and down the covered corridor of the inner courtyard with the other ladies, all of them in the same state of restiveness and expectation, beckoned the eldest of the four servants, one Lai Ta, and asked for more detailed information.

"We only got as far as the outer porch in front of the audience hall," reported Lai Ta. "From there we could not hear what was going on inside. But then the chief eunuch Hsia came out and informed us that our house had met with great good fortune, for the eldest daughter of our house had been raised to the rank of a 'noble and virtuous' Imperial wife of the first rank and appointed mistress of the Phoenix Palace. Later our master himself came out for a moment, confirmed this news, and ordered us to come as quickly as possible and call the old *Tai tai* to an audience of thanks in the palace."

This happy news freed the ladies from all their anxious doubts, and proud joy was visible on every face. The Princess Ancestress and the Princesses Shieh and Chen and Madame Cheng all hastened to attire themselves in the ceremonial robes proper to their rank, mounted four large litters, and proceeding like a shoal of fishes, one after the other, set out for the Imperial Palace. The Princes Shieh and Chen followed behind with Chia Yung and Chia Chiang.

Only one person remained untouched by the joyful spirits which had taken possession of all the inhabitants of the Yungkuo and Ningkuo palaces, both masters and servants, and that was Pao Yu. For he was oppressed with anxiety for his friend Chin Chung, who had come back grievously ill from his two-day visit to the Convent of the Watery Moon. He had always been a delicate youth, and he had to do penance now with a severe feverish cold for his surreptitious nocturnal journeys to Chi Neng's cell, and the sudden change from the warmth of his bed to the cold night air, and since his return from the country he had been confined to bed. Mental excitement contributed to make his condition worse. Urged by longing to see him, Chi Neng had paid him a secret visit one day, but unfortunately she encountered his father, who drove her from his threshold with words of abuse. Chin Chung had come in for a beating too; but the old gentleman had died of excitement a few days later. Now, alas too late, Chin Chung repented of his frivolity. Bitter self-reproach and grief for the loss of his father weakened his physical resistance utterly, he felt more wretched day by day, and was slowly and steadily pining away.

That was why Pao Yu could work up no enthusiasm for the good fortune of his sister, Beginning of Spring. He did not take the smallest part in all the excitements of those days—his father's and mother's and grandmother's audience with the Son of Heaven, and the visits of congratulation paid by relatives and friends. Weary and indifferent, he sat moping in his room, and when anyone teased or reproved him for his strange behavior he became irritable and shut himself off still more from the company of the others.

There was only one thing which could cheer him up a bit, and that was the return of Black Jade. Her father, Ling Ju Hai, had died in the meantime, and after the obsequies had been carried through and the inheritance put in order with the help of her cousin Chia Lien, the two cousins had returned together to the capital.

"Now she will never leave you again," Phoenix had said with a smile to Pao Yu, on Black Jade's return. The reunion of Pao Yu and his now completely orphaned cousin was joyful and sorrowful at the same time, and tears flowed freely on both sides. After the parting of several months, Pao Yu found Black Jade considerably more mature and far more beautiful and attractive than before. She had brought back a whole library of books with her, and also various graceful objects for the writing table, and these she shared out among her cousins and Pao Yu. Wishing to show himself grateful, Pao Yu sought to honor her with a gift of the prayer chaplet which the Prince of the Northern Quietness had given him, but his gift did not please Black Jade at all. It immediately roused her jealousy of the Prince.

"Shall I thank you for a thing that has been worn already by a strange man?" she cried disdainfully, flinging the chaplet on the ground. He picked it up and took it back in silence.

Phoenix and her husband Chia Lien naturally had a great deal to tell each other the first day of their reunion. Phoenix had just finished her long report of her seven weeks in charge of the Ningkuo palace when the little handmaiden Ping stuck her head in the door. When she saw that Chia Lien was there she stopped short and was just about to disappear again.

"What is it?" Phoenix called after her.

"Nothing special. Mrs. Hsueh of the Pear Garden sent Sister Lotus over for some information. I have already given it to her and she has gone away again," replied Little Ping, slipping out again.

"Lotus? Is not that the charming young slave whom Cousin Hsueh Pan bought in Ying tien shortly before coming here?" remarked Chia Lien with a smirk. "When I was over in the Pear Garden just now paying my respects to Aunt Hsueh on my return, I saw a strikingly pretty young thing there. I had never seen her before, and then I heard from Aunt Hsueh that she was that girl, Lotus. She looked really quite enchanting. What a pity that she belongs to Cousin Hsueh Pan. She is far too good for the fool!"

"My word! Here's a man just back from a long journey. He has had a surfeit of beautiful women in Suchow and Hanchow, and still he is not satisfied!" said Phoenix laughing. "Well, then, if you find little Lotus so charming, you shall have her. I have only to exchange her for our Little Ping and bring her over here for myself. I believe Cousin Hsueh Pan is tired of her already. He is one of those insatiable and fickle men who while they are eating one dish always keep watching for the next. He nearly talked his mother to death to persuade her to give him the girl. Aunt Hsueh gave in at last, and handed him over the little one with all due solemnity to be his concubine. And she's not an ordinary slave girl at all, but seems in her whole person and in all her ways to be more like a well-brought-up girl from a good family. But the fellow hardly had her two weeks when he ceased even to look at her, and threw her on the scrap-heap like all the crowd of cheap, ordinary girls he has had. I am really sorry for the poor thing!"

Chia Lien had no chance to reply, for a servant came in to call him to his father, Prince Shieh, who awaited him in the library. When he was gone Phoenix called her little maid, Ping.

"What did Aunt Hsueh want when she sent Lotus over just now?" she asked.

"She wanted nothing and she sent nobody over. I was just fibbing a bit, but it was a white lie," replied the maid with a sly smile. "Lai Wang's wife came to bring you some interest. Could the stupid creature not have found a more suitable time to do it? She had to blunder in just when your husband was there, and she did it purposely so that he should get to know of your business and learn that you have private funds at your disposal. If he knew that he would be even more spendthrift than he is already. Luckily, I was able to intercept old Mrs. Wang just in time and get the money from her."

"Bravo! You have acted most cleverly!" said Phoenix appreciatively. "I was really wondering what on earth should have made Aunt Hsueh interrupt my first chat with my husband so rudely and inconsiderately."

After a little time Chia Lien returned, and just after that in came Mother Chao, his old nurse, to welcome him home after his long absence. She was most cordially invited to sit down, food and drink were served to her, and Phoenix settled down to listen to her conversation. But Chia Lien only half listened to her leisurely chatter; he ate and drank in an absent-minded way, and his thoughts were obviously elsewhere. Would they please excuse him for not taking part in the conversation, but he was in a hurry and had to go over at once for an important discussion with Prince Chen, so he said.

"Do not let us detain you, but what had the old gentleman to discuss with you just a little time ago?" asked Phoenix.

"He spoke about the coming visit of filial reverence."

"Has the visit been already approved by the Court?"

"Not yet formally. But it is as good as certain."

"Is it really?" cried Phoenix, joyfully. "That would indeed be a quite new and unprecedented act of grace on the part of our present monarch, and one of which there is no record either in our historical annals or in our theatrical pieces."

"What is all this talk about?" asked Mother Chao stupidly. "For the past few days I have heard everyone here talking and chattering about a visit of filial reverence, but I have grown dull from old age and I could not make head or tail of all the talk."

"I will explain the matter to you," said Chia Lien. "Our present Son of Heaven is a great advocate of filial reverence. He regards the respectful attitude of children to their parents as a universal law of nature which is binding upon the whole human race regardless of difference of class; and he considers that the maintenance of filial reverence is the most important duty of a wise government, because by it human society can be kept in order in the simplest, most natural way. Our reigning monarch himself shines forth with good example in this respect by surrounding his aged parents, their former Majesties, with every conceivable sign of filial love, day and night. And yet he considers that he does not fulfill his filial duty as completely as he would wish to do, so stern and exalted are his ideals.

"Now, he has come to the conclusion that his wives and secondary wives and other worthy persons who dedicate their lives to the service of the palace are hindered in the expression of their natural feelings of filial reverence and must suffer spiritually by their long years of separation from their fathers and mothers, and that the parents, on their part, who pine for the daughters who have been torn from them have much to endure from this state of things. He has decided that the divinely appointed harmony which should reign in human society is severely injured by this. Moved by these considerations, he has had a memorandum presented to his parents, their former Majesties, in which he has suggested that parents of the Imperial wives shall be permitted in future to come to the palace to visit their daughters on the second and sixth days of each month alternately.

"Their former Imperial Majesties were most deeply moved by this suggestion, the noble motives of which they fully recognized, but they

118

expressed the fear that such private visits of relatives might be detrimental to the majesty and dignity of the Imperial Palace. In a decree which has been published they have now made the alternative ruling that the Imperial wives and secondary wives should be permitted, on request, to visit their parents, provided that the parents have at their disposal suitable separate apartments for the worthy reception and accommodation of an inmate of the Imperial Palace and her suite.

"As can be imagined, this gracious decree has been greeted everywhere with tears of joy. The Emperor's secondary wives Chou and Wu are the first who will avail of this grace of the All Highest. Their respective fathers are already busily preparing a worthy place to receive them on their visit."

"Holy Buddha!" exclaimed Mother Chao. "Then we also shall have to get ready here for a visit from the eldest daughter of the house?"

"Yes, naturally," replied Chia Lien, smiling. "Otherwise why would there be so many important matters to discuss and consult about?"

"That is splendid! Now I shall at last get a glimpse of the world of the great!" cried Phoenix joyfully. "I have always bemoaned my misfortune in having come into the world several years too late. If I were twenty or thirty years older I would not have had to stay at home here, being treated as a stupid, inexperienced child. I too would have seen the first ruler of our present dynasty when he made his celebrated journey through the kingdom, in order, following the example of the Emperor Shun of old, to see for himself how justice was being administered. To really take part in something like that is so much more interesting than any learning from dead books."

"Yes, indeed, something like that happens only once in a thousand years. I well remember what you are referring to," interjected Mother Chao, eagerly. "Our Chia family lived at that time in the neighborhood of Suchow and Hanchow and had charge of the Imperial wharves and dykes. I was present when the Son of Heaven was received in those parts. Oh, indeed, a reception like that swallows a whole heap of money."

"On that occasion my grandfather received the Son of Heaven in his house," declared Phoenix proudly. "He was Commissar for Tributes and for Foreign Relations at that time. All tributes from foreign countries passed through his hands, and all ambassadors from abroad had to dismount at his house first. An immense amount of goods and treasures which foreign ships brought from the southern ports came into the possession of our family in those days."

A servant entered and announced the two nephews, Chia Yung and Chia Chiang, from the Ningkuo palace. They were let in.

"Father sends you word, Uncle, that the land for the reception has already been measured and marked out," announced Chia Yung. "It unites the park of the eastern palace and that of the western one and measures three and a half li wide, therefore it is quite sufficient for a dignified place of reception for the distinguished visitor. An architect has already been instructed to prepare the sketches of the necessary buildings, and he will present his plans tomorrow. As Father assumes that you are tired from your journey, he asks us to say that you need not trouble to come over today; and would you please postpone your visit until tomorrow morning if you wish to discuss anything."

"Tell your father that I thank him very much for his kind consideration and I shall not go over until tomorrow morning," replied Chia Lien. "Tell him that I agree fully regarding the place that has been arranged; it seems to me to be a most fortunate arrangement in every way. It will save us very considerable expense as it obviates the necessity of acquiring a piece of ground specially for this one visit."

Chia Chiang then stepped forward and began to speak.

"I have been instructed to travel to Suchow," he said, "and there to entrust capable agents with the task of finding outstandingly accomplished young dancing girls as well as musical instruments and theater requisites. Two sons of the majordomo Lai Sheng will accompany me, and Uncle asks you to please give me two of your people as well."

Chia Lien measured the youthful speaker with a critical eye. "Can you trust yourself to carry out this task, worthy nephew?" he asked. "True, it is not an immense one, but all the same . . ." he remarked somewhat sarcastically.

Chia Chiang, who was standing right beside Phoenix outside the radius of the lamplight, plucked her dress surreptitiously. Phoenix understood the hint.

"You are overanxious," she said to her husband with a reassuring smile. "Cousin Chen is surely able to judge better than we are who are suitable persons to whom to entrust his commissions. The boys are no longer children, and even if they have not yet probed the mystery of the taste of roast pork, they have at least already seen a live pig running about the road and they know what it looks like in its living state. And after all, Uncle Chen has only sent them into the fray as standard-bearers. He hardly expects them to wage the battle themselves; in other words, to bargain over prices with the agents. That is what our people will be there for. Let them go! They will get on all right."

"Very well, I have no objections," Chia Lien assured her. "But perhaps I can help them with some advice.

"Where are you getting the necessary funds from?" he asked, turning to Chia Chiang.

"Our princely master has already instructed us regarding that," replied Chia Chiang. "We do not need to take any money from the funds here, as the Chia family has a credit of fifty thousand silver taels with the Chen family in Kiang nan, where we shall be stopping on our journey. He will give us a draft for thirty thousand taels, with which we can draw on this credit. The remaining twenty thousand taels will be used later for the purchase of lanterns, colored candles, banners, pennants, cloth for curtains, and other festive decorations."

Chia Lien nodded approvingly. Phoenix decided upon two sons of Mother Chao as travelling companions and assistants for Chia Chiang, then she bade them good-by. Chia Yung went after her and, before she reached the door, said he had to have a private word with her.

"If you want anything from Suchow, dear Aunt, just write it all out on a list," he whispered; "I will give the list to my brother and he will attend to it promptly on the journey."

"Oh, what a silly idea!" she laughed, parrying his offer. "I do not want a thing. On the contrary, I have not got sufficient space for all the stuff which I have! What odd, artful ideas you get!"

And off she went.

Meanwhile, inside the room, Chia Chiang was importuning his elder cousin in exactly the same way. "If there is anything you want, I shall not fail to get it for you along with my other commissions, and lay it at your feet as a small token of my respect," he was saying glibly. But Chia Lien too dismissed the offer with thanks.

"Not so fast, my boy! Beginners like you should stick to the job in hand in your first transactions, and not start distracting yourselves with trifles. If I want anything I shall write," he added smiling, and sent the two young people off.

The next morning Chia Lien went to Prince Chen. Various experts among the friends of the families and some of the older and more experienced members of the household staffs were present, and there was a great consultation, building plans were examined, and questions of labor and materials thoroughly discussed.

That same day a lively scene of building activity commenced at the western side of the Ningkuo palace and the eastern side of the Yungkuo palace. Laborers, carpenters, and builders came in hordes, and a ceaseless succession of carts and handbarrows full of building materials— timber, bricks, glazed roof tiles, gold, silver, copper, and tin—rolled in. At one side outer walls, turrets, and pavilions were pulled down in the Garden of Assembled Perfumes; at the other side the whole former block of servants' residential quarters was torn down in order to make way for one continuous area of magnificent pleasure gardens and pavilions.

Here we must mention that the two estates were separated merely by a narrow private path enclosed by high walls. It was therefore only necessary to knock down the walls in order to turn the whole domain quite easily into one single piece of territory. Moreover, a stream flowed through the Garden of Assembled Perfumes, and it was found possible to divert this stream into the Yungkuo park without difficulty, so that waterworks could be contrived at a reasonable cost. The Ningkuo palace grounds, again, were lacking in artificial hills, rocks, and trees. This lack was overcome by transporting, for the time being, from Prince Shieh's residence and grounds, which were really part of the original Yungkuo park, several hills and pieces of rock as well as a number of trees, bridges, and balustrades, and setting them down again in the Ningkuo palace grounds. In this way a great deal of money which would have had to be spent on new materials was saved, and the aim of achieving a single and continuous new layout of magnificent ornamental gardens was achieved under the expert guidance of the capable old Hu, a former Court architect, in an astonishingly short space of time.

New rocky gorges, ponds, waterfalls, airy pavilions and pagodas, bamboo hedges and flowery groves came into being. The male members of the families of both palaces conscientiously shared the supervision of the work. To be sure, Prince Shieh and Chia Cheng remained out of things for the most part; the latter was too greatly occupied with his ministerial office, while the former loved the leisure of his library, and left it to his son Chia Lien to represent him and to report to him in writing from time to time on the progress of the work. Prince Chen with his majordomo supervised the actual building operations and the rolls of work people; his son Chia Yung supervised the metal work in gold and silver. And so each one had his clearly defined field of activity. As already mentioned, owing to the illness of his friend Chin Chung, Pao Yu took scarcely any part in all the busy doings which were going on in the house. Even the fact that his father, owing to his many other urgent occupations during that time, was unable to watch him and supervise his studies as much as usual, failed to cheer his depressed spirits, as it would assuredly have done at another time.

One morning his inner unrest drove him out of bed just at break of dawn. While he was dressing he was informed that an old servant of his friend had come to call him urgently to the sickbed. Filled with anxious forebodings, he hastened to his friend's house; but he came too late. The sick boy, whom he found lying on his bed with wax-white face and closed eyes, painfully gasping for breath, made no reply to his thrice-repeated cry: "Brother Chin, Pao Yu is here!" Unable to utter one word of farewell, he had breathed out his last remnant of breath in the presence of his friend and set out on his journey to the Yellow Springs.

CHAPTER 14

Pao Yu reveals his talent in the Park of Delightful Vision. Black Jade is annoyed by the bite of a fly.

THE WORK ON THE MAGNIFICENT NEW PLEASURE GROUNDS WAS COMpleted, and one fine day Prince Chen came with his helpers and associates to invite Chia Cheng to view them.

"The work as a whole is finished," he told him, "and now we would like to have your verdict on it, and any suggestions for alterations which you may wish to express. But above all we want your suggestions for the inscriptions which have not yet been made and which are to embellish the principal places in the grounds."

"Hm, these inscriptions are going to offer difficulty," said Chia Cheng, thoughtfully. "Strictly speaking, according to the *Book of Rites*, we must leave to our noble guest the honor of deciding upon suitable titles and inscriptions; but without a personal impression of the landscape and the scenery the Imperial spouse will lack the necessary inspiration for this. If, on the other hand, we await the happy hour of her visit and refrain from putting up any inscription or any motto until then, the scenery, despite all its charms, will still lack something essential."

"Quite so," they replied. "And to surmount this difficulty it seems to us that the best we can do for the time being is to write, in three or four characters, only the basic theme of the various inscriptions and mottoes and to leave the final composition of the text to our illustrious visitor herself to decide at the happy hour of her arrival."

"I agree; let us, then, commence our tour of inspection, for which this lovely spring weather is ideal," decided Chia Cheng, leading the way. It just happened that, as the party approached, Pao Yu was in the new park, which he had been visiting frequently of late at his grandmother's wish, to seek distraction after the many weeks of mourning for his dead friend. Prince Chen, who had gone on ahead of the rest of the company, laughingly advised him to disappear as fast as he could because his stern old governor was coming that way. Much frightened, Pao Yu hurried towards the exit, but just as he got outside, he ran straight into the much-feared parent. There was no way of escape, so he stood shyly at the edge of the path waiting for the company to pass by.

"Come with us!" his father ordered tersely and abruptly. He had heard recently from old Tai Ju that his scion, while not overstudious in school, was showing a truly extraordinary talent for the composition of couplets and antitheses. So he wished to test him out a bit today.

Mr. Cheng stopped first in front of the covered gateway and let the impression of the view from outside work upon him. The roofs of the five-doored gateway, which were covered with copper tiles, stood out like the shimmering scaly backs of lizards or alligators. The balustrades and steps of the marble bridge which led to the entrance were adorned with artistically wrought ornaments in the Western style. Neither the gateway nor the bridge had any whitewash or paint; both above and below everything glittered in the natural white of water-clear marble. White was also the color of the lime-washed wall enclosing the whole, which ran from left and right of the gateway. The wall rose from a base of natural freestones which were ribbed like a tiger's pelt, and cut and placed in such a way, one over the other, that they gave the wall a most pleasing appearance. The whole impression was that of an unusual setting for a beautiful jewel.

Well content, Mr. Cheng moved on. Just inside the gateway the eye was met by a green hill.

"What a beautiful hill!" they all exclaimed, enraptured.

"This hill, which at first shuts out the view, heightens expectation. If one were to see the whole park immediately upon entering, the effect would be monotonous," remarked Chia Cheng.

"Quite so!" the others agreed. "One must have heights and depths to enliven the spirit."

They walked on by a narrow path which wound upwards through a narrow gorge formed by mighty, gray rocks overgrown with moss and creepers. These rocks, with their grotesque shapes, lying this way and that, looked as fantastic as goblins or mighty, fabulous animals. Half-way up, in front of a single mirror-bright sheet of stone, they halted.

"It seems to me that this is the right place for an inscription. What name shall we give to this spot? Your suggestions, please, gentlemen!" urged Chia Cheng.

A dozen suggestions, such as "Stratified Kingfisher Green," "Embroidered Crags," and the like, were heard. Pao Yu was the last to be called upon to speak. He gave it frankly and freely as his opinion that an inscription would be somewhat premature here, where one had just taken the first step into the grounds, but if it were definitely desired to adorn this in itself unimportant spot with a motto, he would suggest the words, reminiscent of an ancient text: "On twisted paths through twilight shades." There was general applause.

"This suggestion of our worthy nephew expresses true natural talent. Compared with him, we others are only clumsy duffers and dry pedants," said the seniors, flatteringly.

"No exaggerated praise, if you please, or the boy will get notions about his bit of knowledge. Better laugh at him; it would be more beneficial to him," objected Chia Cheng, smiling. "At any rate we have still got time to consider the matter."

The path led on through dark grottoes into bright clearings over slopes, some covered with bushes, some with trees, and others, again, with flowers, along by a babbling brook which here wound sleepily through level land and there hopped in gay leaps down towards a valley, to disappear into a narrow fell, and finally to disperse in the form of a steep, foaming waterfall into a small, shimmering lake. A white marble balustrade encircled the shores of the lake, and over its narrow side the triple arch of a marble bridge stretched like the gaping jaws of a sea monster. The pavilion which stood on the bridge and overhung the water was chosen as the next halting place.

All were fully agreed that this charming water pavilion was not only worthy of a poetical name but definitely had to be extolled in a heptametric couplet. Hence, there followed a lively literary debate in which Pao Yu once more had an opportunity of shining. While all the others thought at once of an apt quotation from the celebrated ode, "Pavilion of a drunken old man," in which the poet glorifies a pavilion near the source of the Niang, and wanted to take from this ode the name of Waterfall of Jasper, Pao Yu maintained that this was not a suitable name. On the occasion of receiving such an exalted visit, one must pay heed to etiquette and remember that the ideograph for waterfall also stood for something very indelicate, namely, diarrhea, and might therefore cause disgust in the highest quarters. This argument was quite unanswerable. Chia Cheng stroked his beard thoughtfully and remarked that the boy was full of the spirit of contradiction and that nothing was right to him. First he had been all in favor of old quotations, and now when an old quotation had been proposed he had an objection to raise to it. In the end, Pao Yu's suggestion of "Through Perfumed Glades" as title for the place, where a waterfall emerged from a flowery glade, found unanimous acceptance, and the couplet which he improvised on the spot at his father's wish aroused still more admiration.

The company next made a round of the lake, in the course of which each mount, crag, flower, and tree was the subject of a separate and thorough examination. Suddenly they found themselves before a shady bamboo grove surrounded by a low, whitewashed wall. Inside this green belt lay hidden a friendly little country house, built on piles.

"What a charming little place!" they all exclaimed. They went in. An arbor-covered walk led in zigzag bends from the gateway up to the little cottage, which had only three rooms, two of them opening onto open verandas, and all three furnished tastefully but with the utmost economy of space. From the center room a narrow door led into a back garden full of pear trees and banana plants in bloom. From a foot-wide opening down by the garden wall a clear spring bubbled, which, turning into a babbling brook, wound its way through the garden around the little cottage, and splashed down from the bamboo glade, to hasten, finally, into the near-by lake.

"What a delightful spot! Think of sitting here at the window on a beautiful moonlit night, studying; that would not be spending one's life in vain!" exclaimed Chia Cheng, with a censorious glance at his son, Pao Yu, who at once bowed his head timidly. Once more a lively literary contest arose regarding a suitable motto, and again it was Pao Yu's idea which won the day. He emphasized the fact that the distinguished visitor would make her first rest at this spot and that for this reason the inscription must contain some pleasant personal allusion. The classical quotation which he recommended, "A phoenix comes with grace to rest," aroused the general enthusiasm of the seniors no whit less than did the further stanza which he had to compose at his father's command. His father alone dissented, and was heard to mutter disparagingly something about "mediocrity" and "the brains of an insect."

The way now curved around a green projecting hillock, behind which there emerged into view a rice plantation protected by low yellow clay walls. Adjoining this paddy field was an orchard of some hundreds of apricot trees in bloom. Behind the flame-red cloud of blossoms the straw-thatched roof of a farmhouse peeped through. At the other side of the farmhouse stood a mixed group of trees, such as elms, mulberry trees, and cherry trees. Around them was a green hedge and behind this, on a hill, a country well, complete with bucket and lever. Beyond the well stretched extensive plantations of choice vegetables, each kind in its accurately measured plot.

"That is what pleases me!" exclaimed Mr. Cheng, enchanted at the sight of all the tillage. "A piece of land laid out like that has sense and meaning. I cannot contain my feelings, for the sight moves me to the depths of my being and awakens my longing for a peaceful country life. Let us go in there and rest!"

But at the same moment he discovered by the wayside, behind the path through the hedge, a single block of rock which doubtless lay there to invite the wayfarer to sit down and meditate. This rock awaited an inscription. "No! Come here instead. It is even lovelier here!" he cried from outside, and they all followed him and gathered around the slab of rock. Once more a profound literary discussion arose. "Village of Blossoming Apricot" was proposed unanimously by the elders. But here again Pao Yu was of another opinion, and this time, no doubt emboldened by the previous applause, he put forward his opinion somewhat audaciously, without waiting to be asked for it by his father. This brought him a sharp paternal reprimand.

126

The company now entered the straw-thatched farmhouse. How simple it was inside! Parchment panes were pasted over the window frames, simple wooden bunks served as beds. Every trace of luxury or refinement was washed away, as it were. This was all entirely to Mr. Cheng's taste. But was it to his son's taste too?

"Now, how do you like it here?" he asked, to put him to the test. The seniors, who did not fail to see the hidden intention behind this question, tried to convey to Pao Yu by signs and taps that he should answer in a manner pleasing to his father. But Pao Yu seemed to be slow of comprehension.

"This one cannot at all compare for beauty with the other country house to which we gave the title 'A phoenix comes with grace to rest'" was his glib verdict.

"Stupid boy!" roared Chia Cheng. "Must you, then, always have red balconies and brightly colored pillars? It is plain that, to your depraved taste, nothing is beautiful which is not costly and fine. You have no understanding whatsoever of the pure charm of nature simplicity which this place breathes. In this you betray your utter lack of culture."

Pao Yu had the impertinence to differ, and plunged into a lengthy dissertation on the interpretation of the term "natural," and denying that this piece of ground, which only simulated nature, had any real naturalness. It was an artificial creation made by human hands, isolated, and set down without any natural affinity, in an environment entirely alien to it. True, there were fields here but there was no highroad leading to a near-by market in which the crops could be sold; there was no village in the neighborhood, no temple on the hill. In fact, it lacked this, that, and the other things necessary to maintain the illusion of nature, in contrast to the other country house where there was nothing contradictory to the surroundings and which, despite the artificial bamboo plantation and the artificial watering, nevertheless merited the adjective "natural." In his ardor he became more and more theoretical, until his father lost patience at last and cut short his stream of eloquence with an angry: "Shut up and be off!"

Much taken aback, Pao Yu slipped out the gate, only to be immediately recalled with a harsh: "Stop! Stay here!" He was not allowed to evade dutifully producing the required couplet.

Pao Yu did his best and improvised a most charming couplet, but his father only greeted this latest product of his muse with a muttering, "Worse and worse each time!"

On they went. The path rounded a hill, wound through a flowery field in which there was a rock spring surrounded by willows, led to an arbor of Kashmir thistles, from there to a grove of peonies, and thence through a rose garden to a banana plantation. After various zigzag bends they stood before a rock grotto, overhung with creeping plants, from which they could hear the rippling sound of water. Here the company came to a halt and broke into exclamations of delight. Naturally, this again was the right place for a motto. "Wu ling Spring" and "Grotto of the Strange Hermit" were suggested, while Pao Yu proposed "Bank of the Ferns." "Nonsense!" exclaimed Chia Cheng, cutting short the discussion and walking on through the grotto. At the other side its noisy brook ran into a silent dam.

"Can one not go on farther from here in a boat?" asked Chia Cheng.

"There are to be four boats for picking water lilies and one for rowing," replied Prince Chen, "but unfortunately they are not here yet."

"What a pity!"

"Yes, we must go over the mountain on foot," replied Prince Chen, taking the lead. A steep mountain path wound upwards along the gorge. It was so narrow, indeed, that one had to hold on to shrubs and branches. Then it ran down again, and the wayfarers found themselves on the edge of a silent, lonely fishpond overhung with willow, peach, and apricot trees. At the other end of the fishpond they caught a glimpse, between the green foliage of the trees, of a wooden bridge with a red railing. Crossing this, they came upon a neat but apparently quite tasteless brick house surrounded by a wall.

"Quite devoid of charm!" was the verdict of Chia Cheng.

Yet immediately beyond this plain building the landscape became romantic once more. For the house lay with its back embedded, as it were, in a great boulder-strewn gorge, from which one single rugged peak of rock rose steeply upwards. One felt suddenly and completely transported to an austere highland landscape. Flowers and trees were completely absent. Only mosses, rare herbs, and trailing plants which exuded aromatic and exotic perfumes were visible here.

"This is really interesting," said Chia Cheng, correcting his first impression. "What a pity one knows so little about these plants."

His remark encouraged Pao Yu to display his botanical knowledge. In a long dissertation, interlarded with many learned quotations, he identified the various plants one after another, glibly rolling off the unfamiliar botanical names, until his father at last lost patience and stopped him with a gruff: "Be silent! Who asked you?" Pao Yu, who had rather expected some praise, was so intimidated that he did not dare to open his mouth at all for a long time.

A twin pair of covered corridors led, like two outstretched arms, from this alpine herdsman's hut to an ornate building. This one consisted of five rooms, was completely encircled by an open veranda, and, with its graceful curved roof, its prettily varnished walls, and the green gauze curtains at the windows, it made an even more pleasing impression than the various buildings which had been viewed up to this.

"If a man could brew his tea and peacefully play his lute here, he could even find consolation and escape from the thought that he would die without a son and have no one to offer sacrifice and burn incense for him after his death," sighed Chia Cheng. Then, while the usual literary debate was going on, he turned brusquely to his son, who was still remaining silent.

"Why do you not speak when you should?" he asked. "No doubt you are waiting to be politely requested to grant us the favor of your gracious instruction?"

Pao Yu could not evade the paternal challenge, and once more his motto and his couplet met with the unanimous applause of the seniors. But Mr. Cheng muttered something disparaging about "plagiarism" and quoted the original verse upon which Pao Yu had based his composition. The seniors, however, defended Pao Yu and asserted that at that rate even the great Li Tai Po himself could be accused of plagiarism, since he had based his ode, "The Terrace of the Phoenix" entirely upon an earlier poem, "The Tower of the Yellow Crane." What mattered was the excellence of the new version, and in this case Pao Yu's was decidedly better than the original.

A gruff "Nonsense" was Mr. Cheng's only reply.

After a short walk they reached a high and magnificent castle. A pleasure gallery one story high led from this, in many curves and windings, far into the countryside. The tops of pine trees caressed the edges of the roofs. The marble terraces were lined with orchids. The bodies of dragons and other fabulous animals glittered in gold, silver and bronze.

"The main hall," cried Mr. Cheng. "The only fault one can find with it is a certain excess of magnificence."

"We are aware that the Imperial spouse values simplicity, yet considering her high rank the outlay entailed here did not seem to us to be excessive, but on the contrary called for as our due tribute of respect," the others replied.

On they went until they came to a high triumphal arch made of soft white soapstone. Its frieze was ornamented with a design of dragons in bas-relief.

"What title shall we give this?" asked Mr. Cheng. "Entrance to the Domain of the Blessed Spirits" was the unanimous suggestion. Pao Yu was sunk deep in thought. The remembrance of a similar stone arch which he had once seen though he could not remember when—neither the day, the month, or the year—had been reawakened in him. He was so lost in thought that he still remained silent even when his father asked him for a title.

"Give him until tomorrow!" the seniors urged Mr. Cheng. They assumed that Pao Yu was so exhausted from being asked so often that his brain had now ceased to function, and they feared that if he was too much harried and goaded like an ox in harness his health might suffer, and then they would have to expect the reproaches of the Princess Ancestress. Did not Mr. Cheng think the same?

"Ha, ha, the infant prodigy has reached the end of his wits," he jeered. "Yes, you may be right." Then, turning to the boy: "Very well, I give you until tomorrow, but woe betide you if you have not found a title by then. You will pay for it!"

It was now decided to cut short the tour of inspection somewhat, for there was too much to be seen. Of all the parks and grounds, only about five- or six-tenths had been viewed so far. The company halted once more near a big bridge. Here there was a weir, over which the dammed-up watercourse dropped like a glistening crystal curtain.

"What name shall we give this weir?" asked Mr. Cheng.

"Weir of Penetrating Perfumes," suggested Pao Yu.

"Rubbish! Out of the question!" snapped Mr. Cheng, cutting short the debate and striding on. There followed in gay succession imposing halls and simple straw-thatched huts, massive brick walls and graceful, flowery arbors, silent mountain temples, hermits' cells hidden in dense woods, and witches' caves where love potions might be brewed, pleasure galleries and winding cloisters cut out of rock, angular kiosks, circular pavilions, and many other things worth looking at. But Mr. Cheng did not give himself time to stop everywhere. His legs were tired from walking for such a long time, and he pressed on towards the exit.

A separately hedged off part of the park now emerged into view.

"Let us go and rest in there for a while," suggested Mr. Cheng. They turned aside from the road and, passing under peach trees in bloom and through a rose arbor made of tall bamboo rods, came to a circular moon gateway. Right and left of the gateway was an encircling white-washed wall, shaded with willows from the outside. Along the side of the wall ran a covered pleasure gallery. Apart from a few banana plants which stood among groups of rocks, the courtyard contained only one magnificent specimen of that rare plant, the golden begonia. Its crown spread out like an open umbrella, its branches shimmered like golden threads, the calices of its flowers seemed as it were to spit out vermilion.

"What magnificent blossoms!" they all cried in chorus. "Was such a magnificent specimen ever seen before?"

"It is the foreign kind which is called 'Maiden Begonia,' " remarked Chia Cheng. "The popular explanation for the name is that this variety comes from a distant country of amazons. But that is only a wild legend."

"This explanation does not seem to us so completely without foundation," said the seniors. "The blossoms are indeed quite extraordinary. It may well be true that the plant comes from a country of amazons."

"Very probably the legend originated in the fertile brain of some poet or travelling minstrel," remarked Pao Yu. "The rose tint, the maidenly delicacy and fragility of the blooms may have inspired him with it. And then, in the course of time, his fantastic explanation came to be regarded as truth, because it is such a lovely and plausible explanation."

"Splendid! Well said!" applauded the seniors.

They sat down for a brief rest on the seats in the pleasure corridor and agreed upon the title "Towering Radiance and Shimmering Beauty." Pao Yu too found the title good though not quite adequate, since it only referred to the begonia and left the banana plants unconsidered. The combination of the red of the begonias and the green of the bananas was a deliberate one and therefore required to be expressed in the title. Hence he suggested "Fragrant Red and Nephrite Green."

"Bad," growled Chia Cheng, shaking his head and standing up to go on.

On crossing the courtyard the party came to a circular hall. Its walls were covered from top to bottom with intricately carved, perforated woodwork. This showed the most varied assortment of patterns and pictures—driving clouds, fluttering bats, trees and shrubs, flowers and birds, landscape pictures and scenes from human life, interlaced everywhere with the ever-recurrent lucky signs *fu* and *shou*, signifying "Happiness" and "Long Life." All these things, carved by an artist's hand, veneered with gold leaf and five colors besides, and encrusted with brilliant stones, gave a deceptively lifelike impression. From this artistic background there projected fanlike wall partitions on which there were arranged book-rests, flower vases, pewter dishes, and similar objects. These wall partitions were most varied in form. Some were angular, some were round, some had the shape of banana leaves, others that of sunflower leaves, and yet others took the form of intersected half-circles; and they all fitted into their graceful frames like samplers of tapestry. Then, there were here and there niches in the walls, screened with silk curtains, which gave the impression of being secret, hidden doors; and inside these were precious antiques and works of art such as bronze swords, lutes, porcelain vases, and the like.

The astonishment and admiration of the company knew no bounds and, carried away by their delight in the sights, they had already embarked upon a second round, when Chia Cheng announced that it was time to leave. But he could no longer find the exit. The circular hall contained a number of mirror doors, all similar, and several windows, likewise similar, and the pattern on the wall was so confusingly continuous that it was quite impossible to see where it began and where it ended. But Prince Chen, who knew the place thoroughly, smilingly led the party out of this mazelike hall through the correct mirrored door. Threading their way between flower beds and rose trellises, they passed for a time along a clear watercourse and around the foot of a hill before reaching level ground once more.

"A truly enchanting park, a peak achievement of brilliant invention!" Such was the verdict of the highly gratified company. Pao Yu was glad that the time had come to leave. He was yearning for the company of girls, which he had had to do without for so long. But he had to wait on, for his father had not yet dismissed him.

The word of release came at last. "What are you doing still hanging about here? Have you not had enough? Be off! Your grandmother will be asking for you," said Chia Cheng, suddenly turning to him. He made off in a trice.

The party was hardly out of sight when several of his father's servants came rushing along behind him, and surrounded him, chattering and laughing excitedly.

"Rejoice, young Master! The old master is in a good humor," they informed him with solemn faces. "Your grandmother sent for you several times, but the old master sent her word that he was pleased with you and wished to keep you for a little time longer in his company. Everyone is full of praise of your talent, and they are all saying that your mottoes were much more beautiful than the others. And now you must give us something to celebrate the day."

"Very well, each of you shall have a string of coppers," said Pao Yu, laughing.

"No, coppers are no use to us. We want a proper souvenir," they protested vigorously, and without waiting for his consent they took hold of him and in no time had pulled off the purse, the fan-shaped case, and all the other little things which he carried on his belt.

"Now, that's settled," they declared, "we will be your guard of honor and take you to the old *Tai tai*." And they escorted him in triumph into the presence of the Princess Ancestress. "Oh, they've plundered you shamelessly!" remarked the maid Pearl with a smile, as she poured him tea in the green pavilion.

Black Jade, who had overheard this remark from the next room, came and looked at him attentively.

"You have given them the embroidered lotus-leaf purse that I gave you! That's nice! You may be certain that I will never give you a present again!" she said petulantly, turning her back on him. On returning to her room she took her scissors and began angrily cutting to pieces the still unfinished perfume bag which he had asked her to make for him a short time before. Pao Yu, who came running in after her, looked on regretfully at the work of destruction.

"What a pity to destroy the lovely bag!" he said. "But look! What's this I've got here?" Saying this, he turned back the facing of his coat and, pulling out a lotus-leaf purse, held it towards her, smiling. She looked up. It was the one she had given him. She immediately repented her hastiness and hung her head, silent and ashamed. He must really treasure her gift, she thought, to keep it so safely hidden under his clothing. But to punish her he now began to play the offended party.

"You need not have been so quick with your scissors. But if you think me unworthy of your gift, please take back your purse!" he said coolly, aiming the purse so truly at her that it slid straight down her bosom. Whereupon he left the room. Black Jade burst out crying, took the purse from inside her dress, and was just beginning to cut it up with the scissors. But suddenly there was Pao Yu standing before her again. With a rapid movement he snatched from her this second victim of her ill-temper.

"Spare it, dear little sister!" he begged her, smiling. She let the scissors fall to the ground and, dabbing her tear-filled eyes with her handkerchief, said in a voice choked with sobs: "It is horrible of you to toy with me as you do. Nice one time and nasty the next . . . I can't bear it. . . ."

She jumped up and threw herself on her bed, the better to go on drying her eyes with her face turned to the wall. Pao Yu could not refrain from jumping up after her and assuring her, with many tender words, how sorry he was to have offended her, and that he recognized his guilt and would be better in the future.

Meanwhile the Princess Ancestress had been inquiring where her grandson was. He was in Miss Ling's room, she was told.

"That's all the better," said the grandmother. "His father has been tormenting and persecuting him half the day. Why begrudge him a little time enjoying himself with his cousin, out of harm's way? Do not call him, but only see that they do not quarrel!"

Black Jade, who found Pao Yu's endearments too overwhelming for her liking, had got up from the bed again.

"You tormenter! You do not leave me a moment in peace! I am going to leave you," she said, going towards the door.

"Then I shall go with you," he declared, beginning to fasten the lotus-leaf purse back on his belt. But suddenly she snatched it from him.

"I think you do not like it. You are a plague and a nuisance!"

"Dear *Mei mei,* give it back to me!"

"First say 'please' nicely!"

"Please, please! And you will give me the perfume bag you promised me too, won't you?"

"That will depend entirely on my mood."

CHAPTER 15

On the day of the Lantern Festival the Imperial consort pays her family a visit.

THE FINAL PREPARATIONS FOR THE RECEPTION OF THE MISTRESS OF the Phoenix Palace had now been completed. Chia Chiang had brought back with him from Suchow a troupe of twelve picked dancing and singing girls, who were to prepare a repertoire of twenty dance-plays under the direction of a competent ballet mistress. The troupe was housed in the Pear Garden, in the premises hitherto inhabited by Aunt Hsueh and her family, the latter being temporarily quartered in a quiet and secluded spot at the northeastern extremity of the Ningkuo palace. For attendance on the young artists a few elderly women who in their youth had also been versed in singing and dancing but were now settled, gray-haired matrons, were picked out from among the domestic staff. Chia Chiang was entrusted with the task of seeing to the maintenance of the troupe and rendering an account of the cost of what they consumed.

At the last great session of the festival committee, which took place in the tenth month, the individual committee members had submitted a detailed account of their various departments, and it had been established that there was absolutely nothing lacking. From the brightly colored singing bird and the Manchurian spirit crane, the stag and the hare in the game preserve, the geese and fowls in the farmyards, down to the last bronze bowl and the smallest ornament, everything was in its place. The troupe of dancing girls had completely mastered their repertoire of twenty numbers, and the choirs of twelve Buddhist and twelve Taoist nuns were able to reel off their liturgies at their fingers' end. Yet another general inspection of the festival gardens was made, this time by the Princess Ancestress and her ladies-in-waiting. Now Chia Cheng's great moment had come at last: he composed his petition to the Throne, officially begging the Imperial consent to his eldest daughter's visiting her family. The same day on which he handed in his petition a gracious rescript, consenting to the visit requested, and fixing the date for the fifteenth of the first month, the day of the first full moon in the New Year, namely, the Lantern Festival, was received.

A week before this date the Chief Eunuch Hsia, superintendent of the six Imperial harems, arrived. He examined with the utmost detail the preparations which had been made and inspected the whole of the festival gardens even to the most secluded nooks in which the august visitor was to make herself comfortable and "change her attire." He brought with him a great crowd of other eunuchs who had been specially selected for guard and sentry duties and were now posted at various points. Moreover, the inmates of the two palaces received detailed instructions as to where each person, down to the kitchen staff, was to be for the duration of the august visit, as well as the exact ceremonial which was to be observed at the reception. Furthermore, servants of the Ministry of Public Works from the capital were detailed to clean the streets leading from the Imperial Palace to the princely palace, and posses of special police were sent to keep them clear of traffic and pedestrians.

During the night of the fourteenth to the fifteenth no one closed an eye, and from break of dawn everyone, from the Princess Ancestress down, was ready and waiting ceremonially attired in his or her place for the visitor. In the Park of Delightful Vision the hangings became inflated and welled out like dragons and snakes, the brightly embroidered curtains fluttered like phoenixes, the gold and silver glistened, the pearls and precious stones shimmered, clouds of aromatic fumes ascended from tripod burners and from incense vessels, the fragrant green of young foliage shone from pots and vases. A solemn silence reigned everywhere. Not a hem nor a cough was audible.

The male members of the family had taken their stand outside in the middle of the closed-off street, in front of the western gate, while the ladies, sheltered from the vulgar gaze by high cloth screens, waited close by the gate.

The exhaustion caused by the hours of waiting was already becoming noticeable when a solitary eunuch on horseback came galloping along. Chia Cheng stopped him and asked when the Imperial spouse would arrive.

"Not for a long time yet," was the answer. "At one o'clock she intends to dine, at two she will pray to Buddha in the Hall of Precious Strength from God, at five she will attend the banquet in the Palace of Great Clarity, and after that she will go to see the lantern display in the Imperial Gardens. She can hardly be here before seven this evening."

135

At the suggestion of Phoenix, who had heard the whole conversation through the partition, the older ladies retired indoors for a time to rest. In the late afternoon the loud trot of horses was heard once more. This time ten eunuchs came riding along. They were out of breath and as they dismounted they clapped their hands excitedly. This was the prearranged signal to the many eunuchs who had been distributed over the parklands for several days before, that the august visitor was approaching, and they all rushed to their posts.

A little more time passed in silent expectation, then two outriders appeared riding at an easy trot. They leaped from their horses and, with their faces turned towards the west, took up their position beside the ladies' screen. After a time another pair of outriders came along and joined the first. Then ten more pairs of outriders arrived and, with the first two pairs, formed a double row. From a distance came the sound of music. And now, two by two, the long procession approached: dragon banners, great fans of phoenix and pheasant feathers, ceremonial palace umbrellas swayed to and fro. Next came bearers carrying lighted censers of gold; then, stretched over an arched framework, an immense canopy of yellow silk on which were embroidered seven phoenixes; a crown, robes, girdle, and shoes were borne on cushions; then came more eunuchs carrying basins of warm perfumed water, embroidered hand towels, perfumed handkerchiefs, dusters and similar objects, which they held ready. And finally, borne by eight men, came the great yellow-gold silken State sedan chair, embroidered with phoenixes, with a golden knob at the back and little bells which tinkled sweetly at each side. At its approach the entire crowd which was waiting went down on its knees. Eunuchs came rushing along to help the Princess Ancestress and the other great ladies to their feet again. Then they all surrounded the sedan chair and followed it on foot in orderly procession into the palace precincts. In front of the entrance to a somewhat secluded courtyard situated at the eastern extremity of the Yung-kuo palace the litter was set down. A eunuch hastened up to the door, knelt down, and invited the Imperial spouse to dismount and "change clothes." The eunuch then withdrew to make way for the Imperial ladies-in-waiting, who helped the distinguished inmate out of the sedan chair and escorted her to the apartment in question.

After Beginning of Spring had "changed clothes" she got into the chair again and had herself carried to the Park of Delightful Vision. The park glittered with the multicolored shimmer of innumerable brightly colored lamps and lanterns, the air was heavy with the aromatic perfumes which rose on all sides in spirals of smoke from censers and tripods, and filled with the sweet strains of an invisible orchestra which made itself heard from time to time.

"Much too luxurious, much too costly!" murmured Beginning of Spring, shaking her head, when she saw from inside her sedan chair all the unheard-of magnificence around her.

A eunuch approached the chair, knelt down, and invited Her Highness to enter a boat. Beginning of Spring left the chair and entered the gorgeous State boat, which then glided gently along the glittering watercourse that wound between high slopes. To right and left the cliffs and stone balustrades glittered with the colored lights of innumerable little crystal and glass lamps. The trees and shrubs along the banks, which were still bare of leaves, had been given a springlike appearance by artificial leaves and flowers made of gaily colored fabric and tissue, and everywhere among the branches and leaves bright little lamps and lanterns were glowing. Down below on the water, too, lights rocked and swayed, for everywhere, among the reeds and the lotus leaves and water lilies, glowed little lamps made in the shape of oysters and shells, while others, fastened to the pinions of herons, swans, and ducks, drew fantastic circles of light over the surface of the water. One could imagine oneself transported into a fairy realm of crystal, a sparkling wonderland of pearls and precious stones. The boat itself was likewise a blaze of multicolored lights, and these, playing upon the sumptuous pearl-studded curtains and embroidered damask portieres, and on the wet oars carved of precious wood, made a brilliant galaxy of reflections. The journey ended at a marble landing place which bore the title "Pepper Plant Quay," after which the journey was continued by litter under the stone arches of honor with their dragons in relief, up to the main hall.

On the way Beginning of Spring expressed various wishes regarding mottoes and inscriptions which she desired changed. For instance, she wished the exuberant title on the arch of honor, "Entrance to the Domain of the Blessed Spirits," to be changed to the simple inscription, "Entrance to the Country House of the Filial Visit." Each of these wishes was immediately conveyed by eunuchs to Chia Cheng, who had the required alterations carried out there and then; for all the existing mottoes and inscriptions had only been put up provisionally. They were almost all based upon Pao Yu's suggestions.

It must be remarked here that Beginning of Spring had a particularly tender affection for her young brother. While she was still living at home and Pao Yu was hardly four years old, she used to take an almost motherly interest in the development of his mind, and industriously instructed him in the first foundations of a classical education, and taught him several thousand ideographs. Even after she had been taken into the service of the Imperial Palace, she had never ceased to inquire, in her letters to her father and mother, how he was getting on and what progress he was making in his studies. In making use everywhere of the products of Pao Yu's brain in texts for mottoes, Chia Cheng's idea was to give his sister pleasure. She was to perceive from these that the trouble she had taken with him in her childhood days had not been wasted and had brought forth good fruit. For even if Pao Yu's inspirations did not exactly show genius, at least they betrayed considerable talent and a certain originality.

The main hall shone festively in the resplendent glow of immense candelabra. Everywhere smoldering tripods and incense pots stood about on the grounds, filling the air with aromatic perfumes from the musk glands of the civet and musk ox. It would be impossible to describe adequately the sumptuousness of the interior decorations—to depict and recount in detail all the splendors of the carpets and hangings, the walls and the windows, the staircases and the banisters. It was a real fairy castle, a genuine "cinnamon hall," a "palace of orchids," worthy to be the dwelling place of the Imperial spouse.

Beginning of Spring remarked that there was no inscription over the front of the building. A eunuch explained to her that this was the main hall, and that no one had dared to anticipate her own choice at this, the most important point in the whole of the festive gardens. A head eunuch, who was acting as master of ceremonies, now invited her to ascend the throne and receive the homage of the members of the family. At each side of the steps leading to the throne music began to play. Meantime Prince Shieh and the other seniors had grouped themselves, under the guidance of two eunuchs, on the Terrace of the Moon in front of the entrance to the hall, and stood awaiting a sign to appear before the face of Her Imperial Highness and perform their kowtow of homage in the manner prescribed by Court ceremonial. But Her Imperial Highness released them, and also the ladies, from the performance of this kowtow, and contented herself with a simple levee. In the course of these proceedings tea was handed to Her Highness three times. She then stood up and descended from the throne. As she did so the music ceased. And with this the official part of the reception came to an end.

The Imperial wife now entered a side chamber and changed her attire. She then left the park in a carriage belonging to the house and went, now a simple daughter of the family once more, to visit her parents and her grandmother. This second, private reception took place in the home of the Princess Ancestress. Strictly speaking, Beginning of Spring should now, as daughter and granddaughter, have had to throw herself upon her knees before the old *Tai tai* and her mother. But the old *Tai tai* and the other female relatives approached her with a curtsy and forbade her to conform with the ceremony prescribed by Court etiquette.

After the formalities had been sufficiently complied with the human emotions which the reunion awoke were given full vent. All the assembled female relations welcomed Beginning of Spring in their turn, and as she stood there holding her grandmother's left hand and her mother's right, tears rolled ceaselessly down her cheeks. The relatives were likewise overcome with emotion. All had so much in their hearts which they would have dearly loved to express, but for a long while nothing could be heard but wordless sobbing. Princess Shieh and Phoenix and the three cousins, Greeting of Spring, Grief of Spring, and Taste of Spring, who were modestly standing somewhat in the background, were all seized with the prevalent emotion too, and continuously wiped their eyes.

At last Beginning of Spring mastered her emotions, and forced her voice to a gay and jocular tone as, turning to her grandmother and mother, she said: "Since I was taken away to that place which is closed to you, I have today been permitted to see you again for the first time after a long separation and many difficulties. And now instead of chatting and laughing merrily together, we are all weeping and wailing at one another. We should be enjoying the present moment instead of doing this. Soon I shall have to leave you, and who knows when we shall meet again . . . !"

She could say no more and began sobbing anew. They all pressed around to console and comfort her. She was now brought to an armchair on which she sat receiving the homage of the entire female staff of both palaces, who passed in order of precedence before the doorway and performed their kowtow.

"Our family is so big, it is sad that there is not time to greet everyone," sighed Beginning of Spring.

Her mother asked her whether she wished to receive Aunt Hsueh and her daughter and cousin Black Jade. They were waiting outside but were not venturing to appear unless called, as they considered themselves without rank or dignity. Beginning of Spring had them called in and had a few friendly words for each of them. Meanwhile her attendants were being refreshed in various quarters; only four young eunuchs had remained behind in her vicinity. This absence of guards and retinue allowed the family more unrestricted conversation. Beginning of Spring also exchanged a few words with her father, Chia Cheng, though only through the folding screen, of course, because according to Court etiquette no strange man, not even her own father, was permitted to look with his profane eyes upon a wife of the Emperor.

"The poor peasants who live on salted cabbage and dress in shoddy cotton are better off than we are," lamented Beginning of Spring through the screen. "They can foster and satisfy their natural desire for family life to their hearts' content. But we, on the contrary, though we are made of the same flesh and blood as they, have to endure sorrowful separation. What good to us are all of our splendors and riches?"

Her father too was on the verge of tears, but he spoke words of comfort to her and exhorted her not to quarrel with fate, which had treated her so well, but to acknowledge with gratitude the favor granted to her by the Son of Heaven and to repay it with redoubled dutifulness.

"Who would ever have dreamed that it would be granted to a simple, obscure subject such as I to rear a precious phoenix in his poor, cold household among ordinary birds of the hen and goose species? Next to the favor of the Emperor and the inscrutable designs of nature, such great good fortune is doubtless also to be ascribed to the blessed and benign influence of our ancestors. Therefore, we must show ourselves worthy of our ancestors by redoubled self-sacrifice and devotion to the Throne, the more so now that the Throne has granted us this hitherto unknown favor of a visit to the family. Even if we were to dash our brains out against the ground in doing homage, we should still not have paid the ten-thousandth part of our debt of gratitude to the Son of Heaven—may he see a thousand harvests! Let the Imperial spouse— and this is my most earnest prayer—not think so much of the years she has wasted in the society of her parents, but rather let her dedicate all her mind and all her strength to the service of His Imperial Majesty!"

Chia Cheng then went on to speak of Pao Yu, remarking that most of the inscriptions and mottoes in the park had been planned by him. If she would deign to take notice of one or other of these inscriptions and help to improve upon them, she would certainly make Pao Yu very happy.

"Oh, what splendid progress he has made!" cried Beginning of Spring, joyfully. Then, when Chia Cheng had withdrawn, she asked those around her: "Why do I not see Pao Yu?"

"As a male relative without office or title, he does not dare to appear without being called for," replied the Princess Ancestress.

"Bring him here," the eunuchs were ordered. Soon afterwards Pao Yu appeared, and saluted his sister by falling on his knee and touching the ground with his forehead. But she took him quite unceremoniously by the hand and, clasping him to her breast, fondly stroked his head and neck.

"How big you have grown!" she exclaimed, smiling, but immediately overcome by her childhood memories, she broke down in tears once more.

"The banquet is ready. We beg the Imperial spouse to grant us the happiness of sharing it." With these words they sought to distract her from her grief. Beginning of Spring stood up, ordered Pao Yu to lead

元春

the way, and set out on foot through the new park, together with the entire company, for the main hall, where the banquet was to take place. On the way the most important parts of the park, which was illuminated with innumerable bright lanterns, were inspected thoroughly. Beginning of Spring was lavish with her praise and approval, but she begged her family very earnestly not to indulge in such excessive expenditure when she should visit them again. At the banquet Princess Chen and Phoenix shared the office of handing her food and filling her glass.

After the meal Beginning of Spring asked for writing brush and ink and wrote with her own hand on strips of flowered silk the names and inscriptions which she gave to the most important places in the new park. The grounds as a whole were to receive the name of "Park of Delightful Vision" and the façade of the main hall the inscription "Remembering the Imperial Favor, intent upon Faithful Fulfillment of Duty," and so name after name, motto after motto, text after text came under review. After this, a competition in poetical composition began between the sisters and cousins and Pao Yu. Greeting of Spring, Grief of Spring, Taste of Spring, Precious Clasp, Black Jade, and Li Wan, the young widow of the deceased brother Chia Chu, each received a motto as theme and had to compose a stanza on it. Actually, Pao Yu was given four themes. He was required to extol in stanzas of particularly choice language the four places in the park which pleased him the most. And so the improvising and versifying went on until far into the night. Of the six samples of feminine literary talent, Beginning of Spring declared the efforts submitted by Black Jade and Precious Clasp to be the best; so excellent indeed, she added modestly, that she herself could not compete with them.

Pao Yu too had finished his task with real effort and with the secret friendly help of his two gifted cousins, Precious Clasp and Black Jade. Precious Clasp had helped him with the third stanza by reciting a missing line which he could not remember from a poem of the celebrated T'ang poet, Han Yu; and Black Jade had actually written the whole fourth stanza for him and passed it to him secretly scribbled on a crumpled piece of paper. Beginning of Spring promptly declared this fourth stanza to be by far the best of his efforts. Taste of Spring, who wrote a beautiful hand, now had to copy all the ten stanzas out afresh on paper, after which they were taken by a eunuch to Chia Cheng, so that he might rejoice at these specimens of the literary talent of the younger members of the family.

Cousin Chia Chiang, who was burning with desire to shine with his troupe of dancing girls, was almost beside himself with impatience when at last a eunuch came rushing in behind the dancing stage.

"The literary competition is finished," he announced. "The dance program can begin now. Give me a program quickly."

Chia Chiang handed him a program and a list of the names of the twelve dancers. Beginning of Spring chose four out of the twenty numbers: "The Glorious Banquet," "The Strange Beggar," "Meeting of Phantoms," and "Separated Souls." The audience took their places in front of the stage, Chia Chiang gave the command to raise the curtain, and the twelve girls began to display their carefully rehearsed art. They danced so enchantingly that the audience could only stare as if bewitched; their singing melted all hearts; and in their acting they expressed joy and grief to such perfection that the onlookers, quite carried away, almost took their playing for reality.

After the performance a eunuch appeared behind the stage with a golden plate full of cakes.

Chia Chiang made the dancer, Ling Kuan, step in front of the curtain to perform a kowtow of thanks before the august donor.

"The Imperial wife has declared that Ling Kuan is the best of the troupe," continued the eunuch, "and she desires her to give two or more solo pieces."

Chia Chiang accordingly sent Ling Kuan onto the stage once more and ordered her to give as encores the two numbers "A Walk through the Garden" and "Terrible Awakening from a Dream." As these two numbers did not form part of her special repertoire, the rather independent Ling Kuan performed instead two dance scenes, "Rendezvous" and "Quarrel." Beginning of Spring was again delighted with the girl's ability and rewarded her with an extra fee in the form of two bales of silk from the palace and two purses filled with pieces of gold and silver.

With this the banquet ended. Beginning of Spring stood up to visit some other parts of the park which she had not yet seen, among them a Buddhist temple set on a hill, where she burned incense and prayed to Buddha. She chose as inscription for this temple the words: "On the Boat of Mercy through the Sea of Bitterness."

After this there was a great distribution of gifts in the main hall. Beginning of Spring, seated on a dais, held a comprehensive gift list in her hand and inspected every single present as the eunuchs laid it at her feet. No one in the two palaces, from the Princess Ancestress down to the coolie who collected the garbage and the youngest kitchen maid, went empty-handed. The Princess Ancestress received two house scepters, one of gold, the other of jade, inscribed "May your Wishes come True," an aloe rod, a prayer chaplet of sandalwood beads, four pairs of satin sheets from the Imperial Palace stores with the words "Long Spring," "Riches and Nobility," "Good Fortune," and "Long Life" embroidered on them; also a gold writing-brush case, ten gold bars

143

wrought in the form of the ideographs representing "May your Wishes come True," and ten silver bars in the form of the ideograph representing "Happiness and Blessings." To enumerate all the other gifts would be too lengthy a task. Suffice it to say that the combined household staffs of the east and west palaces received gifts comprising a hundred bales of silk, a thousand ounces of silver, and many bottles of Imperial wine.

It was already approaching three in the morning when the Chief Eunuch, who was in charge, announced that it was time to leave. Once more the eyes of the Imperial wife filled with tears, but she bravely forced herself to smile cheerfully, pressed the hands of her mother and grandmother once more, and begged them not to let the parting grieve them too greatly. The Son of Heaven, in his immense generosity, would surely permit them to see each other again one day, but on the occasion of her next visit they should refrain from such excessive expenditure in her honor. And finally they parted with heartbreaking tears and lamentations. As the Imperial litter disappeared out of sight with Beginning of Spring, her mother and grandmother had to be supported on each side, lest they should sink to the ground with the weight of their grief.

CHAPTER 16

One night the maid Pearl tests Pao Yu's feelings and stipulates her conditions. Black Jade makes fun of Cousin Little Cloud.

On RETURNING TO THE IMPERIAL PALACE, BEGINNING OF SPRING GAVE her Imperial husband a report of her harmonious and pleasant visit to her home. The dragon countenance of the Son of Heaven grew bright with joy and in token of his favor and recognition he sent rich gifts of silk, gold, and silver to his father-in-law Chia Cheng, for himself and his family and also for distribution among the personal attendants of the Imperial spouse.

After all the trouble and exertion which the illustrious visit had caused, the inmates of the east and west palaces permitted themselves a few days of well-earned rest and recreation. The New Year celebrations continued, it is true, but they were less formal than usual. Apart from Phoenix, who continued to carry out her household duties with her wonted energy, everyone sought his or her own comfort and bothered as little as possible about others. Thus it happened that Pao Yu was left to his own devices more than usual, and as the family school was closed for the New Year holidays, he hardly knew what to do with all his free time. He got bored by the monotony of the days, and lack of supervision whetted his desire for freedom.

One afternoon he slipped away from the theatrical performance in the Ningkuo palace. The demon dances on the stage, with their accompaniment of wild cries and the intoxicating music of gongs and drums which could be heard right out on the street, where they held a crowd of loiterers spellbound with admiration, were not at all to his taste. He found this kind of art too rough and ready.

After a hurried, passing glance into the inner rooms, where he said good-by to Princess Chen and various secondary wives, he stole into a somewhat secluded part of the building, a little reading pavilion. In this pavilion hung the picture of a marvelously beautiful woman which was painted in a manner so true to nature that it almost seemed to breathe. I will keep this beautiful lady company so that she will not feel so forsaken on this merry holiday, he thought to himself.

He was all alone, for the servants too had a great deal of freedom that day. The older ones were free to indulge in their beloved card games or spend the day with their relatives in the town; the younger ones were allowed to attend the theatrical performances and fireworks. Today none of them was required to bother much about the little master.

As Pao Yu passed under the window of the pavilion he heard a sound of sighing and groaning from inside. What's this? Can the picture have come to life? he thought in alarm, poking a hole in the window parchment to look in. No, the picture had not come to life; the noise came instead from two real mortals who were absorbed in that pleasurable game which the Fairy of Fearful Awakening had once taught him. In the male half of the couple he recognized his valet, Ming Yen.

"Stop that!" he shouted, pushing the door open with his foot. The lovers separated in haste, hurriedly fastening their clothing. Ming Yen fell on his knees before his master and begged for mercy.

"This is a nice way to behave in clear daylight; if the master of the house hears of it, it will go ill with you," scolded Pao Yu, at the same time taking a good look at Ming Yen's partner. She was not exactly a beauty, this little kitchen maid, but she was charming and pretty enough not to leave a male heart unmoved. She had become red to the ears, and was standing with downcast eyes, silent and embarrassed.

"Why don't you clear out?" asked Pao Yu angrily, stamping his foot. The little creature slipped out like the wind. Pao Yu followed her. "Don't be afraid; I am not a telltale!" he called after her.

"Not so loud, little ancestor. Your shouting will certainly betray us!" cried Ming Yen, following him, in his turn. Pao Yu stopped and let the young girl slip off. After he had questioned Ming Yen about her age and parentage, he said that he would like to take some kind of expedition. Ming Yen suggested a good long walk outside the city walls, but his master thought that too daring. He finally decided on a visit to the home of Pearl, who had got leave to spend the day with her mother. The house was only a bare mile away.

Pearl, who was just taking tea and cake with her mother and brother and half a dozen female cousins, felt not a little surprised and honored by the unexpected visit of her young master. He must surely be very fond of her indeed if he could not do without her for a few hours.

She had wondered what urgent matter had brought him here, but he said he was merely bored and wanted her company. Yet she had to scold him for his folly in daring to leave the house all on his own and she wanted to send him straight back. What if they missed him? Or if he met his stern old father on the way? Or if his horse took fright in the crowded streets and threw him? she asked anxiously. Her brother, who was older than she, calmed her, saying that since the young gentleman was here they were bound in decency to entertain him for a while.

So they took him into the living room, made him sit down on the heated kang, and set before him all kinds of modest titbits which he did not touch. Little comfort though Pearl's simple home could offer him, nevertheless the change pleased him. The easygoing atmosphere of humble folk which this living room breathed was something quite new to the spoiled young aristocrat from a great house, and several of the simple young things who sat with downcast eyes and flushed cheeks around the family board seemed to him quite charming. Pearl herself was touching in her attentions to him. She pushed her own cushion behind his back, put her own foot-warmer to his feet, and set alight in his honor two sweet-smelling offerings of pressed plum blossoms. He noticed that there were red circles round her eyes and signs of tears on her powdered cheeks.

"Have you been crying?" he asked gently.

"No, no! A speck of dust got in my eye, and the lid has got red from rubbing it," she answered brightly. "But you are very smartly dressed! It was not for us, was it?" she asked, changing the subject hurriedly.

"No, it was for that awful theatrical show at Prince Chen's. I have just come from it."

"And you must go back to it as quickly as you can. Our poor hut is no place for you to be."

"I am going, but you must come back soon." She gave him a knowing smile. Then she took the five-colored cord with the stone amulet from his neck and handed it round the family circle.

"Look, this is the wonderful thing I have often told you about. Now you can look at it and wonder at it with your own eyes. Have a really good look at it; you don't have the chance to see such a strange thing as that every day," she declared proudly, fastening the cord round his neck again. After this Pao Yu cut short his brief visit. On

Pearl's advice he hired a small covered sedan chair, which brought him up near the side gate of the Ningkuo palace, so that he might avoid being recognized on the way. Only there did he mount his horse again; and in this way he got in unobserved. Thus his little flight into freedom passed without repercussions, and it would have been scarcely worth mentioning here were it not for the fact that it contributed to strengthening Pearl's self-assurance to a very great extent, as was soon apparent.

In his absence his former nurse, Mother Li, had come hobbling along on her stick to pay him a New Year visit. Although she had long since retired from service because of her age, nevertheless she felt that she was still as important and indispensable as ever. She had scolded the waiting maids and housemaids as usual and held forth loudly about the loose ways that had crept into the household since she had left it; and had gone away at last, still chiding and scolding, having eaten up the delicious mousse which had been sent specially that morning from the Imperial kitchens for Pao Yu, and which Pao Yu had set aside for the maid Pearl.

When Pearl came home in the evening he apologized to her because the greedy old woman had once more snapped up her titbit out of envy. Pearl, in her nice considerate way, had laughed it off, saying: "Thank you for the good intention, but the last time I took that mousse it did not agree with me at all, tasty though it is. So I'm not a bit sorry for it. I should much prefer a few nice roast chestnuts before going to bed. Perhaps you would peel some for me?"

Pao Yu obediently ordered a plate of roast chestnuts, picked out the best, and peeled them for her with his own hands.

"Who was that girl in red, this afternoon?" he inquired casually, absorbed in his occupation.

"She was a cousin of mine. But what are you sighing for? No doubt you are thinking she is not grand enough to dress so strikingly?"

"Quite the contrary. Who has a better right than she to dress in red? Could she not be taken on here?"

"Certainly not. My people find it quite enough to have one slave in the family. You shall have to look around for someone else," retorted Pearl, insolently.

"Do not be so touchy. I did not mean that she should come as a slave, but only to visit, as your relative."

"She is not suitable company for you."

Pao Yu fell silent and went on peeling the chestnuts.

"Why don't you speak?" she went on after a fairly long pause. "I suppose I've offended you? Very well, for all I care, if you're so struck with her, it need only cost you a few ounces of silver and she's yours."

"You misunderstand me. I only meant to say that she deserves far better than an inferior creature like me to pass her life in these spacious halls and extensive gardens."

"That good fortune has certainly been denied her, but she has never had to suffer want and her parents have spoiled her in every way. She is seventeen now and she has already got her full bridal equipment ready in her trunks and cases. For she's getting married this year."

A regretful "Ah!" escaped from Pao Yu.

"Yes, indeed, it's a pity," continued Pearl with a sigh. "We cousins have seen so little of each other all these years that I've been here. And now, just when I am about to return home, she is leaving us."

Pao Yu was so startled that he let the chestnuts roll onto the ground. "What? You want to return home?" he asked, dumfounded.

"Yes. Just when you came this afternoon we were having a family council over it. My mother and my brother were urging me to remain just one more year in service; then they would have got together enough money to buy my freedom."

"Why do they want to buy you free?"

"What a funny question! After all, I am not a daughter of the house. Do you think perhaps that I should end my days here?"

"What if I do not let you go?"

"Oho! Even at the Imperial Court there is no such thing as perpetual servitude. The domestic staff is changed and added to every few years. There are special laws about these things. If even the Court must bow to those laws, then your house must assuredly do so."

Pao Yu could not hide from himself the fact that she was right. Nevertheless he tried to put forward other objections.

"You will find it difficult to get free without the permission of the old *Tai tai*," he remarked.

"Why should she be against it? Am I perchance so special that she could not do without me? That she should perhaps consent to an addition to my mother's allowance, in order to keep me? It seems to me, on the other hand, that I am no better than the average girl and can be easily replaced at any time. At any rate, I have been in the service of your family long enough, first several years with Miss Little Cloud, the old *Tai tai's* granddaughter, and after that who knows how many years with you. It's really time for me to go. Your grandmother will be pleased, on the contrary, I do believe, when she is rid of me at last, and she won't demand a specially big ransom. The fact that I have served you well was only my duty. Others do their duty just as well or better."

Pao Yu fidgeted uneasily on his seat.

"But what if I greatly desire you to remain? Would your mother not desist from her intention if my grandmother asks her to, and offers her an increased allowance?"

"My mother would certainly not dare to resist if the old *Tai tai* insisted absolutely that I should remain, and in that case there would be no need of increasing the allowance by a single copper. But the question is, *would* the old *Tai tai* insist? As far as I know, it has never been the custom of your family to misuse their power and influence in order to intimidate and coerce the weak. From what I know of the old *Tai tai* I doubt very much whether she would depart from this noble family tradition in order to force my mother and me to something which would be of no particular advantage to your family and a human hardship for mine."

Pao Yu remained thoughtful for a few moments.

"If I understand you aright, you are seriously resolved to leave?"

"Yes."

Ungrateful creature! he thought to himself, angrily. Then aloud, with a sigh: "If I had guessed that before I would never have taken you into my service. Now I shall remain behind alone here, a poor forsaken ghost."

He slipped off sadly to his bed and lay down. He did not know that Pearl had only been play-acting a bit, in order to test his feelings for her. In reality, she had declared today at home, when her mother and brother had expressed the intention of buying her back, that she had no desire to be ransomed and would rather die than leave her service. At a time when there was not another grain of rice to eat at home, she herself had decided to be sold into servitude to save her family from starvation. She was lucky enough to have a position now where she lacked neither clothing nor good food, was treated almost like a daughter of the house, and was neither beaten by day nor misused by night; and was she to be so foolish as to give up this pleasant life now to return to the narrowness of her home? Certainly not. She did not wish to hear another word about being bought back, and meantime would prefer her family to regard her as being dead.

An excited family discussion had followed, in the course of which some tears, of which Pao Yu had remarked the traces, had been shed. The result was that the mother and brother gave way and dropped their intention. Pao Yu's unexpected visit had shown them the warm relations existing between servant and master and left them completely convinced and reassured. In short, all that Pearl had just said about leaving and being ransomed was sheer fiction.

Pao Yu had not been in bed for long when Pearl came to his bedside and gave him a cheerful shaking. She noticed tears on his cheeks.

"What has wounded your heart?" she asked gently. "It all depends on whether you are really bent on keeping me. If you are, I could perhaps stay," she added unexpectedly.

He jumped up.

"Oh, is that so? And what can I do to keep you?"

"You would have to promise me three things. If you can do that, I will believe in the sincerity of your wish, and then I will stay, even if they were to cut my throat here."

"Name three, name a hundred conditions, dearest little sister! I will do everything you ask if you will only stay with me. Remain at least until I have turned into fleeting ashes—no, not ashes, for ashes would still contain too big a remnant of my bodily being. Remain until I have turned into a streak of smoke and been blown away by the wind without leaving a trace. Then I will need you no longer; then you may go wherever your fancy urges you. . . . !"

As he spoke he became more and more vehement. She sealed his mouth with her hand and stopped him from speaking more.

"Stop! You need not be so sentimental. You need only fulfill three small conditions."

"And what would they be?"

"Firstly, you must admit your faults when you are reproved."

"I will. And you may wrench out my tongue if I ever talk nonsense again. Go on!"

"Secondly, whether you are really learned or only pretend to be, you must be more unassuming before people, and not mock and criticize so much, annoying your father as you do. In any case, he is not particularly impressed by your achievements and he takes it ill that you speak contemptuously behind his back of worthy older people who have achieved something by dint of ability and whom you like to call 'salaried blockheads.' So, not so overbearing, if you please!"

"You are quite right. And I will never again repeat those silly things that I have said in the immaturity of my youth. Go on!"

"Thirdly, you must have more respect for pious bonzes and holy Taoist priests, and not make fun of them. Moreover, you must be less frivolous and irresponsible in your behavior with young girls, and not run after all the girls you see with painted lips and—in red dresses!"

"All right. I will mend my ways. Anything else?"

"No. It is enough for me if you fulfill these three conditions; if you do, not even a litter with eight bearers will entice me to leave the house."

"Why not? Who knows, you may yet have a litter with eight bearers at your disposal, if you stay here long enough."

"Oh, no. I am not so very eager for that."

They were still talking late into the night when another waiting maid appeared and asked them would they not settle down to sleep at last. It was already the third watch of the night. Pao Yu asked her to hand him the clock. Yes, the hand did in fact point to midnight. Pao Yu washed his face and rinsed his mouth once more, then lay down to sleep at last. Pearl was to learn soon enough, to her annoyance, how lightly he was going to regard the promises which he had just solemnly given her.

The next day brought new life and change to the Yungkuo palace with the arrival of the cousin Hsiang Yun, or Little Cloud. She belonged to the noble family of the Counts Shih and was a granddaughter of the Princess Ancestress. Because of her saucy freshness and exuberant gaiety pretty little Miss Hsiang Yun had always been a very welcome guest, and from childhood a good comrade of her cousin Pao Yu, who was her own age, and with whom she had played many a prank. One occasion remembered with particular amusement in the palace was the time she had disguised herself as Pao Yu and imitated him so perfectly that she could only be distinguished from him by her voice.

Pao Yu happened to be with Precious Clasp when the arrival of his childhood playmate was announced to him. Accompanied by Precious Clasp, he went off at once to welcome her. He found her with the Princess Ancestress, and the sound of gay chatter and merry laughter betrayed her presence from a long way off. Black Jade and the other cousins were all there already.

"Where have you come from now?" asked Black Jade, turning to Pao Yu.

"I was with Sister Precious Clasp."

"Aha, that's why you are so late. Otherwise you would certainly have dashed along here long ago."

"Do you think I exist only to pass the time for you?"

"No, but you may think so if you like. Moreover, I never asked you to while away time for me, and in future I shall willingly do without the pleasure of your company."

And already she was out the door and had run to her room. He ran after her.

"Do not be so terribly touchy," he pleaded. "What bad thing have I said again? Instead of staying here and amusing yourself with us, you go off and make yourself miserable."

"Are you my guardian that you speak like that?"

"Of course I'm not, but I cannot look on and see you torturing your-self."

"If I torture myself, even if I torture myself to death, that's my affair."

"How can one even speak of death now in this joyful New Year Festival time?"

"That is just what I *will* speak of, and now. You are afraid of death, I am sure, and would like to live to be a hundred. Isn't that so?"

"A charming conversation like this would almost make one wish for death."

"Thank you. So you would wish me dead?"

"Who is speaking of your death? I meant mine. How you twist the words in a person's mouth!"

"Cousin Little Cloud is waiting for you!" With these words Precious Clasp broke in on their conversation and snatched Pao Yu away without more ado. Black Jade remained obstinately behind; she sat down by the window and wept, but she had not been there long when Pao Yu came back. As soon as he appeared Black Jade's suppressed weeping changed to loud sobbing. He started trying to pacify her.

"Why are you bothering me again?" she asked, forestalling him. "You have got someone else who can entertain you much better than I can, and who is much cleverer, and more practical, and more educated, and more amusing than I—who is always anxious for your welfare and takes you away in good time when you are in boring company. So what do you want here, please?"

"Do be reasonable!" he pleaded gently. "You know just as well as I do that close relations come before distant ones, and old friendships before new ones. I am much more closely related to you than to Precious Clasp and I have known you much longer than I have known her. We two have eaten together, lived together, learned and played together, for years now, day after day—so you have really no reason at all to feel slighted."

"Pah! I am not so anxious for your favor that I would compete with others for it. I do what suits me. What others think matters nothing at all to me."

"I am just the same. That is why we have such frequent misunderstandings."

"Oh, I understand you thoroughly well. But you will not tolerate any well-meant reproof, and by your whims you are always challenging people to reprove you. To give an example right away: why do you take it into your head to leave off your warm blue fox collar just now in this cold weather?"

"Because your bad humor has made me quite hot," he replied gaily.

"You will catch a fine cold," she sighed. While they were skirmishing in this way Cousin Little Cloud came skipping along.

"You two have each other the whole time; you're together day after day," she said with her comical-sounding lisp. "I come here so seldom, you might really give a little more time to me."

"What a funny pronunciation the little one has!" exclaimed Black Jade, mockingly mimicking her. "If you counted one, two, three her way you would bite your tongue in two."

"Take care that you do not bite your own tongue in two by mimicking her so well!" said Pao Yu to Black Jade in the same tone of mimicry.

"You're terrible. You won't overlook the tiniest defect in your fellow creatures; you must always find fault with us," lamented the victim. "You may put on superior airs with others, but I know someone whom you would never dare to find fault with."

"Oh, indeed? I would really love to know whom you mean," replied Pao Yu.

"If you have enough courage to find fault with Cousin Precious Clasp, you can be really proud of yourself."

"Oh, with her? Very well, just see if I don't. . . ."

Pao Yu tried to cut her short, and began talking about something else. But Little Cloud would not give up and rattled away in mock indignation to Black Jade: "I hope you will one day have a man who will bite his tongue when he speaks and torture you day and night with his stutter. If I live to see that, I will believe, holy Buddha, in you and your power of retribution!"

And with this last shaft she was out of the room in a flash amid the laughter of the others.

Black Jade wanted to dash after her, but Pao Yu stood in the doorway with outstretched arms, laughingly barring her way.

"Be generous and let her off!"

"No, I won't; she will have to pay for this!" said Black Jade heatedly, trying in vain to push him aside.

"Dearest, best sister, I beg for mercy!" pleaded Little Cloud, who had stopped outside.

"Be friends again for his sake," urged Precious Clasp from inside.

"No, I will not!" insisted Black Jade, stamping her foot defiantly. "I see you have all plotted together to make game of me."

"But it was you who began it. Now, do be reasonable and give it up!" Pao Yu tried to persuade her.

And so the lively contest went on for a while, this way and that, until a servant appeared to call them to their evening meal. They broke off their squabble and went off, all four together, hot-cheeked and chattering gaily, to the apartments of the Princess Ancestress. Little Cloud also went to her quarters just as usual, and shared a bed peaceably with Black Jade.

CHAPTER 17

The maid Pearl sulks and takes Pao Yu quietly to task. The maid Little Ping keeps silence and saves Chia Lien from being discovered.

THE NEXT MORNING PAO YU JUMPED OUT OF BED VERY EARLY, PUT on his slippers and dressing gown, and tripped along next door to the bedroom of his two cousins. He found them still in bed fast asleep. The absence of the maids made it possible for him to observe them at leisure. How different they looked even when asleep! Black Jade lay all carefully wrapped and muffled up to her ears in the apricot-colored silk eiderdown, while Little Cloud had let the cover slide off her so much that her right shoulder and her right arm, decorated with two gold bangles, and even a bit of her round smooth thigh lay bare and naked. The blue-black ringlets of her loosened hair fell over the edge of the pillow.

"She cannot be still even when asleep!" murmured Pao Yu to himself. "She'll get a fine cold and then complain of twinges."

And he drew the cover gently and carefully up over her. Thereupon Black Jade turned round and opened her eyes. "What are you doing here so early?" she asked Pao Yu.

"It's not at all so early. Quick, get up!"

"You must go out first."

Pao Yu waited a little while in the adjoining dressing room, then he came back. In the meantime the two cousins had got up and were just at their morning toilet. Pao Yu sat down by the dressing table and looked on as Little Cloud washed herself. When she had finished, the maid Blue Thread was about to take away the washing water.

"Stop!" cried Pao Yu, holding her back. "I would like to have it to wash in."

And he stooped over the basin, wetted his face and hands in the same water which Little Cloud had used, and dried himself with the same towel with which she had dried herself. Then he quickly rinsed out his mouth and cleaned his teeth with blue salts and, this done, turned round again to Little Cloud. She had just finished doing her hair.

"Dear little sister, please do my hair too!" he begged.

"No, I cannot do that."

"But you used to be able to do it before."

"Perhaps so, but I have forgotten how to."

"You must do it! I will not go away from here or put on my forehead band or my cap until you have done my hair! Just to plait the few little pigtails is not so very difficult!"

Finally she gave in and did what he asked; she drew his head nearer

翠縷

to her, plaited the front hair into a ring of little pigtails which when all tied by the ends and drawn up formed a crown-shaped coiffure, and dressed his back hair in a long pigtail with a red braid plaited through it. This braid was decorated with four pearls and it was weighted down with a gold clasp at the end.

"Look here, the fourth pearl does not match the other pearls. I remember that all four used to be alike," remarked Little Cloud while she was plaiting.

"That's right. It is a replacement; I lost the original one."

"Out in the street, I suppose. It's a pity, the lovely pearl is in strange hands now."

"Who knows, perhaps he did not lose it but presented it to someone as a mark of regard," interjected Black Jade.

Pao Yu did not reply, but continued to handle and peep into the bottles and boxes which covered the dressing table. Now he caught sight of an open jar of rouge. He would have liked to stick in his finger, as was his habit, and taste the red stuff, but he was afraid his cousins would catch him at it and scold him. While he was hesitating and staring fascinated at the tempting red paste he suddenly got a slap from behind which made him drop the pot of rouge.

"You shouldn't do that! When will you give up such silliness?" Little Cloud rebuked him.

At that moment the maid Pearl appeared, but immediately withdrew again when she saw how matters stood. She found she was superfluous at such times. While she was doing her own morning toilet Precious Clasp entered her room.

"Where is Pao Yu?" she asked.

"He is busy," replied Pearl with an ironical smile, indicating the next room.

Precious Clasp understood.

"Yes, one can preach to him as much as one likes, but it only goes in one ear and out the other," continued Pearl with a sigh. "They are his cousins, of course, but even with cousins there are certain limits. This boisterous playing about day and night—he knows no moderation!"

Precious Clasp thought she was speaking very sensibly. She sat on the edge of the bed and started a little talk with her, asking about her age and family and other personal things; and the more she chatted with her the more she was charmed by her kind and understanding nature. At last Pao Yu returned. Precious Clasp stood up at once and went off without a word or a greeting.

"Why did she go off so suddenly when I came in?" he asked in surprise.

"Why do you ask me? I cannot know what there is between you two," replied Pearl coolly. Pao Yu did not fail to notice her annoyed expression.

"Why are you in such a bad humor?" he continued, smiling.

"I did not know that I was in a bad humor. Moreover, in future you need not set your foot in my room any more, and when you want someone to serve you, please get someone else! From now on I would prefer to serve the old *Tai tai* again."

Saying this, she threw herself on her bed. Pao Yu sat down beside her and spoke kind words to her, but she shut her eyes tight and did not take any notice of him. He was utterly perplexed.

"What is the matter with her?" he asked the maid, Musk, who came in just then.

"How do I know? You must ask her yourself," answered Musk brusquely, and disappeared again. Pao Yu looked after her, puzzled.

"Ah, well! I'll lie down to sleep too," he said ill-humoredly; and standing up he went into his bedroom and threw himself on the bed. For a while it was quiet in both rooms. Then Pearl heard the sound of regular breathing. She thought he had really gone to sleep, so she got up quietly, went over, and covered him with a blanket. But he pushed the covering away crossly and continued to pretend to be asleep. She saw through his pretense.

"If it suits you that way, I also can pretend to be deaf and dumb in future," she said.

He gave up his pretending and sat up.

"How have I deserved your displeasure again? I have no objection to your scolding me. But to sulk silently without any reason, and not to notice me at all, that's no manners! I do not understand your behavior."

"It is a pity that you lack the necessary insight."

He had no time to reply, for the Princess Ancestress sent for him to come to breakfast. When he returned again after a breakfast taken hurriedly and absent-mindedly, Pearl had made herself comfortable on the divan in the veranda, while Musk was squatting down beside her tranquilly laying out dominoes. They behaved as if they did not see him. He knew that they always made common cause. Enraged and without even deigning to glance at them, he passed them by and went into his own room. Musk got up slowly and followed him in silently, expecting an order. But without hesitation he pushed her out the door.

"Please do not let me disturb you two!" he said angrily. Musk turned away, giggling to herself, and sent him two little auxiliary maids instead. Meantime Pao Yu had again thrown himself on the bed and was buried in a book. When he looked up after a while and wished to order tea he saw the two little things standing quietly and shyly in a corner. One of them, the older, he found most charming.

"What is your name?" he asked.

"Orchid Perfume."

"Who gave you that name?"

"Sister Pearl. My real name is Perfume of Resin."

"Ridiculous!" he murmured. "How many sisters have you at home?"

"There are four of us."

"And where do you come in?"

"I'm the fourth."

"Good. Then I shall just call you Little Fourth. Why these elaborate names? Hurry up and bring me tea!"

The two elder maids who were outside on the veranda had heard the conversation. They pressed their lips tightly together to keep from laughing out loud.

That whole day Pao Yu remained quietly in his room, contrary to his usual custom, and cured his bad humor as best he could by reading and writing. He left all the maids alone, with the exception of Little Fourth. Little Fourth naturally felt very much favored, and being very wide awake, she took the opportunity to fawn upon him and dance attendance on him, thus completely winning his favor. But he was not inclined to pay her much more attention today.

When evening came he felt his self-imposed loneliness doubly oppressive. A few glasses of wine which he had taken at table had excited and stimulated him. His eyes burned and his ears glowed. Normally, in such a mood as this he would have joked and been boisterous with his cousins and the maids. Today it was cold and quiet all around him. He sat alone in front of the lamp indulging in sad thoughts. Should he not go to them all the same, seek their company as usual? No, his pride would not allow that. He did not want to run after them. If he did so, they would treat him with more contempt than ever in the future and take even more liberties in making critical remarks. Better to ignore them completely, as if they were dead, and to be content with his own company for once.

After he had forced himself to this heroic decision a feeling of cheerful composure came over him. He got Little Fourth to pour him out some fresh wine, and took down the work of the great philosopher Chuang Tzu. That was just the right book for his mood. As he was looking through it he came on a passage in the chapter about robbers and thieves entitled "Open the Cupboards" which read: "Away with morality and education! Then there will be no more street robberies. Away with pearls and precious stones! Then thefts will cease. Burn the documents of investiture! Smash up the seals of office! Then people

秋紋
蕙香

will become honest and simple again. Destroy the weighing machines! Smash up the weights and measures! Then there will be no more quarrelling and strife! Do away with laws and regulations! Then people will become sensible of their own accord. Away with the study of harmony and musical instruments! Then people will learn to hear of themselves. Away with calligraphy and color theories! Then people will learn to see for themselves. Away with arithmetic and geometry, with angles and compasses! Then people will become clever and shrewd of themselves. . . ."

When Pao Yu had read thus far, he dipped his brush in the India ink and, inspired by the wine and by the spirit of the wise Chuang Tzu, he wrote on, continuing the theme: "Away with the Pearls and the Musks! Then the inmates of the inner chambers will take care of themselves. Smash up the Precious Clasps! Let the Black Jades return to ashes! Bury all yearnings and passions! Then will the beautiful and the ugly inmates of inner chambers bear with one another and reciprocally and without rancor accept wise instructions one from the other. Should Precious Clasp's divine beauty fade away, I would be cured of the delusion of love. Should Black Jade's splendid mind go to ashes, then I would no longer need to be consumed with admiration for her. These four, Clasp, Jade, Pearl, and Musk, cast out their nets and set their malicious snares and fool and bewitch all who come within their range."

Having written these passages from his heart, Pao Yu flung aside his brush well pleased, lay down in bed, and fell asleep at once.

When he awoke the next morning and turned over on the other side, he saw the maid Pearl lying at his side, fully clothed, on top of the bedclothes. He gave her a push.

"Lie down properly in the bed! You will catch cold like that," he said to her. He had long ago forgotten the little quarrel of yesterday, but she had not. When she remained silent, he stretched out his hand and tried to pull off her jacket. But he had scarcely undone the first button when she pushed back his hand and buttoned her jacket again. He grasped her hand and asked kindly: "What is the matter with you?"

She looked at him astonished. "There is nothing at all wrong with me, but I would advise you to go over quickly to your morning toilet, or else you will arrive too late."

"Over where?"

"As if I need tell you! Let the two of us keep at a distance from each other, for there's only cockfighting between us for the amusement of others. So go along over there, where you find it so pleasant. And if it's no longer pleasant over there, there's always a Little Fourth or a Little Fifth at your disposal over here. What do you want with an awkward creature like me, who stupidly misuses beautiful flower names?"

"Can you not forget about yesterday, then?"

"Never! Not if I were to live for a hundred years! I am certainly not like you, past whose ear all well-meant words are blown away by the wind unheard, and who does not know the next morning what has been said the night before."

Pao Yu seized a jade hair clasp which had slid down near the pillow, and flung it so violently to the ground that it broke.

"May that happen to me too if I do not listen to you in the future!" he said with emphasis.

"Better not to swear!" said Pearl, laughing. "Besides, you do not really mean it."

"If you knew how heavy my heart is!"

"What do you know about grief, anyway? You would have to look into my heart to know that. But enough of this. It's time to get up."

Pao Yu got up and dressed himself. This time he did not go over to Black Jade and Little Cloud but remained quietly with Pearl and let her do his hair. Shortly after he had gone to take breakfast with his grandmother as usual, Black Jade came into his room. Full of curiosity, she ransacked his writing table. There she found the book of Chuang Tzu lying open and beside it the supplementary composition written in Pao Yu's own hand. She did not really know whether to laugh at his outpourings or to be angry. At any rate, she took the writing brush and wrote the following satirical verse as further supplement, under his effusion:

> "Who is the clumsy fool that dares to prattle
> And nibble at the words of Master Chuang Tzu?
> Let him attend to his own business
> And keep his hands off the affairs of others."

Phoenix's little daughter was ill with smallpox, and the doctor had ordered the usual precautions to be taken. Phoenix and her husband Chia Lien had to evacuate their house temporarily on account of the danger of infection, and live separately, Chia Lien in the outer library and Phoenix with her aunt, Madame Cheng. The dwelling was swept out and fumigated in accordance with the prescribed formula, an altar was erected to the goddess of smallpox, and Phoenix devoutly offered sacrifice and prayed before it every day. Everything roasted or baked was banished from the kitchen of the Yungkuo household during the days of the illness. The nurse and the maids who had to attend to the sick child were dressed in new dark red garments. Two doctors took turns in caring for the little patient and were not allowed to leave the house for twelve days.

161

The temporary interruption of marital relations was a hard trial for Chia Lien, and he found the loneliness of his sleeping quarters in the outer library so oppressive that by the third day he was already looking around for some compensation. The company of a few nice young serving boys did not satisfy him for long. Then his eyes fell on the wife of the cook To Kuan. This woman, who was barely twenty, was full of voluptuous charm, and having been married off by her parents to a drunken blockhead whom she did not love, she made it a practice to compensate herself for this as well as she could behind his back. The cook no longer bothered about her doings; he only cared for money and good food and drink, and it was his habit to throw himself on his bed quite early in the evening to sleep off his usual tipsiness. So it was easy for his wife to pick flowers by the wayside or enjoy secret fruits, and there was scarcely a man either in the western or in the eastern palace who had not enjoyed her favors at one time or another.

Chia Lien's mouth too had long been watering for this juicy peach, but fear of Phoenix had restrained him up to now. Under the present circumstances, however, he put aside all his qualms, and as the woman, moreover, was encouraging him by ostentatiously strutting about in front of the windows of his quarters, he easily arranged for a first meeting with her. One evening when the cook was again lying on the kang helplessly drunk and snoring, he slipped into her room. Her proximity was sufficient to make him immediately lose complete control, and no preliminary amorous declaration or skirmishing about was necessary, straight away they undressed and lay down side by side. With keen delight he relished her oft-tried arts of love, which had already made many a man's bones and nerves soft as wax. He felt in her arms as if he were bedded in cotton-wool, and revelled in the union of their bodies.

"You are a real villain!" she remarked laughing, as they lay there. "Your child is ill, your wife is praying to the goddess of smallpox, and you should be mortifying yourself in virtuous solitude. Be off at once!"

"You are my goddess! What do I want with other goddesses?" he stammered, continuing his devout exercise. After this first time he came to her daily and was almost sorry when, after twelve days, the child was well again and the worship of the goddess, as he understood it, was at an end. The altar and the statue of the goddess of smallpox were taken down and in their place a solemn ceremonial thanksgiving sacrifice was offered to heaven and to the ancestors by the assembled family. And Phoenix and Chia Lien returned to their common home.

The maid Little Ping was putting Chia Lien's clothing and bed linen back in their place again, when she discovered between the pillows a long strand of a woman's blue-black hair. She knew what that meant, wound up the strand carefully, hurried off to Chia Lien, and triumphantly held up her find to him.

"Look here, what is this?"

The astonished Chia Lien tried to snatch the strand out of her hand, but Little Ping was quicker than he and dodged him cleverly. He rushed after her, caught her and pushed her down on the divan. There was a violent struggle for the possession of the dangerous piece of evidence.

"Let me go!" screamed the ticklish maid, choking with laughter. "You should be thankful that I have not betrayed you, you rascal! But if you torment me any more I will not spare you but will tell your wife."

"Dearest, best one, do not do that! I will treat you well in the future!" he begged, letting her go quickly, for he had heard Phoenix's voice outside.

"Do not betray me!" he repeated again, in a low voice. Thereupon the redoubtable lady entered. She cast a quick, searching, sidelong glance at her husband and then said to the maid: "Have you moved all my husband's things in here?"

The maid nodded.

"Nothing is missing?" The maid answered in the negative.

"Is there nothing among them which should not be there?"

"What do you mean?" asked Little Ping, laughing. "Is it not enough that nothing is missing?"

"Hm, one cannot know," replied Madame Phoenix also laughing, and looking askance at her husband again. "In two weeks' separation many things can happen. Who knows? Might not a ring, or a cambric handkerchief, or some other tender souvenir be found perchance among his things?"

Chia Lien had become waxen yellow in the face with fright and behind his wife's back cast despairing looks at the maid, like a fowl that is just about to be killed.

"How strange that we should think the same thing, Mistress!" said Little Ping, quite unembarrassed. "Because I feared the same thing as you did I have just looked through his things thoroughly, and have not found the slightest trace of anything. But if you don't believe me, look yourself."

"Nonsense! He wouldn't be so stupid as to put our noses on the scent, so let it be!" replied Phoenix, as she turned round laughing, to go out. Chia Lien breathed a sigh of relief as she turned her back. Little Ping held her nose to prevent herself from bursting out laughing.

"Well, have I acted my part well? You should be very grateful to me," she said to him.

"My heart! My liver! My little meat ball!" he flattered her, embracing her tenderly. Little Ping had again produced the telltale strand of hair and swung it gleefully in his face.

"Look, with this I have you fettered for life!" she cried exultantly. "If ever you are not nice to me, I can go to your wife and betray you."

But with a sudden grab he had snatched at her waving hand and torn the booty from her.

"The thing is safer with me. At best, you will do some mischief with it," he said laughing and stuffed the strand into the leg of his boot.

"Fie! You are very rude!" she pouted, disconcerted. "You are hardly safely across the stream when you break down the bridge. But do not imagine that I will tell lies for you again!" With this she disengaged herself from his tender embrace and slipped out of the room.

"Such a hussy; first you entice, and then, when the fire is alight, you run off!" he called after her.

"Who told you to get on fire?" she called back through the window, laughing. "You do not imagine that I could belong to you? Your wife would certainly have it in for me if she got to know of it."

"Oh, she! You need not be afraid of her. Sometime I'll shatter that vinegar pot in pieces! She'll learn to know me, with her damned jealousy! I've been tired of this tedious spying for a long time past. She watches me as if I were a thief. If she had her way, I'd only associate with men and never speak to any female. Even the very proximity of a woman arouses her suspicion. She, on the other hand, enjoys herself freely and unashamedly with brothers-in-law and cousins and nephews. But just wait, I will pay her back!"

"She has every reason to mistrust you, but you on your part have no reason to be jealous. She is the best and most faithful married woman living. But you are a depraved scoundrel and villain."

"Aha, you have both conspired against me. But just wait, I will have an opportunity someday of stopping your slanderous tongues . . .!"

The approach of Phoenix stopped any further abuse. When she noticed the maid, Little Ping, conversing with him at the window, she said to her teasingly: "If you want something from him, please arrange it inside! Why do you talk with him through the window?"

"That's right. She behaves as if there were a tiger in here who wanted to eat her," interjected Chia Lien, laughing.

"There is no one in there but himself," remarked Little Ping, sharply.

"Oh, but that's all the better," continued Phoenix ironically.

"All the better for whom?" asked Little Ping, irritated.

164

"For you, of course!"

"You would do better not to force me to speak. For if you do, all kinds of nice things might come to light," the maid replied in an injured tone, turning her back on her mistress without drawing aside the curtain for her. Phoenix raised the curtain herself and went into the room.

"The creature seems to have gone crazy," she remarked angrily to her husband. "But if she should take it into her head to want to get the better of me, I would like to advise you also to save your skin."

Chia Lien threw himself full length on the divan and clapped his hands with pleasure.

"What? Is she really so dangerous?" he exclaimed, laughing. "If that is so, I must look at her with quite different eyes in future."

"Of course you are to blame! You must have encouraged her," said Phoenix severely. "Take care that I do not settle accounts with you!"

"Ha, then I had better be off!"

"Stop! Stay here! I have something else to speak to you about."

What she had to speak to him about will be revealed in the next chapter.

CHAPTER 18

Pao Yu falls out with two of his cousins at the same time. Two lovers tease one another with quotations from "The Play of the Western Pavilion."

CHIA LIEN REMAINED STANDING.

"Well?"

"The twenty-first will be Cousin Precious Clasp's birthday. How shall we celebrate it?"

"You must surely know that best yourself. You have had sufficient experience in celebrating birthdays."

"Yes, those of grown-up people; there are definite rules about those. But one cannot yet count Cousin Precious Clasp as an adult, and neither is she a child. That is the trouble."

"It's quite simple. We can celebrate her birthday just as Black Jade's was celebrated last year."

"Of course I had already thought of that. But it won't do, for when Grandmother recently inquired the ages of her various grandchildren, we realized that Precious Clasp is now fifteen, so she is marriageable. Grandmother thinks that we should pay special attention to the importance of this day."

"Good. Then we can arrange for the celebration to be somewhat more sumptuous than that for Black Jade's birthday."

"That's what I think too. I only wanted to have your agreement, so that you would not reproach me afterwards and scold me inconsiderately."

"Very well, very well! I am not as petty as all that. You worry yourself with unnecessary scruples. I am quite satisfied if you do not lecture me about my own affairs; I just mind my own business."

And he turned away laughing.

At the wish of the Princess Ancestress, Precious Clasp, for whom she had a particular affection on account of her even, kindly, and courteous manner, was specially honored on her birthday with a theatrical performance as well as with the usual banquet. The evening before she was permitted to choose the menu and also the theatrical program. Precious Clasp was wise enough to choose certain sweet dishes and sensational and gruesome dramas, which she knew for certain were the Princess Ancestress's favorite dishes and favorite theatrical pieces. The banquet was held in the apartments of the Princess Ancestress. The nice little private stage, on which a troupe of youthful artists from Suchow showed their versatile talents, was set up in the inner courtyard of her residence.

When the performance was about to begin and all the female relatives had assembled, Black Jade was the only one missing. Pao Yu went off to fetch her. He found her lying on the divan in her room poring over books.

"Get up! Get up! It's time for breakfast. And besides, the performance is going to begin at once," he rallied her. "Have you any special wish with regard to the program? If so, I shall have it noted at once."

"No, thank you. If I were to choose, I would choose the whole program. The performance today is not in my honor."

"Have patience a little while! Then your turn will come, and you will be able to choose the whole program. But come now!"

And he laughingly dragged the reluctant Black Jade back with him. The performance lasted from morning until night, and exciting scenes from the adventurous "History of a Journey to the West" were alternated with merry farces such as "Mr. Lu Mislays his Coat" and "The Drunken Lu Brawls on the Wu tai shan," for the Princess Ancestress liked coarse low comedy turns too. After the entertainment she had two of the young artists with whom she was specially pleased brought to her. One of them had played the heroine; the other, the merry buffoon. The whole company gasped with admiring surprise when the two gifted artists declared, when asked, that they were only eleven and nine years old respectively. The Princess Ancestress had them sumptuously entertained and gave each of them a thousand-piece string of money as an extra fee.

"Does not the elder one, in his female attire, resemble a certain person we all know?" remarked Phoenix.

Precious Clasp understood at once whom she meant; she did not mention a name, however, but just nodded her head. Pao Yu followed her example. But Cousin Little Cloud could not refrain from bursting out in her impetuous way: "Why, of course, he is like Sister Black Jade!"

The warning, sidelong glance which Pao Yu shot at her came too late. Everyone noticed now; all scrutinized Black Jade and agreed amid laughter: "Yes, indeed, they are so much alike one could mistake them for one another!"

When Pao Yu was going to bed that night he heard Little Cloud in the next room ordering her maid to pack her things, and saying in reply to the maid's astonished question: "Yes, I am going away early in the morning. I do not wish to stay here any longer. This everlasting criticizing and watching of every word and every look does not suit me."

Pao Yu ran across to her room.

"Dear little sister, you are unjustly angry," he said, trying to placate her. "Black Jade is so terribly sensitive, and that is why I tried to warn you by a look not to mention her name; I was afraid she would take offense at being compared to an actor. I meant it well and you need not be so angry with me on account of it. If it was about anyone else . . ."

"That's enough!" Little Cloud interrupted him indignantly. "Spare me your flowery words! What am I beside your cousin Black Jade? An ordinary girl beside a high-born lady, isn't that so? Others may make remarks about her, but I dare not. If I open my mouth, it's a crime."

"If I have ever thought of slighting you in the least, may I be turned instantly into the dirt of the road, on which everyone may trample!" protested Pao Yu in dismay.

"Make those flowery speeches to inferior people of your own kind, who, in their insensitiveness, know no better than to ridicule and mock their fellow beings, but spare me your common street jargon and do not provoke me to spit out before you!" replied Little Cloud furiously as she ran out of the room to the apartments of the Princess Ancestress, where she spent the night.

Pao Yu, who had run after her in vain, turned back much dejected. He was longing for Black Jade's company; but scarcely had he set foot in her room than Black Jade pushed him out and shut the door behind him. Pao Yu was perplexed.

"Dearest, best *Mei mei!*" he called with gentle entreaty through the door to her.

But Black Jade remained silent and invisible. Pao Yu hung his head and sank into sad thoughts. As there was no sound for a long time, Black Jade, thinking he had gone to his room, opened the door. Then she saw him still standing there like a poor sinner. Now she had pity on him and let him in.

"Will you not at least tell me why you are angry?" he began hesitantly.

She gave a short, dry laugh.

"You ask that? I should take it quietly when I am compared with a comedian and made ridiculous before the whole company?"

"But I did not make such a comparison, neither did I laugh at you."

"No, but your secret exchange of glances with Little Cloud hurt me even more. I know well what you meant by it, that you think more of Little Cloud than of me, that she gives up something and lowers herself when she associates with me. Naturally, she is a high-born lady, a count's daughter, and I am only an ordinary girl of the people! Is not that what you meant? It's a pity that with your good intentions you have found so little reciprocal love from her and have to be reproached by her for going about with an inferior person like me, who, in her insensitiveness, knows no better than to ridicule and mock her fellow beings! I really do not understand your anxious consideration for her. She certainly does not thank you for it."

Pao Yu understood that she had been listening just now to his argument with Little Cloud.

That is what I get for my good intention of trying to play the part of mediator between them! he thought to himself bitterly. Now I have fallen foul of both of them, and have to put up with reproaches from both sides. The wise Chuang Tzu was right when he said: "Why so much activity? It only gives one worry. Why trouble about all sorts of things? One is only annoyed by them. How splendid, on the other hand, only to care about one's own modest necessities of life, and so float on the waves free and alone as a boat adrift!" How useless is my striving and trouble! I do not even succeed in bringing about reconciliation and harmony between two girls! Why should I set myself higher aims?

Sunk in thought, he turned away from Black Jade to go back to his room.

"Go away! You need not come back again and you need not speak to me any more," she called after him.

Without taking any more notice of her he slipped back to his room and threw himself on the bed with a sigh. Pearl's voice startled him out of his brooding.

"We shall probably see more theatrical performances in the next few days, for Miss Precious Clasp is sure to make the best of her opportunity," she remarked, trying to distract him.

"It's all the same to me," he replied, brusquely.

"How is that? In this happy New Year season everyone is merry and in good spirits. Why are you alone out of humor?"

"What is it to me if the others are enjoying themselves?"

"You should get on better with them; then you also would enjoy yourself."

"What have I to do with the others? After all, I am alone, quite alone. No one wants me."

Tears came to his eyes and he gave a loud sob. Then he got up, went to the writing table, took his brush, and worked off his ill-humor by writing a stanza full of the weariness of life and Buddhist renunciation of the world. Having done this, he felt more free and relieved, and lay down peacefully to sleep.

A little later Black Jade slipped into his room full of curiosity, under the pretext of looking for Pearl.

"He's already asleep," Pearl intimated to her quietly. "Here, read this! He has just written it."

Black Jade scanned the page of writing. She was amused at the contents but at the same time felt sorry for the boy.

"It's only a little foolery and means nothing," she said with apparent indifference, but she could not refrain from taking the sheet of paper away with her and giving it to Little Cloud and the next morning to Precious Clasp to read.

> "Do what you want to! Come, go, as you please!
> Weep! Laugh! It's all the same to me.
> What do I care about the world!"

Thus read the stanza, the first part of which was written in the Sutra style.

"Oh, Cousin Pao Yu wants to join the saints and renounce the world!" the three of them cried, looking at each other with embarrassed smiles. Each of them felt a little bit guilty.

"Come, let us go to him together and bring him to reason!" suggested Black Jade. And the three of them set off together to the Chamber of the Fragrance of Culture. Black Jade drew his attention to the fact that his Buddhist stanza was incomplete, and she added the missing conclusive point; and Precious Clasp mentioned the case of a well-known Buddhist sectarian who had resigned the leadership of his sect in favor of his cook, when the latter put him to shame by the correct criticism of a similarly defective stanza which he had composed. Pao

Yu remarked with embarrassed astonishment that his clever cousins knew more than he himself did about a sphere which he had thought quite unknown to them. If they in spite of this did not presume to belong to the "awakened," he concluded that his chance of attaining to even a modest degree of holiness was positively nil. He therefore resigned himself to abandoning all idea of further striving after Buddhist contemplation.

"It was only a jest, the mood of a moment," he explained, smiling. And with this the happy old relationship between the cousins was restored.

When Beginning of Spring, the Emperor's wife, had returned to the Court from her visit to the Park of Delightful Vision, she had expressed the wish that a monument should be erected in the park with an inscription which would commemorate for all time the happy event of her visit. Chia Cheng hastened to fulfill her wish, and entrusted the work to the most skillful stonecutters and engravers he could find.

The Imperial wife reflected, furthermore, that the Park of Delightful Vision, which had been made specially for her visit, would be shut up and sealed by her father after the visit through a sense of dutiful respect, and she said to herself that it would really be a pity if these beautiful places were to be left abandoned and unused in the future. Why should it not be made accessible to her sisters and cousins, who could make rhymes and stanzas so splendidly? Were they not worthy to lift up their minds and hearts amid the beautiful vistas of the park? And should not her brother Pao Yu also share this special privilege? For since his childhood he had been accustomed to the company of girls, and would find himself terribly lonely and neglected if he were suddenly deprived of the accustomed companionship.

Moved by these considerations, the Imperial spouse sent the Chief Eunuch Hsia to the Yungkuo palace with orders to this effect. Mr. Cheng and his wife lost no time in sending people to the park to clean up and furnish comfortably the various places of abode destined for Pao Yu and the young girls.

Pao Yu was very specially pleased with the changes which were to take place. He was just then with his grandmother discussing this and that matter regarding the change-over, when a servant came in to call him to his father. Pao Yu turned pale. His happy mood was swept away immediately. Craving protection, he pressed convulsively against his grandmother's right side as if she were a piece of sugar which was to be crushed to besprinkle a sweet dish. He did not want to go at any price, for he believed it was again to be one of those fatherly reprimands which he feared so much. The Princess Ancestress encouraged him, saying that he had nothing to fear, and that his father probably only wished to give him some instructions on good behavior before he left for the future dwelling. Accompanied by two worthy matrons, who had to act as personal guards, Pao Yu set out on the dreaded journey, but he went so slowly and unwillingly that he hardly progressed three inches with every step. At last, very hesitantly, he entered the parental pavilion. How unpleasant were those half-curious, half-mocking glances which met him as he walked through the rows of servants in front of the entrance. A maid named Golden Bangle was actually so impudent as to pluck his sleeve as he passed by and whisper: "Now, what about it? Would you not like to lick the rouge from my lips? It is quite fresh and has a perfume."

Whereupon an older maid named Bright Cloud gave her a push and said reprovingly: "Ill-mannered creature! You see that he is not in a mood for such jests just now! Be off!"

Inside, Pao Yu found his father and mother sitting opposite each other on the divan engaged in conversation. The three Spring girls, and the younger brother Chia Huan, the son of a secondary wife of his father, were sitting at their feet on low stools. The younger relations, Taste of Spring, Grief of Spring, and Chia Huan, stood up as Pao Yu entered. Mr. Cheng scrutinized the newcomer sharply, then his glance wandered over to the other son, and he compared them. How favorably Pao Yu's prepossessing, cultivated appearance compared with the thick-set, coarse appearance of the bastard! Mr. Cheng went on to reflect that his hair was already beginning to turn gray, and that he could scarcely hope to have another and better offspring than Pao Yu. Nine-tenths of the aversion which he usually felt towards Pao Yu vanished as a result of this silent reflection, and he sounded more gentle than usual when he said: "Her Imperial Highness has deigned to give orders that you are to continue your studies in future, in the company of your sisters and cousins, in the Park of Delightful Vision. But she desires you to pull yourself together and study seriously instead of loafing around. So now, comply with this order and be on your guard!"

Pao Yu managed to murmur a hurried *shih*—yes; there followed a short conversation between mother and son concerning his health, then a gruff "Why is that creature, that plague of my life, still standing there?" scared him quickly outside the door. Now looking happy, he ran nimbly through the lines of servants in the anteroom, cheekily sticking out his tongue at the maid Golden Bangle as he passed.

Chia Cheng fixed the twenty-second of the month as the most suitable day for the move. Meantime the various buildings which had been assigned as dwellings had been put in habitable order. Pao Yu and Black Jade managed to arrange for their quarters to be quite near one another. They each lived on their own, and besides the maids whom they had had up to now each had two elderly chaperons to supervise them and four maids for the rough work of the house.

Thus, on the twenty-second of the month, life and youth entered the hitherto desolate park, and the colorful flower beds and the willow leaves waving in the zephyr breezes could no longer be sad and complain of loneliness. The change of dwelling seemed to alter Pao Yu's whole personality. His dejection vanished and gave place to merry spirits. From now on he passed his days with the girls, reading and writing, strumming the lute or playing chess, painting or reciting verse, while the girls embroidered their phoenix patterns industriously, plucked flowers and identified plants, amused themselves playing dice and other drawing-room games, and sang songs in their gentle voices. He was completely happy and had never before been in such a good mood for writing poetry. Many of his verses and stanzas, though not perhaps showing extraordinary talent, but replete with feeling and keen observation of nature, as, for instance, his "Songs of the Four Seasons," found their way to the public. For there was no lack of flatterers and spongers eager to win his favor, who felt obliged to noise abroad in the streets and market places the fame of the distinguished fourteen-year-old boy poet of the Yungkuo palace, and to display copies of his poems. It became the fashion among the gay young set to decorate fans and walls of rooms with the latest soulful outpourings from the brush of the celebrated Pao Yu; it was considered intellectual to recite his latest poems at social functions; people competed fiercely to obtain a few lines written by his own hand, whether verse, or maxims, or even just short mottoes. Pao Yu felt very important and had his hands full satisfying all the claims made on him from outside.

Who would have thought that in spite of everything his old restlessness would be stirred up again so soon? One day the splendors of the park, which had charmed him so much in the beginning, began to bore him. He found fault with this and criticized that, and felt annoyed and dissatisfied. Also, the society of his companions did not satisfy him; their merry, boisterous playing, their ingenuous, frivolous, girlish ways left him cold. He longed for new diversions, stronger impressions. The fool!

His valet Ming Yen had been trying in vain for a long time to banish his ill-humor with various suggestions and distractions, but at last he got a new idea which succeeded. One day, after a walk through the booksellers' lane, he took home to his master a whole stack of unknown light literature, all novels and romances both old and modern, obscene love stories and tales of the adventures of famous courtesans and the like.

Pao Yu had never before seen such books. When he peeped into them now he became as if intoxicated, and as happy as if they were a valuable find. And the fact that he might only read these books secretly, as Ming Yen impressed upon him, made them doubly fascinating. He hid them as well as he could in his bed and in other safe places, and from now on he spent his time, whenever he was alone and undisturbed, eagerly delving into them.

One day, about the middle of the third month, he sauntered along after breakfast to the bridge leading to the Weir of Penetrating Perfumes, carrying the *Hsi Hsiang Chi,* "Play of the Western Pavilion," in his hand, and sat down to read on a rock under blossoming peach trees at the edge of the pond. As he was sitting there and had just come to a place in the book which described "falling red, gathered up in heaps," a sudden gust of wind blew through the branches and caused a heavy rain of petals to ripple down on him and his book. He was covered all over with the reddish petals and had to shake himself to get rid of the delicate burden. So lovely and charming did these petals seem to him that he would have been sorry to tread on them with his feet. Therefore, he gathered up with both hands the rosy piles which lay round about his seat and carried them to the near-by bank, there to shake them over the surface of the water. And each time that he had shaken out two handfuls in this way, he remained for a while on the bank looking after the flower petals thoughtfully, as they danced about on the waves and were gently drawn by the current towards the weir.

Just as he was bending down to gather together another heap of petals, he heard a girl's voice behind him asking: "What are you doing here?"

He turned around. There he saw Black Jade standing in front of him. She was carrying a spade over her shoulder, on the handle of which hung a flower carrier made of light gauze; in her left hand she had a broom.

"It's good that you have come! You can help me to sweep up these flower petals and throw them into the water. I have already thrown in quite a lot," he said.

"You should not do that! Here the water is tolerably clean, but later on when the petals have drifted farther along with the current, and float into other estates, they will come in contact with all kinds of dirt and refuse. It would be a pity for the lovely, pure petals to become soiled. No, it is better if we take them to the petal grave which I have just dug behind that hill. I shall sweep them up. You stuff them into the bag and then we will carry them to the grave together. In the course of time they will turn into good garden soil. Is not that nicer and cleaner than throwing them into the water?"

174

Pao Yu had to admit that she was right.

"Wait a moment until I put my book away; then we will set to work at once."

"What book have you got?" she asked.

"Nothing special; a commentary on 'The Great Philosophy' of Master Confucius," he replied quickly, trying to hide the book from her sight.

"Show it at once, you rogue!"

"For all I care you may see it, *Mei mei*, but please be so kind as not to say a word about it to other people. Anyway, it is quite a splendid book; the style is wonderful. You will not be able to give a thought to sleeping or eating if you read it. Here."

Black Jade laid down her garden implements and took the book. She sat down on the rock and began to read, and the more she read the more she was fascinated by the book, and she did not stop reading until she had skimmed through all its sixteen chapters in one go. Content and style enchanted her equally, and when she had finished she seemed still to taste in her mouth, as it were, the sweetness she had enjoyed; and, lost in thought, she recited to herself this and that passage which had remained impressed on her memory.

"Well, how did you like it?" he asked, smiling.

"It is really fascinating."

"Yes, isn't it? And does it not apply most remarkably to the two of us? I am the hero full of faults and weaknesses, and you—you are the heroine whose beauty causes the downfall of cities and countries," he quoted jokingly.

His remark made Black Jade flush a sudden deep crimson right up to her ears. She raised her brows and her dilated pupils flashed with anger as she hissed: "What impertinence! I must object to your connecting those common expressions and those improper passages with me! It is an insult! But just wait, I shall tell your parents!"

At the word "insult" fine little red veins became visible around her pupils. Now she turned away quickly and ran off. He ran after her dismayed and held her firmly.

"Dearest *Mei mei*, I beg your pardon a thousand—ten thousand times!" he pleaded. "I see that I have been talking nonsense, but I did not mean to insult you. If I did, may I be drowned in a deep pond and may a mangy tortoise eat me, and may I myself be turned into a big tortoise, and in some future time when you, the wife of a mandarin of first rank, have died of old age, may I for all time carry the socket of the pillars of your grave on my back!"

Black Jade could not help bursting out laughing on hearing this long, comical oath. She was soon appeased again. Casting a roguish glance at him, she said: "Besides, I could reply to you in the same tone if I wished to, and by way of example speak of a certain someone who resembles the famous lance with the silvered wax point."

"If you say such things I also will go and tell tales on you!" he threatened, jokingly.

"I only wanted to show you that I can read just as quickly as you can, and can remember what I read just as easily as you can. It is nothing to me to read ten lines of writing with one single glance. Or do you doubt that?"

"Oh, indeed I believe it. But now we will be sensible again and bury our poor petals."

They set to work again, and swept up and heaped the fallen petals and carried them to the petal grave behind the hill. Meantime the maid Pearl appeared. She had been sent by the Princess Ancestress to fetch Pao Yu. Prince Shieh was not well and Pao Yu was to go to him straight away and wish him a speedy recovery, as was proper. The Spring girls had already visited the sickbed. Pao Yu therefore bade farewell to Black Jade and left the park accompanied by Pearl.

Deep in thought, Black Jade sauntered slowly back to her house. As she was passing by the wall of the Pear Garden she heard from within the gentle sounds of flute playing and charming singing. The music came from the twelve dancing girls from Suchow, who had their quarters in the Pear Garden and were just now practicing a new theater piece. Black Jade was not paying particular attention to the singing, but two lines of one of the songs caught her ear so distinctly that she was able to understand every word. It was about a wonderfully beautiful purple flower, which blooms gloriously, only to be plucked, to wither, and to end miserably in some refuse pit.

Black Jade was touched to the core by the melancholy expressed in these two lines. Involuntarily she slackened her pace and listened hard in an effort to follow the rest of the text. And she could not but silently agree with the sentiments of the next two lines, which spoke of the transience of exterior splendor and good living when inner happiness was destroyed. And she had to sigh, thinking of the superficiality of human beings, who go to the theater only to be entertained and do not think at all of looking into themselves and applying to their own lives the truths which they hear on the stage. While still sunk in meditation, she heard the words:

"As a flower in spring, beauty fades,
As a fleeting wave, youth passes."

She felt deeply moved and frightened. Her head became dizzy, her feet refused to move, she staggered as if she were drunk, and had to sit

down on a near-by rock. There she sat, murmuring to herself again and
again the words she had just heard:

> "As a flower in spring, beauty fades,
> As a fleeting wave, youth passes."

At the same time it occurred to her that in the past she had read in
old stories and also today in the "Play of the Western Pavilion" similar
words about falling petals and running waters, passing spring and lasting sorrow. A feeling of infinite anguish and sadness stole upon her, her
heart shrank, tears dropped from her eyes. She would have so loved to
speak to someone, to let herself be comforted. Suddenly she felt a light
tap on her shoulder. She turned around. A young girl was standing before her. You will learn from the next chapter who this girl was.

CHAPTER 19

*Ni the usurer proves impulsively generous when drunk. A lovelorn maid
gets queer ideas about a lost handkerchief.*

WHEN BLACK JADE TURNED ROUND THERE WAS LOTUS, THE STOLEN
slave girl and daughter of Shih Ying, standing before her.

"Stupid creature to frighten me so!" said Black Jade, angrily. "What
are you looking for here?"

"I am looking for my young mistress, Miss Precious Clasp, but I cannot find her anywhere. And your maid Cuckoo has been inquiring for
you. Madame Cheng has sent you a package of tea from the new
harvest. Would you please come and receive the gift."

Black Jade set out hand in hand with Lotus towards her pavilion.
She accepted the tea from the new harvest, and of the best quality,
which her Aunt Cheng had just sent her and kept Lotus with her for a
while. She found her company pleasant in her present state of mind.
She discussed with her the excellence of this tapestry and the charm of
that piece of embroidery, and did not let her go until they had played
a game of chess and read some passages from a book together. But let
us now leave those two alone for a while and talk of Pao Yu.

When he got back to his dwelling with Pearl he found the maid
Mandarin Duck lying on his divan examining a piece of embroidery
which Pearl had begun.

"Where have you been hiding?" she asked Pao Yu when he entered.
"The old *Tai tai* sent over for you quite a long time ago. You are to
hurry across and visit your sick uncle. Quick! Change your clothes."

While the maid Pearl went into the next room to fetch his visiting
clothes, he sat on the edge of the divan and pushed his slippers off with

his toes. Then he turned round and, taking advantage of Pearl's absence, thoroughly inspected Mandarin Duck, who was lying behind him. She was lying with her face towards the wall and was so absorbed in the embroidery that she no longer noticed him. He found her most bewitching, in her little bright red silk jacket over the green bodice and the white satin sash which encircled her slender waist. And he could not resist bending over her neck eagerly to sniff the fragrance which emanated from her, and to stroke her back playfully.

"Dear *Mei mei,* do let me lick a little of the pink stuff from your lips," he whispered, nestling close up to her and encircling her with his arm and leg.

"Come and look, Pearl!" cried the girl, laughing loudly as she tried to disengage herself from him. "You have been with him goodness knows how long, and you have not yet taught him to behave."

Pearl hurried along with a bundle of clothes in her arms. With one glance she grasped the situation.

"I see that all my good teaching is in vain," she said, turning to Pao Yu. "If that ever happens again I will leave at once."

Pao Yu kept a rather shamefaced silence, changed his clothes, and went off to his grandmother accompanied by two maids. In the forecourt of her pavilion he found his servants already waiting with his saddled horse, to take him to Prince Shieh. As he was mounting his horse while at the same time exchanging a few words with Cousin Chia Lien, who had just come back from a ride, he heard a young man calling up to him from the side: *"Tsing an,* Uncle!"

Pao Yu looked down from the saddle. The young man might have been eighteen or nineteen years old. He was slender and well built, his finely formed face seemed somehow familiar, but Pao Yu could not recall his name or who his family were.

"Why on earth are you staring at him like that? Do you not know him? He is our nephew Little Yun, son of our sister-in-law Five," Cousin Lien informed him, laughing.

"Oh, of course! I remember him now. And the boy behaves as if he were my son!"

"Don't be funny! He is four or five years older than you are," laughed Cousin Lien.

"Hello, how old are you, then?" asked Pao Yu condescendingly.

"Eighteen," replied Little Yun smiling and added with quick wit: "No doubt my worthy uncle is thinking of the proverb of the grandparents who have kept themselves until old age as young as the child in the cradle and of the grandchildren who are old before their years. Now, even if I surpass you somewhat in years, that does not prevent your surpassing me in worth as the sun surpasses the mountain, and since my real father is dead, I would deem myself most happy if you would do me the honor of making me your adopted son."

"At the moment I have no time for you, but come and visit me to-morrow and we shall have a cup of tea and a good chat," said Pao Yu, flattered. "I shall show you the park. But keep clear of the girls."

And with a salute, he rode off, followed by the troop of servants, to the dwelling of Prince Shieh. His attention pleased the Prince, who after a brief greeting sent him off to the Princess. It turned out that Prince Shieh's indisposition was not very serious; he had only caught a slight cold. The Princess kept Pao Yu to dinner, and he found his cousins there also, and so he returned to the Park of Delightful Vision in their company. But let us return now to Little Yun.

Little Yun belonged to a poor branch of the Chia clan, and being the only son of a widow, he was intent upon finding occupation and a livelihood by rendering occasional small services to his rich and fashionable relatives. His visit to the Yungkuo palace today had this end in view.

"Is there anything for me to do?" he asked his uncle Lien when Pao Yu had ridden away.

"I had something in view for you recently, but unfortunately my wife has meantime given this work to Chia Lin, who also needed it urgently. However, there will soon be various jobs in the garden to do, and my wife has promised me that she will give you the task of super-intending them. I cannot do anything for you today, but come round again in the morning immediately after the roll call and you will have an opportunity of presenting your petition to my wife in person. But now excuse me; I have an appointment."

Little Yun thanked him and went off. On the way he said to himself that it would do his prospects good if he could win the favor of the almighty Madame Phoenix by means of some little attention. But where was he to get money for a gift? He decided to look up his maternal uncle, the spice and provision dealer Pu, and to extract something from him.

"I need your assistance, dear Uncle," he said to him. "Do please let me have four ounces of camphor and four ounces of musk on credit. I will pay you promptly at the Mid-Harvest Festival."

Uncle Pu put on a sour grin. "I am sorry," he said, "that I cannot enter into such credit transactions. Only a short time ago one of my employees abused my good nature and took goods on credit from the business and of course did not keep his promise. The result was that my partners and I had to cover the loss out of our own pockets. Since then we have agreed together, under pain of a fine of twenty taels, never again to enter into similar private credit transactions. I have to keep strictly to this. Moreover, the stock of camphor and musk in my modest shop is quite small, and I could not satisfy your requirements completely even if you were to pay cash. You had therefore better look around elsewhere. Besides, it is a well-known fact that money transactions spoil friendship. You are a thoughtless young fellow and none too particular about what is right and wrong. You would take your debt lightly, you would forget to pay, I would have to keep dunning you for it, and you would take that ill of me. My advice to you is this: Help yourself and save money in good time, so that you will not have to borrow at all and your uncle will be pleased with you!"

"You are perfectly right, dear Uncle," replied Little Yun, controlling his feelings with difficulty. "But you must take into account that I lost my father while I was still a child, and for that reason have not had the right instruction and upbringing. My mother has always said how lucky we were in at least having your support and help, most honored Uncle. That is why I thought I could count upon your help. Moreover, I was not aware that I had frivolously squandered away any inherited property, whether a house or a piece of land. Even the best housewife cannot cook rice soup if there is no rice to hand. How, then, could I have put anything aside up to the present when I had not got an income? However, you may count yourself lucky that I do not importune you two or three times a day with this and that request, as many another in my position would do."

"My dear boy, I am in a pretty bad way myself; otherwise I would most willingly give you a hand. But why do you not turn to your rich paternal relations? See that you fill your pockets as full as you can in the Yungkuo palace behind the backs of the gentlemen of the house. Or why not try to ingratiate yourself with their majordomo by dint of flattery, and engage in some rewarding enterprise that will bring in a good commission?"

Little Yun remained silent and turned to go.

"Why are you in such a hurry? You can surely stay for a bite," said the avaricious uncle, just for form's sake. But at the same moment the scolding voice of his wife became audible. "Are you hovering up in the clouds again?" she asked. "I have barely enough food for ourselves in the larder, and there you are, playing the splendid host!"

"If that's so, buy some more provisions for our guest!" he replied, whereupon the ill-tempered female voice was heard once more: "Go over to neighbor Wang and ask her could she help us out with twenty or thirty pence worth of rice; I would pay it back tomorrow," she ordered her daughter.

But Little Yun had had enough of this miserable kind of hospitality, and he contrived to get away, and so he set out on his nocturnal journey home in depressed spirits. As he walked along deeply sunk in his thoughts, he stumbled absent-mindedly against a drunken man who had come reeling towards him. The drunkard grabbed him by the arm and shouted: "Hi, have you no eyes in your head?"

The voice seemed familiar to Little Yun, and right enough it was his neighbor Ni, the well-known usurer and gambler, drunkard and rowdy.

"Let me go, old friend! It is I, your neighbor, Little Yun," he declared, laughing.

The drunken man scrutinized him intently out of glazed eyes. At last he recognized him. He let him free, murmuring a few words of excuse.

"Where are you going, little friend?" he asked.

"Ah, don't ask me. I'm in a bad humor. One's dear fellow beings are so annoying!"

"Speak your mind with confidence! Who has annoyed you? I, the drunkard Ni, stand up for my friends in the whole neighborhood. Anyone who harms one of them will have to reckon with me. I'll pull down his shop and chase his wife and children out on the street!"

Little Yun told him of his futile begging visit to his uncle.

"The wretch! If he did not happen to be your relative, I would make him pay dearly for that!" stormed neighbor Ni indignantly. "But don't worry. I have some small change with me by chance, and I will lend you a few taels, naturally without interest, as is right and proper between good neighbors."

He put his hand in his belt pocket.

"Here are fifteen taels. I hope they are enough."

"You are a good fellow, and I would not like to offend you by refusing your friendly offer; so I accept it with thanks. As soon as I get home I shall write you a receipt."

"What nonsense! If you come to me with a receipt I won't give you a copper."

"As you wish, then. Many thanks."

"That's good. And now I must be getting along, as I have another business call to make; otherwise I would ask you to have a drink. And now, when you go home, would you be good enough to call at my house and tell my people that I shall not be home tonight, and that if they want anything they must send for me in the morning. They will find me at the horse dealer Wang's."

And he reeled on. But Little Yun was delighted with his unexpected good fortune, and his only fear was that as soon as his benefactor became sober he would repent the noble impulse which had overcome him when drunk, and would demand back the sum lent with the addition of a usurious interest. But he would find it easy enough to pay even usurious interest if only Madame Phoenix would give him the hoped-for order.

Very early the next morning he sought out a grocery store in the high street outside the South Gate and bought a package of camphor and a package of musk. Then, well groomed and dressed in his best clothes, he went to the Yungkuo palace. There he was told that Madame Phoenix was just about to go to the Princess Ancestress. Her husband was not at home either. He waited in the forecourt, which several servants were busily sweeping and cleaning with enormous brooms. Just at that moment the wife of the majordomo Chou called out:

"Clear the way. Put by your brooms! The mistress is coming!"

Immediately afterwards Madame Phoenix appeared, surrounded by a swarm of serving matrons and waiting maids. Little Yun stepped up a bit closer and paid her reverence with a deep bow. She did not deign to look at him, but continued to walk straight on, merely inquiring casually how his mother was and why she never came to see her.

"She has not been quite herself these days, but she is very often with you in her thoughts, and is longing to see you," replied Little Yun glibly. He knew that Madame Phoenix was extremely amenable to flatteries.

"Come, come! Don't be too gushing!" she remarked with a smile, slowing down her pace a little. "I am pretty sure she would not have thought of me if I did not happen to mention her."

"Oh, how would I dare to tell lies in your presence, revered Aunt? Only yesterday my mother spoke of you. In spite of your delicate health, she said, you had taken the whole burden of the great household upon your shoulders, and it is only thanks to your incomparable energy that everything runs as if on well-oiled wheels in the western palace. You are simply indispensable and irreplaceable, she thinks."

Madame Phoenix stood still. A benign smile spread over her face.

"And what was your reason for discussing me with your mother behind my back?" she asked, graciously.

"Oh, I had a very sound reason. A good friend of mine, a wealthy dealer in spices, has recently obtained by purchase the post of subprefect in a district of the province of Yunnan. Before setting out with his family to take up his position he sold out his stock and closed down his shop here. When he did this he gave many valuable lots of goods as gifts to his close friends and acquaintances. He remembered me too and gave me a parcel of camphor and musk. I consulted my mother as to the best use I could make of his gift. It seemed to us a pity to sell these valuable drugs below their value, and there did not seem anyone among our close friends worthy of giving them to. Then we remembered that you, esteemed Aunt, always need a great deal of camphor and musk for incense, and we thought that, especially in view of the proximity of the

Boat Festival of the Dragon, you would not disdain to accept this little parcel from us as a small token of our true devotion to you."

And with a deep bow he handed her a beautiful little pinewood box in which a small package of camphor and another of musk were neatly packed. His gift was really very welcome to Madame Phoenix, for she could not have anything like enough incense materials in her household stores for the approaching Boat Festival of the Dragon. With a gracious inclination of the head she indicated that one of her retinue should receive the box on her behalf.

"Thank you for your attention, dear Nephew," she said. "I see that my husband is not mistaken in saying that you possess understanding and tact, and in speaking favorably of you in other respects too."

"Oh, does he really speak of me sometimes?"

Madame Phoenix was on the point of telling him that she had already decided, at the instance of her husband, to give him the task of supervising the intended garden work. But then she said to herself that if she expressed her approval of his appointment so promptly he would probably imagine that her favor could be bought with trifling gifts such as a few ounces of camphor and musk, and would think the less of her for it. She therefore refrained from replying to his question and went proudly on her way.

There was nothing for Little Yun to do but return home still in uncertainty; in the afternoon, however, he set out again for the Yungkuo palace to accept the invitation given him by Pao Yu the previous day. In front of the library, not far from the apartments of the Princess Ancestress, he met Pao Yu's valet, Ming Yen.

"Is your master not coming over from the Park at all today?" he asked.

"I do not know, but I shall go and announce you."

Little Yun passed the long time of waiting looking at the pictures and curios in the library. While he was absorbed in gazing at them, he heard a girl's gentle voice calling for one *Ko ko*. He went out and caught sight of a pretty little maid of about fifteen or sixteen. When she saw him she turned away hurriedly and ran off. As it happened, Ming Yen was just at that moment coming back. He went up to her and asked her whether she had seen her master, Pao Yu. "You see, she belongs to his staff," he explained to Little Yun, who had come running up to him. "I myself have been unable to find him."

"Dear girl, be so good as to announce to your master that his nephew, Little Yun, is here," he asked the little girl. This time she did not run away. Hearing that the stranger belonged to the family had reassured her to some extent, but she seemed still not quite to trust him.

"Come again tomorrow, because I shall hardly have a chance of speaking to my master before this evening, and you surely would not wish to wait until then," she said, briefly and definitely, with the manner of one fully convinced of the importance of her own person. And with this she dismissed him. Little Yun could not help casting a few furtive glances at her as he went away.

When he returned to the Yungkuo palace early the next day he had the good fortune to meet Madame Phoenix as soon as he arrived. She had just got into her carriage to take an outing. When she saw Little Yun she had him called over to her carriage door.

"Look here, my boy, you are being a bit cheeky with me, I think," she said, smiling out the carriage window. "Your gift of yesterday was only an excuse, of course. My husband has meantime told me what you want."

"Oh, has he? How awkward! Yes, that is quite right; I would like very much . . . I am only sorry that I did not come straight to you in person in the beginning, dear Aunt. If I had done so, the matter would have been settled long ago. But one does not realize that Uncle Lien really has so little say in things."

"So that's the way, is it? It was only after having been unlucky with him that you wanted to try it with me yesterday?"

"You do me an injustice, dear Aunt. I regarded it as my duty as a nephew not to go over the head of my uncle. But now that I know how matters stand, I shall apply only to you in future. And will you be so good as to lend me a kindly ear now?"

"Oh, now, straight away? You should have opened your mouth sooner. There are all sorts of trees to be planted and flower beds to be laid out in the park. If you had only said a timely word to me, I would perhaps have entrusted you with the matter."

"Do please do so even yet!"

"That can hardly be managed now. But have patience until next New Year Festival, when we shall have to buy fireworks. I may perhaps consider you then."

"Dear, dear Aunt. Do please try me out right away instead. You may depend upon me to acquit myself well. You will be so pleased with me that you will entrust me with the New Year Festival order straight away."

"My word! The boy does know how to look ahead! Well, you may thank your uncle for having put in a word for you. I would not have bothered about you of myself. So now, to come to the point: Come back again today after breakfast. Call at the Estate Cashier's office, and see that you get started with the garden work the day after tomorrow!" And giving a sign to the coachman, she drove off.

Little Yun was overjoyed. He hoped to fill in the time of waiting until after breakfast by visiting Pao Yu. But Pao Yu was spending the whole of today in the house of his new friend, the Prince of the Northern Quietness.

Punctually at eleven o'clock Little Yun went to the Estate Cashier's Office, armed with the letter of authority which Madame Phoenix had sent to him in the meantime, and there he was handed the handsome sum of two hundred taels. He then hurried home and had a good time for the whole day with his mother. The next morning he settled his account with his neighbor Ni, then went to the nursery garden of Fang Chun outside the Western Gate and bought flower plants and trees to the value of fifty taels. But let us leave him for the time being to his new occupation and return to Pao Yu.

When he had made an appointment the day before yesterday with Little Yun, this was only one of those polite but empty compliments which upper-class people are in the habit of expressing without a moment's thought to people of lower social station. He had of course forgotten the appointment meantime. When he returned home towards evening from his visit to the Prince of the Northern Quietness he felt that he would like a bath. It happened by chance that he was sitting quite alone in his room for a long time, because the maid Pearl had accepted an invitation from Precious Clasp, the maid Musk was ill in bed, and two other maids had gone off to fetch hot bath water. Thus it happened that now when he called two or three times for tea, only the two elderly matrons who had been assigned to him as chaperons answered his call.

"That is all right. You may go," he said, shooing them straight out again with a wave of the hand. He would prefer to get the tea himself, he said. So he went into the kitchen and pottered around the hearth, and was just about to pour a pot of boiling water into the teapot when he heard someone behind him saying: "You will burn your hand. Please let me do it!"

At the same moment a pretty young thing came to his side, took the pot of hot water from him, filled the teapot, and took the tea things into his room. As he sipped his tea he eyed the young maid attentively. He had not noticed her at all before. What lovely curly hair she had, and what a slim, delicate little face.

"Do you belong to my staff too?" he asked.

"Yes."

"How is it, then, that I have never seen you before?"

"There are so many of us, it would be hard for you to know each one. Besides, I am still new, and I have never had any personal services to do for you, such as making your tea."

"Why not?"

"Because the others, the older ones, who have been longer with you, keep those services for themselves."

"That is a pity, for one cannot see you at all then."

"Not unless there is a special order, such as the one on which I came here just now. A certain Mr. Yun asked for you yesterday afternoon. I told him to come back today as you had had no midday sleep yesterday and were tired. Now, today you were with the Prince of the Northern Quietness, and so Mr. Yun has missed you a second time."

"Oh, indeed, so he was here?"

He would have liked to continue the conversation with the dainty little creature, but she suddenly darted off because two older waiting maids were coming along laughing and chatting. They were carrying a splashing tub of bath water. With their free hands they were holding up the edges of their skirts, which had been wetted by the splashes of water. Little Siao Hung ran towards them, amiably anxious to help them carry the tub. When the two older maids reached the room they observed to their surprise and annoyance that Pao Yu was all alone. After they had prepared the bath for him they took the little new maid to task. "What were you doing with him just now when we came?" they asked her suspiciously.

"Nothing at all. I was looking for my handkerchief, which I had lost. He called for tea and as no one else was there to serve him, I gave him his tea. That's all."

"Don't try to hoodwink us, you cheeky creature!" cried the elder girl angrily, spitting in the young one's face. "We can see now why you did not run to fetch the bath water just now, as was your duty, but left it to us two to go instead of you. Your excuse that you hadn't time was just invention and deceit. You wanted to get rid of us so that you would be alone with the young master. But just look in the glass and see if you art fit to show yourself in his presence."

"I'll tell Pearl tomorrow how you pushed yourself forward," the second one put in. "The next thing will be that you will want to serve the young master alone. We others have become unnecessary, isn't that so?"

After the quarrel had been going on this way for a while, a serving matron arrived with a message from Madame Phoenix to the effect that the gardeners would be coming into the park tomorrow and that the waiting maids must keep modestly in the background and not run around out of curiosity and that they must not show their underclothes openly on the washing line before the eyes of the strange men. Moreover, all the part of the park which was to be planted would be screened off.

186

賈芸

"Who is supervising the work?" the two elder waiting maids wanted to know.

"One Mr. Yun," replied the chambermaid. The name was quite new to them. But little Siao Hung remembered very well that the nice young man who had spoken to her yesterday in front of the library door, and had then turned round so noticeably to look after her, was called Yun. Would she really see him again, she wondered. For the little creature was ambitious and wanted to rise in the world. For a long time past she had been hoping to be noticed by Pao Yu, but her elder colleagues always knew how to keep her in the background. And after being caught out today, the very first time she had been alone with Pao Yu, she would have to suffer more envy and more slights than ever from now on. But her forlornness was changed in the twinkling of an eye into joyous anticipation when she heard the old serving matron utter the name Yun, and for the whole day she could not stop thinking of her meeting of yesterday with the nice young man. Then, that night, when she was alone in her room and lay down to sleep, the thought of him did not leave her even in her sleep. Suddenly she seemed to hear a voice outside her bedroom window saying: "I have found your handkerchief, Siao Hung."

She got up and went to the door. There was the young man of yesterday standing before her.

"Where did you find it?" she asked, shyly.

"Come with me. I will show you the place," he answered, drawing her to him and clasping her in his arms. She disengaged herself and tried to run back to her room, but stumbled over a step on the way. This awoke her. What a pity! She had only been dreaming.

CHAPTER 20

A sorcerer bewitches the cousins. The marvellous power of the magic stone brings about their recovery.

AFTER AN UNEASY SLEEP SIAO HUNG GOT UP VERY EARLY THE NEXT day, to go about her work. She was far too excited by her beautiful dream to be able to give the usual care to her toilet. She barely dipped her fingers quickly in the washbasin, carelessly pinned up her long braids in front of the mirror, and fixed a hand towel as apron into the belt of her skirt. Then, with a sigh she took her broom and was once more an ordinary housemaid.

Pao Yu had also kept in his heart the memory of his first meeting of yesterday with the pretty little new maid. He would have liked to call her to do him this or that service, but, in the first place, he was afraid of arousing the jealousy of the older maids, and in the second place, he did not even know the little one's name. He got out of bed very early in the morning feeling in a bad humor, went to the window, and remained leaning out for a while watching the maids sweeping the courtyard. How nicely the vain creatures had decked themselves out! There was not one of them who had not put on powder and rouge and stuck flowers coquettishly in her hair. Unfortunately, he could not discover the little new one of yesterday among them, but he definitely wanted to see her again. He slipped quickly into his clothes and went out into the park. He pretended to have come out to look at the flowers, but in reality he was watching out furtively to the east and the west for little Siao Hung. At last he discovered her leaning on the parapet of a pleasure gallery, hidden under plum blossoms and behind begonia branches, sunk in thought. He went up to her and was just about to speak to her when an older maid came along and told him that it was time to wash. It was really a pity to be disturbed! So he had to leave the little one standing there without having exchanged a word with her, and turn back to the house.

Shortly after he had gone Pearl sent Siao Hung to Black Jade's pavilion. A flower vase had been broken, and she wanted to get the loan of another one from Black Jade. As Siao Hung crossed over the Bridge of Blue-Green Foam on her way there, she noticed that the adjacent hilly part of the park was fenced in and shut off by screens. This was the part where trees and shrubs were to be planted today. Right enough, she saw people at work everywhere digging and planting. And there, at the edge of the drive, she caught sight of Little Yun seated, giving orders. She felt inclined to go over to him, but then her self-confidence failed her, and she stole along by a roundabout way to Black Jade's pavilion. As soon as she had done her errand she slipped into her room and threw herself dejectedly onto the couch. The other maids noticed her depressed appearance, but they thought she was not feeling well, and took no further notice of her.

On the following day the bastard Chia Huan had just returned from the family school and was in Madame Cheng's sitting room busily copying out the Diamond Sutra for her. She wanted a nice legible copy for learning by heart. The bastard felt very important on account of this commission, and was giving orders all around. One maid was to trim and light the wax candle for him, another was to bring him tea, he rebuked a third because she stood in his light, and so it went on incessantly. As he was unpopular with the staff, who had little respect for him, no one took any notice of him except the maid Dawn, who brought him tea.

"Do not give so many orders! You are only making yourself still more unpopular!" she whispered to him, as she poured out his tea. He looked at her angrily.

"I know! You are all for Pao Yu and have conspired against me!" he said sharply.

Dawn showed her teeth and rapped his head with her fingers. "Nasty, snappish cur!" she scolded, and was about to begin a longer sermon when the arrival of Phoenix and Pao Yu prevented her from doing so. The two were coming from a birthday celebration in the house of Madame Cheng's elder brother, Marshal Wang Tzu Teng. Pao Yu's cheeks were red from drinking wine and he felt sleepy. While his mother was asking Madame Phoenix how the birthday celebrations had passed off, and about the guests and the theatrical performance, he let the maids take off his cap, overcoat, and shoes, then he nestled down on the divan beside his mother and leaned his head wearily on her breast. She tenderly stroked his cheeks and neck, and he in turn caressed her.

"How hot you are!" she said. "You have certainly drunk too much again. Make yourself comfortable and stretch yourself out, so that you won't feel ill!"

He followed her advice and stretched himself out behind her on the cushions. At the same time he called Dawn and asked her to massage him a bit. But Dawn did not want to and kept looking at the bastard who was writing near by. Pao Yu took her by the hand and tried to draw her nearer to him.

"Dear elder sister, do look after me a little bit too!" he begged.

"Be quiet, or there will be a quarrel!" she whispered, parrying him and withdrawing her hand, for she had noticed the looks of hatred which the bastard was casting at the spoiled favorite of the family. Actually, Chia Huan had observed, with growing resentment, how Pao Yu was once more claiming the general attention and putting him, the bastard, in the shade. He was devoured with envy and this inspired him to think of a malicious plan. With intentional awkwardness he tipped over the bowl into which the melting wax from the candle was flowing, in such a way that the hot wax splashed over Pao Yu's face. When the latter uttered a loud cry of pain they all rushed over to him and shone the lamps on his face. Then they saw to their horror that his face was covered with a trickling layer of hot liquid wax. Filled with consternation, Phoenix and the maids started to scrape down the wax and to wash the injured skin with tepid water.

"Such a blockhead! And he's no longer a stupid small chick!" she scolded, casting a threatening sidelong glance at the bastard. "He does not yet even know how to manage lights! It just shows how badly his mother is bringing him up!"

Her remark was the cue for Madame Cheng to send for the bastard's mother, the secondary wife Chao, and to overwhelm her with violent reproaches. She should kindly take more trouble with the upbringing of her spoiled offspring, otherwise she need not expect any further consideration and kindly treatment. The scolded woman swallowed her humiliation silently and went away, after having tried to help a little with the injured boy for form's sake.

The left half of Pao Yu's face had been disfigured with ugly blisters. It was lucky that his eye was not injured. His mother was in the greatest consternation; she feared the reproaches of the Princess Ancestress. She had ointment smeared on him and sent him to bed. He himself behaved bravely and generously.

"It does not hurt much at all," he consoled her. "And when Grandmother asks about it I will just say that I got burned through my own carelessness."

"Then we others will have to bear reproaches for not having looked after you well enough. In any case, it is a tiresome affair," said Phoenix.

Black Jade had not seen Pao Yu all this day. When she heard of his accident she visited him, though it was late evening. She got a great shock when she saw his disfigured face, which was covered all over with ointment. Knowing her high-strung nature, he quickly put his hand over the injured places and asked her to go away. But she wanted to know first if he was suffering pain, and she would not be dissuaded from sitting a while on his bed and showing her sisterly sympathy. The next day when he went to his grandmother he most generously took the blame for the accident upon himself. And as Phoenix had rightly guessed, the Ancestress vented all her displeasure on his mother and Phoenix and the maids, who thus had to suffer, though innocent, for the malice of the bastard.

Mother Ma happened to pay a visit the next day. She was well known as a sorceress and also as one who prayed professionally for the sick. When Pao Yu was born she was his godmother and enjoyed the honor of having him call her his adopted mother. When she saw Pao Yu's burns she described magic circles with her fingers over them, at the same time murmuring mysterious charms. Further, she proposed to the Princess Ancestress that she should pray for the speedy recovery of her favorite—naturally, for an appropriate remuneration.

"You must know, old Ancestress, old Bodhisattva of the house," she said to the Princess Ancestress, "that young people of noble descent are particularly prone to be persecuted and afflicted by invisible devils and hobgoblins. The holy writings of Buddha teach that. These wicked demons torment them and scratch them, make the plates and dishes fall out of their hands when they are eating, make them stumble and take false steps. These young people are exposed to the afflictions of the wicked devils at every step during their tender years, and frequently they lose their lives by them."

"Is there, then, no effective charm against them?" asked the alarmed Ancestress.

"Certainly, with the help of Buddha the devils can be driven out. But Buddha demands some good work as a counter-offering. It is written, moreover, in the holy writings, that in the West there is a mighty bodhisattva of light whose special office it is to protect the children of good people from the demons of darkness. But one has first to conjure up this protecting spirit and render him well disposed by means of suitable offerings and sacrifices."

"What, then, does he demand as an offering?"

"Oh, not so much. A couple of ounces of frankincense every day and plenty of oil for a beautiful big altar lamp. For the lamp must not be allowed to go out day or night. It is the symbol of the Spirit of Light."

"Very well. You shall have the money for the frankincense and the lamp. How much oil is required?"

Mother Ma named a whole scale of the sums usually given, which were graded according to the social position of the house concerned. After lengthy bargaining a daily quantity of five ounces of oil was agreed upon. Mother Ma was to receive the money for this each month in advance from the cashier's office.

On the advice of the wise woman the Ancestress ordered, moreover, that Pao Yu's servant should in future carry with him some thousand-piece strings of money to distribute as alms to monks and beggars when he went out. With the assurance that Buddha would reward her charity, the wise woman took leave of the Princess Ancestress. When making a round of the women's quarters in the western palace she arrived at the room of the secondary wife Chao, mother of the bastard Chia Huan. She was sitting on the warmed kang putting slippers together. As she glanced at the heap of brightly colored pieces of satin beside her, Mother Ma remarked: "Ah, I could do with some new material for covering my shoes. Perhaps the *Nai nai* would have some bits left over for me?"

"Look here, there's nothing very good left, but if you do not disdain these shabby remnants, pick out some that you like!"

While Mother Ma was rummaging through the material and making the best pieces disappear into her roomy skirt pocket, Mrs. Chao continued: "Did you deliver to the Temple of the God of Medicine the five hundred copper pieces which I recently sent you?"

Mother Ma said that she did.

"It was terribly little," continued Mrs. Chao with a sigh. "I should so much like to give more and oftener, but just now my hands are tied. I certainly do not lack good will."

"Have patience. Better days will certainly come for you. Only wait until your son is grown up! He will surely have a nice, lucrative position someday."

Mrs. Chao gave an embarrassed smile.

"Ah, please do not speak about that. I do not wish to expect much in that direction, my son's position is so very difficult owing to Pao Yu. The whole household revolves around one person, namely, Pao Yu. But I won't crawl to that woman. . . !"

She significantly stretched two fingers of her right hand up in the air. Mother Ma understood her sign language.

"You mean the second *Nai nai*, Madame Phoenix?"

"Hush!" said Mrs. Chao, frightened, standing up to peep through the curtain and make sure that nobody was listening. There was no one outside. She sat down again, reassured.

"Yes, the autocratic way that person is allowed to rule the house is simply unendurable," she continued in a whisper. "I have no voice in anything; I am hardly a human being beside her."

"Hm. I understand, you are powerless and dare not show any opposition openly. Still, why not try to do so secretly? But I should not say anything."

"Oh, please speak!" interjected Mrs. Chao eagerly. "I am burning to deal just one blow at her secretly. If I only knew how to! I shall not fail to show my gratitude if you will help me."

"Holy Buddha, how can I reconcile my conscience to that? I have such a tender conscience!"

"Now, you are not usually so timid! Or are you afraid that I do not sincerely mean what I say about my gratitude?"

A broad grin spread over Mother Ma's face.

"What, then, would you think of giving me?" she asked frankly.

"You are both clever and wise, Mother Ma, and you know better than anyone that the whole palace, with everything belonging to it, would fall to me, if you succeeded in getting those two, Phoenix and Pao Yu, out of the way. In that case you could demand as much as you wished from me."

"Hm, that is very nice. But assuming that everything goes according to your wishes and you become the mistress, you might go back on your promise. I cannot undertake the business without something in writing."

"If that is all you want I shall most willingly write out a promissory note for you. It will be paid punctually later on, you can rely on that!

Besides this, I can give you some articles of clothing and some pieces of jewelry in advance."

"Yes, I agree to that."

So Mrs. Chao opened her chests and picked out some pieces of clothing and articles of jewelry for Mother Ma, and added to this some broken silver, and moreover she wrote out in Mother Ma's favor a formal promissory note for fifty taels. When the financial side of the matter had thus been satisfactorily settled, Mother Ma got down to work without any more moral scruples, and without distinguishing blue from red or black from white. She took scissors and cut out two human figures from a sheet of white paper. Mrs. Chao had to write on each of them a set of four double cyclic signs—namely, the year, month, day, and hour of the birth of Phoenix and of Pao Yu. Then she cut from a sheet of blue paper two sets of five figures of devils and got Mrs. Chao to sew them carefully with needle and thread onto the first two figures. She had barely time to explain that she would carry out the rest of the charm at home by herself, and quickly to gather up the pieces of paper which were sewn together, when a maid appeared to call Mrs. Chao to a meal. Mother Ma took leave hurriedly and set out for her home.

That afternoon Black Jade went to visit her sick cousin, Pao Yu. On the veranda in front of his pavilion she found several maids busy washing themselves, making up their faces, and painting their eyebrows. From inside came the sound of merry chatter and laughter. Phoenix, Precious Clasp, and the three Spring girls were there entertaining the patient with their pleasant company.

"Ah, here comes another!" they cried in chorus as Black Jade entered.

"You must all have been invited by letter, to arrive in such numbers?" said Black Jade playfully.

"Have you tried the tea which I sent you recently?" Phoenix asked her.

"Oh, I had quite forgotten it. Many thanks for the kind gift."

"It did not taste very good to me," interjected Pao Yu.

"I think it tastes good, but the color is not very special," remarked Precious Clasp.

"It is tribute tea from Siam," declared Phoenix. "I did not like it very much either; I think our Chinese tea is better."

Of course Black Jade had to disagree.

"I liked it. Your stomachs must be out of order, it seems."

"If you like it, you can have more of the same kind," said Phoenix.

"Oh, yes, please. I shall send my maid for it."

"That is not necessary. I was going to send over to you tomorrow for something in any case."

"Oh, indeed? I should very much like to know what service is desired of me in return for the package of tea."

"Who knows? Perhaps you will be asked to prepare to be a little bride for our family," said Phoenix blithely.

"Marvellously witty!" remarked Precious Clasp somewhat acidly, while the others laughed loud.

"Witty? I find the remark in very bad taste and most unfitting," Black Jade burst out violently. She had gone red to the roots of her hair and one could hear her teeth gnashing.

"Now, would you be throwing yourself away if you were to be a bride to that member of the family there?" continued Phoenix calmly, pointing her finger at Pao Yu. "Does his person or his origin not please you?"

Black Jade had stood up and gone silently to the door. Precious Clasp hurried after her and drew her back.

"How can one take offense so easily and just run off?" she said to her. At that moment the two secondary wives, Chao and Chou, who had also come to inquire after Pao Yu's health, entered the room. Everyone stood up politely when they appeared. Phoenix alone remained seated and ignored them deliberately. Shortly afterwards Phoenix and the cousins were called away to Madame Cheng's, to greet the wife of the latter's brother, Marshal Wang Tzu Teng, who had come to visit. The sickroom was soon empty.

"Will you at least stay with me a little while!" begged Pao Yu, when Black Jade too was about to leave him.

"Do you hear that? Your presence is desired here," said Phoenix, supporting his request, as she turned around and with a laugh pushed Black Jade back into the room. Pao Yu caught her by the hand and smiled at her in silent entreaty. Black Jade flushed and tried to disengage herself from him. Suddenly he let her go, grasped his head, and uttered a loud cry of pain.

"Oh, how my head aches!" he groaned. The next moment he gave a great leap into the air and began to run round the room like a possessed person, shouting and stammering out disconnected words. Hearing Black Jade's and the maids' frightened cries for help, Pao Yu's mother, the Ancestress, and their visitor, Aunt Wang, came hurrying. They saw Pao Yu wildly brandishing a naked dagger and a fencing foil as he jumped up and down the room roaring frantically. Shaking with terror, the women snatched up their skirts and ran out of the pavilion uttering loud cries of grief. With lightning speed the awful news spread through both palaces that Pao Yu had gone mad, and in the course of time his father and Prince Shieh, and Prince Chen, and Chia Lien, and many other men and women of the clan arrived at the ill-fated spot.

In the midst of the general tumult, when all minds were concentrated on Pao Yu, Phoenix was suddenly seen running through the park in great bounds. She was armed with a long kitchen knife, with which she was slashing out, here beheading a hen which happened to cross her path, and there stabbing a dog which had come too near her. Her rolling eyes glared with lust for blood as she now approached the group of relatives and servants. Everyone fell back, crying out in fright, but some brave, strong serving men and maids surrounded her, forced the weapon from her grasp, and carried her off to her residence.

There was an excited family council. In great confusion they all talked together. Some suggested this devil-catcher, others that exorcist of spirits; some were for calling a doctor, others for trying magic, and finally it was decided to send for both doctors and magicians. But in spite of a hundred medical endeavors and magic incantations and in spite of thorough sprinkling with holy water, the two possessed persons continued their ravings until their bodies were glowing like fire, and they sank down at last exhausted on their beds. But even lying there, they continued to babble incoherently, and during the night their ravings took on really terrible forms. No one dared to go near them throughout the whole night. The next day the two were shut up in one room in the dwelling of Pao Yu's mother, and guards were posted to watch in turns day and night and prevent the maniacs from escaping. But not far away the Ancestress and Madame Cheng, Prince Shieh, and Aunt Hsueh sat together, never moved a step from the vicinity, and, filled with a thousand fears and sobbing ceaselessly, followed the development of the condition of the two favorites of the house. When three days and three nights had passed without any improvement, Mr. Cheng gave up hope.

"The number of our years is determined by heaven," he said to Prince Shieh, who kept tirelessly putting forward new suggestions. "With only our human strength we can do nothing. The illness of these two defies every treatment. We must leave them to their fate!"

By this time Phoenix and Pao Yu were lying on couches in an exhausted and apathetic condition, and were breathing only weakly. Everyone regarded their case as hopeless, and the elders had decided to make preparations for their death, which was expected at any moment. This news caused renewed lamentation and mourning in the women's apartments. Only one woman was untouched by the general sorrow and, while pretending sympathy, was quietly rejoicing. That was the secondary wife Chao.

On the fourth day Pao Yu suddenly opened his eyes and asked for his things. He could not stand it here any longer, he said, and he wished straight away to leave the house forever. The Ancestress was inconsolable and tried to dissuade him from his intention. But the secondary wife Chao urged her to let him have his way.

"Do not be sad about it, old *Tai tai!*" she said. "Let him put on his clothes and go off. In any case he is no longer any good for his family. He must be permitted to have his way or he will get another attack of madness."

Her remark put the Ancestress into such a rage that one could hear her teeth gnashing and see the foam dropping from the corners of her mouth.

"May the tongue dry up in your mouth, you confounded woman!" she cursed. "You will persecute him to his death! Do not imagine that I am blind! I know well how convenient it would be for you if he died. I know whose fault it is that he trembles before his father like a mouse before a cat, and that his liver is bursting through constant fear. You would like to be rid of him. That would suit you very well! But I will not allow it. . . ." Her voice dropped and she was overcome by a fit of coughing. Mr. Cheng, who was standing beside her, was painfully aware of the reproaches directed at him, and turned away muttering. While the woman who had received this scolding was trying to justify herself and to calm the enraged Ancestress, a servant arrived and announced that the two coffins had been made. The Ancestress now was beside herself. She felt as if her heart were pierced by daggers.

"Who did such a wicked thing as to order those coffins?" she cried in a screeching voice. "Bring whoever did it straight to me that I may have him beaten to death!"

In the midst of the tumult the sound of a wooden clapper, such as pious Buddhists are in the habit of using at prayer, was heard from far down the street, and a loud voice commending, in the name of the Southern Redeemer, certain healing recipes for those possessed by the devil became distinctly audible. The Ancestress forthwith sent servants out the front gate to find the travelling miracle healer and bring him to the house. It was not long before the servants came back with two very odd-looking individuals. One of them was a mangy-looking bonze, the other was a lame Taoist priest. The prominent nose of the former indicated boldness of character, his elongated eyes sparkled like bright stars, the patched bast sandals which he wore left no tracks in the dust, his grimy bald head was covered with scurf. The other walked with a limp, for one foot was shorter than the other, and his shabby habit was dirty and stained with perspiration from top to bottom. From where else could they have come than from the Islands of Spirits in the Western Sea, where the sun sets? Chia Cheng wished to submit the two chance guests to the usual polite questioning about their person and origin, and started by asking them on which mountain or in which temple they had been trained in holiness. But they laughingly refused any information.

"No superfluous questions, please! We have learned that certain inmates of this house are lacking peace of soul, and we have come to cure them."

"You are right. Two members of this house are possessed by wicked demons. What, then, are your remedies?"

"Your house shelters a precious jewel which can cure the two sick people. Why seek other remedies?"

Chia Cheng understood what they meant.

"You surely mean the stone which my child had in his mouth when he was born. The inscription on it certainly asserts that it renders the owner proof against the influences of wicked spirits. But so far it has not shown its magic power."

"That is not the fault of the stone," the bonze informed him. "The stone originally possessed magic power, but its magic has been lost owing to the influences of the flesh and the senses. Bring the stone to us! We will restore its magic powers by incantations."

Chia Cheng obeyed, took the stone from Pao Yu's neck, and passed it to the monk. The monk laid it on the palm of his hand, closed his fingers over it, gave a long sigh, and addressed it thus in a low murmur: "It is now fifteen years since you left your place under the green cliff. Light and shade alternate quickly in this human world. It cannot be helped; you must remain until your earthly destination has been fulfilled. And now I adjure you: become again what you once were, pure and free!"

Murmuring a few more mysterious sentences, he rubbed the stone for a while on the palm of his hand, then handed it back to Chia Cheng.

"Now it has regained its old magic power," he said. "But take care lest it get soiled! Hang it on the balustrade in front of the invalid's bedroom until he is well again, and take care that no female except a relation of his own blood touches it! Follow these instructions, and the sick person will be cured in thirty-three days."

Chia Cheng was about to order his servants to bring food and drink, but the two queer fellows had already disappeared. He followed their instructions exactly, and the health of the two cousins did in fact improve from day to day. It was just as if they were waking up after a long sleep; they got back their appetites and asked for food and drink, and at the end of the thirty-three days they were completely cured. The Princess Ancestress and Madame Cheng were immensely relieved, and the recovery of Pao Yu caused great joy among his cousins, who had been waiting expectantly crowded outside the door of the sickroom. Black Jade was the first who showed her relief by crying from her heart: "Thanks be to Buddha!" Precious Clasp said nothing but only laughed.

"Why are you laughing?" Grief of Spring wanted to know.

"I have to laugh at all the good Buddha has to do. He must make the sick well and bring poor sinners to regeneration. He can do everything; one has only to call upon him. The next thing will be that he will negotiate marriages on request."

"Shame! How can you be so wicked and frivolous!" cried Black Jade, flushing, as, full of indignation, she ran out of the room.

CHAPTER 21

On the Wasp Waist Bridge a lovelorn maid expresses her feelings in commonplace words. The "Courtesan Yang" startles two butterflies in the Pavilion of the Kingfisher-Blue Drops.

At the end of the thirty-three days not only was Pao Yu cured of his mental derangement but the disfiguring burns on his face were also completely healed. He felt stronger and in better form than before, and he was glad to be able to move back at last to his beloved park. And another person rejoiced at his return: that was little Siao Hung; for now she could see her secretly beloved Little Yun again, if only at a distance, for he was still engaged on his garden work. And Little Yun's heart too beat faster every time he saw the graceful figure of the little maid appearing in his vicinity. If only he could manage to speak to her! But he did not dare, for after all Pao Yu had forbidden him at the outset to have any contact with the female inmates of the park. Siao Hung had once noticed a dainty little pale green silk handkerchief in Little Yun's hand. It was her handkerchief which she had lost recently! Perhaps, after all, her dream might yet come true?

One day Pao Yu, remembering the promise he had made quite a while ago, braced himself to invite Little Yun to a cup of tea. Chance would have it that, just as the waiting maid Earring was escorting the guest along, not far from the Wasp Waist Bridge, little Siao Hung was walking over the bridge. Siao Hung stopped and exchanged a few words with Earring. What she had to say was something quite unimportant, but the delay allowed her to look profoundly into Little Yun's eyes, and this hurried exchange of glances caused them both to blush. She had not yet found the pale green handkerchief which she had lost, the artful little creature remarked quite casually as she continued her way.

Pao Yu had ordered that his guest should be brought into the library in the Court of Harmonious Red. While the maid went to announce his arrival Little Yun had an opportunity to look round him. The "court" was an alluring rock landscape, planted here and there with cypresses, banana plants, and one huge golden begonia. Beneath a cypress tree stood two Manchurian spirit cranes preening their feathers with their long beaks. The chirping and shrieking of rare, colored birds in numerous cages resounded from the walls of the pleasure gallery which encircled the round inner courtyard wall. Above the entrance door to the circular main building hung a tablet bearing the inscription "Harmonious Red, Joyful Green." While Little Yun was still pondering over the meaning of these four characters, he was called in. Pao Yu was reclining on a magnificent carved black lacquered divan beneath a red silk canopy edged with gold and embroidered with flowers. In his hand he held an open book which he laid down when the visitor entered.

Pao Yu apologized for the fact that he had been prevented from carrying out his promise until today, two months late, owing to his illness. Little Yun protested politely how sorry he had been about his illness, and what an inexpressible happiness his ultimate recovery was to his whole family. When Pao Yu spoke he only half listened, for his thoughts were distracted as much by the splendor of his surroundings as by the charm of the two waiting maids in attendance. He assumed the elder one, who was so sumptuously resplendent in red and green and silver silk, to be Pao Yu's personal maid, Pearl. As he had heard what an important role Pearl played, he did not dare to allow her to serve him. When she was about to pour out tea, he stood up respectfully and shyly asked to be allowed to pour it out himself. Pao Yu laughingly pushed him down on his seat again, saying he need not be so ceremonious with waiting maids, but in his secret heart he found the obsequious manner of the poor relation somewhat tedious, hence he cut the visit as short as possible and limited the conversation to such superficial, commonplace themes as the weather, servants, garden planning, good food, and the like. Quite soon he felt weary of his guest with his incessant and extravagant praise, and he bade him farewell. The waiting maid Earring had to conduct him out again.

On the way Little Yun deliberately walked slowly and kept watching in all the four directions of heaven for little Siao Hung; but she was nowhere to be seen. He determined to become friendly with the waiting maid Earring in order through her to come nearer to his objective. He asked her about her age and her family, her work and her salary, and every other possible matter. When he had become somewhat more familiar with her in this way he took up courage and asked straight out: "Is the name of the little one who hailed you a while ago on the bridge Siao Hung, by any chance?"

"Yes. Why do you ask?"

"Only this—did she not say something about a lost handkerchief?"

"She has asked me about it again and again, and begged me to help her to find it, but I was not able to; I have more important things in my head."

"I have found it."

"Oh, then, give it to me. She will be grateful to you."

Little Yun put his hand in his pocket and drew out a pale green silk kerchief.

"Here. But can I depend upon you to bring me her thanks?"

"You can depend upon me!"

Feeling very happy, Little Yun walked out the park gateway. He had come considerably nearer his aim today.

After disposing of his visitor Pao Yu had lain down again and begun to daydream. He did not feel in the mood even for reading. The waiting maid Pearl came up beside him and gave him an encouraging cuff.

"How can anyone be so lazy as to go to sleep again? You should go out and take some exercise!"

"I would like to, but I find it so hard to leave you," he replied smiling, taking her by the hand.

"Nonsense! Get up! Get up!" she said, pulling him up.

"But where shall I go?" he yawned. "Oh, I feel so terribly tired and limp!"

"No wonder when you stick in your room the whole day like a silly little girl! Get out into the fresh air; it will cheer you up!"

He got up and stretched himself, then slipped out yawning into the open air. First he made the round of the pleasure gallery by the inner courtyard wall and amused himself there for a while teasing the birds which were swinging in their cages, then he went into the open park, sauntered along by the brook, looked at the goldfishes in their basins, and went on to the game preserve. Here he perceived two young stags bounding away over a hillside. Why did the tame animals take to their heels so quickly at sight of him? While he was pondering over this he caught sight of his nephew Chia Lan in the thicket. The rascal was armed with bow and arrow and was glowing with the joy of the chase.

"What mischief are you up to here?" challenged Pao Yu.

"Oh, I thought Uncle had gone out," stammered the boy, confused. "I was free from school and I wanted to pass the time practicing archery."

"I will knock in your teeth if you ever again attempt to hunt here!"

said Pao Yu severely, and then continued on his way. At last he came to a secret door which was hidden away behind a thicket of high ferns by the edge of a quiet pond. A mysterious humming, which seemed to come from a water dragon lying at the bottom of the pond, filled the air. Pao Yu had arrived at Black Jade's pavilion. He quietly lifted the bamboo screen and stepped into the front garden. There was deep silence everywhere. He crept under the open window, which had only a thin gauze curtain, and peered inside. A wave of heavy fragrance met his nostrils. Before he had perceived the inmate, he heard a deep sigh and then the following words spoken in an undertone:

> Alone all day long on my pillow,
> Where can I put my feelings but in thought. . . .

She is quoting from the "Western Pavilion," thought the listener, amused, peering with difficulty through a slit in the gauze. For he could see distinctly that she was lying on the divan, her limbs stretched out as if in sleep.

"Why do you always lie alone on a pillow just thinking what you feel?"

With these words he burst into the room, smiling. She quickly put her arm over her blushing face and turned towards the wall, pretending to be asleep. He went up to her couch and tried to draw her over to the other side, but he was disturbed in his efforts by two serving women.

"The young lady is still asleep; please wait outside until she wakes up!" the sedate guardians of order informed the intruder. But Black Jade had already turned over onto the other side.

"Who is asleep here?" she asked pleasantly.

"Oh, we only thought . . ." the matrons excused themselves, with embarrassed smiles, and withdrew to give place to the maid Cuckoo. Black Jade had sat up, and began to do her hair.

"What do you mean by surprising me in the middle of a beautiful sleep?" she asked, turning to Pao Yu with a smile.

How bewitchingly beautiful she seemed to him with her cheeks flushed with sleep and the melancholy sweetness of her expression! He pushed his seat nearer to her and gazed at her, fascinated.

"Excuse me, but what were you saying just now?" he asked, absently.

"Oh, nothing in particular."

"I mean just now."

"I do not know what you mean."

"Won't you give me some nuts to crack? But I certainly heard what you said just now. Bring me a good bowl of tea!" he said, turning to the waiting maid Cuckoo.

"I don't think you like our tea. Better let your Pearl get you some!" retorted Cuckoo, pertly.

"It's all right, pour it!"

Cuckoo obeyed, and then turned towards the door.

"Listen! When one day I am united to your beloved little mistress beneath the curtain embroidered with a pair of mandarin ducks, you shall always be allowed to settle the cushions and spread the covers," he called after her jokingly, quoting from the "Western Pavilion."

His words instantly banished the merry expression from Black Jade's face.

"Are you treating me again to the street expressions, the coarse offensiveness, which you read in lewd books? I will not listen to such talk!" she burst out passionately. In one jump she was off the couch and out of the room. He ran after her.

"Dearest, best *Mei mei*, I deserve death!" he called out, quite bewildered. "But I will never again utter such expressions, or if I do, may my tongue rot out. . . ."

The arrival of the waiting maid Pearl prevented him from elaborating his oath.

"Quick! Dress yourself! The old governor wants to speak to you," she announced. The words "old governor" went through his limbs like a stroke of lightning. For the moment all other troubles were forgotten, and he hurried back to his pavilion at Pearl's side in order to get ready for the dreaded visit. His valet Ming Yen was waiting for him at the park gate.

"Do you know why the old man wants to speak to me?" he asked him excitedly.

"No. But hurry up! You will know soon enough."

With his stomach heaving with torturing doubts, Pao Yu hurried on. From behind a projection of wall near the great reception hall a shrill laugh greeted him and Cousin Hsueh Pan suddenly stepped out in front of him. He was clapping his hands wildly and doubling up with laughter.

"Just look how the boy can hurry! One only needs to mention his old man to frighten him out of his wits!" he cried gleefully.

Pao Yu stood dumfounded. He saw that he had been hoaxed and was about to burst out in rage, but Hsueh Pan now greeted him jokingly with a ceremonious bow and tried to appease him.

"I admit my offense and beg your kind forbearance. But I wanted your company so very much. There are a whole crowd of us and you are the only one missing. My birthday will be very soon, on the third of the fifth month, and we are having a preliminary celebration today. Without this little trick I could hardly have enticed you out so quickly.

But it is worth coming to; there are all kinds of delicacies to feast on—crisp fresh lotus roots covered with bread crumbs, giant melons, giant tribute salmon from Siam, Siamese tribute pork fragrant with cedarwood. I have already sent your mother a fine big taste of all these things, but there is still so much, I cannot possibly manage it myself; you simply must help me to eat it. Besides, there is a pretty little boy singer who will make the meal more pleasant for us."

Faced with such enticing pleasures, Pao Yu was soon appeased of course, and he laughingly gave in to the wild cousin's invitation. He returned home in the evening half tipsy. Cousin Precious Clasp, eager for details of the party, paid him a visit, late though the hour was. Let us, then, leave these two to their lively conversation for the time being and return to Black Jade. She had spent the whole day in acute anxiety, wondering how the supposed visit of Pao Yu to his stern father had passed off, and it was long past the hour of the evening meal when she was informed that Pao Yu had at last returned.

She set out hurriedly for his pavilion, for she was very eager to speak to him before bedtime. It happened that Precious Clasp arrived there just before her. She could see her distinctly in the bright moonlight disappearing into Pao Yu's front garden, though she was still quite far away.

Arriving shortly after her, she found to her astonishment that the entrance gate was locked. Nobody opened when she knocked, and a peevish maid's voice called out: "The little master is already asleep. After all, it is now the third night watch. Come back in the morning!"

The waiting maid was in fact already not very pleased at Precious Clasp's late visit, which compelled her to stay up longer than usual. Moreover, she was out of humor on account of a quarrel she had just had with a colleague. It was purely on her authority and through ill-humor that she did not open the door. Naturally, Black Jade could not know this; being of a suspicious nature, she sought the reason for this refusal to let her in in quite another direction.

"But it is I! Why, then, won't you open?" she repeated impatiently.

"It's all the same who you are. The little master expressly ordered that I was not to let anyone in," came the unfriendly reply from inside.

Black Jade was raging and felt like starting to scold aloud, but then she reflected that after all she was an outsider, a guest here, and must therefore show restraint before the staff. This reflection made her painfully aware how alone in the world and how completely orphaned she was, and once more her eyes filled with tears. As she stood thus, perplexed and weeping before the locked gate, she suddenly heard merry laughter from within, and could distinguish clearly the voices of her boy and girl cousins. Her heart contracted convulsively. She felt as if she would cry aloud in her grief. Why did he lock her out so heartlessly? She thought and thought and racked her brains right and left. Did he want to punish her for having reprimanded him today and then run away? But she had not really meant it so seriously. Would he dare to treat her so insultingly for that? The next thing would be that he would refuse to see her at all!

For a long time she stood there, lonely and forsaken, in the shadow of a corner of the wall, and heedless of the night chill which came down from the bluish, glistening hillsides wet with dew and enveloped her. Then she crept away slowly, sobbing wildly. And her sobbing awakened the birds in the branches by the wayside from their sleep and caused them to fly away in alarmed flutters to more distant resting places. She had not gone far when she heard behind her a door creaking on its hinges. She stopped and turned round. Precious Clasp was just coming out of Pao Yu's garden gate. Pao Yu and the waiting maid Pearl were accompanying her a few steps. Black Jade would have liked to hurry back and call Pao Yu to account, but she did not want to betray herself to Precious Clasp and Pearl. So she remained where she was and watched from a distance as Pao Yu parted from his cousin, returned with Pearl, and disappeared inside the garden gate. As soon as the gate had been shut she continued her way in tears.

Her two waiting maids Cuckoo and Snowgoose had long since grown accustomed to the sudden fits of melancholy from which their mistress suffered at frequent and regular intervals. At first they had thought it was homesickness, or grief for her dead parents, and they had made efforts to comfort her; but as the months passed by and these tearful attacks of melancholy continued, they ceased to be surprised, and took these states as inevitable expressions of a somewhat strange disposition. Hence, when Black Jade came home in a broken state this night, they did not take any notice of her condition or ask the reason of her sorrow. But Black Jade shut herself into her bedroom and sat crouched on the edge of her bed for a long time with her hands clasped over her knees, motionless as a statue, until at last she lay down to rest as dawn was breaking.

The following day, the twenty-sixth of the fourth month, the beginning of summer was celebrated. This is the day when the flower spirits come down from their thrones and the corn comes into its glory. According to ancient custom this day was also celebrated in the Park of Delightful Vision with the usual offering of sacrifices, the traditional flower banquet, and boisterous festivity. The youthful female inmates of the park and their waiting maids had put on gaily colored garments, the dazzling splendor of which made the gaudy parrots pale with envy, and brightness and cheerfulness reigned everywhere. Only one person was missing from the merry company, and that was Black Jade.

"Where on earth is Cousin Black Jade?" Greeting of Spring asked. "The lazy thing seems to want to sleep all day."

"Wait, I will go and rouse her!" suggested Precious Clasp, and hurried off. On the way she met the troupe of twelve dancing girls from the Pear Garden.

"The others are over there," she said to them, pointing behind her. "Just go along! I shall follow immediately; I am only going to fetch Black Jade."

As she came near Black Jade's pavilion she saw Pao Yu just entering it. She slackened her pace and reflected a moment. Should she disturb them? No, she would not be so inconsiderate. On this festive day she did not want to upset the sensitive Black Jade, who, she knew, liked to have her cousin all to herself. She promptly made up her mind, turned, and ran back. As she went she noticed a pair of big, wonderfully beautiful butterflies close by the path, fluttering up and down in the gentle wind. How she would love to catch them! She drew her fan out of her sleeve pouch and started to chase them. But each time she thought she was quite near them, the two winged fugitives cleverly dodged her fan, and enticed her farther and farther from the pathway and into the grass right up to the edge of the near-by pond. Here she had to give up the chase. The fugitives escaped from her over the water.

Precious Clasp was about to turn round again when she became aware of the sound of lively whispering coming from the Pavilion of the Kingfisher-Blue Drops. The pavilion, which stood out airily in the middle of the pond, was connected with the bank by means of four covered wooden footbridges. It was surrounded on all sides by high folding screens. Precious Clasp crept across the nearest bridge and listened in through the wood carving of one of the big folding screens, which was pasted up with parchment, and which shut out the view all around. She distinguished two women's voices. Now she heard one of them saying: "Well, tell me at last, is this your handkerchief which you lost that time? If not, I must take it back to Mr. Yun."

"Of course it's mine. Give it to me!" she heard the other reply.

"Just a minute! Not so quick! First out with the reward, for you're not going to get it for nothing! I definitely promised Mr. Yun only to give it up in exchange for the reward."

"Nonsense! Why a reward? After all, it's a duty to give up what one finds in a strange house."

"Very well, then you won't get it."

The dispute continued for a while longer. Then a voice said: "Very well, give him this bangle as a reward! But promise me you won't say a word to anyone about it! Swear it!"

"I swear it, and if I do not keep my word may I get a big boil in my mouth and be miserably suffocated to death by it!"

"Sh! Not so loud! What if anyone should be listening outside! We had better push aside the screen a little so as not to awaken suspicion, and to see better if anyone is coming."

Precious Clasp, who did not want to be caught eavesdropping, retreated quickly across the footbridge, only to return immediately, this time intentionally clattering loudly on the boards. She had recognized little Siao Hung and Earring by their voices, and was astonished at the cunning of these youngest of all the waiting maids, who appeared to be so extremely innocent, yet here, behind their master's back, were gaily knotting the first threads of a pleasant little love game.

"Hi, Sister Black Jade, where have you crept away to? I can't find you anywhere," she called aloud, putting on a completely innocent air. Abashed and startled, the two young girls stared at the unexpected intruder through the space between the two folding screens which they had pushed aside just before. Then they shot out to greet Precious Clasp with due respect.

"Where have you hidden my cousin?" asked Precious Clasp quite naturally.

"We do not know where Miss Ling is," said Earring, surprised.

"But I just saw her by the pond. I thought she must have crept along the bank somewhere here, wanting to take you by surprise, but apparently she saw me coming and evaded me. Or could she have hidden herself here in the pavilion?"

She stepped in and craned her neck and stretched her limbs, as if searching intently.

"She must have just crept into a grotto outside. Let us hope she won't get bitten by snakes!" she murmured. Then she went away again, secretly amused at the little incident and the successful trick which had helped her out of her embarrassment.

Having spent half the night sitting up, Black Jade slept longer than usual today. The others had been in the park a long time before she awoke. She did her toilet in frantic haste, for she did not want to arrive too late at the farewell banquet in honor of the departing flowers, nor to be laughed at by the others as a sleepyhead. She was just getting ready to go out when Pao Yu entered.

"Dear *Mei mei*," he said as gently as possible, "the whole night through I have been turning over your words of yesterday in my mind. . . ."

Just as if he were not present at all Black Jade turned quite unconcernedly to the maid Cuckoo and said: "Look here, tidy up the place thoroughly! Take down the window curtains and the door curtains! Put a light in the incense pot and do not forget to cover it again! You may go to see the banquet, but when it is over come back and await me by the stone lions in front of the door!"

Having given these instructions, she went out into the park, passing by Pao Yu without looking at him. Pao Yu still believed that her strange behavior was due to his joking remarks to Cuckoo yesterday, which she had taken so much amiss. How could he guess that a new cause for her ill-humor had arisen the night before? Why did she bear a grudge against him for so long, contrary to her usual habit, on account of the little offense of yesterday afternoon, he asked himself in vain as he trotted behind her, tortured with uncertainty. Without having spoken one word to each other, each of them arrived separately to join the rest of the company.

Black Jade joined Precious Clasp and Taste of Spring, who were just delightedly watching the strange jumping of a pair of cranes. When Pao Yu arrived a little later his half-sister Taste of Spring took him aside under a pomegranate tree, away from the other two girls.

"What happened yesterday? I heard that our father sent for you suddenly," she asked.

"Nonsense! Whoever told you that must have misheard. I was at Cousin Hsueh Pan's."

"Oh, I am glad it is nothing. But I have a request to make of you. I have saved up a dozen thousand-piece strings of money recently. Would you buy something pretty for me with this money the next time you are in the town? A lovely picture or some old curio?"

"With pleasure. But what? In my strolls inside and outside the city walls, and in the shops and temple markets, I have not seen anything outstanding in the way of pictures or curios for a long time. It is always the same kind of thing—gold, bronze, jade, china, but nothing uncommon. Would you not perhaps prefer a pretty dress or something nice to eat?"

"No, no! But it just occurs to me, I would like to have a plaited willow workbasket or a perfume box made of bamboo root like one you brought home recently, or an earthenware air-draft furnace or something like that. But let this be strictly between ourselves, won't you? For I know from experience that whenever I like something the other girls take a fancy to it too and make off with it."

"But the things you suggest are quite simple, cheap things," said Pao Yu, laughing. "You can buy things like those for a few hundred coppers from any coolie. You do not need me for that!"

"What kind of taste would a coolie have?" replied his sister indignantly. "No, I should like you to choose for me, then I would be sure of getting something uncommon. As a matter of fact, I have a great many more wishes. For instance, I should like a pair of slippers exactly like the ones you got for yourself recently, but mine would have to be a little more daintily worked. . . ."

They went on like this for quite a while, until at last Precious Clasp came along and interrupted the important secret consultation, saying: "Will you two ever have finished talking? We others do not seem to exist for you any longer. After all, you are brother and sister and need not have any secrets from us."

The three of them returned to the rest of the company, laughing merrily.

Pao Yu missed Black Jade. She is avoiding me, but her resentment never lasts more than two days, I know her ways—he comforted himself with these thoughts. As he mused thus, his head bent thoughtfully, his eyes on the ground, he suddenly perceived that the ground was completely strewn with camellia and pomegranate blossoms. How distraught she must be when she no longer finds time to bury her blossoms! he thought. When he looked up again Precious Clasp also had disappeared from his sight. Now they have both forsaken me, he thought miserably. He bent down and gathered up two handfuls of blossoms to carry to Black Jade's flower grave. His path thence wound its way over hills and water courses, through groves and pastures. Just as he was nearing his objective he heard a plaintive girl's voice coming from behind the last shelf of rock. He stood still and listened. It must be some maid who is weeping away her grief for some injustice in this heart-rending fashion, he conjectured, and stepping softly nearer, he peered inquisitively round the shelf of rock. He started back in dismay—for the girl was Black Jade.

Black Jade had not yet got over the insult which she wrongly imagined she had suffered from Pao Yu the evening before. The merrymaking with which the Feast of the Departing Flowers was being celebrated today did not at all harmonize with her gloomy frame of mind, and so she had withdrawn from the circle of her playmates into solitude. She had set out for her flower grave with an armful of fallen petals. While burying the petals in the grave just now she had been overwhelmed with unspeakable grief. Perhaps it was sympathy for the poor blossoms; perhaps it was the thought of the transience of her own blossoming youth. Whatever it was, she was quite overcome with melancholy and broke out into a long lamentation in which she compared herself with a tender blossom and bewailed her inevitably sad destiny— the destiny of a fading flower. And so moving was her melody that in the midst of this song of lamentation, intermingled with tears, the listener by the shelf of rock was seized with emotion, let his load of petals fall to the ground, and broke out in loud sobbing too. What would become of him if all the gentle blossoming maidens around him—Black Jade, Precious Clasp, Pearl, and all the rest—were to fade away and withdraw to those unknown glades where there is no seeking and no finding? These were the thoughts which invaded his mind.

Black Jade, suddenly hearing the echo of her own pain from the wall of rock behind her, stopped short in her lament. They always laugh at me for being foolish, but it seems there is some other fool here besides myself, she thought, turning round. And then she discovered Pao Yu.

"Oh, it's that loathsome one!" she gasped, half aloud. Then, shocked at her own outburst, she quickly covered her mouth with her hand, jumped up, and ran away. He followed her timidly some distance behind for a while, then he ventured to come nearer.

"Please stop!" he implored her. "I know you do not like me, and I will certainly keep away from you in the future, but I would like to speak just one single sentence to you!"

"Very well, but only one sentence," she said, turning round quickly and slackening her pace.

"Will you listen to me even if it is a bit more?"

She instantly resumed a quicker pace. He, following close behind her, heaved a deep sight and then cried out: "Why is it so different between us nowadays from what it was in the past?"

"What do you mean by that?" she asked, stopping.

"Were you not my faithful companion and playmate when you came here? Did we not eat at the same table and rest on the same couch? Were not my favorite dishes your favorite dishes too? Did we not grow up together? And now that you are grown up, you will not look at me and you avoid me for whole days on end. Am I not just as much alone and forsaken as you are? I have a brother and a sister, it is true, but their mother is a stranger. Since we two have no real brothers or sisters, are we not fellow sufferers? Should we not be a comfort and support to each other? And now is it all to come to an end. . . .?"

He could not get any further. Tears choked his voice. She had listened to him silently with bent head. Sympathy welled up in her breast, her anger had more than half turned to ashes. Now she in turn was infected by his tears and began to weep too. Encouraged by her softening of heart, he continued: "I know that I am bad. But what harm have I done you? When I commit a fault you may blame me, and warn me, and scold me, and even beat me, I can bear all that. But that you just do not notice me, that drives me to despair! It makes me

213

demented. Do you, then, really wish me to die a poor sinner whom no Buddhist or Taoist requiem can save from damnation?"

His moving plaint had banished the last remnant of her resentment into the ninth region of heaven.

"Why did you not let your maid open the door to me last night?" she commenced, changing her tone.

"You called on me last night? May I die on the spot if I know anything about that!" he protested, astonished.

"One should not use the word 'die' so thoughtlessly! You know I hate those strong protestations. A simple yes or no is enough for me."

"But really, I knew nothing about your coming. I only know that Cousin Precious Clasp was there."

Black Jade's face brightened up.

"Hm. Then it seems that it was through indolence or bad humor that your maids did not open the door," she remarked after a moment's reflection.

"That must be it!" replied Pao Yu eagerly. "I will investigate the matter at once when I go home. I will give the lazy things a good piece of my mind!"

"Yes, do so, but not for my sake! That this should happen to me is not so very bad. But it might happen sometime to one of your other more favored cousins, and then the scandal would be inconceivable. Isn't that so?" she said, smiling ironically.

And so for the time being peace reigned again.

CHAPTER 22

The better off one is, the more one troubles about one's welfare. The more a woman is cherished and loved, the more love does she demand.

THE FIFTH OF THE MONTH, THE DAY OF THE DRAGON BOAT FESTIVAL, had almost come. The Princess Ancestress had decided to spend this day with Phoenix and Pao Yu and the granddaughters outside the town in the Taoist Temple of the Serene Void. She had declared that the continuous monotony of home life dulled the mind in the long run; she needed a change and looked forward to the much-desired diversion provided by the theatrical performances which just at this time took place at the temple. Phoenix had agreed enthusiastically and added that she was already thoroughly sick of the repertory of the house theater. She undertook to make the necessary preparations for the holiday, which was to last for several days. The temple was comfortably furnished and was closed to the general public during the visit of the distinguished ladies. The majority of the priests were quartered out-side for the time.

Accordingly, in the forenoon of the first of the month the long pro-cession of sedan chairs and carriages set out. At its head came the great sedan of the Princess Ancerstress borne by eight men, and ac-companied by Pao Yu on horseback; then, each in a smaller sedan chair with four bearers apiece, came Aunt Hsueh, Phoenix, and the Widow Chu. There followed Black Jade and Precious Clasp in a blue carriage, the three Spring girls in a red carriage, then four chamber-maids of the Ancestress, Black Jade's maids, Cuckoo and Snowgoose, Precious Clasp's maids, Oriole and Apricot, six maids of the three Spring girls, two of Aunt Hsueh's serving women, Hsueh Pan's young secondary wife Lotus with her maid, two of Widow Chu's maids, and three waiting maids of Madame Phoenix, Little Ping and Little Fong, and the newest recruit Siao Hung, the two chambermaids Gold Ring and Nephrite Buckle belonging to Madame Cheng, who had remained at home herself owing to indisposition, the little daughter of Madame Phoenix and her nurse, then numerous serving women and maidser-vants. A large troupe of servants on horseback brought up the rear. It was an endless procession. The last participants were still climbing into their equipages and disputing about the seats, when the head was al-ready well out of sight. What pushing and shoving, what chattering and tittering! "No, this seat is engaged!" someone said here. "Don't crush my mistress's good dress!" cried another over there. "Don't spoil my coiffure!" was heard here. "Don't sit on my fan!" came a cry of distress from over there. The majordomo bustled to and fro warn-ing the company to be orderly and behave properly in the street, while all along the route the stewards and runners had their hands full keep-ing the streets clear and forcing back the gaping crowd.

A dull boom of salutation resounded from the drum and bell tower as the long procession of sedan chairs and carriages arrived at the Temple of the Serene Void—*Ching hsu kuan*. Before the temple gate the Prior, at the head of a double row of priests swinging censers, had taken up his position to welcome the guests ceremoniously. In the courtyard of the temple, behind the Mountain Gate, between the statues of the patron deities of the town, Prince Chen awaited the guests at the head of a crowd of cousins and nephews from the Yung-kuo and Ningkuo palaces. The Princess Ancestress's sedan was put down, and as the serving women and waiting maids were still far be-hind, Phoenix hurried up to help the old lady to dismount. Just as she set foot on the tiles of the temple courtyard, a little temple boy of about twelve ran past her and carelessly bumped into her. The boy had charge of trimming and cleaning the temple candles. He had been surprised at his work by the arrival of the ladies and wanted to slip out quickly. Phoenix, annoyed at his clumsiness, dealt him a resounding box on the ear.

"Just look out where you are running, little savage!" she rebuked him angrily. The boy, who had fallen and lost his snuffers in his panic, picked himself up quickly and ran off towards the exit. In doing so he got more and more into the crowd, for the occupants of the oncoming sedan chairs had dismounted meanwhile, and the young ladies, together with their waiting maids and serving women, formed such a dense throng at the temple gate that a drop of rain could not have fallen to the ground between them. The women were horrified at the impudence of the young boy who was trying to squeeze through them, and they cried out: "Stop him! Knock him down!"

"What is the matter?" the Ancestress asked Prince Chen.

The Prince rushed to the door, inquired what the hubbub was about, and had the boy arrested by the servants.

"A little candle-trimmer was late at his work and ran into the ladies as they came in," he reported to the Ancrestress.

"Bring him here," ordered the Ancestress. "But be very patient with him! One cannot demand a high standard of manners from the children of such humble people, and one must have consideration."

Dragged along by Prince Chen, the boy fell to the ground trembling and shaking in front of the Ancestress. The Ancestress made him stand up, spoke kind words to him, and asked him various questions, to which the boy was too shy to reply. Finally the Ancestress let him run off after having recommended the Prince to give him a few coppers to buy cakes and help him recover from his fright. Prince Chen did what he was told, and moreover took strong measures together with the majordomo to enclose the premises so that unpleasant incidents of the kind would not occur again. Even the young people and the servants from the Ningkuo and the Yungkuo palaces, who had come out with the others, were not permitted to enter the inner precincts of the temple, which were strictly reserved to the ladies.

The High Priest Chang, who had been standing aside shyly in front of the entrance to the temple all the time, now asked with a smile: "And what about me? May your humble servant pay his respects to the ladies inside? Perhaps the old *Tai tai* may desire my direction and miss me. However, I will certainly not act upon my own authority, but will conform entirely to your princely instructions."

The Prince did not hesitate, for the worthy old man enjoyed a reputation for holiness. Moreover, he used formerly to come and go frequently in the Yungkuo and Ningkuo palaces discharging the duties of exorcist, so he was no stranger to the ladies.

"Of course the temple is open to you, and if you make any more words about it I shall take you by your long beard and pull you in," replied the Prince jokingly, leading him into the inner precincts and up to the Ancestress. The High Priest bowed to the Ancestress and the younger ladies and smilingly offered his greetings: "May the old Ancestress be granted the same abundance of health, happiness, and long life which has been granted her up to the present! Since I have had the honor of offering her my greetings in her palace, it seems to me that her health and appearance have distinctly improved."

"How do you do, holy old man?" replied the Ancestress, smiling.

"The state of health of the little monk depends entirely upon the well-being of the old Ancestress," replied the Prior gallantly, and turned the conversation on to Pao Yu. At his request the Ancestress had her grandson called.

"How magnificently the little brother is getting on!" cried the old man.

"That is only on the surface, unfortunately; he is really a very weak boy," said the Ancestress, sighing. "No wonder, for he studies so hard. His father keeps him down to his books continually and allows him no recreation; he will become ill yet through overwork."

"I do not understand at all why the old master is displeased with his progress. I have had proof again and again of how splendidly the little brother can handle the writing brush and make verses. When I observe him attentively—his face, his figure, his deportment, his way of speaking—he seems to me more and more to be the image of his great progenitor, the Ancestor Prince," he continued.

"You are right," agreed the Ancestress, with emotion in her voice. "Of all my sons and nephews and grandsons, none resembles his Ancestor so much as this child."

The old man's face grew cunning.

"Recently, in the home of a certain noble family, I came across a fifteen-year-old daughter, a perfectly charming, clever, educated young girl. She would be a suitable partner for the little brother. If the old *Tai tai* would honor her humble servant with instructions to that effect, he would willingly place his services at her disposal and open his mouth in the house in question."

"Thank you for the kind offer," said the Ancestress, evasively. "But there is time enough for that. A holy young Buddhist informed us recently that it was the will of Providence that my grandson should not marry too early, so we are waiting until he is somewhat more grown-up. But if you wish to keep a preliminary lookout for a suitable partner, I do not mind. It is of the greatest importance to me that the character of the person in question should harmonize with that of my grandson;

I attach little importance to aristocratic and rich descent; she may well come from a poor family. Therefore, let me know whenever you have suitable suggestions to make!"

Thereupon the old man expressed the wish to be allowed to show Pao Yu's famous amulet to his priestly colleagues. At the order of the Ancestress, Pao Yu took off the chain with the spirit stone and handed it to the Prior. The Prior laid it in a bronze bowl and limped out leaning on his staff. When he returned after a little while he brought back in the bowl about forty or fifty other amulets, presents from the priests to Pao Yu.

"My colleagues thank you for the happiness of letting them see the strange magic stone," he said. "They want to take this opportunity of proving their friendly and humble devotion to the little brother. As they have nothing better at hand, they offer him these little emblems of Taoist piety. He can keep them as souvenirs or pass them on as presents, just as he pleases."

The Ancestress looked with curiosity at the contents of the bowl. They were mostly semicircular gold or jade tablets, pierced with holes, some of them set with pearls, and all of them graven with inscriptions such as "May your wishes all come true," or "Long life and health."

"How did you dare to allow your poor colleagues to go to such expense? We cannot accept these presents under any circumstances!" the Ancestress protested, thanking him.

"Oh, they insisted upon proving their devotion. I could not prevent them from doing so. They will feel hurt if they see that their well-intentioned gifts are disdained."

Of course the Ancestress did not wish to hurt the donors, so she accepted their gifts.

"What shall I do with these things?" asked Pao Yu in a somewhat scornful tone. "I shall give them to beggars on the way home."

"Do not do that!" objected the Prior. "Indeed, I do not fail to recognize your praiseworthy intention, but beggars do not appreciate such things; beggars want money. Keep these little objects! Though they may seem to you outwardly insignificant and worthless, nevertheless they possess beneficent power."

Pao Yu took the hint, and in the evening he ordered that money should be distributed among the beggars in front of the temple gate.

The Prior retired and the ladies went to their living quarters. Three one-story temple buildings had been placed at their disposal. The middle one was intended for the Ancestress, the eastern one for the other ladies, and the western one for the domestic female staff. After a while Prince Chen came to the Ancestress and advised her of the theatrical program. The first piece was to be "The History of the White Snake."

218

"Is not that ancient history?" asked the Ancestress.

"Yes, the play is founded on the old story of how Liu Pang, the founder of the first Han dynasty, killed the white snake and established the rule of justice. The second piece is called 'The Audience Tablets in the Bed'; the third piece is 'The Dream of Nan ko.'"

Prince Chen went down again to supervise the final preparations for the theatrical performance.

Pao Yu, who was sitting above with the Ancestress, passed the time turning over in the bowl the temple souvenirs which had been presented to him, and trying one piece after another on his jade belt. Each time the Ancestress had to give her opinion as to how the piece in question suited him. A lucky orange-colored unicorn, spotted with kingfisher blue, pleased her specially. She took it in her hand to examine it, and remarked: "It is very pretty. I must have seen something like this on one of the girls."

"Yes, you have. Cousin Little Cloud wears a unicorn like that, but it's somewhat smaller," said Precious Clasp quickly.

"You are right, it's Little Cloud," agreed the Ancestress.

"It is certainly strange that I have never yet noticed it on her, although she is so often in and out of our place," said Pao Yu.

"Yes, Cousin Precious Clasp has a good memory," remarked Taste of Spring innocently.

"Especially for matters which concern others," added Black Jade caustically.

Precious Clasp looked away and pretended not to have heard the remark. Pao Yu stuck the golden unicorn quickly into his breast pocket, at the same time looking around shyly to see if anyone had noticed him. He was afraid they might draw conclusions from the fact that he kept just this piece of jewelry after having heard that Little Cloud had a piece exactly the same. But nobody had noticed it, with the exception of Black Jade, and he thought he read approval and agreement from her nods and the expression on her face. In order to escape from his embarrassment he took out the jewel again and held it up to her.

"Pretty, isn't it? I have kept it for you," he said, smiling. "I'll have a string put on it, and then you will wear it!"

Black Jade tossed her head.

"I do not care for it in the least, thank you," she replied coldly.

"Very well, then I shall keep it myself," he said laughing, and hiding it away again.

After they had amused themselves for some hours with the entertainment offered on the temple stage, in the late afternoon the Ancestress quite unexpectedly announced that they would return to the town. When the news of her holiday trip had gone around among the circle of friends and relations, these dear people had hastened to send messengers with all possible marks of attention and with sacrificial gifts, and even to come themselves, as if they thought that it was a matter of a solemn temple ceremony. Now, this was not at all what the Princess had intended. She had only wanted to have some recreation and for once to have a really quiet carefree time with just a few favorite relatives. She was even displeased when Princess Chen turned up belatedly with the new wife of Chia Yung, and she did not receive the two unwelcome arrivals in a very friendly way. Fearing that she might be even more inundated in the following days, she cut short her sojourn and went home in ill-humor.

The enterprising Phoenix, who did not approve of this at all, tried to persuade her the next day to make another trip to the temple, but in vain. It happened that Pao Yu also did not want to go there. He was out of humor too because the Prior Chang had brought up the matter of marriage the day before, and pushed himself forward as a negotiator. Pao Yu did not need this unsolicited mediation; he had made his own choice long ago. He had no desire to appear before old Chang ever again, he declared angrily to his grandmother when he got home. No one could really understand why he was so much annoyed with the friendly old man. Moreover, Black Jade had caught cold on the way home and was a little feverish today. For these three reasons the Princess Ancestress remained firm and let Phoenix and the others go alone.

Pao Yu took Black Jade's slight cold so much to heart that he could not touch a bite the whole day. His anxiety impelled him to visit her constantly and to find out how she was.

"Why won't you go with the others to the plays at the temple instead of sticking at home and being bored?" asked Black Jade, wishing to put him to the test. Her question annoyed him greatly. If anyone else had asked it he would not have been specially upset, but Black Jade should surely know perfectly well that he was avoiding the temple solely on her account and because he wanted to evade the annoying marriage plans of the Prior.

"I see that it is useless for us to know one another. Very well, let us finish with it!" he replied, deeply disappointed. She made matters worse by adding sharply: "Yes, it is certainly useless. Unlike certain other persons, I have nothing at all about me which suits you."

He went up close to her, deeply agitated, and said to her in a voice which trembled: "With these words you have cold-heartedly spoken a curse of damnation over me."

"I do not know what you mean, and I do not understand your agitation at all," she replied. "Evidently you are worried lest the beautiful marriage plan of which the Prior spoke yesterday should fall through, and are making me suffer for your irritation."

Foolish girl! Foolish boy! Why were they shamming and saying the exact opposite of what was in the depths of their hearts? They had belonged to each other secretly long since. Why did they torture themselves and behave as if they were strangers and enemies? They were spiritually so close to each other. Why did they outwardly struggle away from each other? But alas, that has always been the way with lovers, and doubtless always will be.

At the words "beautiful marriage plan" Pao Yu completely lost his self-control. In a sudden fit of passion he tore the spirit stone from his neck and flung it fiercely to the ground.

"I will smash you up, accursed thing! Then I shall have peace at last!" he cried, beside himself. But the good stone was made of such sound material that the fall could not harm it; it did not bear the slightest trace of damage. When Pao Yu noticed this he turned round and began to look for some hard object with the help of which he could smash the stone.

Black Jade bemoaned his absurd action. "What has that deaf and dumb object done to you, that you ill-treat it so? Better ill-treat me!" she said.

Black Jade's waiting maids Cuckoo and Snowgoose had already witnessed many arguments between their mistress and Pao Yu, but no previous discussion had led to so much excitement as this today. In their dilemma they fetched Pearl along to help. The first thing Pearl did was to try to save the threatened spirit stone.

"Do not interfere!" ordered Pao Yu brusquely. "What is it to you if I destroy my property?"

Pearl was startled by the expression of his face as he uttered these words. This rage-distorted, livid face! She had never before seen him in such a condition. She tried gently to pacify him.

"Do you not think at all of your cousin's delicate health when you rage against her so unkindly?" she asked reproachfully, taking him gently by the hand. As if to confirm her words, just at that moment Black Jade's mental excitement caused her to vomit up the invalid soup she had taken shortly before. The maid Cuckoo rushed to help her, quickly holding a handkerchief to her mouth.

"You should not take the little quarrel so much to heart," she said to her. "How can you get well if you vomit up your medicine straight away? Do you not see how our little master suffers when you are ill?"

At the sight of the vomiting Pao Yu himself was overtaken with nausea, and bile rose from his stomach. At the same time he was overwhelmed with remorse for his violent behavior and with sympathy for his poor cousin. His anger had melted away; he was on the verge of tears. As he struggled convulsively on the one hand against his tears and the other against the inclination to vomit, he was such a picture of misery that Pearl was now moved to tears and began to sob loudly. And Cuckoo, who was fanning her mistress to cool her, was in her turn affected by Pearl, so a sobbing, and sniffing and sighing resounded from four directions at the same time, and the whole company was howling. Pearl was the first to pull herself together.

"Look at the silk tassel on your stone which your cousin made for you with her own hands!" she said to Pao Yu, forcing herself to smile. "Is it not enough of a reminder to you to forget your quarrel and be friends again?" Unfortunately, her well-meant words brought about an undesired effect. Forgetting her illness, Black Jade jumped up and tore from Pearl's hand the amulet with the five-colored cord and the tassel which she had made; she seized scissors and began wildly to cut up the tassel. Before Pearl and Cuckoo with united strength were able to wrest the cord from her, the tassel was already badly damaged with many cuts.

"Let it alone! After all, he cares nothing for what I took so much trouble to make for him! He can get someone else to make a new tassel for him," cried Black Jade, sobbing.

"Do not take it badly of her! I am to blame with my thoughtless chatter," pleaded Pearl apologetically to Pao Yu, as she gave him back the cord.

"Please cut it up as much as you like! I won't ever wear the unlucky thing again," declared Pao Yu coolly, and the quarrel would have flared up with new force if Pa Yu's mother and grandmother, who had been called to the rescue by his serving women, had not come between them just at the right moment. When they entered the two cousins became silent, while Pearl and Cuckoo furtively scolded one another, because each believed that the other had called the two *Tai tais* and thereby made the matter worse.

As the two cousins could not be got to utter a word, the ladies discharged their anger on Pearl and Cuckoo and reproached them furiously for not having looked after their master and mistress better and been able to prevent the quarrel. Finally, the Ancestress took Pao Yu by the hand and led him away with her.

The following day, the third of the fifth month, Cousin Hsueh Pan's birthday was celebrated. In his honor a great family banquet and a theatrical performance were given. All the relatives assembled; only Pao Yu and Black Jade were missing. After the happenings of yesterday they were not in the humor to attend a banquet or a theatrical performance. They both excused their absence on the plea of being ill. In reality there was nothing wrong with Pao Yu, and Black Jade was already recovered from her slight cold. The Ancestress had hoped that the two of them would be diverted by the feast and the theatricals and forget their resentments. When the grandson and granddaughter did not appear as expected she thought with annoyance: "What crime have I committed in my former existence that I am being punished with these two bad-tempered grandchildren? Scarcely a day passes that they do not cause me annoyance and agitation. If they would only wait until my eyes are closed and I have drawn my last breath, then, as far as I am concerned, they may quarrel and argue as much as they like!" She stopped and wiped a few bitter tears from her eyes. The news that the Ancestress had shed tears on their account at table moved Black Jade and Pao Yu and caused them to relent somewhat. But still, they preferred to avoid each other. The one sat in her Bamboo Hermitage and sobbed her sorrow to the wind; the other sat in his Begonia Courtyard and sighed his grief up to the moon. Although separated physically, they were together at heart. On the one side Pearl urgently exhorted Pao Yu to make it up again.

"Have you not over and over made peace when there were quarrels among the servants?" she asked. "And today you yourself cannot manage to calm a little girl's heart! The day after tomorrow, the day of the Dragon Boat Festival, are you going to persist in your waywardness and spoil the festival for the old *Tai tai?* Give in and beg your cousin's pardon, so that the quarrel may have an end!"

On the other side the waiting maid Cuckoo lectured Black Jade: "You should not have been so furious. You know his tender spot better than others do. After all, it's not the first time that he has got into a state on account of the stone."

"What do you mean by 'furious'? It seems to me that you are taking sides against me," remarked Black Jade irritably.

"Why did you have to vent your anger over the tassel? By that you incurred seven-tenths of the blame. He had such good intentions towards you, but you grieve him with your exaggerated suspicions."

Black Jade was just going to reply when there was a knock at the outer gate.

"The young master!" shouted Cuckoo joyfully when she had peeped out. "He must be coming to apologize to you."

"Do not let him in on any account!"

"Do you want to do him harm again? We cannot possibly leave him standing waiting in the heat of the sun!"

And already she had hurried out. She opened the gate and let Pao Yu in.

"So there you are! I thought you would never find the way to our door again!" she said jokingly.

"And why not? Why should one take everything so tragically!" he replied, falling in with her lighthearted tone. "And if I were dead, my spirit would come to visit your little mistress not once but a hundred times a day. How is she today?"

"Physically, she is well, but her heart is not yet quite calm and in order."

"I can well believe that," he said smiling, as he walked into the living room. He found Black Jade lying on the divan crying again.

"Are you quite well again, *Mei mei?*" he asked kindly. She wiped away her tears, but remained silent. He sat down on the edge of the couch and continued brightly: "I know you are not angry with me at all. But if I am never seen with you, the others may think that we have quarrelled and that you are really angry with me, and then they would interfere and want to lecture us. I think we could spare ourselves this annoying interference from outsiders. If you have anything against me, blame me, quarrel with me, hit me! Only do not ignore me!"

During his speech he had used the terms "dearest *Mei mei*" and "best *Mei mei*" at least a dozen times. From the remark that other people need not interfere in their affairs, Black Jade understood that he felt specially near and intimate with her. This filled her with secret joy and unsealed her lips.

"You need not come here at all. You only want to annoy me. I at any rate will take care not to come too near you. The best thing is for me to go away altogether," she said, still seemingly quite irreconcilable. But he did not let himself be intimidated.

"Where will you go, then?" he asked blithely.

"Home."

"I'll go with you."

"And what if I die soon?"

"Then I will become a monk."

"Indeed? You used to declare that you also would die in that case. One can see from that that your talk isn't to be taken at all seriously. Besides, you have other cousins. Will you become a monk every time one of them dies? If so, you will have to multiply yourself. What if I tell them of your praiseworthy intention?"

He realized that his statement had been rather silly. He thought of Precious Clasp and blushed. What a good thing it was that no one else was present! There was a long, embarrassed pause in the conversation. At last she tapped him lightly in a significant way on the forehead with her finger.

"You . . ." she began, but could not continue. Instead, she took out her handkerchief and wiped her eyes. His eyes became tearful too, and as he had forgotten his handkerchief he passed his silk sleeve over the moist lids. She noticed it and without a word handed him one of her own handkerchiefs. Touched by this service of love, he clasped her hand tenderly and said: "Enough of tears! My five entrails are already torn asunder from all this howling. Come, let us go to the old *Tai tai* together."

Black Jade pushed his hand away.

"Leave off this coarse caressing! You are growing older every day. When will you learn to behave yourself at last?"

The voice of Phoenix was heard outside. Startled, the two cousins separated hurriedly.

"Now, are you friends again?" asked Phoenix, laughing. "The old *Tai tai* has been grieving up to the heights of heaven about you. She sent me here to see if everything is all right. At first I did not want to come, and I said to her that by the end of three days you would have made it up yourselves, but she got angry at that and gave me a great scolding. And so I am here. Why are you two not to be seen? What has happened to you again? Must you quarrel every three days? The older you grow the more you fly into passions like children. And now come to the old *Tai tai* with me to assure her that all is well."

She took Black Jade by the hand and drew her out with her. Black Jade turned round and called for her waiting maids, but both maids had disappeared.

"Why do you need them? My maids are at your disposal, but let us not delay!" urged Phoenix and dragged the resisting Black Jade with her. Pao Yu followed behind, and so all three arrived at the home of the Ancestress.

"Now, was I not right?" said Phoenix cheerfully. "I did not have to interfere at all; they had already made it up themselves. They had asked each other's pardon and were sitting together quite peacefully, chatting and joking and affectionately clawing each other like an eagle and a female hawk sitting on the same hunting ring."

The Ancestress and all present had to laugh heartily at the odd comparison. Black Jade sat down by the side of the Ancestress; she felt rather embarrassed by Cousin Precious Clasp's presence and did not open her mouth. Pao Yu apologized to Precious Clasp for having been unable to make his birthday kowtow to her brother and bring a present, owing to not being well, but he would make up for the omission later. Then he wanted to know why she was not at the theatrical performance.

"I saw two pieces, and then I could not endure the heat any longer, so I sneaked off," replied Precious Clasp.

Pao Yu wanted to make some reply. Involuntarily, his attention was caught by Precious Clasp's plump white arm, which he had recently seen when she took off a gold bangle for him to look at more closely. And it came into his mind how Precious Clasp generally went by the nickname of "Courtesan Yang," because that celebrated Imperial courtesan of the T'ang dynasty is the only plump lady the Chinese gallery of famous beauties has to show. So, in order to say something, he remarked jocularly: "I am not surprised that people always compare you with the Courtesan Yang, for she also was somewhat plump and sensitive to heat."

His remark greatly annoyed Precious Clasp. She got red and sought for a long time for a suitable reply. At last she gave two short dry laughs and remarked derisively: "If I am so very like the Courtesan Yang, it is really a pity that I lack the suitable cousin, a second Yang Chung. He was certainly a fine fellow!"

It was painful to Pao Yu to have once more laid himself open to correction by a cousin on account of a thoughtless remark, and this time, moreover, before everyone, whereas Black Jade had only corrected him when they were alone just now. Black Jade, who had been secretly pleased at the apt if somewhat crude *faux pas* which he had just perpetrated at the expense of Precious Clasp, and was sorry to see him writhing with embarrassment, decided to come to his help.

"Which play have you seen, then?" she asked turning with a smile to Precious Clasp.

"It was called 'The Tyrant Li Kwei Abuses Sung Chiang and Later Admits His Injustice' or something like that," replied Precious Clasp coolly.

"You are so well versed otherwise in ancient and modern literature and yet you do not know the short popular title of this piece," continued Black Jade, derisively. "As everyone knows, it is called simply 'A Visit of Petition with the Rod.' "

"Yes, very well, let it be 'A Visit of Petition with the Rod'! You, of course, are so well educated and so learned that you must know it too. I really did not know anything until now about a visit of that kind," replied Precious Clasp sharply, and she noted with satisfaction the embarrassment which the sudden blushes on the faces of Pao Yu and Black Jade distinctly betrayed. Her stab had hit the mark. Of those present, a fourth person had understood the import of Precious Clasp's words, and that was Phoenix; and she hastened to clear the uneasy atmosphere with a pleasant joke.

"Is anyone here chewing green ginger on account of the heat?" she asked unexpectedly.

Everyone answered the cryptic question in the negative.

"Indeed? I just thought there might be, there is such a sharp and biting smell here," she said, pretending surprise and making a comic

face. Precious Clasp burst out laughing, and the others laughed with her, although most of them did not know why. The tension had been broken, and the company dispersed in merry mood. When Precious Clasp had gone off with Phoenix, Black Jade remarked with a smile to Pao Yu: "Now are you convinced that other people can have wickeder tongues than I? Compared with them I am positively shy and harmless!"

He found the one just as bad as the other, so he left Black Jade standing there and ran off.

CHAPTER 23

A lost unicorn amulet causes Little Cloud to expose her bare head to the fierce sun. Gold Ring cannot get over the insult she suffers and seeks the death of honor.

ON THE FOLLOWING DAY AFTER THE MIDDAY MEAL IN THE RESIDENCE of the Ancestress, when everybody, employer and servant alike, was taking a midday rest on account of the stupefying heat, and even the birds in the trees and bushes were silent with exhaustion, Pao Yu strode slowly through the back gardens and grounds of the western palace, his hands behind his back. After walking through the western corridor pavilion he came past the self-contained dwelling of Phoenix and on to the home of his mother. Here also the noonday silence reigned over all. Passing by several maids who were drowsing over their needlework, he arrived at the living room of the *Tai tai*. She was lying asleep on a divan of matting. The waiting maid Gold Ring was leaning against the end of the divan, with her legs stretched out limply, dozing.

Pao Yu slipped quietly up to her and plucked at her earring. "Are you so tired?" he whispered. Gold Ring blinked at him sleepily, pointed to the door with a smile, and shut her eyes again. But Pao Yu did not move from her side. When he had furtively ascertained that the *Tai tai* was really asleep, he pulled out of his belt pouch a tube of damp, sticky, perfumed cinnamon paste, squeezed out a little ball, and pushed it between the maid's lips. She liked it and swallowed it down without opening her eyes. He took hold of her hand.

"Look here, shall I ask the *Tai tai* to give you to me?" he asked, quietly. She remained silent.

"As soon as the *Tai tai* wakes up, I shall ask her for you," he continued. Gold Ring opened her eyes and looked at him, smiling.

"You are in a mighty hurry! What about having Lamb's Fleece? If you go into the little eastern garden you can take her by surprise with Master Chia Huan."

"They may enjoy themselves for all I care. I want you!" He had scarcely finished speaking when the *Tai tai* suddenly stood up and dealt the waiting maid a vigorous slap on the face.

"Abandoned creature! I shall just show you! Trying to seduce my son!" she scolded.

Pao Yu had flown out like a streak of smoke the instant the *Tai tai* had stirred. While Gold Ring rubbed her burning cheek in bewilderment, not daring to open her mouth, several waiting maids and serving women came rushing in, ready to serve. The *Tai tai* turned to Nephrite Bangle, the younger sister of the girl whom she had just rebuked. "Tell your mother that she is to take your sister out of the house this very day!" she said. Gold Ring threw herself on her knees and with tears and kowtows implored her enraged mistress to be merciful.

"Hit me, beat me, but do not turn me out!" she implored. "I have already been serving you honorably for ten years. I could not survive the shame of being driven away in the end!" But the *Tai tai*, who was usually so kindhearted, and had never been in the habit of beating her maids, would not be softened this time, and that very day poor Gold Ring had to leave the house in disgrace.

The next day, the fifth of the fifth month, the Dragon Boat Festival was celebrated. Reeds and wormwood were placed over the doors, and everyone wore amulets and magic charms and spells. Madame Cheng gave a family banquet at midday, but nobody was in a really festive mood. Madame Cheng was still out of humor on account of the unpleasant incident of yesterday when she had caught Pao Yu with Gold Ring, and she ignored Pao Yu intentionally. Phoenix, who had been told of the matter by Madame Cheng the evening before, also showed her displeasure and, contrary to her usual manner, was neither talkative nor inclined to laugh. Pao Yu was still suffering from the effect of the painful snubbing to which his cousins Precious Clasp and Black Jade had subjected him yesterday and did not venture to enter into conversation with them, and his bad-tempered silence infected them in turn. And so the banquet proved a most strained and tedious affair and everyone was relieved when it was over, but particularly Black Jade. At no time was she very keen on social gatherings. The more pleasure people find in merry parties, the more keenly do they feel their cold and forlorn state when these parties are over; hence it is best to avoid such social gatherings altogether. Thus she philosophized. She thought of the flowers, whose fading was all the more painful the more one had enjoyed their blooming, and she felt it would have been better had they never bloomed. And so her face was mournful when other people had happy faces, and vice versa.

Luckily, the arrival of Little Cloud next day brought life and merriment into the house. All the cousins were just assembled for the midday meal at the home of the Ancestress when she arrived. The young people jumped up to meet her and overwhelmed her with all sorts of questions. They had not seen her for a month, and of course there was plenty to relate.

"Will you not make your clothing more comfortable on account of the heat?" suggested the Ancestress.

Little Cloud stood up and took off the outer layer of her drapery. And with this the conversation turned to Little Cloud's cleverness in disguising herself.

"Don't you remember that time that she put on Pao Yu's coat and shoes and put his forehead band round her head?" asked Precious Clasp, laughing. "She looked so like him that when the old *Tai tai* came in and saw her back as she stood over there by the armchair, she was deceived and said to her: 'Pao Yu, come here and look at the crystal chains on the ceiling lamps! They are quite covered with smoke and dull the light.' But Little Cloud did not stir from the spot. And how we laughed!"

"Yes, she dresses up splendidly as a boy," added the Ancestress.

"That is nothing for her!" continued Black Jade. "Do you remember that snowy day in the first month of last year when she secretly put on the old *Tai tai's* new red monkey-hair cloak? It was so long and wide for her that she had to tie it up around her hips with two scarves. She played snowballs wildly around the garden with the maids, finally stumbling over a ditch and tumbling down full length in the snow, and everyone thought it was the old *Tai tai*."

The whole company broke out into merry laughter at the memory of this.

"Where on earth is Cousin Pao Yu?" inquired Little Cloud.

"Of course she is only thinking of the naughty companion of her youthful pranks; she has no thought for us others, she is incorrigible," said Precious Clasp jokingly. Thereupon Pao Yu came along and greeted the visitors joyfully.

"He has something nice for you!" Black Jade whispered to her.

"Something nice for me?" asked Little Cloud, incredulously.

"It is true, you can believe it," Pao Yu assured her. "How big you have grown, Little Cloud!"

"You should not call each other by your first names any more," his mother rebuked him. "The old *Tai tai* does not wish it. You are no longer the children you used to be."

"How is your Pearl?" asked Little Cloud.

"Very well. Thank you for your kind inquiry."

"I have brought her something."

She produced a little polished box, in which were four rings. In the red stone of each ring a name was engraved.

"You have given us presents like that in the past!" cried Black Jade, disappointed. "I was expecting you to produce some novelty, but you are not very ingenious. You certainly do not take much trouble to think up something new."

"Oh, please, but on the other hand the presents are very practical," said Little Cloud in self-defense. "For Pearl, Mandarin Duck, Gold Ring, and Little Ping—a suitable ring for each of them, so that one can distinguish them. Otherwise one can hardly tell all the waiting maids and other maids apart. Now, is it not practical?"

"Extremely practical!" they all agreed, amused.

"How she can talk! She's never at a loss for an answer," said Pao Yu, smiling.

"She has no conversation, but on the other hand she wears a golden unicorn like a certain other person," Black Jade interrupted sharply, and went out. Luckily, her remark had been understood only by Pao Yu and Precious Clasp; it was received by her with an understanding smile, and by him with an embarrassed one. Precious Clasp also got up and went to join Black Jade.

"Refresh yourself with a cup of tea and a snack, and rest a while! Then later you can greet your sister-in-law and play in the park," suggested the Ancestress to her granddaughter. Little Cloud took her advice, and after she had greeted Phoenix and the Widow Chu she set out for the Park of Delightful Vision escorted by a swarm of serving women and waiting maids. Shortly before reaching Pao Yu's dwelling, the Courtyard of Harmonious Red, she dismissed her retinue, with the exception of her own waiting maid, Blue Thread. As they came through the rose arbor she noticed something shining like gold lying on the ground. She told her maid to pick it up, and she examined it with curiosity. It was an amulet in the shape of a golden unicorn, very like her own, only somewhat bigger and more finely worked. She took it in her hand and observed it thoughtfully.

How odd! Where can this thing have come from? I have never noticed it on anyone in the house, she thought. While she was still pondering, Pao Yu appeared.

"Look here, why are you two standing there in the strong sun? Why not come in and greet Pearl?" he asked.

"We are just going to her," said Little Cloud, quickly hiding her find. The three of them went into the Begonia Courtyard together. Pearl was sitting on the steps in a shady corner in front of the entrance, leaning against the balustrade and fanning herself to get cool.

She stood up, went to greet Little Cloud and her maid, and led them by the hand into the house.

"I have been expecting you for a long time. I have something nice to show you," said Pao Yu to his cousin, beginning to rummage and search in his pockets.

"Have you put the thing away?" he asked, turning in embarrassment to Pearl, after searching for a long time.

"What thing do you mean?" asked Pearl.

"The gold unicorn amulet which I recently got as a present."

"You always carry it about with you. I have no idea where it is."

"Then I must have lost it outside. Come, help me to look for it!"

He was about to rush out to the park but Little Cloud held him back and showed him her find, with a smile.

"Is this it?"

He seized it with delight.

"You found it?"

"Oh, how can one be so careless! Luckily, it was only a trinket this time, but if you should lose your stone the next time, it might be a great misfortune."

"Oh, the loss of my stone would not trouble me at all. But this article, which you call a trifle, is irreplaceable; its loss would mean death to me."

Little Cloud bent blushing over the teacup which Pearl had passed to her. Then the conversation turned to other things. In the midst of the happy chattering a servant of Mr. Cheng's arrived and announced: "Master Yu Tsun from the Street of Blooming Prosperity has come to visit. The old master asks the young gentleman to come over to salute the guest."

Pao Yu's good humor was instantly over.

"Is it not enough if the old man receives him? Why must I be there?" he murmured ungraciously, while he slowly made himself ready for the visit.

"How can one loiter so long when the old gentleman calls one!" cried Little Cloud, dealing him a rap with her fan by way of encouragement.

"Ah, it is not my old governor who has expressed a wish to see me, but this Master Yu Tsun himself."

"It is all the more flattering for you when such a very distinguished gentleman shows interest in you. He will certainly use his influence for you. That can only be to your advantage."

"Pah! What do I care about patronage and knowing distinguished people? I am an average person and do not want anything more than to be a human being among other human beings."

"You are quite incorrigible! After all, you are growing up. Have you no special ambition? Are you not thinking at all of your future? If you want to pass your State examinations, you must seek the acquaintance of serious people and future ministers in good time. Their conversation is profitable to you, and their friendship will ensure you patronage later on. Being always in the company of girls will not get you on!"

"Would you be so kind as to go to your cousins' apartments, young lady! I would not wish that a serious person like you should be mortified by a sojourn in my unworthy dwelling," said Pao Yu, his tone suddenly grown gruff. Pearl surreptitiously plucked Little Cloud by the sleeve.

"He does not like anyone to bring up this subject," she said to her in a low voice. "Recently he simply ran away when Miss Precious Clasp began to speak of it. It was lucky that it was Miss Precious Clasp, for she did not take it badly. If it had been Miss Black Jade, oh, then there would have been a nice scene! She would not have looked at him again until he had admitted his wrong with all formality and had begged for pardon."

"She is not capable of such a lack of good taste, otherwise I would have broken with her long ago," interjected Pao Yu emphatically.

Just by chance Black Jade was a witness to his last remark. She knew that Little Cloud had set out for the Begonia Courtyard, she presumed that Pao Yu would show her the counterpart to her gold unicorn amulet and in doing so would introduce all kinds of affectionate allusions, as was his way, and she had therefore crept along secretly to listen for a bit under the window. She had just arrived in time to hear Little Cloud recommending him to cultivate the acquaintance of serious men. So when he declared emphatically that she, Black Jade, was not capable of such lack of good taste in conversation, she felt simultaneously moved by four sensations—joy, fear, pain, and regret. She was joyful at not being disappointed in his love and his noble-mindedness; she was frightened at his acknowledging his preference for her so openly before people; she thought with pain of how alone she was in the world since the death of her parents, and how she had no one to confide in regarding matters of the heart. And she had to sigh regretfully because she was wasting away with a malady which would not give her much time to wait, no matter how sure she might feel of his love. She was overcome with grief at the frightening presentiment that she might die too soon to experience the fulfillment of her wish. Her eyes filled with tears and she went away again slowly.

Meantime Pao Yu had finished dressing, and when he went into the park he came upon Black Jade and noticed traces of tears on her cheeks.

"Where are you going, *Mei mei?* You have been crying? Has anyone offended you?" he asked tenderly. Black Jade forced herself to smile. "Crying? I did not know it."

"But I still see the traces of tears!"

He raised his hand and tried to wipe a few damp spots on her cheek with his finger. She recoiled two steps.

"Do not trouble yourself! You are again ready to die, are you not?" she said, derisively.

"Why not?"

"It's nothing to me. But would it not be difficult to part from a certain gold unicorn amulet?"

"What do you mean by that? Do you want to drive me into a rage again?" he burst out hotly.

She saw that she had offended him.

"It was only my chatter," she said, quickly changing her tone. "But do not get so excited! The veins on your forehead are all swollen up with anger! And how you are perspiring!"

She went up close to him and wiped the perspiration from his face with her handkerchief. He submitted to it and looked at her fixedly for a long time.

"Be quite reassured!" he said at last.

"Reassured? About what?"

He gave a deep sigh.

"Are you pretending, or do you really not understand me? Can I have been so much deceived in you all the time that you do not guess my innermost thoughts? If that is so, our daily misunderstandings are not surprising."

"I really do not know what you mean by saying that I should be reassured."

"Dearest *Mei mei*, please do not pretend! You must know. You make your illness worse by your constant worrying."

His reference to her suffering condition hit her like a thunderbolt. How correctly he felt what she herself had realized shortly before with secret fear! She had so much more on her mind which she wanted to say, but she could not utter a word. The tears sprang to her eyes, and with a stifled "Oh" she turned away. He ran after her and took her by the hand.

"Dearest *Mei mei*, do stay for a while! I have something more to say to you."

"I know everything," she said gently, then freed herself and ran off.

He stood where he was and went on talking to himself as in a trance.

"Dearest *Mei mei,* up to now I have not dared to disclose to you what touches my heart to the core, but today I feel the courage in me, and I will speak, even if I have to pay for my impudence with my death. Do you know that I also am ill, ill on your account, and I will not get well again until you are well. Dreaming and waking, I am always thinking only of you. . . ."

"You must be completely possessed by wicked spirits! Hurry up! They are waiting for you!" He was brought back from his ecstasy by the voice of Pearl. Pearl had run after him to bring him the fan he had forgotten, and had been listening for quite a while with growing astonishment to his soliloquy. In his withdrawn state he had not noticed her approach.

"Ah, it's you!" he now burst out, startled, took the fan, and hurried off. Pearl looked after him for a while thoughtfully. It was clear to her that the confession of love which she had just heard could only refer to Black Jade. What would become of herself, Pearl, later on? While she stood there sunk in thought Precious Clasp came along.

"What is Cousin Pao Yu up to?" she called out to the maid. "I have just seen him all dressed up rushing to the park gate with long strides."

"The old Governor has sent for him."

"Oh, woe, no doubt another fatherly reprimand. The poor boy!"

"No, it is not that. He is to greet a guest."

"Is Little Cloud in there?"

"Yes."

"What is she doing?"

"Oh, we have just been chatting a bit."

"I am sorry for the poor girl. Things are not going very well at home. She admitted to me that she often sits up late at night doing needlework."

"Oh, I am sorry for that. And I, stupid thing, was just about to ask her for a new pair of hand-embroidered slippers. I was surprised that recently she sent me back half finished a piece of embroidery—a butterfly-patterned cloth—that she had promised to do for me. She excused herself, saying that she would finish it at her next visit here. Under these circumstances one cannot, of course, expect her to do any more needlework. It's a pity; now I must go without my slippers."

"It is not as bad as that. I shall make a pair for you."

"Really? Oh, that is fine; then I shall bring you the material this evening."

While they were chatting a serving woman came along gasping in the greatest excitement and called out to them: "Do you know that Gold Ring has jumped into the well and drowned herself!"

"But why?" asked Pearl, horrified.

"Just recently she was suddenly dismissed and sent home by the *Tai tai* Cheng, no one knows why. She could not get over it, and she sat about at home the whole day crying. Then she suddenly disappeared. Finally they found her body in the well when they were drawing water. They tried to bring her to life again, but it was too late."

"Why can she have drowned herself? It's strange!" said Precious Clasp thoughtfully, while Pearl shook her head in silence and wept. Precious Clasp went off at once to Aunt Cheng, to hear more details. She found the *Tai tai* alone, in tears. She sat down beside her without speaking.

"Where have you come from?" asked Aunt Cheng.

"From the park."

"Did you see your cousin Pao Yu?"

"Yes, at a distance. He was in visiting dress and seemed to be in a hurry."

"Have you heard that Gold Ring has drowned herself in the well?" continued Madame Cheng, with a deep sigh.

"I heard about it. Why did she do it?"

"She broke something in my room recently and I dismissed her in anger. I intended to take her back again in a few days. Who would have thought that she would take it to heart like that and immediately jump into the well! I am beside myself and am reproaching myself bitterly."

"You should not do that, dear Aunt," said Precious Clasp consolingly. "After all, you were always so good to her! She has certainly not taken her life on account of that. I believe it is more likely that she fell into the well by accident, but if she really threw herself in on account of such a trifle that would be such a foolish thing that one really should not feel sorry for her."

"It may be as you think. But in any case her death grieves me to the core."

"Do not take it so much to heart! Send her relatives a little indemnity! Then you will have done your duty and made restitution, and complied with the obligations of a mistress to her servant."

"I have already sent her family fifty taels. I really wanted to give her a beautiful new funeral robe and thought to take something from my daughter's wardrobe, but she has already worn all her dresses once. And to put a dress which has been worn on a corpse in a coffin is contrary to the Rites. There is nothing for me to do but to send for a tailor to come to the house."

"Why bother so much? Surely the money puts everything right?"

"No, the dead girl was particularly dear to me—almost like a daughter," said Aunt Cheng significantly, beginning to weep again.

"Very well, then, I shall help you out from my wardrobe. I have two dresses which I have hardly ever worn at all and can do without. The dead girl shall have them. She was my size and often wore my old clothes."

"That is very nice of you. But are you not afraid? You say you have already worn the two dresses yourself?"

"Oh, I disregard those superstitious rules," replied Precious Clasp merrily, jumping up. When she came back later to Aunt Cheng with the two dresses for the dead girl, she found Pao Yu in the room. He looked as if he had been crying. When she entered, mother and son suddenly stopped talking. Precious Clasp thought she knew to seven- or eight-tenths what they were talking about; she did not let it be noticed, however, and silently delivered the two dresses which Aunt Cheng later on presented to the mother of Gold Ring.

CHAPTER 24

The degenerate offspring experiences the pain of a paternal flogging.

AND SO MADAME CHENG GAVE TWO BURIAL ROBES TO GOLD RING'S mother, together with several buckles and rings, and also sent a contingent of bonzes to her house to celebrate a solemn requiem for the deceased at her expense.

At the news of Gold Ring's voluntary death Pao Yu felt all his five intestines torn with pain. He had to submit to a stern lecture from his mother. Then when Precious Clasp came in he went off quickly and wandered about his parents' estate aimlessly and quite distraught. As he walked about, sighing and thinking, with his eyes on the ground and his hands behind his back, without noticing the pathways or the surroundings, it happened that he ran into his father at the spirit wall in front of the large reception hall. Frightened, he stepped aside and waited in a humble attitude for his father to pass by.

"What on earth is the matter with you?" asked Mr. Cheng severely. "Just now, when Mr. Yu Tsun wanted to see you, you kept us waiting half the day for you. When you showed yourself at last, you sat there indifferent and apathetic and did not open your mouth. I observed that your depraved thoughts were somewhere else. And now you are running around with a mournful face. What does it mean?"

Normally Pao Yu was not at a loss for a suitable excuse, but this time he could think of nothing. The tragic fate of poor Gold Ring touched him so deeply that everything else was unimportant to him. He would have liked best to follow her to her death. Annoyed at his silence and his confused behavior, Mr. Cheng was about to storm at him angrily when a servant appeared and announced that a representative of the Prince of Chung Shun wished to speak to him.

"Take him into the reception hall!" he ordered his servant, at the same time asking himself, much bewildered, why the Prince, whom he hardly knew, should have sent a messenger to him. He left Pao Yu standing there and hurried away to salute the visitor. He was the Palace Superintendent of the Prince of Chung Shun.

"I come at the order of my princely master," began the Superintendent very formally. "The Prince requests your intervention in a certain matter, the settlement of which is very important to him."

Chia Cheng stood up politely.

"May I ask you kindly to inform me of the princely wishes? I shall not fail . . ."

"For many days my master has missed a young actor named Chi, who plays the part of youthful heroines, and whom he values very much and is accustomed to seeing every day in the palace. All investigations as to his whereabouts have been without result, but in eight of ten houses where the boy has been inquired for he received the same information, namely, that the young actor has recently been a close friend of your esteemed son, the one who was born with a jewel in his mouth. As I did not wish to intrude into your esteemed house without ceremony, I first of all made my report to the Prince. The Prince declared that he would be willing to give up any other actor to your son, but this young Chi, whom he finds pleasing in every way, and who is infinitely important to him, he cannot do without in any circumstances. He therefore politely and urgently requests you to influence your esteemed son to relinquish young Chi. It would contribute greatly to placating my princely lord and relieve me personally of the painful task of undertaking further urgent measures, if you would graciously comply with his request," concluded the Superintendent with a polite bow.

Mr. Cheng sent for Pao Yu without delay.

"Confounded scamp!" he raged at the completely unsuspecting boy. "Is it not enough that you are lazy at home and learn nothing? Must you also do outside the house things which outrage heaven? What do you mean by seducing this young Chi and taking him away from his illustrious master and patron the Prince of Chung Shun? Now the misfortune has come, and I have to pay for your infamous deeds!"

"But I know nothing of all this! I do not know this Chi at all," protested Pao Yu, frightened.

"Do not sham, young man!" remarked the Superintendent with a frosty smile. "If you have not got him hidden in your quarters, at least you know where he is. It would be better for all of us if you would open your mouth."

"I really know nothing," repeated Pao Yu. "I have been falsely accused."

"Oh, indeed? Perhaps I may ask, then, how young Chi's red silk handkerchief comes to be in your belt, young man?"

Pao Yu felt his ears humming and buzzing. To be sure, he had not thought of this piece of evidence. If the Superintendent really knew of such intimacies, then his denials would be of no avail.

"Since you are informed of such small details, esteemed sir, then I am surprised that the fact of young Chi's recent change of address has escaped you," he said as coolly as possible. "As far as I have heard, he has recently settled in the eastern suburb, twenty li distant from the city walls. The district is called 'Red Sandalwood Stronghold' or something like that; he is said to have bought a house and a piece of land there."

The Superintendent's face brightened.

"I shall lose no time but shall go there at once to satisfy myself. If your information tallies, my errand is executed. Otherwise I shall unfortunately have to trouble you again."

Having said this, he took leave. Mr. Cheng accompanied him to the gate, not without having first said sternly to his son: "Do not stir from here! I have something to ask you afterwards."

At the gate Mr. Cheng met his son Chia Huan, who was running along in remarkable haste with several servants.

"Hi! Where are you going? And what is all the hurry for? You are running like a frightened horse!" Mr. Cheng called out to him.

"I have just come from the well in which our poor waiting maid has drowned herself. I have seen the corpse, the swollen head, the inflated limbs! Ugh! Such a terrible sight! I have run as quickly as I could, just to get away at once," said Chia Huan, shuddering with horror.

"What? A waiting maid has drowned herself? That is unheard of!" cried Mr. Cheng, dumfounded. "In my house the servants have always been treated justly and with kindness. Since the days of my illustrious ancestors such a thing has not occurred. Presumably the majordomos have misused their authority in my absence. I cannot, after all, look after everything myself. But on no account must the news of the regrettable occurrence get to the town. The reputation and honor of my house are at stake. And now tell me this! What do you know about how it all happened?" And he turned sternly to Chia Huan. The boy fell upon his knees.

"Do not get excited, Father! No one but the *Tai tai* and her intimates know about the story," he began. "As the *Tai tai* told me . . .

He stopped and looked furtively around him. The servants who were near by understood and stepped back to a proper distance.

240

"Recently, when the *Tai tai* was asleep, brother Pao Yu tried to seduce the waiting maid Gold Ring," he continued in a whisper. "The *Tai tai* punished her by hitting her, and then dismissed her. Gold Ring drowned herself through grief because of this."

His words caused Chia Cheng's face to turn suddenly pale. His complexion became yellowish, like gold paper.

"Stir yourselves! Seize the boy!" he ordered his servants, and rushed into the library. There several friends of the family were waiting for him.

"If it ever again occurs to any of you to admonish me and persuade me to leniency, I shall tear out one by one the last hairs which I still have got despite trouble and annoyance, give over to this worthy son of mine my cap of office, my belt, and all my possessions, and go into a monastery!" he shouted. "Then I shall at last have peace and shall no longer be shamed before my ancestors by my unruly offspring."

The friends of the family, realizing that his outburst of rage was directed against Pao Yu, let their tongues hang out of their mouths with fright, and deemed it wise to get out of the way as quickly as possible. Groaning and snorting, Chia Cheng sank into an armchair.

"Bring the boy here to me! Tie him with a rope! Fetch me the heavy cudgel! Lock the doors! Let nobody, under pain of death, dare to run to the women's apartments and chatter about what is going on here!" Thus ran his various orders, in quick succession. Several of the servants obediently went to the great hall to fetch Pao Yu.

When his father had ordered him, shortly before, not to stir from where he was, Pao Yu had already realized the calamity that threatened him; but he certainly could not have guessed that in the interval his position had been made very much worse by his half brother's talebearing. Tortured with painful uncertainty, he had been pacing restlessly up and down the great hall. If only he could let his mother or his grandmother know! But not one of the servants came within hailing distance. Even his personal servant, Ming Yen, was not to be seen. At last he saw an old serving woman crossing the courtyard. As overjoyed as if he had discovered a precious treasure, he dashed out and stopped her.

"Quick! Run to the *Tai tai* or to the old *Tai tai* and tell them that the old Governor is going to beat me to death! But hurry up! I'm in terrible danger!" he said to her.

Unfortunately, the old serving woman was hard of hearing and only understood a fraction of what he was blurting out in the greatest agitation, and even that fraction she took up wrongly. Instead of *Yao Chin*, "greatest danger," she thought he was saying *tiao chin*, "jumped into the well."

"Let her jump into the well! You need not worry yourself on that account, young gentleman!" she said with a grin. At this Pao Yu realized that he was speaking to a deaf person. He felt desperate.

"Run and call my servant here!" he roared at her.

"Why do you still excite yourself? The family of the dead girl have got a nice lump of hush money, and that settled the matter," came the delicate answer. Pao Yu broke into a frenzy. He stamped his feet and clutched at the air with his hands as if he were seeking some invisible support to cling on to. But his excitement was in vain. Now he saw his father's servants appearing in the distance. He had to get back to the hall as quickly as possible. The servants took him between them and brought him to Chia Cheng's library. The distorted features, the rolling eyeballs, the red eyelids of his father boded ill.

Mr. Cheng wasted no words with a lengthy examination. He limited himself to an angrily snorted greeting of "Loafer! Tramp! Seducer!" and then came the brief order. "Beat him to death!"

And soon they had him strapped to a bench and began to flog him with the heavy bamboo stick. Mr. Cheng seemed to think that the servant whom he ordered to administer the beating was doing it far too mildly. He stamped his feet in rage, grabbed the stick from the servant's hand, and began with all his strength to beat the victim of his paternal anger, until he was out of breath and could continue no longer.

The pampered Pao Yu had never in his life suffered such an experience. His first roars of pain soon changed to a dull rattling in his throat as his breathing became weaker, and after a short while no further sound escaped his lips. He had lost consciousness. In vain the servants and some friends of the family who had remained behind, seized with compassion, tried to intercede for him; Mr. Cheng refused to be moved.

"Ask him what he has done, and then judge for yourselves whether leniency is called for here," he cried, beside himself. "Formerly I have allowed myself—too often, alas—to be persuaded to leniency and consideration. Now you can see what that has led to. If I let him off again this time, the next thing may be that he will become his own father's murderer!"

The bystanders stood in dumfounded silence and sent a message secretly to the women's quarters. Very soon Madame Cheng appeared on the scene. Upon hearing the alarming news she had rushed along in great haste, accompanied by only one waiting maid. When she arrived Mr. Cheng was about to continue the flogging which he had interrupted only to pause for breath. Her appearance acted upon him like oil on fire, and his blows now fell if possible more rapidly and heavily than before. Terrified, the *Tai tai* tried to throw herself in front of him.

"Get away from me!" he shouted furiously. "The measure is full. Today he has to die!"

"Let him die! But do you think at all of the old *Tai tai?*" wailed his wife. "As it is, she is not well on account of the hot weather. The death of her grandson will break her up completely!"

"Do not worry! In begetting and bringing up this degenerate whelp I have failed sufficiently in my duty. I have always, alas, allowed myself to be talked around by you in the past and have refrained from giving him this long-deserved chastisement. But today that is at an end. It is better that the young cur should breathe his last now than that he should live to do still greater harm later on."

With these words he rushed on the boy, who was lying there as if dead, intending to strangle him with the free end of the rope with which he was bound to the bench.

Madame Cheng flung herself into his arms screaming:

"If you are really going to kill him, take the rope and strangle me first. I am past fifty, and he is my only son. I cannot hope for another. Let me die with him, so that in the Realm of Shades I shall at least have the support and succor of a son!"

And she threw herself, sobbing, over Pao Yu's body.

Chia Cheng sank with a sigh into the armchair and covered his eyes to hide his emotion. As the mother clasped the body of her son she perceived with horror that his green silk shirt was soaked through with blood. She drew out her handkerchief and tenderly wiped the bloody scars which covered his thighs and his whole bottom. This made her think of Chia Chu, her first-born, who had died young, and in a loud lament she cried: "My son Chia Chu, I would give up a hundred other sons to have you still alive. Why did you leave me?"

In the meantime the news of the incident had spread to the remaining women's quarters, and now the other ladies hurried along one after the other—the Widow Chu, Phoenix, and the three Spring girls. At the mention of her deceased husband, naturally the Widow Chu could not refrain from breaking into loud lamentations on her part. This dual lament of the women was too much for Chia Cheng, and he also broke into violent sobbing. While tears were thus flowing in three directions, a maidservant appeared and announced: "The old *Tai tai* is coming."

The shuffling of numerous feet was heard outside, and then through the open window came the voice of the old *Tai tai:* "Let him kill me first and then the boy; that will at least be a clean sweep!"

Chia Cheng rushed out, greatly agitated, to receive on the threshold the old lady who now entered, gasping and out of breath, supported by two maids and accompanied by a swarm of serving women.

"What drives my mother out into the open air in this heat? Why does she not order her son to come to her, if she has something to say to him?" asked Chia Cheng, bowing politely. The old *Tai tai* stood still, paused to take breath, and then said with an effort: "I would have had something to say, but as a good son has, alas, been denied to me, I do not really know to whom I could speak my mind."

Chia Cheng quickly fell to his knees.

"Your reproach grieves me beyond words, Mother. I have only given my son a lesson. I owed this to the memory of my glorious ancestors."

"Indeed? To beat to death—you call that a lesson? Did your father ever give you such lessons?"

She could not continue to speak; she was weeping too much.

"Mother, do not take it so much to heart! I admit that I have let myself be carried away by anger; I shall never beat him again," he said, trying to calm her. The Ancestress laughed dryly.

"Oh, please, do not restrain yourself on my account! After all, he is your son. Ill-treat him as much as you wish! But really, you cannot blame us women if we prefer to leave the house under these circumstances. It is better for the sake of peace."

She gave instructions to her retinue to get the large sedan chair ready.

"I wish to travel to the southern capital at once with the *Tai tai* and my grandson," she declared briefly and definitely.

"But, Mother, surely you will not do that! I am beside myself!" cried Chia Cheng, astounded.

"It is better that I go; then you can have quietness and need not let yourself be talked out of things again by anyone," persisted the Ancestress. And once more she ordered her retinue to pack quickly and get ready the carriages and the sedan chairs. Chia Cheng hit his forehead on the ground despairingly and acknowledged his guilt, but the Ancestress took no notice of him. Her grandson's pitiable condition absorbed all her attention, and she broke out again into violent sobbing. Madame Cheng and Phoenix, by their united efforts, succeeded gradually in calming her. Now several waiting maids and serving women began trying to help Pao Yu to his feet.

"You stupid creatures, kindly open your eyes!" scolded Phoenix. "Do you not see that he cannot walk in that condition? Fetch a stretcher quickly!"

Thereupon, they carried Pao Yu on the stretcher to the home of the Ancestress. Chia Cheng joined the procession of women who accompanied him. On the way he had to listen to the ceaseless laments of his wife, which cut him to the soul and finally cooled the remnants of his anger. He realized that he had gone too far and endeavored once more to talk the Ancestress round in a conciliatory way.

"You should have thought of me before you maltreated the poor boy so wickedly! You are a bad son. What do you want here? Do you want the further pleasure of looking on at his death? Get out of here! I do not wish to see you!" she rebuffed him indignantly.

Chia Cheng slipped away disconcerted. In the meantime Aunt Hsueh, Precious Clasp, Lotus, Black Jade, and Pearl had also arrived on the scene. They all pressed around the ill-treated boy and helped to wash his burning wounds and to cool him with their fans. But Pearl was longing to find out the reason for the ill-treatment, so she went out and searched for Pao Yu's servant, Ming Yen.

"Why did you not inform the *Tai tai* and the old *Tai tai* in time?" she asked him reproachfully.

"I just happened not to be with him and only heard about it when they were in the middle of the flogging," declared Ming Yen. "There were two reasons for the chastisement—the matter of the actor Chi, and the suicide of Gold Ring."

"How did the old master get to know of these things?"

"Hsueh Pan was jealous of young Chi and out of envy spread the story of his association with Pao Yu through the town, and so the fire ran on until it reached the old master. And as for the matter of Gold Ring, apparently Chia Huan has been gossiping. At least I heard that just before the flogging he ran across the old gentleman and privately whispered something in his ear."

Pearl kept these things in her heart and returned to the bedside of her master to help to nurse him devotedly.

CHAPTER 25

The Begonia Club meets in the Hermitage of Clear Autumn Weather.
The Princess Ancestress entertains the godmother from the country in
the Park of Delightful Vision.

THE TOUCHING SYMPATHY OF HIS TWO COUSINS PRECIOUS CLASP AND Black Jade afforded Pao Yu comfort in his sufferings. Precious Clasp herself brought him a healing powder which Pearl had to dissolve in wine and spread on the injured places. And when, towards evening, he woke up, still quietly weeping, out of a light sleep, he found Black Jade sitting by his bed and had to promise her that he would get well. She had many other things on her heart which she wanted to say to him, but unfortunately their short time together was disturbed by the intrusion of Phoenix and Madame Cheng, before whom Black Jade quickly fled. Soon after she had gone Pao Yu dropped off to sleep once more. When he awoke again Pearl put before him the two bottles containing essence of olives and essence of roses which his devoted mother had left to strengthen him. Pao Yu drank the lightly perfumed drink with great relish; then he thought of Black Jade. He felt a great longing for her and wanted to see her without fail, but Pearl's presence would be inconvenient. Accordingly, under the pretext of wanting her to fetch a certain book from Precious Clasp, he first got Pearl out of the way. Then he called the waiting maid, Bright Cloud. "Go to Miss Ling and see what she is doing!" he ordered her. "If she asks how I am, say I am getting on well."

"But I can't just go up to her like that without any excuse," objected Bright Cloud. "Don't you have any message for her?"

"I cannot think of any."

"Well, just let me ask her for something or take something to her. Then the matter will be correct."

Pao Yu thought it over. Then he reached out for two handkerchiefs which were lying near by and gave them to her.

"Here. Take these two handkerchiefs to her in my name!"

"What will she do with these two handkerchiefs, which are no longer new? She will be angry and think that you want to make game of her," said Bright Cloud doubtfully.

"Do not worry about that! She will know well what to think about it," Pao Yu reassured her with a smile.

So Bright Cloud took the two handkerchiefs and ran to the Bamboo Hermitage. Black Jade was lying in complete darkness, without any lamp to light her. Bright Cloud was shown into the bedroom where she lay on her bed, sadly daydreaming.

"Who is that?" she asked.

"It is I, Bright Cloud."

"What do you want?"

"The young master sends you these two handkerchiefs."

What shall I do with them? thought Black Jade to herself, taken aback.

"Let him keep them or give them to someone else," she said aloud. "I have no need for new fancy handkerchiefs."

"They are not new ones, but used everyday ones."

Black Jade was still more puzzled; she wondered for a while what the reason of this strange gift might be, and then suddenly it became clear to her.

"That is all right; leave them here!" she said quietly.

Bright Cloud put them down and went away. When she had gone Black Jade ordered the lamp to be lighted, ground some Chinese ink on the ink-stone, dipped her brush in it, and wrote on the plain handkerchiefs three improvised quatrains in which she expressed without any shyness or hesitation the secret longings of her lonely maidenhood.

246

In the ardor of composition and writing she was overcome with feverish excitement, her face burned, and her whole body glowed. She got up and stood before the mirror, pushed aside the cotton curtain, and looked at herself in the shining glass. The peach-blossom color of her cheeks frightened her. Was that only due to her illness? She lay down again, put out the lamp, and went to sleep, but her thoughts still remained on the two handkerchiefs which she held clasped in her hand.

The following morning, urged by longing, Black Jade went off very early to the Begonia Courtyard and, hidden by branches and bushes, watched from a distance the coming and going there. She saw the three Spring girls and the Widow Chu coming to pay a visit, and later on, accompanied by a large retinue, the *Tai tai,* and the old *Tai tai* leaning on the arm of Phoenix; and after them Princess Shieh, and Aunt Hsueh with Cousin Precious Clasp. And she thought to herself how lucky Pao Yu was to have so many relatives to concern themselves about him, and she pitied herself, the poor forlorn orphan. Thus she stood for a long time, spying and watching from her secret observation post, until she was tracked down by her maid Cuckoo.

"Come and drink your medicine, Mistress, and do not let it get cold!" the maid warned her.

"Ah, there's time enough for that. Anyway, it can't make any difference to you whether I take my medicine or not."

"But you must get rid of your bad cough! To be sure, we are in the fifth month and the middle of the hot summer, but in spite of that you must beware of catching cold. To stand this way on the wet grass early in the morning is really unwise. Come and lie down for a while!"

Black Jade reluctantly took her advice and, leaning on her arm, returned slowly to the Bamboo Hermitage. As she walked through the front garden, where the bamboo branches cast dappled shadows, now dark, now pale, on the green mossy ground, she thought involuntarily of that passage in "The Play of the Western Pavilion" which describes a hidden little glade with its dove-speckled, bluish moss. And with a sigh she compared herself to the heroine of the famous play. She also was unhappy, it is true, but at least she had a mother and a little brother by her side; while I, unfortunate one, have neither. Thus she thought sorrowfully to herself. The noise of her parrot in the veranda, which came fluttering onto her shoulder with a hurried flapping of its wings and joyful shrieks, startled her out of her meditation. "Be quiet! You frighten me to death and fill my hair with dust!" she said to him.

The parrot flew back gracefully to its perch and shrieked: "Raise the curtain quickly, Snowgoose, the young lady is here!"

Black Jade stood in front of him, tapped his perch, and asked: "Have you had your proper food and drink today?"

The parrot gave a deep sigh, in just the tone that it had learned from listening to its mistress, and then recited:

> "I bury the flower petals today;
> They laugh at my foolishness.
> When I die,
> Who will tend my tomb?"

The maid Cuckoo had to laugh out loud.

"Just listen, how well he has memorized your own words, Mistress!" she cried.

Black Jade made her take the perch down and hang it on a nail in front of the moon window. Then she went inside, took her medicine, and sat down by the window. She sat there for a long time, staring at the cooling shadows which fell into the room from the bamboo branches outside, dappling the floor and the wicker furniture with bluish green spots, and gave herself up to her melancholy thoughts. At intervals, for a change and to pass the time, she conversed with her parrot, baiting him and teasing him, and ardently repeating this or that favorite verse to him.

Thanks to the loving care which surrounded him on all sides, Pao Yu's recovery made rapid progress. In order to protect him from further ill-treatment by his father, his grandmother gave instructions that she was to be informed at once every time that Mr. Cheng wished to see his offspring, whether it was to examine him or to present him to prominent guests. Then the servants were to give the message in her name to Mr. Cheng that Pao Yu was still in urgent need of care and not fit for visiting. Pao Yu rejoiced when he heard of his grandmother's instructions, for these formal conversations with serious men, these solemn formalities, and this troublesome, hurried dressing up in his best clothes were exceedingly repugnant to him. And the fact that he was to be free for the present from the dreaded daily morning and evening visits to the stern old gentleman relieved him immensely.

Every morning now he only had to go to his mother and his grandmother to inquire dutifully after their health. Then, for the remainder of the day, he could do and behave as he wished. He was able to follow his favorite pursuits and his amorous inclinations and enjoy himself with cousins and waiting maids to his heart's content. Now and then Precious Clasp or Black Jade felt obliged to rebuke him for his frivolous manner of living, and to exhort him to earnest endeavor. But then he would get angry and reply: "It is a pity that even the pure, merry atmosphere of the girls' apartments in this unhappy house is spoiled by the dirty, ill-humored gossip of men! I do not want to hear anything of tiresome words such as office, and dignity, and State, and fame! These boring things were invented long ago by place-hunters and pedants in

248

order to keep stupid, uncouth men in their place. What have gentle, innocent girls like you to do with such dull things? It is an ingratitude and an offense against kind nature, which has made you for more beautiful purposes, if you occupy yourselves with these nasty things."

In the end none of his cousins or waiting maids dared to come to him with admonitions or suggestions any more. It was just this that he esteemed so highly in Black Jade—that she had always tactfully spared him any unpleasant questioning regarding his calling, or future, or such worldly matters.

Many months passed thus for Pao Yu in pleasant routine and in merry company, happy play and eager verse-making in the Park of Delightful Vision. His life became even more pleasant and carefree owing to the fact that his father was called away to a distant province as Chief Magistrate.

One day Pao Yu received from his half sister, Taste of Spring, a written invitation to take part in the formation of a poetry circle. He set out at the appointed hour for her dwelling, the Hermitage of Clear Autumn Weather, where he found all the cousins already assembled. There was unanimous enthusiasm for the proposal, and it was decided to hold a poetry meeting on the second and sixteenth of each month. Each member was to be host in turn and entertain the other members with wine and light refreshments. The Widow Chu, who on account of her prosaic and practical disposition was not exactly made for poetic composition, was entrusted with the business management of the club. Greeting of Spring, who excelled in calligraphy, was given charge of making the fair, clean copies of all finished compositions, for the club archives. Grief of Spring was appointed judge of rhyming on account of her skill in making rhymes. Each member received a literary club name which occasionally was derived from the name of the place where the member lived. The club itself was called *Hai tang*, or Begonia Club, in honor of the two pots of white begonia which Pao Yu had just by chance received as a present that day. The begonia was also the theme for the first composition at this foundation meeting, for Black Jade had insisted that the club should begin its activity at once. On this occasion the chairman of the club, the Widow Chu, awarded the first prize to Precious Clasp for the depth of feeling which she revealed in her poetry. The opinions had been divided. Other members wanted to award the first prize to Black Jade on account of the perfection of form of her composition.

At the next meeting the youngest member, Little Cloud, was to act as hostess. At Pao Yu's instigation she had been invited by the Ancestress on a long visit again and was living with Precious Clasp. Precious Clasp shared the duties of entertaining with her in a sisterly way, and furnished the table with some baskets of delicate if not exactly expensive crabs at her own cost.

This time the theme was the chrysanthemum, and it was to be treated in twelve variations. Following the natural course of events, the first subtheme chosen was the motto: "One thinks of chrysanthemums," then "One looks for chrysanthemums," "One plants chrysanthemums," "Happy observation of the flower," "Chrysanthemums in a vase," "Chrysanthemums in song," "Chrysanthemums in pictures," "Questions to chrysanthemums," "Thanks to chrysanthemums," "Chrysanthemums in the shade," and finally "When chrysanthemums dream" and "When chrysanthemums die." Little Cloud fastened the list of the twelve themes on the garden wall, and every member was permitted to pick one or several themes, at choice. After the compositions had been handed in and fair copies made by Greeting of Spring, they were subjected to a scrupulous examination by the Widow Chu. She crowned as the three best works in order of merit the poems "Chrysanthemums in song," "Questions to chrysanthemums," and "When chrysanthemums dream." The Princess of the Bamboo Hermitage was announced as the author of all three compositions. This was Black Jade's club name.

It just happened that that same day Godmother Liu from the country arrived on a visit at the Yungkuo palace. The vigorous old peasant woman was a distant relative of Madame Cheng and had been to visit once before, three years ago. She brought with her as presents some bags full of dates, melons, gourds, and various other country produce. Actually, she had only come to visit Madame Cheng and Phoenix, but when the Ancestress heard of her arrival and was told of her jolly disposition, she expressed a wish to make the acquaintance of this godmother from the country.

"You should deem yourself lucky; the old *Tai tai* wishes to make your acquaintance," the wife of the majordomo Chou Jui, who had escorted her in and announced her, told the visitor. "Come and follow me!"

"But I cannot possibly let myself be seen in this poor peasant attire!" objected Godmother Liu, horrified. "Go and tell the old *Tai tai* that I have gone home already."

"Do not worry!" the other reassured her, laughing. "Our old *Tai tai* is goodness itself and kind and generous to simple people. The waiting maid Little Ping will take you to her."

Trembling and hesitant, Godmother Liu followed the waiting maid Little Ping into the living room of the Ancestress. Pao Yu and the

探春

young ladies from the Park of Delightful Vision were gathered there too. Godmother Liu was quite dumfounded by all the splendor of the garments and the glitter of the jewels and needed a little time to collect herself. She noticed a dignified old lady reclining on a divan in the midst of the beautifully dressed young people. That must certainly be the Ancestress, she thought. She bowed as low as her old bones would allow her to, and said solemnly: "I wish the old Bodhisattva a long life of peace!"

The Ancestress replied kindly to her exuberant greeting and asked her to sit down.

"How old are you now, Cousin?" asked the Ancestress.

"Seventy-five," replied the old woman, standing up briskly.

"So you are older than I am! See how healthy and strong she has remained!" said the Ancestress admiringly, turning towards the bystanders. "Who knows how decrepit I may be if I ever reach her years!"

"There must be distinctions; wise Providence sees to that. Our kind is, after all, born for work, the old *Tai tai* for gentle living. What would become of farming without people like us?" said Godmother Liu.

"Are your teeth and eyes still sound?" the Ancestress asked, continuing her inquiries.

"They are in the best of order. Only a back tooth on the left side has become a little loose recently."

"What a useless creature I am compared with you!" sighed the Ancestress. "My eyesight is getting bad, my hearing is weak, my memory plays tricks on me. I avoid the company of strangers in order not to show my physical weakness. All I do is eat what my shaky teeth allow me to, and sleep, and entertain myself with my children and grandchildren when I need diversion."

"One can see from that how high you stand in the favor of heaven; I wish life were as kind to me!" said Godmother Liu.

The Ancestress was so charmed by the country simplicity and the ingenuity of her visitor that she promptly invited her to remain for a few days as her guest. Phoenix saw to it that she had comfortable quarters.

The next day the Ancestress would not let herself be dissuaded from personally showing her guest the beauties of the Park of Delightful Vision. Here daughter-in-law and grandchildren helped to show her around. Godmother Liu could hardly get over her astonishment.

"We country people have an old custom of hanging up pictures of magnificent palaces and parks on the walls of our rooms at New Year," she said. "Up to now I always thought that such splendors existed only in the imagination of the painters, but now I see that here in this splendid park everything is even more beautiful than in our pictures. I wish

I could take pictures of this park home with me to show to my people in the country. They would open their eyes in surprise."

The Ancestress smilingly pointed to her granddaughter Grief of Spring, and promised that her artistic hand would produce some beautiful views of the park for her. The midday meal was taken in the Clear Autumn Weather Hermitage, the home of Taste of Spring. Phoenix, always ready for a joke, had secretly arranged with Mandarin Duck, the favorite waiting maid of the Ancestress, to amuse the company at table at the expense of the good lady Liu. Even at gentlemen's dinner parties in the Yungkuo palace it was a favorite custom to make a new guest at table the object of general amusement. Accordingly, before the meal Mandarin Duck took Godmother Liu quietly aside and informed her of various alleged "customs of the house," and instructed her that she must keep silent about such and such and say such and such things if she was not to cause displeasure and excite laughter.

Godmother Liu was given her place at the table beside the Ancestress. The waiting maid Mandarin Duck, whose task it was today to pass warmed handkerchiefs to the Ancestress from time to time or to chase away the flies with a feather duster or to wield a cooling fan upon her mistress, had taken up her position behind the Ancestress's back, whence she was able to keep an eye on old Liu and give her a surreptitious wink now and then.

As soon as they had taken their seats the first thing to be laid before the guest was a pair of heavy, old-fashioned, ivory chopsticks with golden tops.

"What shall I do with these heavy things?" Godmother Liu blurted out in alarm. "They are even more difficult to manage than our iron chopsticks in the country."

There was suppressed giggling all around. Then the maids brought along big serving trays with many different kinds of food in little dishes and bowls. Phoenix chose a bowl with dainty pigeons' eggs, which she put before the guest. The old *Tai tai's* saying "please!" politely gave her guest a sign to begin the meal. Remembering the instructions she had received from Mandarin Duck beforehand, Godmother Liu rose at once from her seat and recited the following words loudly and solemnly over the table:

> "I am old Mother Liu,
> Into my mouth fits a whole cow.
> A good, fat mother swine,
> I eat alone, and in no time!"

As soon as she had said her piece, she slapped herself several times on the cheeks, sat down again, and silently set about eating her dish of pigeons' eggs. The party were astonished at first at her strange behavior, but they soon guessed that the good old lady was the victim of alleged "customs of the house." Soon hearty laughter spread down the table. Little Cloud had to splutter out the tea which she had just taken in her mouth. Black Jade had to hold on to the edge of the table, she was so shaken with laughter. Pao Yu fell on the breast of the Ancestress, and the Ancestress clasped him crying out: "My heart, my liver!" her voice stifled with laughter. Madame Cheng, who guessed that the originator of the lark was the jester Phoenix, silently threatened her with her raised finger. Aunt Hsueh also had to splutter out a mouthful of tea, which spilled over Taste of Spring's frock. And Taste of Spring in her turn spilled the contents of her teacup, which she was holding in her hand, over Greeting of Spring's skirt. They were all doubled up with laughter. This one and that one slipped out quietly from the table to laugh her fill undisturbed outside and put on a clean dress which the maid had ready. Only Phoenix and the waiting maid Mandarin Duck remained impassive and continued to serve old Liu with dignity and kindness, as if nothing had happened, while old Liu herself seemed not to have noticed that she was the cause of the general merriment. She calmly took the heavy chopsticks in her hand and set to work on the pigeons' eggs.

"Oh, what pretty little hens you must have to lay such dainty little eggs as these! I, too, would like to have a specimen of this kind of hen," she remarked; and her remark let loose another burst of laughter.

"These rare eggs cost a good deal of money, too—a silver tael each," declared Phoenix importantly. "Eat them and do not let them get cold!"

Godmother Liu made a great effort to catch the slippery little things between her awkward chopsticks. They scorned her efforts and rolled again and again with an audible plop back into the bowl. At last she succeeded in getting one close to her mouth. She stretched out her neck to snap at it, but at the last moment it escaped from her chopsticks and rolled onto the floor. She put down the chopsticks and was about to catch the runaway egg with her hand, but a maid got there before her, picked up the egg, and put it aside.

"It's a pity!" sighed Godmother Liu. "One tael apiece, and only to look at!"

"Who gave those heavy chopsticks to our guest!" asked the Ancestress reproachfully of those around her. "After all, we are not having a solemn banquet today. Of course, it's another nasty trick of our hobgoblin Phoenix! Fetch other chopsticks quickly!"

They obediently laid a more manageable pair of chopsticks in front of the guest. These were made of ebony and mounted with silver.

"These silver things do not seem to me to be much better than the gold ones I've had," muttered Godmother Liu suspiciously. "There's nothing like our simple country prongs."

"The silver tops are there as a protection against poisoning," explained Phoenix. "When there is poison in the food the silver becomes tarnished, and so one is warned."

"Oh, my goodness! Can there be poison in such splendid food?" Godmother Liu burst out. "Then our food in the country must consist of pure arsenic. Now, such poisonous food pleases me very well, and I would willingly die eating it."

The Ancestress was glad to note her good appetite; she had heaping portions put before her and even gave her the best bits off her own plate.

After the meal they took a siesta in Taste of Spring's bedroom. The waiting maid Mandarin Duck stole along to Godmother Liu's side and asked her not to be offended at the tricks they had played on her at table.

"What is there to be offended at?" replied Godmother Liu, laughing. "I took part in them of my own free will and play-acted for your Ancestress, in order to cheer up her old heart a bit. That was all arranged beforehand with Madame Phoenix. When I am really angry I am in the habit of keeping my mouth shut."

When the Ancestress looked out the window, after her siesta, at the beautiful group of pine trees in the courtyard in front of the back pleasure veranda, the wind wafted to her ears the gentle murmur of distant music.

"It sounds like music from a wedding procession. Are we, then, so near the street here?" she remarked to those around her.

"Oh, no. The street is much too far away from here. It is probably our dancing girls rehearsing in the Pear Garden," said Madame Cheng.

"Let them come and rehearse here before us! They will be glad to be allowed to walk in the park, and we shall enjoy their art," suggested the Ancestress cheerfully.

Phoenix sent at once to the Pear Garden and was preparing to set up an improvised dancing stage composed of tables covered with red carpets, in the courtyard.

"No, not here! Order them to go to the Lotus-Root Pavilion by the pond! There is enough room there; and besides, the splashing of the near-by waterfalls will make splendid accompanying music. We will watch their performance from the bank, and will also take a glass of wine in the Damask Kiosk!" said the Ancestress.

Her suggestion met with unanimous applause.

"Very well, let us go over!" said the Ancestress, turning and winking at Aunt Hsueh. "Our young girls do not like strange visitors to stay a long time with them profaning their maidenly apartments. Is that not so?"

"Oh, please do remain here as long as you like!" protested Taste of Spring.

"No, no, two other 'Jades' of grandchildren might be jealous," said the Ancestress jokingly, alluding to the sensitive Black Jade and Pao Yu. "Now let us have a little drink, and then we shall invade the two of them!"

Laughing and chattering, the company stood up and went to the boat-slip near the Duck-Plant Bank. Two boats were already awaiting them there, staffed by hired ferrywomen from Suchow, with long wooden poles. The Ancestress, Madame Cheng, Aunt Hsueh, Godmother Liu, Widow Chu, and Phoenix as well as the two waiting maids, Mandarin Duck and Nephrite Bangle, took their seats in the first boat. The high-spirited Phoenix sat at the bow and took hold of a pole in order to have a hand in running the boat.

"It's better to leave that alone! Poling is not child's play, it has to be learned!" cried the frightened Ancestress from the cabin. "It's true, we are not on a huge river here, but the water is deep enough to drown one. Be good enough to come in here at once!"

"I am not the least afraid! The old Ancestress need not worry!" replied Phoenix, laughing and pushing off vigorously from the bank. In the beginning it went well, but when they were in midstream the heavily loaded little boat began to toss, and Phoenix became dizzy. She quickly gave the pole to the ferrywoman who was standing near by and squatted down on the deck boards; otherwise she would have fallen over. Pao Yu followed in the second boat with his sister and cousins. The female servants ran along the near-by river-bank. Pao Yu was drawing his companions' attention regretfully to the many withered lotus leaves, and said they should get the gardeners to sweep them up. Precious Clasp agreed with him, but once more Black Jade was of a different opinion.

"On the whole I do not think much of the poems of Li Shan," she remarked thoughtfully. "But one line of his I find splendid: 'Leave the withered lotus leaves as they are; they make us understand the lament of the rain.'"

"That is definitely a magnificent line," agreed Pao Yu fervently. "So let us leave the withered leaves where they are."

The boats glided into the Sandbank Harbor of Blossoming Purity. Shadowy darkness lay over the river-bank, which was densely timbered with trees. The withered reeds, the faded green of the water-chestnut trees, exhaled autumnal melancholy. Precious Clasp's pavilion was not far from the river-bank. The Ancestress decided to pay a visit there in passing. A narrow, steep "Cloud Path" led over stone steps up to the Jungle Court. In the front garden the visitors' nostrils were assailed by a strange, strong perfume. There the wonder plant, the spirit creeper, grew, its beautiful fruits peeping forth from under frost-blue foliage, and hanging in heavy clusters and tresses like reddish and bluish corals.

On entering the pavilion the Ancestress felt as if she had been transported to a snow grotto, so drab and inhospitable did the interior appear to her. Not a bit of decoration, no curios, and no knickknacks. Only on the writing table a simple pottery vase with some chrysanthemums in it. The green gauze curtain above the bed, the few cushions and covers, were of the simplest kind. A few books and tea bowls completed the scanty equipment. The Ancestress sighed.

"Such simplicity!" she said, shaking her head and turning towards her attendants. "Everything is lacking here. Why did you not make it more attractive for the child? We have everything available in the house! I cannot look after every single thing myself. Mandarin Duck must fit up the room with some pretty works of art. You should really have seen to this long ago," she said reproachfully, turning to Phoenix.

"But she attaches no importance to furnishings," replied Phoenix, smiling. "She sent me back all the articles I had placed at her disposal."

"At home, too, she never thought much of jewelry or trinkets," said her own mother, Aunt Hsueh, reassuringly.

"It's unbelievable!" said the Ancestress. "Her desire for simplicity and economy may indeed be very praiseworthy, but what kind of impression does such a tasteless room make on visitors? Besides, she is a young person who must enjoy lovely things. If the youth are so abstemious, then we old people should really be contented with a stable. Luckily, I have some nice things I can do without, which my grandson Pao Yu has not seen yet; otherwise he would have taken them away from me long ago."

She turned to Mandarin Duck. "Bring the young lady the marble bowl with the country scenes, and also the cheval mirror with the green silk hangings, and the stone tripod for burning Chinese ink! Also change this shabby gauze curtain for the white silk hand-painted one!"

"The articles are stored in the lumber-room in the eastern tower, but I do not know which box they are in. It will take some searching to find them," remarked the waiting maid.

"One or two days do not make any difference. But I will not allow the matter to be forgotten."

After a brief delay in the inhospitable Jungle Court they went on to the Damask Kiosk. There the twelve dancing girls from Suchow paid their respects and asked what the company wished the program to be.

"Only perform something which you have practiced well," ordered the Ancestress, whereupon the troupe of dancers went off to the Lotus-Root Pavilion across the pond in order to stage their performance there. In the Damask Kiosk a merry drinking party now started with the favorite game of improvising rhymes, at which the unrestrained doggerel and the peasant coarseness of Godmother Liu, who was proof against drink, provided ceaseless merriment. Godmother Liu partook heartily of the good wine and the delicious pastries handed around with it, and fell more and more into a state of bibulous exhilaration; and when the captivating strains of dance music sounded across from the water pavilion, her delight knew no bounds and she accompanied the music with violent gesticulating of her hands, rhythmical stamping of her feet, and swaying of her body. Pao Yu secretly nudged Black Jade to draw her attention to the comic gestures of the old lady, whereupon Black Jade remarked wittily: "In our old writings they speak of the calming influence of holy music, which even tames the wild animals and makes them dance sedately in sets. One can say of this music that at least it can enrapture a cow."

When the dancing performance was finished, the company rose from the table. The Ancestress took Godmother Liu by the hand and, making an extensive tour, showed her the remaining splendors of the Park of Delightful Vision. The inquisitive old lady could not get over her astonishment, and ceaselessly questioned and asked for information, now about this kind of mineral, and now about that plant or tree. Once she remarked pensively: "Who would have thought that here in the town not only do the people acquire fine polish and education, but even the birds attain to knowledge and the power of speech under your salutary influence!"

And when she saw the surprised expressions around her, she continued: "The green bird with the red beak sitting there on the golden perch is a parrot, and I know already what he can do. But now I would very much like to know whether the big blackish gray fellow over there in the cage, which looks like a phoenix, has been taught to talk by you?"

With amusing remarks such as these she provided gaiety and merriment again and again.

The company had arrived at the Kingfisher's Cage Hermitage, where a beautiful young nun named Miao Yu lived. The highly educated eighteen-year-old girl came from a noble mandarin family of Suchow. After the death of her parents she had renounced the world and dedicated herself to the service of Buddha. On the occasion of the visit of the Imperial spouse she had been transferred to the park from her convent in front of the city gates. In the seclusion of the Kingfisher's Cage she now lived the life of a holy anchoress with two elderly attendants and a young maid, and strove zealously, by severe mortification and deep meditation pleasing to God, to subdue the refractory flesh and, despite her youth, to work her way up step by step to an early sanctity. The nun was as well known for her beautiful crochet work as for her skill in preparing tea. Therefore, immediately after the salutations, the Ancestress asked for a bowl of her celebrated tea. The nun brought her, with her own hands, on a lacquered tray decorated with begonia petals, clouds, dragons, and *shu* signs, a five-colored bowl of best K'ang Hsi china of the Ch'eng Hua period, filled with that fine kind of tea which is known as "Lao Tzu's eyebrows."

"What kind of water is it made with?" asked the Ancestress.

"With rain water collected last year," the nun declared. The Ancestress drank half the bowl and left the other half for Godmother Liu to drink. Then she wanted to know how she liked the tea.

"Quite well, only it's a little insipid and heavy. It should have been allowed to draw a little longer," Godmother Liu admitted frankly. Her verdict provoked laughter on all sides and greatly annoyed the nun. While the rest of the company were being served by a hermitage maid with the same kind of tea in white covered cups of the new, thin "eggshell" china of State manufacture, Precious Clasp and Black Jade were favored by the nun with another specially exquisite kind of tea. She plucked the two girls by the lapels of their gowns and led them into a private room apart. The inquisitive Pao Yu could not refrain from sneaking after the three and observing through a slit in the door what the nun was doing.

He saw how she gave Precious Clasp a seat on a wooden guard-bed and Black Jade on a prayer mat, then put a pot of water on a windfurnace and finally poured the boiling water into a tea pot. He flung open the door and burst into the room saying: "Just look, you are enjoying your best tea here in secret!"

"Certainly, and there's nothing for you to look for here!" replied the cousins, laughing. Pao Yu would not be intimidated, however, but remained where he was and insisted on having a sample of the "favorite tea" put before him, too. The nun was just collecting cups for her guests when the hermitage maid came in with the same bowl out of which the Ancestress and Godmother Liu had previously drunk. The nun would not have it.

"No, not that one! Put it aside; it is not to be used again," she declared. Aha! Obviously she considers the bowl desecrated because old

Liu drank out of it, said Pao Yu to himself. At last the nun found two suitable tea vessels for the two girls. One was a precious antique pewter goblet of the Sung dynasty, as the following engraved inscription showed: "In the fourth month of the fifth year of the Yuan Fong Period of the Sung dynasty Su Tung-po was received into the Han Lin Academy." The three-legged goblet with handle had obviously belonged originally to the famous poet, Su Tang-po. The nun presented it to Precious Clasp. The other vessel, which was also of metal, resembled one of those alms bowls used by Buddhist begging monks, except that it was somewhat smaller. The inscription showed it to be of still greater antiquity, for in that characteristic seal script which stood out like drops, one read: "Wen Chiao, who lighted up a rhinoceros's horn." Presumably the bowl once belonged to Wen Chiao, a literary and political celebrity of the eastern Chin dynasty, of whom tradition relates that he conceived the brilliant idea of illuminating the depths of a river by means of a light inside a rhinoceros's horn, which he let down into the water. The nun presented this historic receptacle to Black Jade. Finally, she poured tea into a beautiful green nephrite bowl which she herself used every day, and passed it to Pao Yu. Pao Yu was disappointed.

"My two cousins have got such wonderful antique, precious things to drink from, and I have to be satisfied with a simple, everyday piece of china. This means, I suppose, that my cousins are very special people and that I am just an ordinary fellow," he pouted in joke.

"You call that everyday ware?" said the nun, turning to him, much offended. "I do not wish to be at all presumptuous, but I believe that you will not find such everyday ware in your own home."

"In your select proximity ordinary precious objects such as gold, pearls, and nephrite become everyday trifles," said Pao Yu gallantly, seeking to make amends.

The nun was placated once more and compensated him by giving him a monster tankard made of knotty bamboo roots plaited in varied snake coils, which she rummaged out for him. Pao Yu found the nun's favorite tea, which he sipped out of the huge "seaman's goblet," incomparable and could not praise it highly enough.

"Is this tea also prepared with last year's rain water?" Black Jade wanted to know.

The nun smiled contemptuously. "That just shows what very ordinary people you are!" she said. "People like you cannot even distinguish the quality of tea water! Five years ago, when I was living in the Temple of the Dark Funeral Incense Fumes, I obtained the water which made this tea from the snow that covered the plum blossoms. I collected the snow in that blue glass jug with the specters' heads, and

kept the jug untouched, deep down in the earth, for five years. Only this summer I dug it up and took out the snow water. Today is the second time that I have prepared tea with some of this precious water supply. How could you think that one could get from ordinary last year's rain water such a pure, fine taste as this precious tea possesses?"

Black Jade was afraid of irritating the irascible nun still more by any unguarded remark, and she therefore took her leave shortly afterwards with Precious Clasp. Pao Yu remained behind a little longer. He turned the conversation to the subject of the K'ang Hsi china bowl, out of which old Liu had drunk a while since.

"I admit that the bowl is soiled and desecrated, but would it not be an utter shame simply to throw away the beautiful article as rubbish?" he remarked. "In my opinion it would be best to give it to that good, simple peasant woman. She could sell it and make a nice profit on it. What do you think?"

"Yes, certainly, one could do that," said the nun after reflecting for a moment. "It is lucky that I have never used it myself, otherwise I would have broken it to fragments at once. Well, as far as I am concerned, you may take it and give it to the old woman yourself!" Pao Yu went off with his china bowl for booty. Outside, he handed it to the waiting maid Mandarin Duck with the request that she should give it to Godmother Liu the next day as a parting gift to the guest for her journey. The Ancestress as well as the rest of the company had already stood up to go. The nun accompanied them as far as the temple gate, then she hurried back quickly and bolted the gate behind the undesired guests from the profane world.

In the further course of the sight-seeing tour Godmother Liu became separated from the rest of the company and lost her way. She had suddenly felt violent stomach pains, accompanied by sinister internal rumblings, and a serving woman had to take her hurriedly to a little secluded nook in the northeast corner of the park. As was inevitable after a meal so heartily partaken of, the session there lasted rather long, and when she reappeared her escort had long since gone away. Tired from so much running about, she had taken the welcome opportunity to steal away to her room and take the midday nap which she had missed. There was no trace of the rest of the company either. Alone and abandoned, Godmother Liu now wandered at random through the paths and enclosures of the vast and unfamiliar park, flowers dancing before her eyes and her limbs heavy with wine, until, after asking the way of a wall painting of a beautiful young girl which she had mistaken for a living person, and run her head against the painted scenery on a spirit wall, she at last found herself in a magnificent, circular hall, glittering with gold and precious stones, a bewildering maze of woodcarving on the walls, and numerous niches concealing vases and weapons and lutes, and all kinds of works of art. There she had first of all a one-sided conversation with an old woman dressed exactly like herself, whom she took to be a distant cousin from her own village, until she remembered at last that she had heard in the past of great wall mirrors which were said to be found in the houses of the rich, and it dawned on her that she had just been talking to her own reflection. After she had long been looking in vain for an exit, a mirror panel, furnished with Western door mechanism, yielded to a chance pressure of her hand and admitted her to a luxuriously furnished bedroom. Dulled by wine and exhausted by her wanderings, without much ado she made herself comfortable on the soft cushioned couch under the magnificently embroidered damask canopy. When the missing guest was at last discovered by Pearl after much searching, and, being sober once more, had asked to which of the young ladies the magnificent room belonged in which she had slept off her tipsiness and had felt as if in heaven, she learned to her horror that she had wandered into the bedroom of the son of the house. Luckily, no one in the house with the exception of Pearl knew of the daring escapade of the old woman, for the whole staff of the Begonia Courtyard had gone out that afternoon, and Pao Yu, whom Pearl dutifully told, very considerately took care that the matter should not become known. He agreed with Pearl to say that the old lady had lost her way in the park and had been found asleep on a mossy rock. It can well be understood that a powerful fumigation with frankincense of sandalwood and musk was required to dispel the unseemly traces which the tipsy guest had left behind her in Pao Yu's bedroom. The Ancestress, who otherwise was accustomed to seeing at most two or three interesting parts of the park at one time, felt quite worn out the next day from the exertions which she had undergone for the sake of Godmother Liu. But in view of the lively entertainment which her guest had given in return, she did not regret her exertions, and on bidding farewell to the godmother from the country she loaded her with rich gifts and expressed the wish that she should come back again very soon.

CHAPTER 26

Pao Yu sets out to burn incense in the dust of the highway in memory of a dear departed. On the Day of the Thousand Autumns Phoenix unexpectedly turns into a vinegar barrel.

PHOENIX'S BIRTHDAY WAS CELEBRATED ON THE SECOND DAY OF THE ninth month. At the suggestion of the Ancestress everyone abstained this time from giving individual gifts, and instead all the ladies and girls of the two palaces as well as all the female servants had each to contribute, according to her means and position, from one tael to twenty taels to a common birthday fund. This fund went to defray the expenses of the various amusements of the day. The management of the funds was entrusted to Princess Chen. Besides the usual festive banquet, there were many other pleasures: a troupe of actors performed plays, a troupe of jugglers showed their hundred tricks, and a storyteller recited amusing stories.

The company had been assembled for quite a long time; only Pao Yu was missing. When he was sent for word came back that he had gone into the town. They could hardly believe this, so they sent for Pearl, from whom they expected more information.

"He said yesterday that he would have to go to the 'Prince of the Northern Quietness' today on an urgent matter," Pearl was able to tell them. "I tried to dissuade him, but in vain. He rode off very early today."

Everyone thought it very tactless of him to go off just then, especially as a meeting of the Begonia Club had also been fixed for that day.

"Curiously enough, he did not put on his visiting suit but just wore his everyday clothes going out," added Pearl. "Very likely he had to pay the Prince a visit of condolence on the death of a secondary wife, but I do not know anything more."

"That would excuse him to a certain extent," people said, modifying their first judgment.

It was in a sense true that Pao Yu had gone out on account of a death, but he did not tell anyone around him who the dead person in question was. The day before, he had only given a brief order to his valet Ming Yen to have two horses ready early the next morning at the back gate of the park. And the servant Li Kwei had been ordered to say, if anyone should ask for Pao Yu, that he had gone to visit the Prince of the Northern Quietness, but that they should not send for him, as he would be back in good time.

Quite early, then, on that morning he appeared at the back gate of the park, dressed in the simplest attire, and without saying a word he mounted his horse and rode off at a smart trot, his body bent right over the saddlebow. Ming Yen had to use his whip in order to keep pace with him. Asked where he was going, Pao Yu had replied: "Straight on, out through the northern city gate!"

"But there is nothing interesting out there; the district is desolate and lonely," Ming Yen had declared. Pao Yu had nodded and replied: "The more desolate and lonely it is, the better."

Ming Yen was very much puzzled by the strange, distraught manner of his master. They had ridden six or seven li at a quick trot, and were now out in open, thinly populated country, when Pao Yu stopped his norse.

"I wonder whether incense could be procured in this neighborhood?" he asked, turning to Ming Yen.

"It's possible; but the question is: What kind would it be?"

"I need sandalwood, lavender, and olibanum incense."

"Such fine varieties as those will be difficult to get in this deserted region," said Ming Yen, laughing. "But don't you usually carry some incense with you in your belt pouch?"

Pao Yu rummaged in his lotus-leaf bag and did in fact find two little fragments of Cambodian aloewood. "Good, we've got incense!" he said, gratified. "Now, I only need a brazier."

"How can you expect to get a brazier out here in this wilderness?" asked Ming Yen, shaking his head dubiously. Then an idea occurred to him.

"If we ride on just another two li, we will come to the nunnery known as the Temple of the Water God, and there we can get everything we want."

"That's splendid!" said Pao Yu, and whipped his horse up to a swift trot. Ming Yen wondered to himself how it was that his master, who usually seemed rather contemptuous of the Temple of the Water God, was apparently so eager to visit it today.

The old Abbess of the Temple of the Water God, who was in the habit of dropping in at the Yungkuo palace now and then, was much surprised and felt as greatly honored at the unexpected visit of the aristocratic young grandson of a prince as if a living dragon had descended onto her threshold straight from the skies. But Pao Yu took no special notice either of her or of the Water God. He only glanced hurriedly and without any show of reverence at the statue of the god within the temple, which, though only roughly fashioned of clay and plaster, was nevertheless quite imposing; then he went straight off to the garden at the back of the temple. He procured a burning brazier from the Abbess, and chose a spot beside the temple well as the site for his offering. Now Ming Yen guessed the connection and understood why his master seemed to be thrilled with joy just now when he had mentioned the Temple of the Water God. Pao Yu's pious act of devotion to the dead naturally referred to Gold Ring, who had lost her life through his fault. It was on Phoenix's birthday a year before that the poor creature had thrown herself into the well.

While Pao Yu was lighting his two fragments of Cambodian aloe-wood over the burning coals, weeping, and devoutly prostrating himself in silent salutation to the dead, his sympathetic servant also fell upon his knees and, striking his forehead several times on the ground, began to pray thus: "I, Ming Yen, who have served my young master faithfully all these years, have always until now known the secrets of his heart. Only today he has not confided in me, and has been silent with regard to the reason of his burnt offering. Propriety forbids me to importune him with curious questioning. But I have no doubt that you, Spirit in the Realm of Shades, for whom this offering is made, but whose name I do not know, once lived among the people as a sensible, clever, chaste, splendid, and incomparable young lady or little sister. As my little master cannot speak out in my presence regarding the matters which weigh on his heart, let me pray instead of him, and give ear to my supplication since you are a spirit and have the power of spirits. Graciously listen to my little master, who remembers you so faithfully; protect and guard him when he enters into the Realm of Shades, and help him, that in a future existence he may be born again as a girl, and so may be able to play and joke and be happy with such as you to his heart's content!"

When he had finished his prayer he made a few more kowtows. Then he hurriedly rose from his knees. Pao Yu had listened to him with increasing amusement and during his prayer had given him a friendly push with his foot.

"Cease your nonsense!" he whispered to him, shaking with laughter. "How awful if anyone should hear you! You make me a laughingstock before the people!"

Thanks to the innocent simplicity of the good Ming Yen the sorrowful ceremony thus lost nine-tenths of its bitterness, and after hurriedly refreshing themselves with a frugal snack in the convent, master and servant set out for home in cheerful spirits.

Pao Yu quickly exchanged his dusty everyday clothes for exuberantly colorful festive attire and went to the birthday party. All were assembled in the large, newly built Hall of Blossoms, from which the merry piping of flutes and the sound of shrill singing could already be heard in the distance. As he was striding through the corridor pavilion near the entrance to the hall he came upon the maid Nephrite Bangle, the sister of the dead girl, Gold Ring. She was sitting under the projecting roof,

266

weeping. When she saw him she turned away with a deep sigh and then said, with a sad smile: "Hurry in! You are being waited for as if you were a magic phoenix who brings healing!"

"Guess where I have been!" he said to her gently. Nephrite Bangle shuddered and silently wiped away her tears.

When he appeared in the Hall of Blossoms Pao Yu was indeed received and greeted with as much amazement as if he were a fabulous creature. Everyone surrounded him, overwhelmed him with questions, and heaped reproaches on him. He should have said beforehand where he wanted to go to and how long he would be away, and it was certainly no manners simply to run off on his sister-in-law's birthday, and they had been worried about him, and so on. Pao Yu replied calmly that he had paid a visit of condolence to the Prince of the Northern Quietness, whose favorite wife had died. But it was difficult to pacify the Ancestress, and she threatened that if he ever again went out of the house without saying a word, she would tell his father and have him thrashed. Pao Yu solemnly promised to be better, and with this the incident was closed and the merry party continued. Who would have thought that in the course of the day the festive spirit was again to be overcast by a new and this time more serious occurrence?

The theatrical troupe was just performing "The Thorn as Agraffe," that well-known play about the poor girl and the rich suitor. It was a really touching piece which made the Ancestress weep and laugh alternately, sigh one moment and swear the next. When it came to the scene in which the hero offers sacrifice to his drowned sweetheart, Black Jade remarked to Precious Clasp: "This young man is an utter fool! Has he really got to run to the river-bank in order to offer sacrifice to the beloved with water from the river? Could he not satisfy his feelings just as well at home with a bowl of water from the well? Water is water. What is in one's heart is what matters!"

Precious Clasp did not reply, but Pao Yu distinctly felt the pointed allusion to himself which was hidden in her remark. How closely the action on the stage coincided with what he had gone through today, and how correctly his clever cousin had seen through him once more! But he, pretending not to have noticed anything, asked for another goblet of wine, and drank to the health of sister-in-law Phoenix.

Phoenix, who usually did not drink much, and did not enjoy ceremonial dinner parties where one had to sit quiet for such a long time, was obliged today at the express order of the Ancestress to sit in the place of honor for longer than she wished, receiving the homage of the company, as the most important person present. All the female relations, as well as some privileged ladies of the female retinue, down to the waiting maid Mandarin Duck, came up one after another and drank to her health, and she could not avoid allowing her glass to be filled afresh each time in response. The effect of this unaccustomed quantity of wine soon became evident. She suddenly felt rumbles in her stomach and had to go to her apartments leaning on the arm of her waiting maid Little Ping in the middle of the performance by the troupe of jugglers.

Now, as she approached the corridor pavilion of her home, she could see from a distance how one of her maids, who had been keeping a lookout in front of the entrance, turned quickly as lightning at sight of her and ran into the house. The strange behavior of the maid immediately awakened her suspicions. She called out to her to stop, but the maid behaved as if she did not hear her and disappeared inside. Then she became really suspicious. She ran into the inner courtyard of her house as quickly as her legs would carry her and sat down on the steps of the stone terrace. Then she called out the maid in question and ordered her to kneel down before her. She next sent Little Ping to fetch two doorkeepers from the inner gate, who were to bring ropes and whips with them.

"Tie up the miserable bitch, the wretched hussy, who no longer has eyes for her mistress, and beat her until she is half dead!" she ordered the two servants harshly. The maid, almost swooning with fright, despairingly beat her forehead on the stone flags and whined for mercy.

"Am I a ghost or why did you run away when you saw me coming?" shouted Phoenix.

"I did not see the *Nai nai* at all; it just occurred to me that the house was empty and unwatched, and that is why I ran in," the maid tried to excuse herself.

"Oh, indeed? If the house was empty, what were you loafing about outside the entrance for? Besides, I shouted myself hoarse calling you. You were not far away, you are not deaf and must have heard me, but in spite of that you ran on. Spare yourself the trouble of lying. My patience is at an end."

And she dealt the maid two such powerful slaps on the face that both her cheeks immediately swelled up and turned purple.

"You will sprain your hand, *Nai nai!*" cried the waiting maid Little Ping, trying to pacify her.

"Very well, strike her instead of me!" hissed her angry mistress. "And if she still remains stubborn, I will have her tongue singed with a hot iron."

"I will confess," howled the maid in terror. "The master is in the house. He ordered me to watch out for you and to warn him as soon as you returned."

Aha, now we are getting somewhere, thought Phoenix.

"Why should you keep a lookout for me? Was he anxious lest I could not find the way alone?" she persisted. "Out with the truth, or I will prick you with pins!"

In order to show that she was in earnest she drew from her hair a long, pointed hairpin, which she waved threateningly in the face of the kneeling girl. The maid drew back her head in terror and moaned: "Do not stick me! I will tell you everything! But please do not betray me! When the master came home today he took two pieces of loose silver, two agraffes, and two pieces of satin out of the treasure trunk. I had to take them secretly to the wife of the servant Little Pao and bring her back to the master. She is still inside in the master's room. I was to keep watch outside. What has taken place in the room I do not know."

Phoenix had to pause to get over an attack of faintness, then she picked herself up and rushed to her husband's pavilion. On the way there she noticed that another maid was cautiously spying out the courtyard gate, and on seeing her quickly drew in her head and made off. Phoenix called her by name. This maid was cleverer than the first one. When she saw that she was detected she turned round quickly, hurried up to Phoenix, and said quite coolly: "I was just on my way to you, and now you come along yourself!"

"What message did you have for me, then?"

The maid reported that the master was in the house and had Little Pao's wife with him, and so on.

"And why did you not tell me that at once instead of only doing so now to save yourself when you see you are found out?" said Phoenix, giving her a slap. Then she ran on and crept under the window of her husband's bedroom. Scraps of an animated conversation reached her ear. Now she distinguished a woman's voice: "Just wait, sooner or later that Princess of the Underworld will die; then your sufferings will be at an end!" To which the voice of her husband replied: "Yes, but what then? Shall I marry another then, and have all the old misery begin over again?"

The woman's voice continued: "After all, you have Little Ping. Make her your first wife when the other one dies. Then you will have no more worries."

To which he replied: "She is dead bent on seeing that I have nothing to do with Little Ping. I know that Little Ping suffers because of her suspicions, but she does not dare to do anything. That woman is just my fate, my unlucky star."

Phoenix was trembling with indignation. Little Ping, whom she had always regarded as fidelity personified, had now been unmasked as a secret enemy by the conversation she had just overheard! She was unable to contain herself any longer and, suddenly turning round, dealt the puzzled Little Ping two slaps on the ears. Then she stormed into her husband's bedroom, pushing open the door with her foot. Without wasting a word she rushed at the rival and commenced beating her with all her strength. When she could continue no longer, she planted herself before the door in order to prevent her husband from escaping, and shouted at the woman: "You crazy hussy, so you want to steal my husband from me and would like to kill me into the bargain? Those are fine plans! Come here, Little Ping! You are no better than that woman and you are involved in the same guilt as she is. You have meanly betrayed me behind my back!" And once more she boxed poor Little Ping's ears right and left. The outraged Little Ping in her turn vented her anger on the wife of Little Pao by dealing her a couple of blows.

"Could you not get on with your dirty game by yourselves? Why did you have to drag me into it?" she shouted.

Chia Lien, who was somewhat drowsy from all the wine he had been drinking, had at first looked on in confusion at the scene which was being enacted with such dramatic rapidity before his eyes. When Phoenix had thrashed his paramour just now, he had felt angry and ashamed, but respect for his wife had nevertheless restrained him. Now, however, seeing the maid Little Ping also dealing out abuse and blows, he felt impelled to give up his passive attitude and come to the aid of his doubly maltreated paramour.

"What do you mean by hitting out like that?" he said roughly to Little Ping, pushing her with his foot. While Little Ping drew back frightened Phoenix pommelled her in the back, rebuked her for cowardice, and again pushed her forward. In desperation she ran out of the room into the kitchen, and was in the act of gashing herself with a kitchen knife when she was stopped just in time by the maids who were near her. Meanwhile, Phoenix in the bedroom was venting her rage on her faithless husband. She rammed her head wildly against his chest and shouted in his face: "You have been conspiring against me with that woman! I heard you raging against me in here. You will drive me in the end to take my life."

Her raging drove him into a frenzy. He pulled down a sword from the wall and shouted back at her: "If you really want to die, I can do you a favor and kill us both together. For I also am tired of life and would willingly sacrifice myself with you for the sake of peace."

In the midst of this scene Princess Chen appeared escorted by several women.

"What is the meaning of this row? Why, just now the most beautiful harmony was reigning!" she cried in amazement.

The presence of others and the fiery influence of the wine caused Chia Lien to enjoy more than ever striking the exalted pose of the angry husband, and he waved his sword so wildly around him that it really looked as if he wanted to kill his wife. The appearance of Princess Chen had quite the opposite effect on Phoenix. Her defiant ferocity changed instantly to an attitude of meek dejection, she crept away behind the Princess's back and fled weeping from the dangerous battle zone to the safe proximity of the Ancestress.

"I was just going to my house to change my dress, when I heard my husband inside talking to someone," she reported in tears, touching up the narrative a little in her own favor. "I did not venture to go in at once, but remained standing at the window for a bit. Then I distinguished the voice of Little Pao's wife and to my horror heard the woman discussing a horrible plot against me with my husband. They wanted to poison me and after my death he was to make Little Ping his chief wife! You can imagine my indignation! In spite of that I kept control of myself, went in quite quietly, and confined myself solely to taking the disloyal Little Ping to task, and giving her two cuffs on the ear. Had I not a perfect right to do that? And what does he do? He snatches a sword down from the wall and tries to kill me!"

"That is really going too far! Bring the rough, low fellow here to me at once!" ordered the Ancestress indignantly. She took Phoenix's narrative to be quite true. But her order was unnecessary, for Chia Lien came storming in, the naked sword in his hand, followed by a crowd of frightened people. Princess Shieh and Madame Cheng stood barring the way of the raging man.

"What barbaric behavior this is! Have you no consideration for the old *Tai tai?*" they shouted at him.

"It is all due to the fact that the old *Tai tai* has always made a favorite of her! But I will not put up with her impudent insults!" he shouted back, blinking askance at them with bleary, drunken eyes.

His mother succeeded in taking the sword from him.

"Quick! Be off! Get out of here!" she cried, trying to push him towards the door. But he struggled and gesticulated savagely, and filthy language streamed from his mouth like spittle.

"Fetch his father here!" ordered the Ancestress, enraged at his shocking behavior. "He will inspire him with respect."

Her threat was sufficient to bring Chia Lien to his senses. He stumbled out the door and took himself off, muttering, to the outer library. Meantime the ladies endeavored to calm Phoenix.

"It is not as serious as all that. A little squabble, such as young people often have," remarked the Ancestress soothingly. "It is I who am really to blame. I should not have induced her to drink wine. No wonder that it rises up in her afterwards in bile, sour as vinegar."

They all had to laugh at her good joke, for the word "bile" not only means sick vomiting but also jealousy.

"Calm yourself!" continued the Ancestress, turning to Phoenix. "He will have to beg your pardon formally tomorrow; I will see to that! But you must keep away from your house today and leave him alone, otherwise he may get into a fury again. But what has come over that hussy, Little Ping, that she should carry on this base intrigue behind your back? I always thought she was good and respectable."

"Little Ping is innocent," said Princess Chen, with a smile, in defense of the absent maid. "Instead of coming to blows with each other the couple have vented their rage on an innocent person. She does not deserve a word of blame. She has been bitterly wronged."

"Oh, I am sorry for that," said the Ancestress regretfully. "She certainly never gave me the impression of being a bad girl, eager to be seduced. Of course she must be compensated for this. Amber, quick, run to Little Ping and tell her I know now that she has been wronged, and I shall make her mistress beg her pardon tomorrow. But today, her mistress's birthday, is not the right time to do so. Meantime, tell her not to fret, and to have patience until tomorrow."

Little Ping had run to the Park of Delightful Vision and been consoled alternately by Pao Yu and Pearl. Pao Yu had received her kindly in the Begonia Courtyard, had let her put on one of Pearl's gowns instead of her own which had been soiled with wine and tears, placed Pearl's dressing table at her disposal, and refreshed her with a bowl of punch. Then, when Amber brought the comforting message from the Ancestress, Little Ping felt her face glowing with renewed beauty and her tears turned to joy. She spent that night with Widow Chu in the Rice Farm Courtyard, while Phoenix remained with the Ancestress.

The following morning the domestic quarrel of the day before was satisfactorily settled with due formality according to the instructions of the Ancestress. Chia Lien was called to the Ancestress, and had to beg her pardon on his knees, and in doing so he pleaded drunkenness as an excuse for his conduct. Then he had to go to Phoenix, who was standing there, her eyes red from weeping, her hair undone, without jewelry, unpainted and unpowdered, looking miserable and lovely at the same time, and had to bow to her and beg her pardon. His penitent words: "I have done you wrong, *Nai nai*, and I beg you not to be angry with me any longer," caused a sigh of relief from all those present.

"You must not be, otherwise you will make me angry," said the Ancestress, turning with a smile to Phoenix. When peace had been restored between the husband and wife, Little Ping was sent for. Chia Lien bowed politely to her too and begged her pardon for the injustice done to her yesterday by himself and his wife.

"Will you not say a kind word to her too?" the Ancestress urged Phoenix. But already Little Ping had prostrated herself on the ground before her mistress, and as she kowtowed she said with deep humility: "I deserve death for having caused my *Nai nai* annoyance yesterday, the day of her thousand autumns!"

Phoenix, moved to tears, drew her to her feet. She felt thoroughly ashamed. How on earth could she have forgotten herself so utterly, yesterday, as to beat the good girl? It was certainly all because she had drunk too much wine.

"In all the years in which I have served you, you have never once raised your little finger against me!" continued Little Ping, likewise moved to tears. "You have always been good to me. Therefore I will bear you no grudge for the little incident of yesterday."

"Well, everything is right again now! And anybody who makes a fuss about the story after this will get a sound thrashing." And so the Ancestress closed the ceremony of reconciliation and dismissed the participants, after having received a parting kowtow from all three of them together. But when the husband and wife were alone in their home once more, Phoenix could not refrain from remarking: "Is there really something so repulsive and loathsome about me that that hussy dares to call me princess of the underworld and a nightmare? And you backed her up in wishing me dead! When an inferior woman like that is more pleasing to you than I am, how can I keep face and continue living beside you?"

She talked with increasing excitement and broke out into sobs.

"Are you beginning again? Did you not have enough of a scene yesterday?" he growled, peevishly. "I have humiliated myself before the people and asked your pardon on my knees. Is that not enough for you? Do you want me to go down on my knees again, so that your face may brighten once more? One should not be too arrogant, else one gets just the opposite of what one wants."

Phoenix saw he was right, so she remained silent.

"Let it be now! I admit that I have been wrong!" he continued, amiably, when suddenly a maidservant came rushing in and announced excitedly: "The wife of Little Pao has hanged herself." After the first shock Phoenix pulled herself together quickly.

"Well, enough of this! What is there really so exciting about it?" she asked callously. The majordomo Ling's wife, who looked after the female staff, came in timidly and confirmed the news.

"The members of her clan intend to lodge a complaint with the authorities," she added, reluctantly.

"I do not mind. I intended to do the same myself," said Phoenix, coldly.

"I tried as hard as I could to dissuade them from their intention. Perhaps they could be indemnified with money," continued Mrs. Ling.

"Money? I have no money for that. And even if I had, I would not think of doing such a thing. Let them lodge their complaint, and you may spare yourself the trouble of trying to mediate," declared Phoenix resolutely.

Chia Lien winked surreptitiously at Mrs. Ling. She understood the hint and took her leave, but waited for him outside the door. He went out after her.

"I will see what can be done!" he said to Phoenix.

"But do not give any money!" she called after him.

The outcome of the consultation between Chia Lien and Ling's wife was that she was authorized to offer the relatives of the deceased two hundred taels as hush money. Chia Lien had a bad conscience and wanted to avoid a scandal at any cost. He arranged with Mrs. Ling that the money was to be taken from the housekeeping funds and drawn out under cover of current expenses by means of falsified accounts. The matter was hushed up in this way without Phoenix having to know anything about it. The relatives were satisfied, pocketed the nice sum of money, and swallowed their resentment. Moreover, Chia Lien took Little Pao aside, consoled him with a few ounces of silver and some words of condolence, and promised to help him to get another wife. This pleased the servant Little Pao quite well, and so the painful matter was settled.

CHAPTER 27

The windy and rainy mood of a gloomy autumn evening inspires Black Jade with an elegy on the wind and the rain. The maid Mandarin Duck renounces the bliss of a Mandarin Duck union.

BLACK JADE WAS ACCUSTOMED TO EXPERIENCING AN AGGRAVATION OF her old complaint in the spring and autumn. During these autumn days she was troubled more than usually with her feverish symptoms and her bad cough; she had to stay in bed often and seldom emerged from the Bamboo Hermitage. She suffered greatly from being alone so much and was always watching out longingly for the distraction of a visit from any of her cousins. But when the longed-for visitor came she grew weary after only a few sentences of conversation, and was glad when the visit came to an end. Her companions, aware that she was ill and even in normal times a somewhat oversensitive person, did not mind this lack of ceremony and of cordial hospitality.

One day Precious Clasp came to visit her and turned the conversation to Black Jade's ailment. She did not think very much of the family doctors and medicines she had had up to the present, and she thought that Black Jade should try for once to have herself examined and treated by some real authority. Trying to drag herself around like this was simply no life.

"No doctor can help me!" said Black Jade gloomily. "I know my ailment, and there is no remedy for it. Even on the days when I am well, am I really a completely normal person?"

"Food is our life!" continued Precious Clasp eagerly. "It is owing to the wrong kind of food that your vital forces are failing."

"Our life and death are predetermined," sighed Black Jade. "We cannot overcome our fate. This time the illness has been more severe than usual. . . ."

A violent fit of coughing prevented her from speaking further. Precious Clasp was sincerely sorry for her.

"I looked at your prescriptions recently," she said. "In my opinion you are using too much ginseng and cinnamon. They may well stimulate the vital forces, but too much of them is harmful. And do not take your ginseng and cinnamon infusions too hot! Above all, you must keep your liver rested and cool, for too much heat in the liver injures the substance of the organ and impairs the digestion, and thereby endangers life. You should eat an ounce of best swallows' nests and half an ounce of ice sugar every morning, stirred into a warm brew of silver flakes. That will strengthen you more than any medicine."

"How kind of you to trouble so much about me!" said Black Jade, touched. "I really do not deserve it. Formerly I believed all kinds of bad things about you. But since you enlightened me in such a sisterly way recently about bad books, and showed me so much loving sympathy today, I realize that I have misjudged you up to the present. You must excuse me on account of my being so much alone and deprived of the advice of parents or brothers and sisters. I am now fifteen years of age, but until now no one has found such friendly and understanding words for me as you have. In the past I was always somewhat incredulous when Little Cloud sang your praises, but now I am convinced that she was right. It is quite true that this doctoring with cinnamon and ginseng infusions has never done me much good. Grandmother, Aunt Cheng, and Cousin Phoenix have never said anything to me about swallows' nests and ice sugar, and the serving women and waiting maids do not trouble about me at all. They do not regard me as really belonging here, and look upon me as a stranger whom they only serve unwillingly. I doubt very much if I will be allowed to have the daily ration of swallows' nests and ice sugar which you think is necessary."

"Confide in me! I am in the same position as you are," said Precious Clasp.

"But you have still got your mother and your brother, who is older than you. Your family still possess a house and a piece of land of their own! You are not thrown upon the charity of strangers! If it suits you you can go away any time you like and live on your own property. But I have no home; I have no means to dress and feed myself. Naturally, under these circumstances I am not fully accepted by the servants and get but little respect. You are in a much better position than I am!"

"Well, what more do you need for your future than a little bridal jewelry? It is a pity that it is not yet time for that," said Precious Clasp jokingly.

Black Jade blushed.

"I confide my troubles to you because you seem so kindhearted, and then you mock me! That is not right," she said smiling.

"It was only a joke!" said Precious Clasp, cheerfully and unconcernedly, excusing herself, "but perhaps there was some truth in it, who knows? In any case, have confidence in me! When anything worries you, when you have anything to complain of, tell me about it, and I will help you as far as is in my power. But as for my brother, Hsueh Pan, whom you have just mentioned, well, you know yourself how much he is worth and how little support I have from him! Of course I am in a somewhat better position than you are, because I have still got my mother. One can talk things over and share one's joys and sorrows with her. But, to make up for that, you have intelligence. After all, you are not a silly dairymaid who cannot help herself and only knows how to sigh. You can open your mouth to me with confidence. I will talk to my mother tomorrow about the swallows' nests; I think she has still got a supply. I will send you a few ounces; and one of my maids will prepare the dish for you every day; you need not trouble the other servants at all. But now I will go. You must be exhausted."

"Come back in the evening!"

Precious Clasp promised to do so and went away. Black Jade partook of a few mouthfuls of thin rice soup, then she stretched herself on her bed and lay there in a dreamy state throughout the long gray autumn afternoon. How gloomy it was outside! The sky had become overcast; a fine drizzle made it seem already dusk. How sad the monotonous dripping sounded on the bamboo leaves in front of the window! Black Jade lay there for hours, and waited in vain for Precious Clasp's return. She will not go out in this weather, she said to herself.

When darkness fell she had the lamps brought and picked a book at random from the bookshelves. It was a collection of well-known poems set to music. On turning over the pages she came upon headings such as "Pain of Parting" and "Autumn Suffering in the Maiden's Chamber" and such like. These elegiac poems suited her mood and inspired her to compose one of her own, which she called "Elegy on the Wind and the Rain Written Sitting by the Window on an Autumn Evening."

She had just finished her long poem, consisting of ten seven-word couplets, and had lain down again, when Pao Yu was announced. And he walked straight in, a broad-rimmed weather-hat of plaited bast on his head, and a wide cloak made of reeds, like those worn by fishermen, over his clothes.

"Oh, what kind of fisherman is this!" Black Jade greeted him, laughing.

"Do you feel better today? Have you been taking your medicine regularly? How is your appetite?" he inquired anxiously, as he laid aside his rain-wear. He took the lamp in his right hand and held it close to Black Jade's face, shading with his left hand the side nearest her.

"You look distinctly better today," he declared contentedly after a searching inspection, during which Black Jade, on her part, had been observing him also more closely. He wore a short red damask smock, no longer quite new, which was tied around the hips with a green cotton sash. Under the smock green satin breeches, embroidered with flowers, reached to his knees. Thickly quilted stockings of a woven golden material covered his legs, and beautiful, comfortable satin slippers embroidered with flowers and butterflies enveloped his feet.

"Only the upper part of you is protected from the rain. How is it that in spite of this your stockings and slippers are clean and dry?" asked Black Jade.

"Oh, on the way here I wore a pair of stout wooden rain-shoes made from the wood of wild apple trees. I left them outside under the projecting roof," replied Pao Yu, smiling.

"Where, then, did you get that beautiful fine weather-hat? It is so light and pliable, not at all the usual prickly kind that one gets in the market," inquired Black Jade further.

"All three articles—the bast hat, the reed cloak, and the wooden shoes—are presents from the Prince of the Northern Quietness," Pao Yu declared proudly. "He wears the same outfit himself in bad weather. Do you like it? If you do, I shall get the same kind of costume for you. The rain-hat is the most valuable of all. The top is made of bamboo pith and is removable. One can take it out and shape it to one's liking. In winter, in snowy weather, one can take it out and turn back the remaining wide brim over a warm fur cap. Practical, is it not? Would you also like to have a rain-hat like that?"

"No, thank you! I would not like to go about dressed up like a fisherwoman on the stage. . . ."

She stopped short and a hot flush spread over her face. Too late it occurred to her that she had just now greeted Pao Yu as a fisherman. Pao Yu took no notice of her embarrassment, which she tried to hide by convulsive coughing. He had found on the table the poem she had just finished, and was reading it through eagerly.

"Splendid!" he exclaimed involuntarily.

In a second she had grabbed the sheet of paper and burned it over the lamp.

"Too late!" he laughed. "I know it by heart already!"

"I should like to sleep now. Please go away!" she said.

He turned up the lapel of his coat and took out a gold pocket watch the size of a walnut. The hands already pointed to the hour of the boar, the tenth hour.

"You are right. It is high time for you to go to bed. You must be worn out."

He quickly put on his rain wear and took his leave. At the door he turned around once more. "Have you a wish for anything special to eat tomorrow?" he asked. "If so, I will tell the old *Tai tai*. You can rely on me more than on those old women."

"Give me time until the morning. Perhaps I shall think of something nice during the night. But now hurry up! See how it's pouring outside! Have you anyone to accompany you?"

"We are here," answered two serving women, who were in the act of opening a huge umbrella and lighting a pole lantern outside the door.

"You think of lighting a lantern in this weather? It will soon be soaked through and go out," said Black Jade.

"It's a horn lantern, made of a ram's horn, and it's rainproof."

Black Jade took a glass lantern from the bookshelf, got her waiting maid to put a lighted wax candle into it, and handed it to Pao Yu. "Please take this glass one instead. It is brighter than your dull horn, and it also is rainproof."

"No, thank you, I have a glass one like that myself, but I was afraid that the bearers might slip on the slippery damp path and break the lamp. That is why I did not use it."

"Do take this one! Better for the lamp to be broken than for you to slip in the dark and be hurt. You are not used to those awkward wooden shoes. Have the horn lantern carried in front and take the glass one in your hand yourself! You can send it back tomorrow."

How touchingly concerned she is about me, thought Pao Yu, as he politely took her glass lantern and now really set off. A serving woman walked in front with the horn lantern, the other serving woman followed with the umbrella, and behind them walked Pao Yu leaning on the arm of a maid who had to carry the glass lantern. Another maid carrying an umbrella brought up the rear.

Scarcely had he gone with his retinue when a serving woman with umbrella and lantern arrived from the Jungle Courtyard. She had been sent by Precious Clasp and brought a big parcel of swallows' nests, plum dumplings, and foreign candied sugar.

"Here, enjoy these! And when you have finished them, my young lady will send you more," said the messenger from the Jungle Courtyard.

"It is too kind of you to have taken the trouble to come out so late! Please refresh yourself in the waiting maids' room with a bowl of tea!"

"Thank you, but I cannot wait, I have still some things to do."

"I understand, you intend to have a turn in the gambling house. On these long dull evenings one likes to pass the time with a little game," said Black Jade, smiling.

"The young lady has guessed rightly. Recently I have been enjoying some pleasant and most respectable society. We gather every evening for a game, and just today I am to preside at our club. So I should not like to be late."

"Oh, I am so sorry that you have sacrificed your little game for my sake and taken the trouble to come over to me in this rainy weather. Naturally, I must compensate you for that."

Black Jade ordered her waiting maid to give a few hundred coppers to the serving woman, and to fortify her with a bowl of punch against the bad effects of the rainy weather. The serving woman thanked her with a kowtow, but confined herself to accepting the coppers only, and trotted away in a great hurry with her umbrella and lantern.

When she was gone the waiting maid Cuckoo had to help her mistress to undress, and she cleared away the parcel and the lamp. But in spite of being so tired, Black Jade could not get to sleep. She felt obsessed with the thought that Precious Clasp had an advantage over her, the orphan, in having a mother and a brother, and that Pao Yu, despite his declaration of friendship, would reject her in the end. The monotonous sound of the rain pattering down ceaselessly on the bamboos and the banana leaves made her feel desperately depressed. A shudder passed through her and she buried her face in her pillow, weeping. Half the night had long since passed when at last, about the hour of the fourth beat of the drum, she fell asleep.

The next morning Phoenix was summoned to Princess Shieh. After a hurried toilet she went off in her carriage to her mother-in-law. The Princess first sent her attendants away, then she started in a low and confidential tone: "I need your advice in a somewhat delicate matter. My husband has cast his eyes on the old *Tai tai*'s favorite waiting maid, Mandarin Duck. He would like to make her his 'side-chamber' and has asked me to undertake the necessary steps with the old *Tai tai*. In itself, the matter is not of so much importance, but I rather doubt whether the old *Tai tai* will give up Mandarin Duck. I do not quite know what attitude I should take. What would you advise?"

"It is a ticklish order, and you will run your head against a nail in carrying it out," replied Phoenix promptly. "The old *Tai tai* will lose her appetite completely if she is separated from Mandarin Duck, who is indispensable to her. Moreover, the old *Tai tai* has said often that your husband is really too old now to have a 'side-chamber to the left' and a 'side-chamber to the right.' This causes him to neglect the management of the palace, and besides, this merry life of pleasure is not beneficial to his health, in her opinion. You can see from this that the old *Tai tai* is not overly pleased by your husband's ways. He would do better to get well out of the tiger's way, rather than to tickle its nose with a blade of grass just now. Do not be angry with me, but you cannot count on me in this matter. I consider it would be useless for me to intercede. Your husband is no longer a young fellow, he has children and grandchildren. What would the people think? It would give rise to nice gossip; you should bring him to reason and talk him out of his intentions."

The Princess did not seem very pleased at her words.

"Other aristocratic gentlemen can keep three 'side-chambers' and four concubines, and is my husband not to be allowed this?" she asked with a frosty smile. "If I tried to dissuade him, I would be unlikely to make any impression on him. You know how obstinate and irascible he is. Who is asking you, in any case, to intercede with the old *Tai tai*? I shall go to her myself, of course. I merely wished to ask your advice. As far as Mandarin Duck herself is concerned, if she were the old *Tai tai*'s favorite waiting maid ten times over, she would hardly decline such an advantageous match."

Phoenix considered it advisable to give in. She knew that partly for the sake of peace, and partly out of cunning, the Princess did not dare to oppose her husband in any way. For, as the wife of the family Elder, on whom the business management of the estate devolved and through whose hands all income and outlay went, she knew how to make a good thing of it and to feather her own nest under the pretext that her husband was somewhat extravagant. In view of such important advantages it would naturally not occur to her to annoy her husband. Presumably some personal profit was the motive of her attitude in this matter today also. So Phoenix immediately altered her opinion and pretended to be in full agreement.

"You are quite right; in my youthful inexperience I had not thought of that at first," she said, skillfully changing her course. "The old *Tai tai*'s remarks about your husband, which I mentioned just now, I only know from hearsay, of course. It was really too simple of me to take such foolish talk seriously. Parents often talk like that in anger when their children do something wrong, and very quickly make a harsh judgment and threaten to beat them to death. But as soon as they see their children again, parental love conquers, and the first anger blows over. Why should not the old *Tai tai* fall in with the harmless wish of her son and give him a waiting maid to whom he has taken such a fancy? We should get to work at once. Luckily, the old *Tai tai* is in a good humor today. Shall I go on in advance and prepare the ground for you? Then, when you come along I will see that the other people there clear off, leaving you to discuss everything alone and undisturbed with the old *Tai tai*."

The Princess was visibly pleased at her altered attitude.

"Very well, go on ahead, but do not mention anything to the old *Tai tai* yet! We must gently win her over by indirect means through Mandarin Duck herself. But first let us get to work on Mandarin Duck! She will probably resist and be bashful and coy in the beginning; I shall do my part later to dispel her doubts. Once we have Mandarin Duck's consent, the old *Tai tai* will not resist either, remembering the old rule: 'Never keep anyone who wants to leave.' "

"Splendid! Those are the right tactics!" agreed Phoenix eagerly. "Mandarin Duck will certainly co-operate. Indeed, she would be utterly stupid if she were to refuse such an opportunity, which would raise her from the position of a servant almost to that of a mistress, and wish to remain in service instead, with the prospect of becoming at some future time the wife of a fellow servant."

"Quite right! Certainly she can only congratulate herself on this match. So go on ahead and speak to her! I shall take my breakfast quickly and follow you immediately."

The clever Phoenix had in the meantime thought of something else. She was not at all so certain that Mandarin Duck would be amenable.

If I fail to win over Mandarin Duck, the Princess will probably blame me and reproach me afterwards, she thought to herself. Better for us to go together. Then I shall be free of the responsibility of any possible failure.

"Aunt Cheng sent me two baskets of freshly baked quails for the breakfast table a little while ago; I was about to set half of them aside for you in any case," she said smiling. "Besides, the hem of your sedan chair curtain is torn. I chanced to hear your bearers talking about it just now as I was coming through the main gateway. They were carrying it away to have it repaired. Would it not be best if you come with me now in my carriage; we could have breakfast together, and then go on to the old *Tai tai*."

The Princess saw the point of her suggestion; she dressed quickly and got into the carriage with her. Finally, Phoenix was cunningly able to arrange that the Princess should go on alone to the old *Tai tai* and that she should follow her later. Accordingly, the Princess went off to the Ancestress, exchanged a few conventional words with her, and left her soon again on the pretext that she wanted to visit Madame Cheng; in reality, however, she slipped off to the room of the maid, Mandarin Duck. Mandarin Duck was just sitting there doing needlework. When the Princess appeared she rose politely.

"Oh, what a lovely piece of embroidery you are doing! Please let me see it!" said the Princess. And she took the embroidery out of the girl's hand, examined it for a while with exclamations of delight, and returned it to her again. Then she submitted the young girl to a searching inspection, noting the fact that she was wearing a silk tunic of pale violet—the color of lotus root—and water-green trousers, and that she had a supple wasp waist, round, gently sloping shoulders, a narrow face oval as a duck's egg, hair that shone like lacquer, a small finely arched nose, and a delicate mole on each cheek. Mandarin Duck felt somewhat unpleasantly surprised at the close inspection and conjectured at once that there must be something special behind it.

"What brings the *Tai tai* here at such an early hour in the morning?" she asked, with a smile.

The Princess let her retinue understand by a glance that she wished to be alone, whereupon the attendants went away. Then she sat down and took Mandarin Duck by the hand in a friendly way.

"I have come here specially to congratulate you."

Mandarin Duck thought she could guess up to three-tenths of what it was all about. She bowed her head, blushed, and remained silent.

"My husband has regretted for a long time past that he has no one in his permanent environment on whom he can really rely," the Princess continued. "It is repugnant to him to obtain what he wants in the usual way through a professional negotiator, for money. He has a prejudice against what one gets through such negotiators, and he thinks that a strange girl bought in this way might disappoint later through this or that physical or other defect and reveal all kinds of bad manners and seductive monkey tricks after two or three days. Now, for the past six months he has been dispassionately observing our girls here, and after thorough scrutiny he has come to the conclusion that of them all there is only one he would consider having, and that is you. He finds to his satisfaction that meekness, reliability, and all the other feminine virtues are incorporated in you. Therefore, he now wishes to take you into his chambers. Your position would, of course, be quite different from that of the kind of girl one buys through some broker. You would have the rank of a secondary wife with the title of 'Aunt' and enjoy corresponding honor, respect and power. Does it not mean to you the fulfillment of everything you could possibly wish that my husband has chosen you and now offers you a position which will place you beyond all the intrigues and envy of your kind? So now come with me to the old *Tai tai* to obtain her consent!"

She had stood up and was just taking Mandarin Duck by the hand to lead her out. Contrary to her expectation, however, the blushing girl withdrew her hand and refused to go with her.

"You need not be bashful, and whatever is to be said to the old *Tai tai* I shall say myself; you only need to follow me," the Princess said with gentle persuasion.

But Mandarin Duck still kept her eyes on the ground and did not move from the spot.

"Surely you have nothing against it?" persisted the Princess. "You would indeed be silly if you turned down the prospect of being the *Nai nai* of a gentleman and preferred to be the wife of a servant. If you say yes, you may expect to have a most pleasant life. You are aware, of course, that I am of a kind and peaceable nature, and my husband also will treat you in the best way, the more so if you make him happy with a little girl or perhaps a little boy by the end of one year. Then you will be in exactly the same position as myself, and will be able to command the staff just as I do, and the servants will obey your slightest wish. So be reasonable and do not miss this favorable opportunity! It will never be offered to you again. How is this? You still keep silent—you, who are usually so wide awake? Have you anything on your mind? Do speak out! Ah, I understand, you are shy to say 'yes' yourself and would prefer to leave it to your parents. Very well, I shall come to an understanding with your family." With this the Princess broke off the difficult negotiations for the time being and went to look for Phoenix.

Meantime Phoenix had begun by questioning her waiting maid Little Ping. Little Ping had shaken her head doubtfully and confirmed her own misgivings regarding the success of the plan.

"I have tried in vain to dissuade the Princess," Phoenix said to her. "Now she will have to put up with the public disgrace of possible failure. But she will be here at any moment. Go to the kitchen and have the quails roasted for breakfast, and see that there are some other suitable dishes to go with them! While the Princess is with me you need not come in; you can go into the park for the time being! Come back again when she is gone!"

Little Ping carried out her orders in the kitchen, and then she went for a walk in the garden. There she met Mandarin Duck. When the Princess had left her, Mandarin Duck had thought it wisest to make herself invisible for a time. "If the old *Tai tai* should ask for me, say I am ill!" she said to her companion, Amber, and then she disappeared into the park.

"Ah, here comes the new aunt!" she heard herself jokingly called by Little Ping.

"Are you taking part in the conspiracy against me with your mistress?" replied Mandarin Duck, flushing angrily.

Little Ping regretted her thoughtless joke and, smiling, drew the other over to a ledge of rock under a plane tree, and assured her that Phoenix was not taking part in the conspiracy at all but, on the contrary, was on her side. Mandarin Duck, her cheeks red with excitement, replied: "With Gold Ring dead, we are barely a dozen waiting maids here now—Pearl, Amber, Gray Cloud, Bright Cloud, Cuckoo, Nephrite Bangle, Musk, Blue Ink, Little Cloud's maid Blue Thread, you, and myself. Formerly we always told one another everything and confided in one another. Recently all you others go your own way, only I keep to the old ways and stick to the rule of confiding in you when there is something special on. And so I will also now confide to you my solemn decision: Quite apart from the fact that Prince Shieh now wishes to make me his secondary wife without more ado, and even if he wished to make me his chief wife in case of the death of the Princess, and even if he were to submit his offer of marriage according to all the rules of good form through three negotiators and the sending of the six kinds of bridal gifts, nevertheless I would not consider it! . . ."

"Why, what kind of secret discussions are going on here?" a voice blurted out from behind the trunk of the plane tree, and Pearl, who had slipped along unnoticed, sat down laughing beside the two others on the rock. Little Ping explained matters briefly to Pearl.

"What an old libertine!" said Pearl, disapprovingly. "Of course he has no more prospects with women of his own station, so that's why he does it this way."

"I know how you could foil him in his project," said Little Ping.

"How then?" asked Mandarin Duck curiously.

"Simply tell the old *Tai tai* that you have already given yourself to Mr. Chia Lien! The father cannot very well take his son's sweetheart."

Mandarin Duck took her suggestion, which was meant as a joke, extremely badly. "You stupid thing!" she hissed. "You have seen only

鴛鴦

recently how Madame Phoenix raged when she caught her husband with Little Pao's wife. I would only expose myself to the greatest unpleasantness."

"I have a better suggestion," interjected Pearl, laughing. "Say to the old *Tai tai* that she should make the Prince believe that she has already promised you to my little master. The Prince will have a fit!"

"Fie, you two depraved creatures, to make game of me in my predicament and repay my confidence with mockery!" wailed Mandarin Duck, overcome with anger and shame.

"Do not take it so badly, dear sister!" said the two, trying to calm her. "We were getting on so well together. A little joke like that among good friends is not really so wicked. But, seriously, what are you thinking of doing?"

"I'm not thinking of doing anything at all! I am just not going to appear! That will be enough!"

Little Ping shook her head doubtfully.

"That won't help you much. The Prince is a stubborn person and will not give way. If he does not succeed now, then it will be later on. The old *Tai tai* will not live forever, and cannot protect you your whole life long. When she is dead he will take possession of you by force. That would be still worse, whereas now the matter would still have some formality at least."

"Pshaw! He would not succeed so quickly. First of all, as her son, he would have to do the three years' mourning and during that time would have to put all thoughts of marriage out of his head. Meanwhile I would gain time to know what to do. If the worst comes to the worst I will cut off my hair and go into a convent."

"You have courage!" the two companions sighed admiringly.

"I will take a chance!" declared Mandarin Duck firmly. "The Princess intends to apply to my parents, as she said just now. My parents live in the southern capital. Ha-ha! She can be looking for them there for a long time!"

"But they are not lost to the world. As far as I know they are stewards of a house there; they will find them, all right," objected Little Ping. "Besides, you have your elder brother and your sister-in-law here in the neighborhood. They can turn to them too. It is a pity that you were born and grew up here in the house, and are therefore not so free as we are, who only came to belong to it later."

"Ha, that makes no difference to me! The stubborn ox cannot be made to drink. . . ."

"Be quiet, here comes your sister-in-law!" said Pearl, interrupting her talk.

"They have sent the right person! That is just a suitable errand for this capable universal camel-dealer!" muttered Mandarin Duck contemptuously. Meantime the sister-in-law had come up to them. The three stood up and wanted to make room for her on the ledge of rock.

"No, thank you. Do not stir!" said the sister-in-law. "I only want to discuss something with our girl."

"What is the hurry? Do take a seat. We are just passing the time guessing riddles; you can guess with us," prattled Pearl and Little Ping, pretending not to understand.

"Don't mind this nonsense! What is the matter, then? Out with it!" said Mandarin Duck, turning to the sister-in-law.

"Come with me! Not here!" said the sister-in-law, beckoning her. "I have a pleasant bit of news for you."

"Ah, you've come on the instructions of Prince Shieh, of course?"

"Well, come along, then, so that I can tell you details of your wonderful luck!"

Mandarin Duck stood up, drew up a mouthful of saliva from her throat, and spat it right into her sister-in-law's face.

"Kindly keep your dirt to yourself and be off—and get as far away from me as possible!" she began angrily. "I won't listen to this stupid talk of good luck and pleasant news! You really behave as if I were to be envied for the prospect of pining away my life at the side of an old tyrant, a profligate old man! That means wanting to chase me into a fiery pit with your eyes open! But I will not be misled by anyone, and I will decide my own weal or woe for myself!"

The dumfounded sister-in-law had not expected such a quick and thorough rebuff, and went away grumbling and sulking. Pearl and Little Ping tried for some time to calm the excited Mandarin Duck; then, turning to Pearl, Little Ping said: "From where did you come so unexpectedly just now? We didn't notice you coming."

"I had been with Miss Grief of Spring to fetch Pao Yu but I arrived a moment too late for he had already gone back to the Begonia Courtyard, so they said. That seemed doubtful to me, for I would have met him on the way. I thought he would be with Black Jade, but he was not there either. On the way back I saw you in the distance, so I hid myself in the bushes and slipped along quietly, and did a little eavesdropping. I am only surprised that your four eyes did not discover me."

"And I am surprised that your six eyes did not notice me," a voice was suddenly heard to say behind their backs. Three startled heads turned around as Pao Yu stepped out laughing from behind a projecting rock.

"Where did you come from? My eyes are worn out watching for you!" said Pearl.

"I saw you long ago and disappeared just for fun. The way you stretched your neck this way and that way and ran here and there searching desperately—it was too funny! Finally I chose your own nook here to hide in."

"Let us look around quickly! Perhaps someone else will suddenly emerge," said Little Ping in joke.

"So now he too has spied on us successfully," said Mandarin Duck, stretching herself out on the rock and yawning. Pao Yu shook her to make her sit up.

"You will get cold on the bare stone. Better come in with me. It will be more comfortable, and you can refresh yourself with a bowl of tea." And the four of them went off to the Begonia Courtyard.

Meantime Princess Shieh had got information from Phoenix about Mandarin Duck's family and learned that the parents had a position as house stewards in the southern capital and that it would not be easy to get hold of them, but that on the other hand an elder brother and his wife were within reach at any time, for both of them were in the service of the Ancestress. The brother, whose name was Wen Hsiang, was a buyer, and his wife was chief laundress. The Princess had had the wife called at once and had sent her to importune and harangue the obstinate Mandarin Duck, with the unfortunate results already reported.

"She abused me, using expressions which I cannot repeat before the *Tai tai,* and Pearl too attacked me," the sister-in-law complained, as she reported to the Princess the rebuff she had received. Because Phoenix was present she did not dare to mention that Little Ping also had attacked her. "The old master should look around for another woman. That nasty female would only bring him the greatest unhappiness."

"How did Pearl know about the business? Was anyone else present?" asked the Princess, suspiciously.

"Yes, Little Ping."

"Little Ping? What was she doing there?" interjected Phoenix, feigning ignorance. "Did she also take sides against you? You should have given her a box on the ear, the deserter! I have been looking for her half the day."

"I don't mean that she was actually present. I saw her from a distance, and I may have made a mistake," said the other, embarrassed, trying to correct herself. She did not want to incur the disfavor of the dreaded Phoenix. Happily, it escaped Princess Shieh that Phoenix had been playing a double game.

When she told her husband in the evening of the failure of her mission, Prince Shieh sent for his son Chia Lien.

"Go to the southern capital and bring old Chin Tsai, Mandarin Duck's father, here to me!" he ordered. "Somebody can surely be found to hold his job for him in the meantime."

Chia Lien felt little desire for this journey and tried by every possible excuse to get out of the request.

"The journey will be useless. According to recent news old Chin Tsai has been dying of consumption for some time," he lied. "His coffin has been ready for a long while. Perhaps he has died already. And one cannot do much with the mother, she is deaf . . ."

"Get out of my sight, you ill-bred jailbird's brat!" the Prince interrupted him angrily, and showed him the door. Then he had Mandarin Duck's brother brought in. But the next morning the brother had to report failure to his master. Mandarin Duck had definitely refused. The Prince raged.

"I know, it has been like that since ancient times; women prefer the young to the old," he complained. "Probably she has designs on my son or on Pao Yu. But she must give up any such ideas. I would like to know what rascal here would have the impudence to want her after I have stretched out my hand for her. And if she thinks she could marry outside the house with the help of the old *Tai tai*, she should think twice about it. Whoever she marries, she remains within my reach. Unless she prefers death or a convent, I will still force her, if not by fair means, then by foul. She would do better to change her obstinate mind and agree. Go and tell her that! And take care not to tell me lies. To make sure, I will get my wife to speak to her again. If you come back to me with a 'No' and my wife brings a 'Yes,' I warn you to mind your skull."

Wen Hsiang promised to do his best, went to his sister, and repeated the Prince's words to her. Mandarin Duck was speechless at first at the threat. But after a moment she had pulled herself together.

"Very well, I will give in and will go to the old *Tai tai* at once to inform her of my decision, and your wife shall accompany me there," she declared firmly.

Pleased at her apparent change of mind, the brother fetched his wife, and so Mandarin Duck, accompanied by her sister-in-law, went to the Ancestress's apartments. She found the old *Tai tai* in the midst of a big family circle: Madame Cheng, Aunt Hsueh, Widow Chu, Phoenix, Pao Yu, Precious Clasp, and the three Spring girls were present, as well as a swarm of waiting maids and serving women and several wives of the majordomo. Princess Shieh was missing.

Mandarin Duck went fearlessly up to the Ancestress, threw herself with a loud cry at her feet, and began to relate the outrageous demand which Prince Shieh had made of her, how he had importuned her, first through the Princess, then in the park through her sister-in-law, and finally through her brother; how he had pressed her, tried to intimidate her by threats, insulted her, and accused her falsely of an association with Pao Yu and Chia Lien, and had threatened never to let her out of

reach of his claws as long as she lived, even if she were to marry someone somewhere else, and even if he had to fetch her down from the
clouds. But she now solemnly declared before all present that she would
remain unmarried all her life long, and that if the old *Tai tai* should try
to force her to marry, she would prefer to take a knife and cut her
throat. She wished to serve the old *Tai tai* faithfully as long as she lived,
and if the old *Tai tai* should die one day, she would follow her voluntarily into the Realm of Shades or else cut off her hair and become a
nun.

"Heaven, earth, sun, and moon, all good and wicked spirits, be witness that I sincerely mean it, and may I suffocate from thick boils in my
throat if I lie!" she cried solemnly.

At the same time she quickly pulled out a scissors which she had
hidden in her sleeve, loosened her hair, and began wildly cutting off her
beautiful long braids. Luckily, she did not get very far in her work of
destruction, for some of the waiting maids and serving women standing
by fell excitedly upon her and stopped her.

The Ancestress trembled all over, she was so excited and startled by
the unexpected scene.

"What! They are trying to take away the best, the truest, and the
only dependable support I have!" she cried indignantly. And then, turning to Madame Cheng, she said: "That shows all your falseness! Outwardly you are a wonder of goodness and filial devotion, but behind
my back you plot vile actions! Do not begrudge me just what is dearest
to me!"

Madame Cheng, who had been addressed so ungraciously, though in
reality she was not implicated, stood up and endured the undeserved
reprimand of the Ancestress humbly and in silence like a well-behaved
daughter-in-law. The other ladies present were likewise hindered
through respect from uttering a word of reply. Just at the beginning of
the scene the Widow Chu had pushed the young girls out the door in
order not to let them hear Mandarin Duck's painful revelations. But
Taste of Spring, Madame Cheng's stepdaughter, had stood under the
window and attentively followed the further development of the scene.
It grieved her to see how her stepmother had been wrongfully reprimanded, and how no one had dared to say a word in her defense.
Bravely and resolutely she went in again and walked up to the Ancestress, with a smile. "The *Tai tai* is not to blame," she said. "After all
she cannot be held responsible for the deeds of the elder brother-in-
law."

"The child is right. Really, I have become rather thoughtless with
age," the Ancestress admitted with a smile, and turning to Aunt Hsueh
she continued: "Do not laugh at me! I have wronged your good, kind

sister. My reprimand should really be made to my other daughter-in-law, the wife of my elder son, who has taken part in this intrigue through fear of her husband."

And then turning to Pao Yu, she said: "Why did you not draw my attention to the fact that I had done an injustice to your mother?"

"The respect due to my uncle and aunt forbade me to take sides with my mother. Naturally, I was wrong and must ask her pardon."

"You are right. Kneel down and ask her not to be angry, and to forgive me on account of my age and for your sake."

Pao Yu knelt down obediently in front of his mother and was about to begin the required speech of apology, but Madame Cheng drew him to his feet with a smile and, as a devoted daughter-in-law, refused to accept an apology from his mouth excusing her mother-in-law.

"Now, Phoenix, what do you think?" said the Ancestress, turning to Phoenix.

"Oh, if I were perchance not your granddaughter but your grandson, I would certainly have been after Mandarin Duck long ago myself," said Phoenix, cleverly evading the delicate question with a joke, for she could not very well take sides openly against Prince and Princess Shieh.

"Very well then, I will give her up to you. You can have her," declared the Ancestress.

"Thank you, but give me time until my next rebirth. Perhaps I shall come into the world as a man next time, and then I shall fetch her."

"Take her and give her to your husband! Then your father-in-law will surely lose all further desire for her."

"Oh, she is too good for my husband. Two stale rolls like myself and Little Ping are good enough for him."

The whole company burst out in loud laughter. Then Princess Shieh was announced.

The Princess had come along quite unsuspecting, and only outside the door was she secretly informed of what had happened by some serving women. In her dismay she would have liked to get away again at once, but it was too late, for she had already been announced inside and Madame Cheng had come out to greet her. For good or ill she had therefore to make the best of the painful visit.

There was an embarrassed silence as she entered. The Ancestress made no reply whatever to her *tsing an*. Phoenix had already gone away on some excuse, and so had Mandarin Duck. Aunt Hsueh and Madame Cheng took their leave shortly afterwards, one after the other, tactfully, in order to avoid witnessing the humiliation of the Princess.

"You have played marriage broker for your husband," the Ancestress began, when she was alone with the Princess. "It was no doubt very kind and self-sacrificing of you, but it seems to me that your consideration for your husband goes a bit too far. You have children and grandchildren, and yet you still let yourself be tyrannized by your husband?"

"I have already called him to account at various times, but unfortunately without success. It is so difficult to advise him; the old *Tai tai* knows that herself," said the Princess in embarrassed self-defense.

"Then you would no doubt even go so far as to commit a murder for your husband, if he were to suggest it to you?" asked the Ancestress sharply. "You know how dependent I am on Mandarin Duck. My second daughter-in-law is ailing and cannot give me much attention. Phoenix is indeed helpful, but she has to look after everything in the house, therefore she cannot devote much time to me. So I have only Mandarin Duck to count on. She is zealous and efficient; she knows what I need and knows my peculiarities and my wishes, and in the course of her life which she has spent in this house she has devoted herself entirely to me. In short, she is indispensable to me. I am old and cannot very easily get accustomed to a new maid. I was just about to send word to your husband that if he must have another wife, he may buy one at my expense; I shall place eighteen thousand taels at his disposal for the purpose; but he shall not get Mandarin Duck under any circumstances. She is more precious to me for the remainder of my life than he is, for all his filial devotion, even if he were to exert himself for my well-being day and night. And that is enough about that! It is a good thing that you have come yourself, for you can deliver this message from me to him personally straight away. That is surer than if he were to hear it through my servants."

And with this the matter was settled for the Ancestress. She had the other ladies recalled and enjoyed herself with them over a game of mah-jongg.

While they were in the middle of the game Chia Lien came sneaking along cautiously. He had been sent by his father, Prince Shieh, to spy out the result of the Princess's mission. Just in the nick of time he ran into Little Ping outside the door. She told him how matters stood and warned him not to appear before the old *Tai tai*. She had been very angry indeed a short while ago and now, during the game, Phoenix had at last succeeded in getting her out of her bad humor to some extent by her funny tricks.

"Well, since she is in a good humor again I can venture to show myself," Chia Lien insisted, and in spite of being warned came nearer to the waiting maid. When Phoenix saw him sticking his head inside the door she gave him a warning look, which meant to say that he should disappear as quickly as possible. At the same moment Princess Shieh deliberately stepped in front of the Ancestress, on the pretext of having to pour out some tea, in order to screen him from her eyes, but the Ancestress had already caught sight of him.

"Who is outside? It seems to be one of the sons of the house," she said.

"I shall go and look," said Phoenix, and slipped out in order not to be there when her husband was rebuked. Chia Lien, having once been discovered, could not very well deny his presence. He walked up to the Ancestress as coolly as possible and with a smile offered his *tsing an!*

"I only wanted to know whether the old *Tai tai* will be present on the fourteenth, when the majordomo Lai Sheng gives his banquet in honor of the promotion of his son. If so, I want to have the large sedan chair put in order in good time," he began.

"If that is all you have to say, then you could come in without ceremony and need not first creep around outside like a ghost," replied the Ancestress crossly.

"I did not want to disturb the old *Tai tai* at her game and only wanted to ask my wife to come out," he said in embarrassed excuse.

"You could very well have waited until your wife went home. This ghostlike lurking and sneaking around is not mannerly! You frighten me unnecessarily! And now kindly let your wife finish her game with me and do not disturb us any more! Run off now and weave some more plots with Little Chao's wife against your wife!" retorted the Ancestress indignantly.

"Little Pao, not Little Chao," Mandarin Duck corrected her, while they all laughed at the confusion of the name. The Ancestress, too, smiled.

"Well, Little Pao or Little Chao! I have no memory for such treacheries!" she burst out heatedly. "In my time I came here as the young wife of a great-grandson of this house. Now I have great-grandsons. In the fifty or sixty years since then I have lived through much and seen many things, but such a base scandal as this I have never before experienced. Off with you! Out of my sight! What are you doing, still lurking around here?"

Silent and abashed, the culprit withdrew.

"I warned you, and yet you stumbled right into the net!" Little Ping called after him derisively outside.

"The old man is to blame for the whole scandal, and we two have to suffer for it!" said Chia Lien peevishly to Princess Shieh, who had hurried out after him.

"Fie, how can you be so unfilial! Other sons suffer even death for their fathers!" his mother too rebuked him now. "Take care not to

293

irritate your father these days! If you do you will get a thrashing into the bargain!"

"Will you please go to him first?" her son begged her dejectedly. "I don't dare."

So Princess Shieh went off to her husband alone and informed him of the sad result of her mission. The Prince realized that further steps would be useless, so he swallowed the insults which had been aimed at him, but he was so annoyed that, under the pretext of being ill, he did not show himself to the Ancestress for some time, and left his wife and his son to make the daily duty visits on his behalf. Moreover, he sent out his servants to look around for another suitable wife for him elsewhere. At last he succeeded in finding, for the price of eight hundred taels, a fresh seventeen-year-old to wed and conduct to his chambers.

CHAPTER 28

The Mad Robber Count has improper designs and experiences a flogging. The Cold Knight sets off on a journey to avoid trouble.

THE SON OF LAI SHENG, MAJORDOMO OF THE YUNGKUO PALACE, HAD attained to a high official position thanks to the patronage of his former princely masters. The proud parents had decided to celebrate the happy event duly by a banquet in their home lasting three days. The first day was reserved for the noble gentlemen and ladies and young girls from the Yungkuo palace and the Ningkuo palace, as well as some important guests from mandarin circles. On the second day the relatives and friends were to be feasted, and on the third day former colleagues from both palaces. The Princess Ancestress had graciously accepted the invitation, and on the fourteenth, accompanied by many members of the clan, both male and female, she personally graced with her presence the home of the former majordomo and his wife. The garden, with its beautiful pavilions, was reserved to the ladies, while the gentlemen were entertained in the reception hall.

Among the guests was a certain Liu Hsiang Lien, a close friend of Pao Yu and of the late Chin Chung. This orphaned scion of an ancient noble family was a merry fellow who was not much addicted to his books, but rather favored hunting and and military pursuits, flute and lute playing, wine and dice; neither did he disdain the abodes of flowers and willows. The handsome, well-built young man possessed, moreover, a great liking and talent for the theater and occasionally appeared in amateur performances as the gifted impersonator of the youthful heroine of sentimental "Wind and Moon" pieces. On the occasion of some

柳湘蓮

such amateur performance the libertine Hsueh Pan had seen and admired him, and had been unable to dismiss him from his mind ever since. He had a burning desire to make his acquaintance and become friends with him, erroneously believing him to be one of those loose-living theatrical youths who are ready to be seduced for an amorous game of "Wind and Moon." Therefore, his joy knew no bounds when he met him by chance at the feast, and he firmly decided to make friends with him then and there.

The host had engaged a troupe of actors to entertain his guests, and at the special wish of Prince Chen, who was merry from wine and who also was an admirer of his art and his person, young Liu had performed in two acts of one of his own pieces. Afterwards the Prince had made him sit beside him at the table for distinguished guests, and drawn him into a long and affable conversation. And so Hsueh Pan, who was sitting near by, became acquainted with him and, as he grew more and more exhilarated by wine, importuned him so obtrusively with insidious questions and amiable attentions that it gradually became irksome to young Liu, who availed of a favorable moment to rise from the table, and quickly decided to leave the party.

The host's son asked him to stay a while longer as Pao Yu, who was over there with the ladies, specially wished to speak to him alone after the company had risen from the table—a wish easily understood, as Pao Yu had to be wary of exposing himself to the chatter of his watchful cousins or to the mockery of the tipsy gentlemen. But if he, Liu, really must go already, perhaps he would wait just a little until the host's son had called out Pao Yu. Young Liu agreed to this, and his host sent a serving woman over to Pao Yu to call him away discreetly from the ladies.

Pao Yu took his friend to the library, which was somewhat secluded and where two people could chat undisturbed.

"I am worried about our good Chin Chung's tomb. Have you been out there recently?" began Pao Yu.

"Yes, quite recently, when out hunting with falcons. We were hunting scarcely two li away, and I took the opportunity of visiting the tomb secretly. I was afraid that it might be washed away or swimming in water after the heavy rains of last summer. My misgivings were well founded; it looked very much in need of repair, so I went out there again two days later with two coolies, and put it in order. The job cost me a few coppers."

"Ah, now I understand. Last month I sent my servant Ming Yen out there and ordered him to lay on the tomb as an offering ten ripe lotus kernels which I had plucked from the pond in the park with my own hand. On his return I asked him in what condition he had found the tomb and whether it had suffered very much from the summer rains. He said that, on the contrary, it looked much better than it had looked before, in fact like new. I thought at once that it must have been the work of some friend. Now I know that it was you. Unfortunately, I find it most difficult to get away from home, I am continually under observation; every step I take is watched and criticized. Therefore, I could not see to the tomb personally. And the silly thing is that I cannot even spend money on my own, although there is really enough money in our family."

"Do not worry on that account! After all, you have me. Call on me with confidence any time you want something from outside! Moreover, I have seen to it that on his next anniversary, the first of the tenth month, our dead friend shall receive a worthy burnt offering."

"I am glad of that. I was going to send Ming Yen to you about it; but you are such a drifting water plant, one can never know where to look for you."

"That is true, and now I have another long journey before me. This time I shall certainly not be back for three or four years."

"So long? What, then, is driving you away?"

"I cannot explain it to you now, in such a hurry. You will hear of it later. But now I would like to go."

"Could we not have another talk again this evening when the company has dispersed?"

"Unfortunately, it cannot be! I do not want to stay here any longer, or else there will be a quarrel with your cousin Hsueh Pan—you understand?"

"Yes, I well understand. Indeed, it is best for you to get out of the way. But before you set out on your long journey, we will see one another to say good-by, won't we? Promise me!"

"Of course I shall say good-by to you before I go. And please do not speak to anyone about my journey! Now go in again and let me disappear unobtrusively!"

They separated, and young Liu went towards the gateway. He was just about to leave through the gate when he encountered Hsueh Pan, who shouted: "Where is little Liu hiding? Who has let little Liu go out?" as he watched and searched for him. Young Liu's eyes flashed angrily when he saw the drunken fellow and heard him bawling. He would have liked best to knock him to the ground with a powerful blow, but consideration for his host prevented him from committing a violent outrage on his premises. Meantime Hsueh Pan had noticed him, and now greeted him as if he were a jewel he had lost and found again.

"Where do you want to go, dear little one?" he babbled, catching him by the arm.

"I'm going to take a little exercise, I'll come back again," replied young Liu.

"Ah, don't go away! There's no life here without you. Stay for my sake! I will do anything for you that you ask. Do you want money? Do you want a position? Your elder brother can get anything for you if you are just a little nice to him."

Young Liu felt greatly disgusted with the tiresome fellow. If he could only fix him once and for all! Then a good idea came to him. Assuming friendliness, he drew the other aside into a corner.

"Do you really want to be my friend, or are you only pretending?" he asked in a low voice.

"But, dear, good brother, how can you still ask such a thing?" replied the other joyfully, eying him askance. "If I do not mean it sincerely, may I fall dead immediately!"

"Very well. But here in this house we are hampered. Let us wait a little while. I will go away alone first. Follow me to my home a little later on! We will have a bit of a carouse tonight at my place. Besides, I have two charming young things there for company. But come alone, without servants! I myself have people to serve us."

Hsueh Pan became almost sober again with joy at his words.

"Really? Do you want to?"

"How can you still be doubtful?"

"But where shall I find you?"

"I live outside the city walls in front of the North Gate. You could stay the night with me."

"Oh, if I only have you I shall not think any more of home."

"Very well, I shall await you by the bridge at the North Gate. And see that you are not noticed going away from here!"

Hsueh Pan promised, and the two returned to the table and continued the carouse for a while longer. In his excessive joy Hsueh Pan tossed down so much wine that within a short time he was nine-tenths drunk. Young Liu soon left the table again, sent his servant home, and rode alone to the bridge in front of the Northern Gate. After the time required to take a moderate meal, he saw Hsueh Pan approaching at a trot on his big saddle horse. He was a ridiculous sight as he rode along, swaying to and fro in the saddle, his round head ceaselessly turning to right and left like a peddler's drum, his mouth open and his staring wine-drunk little eyes peering frantically about him. In the dusk he naturally failed to see Liu, who had stopped by the bridge, and quickly rode past him farther and farther along the highroad, out into the open country. In spite of his angry mood, Liu had to laugh at the blundering fellow, and he followed him at a discreet distance. As the district became more lonely and deserted, Hsueh Pan turned round his horse in a circle and made for the road back. Then at last he caught sight of young Liu.

"You are a decent fellow, you have kept your word!" he called out to him joyfully.

"Farther, farther! We go straight on for a while," Liu urged him, laughing, and trotted quickly ahead of him along the highroad. Hsueh Pan trotted after him, panting with exhaustion. At a very lonely spot, near a pond surrounded by reeds, Liu stopped, dismounted from his horse, and tied it to a tree.

"Get down! Here at this spot we will confirm our union by a solemn oath. Accursed be he who breaks faith and betrays the other. You swear first!" he cried grimly to Hsueh Pan.

"Agreed!" babbled Hsueh Pan, slipping down from the saddle and likewise tying his horse to the trunk of a tree. Then he knelt down on the ground and began solemnly: "I hereby vow eternal fidelity. Should I change my feelings and become a traitor, may the punishment of heaven and the vengeance of earth fall on me . . .!"

He had not yet finished his oath when he heard behind him a whizzing sound and immediately felt a powerful blow on his neck as if from an iron cudgel. Everything went black before his eyes, and golden stars danced through the darkness. He lost his balance and toppled over.

"Weakling!" snorted Liu contemptuously at the man lying in the dust. "He has felt only three-tenths of my anger as yet and already he is finished. Wait, there's more to come!"

He dealt him a few blows of his fist in the face and several kicks in the body, which brought the other down again and again as often as he tried to raise himself up.

"You call that friendship?" groaned Hsueh Pan. "If you did not wish to associate with me, why could you not say so in a friendly way? Why this deceit and maltreatment?"

He was about to go on to angry scolding, but Liu rudely cut him short.

"For whom have you taken me, the great Liu, in your blindness?" he shouted at him angrily. "If you try any impudence, you will get a lesson!"

And he gave him thirty or forty strokes of his horsewhip, then dragged him by the left foot to the muddy bank of the near-by reedy swamp and flung him down flat in a stagnant pool some steps from the edge.

"Do you know me now? Will you make an apology?" he asked him furiously.

Hsueh Pan, half sobered by the rough treatment and the cold dousing, was fully occupied in dragging himself out of the mud and slime, and only answered with miserable grunts and groans. Liu threw the riding whip onto the bank and belabored him anew with a few heavy blows of his fist.

Hsueh Pan heaved himself up onto dry ground with such an effort that his sinews almost snapped, and howled: "I admit that you are a respectable, honest fellow! I misjudged you. But that is the fault of others, who led me astray with their talk. . . ."

"Leave the others alone!" Liu interrupted him angrily. "Kindly keep to the point and to the present time!"

"Well, I admit my error. You are a good, respectable man, a perfect man of honor."

"That does not yet satisfy me. If I am to grant you mercy, kindly express yourself somewhat more courteously and humbly!"

"Dear younger brother!" panted Hsueh Pan. He got no further. The other had once more dealt him a blow on the face.

"Dear elder brother! . . ." Slap! Two blows again fell on his face.

"Good old master!" whined the humbled Hsueh Pan. "Graciously have pity on me! My foolish eyes were struck with blindness. From now on I shall respect and honor you."

"Drink two mouthfuls of this puddle water!" ordered Liu, to fill the measure of his humiliation.

Hsueh Pan put on a grimace of disgust.

"That dirty water? But no one could drink that!" he ventured to reply, and again Liu dealt him another blow of his fist.

"Very well, very well, I shall drink it," Hsueh Pan hastened to say, in order to ward off further ill. And he complied with the order by sticking his head down in the slimy pool and filling his mouth with the revolting fluid. But he did not get as far as swallowing it. He belched and had to vomit out the liquid together with the contents of his stomach.

"You are lucky that the air here does not suit me any longer," declared Liu brusquely, and, repelled by the stench of the place, he turned hurriedly away, loosened his horse, and trotted off.

The sudden disappearance of Hsueh Pan and young Liu from the table had not passed unnoticed. When they did not return, the whole house was searched for them, but they were not found. At last the news spread about that they had been seen trotting off quickly in the direction of the northern city gate. Thereupon Prince Chen sent his son Chia Yung with several servants out to the northern gate to look for them. About two short miles beyond the bridge by the gate, near a pond surrounded by reeds, the searchers found Hsueh Pan's horse tied to a tree. The rider cannot be far from where the horse is, they thought to themselves. And right enough, they now heard a miserable groaning and long-drawn-out cries for help coming from the edge of the pond. They dismounted and hurried to the spot whence the calls came. There they found Hsueh Pan lying among the reeds, his clothes wet through and dirty, his face disfigured, bruised, and covered with welts, lying like a water hog on the ground among the reeds. Chia Yung, who at once guessed nine-tenths of the truth, had his helpless uncle, who was groaning with pain, assisted to his feet by his servants.

"See how the great uncle now seeks out swampy puddles and muddy pools for the scenes of his amorous adventures," Chia Yung teased him. "He has probably bewitched the water-dragon Prince with his charm? Apparently he knocked against the dragon's horns in doing so."

Hsueh Pan was so ashamed that he would have liked best to creep into a crack in the ground. In his present bruised condition it was impossible for him to think of climbing into the saddle. There was nothing else to do but hire a sedan chair from the near-by Temple of Kuan ti, the god of war, and take Hsueh Pan back to town in it. At his urgent entreaty he was not taken back to the banquet, as Chia Yung had maliciously wanted, but was carried straight home.

So Chia Yung returned alone to the banquet table in Lai Sheng's house, and his report of his adventures made Prince Chen smirk and grin knowingly.

"Being trapped like that will do him no harm at all!" said the Prince maliciously.

When he went to visit him in his home later in the evening, he was informed that Hsueh Pan was ill and could not see anyone. When Aunt Hsueh and Precious Clasp arrived home somewhat later, Hsueh Pan's secondary wife Lotus met them with tear-stained eyes and pointed to the bedroom where they found Hsueh Pan lying in bed with bruised limbs and swollen face, doctoring himself as best he could. Luckily, he had come out of the scrap without any severe internal injuries or broken bones.

Aunt Hsueh was beside herself and abused her son and his torturer in turn. Actually, she wanted to complain to Madame Cheng and have young Liu arrested immediately, but Precious Clasp was able to dissuade her from this and pacify her. It was nothing but a little scuffle between drunken boon companions, she said. Such things occur often and one need not make much fuss about them.

"Besides, everyone knows our family heir as one who defies heaven and has contempt for the law," she continued. "If you were to let it come to a lawsuit, people would take sides against you and him. If you insist on getting satisfaction, have patience for a few days until Hsueh Pan is well again. Prince Chen will certainly show his gratitude for the banquet today by a counter-invitation. All the guests of today will be present, and also brother Hsueh Pan and that fellow Liu. Liu can then apologize before all those present. That is much better than letting it come to a public scandal."

"You are right, my child," agreed Aunt Hsueh. "The first outburst of anger clouded my understanding."

"In reality he deserves what he got," continued Precious Clasp, with a laugh. "Up to now he has had no respect either for you or for other people and has been behaving very badly day after day. He will only be taught wisdom by adversity. Two or three such bitter experiences and he will be cured!"

That night Hsueh Pan could not sleep a wink. He raged against his enemy, swore vengeance, and next day sent his servants with orders to tear down Liu's house and flay him or, better still, strike him dead immediately. But the servants returned without having performed their task. Young Liu had acted in drunkenness yesterday. On becoming sober he had regretted his action and had fled from the town through fear of punishment, so his neighbors had told them. How Hsueh Pan received this information you will hear in the next chapter.

CHAPTER 29

The libertine, shamed and disgraced, seeks distraction in a business expedition. A superior girl practices the art of poetry, studying the best masters.

THE NEWS OF THE FLIGHT OF HIS OPPONENT HAD THE EFFECT OF making Hsueh Pan's anger abate gradually. His physical state, too, had improved in the course of a few days, but shame over the outrage he had suffered continued to prevent him from appearing before his relatives and friends.

The tenth month had arrived. This is the time when travelling traders complete their annual accounts and set out for home, to spend the New Year Festival with their families. During those days many farewell dinners were given in the Yungkuo and Ningkuo palaces for the business managers who maintained various kinds of shops in the town on behalf of the two princely houses, and who were now departing for their homes. Among these business managers was one Chang Te Hui, who conducted a pawnbroker's shop for Hsueh Pan, and moreover himself possessed a private fortune of three thousand ounces of gold.

"The market has become very difficult today for mourning finery and perfumed fans," he remarked casually at the farewell dinner which

Hsueh Pan gave for him. "The prices of these articles will rise appreciably next year. I intend to put in good supplies in time, and then, in the first months of next year, to sell my goods at a profit when touring the provinces. Even after deducting the inland customs taxes, I shall probably make a good profit. Therefore, I shall stay away longer than usual this time and shall hardly be back before the Dragon Boat Festival on the fifth of the fifth month. Until then you must entrust the management of the pawnshop to my servants."

When Hsueh Pan heard him telling this, he thought to himself: Wouldn't it be wisest to join with him and invest some capital in his undertaking? I have suffered a shameful exposure here and it would do me no harm to disappear from the place for six months or a year and so escape unpleasant gossip. After all, I cannot very well go on indefinitely keeping out of people's way on the plea of being ill. Besides, this would afford me a good opportunity of finding a useful occupation. I am certainly old enough to really begin to do something. I have no taste for either books or soldiering, so a little trading should suit me better. To learn to use scales and abacus, and to get to know the country and the people, and new districts and customs, is also a valuable experience. Even if this journey does not bring me financial profit, it offers the advantage of a welcome change of occupation and scene.

Having debated with himself in this way, he calmly informed his business friend Chang of his decision after they had stood up from table. Would Mr. Chang please postpone his departure for two days, so that he could join him? The same evening he put the matter to his mother. Aunt Hsueh found his intention praiseworthy in itself, but, on the other hand, she feared that he would get into mischief on the way, with unpleasant consequences for himself, and uselessly squander the capital which he would take with him. So she did not wish to let him go. He was the mainstay of her old age, and after all he did not need to make money by such small trading efforts, she objected. But Hsueh Pan was fully determined not to be turned aside from his decision.

"You are always finding fault with my lack of knowledge and experience," he said. "One time you say I don't know this, and another time that I don't understand that. And now, when I want to break with my previous aimless life, enter a useful occupation, and become a competent person, you are against that too. How, then, am I to please you? After all, I'm not a girl who can be kept shut off from the outside world for her whole life. Besides, this Chang is a seasoned, experienced, and worldly-wise businessman whose company and conversation can do me nothing but good. He will certainly see that I do not get into any mischief, and his advice will be most helpful to me. My decision stands firm. I refuse to be deterred. Just you wait and see! I shall come back next year with my fortune made. You don't know me yet!"

Aunt Hsueh discussed the question with her daughter Precious Clasp. "Yes, his intentions sound quite laudable. If only he does not fall into his bad old ways again while he's away!" said Precious Clasp. "But you can't very well keep him tied to your apron strings. After all, he's a grown man, so why should he stick at home? Let him go out confidently and see a bit of the world. If he wants to mend his ways and become a useful member of society, do at least let him have a try! Moreover, in Mr. Chang he has a reliable adviser by his side. Besides, it can do him no harm to have to stand on his own feet for a change and do without the backing of his family, and be away from the friends who lead him astray. He will have to keep his eyes open and become self-reliant. Take courage and let him have the eighteen hundred ounces of silver which you have set aside for him in any case, and let him be off!"

"You are right. Let us hope he will take up a useful occupation!" agreed Aunt Hsueh, after lengthy consideration.

The next day she invited the business manager Chang to the house and had a meal served to Hsueh Pan and himself alone in the library. During the meal she herself, speaking through an outside window, informed the guest of her approval of the journey, adding a hundred practical hints and a thousand salutary warnings, which the guest promised, with two mouths at the same time, to take to heart. Hsueh Pan was supremely happy. The fourteenth day of the tenth month was picked out in the calendar as a lucky day for the departure. The intervening two days were filled with busy preparations for the journey, mother, sister, secondary wife, and two elderly serving women all helping zealously. Three big carts were filled with the luggage alone. As saddle animals Hsueh Pan was given a big mule, ice-gray in color, which belonged to his own family of Hsueh, and also a strong hack from the princely stables. For staff he was given five people, three experienced older servants and two young fellows. On the thirteenth there was a great leave-taking of the relatives. Then, early on the morning of the fourteenth, he set out on his journey. Mother, sister, and Lotus accompanied him as far as the inner gateway, and remained peeping out after the departing figure for a while, then turned back with sighs, half saddened and half relieved, to their apartments.

After Hsueh Pan was gone Aunt Hsueh had all the ornaments and furnishings taken from his gentleman's apartments into her own dwelling, and locked up his suite. Moreover, she arranged for Lotus to come to live in her suite and sleep with her at night. But Precious Clasp begged to be allowed to have Lotus live with her in the Park of Delightful Vision. There was plenty of room, and she could very well do with a companion and partner for the long winter evenings, so she said. Aunt Hsueh consented, and so Lotus packed her blankets and cushions and clothes and toilet articles and moved over to the Jungle Courtyard. Lotus was very pleased with the change; indeed, she had already intended to ask Aunt Hsueh's permission to go over now and then for a day to keep Precious Clasp company in the Park of Delightful Vision; and now she was actually to be allowed to live there permanently.

"I should so love you to teach me the art of poetry, if you have time and inclination," she said, radiant with joy, to Precious Clasp the very day she came over to her.

"My word, you are greedy! You are like the old Emperor Kuang Wu-ti, of the Han dynasty, who had hardly conquered the land of Lung when he began coveting the land of Chu also. Naturally, I shall be delighted to teach you the art of poetry, but not straight away on the first day. Today you must first of all pay your farewell visits to the old *Tai tai* and to the other ladies over there, one after the other, and then pay your first visits to all the young ladies here. If people ask you the why and wherefore of your presence here, you can say that I wanted you as companion."

Lotus was just about to set out on her round of visiting when the waiting maid Little Ping appeared on the scene.

"Here's my new companion since today," said Precious Clasp, pointing to Lotus. "I was just on the point of duly announcing her change over here to your mistress Phoenix."

"Why the formality? I have nothing against it."

"Oh, yes, but we must have order. It's on account of the gate watchmen at the entrance to the park, so that they may know that they have to let one more person in before they close the gates in the evening. But now you yourself can notify your mistress, and I shall not have to send over specially."

"Very well, I shall see to that. Has she already bidden farewell to her old neighbors and presented herself to her new ones?"

"She is just going to do so now."

"Tell her she'd better not visit us. Mr. Chia Lien is lying sick at home."

When Lotus had gone Little Ping took Precious Clasp aside and asked her in a whisper: "Have you heard about our latest scandal yet?"

"No. I was so busy in the last few days helping my brother to get ready for his journey that I could not bother about anything else. I haven't seen my cousins in the last few days either."

"Then you have not heard anything much about the severe flogging which Mr. Chia Lien got recently from his father, Prince Shieh?"

"No, I only heard a whisper of it, and that is one reason why I was going to visit Phoenix. What was the reason for it?"

"Naturally, that Mr. Yu Tsun is once more at the bottom of it—that dubious 'Gentleman from Nowhere,' who once got stuck halfway to the capital, half dead from hunger, and unfortunately did not pass out. In the ten years that he has been coming in and out of here, he has brought nothing but misfortune to our house. Well, I'll tell you the story. One day in the spring Prince Shieh chanced to see some beautiful old fans. From that time onwards he lost all liking for his own fans, and sent out his servants to find him old fans like those he had seen.

"Well, they do in fact hunt up a wretched old eccentric of a fan collector who has in his possession no less than twenty valuable old specimens. The old gentleman in question, who was commonly known as 'the stony eccentric,' must surely have had a quarrel with the Prince in some former existence. Be that as it may, though he's so poor that he has hardly a bite to eat, he will not part with his fans at any price. The Prince makes every conceivable effort to get at least a sight of the things. After two or three polite requests the eccentric at last expresses his willingness to receive the Prince and show him his treasures. They were all rare, unique examples, their handles and ribs made of marbled tear-bamboo or carved from coco-palm wood, elk's horn, and similar rare materials, and covered, moreover, with paintings and inscriptions made by the hands of historically famous persons.

"The Prince was firmly resolved to buy them, but when he asked the price, the eccentric owner shook his head and declared that even if he were offered a thousand batzes apiece, he would not give them up. The Prince went away foiled in his purpose, but he sent his son there every day to continue negotiating. He increased his offer gradually to five hundred batzes, but still the eccentric would not part with his fans. He would rather give up his life, he declared. The Prince was furious with his son and abused him for being an incompetent ass because he could not carry off the deal. Now, so far it is not too bad, and the matter would have blown over if that wretched Mr. Yu Tsun had not quite unnecessarily poked his nose into it. He suddenly brings a false charge against the queer old fellow, alleging that he has defrauded the State of this and that amount in rates and taxes, drags him to his yamen, puts him on trial, condemns him, and confiscates his goods and chattels, including the beautiful fans, by way of recovering the alleged debt due for taxes. Then he passes the fans on to the Prince at a low taxation value. The unfortunate owner died, so they say, of agitation and grief.

"The Prince then said contemptuously to his son: 'You have been telling me all along that this deal was impossible. How is it, then, that other people have been able to carry it through?' Whereupon Mr. Chia

Lien replied scornfully: 'That's a fine achievement indeed—to make a good, innocent man wretchedly unhappy for the paltry matter of those fans!'

"His thoughtless remark annoyed the Prince extremely. He was already on rather bad terms with his son on various grounds. To make a long story short, he had him severely flogged, not only on the back parts as he lay down, but all over his whole body, even his face, while he stood. He has bleeding wounds in two places from it. That is why the Mistress has sent me over here now. She wants some of that good ointment which you have."

Precious Clasp got the waiting maid Oriole to fetch the desired ointment; and she thought it better not to visit Phoenix under these circumstances.

After supper, while Precious Clasp went to the Ancestress, Lotus made a dash over to the Bamboo Hermitage to greet Black Jade. After a few preliminary words Lotus expressed her ardent desire to learn to write poetry, and she earnestly begged Black Jade to instruct her.

"I am not very accomplished myself, but I shall be able to teach you something at least," agreed Black Jade, in smiling acquiescence, "but first do me reverence and acknowledge me as your mistress!"

Lotus bowed politely before her and promised to be a good and docile pupil. Black Jade began her instruction straight away with a lecture on verse measure and structure, and on the importance of seeing that the correct words stand in correct sequence and relation to each other in the different lines and that they are contrasted in sense and sound; that, for example, an abstract word should be set against a concrete word, and a flat tone against a sharp one. Only poets who were competent to make a quite new, original poetic form were free of these rules.

"Is originality of expression the thing that matters, then?"

"Not so much of expression as of thought. One's thought must be genuine and original. Form and expression are only decorative accessories, so to speak. The language must not kill the spirit—that is the general principle."

"I love the poems of Lu Fang Kung," said Lotus naïvely, and she quoted two lines of this obscure poet.

"How on earth can anyone read and esteem such insipid stuff!" said Black Jade disdainfully. "But of course you have no judgment as yet; you lack the necessary book learning. If you really wish to study seriously, listen to my advice: Begin with Wang Wei.[1] I have got his 'Collected Works' here. Pick out a hundred of his poems in the five-word

[1] Wang Wei, 699–759.

pattern and impress them word for word on your memory. Then read a hundred and twenty of the seven-word poems of old Tu Fu.[2] Go on then and read thoroughly two hundred seven-word poems of the great Li Tai Po.[3] When you have made yourself familiar with these three masters you will have acquired a solid foundation. Then you may go on later to Tao Chien[4] and the other poets. If you proceed on these lines, within a year you will be able to take part yourself in poetry writing like a tried expert."

She got the waiting maid Cuckoo to fetch the volume of Wang Wei for the poetic aspirant.

"Take it with you and study particularly the passages which I have marked in red. And if any line does not seem quite clear to you, do not hesitate to ask me; I will gladly explain it to you."

Lotus went off very happy to the Jungle Courtyard with her volume of Wang Wei. All that evening and late into the night she sat under the lamp studying it, poem by poem, verse by verse. She seemed oblivious to all that was going on around her. Precious Clasp had to call her again and again before she went to bed at last. And she continued like that day after day with tireless zeal.

One morning, as Black Jade was at her toilet, Lotus came again to the Bamboo Hermitage, the volume of Wang Wei under her arm, and, after proudly reciting a verse from it, asked if she might have a volume of Tu Fu next.

"How many poems do you know by heart already?" asked Black Jade, smiling.

"All the poems which you had marked in red."

"And have you tried writing any yourself yet?"

"A little."

"Let's hear it!"

Thereupon Lotus treated her teacher to a first sample of what she could do, and then entered into an ardent literary discussion, in which Pao Yu and Taste of Spring, who happened to come in, also joined. Taste of Spring at once declared that Lotus must become a member of the Begonia Club.

"Oh, but I can only blunder along as yet; good will is all that I have," protested Lotus modestly.

"Don't let that worry you! All of us can only stumble along," said Black Jade and Taste of Spring simultaneously, laughing. "Who says that we can really compose poetry? People would positively laugh their

[2] Tu Fu, 712–770.
[3] Li Tai Po, 701–762.
[4] Tao Chien, 365–427.

teeth out of their mouths if our amateur efforts were to penetrate beyond the precincts of the park and become public."

"Oh, don't pretend to be too modest!" protested Pao Yu. "When our club came under discussion at a party recently, some of my friends asked to see some samples of our art; I wrote out a selection of our poems for them and submitted them to their judgment. They were received most enthusiastically, and a great many copies have been made and distributed."

"Is that true?" interjected Black Jade and Taste of Spring simultaneously.

"Of course it is. I don't gabble lies like your parrot there on the perch."

"Well, you shouldn't have done that!" scolded the two young girls. "It was most indiscreet of you. Whether the images painted by our ink brushes can be considered real poems or not, they were definitely not meant for publication."

"What harm is it, anyway? What would we know today of the many beautiful poems written by young girls in the past, if they had not been made public by indiscretions?"

The discussion was interrupted by the appearance of Grief of Spring, who wanted Pao Yu to give his verdict on the big painting of the park on which she had been working for many weeks past at the order of the Ancestress. Lotus also went off with a volume of Tu Fu, after Black Jade had given her, at her request, another theme to work on. She was to compose a poem consisting of eight seven-word lines on the beautiful harvest moon of last night, with the basic rhyme *an* recurring six times.

She sat up far into the night, partly over her Tu Fu and partly over her own composition, and so engrossed did she become that she completely forgot to eat, drink, or sleep.

"You will make yourself ill; it is really absurd of you," scolded Precious Clasp. "You are a bit weak in the head by nature already, and now you will go quite crazy! But it's all Black Jade's fault, and I'll take her to task for it!"

"I'll come right away, dear young lady; but please don't disturb me now!" replied Lotus absently; and she went on writing until she had finished her work. The following day she showed it to Black Jade for her verdict.

"The thought is not bad, but the language is inadequate. That is because you lack education and are not well read. It all sounds too forced. But do not be discouraged. Try again!" This was her teacher's verdict.

Lotus walked thoughtfully into the park. She did not trust herself to return to the Jungle Courtyard. Precious Clasp would be sure to laugh at her over her bad marks. So she lingered by the fishpond, wandered under the trees, rested on blocks of rock, staring absently into space, or, bending low, traced ideographs in the sand. Her peculiar behavior was soon noised abroad among the other inmates of the park. In no time the Widow Chu, Precious Clasp, Taste of Spring, and Pao Yu hurried along and, hiding behind a shelf of rock, watched her every movement with anxious attention, as she knit her brows, frowned or laughed to herself. It all seemed very strange to them!

"She's a bit crazy," whispered Precious Clasp to the others. "She sat up last night until the fifth night watch, muttering to herself and writing, writing and muttering. It was already dawn when at last she lay down to sleep. As soon as there was light I heard her moving about again, making a hurried toilet and then running off to Black Jade without taking any breakfast. And now there she is at it again! I ask you, is that normal?"

"She is an unusual person and no doubt divinely inspired," said Pao Yu, reverently. "Up till now we have laughed at her and considered her commonplace. Now her true nature is breaking out."

"You would do better emulating her instead of merely admiring her; think how it would help your studies," said Precious Clasp teasingly. He bore her hint in silence. At this moment Lotus threw back her head with a jerk, jumped up, and ran off in the direction of the Bamboo Hermitage.

"Come! Let us run after her and see what she's up to next!" suggested Taste of Spring. And they all followed her to the Bamboo Hermitage. They arrived there just in time to see Black Jade looking through the new version of the poem about the moon and criticizing it. She found it still insufficiently polished and demanded a third version. Lotus was crushed. She had imagined that this time she had really got it right. The others encouraged her, and so she set to work for the third time, seated on the stone terrace in front of the bamboo hedge, her eyes and ears closed to all that was going on around her.

"Do take a rest!" Taste of Spring called out to her from the window.

"Rest doesn't fit in with the rhyme!" replied Lotus absently.

"She is really possessed by the demon of poetry; Black Jade has to answer for that!" remarked Precious Clasp amid general laughter.

"Why should I not teach her, since she asked me to do so?" asked Black Jade in self-defense.

"Let's take her over to Grief of Spring and show her the new painting; that will distract her," suggested the practical Widow Chu. They followed her advice, took Lotus, and laughingly bore her off, past the Lotus-Root Pavilion, to the Little Castle of Warm Perfumes. Grief of Spring was just resting from her painting and had dropped off to sleep on a divan. The picture, which stood on an easel, was covered with a cloth. They awoke the sleeper, drew the cloth off the easel, and looked at the picture. One-third of it was finished, and showed only three of the ten pavilions in the park. The girls pointed out to Lotus the various beautiful young girls who had been painted into the landscape.

"Every girl who can compose poetry is put into the picture," they explained to her in jest, "hurry up and study, so that you also will figure in it!"

The slight distraction with the picture did not divert Lotus for long. She spent all the rest of the day and almost the whole night at her composition. Even in her sleep she kept on searching for suitable words and rhymes. Once Precious Clasp heard her exclaim: "Ah! Now I've got it! She won't be able to find any fault with it this time!"

She will never learn to compose poetry, but she *will* go off her head trying to do so, thought Precious Clasp to herself, with a sigh. Curiously enough, however, the right formation of the eight lines, which had eluded Lotus in her waking hours, actually came to her in her dreams. When she took over the fresh copy to the Bamboo Hermitage the next morning, she found Pao Yu and all the young ladies of the park already gathered there expectantly, for Precious Clasp had spread the news of the zealous apprentice's audible dream ravings.

"Here! Examine it, and if you don't find it good, I'm through with poetry-writing forever!" Saying this, Lotus walked in and handed Black Jade her manuscript. They all bent their heads inquisitively over the sheet of paper.

"Not only faultless but new and original in form and content," was the general verdict, and it was unanimously decided to accept Lotus as a new member of the Begonia Club as a result of this proof of her talent.

CHAPTER 30

A quack doctor treats Bright Cloud with "tiger and wolf medicines."
Despite being ill, Bright Cloud heroically sacrifices herself for Pao Yu
and mends his peacock-plume cloak.

Soon after Lotus had been received into it, the Begonia Club acquired a big influx of new members. One fine day in the tenth month a whole lot of new relations came to the Yungkuo palace— two Misses Li, cousins of the Widow Chu, together with their mother; a younger cousin of Precious Clasp named Precious Harp, together with an elder brother, and finally an impoverished sister-in-law of Princess Shieh with her daughter Wreath of Clouds—in all, seven persons. The three parties had met by chance on the way there and, having ascertained their mutual relationships, had continued the journey together. The Ancestress, who could never have enough relatives around her, welcomed the new arrivals most warmly and kept the whole lot of them as permanent guests of the house.

She was particularly enchanted with Precious Harp, who if possible even surpassed her cousin Precious Clasp in charm. She got Madame Cheng to adopt her, but took her to live in her own apartment. While her father was still living in the capital the young girl had been betrothed to a young man named Mei, son of the member of the Han Lin Academy, and now had come to town escorted by her elder brother for the celebration of the marriage, which was to take place soon. Her brother was lodged with Aunt Hsueh and lived in the rooms formerly occupied by Hsueh Pan. The other three young girls found accommodation in the Park of Delightful Vision—Wreath of Clouds with her cousin Greeting of Spring, the daughter of Prince Shieh, and the two Li girls with their cousin the Widow Chu in the Rice Farm.

To the great joy of the Begonia Club, all the four new cousins were well versed in literature and poetry, and were heartily welcomed as new members of the club. The membership of the club thus rose to fourteen —the Widow Chu as chairman, the three Spring girls, the two cousins Precious Clasp and Precious Harp, and the two sisters Li Wen and Li Ki, Black Jade and Pao Yu, Little Cloud, Lotus and Wreath of Clouds, and Phoenix as honorary chairman. True, the latter did not understand the art of verse-making, but she had been prevailed upon to accept the honorary chairmanship so that her powerful financial help might make the various club fixtures possible. In this she had come up to expectations, and immediately on joining the club she had replenished its scanty funds with a handsome subscription of fifty taels.

The Widow Chu was the oldest member in years; after her came Phoenix. The age of the other members ranged from fifteen to seventeen. As most of them had not known each other long and had not got the dates of each other's birthdays very accurately in their heads, there was much amusing confusion over forms of address, and it often happened that a younger member addressed an elder one as "younger sister," and vice versa. And so in these winter months, the Begonia Club became extremely active, and literary rivalry reached a new peak in the Park of Delightful Vision.

One day Pearl had asked for an extended leave at the wish of her dying mother, who wanted to have her near her in her last hours. During her absence the waiting maids Bright Cloud and Musk had to take her place in personal attendance on Pao Yu. "See that your master

李純

goes to bed early and rises early and does not get into any mischief," Phoenix had impressed upon them.

The first night after Pearl had left Pao Yu called her name twice in his dreams.

"What is it?" asked Musk, yawning, from near by.

"I want tea."

While Bright Cloud remained lazily in bed, Musk got up and hurried into the kitchen. As she had only got on a red quilted petticoat, he made her put on his warm sable fur. She brought him a bowl of tea and poured out half a bowl for herself.

"Bring me a drop too," begged Bright Cloud.

"My word, you put on as much airs as if you were a daughter of the house."

"I will dance attendance on you tomorrow in return. You need not stir the whole day."

Musk did as she asked and brought her a bowl of tea. "And now I want to slip out for a moment," she said. "Go on chatting. I will be back at once."

"Beware of the ghosts outside!" Bright Cloud called after Musk.

"There's clear moonlight; you need not be afraid. We'll be talking until you come back," said Pao Yu. A significant clearing of the throat gave Musk to understand that he wished to be left alone with Bright Cloud. Already Musk had reached the back door and slipped out under the felt curtain into the moonlit courtyard.

Bright Cloud suddenly felt tempted to slip out after her and give her a bit of a fright. As she was strong and healthy by nature she did not trouble to dress first, but climbed down from her alcove just as she was, with only a short petticoat on, and slipped out the door.

"Don't catch cold!" cried Pao Yu warningly after her, but she was already out the door. She was hardly outside, however, when she felt a cold wind cutting through her flesh and bones. She shivered, but remained outside all the same. She was just about to creep up on Musk from the back and frighten her by calling out at her, when she herself was startled by Pao Yu's voice, calling her back from within. She hurried to his bedside.

"You frightened me to death!" she said to him, laughing.

"I did not want to frighten you, I only wanted to save you from catching cold. Besides, if you go fooling about outside at night you may disturb other people's sleep and cause gossip. I don't want it to be said that the devil broke loose here as soon as Pearl's back was turned. Come over here and straighten my blanket!"

Bright Cloud went up to his bed to straighten his blanket and in doing so let her hand slip a little under it.

314

"Ugh! How cold your hand is!" he cried with suppressed laughter, and rubbed her cold, red cheek.

"Come in under the blankets and get warm!" he whispered to her, but unfortunately at that moment the door creaked and Musk came back. She was out of breath and reported excitedly that she had just got a fright outside. She thought she had seen someone cowering in the dark shadow of a rock, and she was going to call for help, but it was only a pheasant, and it flew away at her approach.

"Wasn't it lucky that I did not scream? That would have caused a nice uproar in the house. Where was Bright Cloud hiding herself? I was sure she would slip out after me."

"I scared her back; otherwise she would have given you a fine fright."

"It wasn't even necessary; she took care of that herself," remarked Bright Cloud, climbing up into her alcove again.

"Surely you did not go out like that, like an unsaddled race horse?" asked Musk.

"Of course she went out like that," said Pao Yu.

"How silly of her! She has probably caught a nice cold!" As she said this a double sneeze resounded from Bright Cloud's alcove.

"Now the trouble begins," sighed Pao Yu.

"She has not been well all day; and she had no appetite, either, but instead of minding herself, she goes playing hide-and-seek and running about ridiculously undressed. It will serve her quite right if she is ill in the morning!" scolded Musk, as she poked the stove, shovelled out the hot ashes, and put on two logs of aromatic Cambodian wood. After she had trimmed the wick of the lamp behind the dividing screen, she snuggled down once more on her couch near Pao Yu's canopied bed. Close by, the big clock struck twice, tang, tang. From the serving women's room came a strong twice-repeated sound of throat-clearing, and a voice called over in a tone of annoyance:

"Will the young ladies please keep quiet and go to sleep at last? There will be time for chattering again tomorrow!"

A little more suppressed giggling and whispering, then silence returned at last to the Begonia Courtyard.

The next morning Bright Cloud awoke with a heavy cold. Her nose was obstructed, her voice was hoarse, her limbs were heavy and stiff. According to the rules of the household every illness, however trifling, had to be reported at once to the *Tai tai*, and the old *Tai tai*, who was very apprehensive about infection, was in the habit of getting sick servants out of the palace immediately and sending them back to their families. Pao Yu, already deprived of Pearl, was unwilling to have the pretty maid Bright Cloud also removed from his vicinity. He therefore decided to keep her at home and to get a doctor for her, unknown to the Ancestress.

"But Madame Phoenix at least should be told. Otherwise she may find out that the doctor has been here, and take it amiss that she has not been told about it," objected Bright Cloud.

Pao Yu agreed, and sent a serving woman to Phoenix. Bright Cloud had caught a slight cold, it was nothing at all serious, and he begged— so the message ran—to be allowed to look after her at home as he could not well do without her; he would get a doctor in by the side gateway, and would she, Phoenix, please not make any fuss about the matter. Phoenix sent back word that she had no objection, but if there was not an immediate improvement the patient must definitely leave the house and go back to her family, for the danger of infection was particularly great in these winter days and the health of the young ladies was very precious.

"She really carries on as if I had the plague!" exclaimed the offended patient, peevishly. "Very well, then, I'd prefer to go away at once in order to save the grand ladies here from any more headaches."

She sat up and was about to start packing her things, but Pao Yu pressed her gently back on her bed.

"Do not be so quick to take offense!" he said placatingly. "Phoenix feels responsible to the old *Tai tai*, and wants to feel that she has done her duty in case anything should happen, but she did not mean it so strictly as all that."

At that moment the doctor whom he had sent for appeared on the scene, escorted by three elderly attendants. Pao Yu hid hurriedly behind a bookcase. The serving women let down the red embroidered curtain in front of Bright Cloud's alcove, then the patient had to stretch her hand out through the curtain. The doctor looked for a while at the hand and the two fingers, the nails of which were two or three inches long and dyed red with China balsam. Then he felt the pulse after a serving woman had wrapped a clean handkerchief around the patient's wrist.

"Internal congestion, external irritation; a slight cold due to the bad weather." In these words he explained his diagnosis to the serving women when they got outside the door. "Fortunately, the young lady is observing moderation in eating and drinking, therefore the cold has not done her much harm apart from a slight deterioration in her breathing and in the circulation of the blood. A little dose of medicine, and she will be all right again."

The chamberwoman escorted him out of the park again. Widow Chu had taken care that he should not catch sight of any of the youthful female inmates of the park on his way out. Having reached the park gate, he stepped aside into the gatekeeper's lodge to write his prescription. When he was about to go, a serving woman asked him to wait a moment. The young master wished to see his prescription and might want to speak to him.

"Oh, was the patient a young gentleman? The apartment, with its lowered bed curtain, gave me the clear impression of being a young girl's room. I thought I had the honor of treating a young lady of the house," remarked the doctor, astonished.

"This is your first time here, so naturally you could not know the constitution of the household," a serving woman explained to him, with a smile. "You have just been in the residence of our young master, and your patient was not a young lady, a daughter of the house, but one of the young gentleman's waiting maids. You would hardly have received admission so easily to the bedroom of a young lady." And she took the prescription and ran off with it to the Begonia Courtyard, to show it to Pao Yu. Pao Yu read it. There was something in it about purple thyme, ironwood, sage, and lemon, and "broth of horse's tail," and the like.

"Damn it all!" he exclaimed. "What does the fellow think he's doing? He has prescribed stuff here which might be all right for one of us, but not for a frail young girl! Send him about his business at once and get a better doctor!"

"We shall send for Doctor Wang at once," promised the serving woman who had been responsible for the first doctor's having been called. "Who would have thought that that one would be such a quack? But we certainly cannot let him go without paying him something. For it was we who sent for him, and not the majordomo."

"How much do you think we should give him?" asked Pao Yu.

"A tael would be about right."

"And how much does the other one, Doctor Wang, get?"

"Doctor Wang, like Doctor Chang, is one of our regular house doctors here. He need not get a special fee for this particular visit. He draws his regular salary at the four annual festivals."

"Very well, go and take the quack his tael," Pao Yu ordered Musk.

"Yes, I would if I knew where Pearl has put our housekeeping money," said Musk.

"As far as I know, she keeps it in her little cabinet with the shell and mother-of-pearl incrustation. Come, let us look!"

Together they went into Pearl's room, which was crammed with furniture and belongings, and opened the cabinet in question. They found the top section full of painted fans, purses, bags, perfumed pomades, handkerchiefs, and similar small articles. On the lower shelf lay some thousand-piece strings of money. Besides these compartments there was a drawer. In this they found an open cashbox made of plaited bamboo containing several pieces of broken silver and a small money weight. Musk picked out one piece of silver at random and put it on the scale.

"Is that much a tael?" she asked Pao Yu uncertainly.

"You ask me in vain," said Pao Yu with an embarrassed smile, for he was no wiser than she was in the matter of weighing money.

"I will ask the others."

"Whatever for? Just take that piece. If it's a bit more or less, what does that matter? We are not peddlers here."

Musk put away the scales and weighed the piece of silver thoughtfully in her hand.

"Well, let's only hope it's not less than a tael," she said hesitantly, "else that poor devil of a quack might get a false impression of us; not that we do not know how to weigh the stuff—that would hardly occur to him. But he would probably think that we gave him so little deliberately because we are hard up and have to count our pence."

"That's half a five-ounce bar," put in a serving woman, who had been listening, from the door. "The piece you're holding in your hand weighs a good two ounces. You may pick a smaller piece with an easy conscience."

"Ah, why should we search any more? Here, keep the extra bit for yourself!" said Musk bumptiously.

"And let Ming Yen go fetch Doctor Wang at once!" added Pao Yu.

After a little time Doctor Wang arrived and examined the patient anew. His diagnosis was not much different from that of his colleague, but his prescriptions were considerably different. This time the harsh purgatives and sudorifics were omitted, and in their place there was mention of archangel root, peony root, and similar mild drugs. Moreover, the dosage of the individual drugs was not so great as in the first prescription.

"This pleases me better; it looks more like the right medicine for young girls," said Pao Yu complacently to his two waiting maids. "Those purgatives and sudorifics must definitely not be used too freely. When I was a child and used to get head colds and constipation, the doctors never treated me with 'horsetail broth' and chalk and lemon and 'tiger and wolf' medicines of that kind. What was too rough for me is definitely not the right thing for the tender constitution of young girls."

An old serving woman brought in the various medicines. Pao Yu instructed her to fetch the silver vessel in which medicines were usually prepared and to concoct the brew at once in Bright Cloud's room over the charcoal fire.

"Do please have them prepared on the proper stove in the kitchen, otherwise this whole room will stink of medicine fumes, and that would be unbearable!" protested Bright Cloud.

"Oh, but medicine fumes are much more precious than all flower perfumes put together," Pao Yu remarked persuasively. "Could there be anything better or more noble than those herbs which holy hermits have cultivated, and picked, and prepared in their solitude? Here, where otherwise everything is beautiful, there is one thing which I have always missed—the fragrance of healing herbs and wonder-working drugs. Only now will the right harmony be achieved, and my contentment be complete."

And so it was that, when he returned after a lengthy visit to the house of the Ancestress, he found his apartments filled with the penetrating odorous fumes which poured out of Bright Cloud's room. Bright Cloud bravely swallowed her hot broth and took a second dose of it in the evening, but without any real success. True, she sweated a bit in the night, but the next morning she complained as before of headache and fever, obstructed nose and coated tongue. Doctor Wang turned up to examine her for a second time and changed this and that item in his prescription, increasing one and reducing another. When the revised prescription also failed to produce results, Pao Yu gave the peremptory order: "Fetch the snuff!"

Musk sprang to her feet and brought him a little gold-edged crystal snuffbox decorated with two golden stars. Pao Yu raised the lid. The inside had a picture of a naked woman with golden hair and wings on her shoulders, painted on European enamel. The box contained genuine European snuff of the very best quality. Bright Cloud became completely engrossed in examining the picture.

"Here! Sniff it! It must not remain long uncovered or else the aroma fades!" Pao Yu urged her.

Bright Cloud quickly lifted out a pinch, put it to her nose and sniffed, then took and sniffed several more pinches in the same way. Suddenly she perceived a sharp, biting, prickly sensation from deep within her nostrils right up to her temples, and immediately had to sneeze so forcibly five or six times in rapid succession that her eyes and nose were flooded.

"Ugh! How it bites! Quick! Fetch me paper!" she cried laughing. A little maid jumped up and brought her a whole bundle of fine tissue paper. Bright Cloud pulled out sheet after sheet and wiped her nose with it.

"Well, how's that?" asked Pao Yu anxiously.

"Oh, that was fine!" she cried, delighted. "I really feel much better already. Only my temples are still aching."

Pao Yu was quite proud of the rapid success of his own medical treatment. He did still more, and procured for the patient a little of the European ointment which Phoenix was always in the habit of rubbing on for headaches. Then he left the sickroom and strolled out into the park to seek some relaxation with Grief of Spring, who was sitting before her easel, painting.

On the way he met Snail, Cousin Precious Harp's little chambermaid, who was on her way to Black Jade's home, the Bamboo Hermitage. Her mistress and Precious Clasp were there, she said. Thereupon he changed his mind and accompanied Snail to the Bamboo Hermitage.

"Here's another visitor! All the seats are already engaged!" This was the laughing greeting which met him as he entered Black Jade's bedroom.

And in fact he found no less than four cousins—Black Jade, Precious Clasp, Precious Harp, and Wreath of Clouds—gathered round the glowing brazier. Cuckoo, the waiting maid, was sitting not far from the window on the edge of the bed doing some needlework.

"What an enchanting picture!" cried Pao Yu admiringly. "One could call it 'A Gathering of Girls in Winter.' And how cozy and warm you are in here!"

He settled down comfortably in an easy chair covered with squirrel fur which Black Jade was in the habit of using. His glance fell on a jade vase in which five hyacinth flowers made a fine show.

"Where did those magnificent hyacinths come from? They were not here yesterday, were they?" he asked.

"They are a present from the wife of your majordomo, Lai Sheng," explained Black Jade. "She gave Precious Harp two vases of hyacinths like that one, and two of calycanthus. Precious Harp has handed on a vase of hyacinths to me and one of the vases of winter sweet to Little Cloud. Do you like the hyacinths? You may have them."

"No, thank you. I have some in my place, but they are not as beautiful as yours. Anyway, you cannot well give yours away!"

"Why not? I have an abundance of perfumes here already—medicinal odors. My drug vessel never leaves the fire the whole day. It would really be a pity if the beautiful pure perfume of the flowers should be spoiled by these medicine fumes. All these strong perfumes are a bit too much of a good thing; they make me feel quite weak."

"The drug caldron has been simmering over in my quarters too since yesterday," he said, laughing, and told of Bright Cloud's cold. "And don't you think that hyacinths and calycanthus would be most delightful and fitting themes for our next club session?" he added.

At this the conversation turned to poetical composition.

"The next time the club holds its session in my place you will all get a surprise," said Precious Clasp, putting on a stern air. "Each member

320

will have to produce four five-word rhymed octets, and four verses each of twelve lines in flowery language and unrhymed verse, on eight different themes. The first theme will be: '*Tai chi tu*—Thou great Destiny,' and no one will be let off!"

"Don't believe her! She's only joking!" interjected Cousin Precious Harp, smiling. As the daughter of a big businessman she was already widely travelled despite her youth, and was generally admired by the cousins for her knowledge of the world and her more emancipated views. "Why should we bother with tedious philosophical themes from the *I Ching*, the Book of Changes? Besides, we would not produce anything very brilliant from it; at the best it would be stilted and artificial. Which just reminds me of something. When I was eight years old my father took me along on a journey to the coastal cities of the Western Sea, where he used to purchase foreign goods. There I made the acquaintance of a beautiful fifteen-year-old European girl. She was just like those beautiful women whom one often sees in European paintings. Golden hair fell in loose locks over her shoulders. Her jewelry consisted of corals, brilliant agates, and green cat's-eyes. She wore a fine vest of gold mesh. In the belt which held in her long-sleeved dress of Western damask she wore a small jewelled dagger in a golden sheath. She was wonderfully beautiful to look at, even more beautiful than those women in the pictures. It was said that she knew our Chinese poetry and our Six Classical Books, and that she even understood Chinese literature. My father asked, through the Consul, to see some examples of her Chinese poetry. He and all his friends found them astonishingly good."

"Oh, show us a sample of them!" begged Pao Yu excitedly.

"I am sorry that I cannot. I have put the poems away at home, in the southern capital."

"What a pity!" he sighed, disappointed. "How lucky you are to see something of the world. That luck will never be mine."

"Do not be taken in by her!" cried Black Jade. "She has brought so much luggage here; why should she leave just those poems at home? I simply do not believe in the existence of those poems!"

"That's just like Black Jade. She won't be taken in! But this time she is definitely too skeptical," remarked Precious Clasp.

"Let Precious Harp prove her assertion by visible evidence; until then I will not believe her," insisted Black Jade.

"Have patience for a few days until she has unpacked and tidied all her things; then the poems will come to light," retorted Precious Clasp. "Do you not know one or another of them by heart? Do, please, recite one of them to us as best you can!" she said, turning to her cousin.

"Gladly. I can remember a rhymed five-word octet. Quite an achievement for a European girl," replied Precious Harp.

"Come, let us hear it! No! Wait until I call Little Cloud; she must hear it too," said Precious Clasp.

"Run over to the Jungle Courtyard and ask the young lady to come over," she bade the waiting maid Snail. "Tell her that there's a beautiful European girl who can compose poetry in Chinese, whom we are admiring over here. And tell her to bring back the other poetry-mad girl with her."

After a short time Snail came back with Little Cloud and Lotus.

"Where is the European beauty?" cried Little Cloud while still a long way off.

"She is not yet here bodily, but you can already hear her speaking," came the laughing answer.

Precious Harp once more repeated for the benefit of Little Cloud and Lotus what she had just recounted about the beautiful girl from the distant West. Then she recited:

> "Last night I dreamt the dream of the red chamber.
> Tonight my songs rise in a rain-drenched land.
> Cloud islands gather above sea foam,
> Mountain mist drifts on thickets and pine trees.
>
> Under the eternal moon there is no more time,
> Only the ceaseless rise and fall of changing moods.
> Can I ever forget the springtime of childhood
> South of the bed of the river Han?"

"Splendid! She can compose poetry almost better than we Chinese!" was the general verdict. The talk went on a little longer; then the secondary wife Chao came to inquire how Black Jade was, and the company broke up.

Early the next morning Pao Yu set out under a gray, overcast, wintry sky for the apartments of the Ancestress to give her his usual morning greeting. The Ancestress had not yet got up, but she allowed him to come into her bedroom. Cousin Precious Harp, whom he perceived lying beside the Ancestress with her face to the wall, was still fast asleep.

"Is it snowing?" asked the Ancestress with a glance at Pao Yu's rough weather-cloak of reddish brown monkey-hair felt.

"Not yet, but it certainly looks as if it will."

"Bring him the peacock-feather cloak!" the Ancestress ordered her waiting maid, Mandarin Duck. The maid brought in a magnificent cloak, which shimmered gold, blue, and green, and which he saw now for the first time. It was even more beautiful than the fur-trimmed duck-

寶琴

feather coat which the Ancestress had recently given to her new favorite, Precious Harp.

"This is the golden bird-droppings cloak," declared the Ancestress jokingly. "Here, I'm making you a present of it. It comes from Russia and is worked in peacocks' feathers and silk yarn. Go and show it to your mother!"

Pao Yu performed a kowtow of thanks and went off proudly with the precious garment. Outside he passed Mandarin Duck. She looked away deliberately. Since the day on which she had made her solemn vow of chastity she had avoided him and no longer spoke to him.

"Have a look, how does this new cloak suit me?" he asked her, smiling. She only waved him off with a gesture of the hand and disappeared immediately into the Ancestress's bedroom.

After his mother and his waiting maids had duly admired him he returned to the Ancestress and dutifully reported to her that his mother had warned him to wear the new garment with very special care and not let it get damaged.

"She is quite right. You must take good care of it. It is the only one of its kind that I have got, and you will never get another. Always be quiet and reserved, be temperate in drinking, and come home nice and early!"

"*Shih, shih,*" he promised eagerly, and took his leave. He could hardly wait to show himself in his magnificent new garment to his acquaintances in the town, who had invited him to visit them that day. When he came home in the evening his waiting maids were startled to hear him uttering dejected sighs and stamping angrily with his foot.

"What's wrong?" asked Musk.

"The new cloak! It is really terrible! The old *Tai tai* gave it to me this morning in a fit of good humor, and now I find that there is a big burn on the collar!" he lamented disconsolately. "A good thing that it is so late in the evening; so I shall not have to show myself over there any more today."

The waiting maid Musk inspected the damage, and she did in fact find a singed spot about the length of a finger.

"Apparently someone came too close with a hand-warmer," she remarked. "But it is not so bad. We'll just give it to the tailor and let him repair it."

She wrapped up the cloak and handed it to a serving woman.

"Take this quickly to the tailor," she said, "and tell him he must have it repaired by tomorrow morning. And make sure that the old *Tai tai* and the *Tai tai* hear nothing about it."

After a little while the serving woman came back with the cloak. "I tried several tailors and tailoresses," she reported, "but no one knows this kind of embroidery, and none of them would undertake it."

"Then simply do not wear it tomorrow," Musk advised him.

"That will not save me, for both Grandmother and Mother expressly wished me to wear it tomorrow, on Uncle Wang's birthday. They will be frightfully angry when they hear that I damaged it the very first day."

"Let me see it!" cried Bright Cloud from her alcove, turning round in her bed.

Musk handed her the cloak and held the lamp up beside her.

"What is needed is peacock-gold silk thread. The difficult part is the border. It needs invisible mending," declared Bright Cloud after a thorough examination.

"We have got the right yarn all right, but who is there in the house except you who can do invisible mending?" remarked Musk.

"I will try to do it!"

"But surely you are not going to risk your health, now that you are just getting well?" protested Pao Yu.

"Don't bother. That is my own business."

She sat up in bed, tidied her hair, and slipped a house frock over her nightgown. She felt giddy, her eyes swam, and she would have liked to sink back on her pillows. But for Pao Yu's sake she gritted her teeth, got Musk to hand her needles, scissors, and various balls of embroidery yarn, and set to work bravely.

"This thread is about the best," she said after lengthy searching and comparing. "True, it does not match exactly, but the difference will not be noticeable."

"I think so too," agreed Pao Yu. "It would be hard for us to dig up a Russian tailor here."

She pushed a bamboo darning knob the size of a teacup under the damaged spot, deftly cut away the singed material with a sharp gold knife, and began darning diligently to and fro, stitch by stitch, artistically reproducing the original pattern. After she had used three or four needlefuls of thread she sank back exhausted on her pillows and had to rest for a while.

"Would you like a little hot broth?" asked Pao Yu anxiously, putting a squirrel fur around her shoulders and pushing another pillow behind her back.

"Spare your trouble, little ancestor! Please go to bed instead, or you will not be able to open your sleepy eyes in the morning. For it's already midnight and long past your bedtime," she rebuffed him impatiently.

He did as she bade him and crept under his bedclothes, but for a long time he could not sleep. The clock was striking four in the morning before the valiant Bright Cloud had finished her task. After brushing away a few stray ends of thread with a little brush, she showed her work to Musk.

"This is splendid!" cried Musk. "Unless you look very hard you can't discover a trace of the mend."

"It is really quite impossible to distinguish from the original pattern," Pao Yu, who had slipped quickly out of bed, agreed with enthusiasm.

"Oh, no, it hasn't turned out to be as beautiful as all that, but I can't do another stitch however hard I try," murmured Bright Cloud weakly; and with this she fell back unconscious on her pillows.

Pao Yu and Musk between them brought her back to herself by energetic thumping and massaging, and neither of them left her bedside until the next morning when Doctor Wang came and felt her pulse once more. The doctor was surprised at the relapse the patient had suffered after having already shown a marked improvement; he thought she must have either eaten too much or overtired herself, and he prescribed another blood- and nerve-strengthening medicine consisting of china-root, foxglove, archangel root, and similar herbs. Thanks to her sound constitution and to the fact that she had always been moderate in eating and drinking, had avoided all too highly spiced foods, and had dieted strictly, particularly during her illness, as prescribed by the rules of the house, Bright Cloud recovered rapidly and was well again in another week.

CHAPTER 31

The waiting maid Cuckoo slyly tests Pao Yu's feelings and upsets his mental balance by hinting at a parting. A kindly aunt pacifies a lovelorn maiden with gentle words.

ONE DAY IN THE SPRING PAO YU WENT OVER TO THE BAMBOO HERMIT-age to inquire after Black Jade's health, but Black Jade was just having her midday nap. Loath to disturb her, he went out instead to the waiting maid Cuckoo, who was sitting in the open pleasure veranda in front of the house doing some needlework.

"How is your little mistress? Is her cough better?" he asked.

"Yes, thank you, it is a bit better."

"*A-mi-to-fo!* It's a relief to hear that."

"Since when do you invoke Buddha? That is something new to me!"

"Ah, well, in distress one clings to the doctor."

晴雯

He remarked that she was wearing only a thin black silk skirt and a dark green satin vest over it.

"Do you not find that attire too light for this between-seasons weather?" he asked, stroking her with his hand. "You will catch cold sitting here exposed to a draft."

"Don't do that!" she said, angrily recoiling. "Now, understand once for all: when we talk together there must be no more of this fondling. You are not a little boy any longer. What will people think if they see you? They will pass remarks about your behavior behind your back and lose respect for you. Our young lady has strictly forbidden us to go on with any fondling. Do you not notice how reserved she is with you herself?"

And getting up, she gathered her needlework together and went into the house. He looked after her as utterly dumfounded as if a pail of cold water had been thrown over him. Then he crept off and sat down on a piece of rock on the way, overwhelmed by a thousand sorrowful thoughts. So great was his despondency that his eyes filled with tears. He had been sitting there lost in thought for the time that it would take to eat a moderate meal when the waiting maid Snowgoose came by. As she saw him sitting there so forlorn on the rock under the peach tree, with his face propped on his hand, staring absently into space, she stood and looked at him and said with a smile:

"What are you doing here, all alone and forlorn? Is it not too cold for you, sitting on that stone?"

"What is it? What do you want with me?" he asked, starting up in alarm. "You're a girl too, aren't you, so you also have no doubt been forbidden to have anything to do with me. What would people say if they saw us together? Away with you at once!"

Snowgoose turned away perplexed and went into the house. The young lady must have been reprimanding him again, she said to herself.

"Here is the ginseng which Madame Cheng sends the young lady," she said to Cuckoo. "The young lady is still asleep? Who, then, has just been upsetting the little master so much that he's sitting outside there now, crying his eyes out?"

"Where is he sitting?"

"On a stone under the peach tree behind the honeysuckle arbor."

Cuckoo promptly laid aside her needlework and hurried out. She could scarcely keep from laughing out loud when she saw the poor boy sitting on his rock.

"My word, you have chosen a nice cool spot to sit down and rest in! Let us hope you don't catch cold from it! How on earth could you be so touchy over the two well-meant words I said to you just now?"

"I touchy? I am nothing of the kind! You were quite right. But I was only saying to myself, the others may come to think as you do, until in the end no one will be left to speak to me any more; and that thought naturally was painful to me," he replied with a sorrowful smile.

She sat down close beside him.

"Why do you come up so near me since you bolted off just now when I came too near you?" he asked.

"Ah, do drop that and let us forget it! What I wanted to ask you was this: Sometime recently you began talking to my little mistress about swallows' nests, and you were interrupted just as you had begun by the secondary wife Chao's coming in. I would very much like to know what more you wanted to say about the swallows' nests."

"Oh, nothing much. I had told my grandmother that your little mistress required some swallows' nests every day as medicine; for Precious Clasp is also only a guest here and cannot keep on providing her with a sufficient amount. As far as I know, Grandmother conveyed my wish to Phoenix. That is what I was going to say to your little mistress the other day when I was interrupted."

"So she owes it to your kind intervention that she now receives an ounce of swallows' nests every day from the kitchen? She could not make out why the old *Tai tai* had suddenly become so attentive to her."

"Well, if she's good and eats her portion every day, let us hope that in two or three years she will be quite healthy," said Pao Yu.

"But the question is: Will she have enough money to continue the cure when she goes home next year?" remarked Cuckoo.

"Home? Whom are you talking about?" he asked in alarm.

"Miss Black Jade, of course; for she is going back to her own town of Suchow next year."

"Oh, come! You are talking nonsense. Her parents are both dead and that is just why we have taken her in here. What would she do in Suchow?"

"Oh, don't imagine that there are no other distinguished houses besides your Chia clan!" retorted Cuckoo cheekily. "Certainly the old *Tai tai* did take in the orphan at the time in order to give her a substitute for her parental home. But now the young lady is grown up and marriageable. Therefore it is only proper that she should go back to her own family. Her parents are dead, but she has got other relatives. Even if they are poor, they are nevertheless members of a highly respectable clan in which the fragrance of a noble culture has been passed down for generations, and these people would expose themselves to mockery and contempt if they allowed their own relative to continue to eat at a strange table. In short, next spring or at the latest next autumn Miss Black Jade will leave this house. And if they do not send her away from here of their own accord, well, then the Ling family will come and take her away. One evening recently the young lady gave me instructions to ask back from you all the little gifts and souvenirs which she has given to you in the course of the years. And she will likewise send back to you one of these days all the gifts and souvenirs which she has received from you."

Pao Yu felt as if a thunderbolt had struck him right on the top of his head. He was unable to utter a word. Cuckoo was just about to continue when Bright Cloud came along. She was looking for him.

"I had a message to give him from my young lady. He does not seem to have quite grasped it yet. Take him away!" declared Cuckoo curtly, and left the two alone.

Bright Cloud perceived with amazement the distraught, absent-minded expression of Pao Yu's face, the flush on his cheeks, the drops of sweat on his forehead. She took him by the hand and led him back to the Begonia Courtyard.

"What has happened?" asked Pearl, horrified.

"He's got a feverish cold. Apparently he was hot and got into a cold draft," said Bright Cloud with a shrug.

If only it were merely that! But the pupils of his eyes were so strangely fixed, saliva dropped from the corners of his mouth, he seemed completely in a daze, and allowed everything to be done to him—let himself be put to bed, then propped up with pillows and given tea, all without showing any movement of his own will. His waiting maids were utterly dumfounded by the alteration in his whole being, and in their perplexity they called Mother Li, his old nurse, to his bedside.

Mother Li observed him attentively, addressed various questions to him without receiving any answer, felt his pulse, and dug her sharp fingernails deeply into his lips and other parts of his body. But though she pressed so hard that the marks of her nails were deeply imprinted on his skin, he seemed to feel nothing and remained absolutely listless. Then she raised a loud lament, rocked her head to and fro like one possessed, beat wildly with her fists on the bed and the pillows, and cursed herself for having nursed him in vain in his infancy and devoted her life to him to no purpose. Pearl, who thought the world of old Li and her opinions, became infected by her outbreak of despair and joined in her lament. At this point Bright Cloud at last spoke up and confessed that Pao Yu's condition had nothing to do with catching cold, but that he must have been driven distracted by something which Cuckoo had done to him just now in the Bamboo Hermitage.

On hearing this, Pearl dashed off at once to the Bamboo Hermitage to take Cuckoo to task. She found her giving Black Jade some medicine. Without salutation or ceremony she flew at Cuckoo, crying: "What have you just been saying to our little master? Go over and look at him and see for yourself what you have done! See how you can answer for yourself to the old *Tai tai!*"

With these words she threw herself into the nearest armchair. Black Jade was taken aback by her unmannerly, excited behavior, in such strong contrast to her normally precise and polite ways.

"What has happened?" she asked, full of misgiving.

"Ask that of your Cuckoo!" replied Pearl, weeping. "I don't know what she has been saying to our poor little master. At any rate he's completely distracted. He can neither speak nor see, and his whole body feels cold. Mother Li has just been prodding him in vain with her fingernails, but he felt nothing; his body seems to have gone dead. Mother Li has given him up already; she's sitting over there lamenting his end."

When Black Jade heard this, her agitation was such that she vomited the medicine she had just taken and shook so badly with coughing that it seemed as if her lungs would burst and her entrails come apart. Her face became a deep crimson, her eyes, suddenly bloodshot, protruded from their sockets, she sat there bent over, and her breathing was so weak that she could not even raise her head. With horror Cuckoo perceived the consequences of her thoughtless behavior.

"What did I say, anyway?" she whimpered. "I only said a few words to him in joke, and he took them seriously."

She tried to attend to her mistress and began to clap her back, but Black Jade pushed her away angrily.

"Stop thumping me! Instead, get me a rope with which to hang myself!" she gasped laboriously.

"Surely you should know him by now, and understand that in his simplicity he takes everything said in joke for the truth!" said Pearl reproachfully.

"If your words were not meant seriously, go and clear up the misunderstanding; perhaps that will bring him back to his senses," Black Jade ordered her maid.

Cuckoo set out obediently for the Begonia Courtyard together with Pearl. Pao Yu's mother and grandmother had meantime arrived there.

"What did you say to him, you wretched bitch?" the Ancestress burst out angrily as Cuckoo appeared.

Cuckoo was just about to stammer some words of self-defense when Pao Yu perceived her and instantly awoke from his state of trance. A deep sigh and a mournful "Ah!" burst from his lips. Then he broke into sobs. Everyone breathed a sigh of relief.

"Beg his pardon!" urged the Ancestress. She thought that Cuckoo had offended Pao Yu in some way, but to everyone's surprise Pao Yu took Cuckoo affectionately by the hand and drew her closer to him.

"Do not say any more about going away," he whispered, "but if it must be, let me go with you!"

His words were incomprehensible to the others. They pressed Cuckoo to speak up, and then they learned at last how Cuckoo had put Pao Yu to the test for fun and driven him completely demented by her talk of bidding farewell and returning to Suchow, which of course she did not mean seriously at all.

"So that is all it was? I was wondering what on earth could have happened," said the Ancestress, melting into tears of relief. "You are such a clever, sensible girl normally, and you must know that he is a simpleton! How on earth could you make game of him so irresponsibly?" she said reproachfully to Cuckoo.

At this moment a servant announced: "Mrs. Ling Chih Hsiao is outside and would like to know how the little brother is."

The mention of the name caused a violent change in Pao Yu.

"How frightful!" he cried. "There, her relatives have come already to take her away! But you must not let them! Away with them! Away with them!" he cried in a frenzy of excitement.

Pretending to comply with his wish, the Ancestress gave orders that the wife of the majordomo Ling should be sent away again.

"Do not be uneasy! The Lings whom you mean are all dead. Your cousin has not got any relatives left who could take her away," she said in an effort to pacify him.

"Yes, but who then are these other Lings? I do not want anyone of the name of Ling to come near me except my cousin!" he cried, still trembling with fear.

"You shall have your way. No other Lings will come near you!" said the Ancestress, and she gave instructions that the family of the major-domo Ling were not to enter the Park of Delightful Vision in future and were never to be mentioned in Pao Yu's presence. No one dared to laugh at this strange instruction.

Pao Yu's glance chanced to fall on the European mechanical ship of gilded tin which was hanging on the wall.

"Look, there's her ship! It's coming to fetch her!" he shouted in a new access of feverish hallucination, pointing with his finger at the ship on the wall.

At a sign from the nurse Pearl hurriedly removed the toy from the wall in order to withdraw it from his sight, but he stretched out his hand, made Pearl give it to him, and hid it under the bedclothes.

"Now she can't sail away!" he said contentedly, at the same time holding Cuckoo convulsively fast as if he would never allow her to leave his side again. At this point Doctor Wang was announced.

Doctor Wang felt Pao Yu's pulse, and then, while Cuckoo listened conscience-striken, with bent head, treated the company to a long and learned professional diagnosis concerning furring of the tongue, and constipation, and deficiency of the flow of blood to the brain owing to mental excitement, with their accumulated result of mental derangement.

"Enough of that learned stuff!" interrupted the Ancestress impatiently. "We others are lay folk and cannot follow your theories. What we want to know above all is this: Is his condition serious?"

The doctor reassured her and with a courteous smile promised speedy recovery.

"Good! Then go and write your prescription in the next apartment. If it is successful you may be assured of an extra fee, and I shall see that my grandson presents it to you personally with a kowtow of thanks. But if it is unsuccessful, woe betide you! I will send out my people to pull down the whole school of medicine where you studied!" threatened the Ancestress laughing.

At the mention of an extra fee the doctor was overjoyed, and made many deep and ceremonious bows and murmurs of *pu chan*, "too great an honor," even continuing his *pu chans* long after the Ancestress had come out with her frightful threat—a circumstance which naturally evoked hearty laughter among all present.

The medicine prescribed by Doctor Wang effected a real improvement, and the Ancestress, reassured to some degree, was able to leave the sickroom with her ladies. As Pao Yu did not permit the waiting maid Cuckoo to leave his side, Amber was allotted to Black Jade in her stead for the time being.

And so it happened that that night the three waiting maids, Pearl, Bright Cloud, and Cuckoo, watched by Pao Yu's bedside as well as the nurse Li and several elderly serving women. He slept, but at times raved wildly in his dreams and cries such as "Has she gone already?" or "There are her people coming to fetch her away!" betrayed the fact that even in his sleep he was still with Black Jade. Several times during the night the Ancestress asked for reports from the sickroom, and when she heard of his delirious dreams, she ordered that the patient should be given the best cinnamon pills and wonder-working powders in the domestic medicine closet—efficacious remedies which had power to drive away evil spirits and purify the choked-up doors of the body and make them free so that good spirits could find entry.

The next day Pao Yu felt distinctly better and was back in his right senses once more, but because of his fear that Cuckoo might leave him, it pleased him to go on playing the invalid a while longer. Of course he could not continue indefinitely deceiving those around him by these artful pretenses, and when Little Cloud came to visit him one day and in her merry way mimicked his condition during those critical days by means of all sorts of grimaces and tomfoolery, he forgot his pretense of suffering so far as to sit up in bed and laugh heartily. He had not thought that his recent condition had been so funny, he said. That made the household feel fully assured that he must really be well again.

"Why did you put me into such a state of fright recently?" he asked Cuckoo one day when they were alone.

"Why, I only did it for fun. How on earth could you have taken it seriously?"

"All the same, what you said did not sound so very unlikely."

"You can be easy in your mind. Not one of Miss Ling's closer relatives is still alive, and all the distant relatives live far away from Suchow, scattered through the various provinces. And even if someone should turn up one day to fetch away my little mistress, it is quite certain that the old *Tai tai* would not let her go!"

"And even if the old *Tai tai* should be willing to let her go, I would definitely not allow it!" he added passionately.

"Come now! Who knows if you will still think the same way in two or three years? For you are now grown up, and already engaged."

"Engaged? I didn't know that!"

"Oh, it's said that the old Ancestress intends Miss Precious Harp for you. For what other reason would she make such a favorite of the young lady?"

"Ha! Ha! So I am still taken for a fool? Yet it seems to me that I am not quite such a fool as you are. I happen to know that Cousin Precious Harp has already been engaged for a long while past to young Mei, son of Mei, the member of the Han Lin Academy. So you can't fool me this time! Do you not know of the solemn vow that I have made to your little mistress? No! No! I am lucky enough to have just recovered from my last fright, and already you want to start trying to hoax me again? I only wish that I could tear the heart out of my breast here and now and show it to you and to your mistress in order to convince you both how sincerely I mean it. Then I would die happy. And when I am dead may I be burned to ashes and go up in smoke, and may the wind carry me in all directions. That is what I would wish!" He had said all this with rising excitement; he was gnashing his teeth; his eyes were full of tears.

"Don't get so excited! I only wanted to put you to the test a bit, I was worried about my little mistress. True, I have not always belonged to her since I left home, but she has always been so good to me. That is why I am so very fond of her, and I dread the thought of being parted from her," said Cuckoo, holding his mouth shut with one hand and wiping the tears from her eyes with the other.

"You silly little thing! You're grieving without reason," he said, now in his turn laughing, trying to calm her. "Let me confide one thing to you: in life and in death, we three shall stay together!"

Cuckoo remained thoughtfully silent. A serving woman appeared to announce that Chia Huan and nephew Chia Lan were outside and would like to inquire about the health of the little master.

"Oh, let them not trouble about me; I want to go to sleep now. Send them away again!" muttered Pao Yu.

"You would do better to send me away. It is time I was looking after my little mistress again," interjected Cuckoo.

"You are right. I was thinking of that myself last evening, for I am now quite well. Go then!"

Cuckoo immediately set about packing her bedclothes and other things.

"You have got three hand mirrors," he remarked. "Would you leave me that one there as a souvenir? I will always place it beside my pillow when I go to bed and take it with me when I go out."

Cuckoo did as he wished; then she took leave of him and of all the other inmates of the Begonia Courtyard, and returned to the Bamboo Hermitage.

All the time that she knew Pao Yu to be ill in bed, Black Jade had suffered with him, and during Cuckoo's absence she had shed many a secret tear. Now, when she saw Cuckoo coming back to her and heard her report of Pao Yu's recovery, she herself suddenly felt a great deal better and more cheerful.

"He means it really seriously," said Cuckoo with a smile to her mistress as they went to bed that night. "That sudden bad turn he took was solely due to my having let drop a few words about our going away and bidding farewell."

Black Jade pretended not to have heard her remark. After a fairly lengthy pause Cuckoo continued, as if talking to herself: "Why get restless and want to change when one is so safe and well looked after here? The chief thing is that you two have known and understood each other from childhood. Everything else will come right in time."

"Will you not go to sleep at last? Are you so little tired from the last few days that you must go nibbling idly at ants' eggs?" asked Black Jade, interrupting her soliloquy. But Cuckoo refused to be rebuffed and continued: "Oh, it's not just idle chatter; what I want to say to you comes straight from my heart. Believe me, I have felt for you all these years, in your loneliness and desolation. How I wish that the main affair of your life would happen very soon, while the old *Tai tai* is still alive! As long as the old *Tai tai* is in command you have nothing to fear, but once she is dead, who knows? These aristocratic young people simply are as they are: today they look to the east, tomorrow to the west; they like best to do with not less than 'three chief rooms and five side-chambers.' Today they bring home a wife beautiful as a heavenly fairy; after three or five nights they are tired of her, and begin looking out for another, and then they either hate the first wife or else banish the thought of her into the farthest corner of their minds. When this happens it is a good thing for a young wife to have the backing of an influential crowd of relations. Therefore I think that it would be a good thing for you if your main affair was settled while the old *Tai tai* is still in authority here. You are clever, you will understand what I mean when I advise you to make up your mind now and keep to your decision, bearing in mind the proverb:

> Ten thousand gold batzes
> Are more easily won
> Than a single heart."

"You seem to have gone out of your mind," said Black Jade, cutting short her flow of talk. "How on earth can a person change so suddenly, all in a few days? You have become quite intolerable. But just you wait! I will ask the old *Tai tai* tomorrow to take you away from here."

"Why? I only meant well by you. I merely want you to look out for yourself while there is yet time. Surely there's no harm in that?" said Cuckoo, in laughing self-defense, and soon after fell asleep.

But Black Jade remained awake for a long time. In her heart she felt quite differently from what the brusque tone she had just put on would lead one to believe. She was profoundly moved by the sensible words of her good waiting maid and she had to agree with her in her heart. She lay awake the whole night, tossing and turning fretfully and weeping silently into the pillow; only as dawn was breaking did she get a little sleep.

She got up next morning so exhausted and underslept that she found it an effort to wash herself, and rinse out her mouth, and eat her swallows' nest cream. That day Aunt Hsueh was celebrating her birthday. Black Jade went over to offer her congratulations and at the same time took her a piece of her own needlework; then she came straight back to her Bamboo Hermitage. She was quite unable to attend the usual banquet and theatrical performance. Pao Yu was also absent from among the birthday guests. At the festive banquet for the male guests, which lasted more than three or four days, nephew Hsueh Kuo did the honors in place of the absent Hsueh Pan.

For a long time past Aunt Hsueh had had an eye on Wreath of Clouds, Princess Shieh's poor niece. True, the young girl was penniless, one of those who "have only a thorn for a hair-clasp," as the saying goes. On the other hand, she was graceful of form, and quiet and pleasing in her ways, in fact, she had the making of an ideal wife. Actually, Aunt Hsueh had been thinking of her for her son Hsueh Pan, but then she said to herself that the young girl was really too good for that scoundrel and wastrel and would only suffer misery if married to him; so she changed her plans and decided to win Wreath of Clouds for her nice young nephew Hsueh Kuo instead.

She first informed Phoenix of her plan, and Phoenix in her turn confided the matter to the Ancestress. The Ancestress gave her willing consent and evinced eagerness herself to play the part of the sponsor and go-between who brings the mountains together. She sent forthwith for Princess Shieh and asked her consent to the project. The Princess said to herself that a union of her poor niece with the rich family of Hsueh Kuo could not be other than advantageous, and as the suitor, moreover, was a good-looking, well-behaved young man, she consented without any lengthy deliberation. The Ancestress now sent for Aunt Hsueh to be the third party at the marriage conference. For the sake of good form, quite a lengthy discussion of pros and cons now developed between Princess Shieh and Aunt Hsueh, with apparent resistance and rejection, and raising of this doubt and that objection until, thanks to the energetic persuasion of the Ancestress, agreement was eventually reached. The parents of the bride were now informed and called upon to appear. Sometime previously they had taken refuge in the Yungkuo palace, owing to their poverty. Could they have wished for anything better than this advantageous union with the well-to-do family of Hsueh? They were only too willing to give their consent.

The Ancestress was very pleased with her achievement.

"There's another business happily concluded! All my life I have enjoyed carrying through negotiations of this kind, and now what about my marriage broker's commission?" she said jokingly to Aunt Hsueh.

"Naturally, the commission has been well earned. I trust that ten thousand silver pieces will suffice," said Aunt Hsueh, taking up the jest. "But how would it be if the old *Tai tai*, having negotiated the marriage, would also do us the honor of giving the wedding feast?"

"No, thank you; I should prefer not to," replied the Ancestress, laughing. "Let other hands and feet than mine stir themselves this time!" Thereupon she sent for Princess Chen and instructed her to make all the necessary preparations for a worthy wedding feast, neither too economical nor too luxurious, and to render her a conscientious and detailed account of all the outlay.

During her sojourn in the Yungkuo palace Wreath of Clouds had attached herself most of all to Precious Clasp and had found in her a friend as sympathetic as a sister. True, she lived with her cousin Greeting of Spring, but the latter bothered just as little about her poor relation as did her stepmother, Princess Shieh. She was made to feel quite clearly that she was poor and did not belong to the respected mandarin class as the other young girls in the Park of Delightful Vision did, and she was poorly equipped and often was without even the most necessary things. She lacked the courage to beg from her cousin or from her proud aunt, Princess Shieh, and at such times of need it was always Precious Clasp to whom she turned in her embarrassment and who helped her out secretly with this or that.

One day Precious Clasp met Wreath of Clouds by chance in the park. They were both going in the same direction—to visit Black Jade. Coming to a narrow pathway, Precious Clasp let the other step in front, and so she noticed what very thin clothing she wore.

"Why do you not dress more warmly in this cold early spring weather?" she asked her.

Wreath of Clouds bent her head, embarrassed, and did not answer.

"Your pocket money has run short again, I suppose?" she asked, smiling. "Yes, I know, Cousin Phoenix has taken to pinching and reckoning of late."

Wreath of Clouds nodded eager agreement.

"I have to give half of my meager two taels a month to my parents at Aunt Shieh's wish. Then there are the little gifts which I have to give to serving women and waiting maids to induce them to condescend to serve me at all and not overlook me completely. So what is there left with which to buy things?" she complained. "Of course my pocket money always runs out right at the beginning of the month. And the fact is that I have taken all my warm lined clothing secretly to a pawnshop and pawned it."

"So I thought. Well, I shall have a talk with Mother. And meantime, will you turn back and send me your pawn ticket as quickly as possible, and I will have it redeemed secretly, and you will have your warm things back by this evening. You could easily catch a bad cold by running about so lightly dressed. Where is your pawnshop, by the way?"

"It is on the main road west of the Drum Tower, and is called the Hall of Enduring Well-Being, or something of the kind."

"Oh, indeed? Then the money will at least remain in the family. The employees in the pawnshop will think that if their employers do not come to them in person, at least they honor them with their clothes."

Wreath of Clouds flushed with embarrassment. So she had gone to a pawnshop which was run by the Hsueh family, of all people!

When Precious Clasp reached the Bamboo Hermitage she found her mother Aunt Hsueh together with Black Jade.

"How marvellous are the ways of destiny! Aunt Hsueh has just told me of the engagement of her nephew to Wreath of Clouds. Who would have thought it would all happen so quickly?" said Black Jade to Precious Clasp.

"Yes, my child, if the old man in the moon wills it, two people find each other even if they are a thousand miles apart," remarked Aunt Hsueh with a smile. "The old man in the moon secretly seeks out his young people and binds them together with the magic red cord which he winds around their feet. When that happens, countries and seas and years may lie between them, but his chosen young people must become man and wife in the end. None of it happens by human will. And on the other hand, two human beings may live ever so close together, and they may be solemnly destined for each other by parents and relatives, but if the old man in the moon does not knot his red cord, then, in spite of everything, they do not get each other. Who knows how quickly it may one day happen to you two girls, even if your future husbands are in the Southern Mountains or by the Northern Sea?"

"All the same, a little motherly help could not harm us, perhaps," said Precious Clasp, with a laugh, nestling against her mother's breast.

"Imagine a big girl like her being petted like that! How lucky she is!" sighed Black Jade, smiling sadly. How happy she would be if she could nestle on a motherly breast, she thought. And her eyes filled with tears.

"Don't weep, dear child!" said Aunt Hsueh, moved with pity, flicking her face with a feather duster. "I can quite understand how sad it makes you to have to look on at the caresses between a mother and daughter. But believe me, I feel for you no whit less than I do for my own daughter, but I dare not show my feelings openly, there are so many malicious tongues in the house. No one would understand that one could adopt a defenseless orphan out of pure human sympathy— no, it would be interpreted as currying favor with the old *Tai tai*; for the old *Tai tai* also has a special preference for you."

"Oh, if that is the way it is with you, Aunt, may I not look upon you as a mother?" asked Black Jade.

"Why not? If you do not scorn me, I will willingly adopt you," replied Aunt Hsueh affectionately.

"No, that would not do," interjected Precious Clasp, smiling slyly.

"Why would it not do?" asked Black Jade, surprised.

"Well, naturally, because of my brother Hsueh Pan. For after all, he is not yet married. Why do you think it was that Cousin Wreath of Clouds has been betrothed to Cousin Hsueh Kuo and not to him?"

"Why? Presumably because he is away or because his horoscope does not agree with Wreath of Clouds'," replied Black Jade guilelessly.

"No, no, that's not the reason. Hsueh Pan's bride has already been chosen, and as soon as he comes back from his travels her name will be made known. Now can you guess why Mother cannot very well adopt you as a daughter? Just think hard!"

Precious Clasp winked gleefully at her mother as she said this, but Black Jade, who now understood, took her jest seriously. Horrified, she hid her face on Aunt Hsueh's breast, murmuring distractedly: "I won't! I won't!"

"Don't let her frighten you! She is only hoaxing you!" Aunt Hsueh reassured her, embracing her tenderly.

"Really, you may believe it! Mama is going to speak to the old *Tai tai* tomorrow and ask for your hand. Why should she waste time looking elsewhere when the right bride is here?" continued Precious Clasp, persisting with her jesting.

"Oh, you're crazy!" exclaimed Black Jade, laughing and going for Precious Clasp with outspread fingers as if about to claw her. Aunt Hsueh parted the two young girls, saying to her daughter as she did so: "Enough of this nonsense! Since I think even Wreath of Clouds too good for your scamp of a brother, how would I ever dream of delivering this delicate and sensitive child into his claws? No! The old *Tai tai* said only recently that she intends her grandson Pao Yu for your cousin Black Jade. And it is best so, too; for Pao Yu is so full of peculiarities that he must have a wife who knows and understands him thoroughly, and surely only Cousin Black Jade can do that. The old *Tai tai* will on no account give him a strange girl as wife."

Black Jade had listened with growing tension, making faces at her cousin the while. Now she flushed up to the roots of her hair.

"Phew! You deserve a good spanking for enticing your mother to talk about things which should not be mentioned!" she said to Precious Clasp in jest, pretending indignation.

"Oh, if that is Madame's opinion, would she not go one step further and herself put in a word for my little mistress with the old *Tai tai?*" interjected Cuckoo eagerly, turning to Aunt Hsueh.

"Listen to the girl. She can hardly wait to see her young lady leave her maiden's quarters! Probably she wants to marry herself, eh?" remarked Aunt Hsueh. Cuckoo turned away blushing.

"Kindly do not meddle in matters which do not concern you, you cheeky little creature!" Black Jade called after her, with a voice of pretended sternness. But immediately she herself had to burst out laughing.

"*A-mi-to-fo*, holy Buddha, what a cussed creature, *chai tzu* . . ."

she was in the act of continuing. But she did not get beyond the *chai;* the *tzu* turned into a hefty sneeze, to the amusement of all present. She was about to finish the sentence she had begun when Little Cloud burst in, waving a piece of paper in her hand.

"Can you tell me what this funny document means?" she asked. "It looks like a bill."

Black Jade was the first to look at the paper. She could not make it out either, and then Precious Clasp glanced at it. To her horror she recognized Wreath of Clouds' pawn ticket, of which she knew already. She hurriedly snatched it from Little Cloud and tried to hide it. Aunt Hsueh too had already stolen a glimpse at it.

"It's a pawn ticket," she explained to Little Cloud. "It must belong to some serving woman. Where did you find it? The owner will miss it."

"A pawn ticket? What may that be?" asked Little Cloud naïvely.

"What a little noodle! She doesn't yet know what a pawn ticket is!" the women and waiting maids who were standing about exclaimed, giggling.

"What is there so funny about that?" said Aunt Hsueh reprovingly. "This ignorance is only to her credit. It shows that she is a real Miss 'Thousand-Gold-Piece,' a genuinely innocent young girl who knows nothing as yet of this wicked world. I trust that the other young ladies here are all just the same kind of little noodles."

"Of course, of course," replied the serving women fervently, as if with one voice. "After all, Miss Black Jade didn't know either, so the other young ladies surely cannot know. Indeed, we feel sure that even our little master, although he has been outside the house so often already, has never seen a pawn ticket either."

Aunt Hsueh then explained briefly to the three young girls the nature and meaning of a pawn ticket.

"Oh, goodness, what funny ideas people come on in order to obtain money!" cried Black Jade and Little Cloud, astonished, and their remark induced a further outbreak of giggles and exclamations of "little noodles" among the serving women and waiting maids.

"Where, actually, did you pick up the ticket?" Aunt Hsueh wanted to know. Little Cloud was just opening her mouth to answer when Precious Clasp forestalled her: "Anyhow, the ticket is expired and invalid long ago. Lotus just kept it for fun." Of course her aim was to prevent the truth from coming out and to save Cousin Wreath of Clouds embarrassment. Aunt Hsueh was satisfied and desisted from further questions; but later, when they were by themselves, Precious Clasp began questioning Little Cloud once more. Little Cloud then confessed that she had just noticed Wreath of Clouds' maid surreptitiously slipping the ticket across to Precious Clasp's maid Oriole, and had seen

341

Oriole putting it into a book. Being curious by nature, she had taken out the ticket unobserved and, as she did not understand what it meant, had brought it in to have its purpose explained.

"So Wreath of Clouds has pawned things? But why did she have her ticket sent over to your maid?" asked Little Cloud. Realizing that she could no longer hide the true facts of the case, Precious Clasp confided the story to the two cousins. They were both sorry for Wreath of Clouds and indignant that she was treated so shabbily by her rich aunt the Princess and her cousin Greeting of Spring.

"See if I do not give Cousin Greeting of Spring and her ill-behaved staff a good piece of my mind," declared Little Cloud angrily.

She would have liked to carry out her intention straight away, but the others succeeded in dissuading her from such hasty action, which would only have brought unpleasantness to herself. They all agreed to avoid useless lecturing and instead to be nicer to Wreath of Clouds themselves and to find a pretext for getting her away from the unpleasant company of her cousin Greeting of Spring by taking her to live with Precious Clasp, Little Cloud, and Lotus in the Jungle Courtyard.

CHAPTER 32

Chia Lien secretly takes the second Miss Yu to wife. The third Miss Yu aspires to the hand of the Cold Knight.

CHIA CHING, THE PRINCE HERMIT, WAS DEAD. THE NEWS OF HIS decease reached the Yungkuo and the Ningkuo palaces exactly on Pao Yu's birthday, as it happened. It also chanced that just at that time the Princess Ancestress and the older ladies and all the male seniors of both palaces, among them Prince Chen and his son Chia Yung, were away taking part in the funeral procession to the Imperial burial grounds of a recently deceased Imperial wife. Princess Chen had to leave the birthday banquet forthwith, remove her jewelry and her festive attire, put on a simple white mourning robe, and hasten out into the mountains in front of the city, to the hermitage of her dead father-in-law, in order to comply with the initial formalities such as viewing the corpse, having it prepared for the bier, and so on. For she was the only representative of the family at home. True, she sent express messengers to her absent husband, but it would be several weeks in any case before Prince Chen could be back from the Imperial burial place to help her. Therefore, she had to resign herself to taking up her quarters for a time in the near-by Temple of the Iron Railings, where the family vaults of the Chia clan were situated and where she had the corpse laid temporarily on a bier;

and she had to carry through the prescribed funeral rites alone there, until her husband could come and relieve her and make the final arrangements for the obsequies. She had taken the majordomo Lai Sheng and his wife with her to help her. In order not to leave the Ningkuo palace entirely without the supervision of a respected older person, she had induced her stepmother to come and take over the management of the household during her absence.

Her stepmother, the Lady Yu, had brought with her two unmarried daughters. They were both equal in beauty but far from alike in character, as will be noticed later. When the older ladies and the male senior members of the Chia clan came home subsequently, having been graciously excused by the Emperor from further attendance at the Imperial burial place, and the various services took place before the bier of the Prince Hermit in the great hall of the Ningkuo palace, the sight of the two beautiful Yu girls inevitably awoke in Chia Lien's breast such burning desire that his mouth literally watered. For a long time past he had been tiring of his first wife, the more so since Phoenix had been ailing frequently of late and was often confined to her sickbed. Chia Lien found both the Yu girls equally desirable, but since the younger one had given him unmistakably to understand that she did not care for him, he confined his attentions to the elder one, and had the satisfaction of seeing that his feelings were reciprocated. To be sure, their relations at the beginning were confined to hurried meetings and surreptitious exchanges of glances and words. For there were always too many observant pairs of eyes in the neighborhood, which effectively prevented him from attaining the goal of his desires.

So he breathed a sigh of relief when at last the obsequies in the house came to an end and the coffin of the Prince Hermit was taken to the family burial place at the Temple of the Iron Railings. While the other relatives might return to the town the same day, the funeral rites required that the closer relatives of the deceased, namely, Prince and Princess Chen, their son Chia Yung, and their daughter-in-law, had to remain a full hundred days longer in the family temple, to carry out the further obsequies. A large proportion of the palace staffs likewise remained out there with them, while at home in the Ningkuo palace the Lady Yu, with her two daughters, took over the running of the household once more.

It is now or never, said Chia Lien to himself, and he resolved to achieve his goal during these hundred days. Naturally, he required a suitable pretext for approaching his beloved, whom he knew to be less watched and observed than usual in the semideserted Ningkuo palace. For this reason he rode out quite often to the family temple to keep Prince Chen and his family company for one or two days, and nearly always there was some order of the Prince, or this or that domestic request on the part of the Princess, which offered him the desired excuse of entering the eastern palace on his return and seeing and speaking to the beloved.

One day, when he was once more out at the Temple of the Iron Railings, the Prince's deputy majordomo, Yu Lu, called to discuss some business with his master. A balance of six hundred ounces of silver was still owing for the white funeral cloth and the green smocks for the coffin bearers, and the two cloth merchants had called yesterday to complain and demand payment, he reported.

"Well, just get the money from the household cash. Why bother me about it and make this unnecessary journey here?" said the Prince.

"The bursar could not pay me the sum. The cash has been exhausted, owing to the many heavy expenses of the recent weeks of mourning. The ready money available is earmarked for covering the expenses of the last hundred days of mourning here in the Temple of the Iron Railings. That is why I have come for your instructions."

"Well, just see where else you can get the money from; you are old and wise enough to do that," said the Prince.

"Hm, if it were only a matter of one or two hundred ounces, I would know how to get over the difficulty, but six hundred straight away . . .!" Yu Lu answered hesitantly, much embarrassed.

The Prince considered the matter for a while, then he turned to his son, Chia Yung, and said: "Go to your mother and ask her what became of the five hundred ounces which came in recently as a funeral gift from the Chen family of Kiang nan. As far as I know, the money has not gone into the household cash."

Chia Yung went to the Princess and came back after a while with the message that two of the five hundred ounces were already spent, and the remaining three hundred were in the safekeeping of Mother Yu.

"Very well. Then you must go to your grandmother, ask her to give you the three hundred, and hand them to Yu Lu to pay his cloth merchants' bill. He will rake up the balance himself. At the same time have a look around and see how things are going at home, whether there is anything that calls for discussion; and see also how your two aunts are, and give them our greetings."

Chia Yung and Yu Lu were just about to take leave when Chia Lien appeared.

"Well, what's the important discussion?" he asked, and when the Prince informed him, he thought to himself, this is just my chance; I must seize it.

"Why should you go borrowing from outsiders, dear Cousin, when it is a matter of such a trifle?" he continued aloud. "I happen to have

344

quite a large sum lying at home. I place it at your disposal with pleasure."

"That is splendid! Would you be so good, then, as to give my son a written order, so that the money can be handed over to him."

"Hm, I should prefer to do that myself. Besides, I have been long enough away from home and must think about returning in any case. I should like to see how Grandmother, and Mother, and my aunts are, and to make sure that everything is in order at home."

And so it came about that Uncle Lien and Nephew Yung set out together, accompanied by a few servants, to ride back to the capital. On the way the uncle contrived, as if by chance, to lead the conversation on to the subject of Cousin Yu Number Two. He could not find nearly enough words with which to praise her good qualities and her virtues, her beauty, her good character, and her blameless behavior, and so extravagant were his eulogies that the nephew very soon realized what he was driving at.

"My uncle seems to be very much taken with her," remarked Chia Yung with a smile. "How would it be if he were to make her his 'lady of the side-chamber' and if I were to act as go-between?"

"Do you mean that seriously, or are you joking?" asked Chia Lien, pretending surprise.

"I am serious, of course."

"That's very friendly of you. But there are various difficulties. What would my wife say to it? And would your grandmother approve? Moreover, I heard that your second aunt is already engaged."

"That is true. But since the father of her betrothed, a tenant farmer on the estate named Chang, lost his fortune ten years ago in a lawsuit, the two families have broken off relations. For a long time past Grandmother and Father have planned to have this engagement cancelled by the payment of a small indemnity in cash, and to seek another suitable husband for my aunt. The Chang family are poor; they will be very glad to renounce the betrothal for a few ounces of silver. And I have not the least doubt but that Grandmother and Father will joyfully give their approval to such a distinguished suitor as you. The only doubtful point is the question of what Phoenix would say to it."

This Chia Lien did not know either, and his only answer was a forced smile.

"Wait! I've got an idea!" exclaimed the nephew, after thinking for a while. "We shall certainly require some courage, and you must not shrink from spending a bit of money too, if the matter is to succeed."

"Out with it!"

"My plan is simply to hoodwink Phoenix. She must not hear anything of your intention. I will carry through the whole business with the utmost discretion with my father and my grandmother. As soon as they have consented, I shall buy a little house for you close behind our palace. I shall furnish it nicely and cozily as a love nest for you, and hire two or three discreet and reticent serving women. Then one happy day I will conduct my aunt there secretly and unseen by either spirit or mortal, and install her in your love nest as your secondary wife. You will then live alternately with Phoenix and with your new wife for the future. If Phoenix gets to know of it in the course of time and makes a row, why, you need only say that you were moved to act as you had done by the very understandable wish to beget the son and heir that your principal wife had failed to give you. Faced with the accomplished fact, with the rice in the pot already cooked, Phoenix will no doubt put up with it. And then, in the end, you will ask the blessing of the old *Tai tai.*"

In his infatuated state Chia Lien found the plan splendid. It did not even occur to him that according to traditional observance it was improper for him to think of marriage in this mourning period. Still less did he reckon with the sternness of his father, Prince Shieh, and the jealousy of his wife, Phoenix. Nor did he guess, moreover, that his cunning nephew had his own advantage in mind in making this suggestion. For the nephew too was madly enamored of his beautiful aunt, but within the parental home he could not well make overtures to her. In the solitary love nest behind the palace, however, he would have a splendid occasion to do so. He would only have to watch his chance when Uncle Lien was not there, and this opportunity would offer itself often enough. But none of these things crossed the mind of the infatuated uncle.

"You are really a bright boy, dear nephew!" said the latter, beaming with joy. "By way of thanks I shall give you a present of two pretty waiting maids."

Meanwhile they had reached the main gateway of the Ningkuo palace, and here they parted with mutual promises of the strictest secrecy. The nephew was considerate enough to allow the uncle to go alone to Grandmother Yu in order that Chia Lien would have the field to himself later when he would meet Aunt Number Two. Meantime he himself turned in to the western palace to greet the old Ancestress.

In front of the great hall Chia Lien dismissed his retinue of servants, dismounted from his horse, and went alone and unannounced to the ladies' quarters. As a near relative who was on close terms of friendship with Prince Chen, the master of the house, he could take this liberty without causing unpleasant surprise among the staff. On walking unannounced into the living room of the ladies Yu, he had the good luck to find Miss Yu Number Two alone. She was reclining on the couch busy with her needlework, in the company of two waiting maids.

Chia Lien walked up to her eagerly and saluted her politely. Miss Yu, suppressing a smile, rose to return his greeting, and invited him to sit down by her side. Chia Lien gave her to understand at once how happy he considered himself to see her again.

"But where are your mother and sister?" he inquired.

"They are in the back, in the storerooms," she replied.

Meanwhile the two maids had disappeared to get tea. Chia Lien availed of this opportunity to gaze deeply into the eyes of the beautiful cousin, whereupon she bent her head a little, but continued to smile ingenuously. He did not wish to push his advances too directly and crudely. His glance fell on her hand, which was toying with the ornamental silken ribbon of a handbag of lotus-leaf shape.

"Oh, I have left my betel-nut bag out at the temple," he said, feeling around his belt. "Perhaps my good cousin would give me a few nuts out of her bag?"

"I happen to have betel nuts in my bag, but it is my custom to eat them myself and not to share them with other people," she replied.

He sidled closer up to her and reached for her bag, to help himself to some. Fearing the maids might surprise her in this equivocal situation, she hurriedly flung him the bag. He caught it deftly, took out a nut, and put it in his mouth. Then he tried to push the bag back onto her lap. Just at that moment the two waiting maids came in with the tea things, so he hid it for the time being in his sleeve pocket. While he was drinking his tea he managed quietly to unfasten a dragon-shaped clasp of jade from his belt and to knot the ribbon of her bag around it. Then, when the maids were not looking, he threw the bag over to her unobserved. She pretended not to notice.

After a while the jingling of the bead curtains was heard and in came Mother Yu with daughter Number Three and two little waiting maids. Chia Lien hurriedly gave his fair neighbor to understand by his glances that she was to hide her bag, but she took no notice of him. It was now high time for him to stand up and salute Aunt Yu and Cousin Three. Then, when they were all seated again, and he could steal a glance at Cousin Two, he noticed that her bag was still there, but its silken ribbon had disappeared together with his dragon clasp. She herself looked as gay and unconcerned as if nothing had happened. So now he was reassured.

They talked about all sorts of things, then he brought forward the business reason of his visit, and had the three hundred ounces of silver handed to him. At this point Nephew Chia Yung appeared on the scene.

"The old Governor would like to speak to you," he said, winking gleefully at his uncle. Chia Lien was about to take leave in haste when he heard his cheeky nephew turning to the Lady Yu and saying: "Now, what do you think, Grandmother? Wouldn't this uncle here be just the right man for Aunt Two? Hasn't he got all the qualities—height, figure, good appearance, and so on—which Father said recently he would require of her future husband?"

Saying this, he pointed his finger quite unconcernedly at his Uncle Chia Lien and made cheeky faces at his Aunt Two. Taking the part of her sister, who was visibly embarrassed, Aunt Three opened her mouth and began scolding, half in joke and half in earnest: "What an impertinent little monkey! If Mother had not happened to speak of this herself already, I would give him a good hiding!"

But the little monkey had already slipped giggling out the door. Immediately afterwards his uncle too took his leave, all smiles.

That same day Chia Yung returned to the Temple of the Iron Railings and, after having made his business report to his father, presented Uncle Chia Lien's marriage proposal and strongly advocated the suggested union between his uncle and his aunt. Prince Chen considered the matter, then he said with a smile: "It seems all right to me. But is the girl herself willing? Go back to the city tomorrow and make sure on this point!"

He then visited his wife and asked her opinion.

At first Princess Chen was decidedly against the plan, which seemed to her a rather dubious one. That this marriage should take place during the mourning period, that a secondary wife should be taken without the knowledge and consent of the principal wife—these circumstances constituted breaches of the Rites, and were contrary to all conceptions of correctness and good form. But as she was used to assent to everything which the Prince had once taken into his head, she gave way in the end. Moreover, this Miss Yu was not her blood sister but only a stepsister; she therefore did not have to be too scrupulous about taking responsibility for the possible unpleasant consequences of this incorrectly effected union.

Accordingly, early next morning Chia Yung hastened back to the Ningkuo palace at his father's request to obtain the consent of the ladies Yu. He had himself announced to Grandmother Yu and, when admitted to her presence, informed her of the Prince's wish, and with much emphasis and many flowery phrases, put forward all possible points in favor of the match—what a fine life Aunt Two would have with Chia Lien, who would make her his principal wife as a matter of course when Phoenix would die—an event which was to be expected sooner or later; and that the Prince would defray all the costs of the wedding and provide a handsome home and fine furniture, and would also see that she, Grandmother, had a carefree old age; and he would help, moreover, to obtain a good match for Aunt Three. He held forth on all these things and with such eloquence that Mother Yu was completely won over. The business was to cost nothing, and besides, Chia Lien was a fine-looking, fashionable young man. It would be madness to refuse such an advantageous offer. Grandmother Yu consulted for a short time with her daughter, and that same day Chia Yung was able to bring his father the desired word of consent.

Chia Lien was now summoned to the family temple, and informed of the approval of the other side. He was overjoyed, and his gratitude towards his friendly helpers, Prince Chen and his son, knew no bounds. Wedding garments and lingerie were bought in haste and all the other wedding preparations were made. Two li from the back walls of the princely abode, in the quiet little Lane of the Flowering Branch, a suitable "love nest" was acquired. It was a small country villa of twenty rooms. Little Pao, who, after his wife had killed herself, had married the merry widow of that crazy fellow the cook To who had died of drink, was engaged as a servant. He had left the palace service some time previously. Chia Lien could not have hit upon a better choice, for Little Pao had received a hundred taels in hush money from him some time previously, as well as the pretty Widow To, in compensation for the loss of his wife, and he was therefore deeply indebted to him. Moreover, his wife's former tender relations with Chia Lien were likewise a bond between herself and their new master. Therefore, Chia Lien would be able to rely upon his servants for true devotion and reticence. And old Chang, the impoverished father of the original fiancé of Miss Yu Number Two, was compensated with a sum of twenty taels, for which he signed the required deed of relinquishment.

The third day of the new month was picked out in the calendar as a suitable day for the wedding. Mother Yu and Daughter Three had inspected the new home the previous day and found it in the best possible order. And now the bride was fetched in an ordinary litter, unseen by either spirit or mortal, in the fifth hour of the morning of the third, and taken to the love nest in the Lane of the Flowering Branch. A little time later Chia Lien arrived, equally unobtrusively, seated in a small sedan chair and dressed in his everyday attire, paid his respects to heaven and earth and to his Aunt Yu, who was present, burned incense and little paper horses, and drank with his new bride from the same wedding beaker in a festively illuminated bridal chamber, then later revelled with her in that unrestrained manner of phoenix couples which is all too well known.

The news of this secret marriage did not penetrate beyond the circle of the few initiated persons. From now onwards Chia Lien covered his fairly frequent absences with the pretext to Phoenix that his presence was required in the Ningkuo palace, and in view of his close friendship with Prince Chen the unsuspecting Phoenix believed him. Everything went as he had desired. Chia Lien allowed his new wife fifteen taels per month and, when he himself could not be with her, permitted her to take her meals with her mother and sister so that she would not feel too lonely. His intimacy with the new wife was so great that he gradually took away secretly from his home in the Yungkuo palace all the objects of value which he had collected for himself in the course of the years, and gave them into her keeping. Moreover, he was so rash as to tell her, during the hours they lay together, every conceivable intimate detail about the character and person of his principal wife. The second Yu was naturally extremely gratified, and in her dreams already saw herself as the successor of Phoenix and the future mistress of the western palace.

Two months of secret and undisturbed happiness had passed in this way when Prince Chen returned home one evening to the eastern palace from the Temple of the Iron Railings, the hundred days of mourning service there having come to an end. After his long absence he had a wish to see his two beautiful sisters-in-law that same evening. Having made sure that Cousin Chia Lien was not there, he set out for the Lane of the Flowering Branch accompanied only by two trusted farmhands.

While he was chatting and drinking punch with Mother Yu and Sister-in-law Three in the lamp-lit living room of the west wing, Sister-in-law Two having withdrawn immediately after greeting him, Chia Lien arrived. When he heard that his princely cousin was there, he thought his own thoughts, and quietly went straight to his *Nai nai*, for he wished to leave his cousin undisturbed. Besides, he felt tired and planned to go to bed early. He settled down comfortably, ate his evening meal, and drank to the point of exhilaration. The *Nai nai* drank sturdily with him, and when he saw her sitting in front of him in her red undergarment with her hair loosened and a springlike flush on her cheeks, she seemed to him more beautiful than ever, and he embraced her and said to her flatteringly: "People will keep on talking in the highest terms of my principal wife, but when I compare you with that wicked witch, it seems to me that she is not even worthy to untie your shoes."

"Ah, of what use is one's little bit of beauty, when all is said and done!" she replied with a sigh.

"What do you mean by that? I do not understand you," he said.

"Oh, I was thinking of my sister," she replied, suddenly bursting into tears. "We two have now been living as man and wife for the past two months. You know how devoted I am to you, and I know what you are to me. But what is to become of my sister? What is she to do here with us? That troubles me. We should put our minds to securing her future too."

"I understand perfectly well. I myself have already been thinking about that, so please do not worry!" he said with a reassuring smile. "You shall see that I am not a jealous, selfish man. Now, how would it be if your sister were to take Cousin Chen? Come, let us go straight over and discuss it with him quite openly. Luckily, they are all there together."

So they went over to the living room in the west wing. Their unexpected appearance embarrassed the belated visitor and Mother Yu very considerably, but Chia Lien was able tactfully to restore a relaxed atmosphere by a few friendly words.

"After all, we are good friends and cousins and we do not need to stand on ceremony with each other," he said blithely to Cousin Chen. "Heaven knows how much you have exerted yourself on my behalf, and I owe you an endless debt of gratitude. Under the circumstances it would be strange indeed if we were to be embarrassed before each other. You are always welcome here."

And there and then, to show his devoted gratitude, he went on his knees and was about to kowtow, but Cousin Chen raised him to his feet at once.

"I am most willingly at your service, dear Cousin. Please tell me what I can do for you!" he said.

"Oh, I would only like to drink a glass of wine with you," replied Chia Lien. He motioned to Little Pao's wife to pour out the wine, then, turning to the third Yu, he continued with a smirk: "Well, how would you like to drink a goblet together with Cousin Chen? I on my part will raise my glass and drink to your mutual happiness!"

At these words the third Yu became beside herself with rage, and with one leap sprang up on the divan.

"Spare me your flowery rigmaroles! I know what all of you are like in this noble house!" she shouted at him with the utmost scorn, from her perch. "We are at your disposal as whores, nothing else! First you get hold of my sister with your stinking money, and now it is to be my turn! But that's where you're wrong! . . . Very well, then, I am willing, and as long as we are treated decently, we shall keep quiet. But look out if you give us the slightest cause for complaint! I'll run to your first wife and make a row. Then we shall see if she really has all the brains and ability she is credited with! And now let's be merry and drink to our hearts' content!"

She poured out a full glass for herself, drank it half empty, then poured the other half down Chia Lien's throat. The two cousins were speechless at her behavior. They were quite well accustomed, to be sure, to the loose tone of low haunts, but to hear such unrestrained language from a maidenly mouth—that was something quite new to them. The third Yu did not let their embarrassment deter her, however, and continued brazenly with her loose talk and her strumpet's airs.

"Come! Don't be timid! Help me to amuse the gentlemen!" she pressed her sister, who had remained shyly in the background. "After all, we are all one family here together, and it's so nice being all to ourselves. Why shouldn't we have a jolly time? Hoop-la! Let's be merry!"

Prince Chen cursed his thoughtlessness in starting it all. This wild girl was positively frightening. He tried to reach the door, but the third Yu would not let him escape. In order to show that she meant the word "merry" seriously, she took off her jewelry, loosened her hair, and without the least embarrassment stripped off her upper clothing. Then she sat down dressed only in her red undergarment. Even that she had half opened, so that only a thin pale green chemise covering the snow-white twin waves of her breast, green knickers, and red slippers were visible. No, she was certainly not stingy with her fresh charms—charms which could not fail to bewilder and infatuate any man's heart.

And she went even farther in the exhibition of her unrestrained temper, keeping the senses of her two male companions in a whirl. She was all movement; she did not remain seated long enough to complete one sentence, but kept jumping up, and sitting down, and changing her place continually, so much so that her earrings never stopped swaying like swings. Between times she poured herself out one glass of drink after another, while her eyes gleamed more and more seductively in the lamplight, like the humid glistening of autumn dew; the flush on her cheeks mounted up to her temples like red waves; the blue-black streaks of her tapered eyebrows, which were shaped and outlined like narrow willow leaves, played in a language more eloquent than words; the fragrance which streamed from her vermilion lips was like the perfume of sandalwood. Her well-calculated game bewitched both her brother-in-law and her cousin to an equal degree, repelling and attracting them at the same time. Silent and fascinated, they sat, and stared, and listened, transfixed with horror, to the ceaseless flow of audacious jests, and boisterous banter, and ironically malicious taunts, uttered at times in the coarsest jargon of the streets, which leaped from those beautiful, delicate, maidenly lips. At last the third Yu had had her full fling. She jumped up, pushed the visitors out the door, bolted it behind them, and lay down to sleep.

From that time on Prince Chen never again ventured unasked into the proximity of that difficult sister-in-law. But it was all the oftener that she summoned, now himself, now his son, and again Chia Lien to her presence, though only, to be sure, when she felt she had a cause for complaint, or wished to ask for something. If she had been most exacting already and eager for the latest fashions in clothing and personal adornment, her demands now knew no bounds. If she was given silver jewelry, she demanded gold; if they loaded her with pearls, she demanded diamonds. If a frock did not please her she took a pair of scissors and slit it open and chopped it into bits, regardless of whether it was old or new, cheap cotton or costly satin. If a dish placed before her at a meal did not please her, she just tipped the whole table over and let all the plates and dishes of food roll over the floor. When this happened, brother-in-law, cousin, or nephew had to take turns in coming to the rescue, and procuring immediate help at her imperious orders. But above all they had to pay, and pay again. And if they showed unwillingness to serve her she made the most violent scenes, heaped abuse upon them, and threatened to betray and expose them to the redoubtable Phoenix. In short, she knew how to exploit the situation to the fullest advantage, and to make life as difficult as possible for those three male relatives of hers who had entangled themselves in a painful family secret.

The second Yu felt, even more than the others, that this situation was untenable, and she pressed her clandestine husband to try to arrange for an early marriage, which would at last rid the house of the tormentor and restore peace to the love nest in the Lane of the Flowering Branch.

"I have already discussed the matter with Cousin Chen," replied Chia Lien, "but he finds it too difficult to part with your sister. I have put it to him that she is a succulent but indigestible piece of wild mutton for him; a beautiful but at the same time thorny rose, and that it is best he should give her up; but he could not bring himself to do that. So what's to be done?"

"We will speak seriously to her tomorrow," suggested the second Yu. "Just you leave it to me! Even if she rants and rages, I will make her see reason in the end."

The next day they gave the third Yu and her mother a formal invitation to midday dinner.

"I can very well guess why you have invited me," said the shrewish younger sister—today by chance in a softer mood—to the elder, with tears in her eyes, thereby forestalling her. "I expect you will want to reason with me again, but you need not beat about the bush; I'm not a thickhead. I can see through you and I know what you are aiming at. You and Mother are comfortably settled here and well looked after, and now you want to have your peace and to pack me off somewhere else. From your point of view that is certainly right and reasonable, but for me marriage is a solemn decision. I cannot bind myself for life to the first man who turns up. Very well, find me the right man whom I can love, and I will follow him as my husband. But spare me proposals such as Cousin Chen's. Whatever his money and position, I do not love him and I will not have him."

"Who, then, is the right man for you? Speak up and tell us!" urged Chia Lien. "Then you may leave all the rest to us. Neither you nor your mother will have any expense or trouble!"

"Ask my sister. She knows exactly whom I mean," declared the third Yu briefly and resolutely.

"Oh, I can already guess who it is, and I must admit that you have good taste," cried Chia Lien, laughing outright.

"Who is it? Who is it?" asked the second Yu, eagerly.

"Why, who else can have got within range of her eyes except Cousin Pao Yu?"

The third Yu smiled contemptuously.

"Pah! As if you few cousins were the only men available for us sisters, even if there were a dozen of us! How absurd! Fortunately, there's more choice than that in the world for us."

"Well, whom else would you consider?" she was asked eagerly from three sides at once.

"Let my sister think hard and throw her mind back five years!" retorted the third Yu.

The conversation was interrupted by the appearance of Chia Lien's trusted servant, Little Hsing, who had come to call him to his father, Prince Shieh, on an urgent matter. So Chia Lien had to break off the important consultation for the time being and set out on horseback. He took as escort his servant Little Lung, and left Little Hsing at the disposal of his second wife until his return.

The second Yu availed herself of the opportunity to question Little Hsing about life in the western palace. How old Madame Phoenix was; whether she was really as bad as she was made out to be; the age and character of the Ancestress and the various young girls in the Park of Delightful Vision; these and many other things she wanted to know exactly. Grinning obsequiously as he sat eating, and drinking tea, Little Hsing gave her the information she desired. The staff had more respect for Phoenix than for Chia Lien; all feared her sharp tongue and the poison of her crooked designs; her husband, on the contrary, was a good-natured fellow; and as for Little Ping, Phoenix's personal maid, she never dared to oppose her stern mistress openly, but behind her back she put right many wrongs and was generally beloved by the whole staff as a kindhearted protectress. He told, moreover, how Phoenix contrived to hoodwink the old *Tai tai* continually and keep her in good humor by always ascribing everything favorable to herself and blaming everything unfavorable on others; denying her own mistakes and harrying others for theirs, and fanning the flames against them; and how greedy she was for money, which she would like to heap up mountains high if she could, and that apart from the old *Tai tai* there was no one in the whole house now who could stand her. With sly calculation Little Hsing came out with these and similar things, which he knew would sound sweet in the ears of the future mistress.

"My word, that's a nice way to let your tongue run about your mistress behind her back! What will you not say about me one day, for I am quite a lot worse than she is?" said the second Yu, laughing.

Little Hsing promptly fell on his knees before her.

"May I be struck by lightning if I ever carry on against you!" he protested. "With you, *Nai nai*, it is quite different, of course. We servants would have counted ourselves lucky if our master had made a lady like you his first lady from the very beginning. We would not have had to put up with so many blows and scoldings the whole time, and to live in fear and trembling as we do. Whether we talk openly or behind your back, we cannot praise and bless your gentleness and kindness of heart highly enough. We compete eagerly for the honor of being brought out here with our master, for then we have the opportunity of waiting upon you!" he flattered her.

"Oh, you crafty knave! That's enough now, stand up! You need not be afraid. I was only joking just now. I am not so bad at all. But tell me, how do you think it would be if I simply went over one day and made the acquaintance of your severe mistress?"

Little Hsing held up his hands in horror.

"I warn you a thousand, ten thousand times! Do not do that! Take my advice, *Nai nai*, and beware of allowing her to set eyes on you! I warn you, she's a two-faced woman. She bewitches you with smiles and sweet words, and at the same time she's planning vile things and throwing her snares around your feet to trip you up. She carries sharp daggers and knives around with her in secret. Not even your sister, for all her able tongue, would be a match for her, let alone such a noble, fine, gentle-natured lady as you! No, she is no company for you!"

"I did not have any intimate acquaintance in mind; I meant merely a formal courtesy visit."

"Whether formal or friendly, I warn you, *Nai nai!* Do not think that I've been drinking and don't know what I'm saying! But believe me, she has only to see you, with your charms, which are greater than hers, and your friendly ways, which are more winning than hers, and she will see you as her deadly enemy. If other people have just an ordinary jugful of the vinegar of jealousy in them, she has a whole barrelful. My master has only to look once too often at one of her waiting maids, and that is enough excuse for her to berate and punish the poor creature most cruelly in his presence."

"My word, she seems to be a real devil. Now tell me something about the Widow Chu and the young girls in the Park of Delightful Vision."

"Well, here goes! The Widow Chu is a nice, good soul, who concerns herself with nothing else but superintending the young ladies' studies and teaching them needlework. As for our four young daughters of the family, the eldest, Beginning of Spring, the Imperial wife, is goodness and virtue itself. The second one, Miss Greeting of Spring, is a bit stupid and for this reason goes by the nickname of 'Blockhead.' The third, Miss Taste of Spring, has the nickname 'Rose' on account of her rosy cheeks and also because, though she's very charming, she can also be terribly prickly. It's a pity that she is not the child of the good *Tai tai* Cheng but of the wicked secondary wife Chou. That's a real case of a phoenix chick being laid by mistake in a raven's nest. The fourth of the girls, Miss Grief of Spring, a younger blood sister of Prince Chen, is a very well-behaved, good child. Besides these, we have two foster daughters in the house, two very unusual young girls. The one, Miss Black Jade, is the child of the late Aunt Ling, the other, Miss Precious Clasp, is the child of our Aunt Hsueh. They are both equally beautiful and highly educated. When we servants catch sight of one of them in the distance, we hold our breath."

"Oh, indeed? And why is that?"

"For fear that the one, the delicate Miss Black Jade, might be blown over if we breathed too hard, and that the other, the delicious Miss Precious Clasp, might melt away if we breathed too hotly."

Everyone in the room had to burst out laughing at this droll explanation.

But our esteemed readers will want to know at last whom the third Yu really did want for a husband. Just be patient. You will learn this in the next chapter.

CHAPTER 33

A fiery maiden, ashamed of her unrequited passion, takes her life. The Cold Knight strides with a cold heart through the Gateway of the Great Void.

LITTLE PAO'S WIFE GAVE THE WITTY LITTLE HSING A SLAP AND SAID to him, laughing: "From the way you let all that, truth and invention, run off your loose tongue, anyone would think you had picked it up from young Master Pao Yu instead of from your master, Mr. Chia Lien."

"What does that young boy Pao Yu do with himself generally?" asked the third Yu.

"Oh, it would be better to ask, what does he not do! Certainly nothing very brilliant," replied Little Hsing with a meaningful grin. "He is utterly degenerate and has no interest either in books or in arms. In the beginning his father, Mr. Cheng, used to take some trouble with his upbringing, but he has given that up long since. So the boy is left completely to his own devices. Outwardly he is a very nice-looking, bright lad, and does not look at all as if he is wanting in the top story, but when you have a good look at him you can see that he's a weak-witted fool. He seems so timid before strangers that he can hardly get out a sentence. He's a real little sissy of a mother's darling and never feels at ease unless he has a crowd of girls around him to fool about with and to pet and cuddle. The poor soppy fellow lacks all seriousness and firmness of character. With us servants, for instance, he's different every time, according to his mood. If he's in a good humor he jokes with us as if we were his equals and there was no such thing as difference of class. If he's in a bad humor he retires into his shell and other human beings simply do not exist for him any more. At such times he doesn't even reprimand us if we behave improperly. Naturally, in these circumstances it's impossible to have any respect for him."

"You servants are certainly a difficult lot to handle," said the third Yu, smiling. "When you finally have a really goodhearted and conscientious master or mistress you grumble and are discontented with them."

"It's a pity about him, for he's a nice boy otherwise," sighed the second Yu, compassionately.

"Oh, don't listen to all this servants' gossip!" continued the third Yu. "Why, we have met him once or twice ourselves, and have been able to form our own judgment of him. There is certainly something effeminate in his nature and behavior, but that is not surprising when a boy grows up only among women and girls. But to call him weak-minded and a fool—no, that is quite ridiculous and unjust! Don't you remember when we met him just recently at the funeral services at the bier of the Prince Hermit? We girls were all standing together in a group. Then when the monks filed in and took up their position all round the coffin, Pao Yu came in and stood right in front of our group. That was remarked upon unfavorably by everyone. Had he no eyes in his head, and was it not most inconsiderate to stand so awkwardly right in our way, blocking the view from us, people said. But afterwards he told us the reason for his strange behavior. He knew perfectly well what was correct, and he had very good eyes in his head, so he said, but he had deliberately pushed himself in between us and the monks so that we should not be treated too directly to their unsavory odor. And later, when you asked for a drink of tea and the serving woman began to fill up the bowl for you which he had just drunk out of, he stopped her and ordered her to rinse the bowl with water first. From these two little incidents, which I observed dispassionately, I could see that he is, in fact, a person of very fine feelings, and that in the presence of young girls he has only eyes and thoughts for us and forgets everything else on our account. Naturally, outsiders who do not know his nature cannot understand his behavior."

"Hearing you talk that way, it seems to me that you and he are already of one mind," said the elder Yu gaily. "How would it be if you and he were to become betrothed?"

Because of the presence of the servant Little Hsing, the third Yu chose to remain silent, and sat with bent head, nibbling melon seeds.

"Yes, he would suit the young lady quite well," interposed the presumptuous Little Hsing, "but unfortunately he is already disposed of. It's an open secret, after all, that Miss Ling is his intended. Of course they're both very young yet, and besides, Miss Ling has been very sickly of late. But in two or three years the old *Tai tai* will no doubt open her mouth and settle the matter."

While he was saying this the servant Little Lung came back from the Yungkuo palace. "Prince Shieh is sending his son Chia Lien on an important mission to Ping an Chow," he reported. "He will set out in three or four days and will be away for about two weeks. He therefore asks to be excused for today, as he is occupied with urgent preparations for the journey, and he asks the *Nai nai* please to go ahead alone with the matter she knows of. As soon as he comes back he will take it up again." The two servants, Little Lung and Little Hsing, now withdrew. The second Yu bolted the hall door behind them and she, her mother, and her sister went early to bed, but before going to sleep she questioned the younger sister persistently until she found out from her the name of the man whom she wanted for her bridegroom.

When Chia Lien made a brief dash over early the next day and wanted to know the name of the third Yu's chosen man as quickly as possible, the second Yu replied with a laugh: "There's no hurry; the man in question is far away now, heaven knows where and for how long. My sister declares that even if he stays away a year, she will wait for him a year; if it is ten years until he returns, she will wait patiently the ten years, but that if he dies in the meantime she will have her hair cut off and go into a convent; but she will never marry any other man, whatever happens."

"Who, then, is this fellow who has taken her heart so completely?" asked Chia Lien, impatiently.

"Oh, that is a long story, but I will make it as short as I can. It began five years ago in Grandmother's house on her birthday. There was a theatrical performance in celebration of the day. The performers were not professional actors, but all sons of good families. Among them was one who played the part of the youthful heroine. He is said to have fled from the town a long while ago on account of some trouble or other, and to be travelling in distant parts. His name is Liu Hsiang Lien."

"Oh, so that's the man! A fine, handsome fellow. Your sister has good taste and good eyes; one must say that for her. But he's of a cold, proud nature. He has no time for ordinary people, but he gets on splendidly with Pao Yu. Last year he had a fight with our wild cousin Hsueh Pan, and to save our family from further awkward incidents he simply disappeared from the town immediately afterwards without leaving a trace. Perhaps one could find out something about his whereabouts through Pao Yu's servant, but he is certainly a drifting water plant. It may well be years before it occurs to him to show his face here again, and your sister may perhaps wait in vain. She would do much better to put him right out of her mind."

"You seem not to know me yet, brother-in-law," interrupted the third Yu, suddenly coming in from an adjoining room. "I'm in the habit of saying what I mean. It is either Mr. Liu or no one, and that's that! From today on I will devote myself to prayer and fasting and looking after my mother, while I wait for him, even if I have to wait a hundred years. And if I do not mean this sincerely, may my fate be the fate of this clasp!" she continued solemnly. Drawing a jade clasp from her hair, she broke it in two, then disappeared into the adjacent room again.

Chia Lien had to resign himself to her decision. He tried to find out something about the whereabouts of the Cold Knight through Pao Yu's personal servant, Ming Yen, but Ming Yen knew nothing; and his inquiries in the young man's former locality were equally fruitless.

Shortly afterwards Chia Lien set out on his journey to the prefecture of Ping an Chow, after having spent two more nights secretly in the Lane of the Flowering Branch.

He had been three days on the way when a trading caravan came towards him. As the two parties drew close he perceived to his astonishment that his cousin Hsueh Pan was one of the dozen men on horseback escorting the caravan. And what astonished him still more was to see, riding peacefully by his side, his former enemy, the Cold Knight. After mutual greetings, both parties turned in to rest in a near-by inn.

"How comes it that I see you two former tilters and adversaries so peacefully united now?" asked Chia Lien.

"My caravan was attacked and looted by a band of robbers in the neighborhood of Ping an Chow. Then just by chance and in the nick of time along came Brother Liu to our rescue with his party. He put the robbers to flight, recovered the booty from them by force of arms, and saved the lives of myself and my people. As he scorned my thanks, I offered him blood brotherhood. And so we have become true confederates and blood brothers forever and have been travelling part of the way together. But our ways must soon part again. I am going back to the capital, and he is going two hundred li farther south to visit an aunt of his. As soon as I have finished my business at home I intend to obtain a bride and a house for him and to persuade him to settle down permanently in the capital."

"A bride? Oh, that is splendid! I can suggest a suitable party straight away," interposed Chia Lien eagerly. And he told of his secret marriage to the second Yu sister and of the younger sister who was still unwed. He refrained, however, from saying that the third Yu sister had herself chosen the Cold Knight as her husband, and he also prevailed upon his cousin not to breathe a word of the whole story when he got home.

"You should have hit upon that sly plan of yours long ago! It serves my strait-laced cousin Phoenix quite right!" said Hsueh Pan maliciously; and gave his ready approval to the new marriage plan too. But the Cold Knight declared: "That is all very well, but I have firmly resolved to marry only a really outstanding beauty. I set less value upon money and lineage than upon this. I shall have to make sure on this point before I can agree to your suggestion."

"Oh, you can be quite easy on that score," Chia Lien assured him zealously. "But what are words? You must see her for yourself, and then you will be convinced! It would be hard to find another girl who could compare with her for beauty."

"Very well, I agree; and I shall be in the capital in about two months' time, but I want to visit my aunt first," declared the Cold Knight.

"I accept your word, but you are a restless fellow, a drifting water plant. Would you not prefer to back up your word in a visible way with some kind of betrothal gift?" suggested Chia Lien with a smile.

"Do not worry, brother-in-law; you may rely upon my word. I am not in funds just now, and besides I am travelling. Where would I get a suitable gift right away?" replied the Cold Knight.

"Let me procure the gift!" suggested Hsueh Pan.

"It need not be expensive gold and silver and jewelry straight away. Any little trifle which you are wearing will do just as well. Only it is best that it should be a personal souvenir of yourself, for otherwise she may possibly not believe me," insisted Chia Lien.

"Very well, then. She shall have my twin-blade sword. It is an old heirloom of my family which I have always treasured faithfully," said the Cold Knight.

They drank a few more glasses together, then broke up and went their opposite ways. Chia Lien carried out his mission to the Prefect of Ping an Chow and was back again in the capital after two weeks.

His first visit was to the Lane of the Flowering Branch. Apart from two surreptitious and completely fruitless visits from the princely brother-in-law, nothing of any consequence had happened during his absence. The three ladies Yu had remained quietly at home behind closed doors and passed the time busy with their needles. Chia Lien proudly reported his successful meeting with the Cold Knight and handed over to the third Yu her betrothal gift, the "duck couple" sword with the twin blades.

She examined her strange betrothal gift more closely. One single sheath studded with pearls and jewels concealed two completely identical, coldly glistening, sharp-edged blades. The symbol *yuan*, signifying "little drake," was engraved on the one, and the symbol *yang*, signifying "little duck," on the other.

The third Yu was overjoyed. She took the twin sword and carried it into her maiden chamber, where she hung it on the wall over her bed, for she wished to have it continually before her eyes so that the sight of it might strengthen and support her until the day when the beloved himself would come to lead her to his home.

Chia Lien remained for two days with his *Nai nai* in the Lane of the Flowering Branch; only then did he go to the western palace to present his report to his father and to greet Phoenix. She had recovered meantime from her long illness and was able to go out again, and to resume her accustomed activities in the household. Finally he visited Prince Chen and informed him of the successfully concluded betrothal of the third Yu. The Prince listened to him rather indifferently and unsympathetically. He was out of humor because of the failure of his own efforts to win the favor of his beautiful sister-in-law. So he confined himself to putting his hand in his pocket and taking out a few dozen taels as his subscription towards the young lady's dowry, leaving all the rest of the arrangements to his cousin Chia Lien.

In the eighth month the Cold Knight did in fact turn up once more in the capital. On his first day there he visited Aunt Hsueh and his new friend Hsueh Pan, who was in bed with a severe cold in the head. Aunt Hsueh no longer bore him any grudge for his past quarrel with her son, and now regarded him only as his friend and rescuer and loaded him with thanks and attentions. In order to pay off some part of their debt of gratitude, mother and son had undertaken to meet all the expenses of the coming marriage out of their own pockets, an arrangement in which the Cold Knight gladly acquiesced.

The next day he paid a visit of friendship to Pao Yu and wanted to hear more details about Chia Lien's secret marriage to the second Yu, but Pao Yu too knew only a little about it, from hearsay through Ming Yen.

"And in any case I should prefer to keep as clear of the delicate matter as possible," said Pao Yu, parrying his questions. "But tell me about yourself. I hear that you met Cousin Chia Lien on the way to Ping an Chow and had an important conversation with him. What was it about, by the way?"

The Cold Knight told of his betrothal to the third Yu, which had been agreed upon on the journey. "Oh, you are to be congratulated!" Pao Yu assured him fervently. "She is really a ravishing beauty—a worthy partner for you."

"Oh, indeed? If she is as beautiful as all that I cannot understand why a poor fellow like me should fall to her lot. Besides, I am by no means on intimate terms with her brother-in-law," said the Cold Knight thoughtfully. The suspicion that a former light-of-love of Prince Chen's was being foisted upon him suddenly crept into his mind. "It really puzzles me that I was pressed into this engagement in the course of our brief chance meeting on the road. I cannot imagine a girl like that running after a man. I cannot help feeling suspicious about the whole thing, and now I am almost sorry that I handed over my sword as a pledge. I should have preferred to make some inquiries myself first."

"Your doubts are certainly quite unfounded. First you insist upon getting an outstanding beauty, and now when you have got her you begin to falter. Take her, and do not hesitate any longer!"

"Are you so sure, then, that she is beautiful? For it seems to me that you do not appear to know much more than I do about her person and her family."

"She is a stepsister of Princess Chen, whose maiden name was Yu. During the recent funeral solemnities in the eastern palace I met her and her mother and sister I do not know how many times, so I surely must know."

The Cold Knight stamped his foot angrily.

"Do not talk to me about your eastern palace!" he cried. "The only creatures there that are not disreputable are the two marble lions in front of the main gateway. No! The whole business seems most shady to me. I will not go through with it!"

But he immediately repented of his offensive outburst when he noticed the embarrassed flush on his friend's cheeks.

Bowing ceremoniously before him, he hastened to apologize. "I have

362

let my tongue run away with me, and I deserve death for my bad manners," he said. "But tell me at least something about her character."

"Oh, please, why do you keep on asking me? Apparently you are better informed than I am. Besides, I myself may perhaps be disreputable and untrustworthy?"

"Please do not be resentful. I forgot myself."

"Very well. We shall say no more about it!"

The Cold Knight perceived that he would get nothing more out of his offended friend, so he bowed once more briefly and formally and took his leave. He was determined to cancel the overhasty betrothal, which seemed to him more and more questionable.

He set out straight away to report his decision to Chia Lien, who at this hour was with the second Yu in the Lane of the Flowering Branch. The unsuspecting Chia Lien received him in the most friendly and familiar manner, and led him straight into the drawing room of the ladies of the house, where he introduced him to his future mother-in-law. He was not a little surprised at the stiff and formal manner in which his presumptive brother-in-law bowed to Mother Yu, and still more surprised when he heard him addressing her not as "mother-in-law" but as "old aunt," and referring to himself not as "son-in-law" but simply as "the later born one." But he was dumfounded when during tea the Cold Knight suddenly said without any warning: "Our recent agreement was an overhasty, chance arrangement. My aunt, whom I visited shortly afterwards, had already chosen my future bride and she wishes me to marry her in the fourth month. Respect for my aunt demands that I should fall in with her wishes. In these circumstances I must reluctantly renounce our agreement and request the return of my pledge. If it had been any kind of ordinary ornament, I would not insist upon its return; but that sword is precious and sacred to me as a heritage handed down by my fathers and ancestors. I must therefore reluctantly ask for its return."

Chia Lien could hardly believe his ears when he heard him speaking in this way.

"My brother is mistaken; an agreement is an agreement," he cried, aghast. "That is just why I insisted upon a betrothal gift—so that there would be a visible pledge if you should regret your word. How would it be if every betrothed man could back out of his betrothal whenever he liked? No! What you ask is impossible!"

"I am ready to make any satisfaction that my brother may stipulate, but I must have my sword back," insisted the Cold Knight with a smile.

Chia Lien was about to make some reply, but the Cold Knight stood up and asked him to step outside in order to avoid continuing the dispute in the presence of Mother Yu. The two were just about to leave the room when the door leading to the adjacent room suddenly opened and the third Yu walked in. She had been listening to the whole argument from the next apartment. So she had been waiting and waiting for the beloved, only to hear now that he wished to have nothing to do with her! Perhaps he had heard an unfavorable report of her in the Yungkuo palace? Perhaps she had been described to him as a shameless hussy, unworthy to become his lawful wife? If she let him go now without further ado, there would probably be a fierce quarrel outside on her account between himself and Chia Lien. She did not want that. Suddenly resolved, she tore the double sword down from the wall, drew out the "female" blade, and, hiding it under her right arm, walked into the room, carrying the "male" blade in the sheath.

"Your quarrel is unnecessary; I return my betrothal gift voluntarily," she said in a voice choked with tears, handing the Cold Knight the sheath with the male blade. At the same time she drew out the hidden female blade and, with a powerful thrust, pressed it into her delicate throat. The others sprang forward aghast and tried to stop her, but it was already too late. The petals of the broken peach blossom were already falling in red splashes over the ground; the crumbling nephrite hill would never rise again!

After the first shock the mother of the dead girl raised a loud lamentation and broke out in bitter curses and revilements of the Cold Knight. At the same time Chia Lien took hold of him and ordered his servants to bind him with ropes and drag him before the Court, but the second Yu dried her tears in haste and made him desist from his intention.

"My sister did what she did of her own free will; the gentleman has exercised neither pressure nor force upon her," she said. "To bring the matter before the Court would not undo what is done, and would only bring discredit on our house. Let the gentleman go his way!"

Chia Lien had to admit that she was right, and he let the Cold Knight go. But the latter remained standing where he was, as if stunned, wiping away the tears which ran slowly down his cheeks.

"What a magnificent, heroic girl! Who would have thought such a thing could happen? I curse myself, bringer of woe!" he murmured to himself, lost in thought. And he remained there as if rooted to the spot until a coffin was brought and the hapless girl was laid in it. Then, with his hand on the coffin, he broke into loud lamentations, which continued for some time. Having thus paid the dead girl her due tribute of reverence, he took his leave and walked slowly away. Sunk in thought and tortured with self-reproach, he walked on and on, heedless of either road or goal.

Suddenly he heard a gentle sound like the rustling of silken garments

尤
三
姐

and the tinkling of golden bracelets and jade belt ornaments, and lo and behold, there stood the third Yu before him. In one hand she held his double sword, in the other a parchment scroll, and she said to him in a tone of lamentation: "In the vain folly of my love I waited for you for five years. Fool that I was, I did not know that your heart was as cold as your glance. I have had to pay for my foolish passion with my life. I am now in the service of the Fairy of Fearful Awakening, who reigns in the Realm of the Great Void. It is my task to register, with my comments, in the archives of unpaid love-debts, notable cases of unhappy love. I have come to bid you a last farewell, for to see each other again is denied us."

With tears in her eyes, she bowed to him in salutation. He threw himself upon her and tried to embrace her and hold her fast, but she pushed his hands gently away from her and eluded him. Thereupon he began to sob loudly, and the sound awoke him, for he had only been dreaming. When he raised his eyes he saw around him the ancient, crumbling walls of a ruined temple. By his side sat a man attired in the dirty robe of a Taoist priest. He was lame in one foot, and was busily engaged catching fleas.

"Who are you, Master, and where are we?" he asked the peculiar-looking stranger.

"I do not know that myself, and in any case it does not matter; I only know that we have just been having a brief rest," came the strange reply. Suddenly illuminated with inward light, the Cold Knight shuddered with icy horror, and, drawing his sword, he raised it to his head and cut off his hair. Then he followed the uncanny stranger, he knew not whither.

CHAPTER 34

Phoenix cross-examines the servant and so finds out the master's deceits. The unhappy Yu girl allows herself to be lured into a trap.

THE THIRD YU WAS COFFINED ON THE VERY DAY OF HER DEATH AND was buried very quietly outside the city walls. The news of her sudden death was brought to Aunt Hsueh's ears by a waiting maid. Aunt Hsueh was profoundly grieved and dismayed. She had been delighted to help arrange the wedding with the third Yu out of gratitude to the Cold Knight for having saved Hsueh Pan's life on the highroad. She had intended, moreover, to give him a complete house with furniture as a wedding present.

"What do you think of this sad, puzzling occurrence?" she asked her daughter Precious Clasp with a sigh. "The poor thing was engaged to the Cold Knight, your brother's sworn friend. And now, shortly before the marriage, she has taken her life! And her fiancé has since disappeared without leaving a trace!"

"That confirms once more the truth of the old saying that human fate is as incalculable as the course of the wind and the form of the clouds. Between evening and morning our fate can suddenly change for good or for ill. It was her predetermined destiny," concluded Precious Clasp philosophically. "But what is the use of brooding and complaining? She is dead and it cannot be helped, and we cannot bring her back again. Get over it and turn your attention to our own lives and our own affairs! Brother Hsueh Pan has already been back from the South some weeks and meantime has probably sold the goods he brought back. It is high time for him to give a feast for his associates, who spent months travelling with him, and shared his hardships and dangers, to celebrate the happy return home. You should speak to brother Hsueh Pan and urge him to comply at last with this duty, proper to his position."

Mother Hsueh was about to reply when the subject of discussion himself appeared. He looked quite distraught and cried excitedly to the two women: "Have you heard the sad news yet? Cousin Yu dead! Brother Liu disappeared!"

"We have just been speaking about it. What a sad case!" sighed Aunt Hsueh.

"They say he has gone off with a strange Taoist monk."

"That makes the story all the more weird. How on earth could such a sensible young man as that Liu get such a crazy idea? As he is your friend and is all alone in the world, you must exert yourself for him and have him searched for. He will scarcely go far with that wretched begging monk. Presumably he is hiding in some temple in the neighborhood."

"My men and I have already searched for him everywhere inside and outside the town; but there was no trace of him anywhere."

"Good, then you have already satisfied your obligations as a friend. But do not neglect your own affairs because of all this. You are bound in gratitude to prepare a worthy feast for your men, who travelled three thousand li and shared all troubles and dangers faithfully with you for four or five months. They well deserve it."

Hsueh Pan agreed with her, and that same day he sent out invitations to a number of his business managers and travelling companions summoning them to a banquet. When the guests were assembled round the table, one of them called out during the banquet: "Two of our good companions are still missing from the table."

"Who, then?" they were asked.

"Mr. Chia Lien and our host's sworn friend, the Cold Knight. Why have they not been invited?"

Hsueh Pan's face darkened and he sighed deeply.

"My cousin set out for Ping an Chow again a short time ago," he said, "and as for my friend Liu, the mere mention of his name gives me pain. It is a very strange story. He suddenly renounced the world and disappeared in the company of a stranger, a Taoist priest." And he related all he knew of the tragic outcome of the engagement of his friend, and of his sudden disappearance.

"How strange!" they all said, and one of the business managers went on to tell: "A similar case was spoken of recently by the customers in the shop. The story was of a monk who with three or four sentences bewitched somebody and made him invisible. I do not know any more details; we were busy serving and had no time to pay attention to the idle gossip of customers."

"Oh, what nonsense! This is sure to be quite a different kind of case," said another, skeptically. "A courageous, sensible, strong fellow, used to arms like Mr. Liu, would certainly never allow himself to be bewitched by a wandering monk. Presumably he only pretended to join him in order to get behind his magic tricks and hocus-pocus. He will undoubtedly get the upper hand of the swindler in the end."

"That is probably what has happened!" agreed Hsueh Pan warmly. "Really, these mountebanks who bluff and dupe people with their tricks should be put down with an iron hand."

"Have you not had a search made for your lost friend?" they asked him.

"Yes, of course, I have had him searched for everywhere, both inside and outside the city walls; but—and you may laugh at this—he cannot be traced anywhere," declared Hsueh Pan, becoming despondent once more. The company around the table fell into an embarrassed silence; nothing could be heard but long and short sighs, no one could be merry any more, and after just a few more glasses of wine the party broke up in depressed mood.

A few days afterwards Pearl went to visit Phoenix in a free hour to inquire after her health, but she did not stay long. She thought she perceived a certain uneasiness in the air, she noticed excited, whispering waiting maids and caught something about cross-examinations to which these porters or those servants had been subjected by Phoenix. Therefore she did not want to be in the way. She had hardly gone when Phoenix sent for Little Wang, the gatekeeper of the second gate.

"Well, how was it? What have you heard?" she asked the waiting maid Little Ping before Little Wang arrived.

"The maid who secretly informed me has been eavesdropping just now at the second gate on a conversation between Little Wang and two of the master's servants. It was about a second *Nai nai*, who was much more beautiful and much kinder and more friendly than the old *Nai nai*, by which they meant you. . . ."

Little Wang was announced. Phoenix asked Little Ping to be silent and ordered that Little Wang should come in. He remained standing timidly on the threshold of the antechamber in a respectful attitude, his hands hanging down by his sides.

"Come nearer! I wish to question you," ordered Phoenix, whereupon he advanced to the threshold of the inner chamber.

"What do you know about the person with whom my husband associates outside?"

Little Wang bent one knee.

"The slave performs his service at the second gateway day after day. How can he know what the master does outside?"

"Naturally, you know about nothing!"

Little Wang went down on both knees.

"Very well, then, I was present by chance just now when Little Hsing and Little Hsi were gossiping at the second gate. I only told them to be quiet; I understood nothing of what they were talking about. You should question Little Hsing. He always accompanies the master when he goes out."

"Ah, you are just as good for nothing as the other pack!" cried Phoenix angrily. "You are all tangled and matted together like creepers. But do not imagine that you can deceive me! Run and bring Little Hsing here! I shall cross-examine him first, then you shall have another turn!"

"*Shih, shih!*" stuttered Little Wang; and, having made a kowtow, he picked himself up quickly and ran out, returning very soon with Little Hsing. Little Hsing stood timidly hesitant on the outer threshold.

"Come in!" Phoenix ordered him. "That's nice business you have been up to with your master! Now, out with the story!"

The severity of her face and voice shattered the air of confidence which he had put on up to now. In his confusion he could think of nothing better to do than to fall upon his knees and press his forehead to the ground.

"You are not implicated in the case yourself," continued Phoenix in a milder tone; "but why did you not notify me at once? I cannot help reproaching you. Now, please, out with the whole truth. Then I will spare you. But woe betide you if you only come out with empty evasions! Better make sure first that your brain-box is well screwed on!"

Shaking with fear, Little Hsing slid a little nearer, and made another kowtow.

"The slave is not at all aware of what harm he is supposed to have done with the master," he said now, as calmly and boldly as possible.

"Give him a couple of blows!" ordered Phoenix, blazing up in anger. Little Wang rushed up and was just about to carry out her order when she stopped him.

"No, let him box his own ears! There will be time enough later on for other hands to belabor this tortoise."

Little Hsing bent to the right and to the left, dealing himself, with a swift sweeping movement, a good dozen heavy clouts on the ears, until his mistress called "Stop!"

"Well, what do you know about this new *Nai nai*, whom your master is said to have picked up in the city?"

Little Hsing pulled off his cap and beat his bare forehead a couple of times on the earthenware tiles of the floor so forcibly that the thuds resounded dully like mountain echoes.

"I beg for mercy and I will certainly not lie again!" he declared.

"Stand up and speak!"

Little Hsing picked himself up and told what he knew—how one day the house steward Yu Lu went out to the Temple of the Iron Railings to Prince Chen for money; how Mr. Chia Lien had accompanied him back to the eastern palace, and how he and Mr. Chia Yung had discussed the two sisters-in-law of Prince Chen on the way and how Mr. Chia Lien had indulged in admiring praise of their superior qualities and virtues; how Mr. Chia Yung had offered his services to procure the second Yu girl as a secondary wife for him. He had got thus far with his confession when Phoenix, almost choking with rage, burst out: "So it's that one! And a relative into the bargain! Such miserable, faceless, tortoise behavior!" Little Hsing, alarmed, paused in his report, made a hasty kowtow, and then stared resignedly in front of him.

"Get on! Why do you not talk?" Phoenix urged him.

"But will the *Nai nai* not hurt the slave if he speaks on?" asked Little Hsing, wanting to be sure first.

"Nonsense! Go on!"

And Little Hsing continued to relate how his master had entered joyfully into his nephew's plan.

"How the plan was subsequently carried out is not known to me."

"Of course, a servant cannot know everything that the master does or does not do. Go on!"

"Then, later on Mr. Chia Yung procured and furnished a house for Mr. Chia Lien. . . ."

"A house? Where, then?" he was again interrupted.

"Behind the eastern palace."

"Aha! And we noticed nothing of all this! We must have been simply dead!" said Phoenix, turning a reproachful glance on the waiting maid Little Ping.

"Then Prince Chen paid an indemnity to the family Chang; I do not know the exact amount," continued Little Hsing.

"The family Chang? What, then, has that family got to do with the matter?"

"You must know that the second *Nai nai* . . ."

He stopped short and gave himself a resounding box on the ear. How could he so forget himself as to mention a second *Nai nai* in the presence of the *Nai nai?* This comical act of voluntary self-chastisement made Phoenix smile in spite of the seriousness of the situation, and the waiting maids and serving women to the right and to the left quickly put their hands over their mouths and had to laugh too.

"The younger sister of Princess Chen," he corrected himself, "was originally betrothed to a certain Chang Hua of the family of Chang. The family has recently been in very poor circumstances and was therefore willing to renounce the engagement on payment of an indemnity."

"Did you hear that? See what revelations are coming to light!" exclaimed Phoenix, shaking her head and turning to her attendants. "And yet this impudent fellow asserted in the beginning that he knew nothing!"

"Mr. Chia Lien had the house newly painted and beautifully papered and furnished, and then he brought home the second Yu."

"Who escorted her?"

"Only Mr. Chia Yung and a few waiting maids and serving women."

"Not Princess Chen?"

"No, she only paid her a visit two days later and brought several presents with her."

"So this is the alleged business which kept him for days on end in the eastern palace!" hissed Phoenix. "Is anyone else living with that person?"

"Her mother and also, until a short time ago, the younger sister who cut her throat."

"Why, actually, did she do that?"

Little Hsing told of her unhappy love and her betrothal to the Cold Knight, which had been broken off.

"He did well to free himself in time from that disreputable crowd!" said Phoenix derisively. "Anything else?"

"I know nothing more; and every word I have reported is certainly true. The *Nai nai* can make inquiries, and if she can convict me of a lie, she may have me beaten to death if she likes!"

"I would have reason enough for that, you ape. Stand up!"

Little Hsing kowtowed once more, stood up, and slunk out. He was already on the outer threshold when Phoenix called him back.

"You seem in a mighty hurry to be off to your new *Nai nai*. You would like to divulge everything to her and earn a reward, wouldn't you? But you will do nothing of the sort! From today on you will not stir a step to go to that house but will remain permanently at my disposal. Is that understood?"

"*Shih*," promised Little Hsing and withdrew again, to be called back once more.

"Now, you are going to run off and repeat everything to your master, are you not?"

"Your servant will not dare."

"I would not advise you to, if you value your skin. Off with you! Clear out!"

Now Little Wang was called in. Phoenix looked at him sharply for a moment, and then she said: "You are a good fellow, Little Wang. I am pleased with you. And in future always be sure to tell me when you hear something outside! Can I rely on you? Very well, you may go."

"Now, what do you think of that? A nice story, is it not?" she said, turning to Little Ping. Little Ping only smiled. Phoenix threw herself on the divan, took a sip of tea, and settled down to think. Suddenly she raised her brows. She had thought of a plan; she beckoned Little Ping.

"We must act, and at once, before my husband is back from his travels," she said, and began to explain her plan to the waiting maid.

During the next few days the residence of the absent Chia Lien became a hive of activity. A crowd of builders, carpenters, painters, joiners, and other artisans arrived, and on the instructions of Phoenix they put in order the empty eastern wing, consisting of three rooms. The rooms were fitted with the same kind of wallpaper, carpets, furniture, covers, curtains, and other equipment as the rooms which Phoenix herself occupied. On the day that the work was completed and the workers left the house—it was the fourteenth of the ninth month—Phoenix sent a message to the Ancestress that she intended to visit this and that temple to burn incense and pray on the following day.

The next day she got into her carriage and, accompanied by the waiting maids Little Ping and Little Lung, as well as the wife of the porter Little Wang and the wife of the steward Chou Jui, went off, not to the temples named, but to the house of the second Yu in the Lane of the Flowering Branch. Little Hsing was taken along and had to show the way and announce the visitor. The second Yu was more than a little surprised when quite suddenly the wife of Little Pao came running in, terribly excited and trembling all over, and announced: "The great *Nai nai* is coming to visit!"

She pulled herself together at once, however, ran to the door and accompanied her visitor courteously into the reception room, politely laid cushions for her in the place of honor, and had tea served to her. She excused herself on the plea of her youthfulness for all that had happened. Everything, she said, had been done over her head and through her mother and Princess Chen, and she assured Madame Phoenix of how honored and happy she was at the visit, and how eager to hear the instructions of the "elder sister" and to serve her with dutiful respect.

Phoenix was dressed completely in white and silver gray, to give the impression that she was mourning for the deceased third Yu, for whom she in fact cared less than nothing. To the kowtow of submission which the other performed before her she replied with a slight bow, and said:

"Purely out of understandable tenderness and care for his health, and also to spare his parents annoyance and trouble, I always warned my husband against spending the night away from home 'between flowers and beneath willow trees.' Unfortunately, he has completely misunderstood my well-intended advice. Now, if it were a question of some dubious person, he would perhaps be right in concealing an attachment from me. But the fact that he has chosen a highly respectable woman such as you, dear sister, for his 'side-chamber' makes it a different matter and quite in order. No one in his senses could blame him for it. Such things are, after all, customary in other families. I myself have always actually advised him to such a step; I have even offered him Little Ping. It is indeed my own wish that he should have a little boy and legitimate heir, who would one day be a support and comfort to myself in my old age. It was quite wrong of him to keep this matter secret from me through quite unfounded fear of my jealousy. I am neither narrow-minded nor jealous, and call heaven and earth to witness that. I only heard of the matter just by chance a few days ago. My husband is away travelling at present, so I cannot speak to him myself. In order to show you meantime, dear sister, how greatly my husband has misjudged me, I have come to you today to invite you, earnestly and lovingly, to give up your isolation and come over to me. Let us live together in future and unite in a sisterly way in caring for our husband's health and well-being; we owe this to the strict requirements of good form and propriety. This living separately is profitable neither to your reputation nor to mine, nor to that of our husband. How do I stand in the eyes of the servants who as it is detest me because I keep a somewhat strict eye on them? No, the present situation is untenable. So do me the favor, dear sister, of moving over to my place! As regards accommodation, and food, and clothing, and service, you will have exactly the same as I have. You are such a sensible woman, you will be a valuable and inestimable support to me, and there will be an end once and for all to the servants' gossip. When our husband comes home and sees us peacefully united he will feel penitent and will realize that he has shamefully misjudged me. But if you do not wish to move over to me, then I am determined to move over to you, dear sister. And in this event I hope you will put in a good word for me with our husband, so that he will not tear us apart again. I shall be most glad to do everything for you, to do your hair and prepare your foot bath, and perform every service which you may ask, if only I can be with you."

She had spoken with growing emotion, which was meant to simulate sincere feeling, and she now began actually to sob and weep. Her emotion seemed so genuine that the second Yu was quite touched and her eyes too filled with tears. At a sign from her mistress the wife of the steward Chou Jui now had to take out of her cotton bag four pieces of beautiful silk cloth and a pair of gold bangles and of earrings set with pearls, and pass them to the second Yu as a token of friendship. The second Yu was now fully convinced that Phoenix must be a most kind-hearted woman and that everything which Little Hsing had recently told about her wicked character must be slander and servants' gossip. She gave up her previous reserve, became talkative, opened her heart wide, laid bare her thoughts, and trustfully accepted the invitation to move over to the western palace that very day.

"But what will become of my household here?" she asked.

"That is very simple. Your new dwelling is ready and furnished, so we only need to take over your clothing and linen and other personal belongings. All the furniture can be left here."

The second Yu indicated the few trunks and objects which represented her personal belongings, dressed herself ready to depart, and allowed Phoenix to take her by the hand and lead her to the carriage. On the journey in the carriage Phoenix said to her confidentially: "Over here our household rules are rather strict. So far the old *Tai tai* knows nothing of this story. If she now learns that our husband has married secretly in the middle of the mourning period, she will be very angry and probably have him nearly beaten to death in punishment. Therefore, it is better for me not to present you to the old *Tai tai* straight away and not to take you into my own home yet, but to put you up in the park for the time being. You will be well looked after there and quite safe from prying eyes. In the meantime I will take further measures and carefully prepare the old *Tai tai*."

"Do exactly as you think best!" replied the second Yu submissively. As prearranged, the carriage entered the precincts of the western palace, not through the main entrance but unobtrusively through a back gate.

374

Soon after passing in Phoenix dismissed her attendants and smuggled the second Yu through yet another side gate into the Park of Delightful Vision and took her thence, unobserved, to Widow Chu's in the Rice Farm. She told the widow about the matter and asked her to keep the second Yu with her for a few days. At the same time she ordered the servants in the park, under the threat of severe punishment, to keep strict silence and to watch the newcomer's every step, and under no circumstances to allow her to leave the park. Furthermore, she deprived the second Yu of her former servants and gave her instead one of her own maids named Shan, to whom she gave her own special instructions.

Three days later the second Yu wanted to send the waiting maid Shan to Phoenix to get some new hair oil. She met with unexpected resistance.

"Indeed, you have strange ideas!" said the maid very cheekily. "Madame Phoenix has more important things in her head and cannot trouble about such trifles. She is on the go the whole day taking orders from the old *Tai tai* or Princess Shieh or the *Tai tai* Cheng; then she has to look after all the young ladies in the park, and the many guests and visitors, and finally, she is responsible for all the several hundred servants. Everyone turns to her; she is besieged on every side with questions and requests. At a moderate estimate she has to settle every day one to two dozen big matters and thirty to forty smaller ones. Thousands go through her hands every day. How, then, can I trouble her with such trifles? You must get accustomed to having patience. Just remember that you did not marry into our house in an open, correct manner; all the more reason, then, to be unobtrusive and quiet! Be thankful that she has treated you in such a friendly way up to the present, and do not lose her favor by your folly. Otherwise it may go badly with you!"

There was nothing for the second Yu to do but to put up with the reprimand and be silent. Gradually the maid Shan began to show all kinds of negligence in her service—she served the meals unpunctually, and what she did put on the table either at midday or in the evening usually consisted only of stale leavings. Two or three times the second Yu ventured a remark, but each time she was so intimidated by offended looks and indignant demeanor that she did not venture another word of complaint and put up with everything.

Phoenix herself came over once a week. On these visits she was outwardly all friendliness and kindness, and loving expressions such as "dear sister" and "good sister" simply flowed from her lips.

"If you have any complaint to make about the service, let me know at once!" she said. And she put on an act of lecturing the staff of the Rice Farm, saying that she would see through it and take ruthless measures if they failed in their duty and were negligent in their service behind her back. The kindhearted Yu was sorry for the servants who were thus rebuked, and whenever she thoughtlessly opened her mouth to complain about this or that, she shut it quickly again, wishing to spare her servants and not to make herself unpopular. And so everything remained just as it was after these visits of inspection.

Meanwhile Phoenix was making secret inquiries about the past life of the second Yu through her confidant, the porter Little Wang, and so she learned of the latter's first engagement to young Chang Hua, who was now nineteen years of age and an utter wastrel and loafer. His parents had cast him off long ago on account of his dissolute way of life; consequently he himself knew nothing as yet about the cancellation of his engagement and the indemnity of twenty taels which Prince Chen had paid to his parents.

Now Phoenix sent Little Wang secretly to Chang Hua and won him for her little game by a payment of twenty taels. He was to serve a writ accusing Chia Lien of having enticed away his betrothed and married her in the middle of a period of public and family mourning without the knowledge of his legal wife and of the family elder, after having obliged her by coercion and money to cancel her previous engagement to him, the plaintiff. Chang Hua had hesitated to make a direct accusation against a member of the powerful Chia clan, whom he did not wish to quarrel with. It was therefore agreed that Little Wang should take the accusation upon himself as the alleged go-between and instigator. Phoenix was less interested in actually carrying through the lawsuit than in exposing the "gang," namely, the chief culprits of the story— her cousin Prince Chen, his wife, and their son Chia Yung—and frightening them by the imminent prospect of a public scandal. Moreover, she intended to step in just at the right moment if the action should take an unfavorable turn.

Chang Hua accordingly appeared one day before the public session of the Court, called attention to himself by the customary cry of "Injustice," and handed in his writ. In response to the writ the magistrate sent his greencoats next day to the Yungkuo palace to arrest the accused porter Little Wang and hail him before the Court. Through respect, the greencoats did not enter the lordly mansion themselves, and were about to send a servant to the custodian of the inner gate politely requesting him to come out. But that was not at all necessary. Little Wang had reckoned on their coming and was already waiting cheerfully for them in the street in front of the gate.

"No doubt, honored brothers, you have come for me. Very well, seize me and hold me fast!" he invited the greencoats peaceably and good-humoredly, for he knew in advance that no harm would come to him.

"But, good elder brother, how can we do it! We only want you to come with us without any fuss," they invited him just as politely, and escorted him to the Court. The magistrate showed him the indictment handed in yesterday. Little Wang read it, kowtowed, and declared: "That is quite correct. But I myself have nothing to do with it. Chang Hua has merely drawn me into it, because we have been on unfriendly terms for a long time past. You will have to arrest other people."

The plaintiff Chang Hua likewise kowtowed and explained: "That is also correct; but I did not dare to take action against the employers, therefore I named the servant."

"Stupid fellow! We are standing here in an Imperial Court, before which we are all equal, whether master or servant; so now cite the names!" replied Little Wang. Chang Hua now named Chia Yung, the son of Prince Chen, as being really the guilty person. The magistrate therefore could not do otherwise than issue a summons against Chia Yung.

The same evening Phoenix secretly sent the magistrate three hundred taels to his house with a message requesting him for this and that reason to proceed without consideration against her accused clan and to take a really high hand with them. She was very anxious—so the message ran—to give her people a proper scare. And the magistrate, as a good friend of her uncle, Marshal Wang Tzu Teng, felt obliged to comply with the request which she had backed with such a considerable gift.

Prince Chen and his son were terribly shocked when news came that this obscure individual, Chang Hua, had dragged their honorable name before the magistrate's Court. Prince Chen foamed at the mouth over the colossal impudence of the fellow. He had vainly believed that he had silenced the family Chang once for all with the indemnity of twenty taels. Now he would have to dig deep into his pockets again and quickly produce two hundred nice shining silver pieces to buy the magistrate's favor. Just as he and his son were discussing the annoying affair and the counter-measures to be taken, who should appear quite unexpectedly but Cousin Phoenix.

The father and son would have given anything to escape this meeting, but it was too late.

"That's a pretty business you two have been up to with my husband!" she said, bursting in on them.

While she caught Chia Yung by the hand, as he murmured an embarrassed *tsing an*, the Prince succeeded in squeezing past her and gaining the exit.

377

"An urgent business engagement!" he excused himself with a glib smile. "But my son will keep you company for the present and see that you get the best things from the kitchen."

In a trice he was out the door and had mounted his horse and gone off. In the meantime Mother Yu had appeared from the next room. Seeing the visitor's angry face, she guessed there was trouble brewing.

"You seem to be out of humor. May one ask . . .?" she began. In reply, Phoenix spat right into her face.

"You are welcome to ask!" she hissed. "Am I to accept it quietly when you smuggle in your jilted daughter and secretly pawn her off on my husband? If you had just done it openly and honestly, and in the proper manner with three negotiators and six witnesses. But no, you did it on the sly, and, what is doubly incorrect, in a time of public and family mourning! And now we shall have the devil to pay! A man has appeared and has brought the matter publicly before the Court, just so that everyone will hear what an abominable, narrow-minded, jealous woman I am! People will point their finger at me and persuade my husband to divorce me! What have I done to you that you treat me so meanly? Is the old *Tai tai* perchance behind it all? Did she inspire the whole base plan, in order to get rid of me in this way? Well, it will all come to light in time. First you will come to the Court with me, and let each of us render an account to the judge, so that the truth may triumph. And then let us appear before the assembled clan at home and let us each justify herself. If the clan finds me guilty, very well then, they may write the letter of divorce for me and I will leave the house voluntarily."

She began to weep loudly, and to drag Mother Yu by the hand to the door as if she wanted to set out for the Court with her straight away. Utterly dismayed, Chia Yung got in front of her, threw himself at her feet, performed a kowtow, and begged for mercy.

"May lightning strike you and split you in five, you crazy creature," she roared at him. "Shame on you, you good-for-nothing, shameless intriguer and disturber of family peace, scorner of laws and rights and of all order of heaven and of earth! The spirits of all your ancestors and the shades of your late wife will turn away from you in abhorrence and disgust. And a creature like you has the impudence to want to harangue me!"

She raised her hand and dealt him blows right and left. Chia Yung bent down again quickly to make another kowtow. "Do not excite yourself, Aunt!" he begged. "For the sake of the one day in a thousand that I am good, please relent! Spare your nerves and your gentle hand! If I deserve blows on the ear, I can deal them myself."

And he gave himself a few powerful slaps. Then he started to upbraid himself: "May such a thing never happen to me again! To count up to four and skip the three! To follow the uncle and to overlook the esteemed aunt, that indeed is no manners! What, then, has the esteemed aunt done to you, that you should join with others in being so abominable and irresponsible towards her?"

The bystanders had difficulty in keeping from laughing aloud when they heard him abusing himself in this way. But Phoenix threw herself on Mother Yu's breast with a pathetic outcry, calling upon heaven and earth.

"Come! Come with me to the Court! Otherwise the constable may come and fetch us by force!" she sobbed. "And afterwards let us go together to the old *Tai tai* and have the clan judge us. I shall bow to their judgment and leave the house at once if the verdict is against me. I have already fetched your daughter away and lodged her in the park for the time being. I have, as a matter of fact, furnished a permanent home for her in my own house, where she will want for nothing and fare exactly as I do as regards clothing, food, and service. But up till now I have not dared to let her be seen by the old *Tai tai*, as I wished to spare the old lady annoyance and excitement. But the matter cannot be hushed up any longer. Now that it has become a public scandal the old *Tai tai* will have to hear the truth. It is terrible that she has to experience such a disgrace in her old age! What has happened to the good name of our family? It is gone! And besides, there is all this unnecessary expense! I have secretly taken five hundred ounces from the funds and passed them to the magistrate in the hope that he will dismiss the case. It's a pity to lose that good money! And I do not even know yet if what I did is of any avail. The magistrate seems to have taken my gift badly, for he has held my messenger and put him in chains. Oh! Oh! What will the illustrious ancestors of our house in their Realm of Shades think of us . . .?"

She again wept aloud and even hit her head against the wall as if she wanted to take her life.

Mother Yu felt crushed and kneaded to noodle dough by this outbreak of despair. Her dress was wet with her tears. Now she in her turn stormed against Chia Yung. "Ill-behaved creature!" she cried. "You have made a fine mess of things, you and your father! And I had warned you beforehand . . .!"

"Well, if you were against it, why did you not open your mouth and say a word to me?" interjected Phoenix. "Your mouth is not stopped with eggplant apples or constrained by a bit and curb. I certainly would not have let it come to this public lawsuit and scandal if I had been informed in good time. You could well refrain from reproaching others, and reproach yourself instead, for your stupidity and your culpable silence!"

Oh, how cleverly she knew how to twist things round, after having herself goaded Chang Hua into bringing an action! The various secondary wives and serving women and waiting maids who were standing about felt so full of pity for Mother Yu, seeing her so cruelly driven into a corner, that all together they fell at the feet of the angry Phoenix, appealing to her great wisdom and understanding, and implored in chorus for peace and mercy, for she had now trampled on the poor old lady long enough. True, their entreaties had the effect of making Phoenix stop shouting and she put her tousled coiffure in order again; but she was very far from being pacified. She disdained the tea which was offered to her and threw it straight away on the floor. She was itching to call Prince Chen to account next.

"Fetch your father here! I want to ask him a few questions personally," she ordered Chia Yung peremptorily. "I demand an explanation from him as to whether he considers it to be consistent with the *Li*—the requirements of propriety and good custom—for a nephew of the deceased to go off gaily and marry in the middle of the period of mourning for the family elder. A little instruction can do him no harm and may deter him from giving bad example to you young people in the future."

Chia Yung quickly threw himself on his knees, hit his forehead on the ground, and protested: "My parents have had nothing to do with the whole business. I alone am guilty. I was the sole instigator. The esteemed aunt may chastise the unworthy nephew as much as she wishes and he will bear it in silence! But let her please spare his parents! He could not survive it if she does not! He also trusts and implores that the honored aunt may manage to stop the action. The stupid unworthy nephew does not feel that he is equal to such a task and depends entirely on the wisdom of the honored aunt." He accompanied his humble speech with repeated kowtows. Phoenix was pacified to some extent. She raised him up, and then, sighing and wiping away her tears, she turned to Mother Yu: "Do not be angry with me! In my youth and inexperience I have let myself go somewhat, and offended you greatly, but the painful news had so surprised and dumfounded me! Forgive me! And now we must act wisely and reasonably. First of all, this unpleasant action must be settled. You must have a word with Cousin Chen about it without fail."

"Do not worry! The matter will be arranged by us to your satisfaction," said Mother Yu and Chia Yung as if with one voice. "The five hundred ounces which you have already spent will, naturally, be made good to you. On no account must you suffer any further monetary loss in this matter. It would indeed be irresponsible for us to allow such a thing. But we have yet another request to make of you. May we count upon you to set the matter right as far as possible with the old *Tai tai* and not to put us in too unkindly a light with her?"

"Ha, you are asking a bit too much of me!" replied Phoenix coolly. "First you do me a grievous wrong, and then you ask me to come forward and plead for you. Surely, rather a lot to ask! Now, I am of a very kindhearted nature, and, moreover, I am sincerely happy to have a sister and companion coming to my house; I have not been able to sleep for many nights, so great has been my joyful anticipation. If only this obscure fellow, this confounded Chang Hua, had not come between us with his lawsuit! How stupid of Cousin Chen to run away like that! I wanted to discuss with him some means of getting rid of this mischievous litigant!"

"Do not worry, we shall be able to cope with the fellow all right," Chia Yung assured her zealously. "That poor devil of a starving wretch will be glad to withdraw his accusation for a small indemnity. We will see to that. He will give us no more bother in the future, we can assure you!"

"That's all right, if only it works! As long as the money lasts he may perhaps keep his mouth shut, but as soon as he is without a penny again, he will resume the quarrel. In the long run it is useless to waste money on him; we shall have no peace from him whatever we do," said Phoenix skeptically.

"Well, one could give him the choice of either the money or the woman," said Chia Yung, with a smile. "If he positively insists on his claim and demands the woman, we shall just oblige him and hand over my second aunt. I would undertake to persuade my aunt to comply."

"Under no circumstances!" interrupted Phoenix quickly, for she saw that her further plans were being jeopardized. "I do not wish under any circumstances to be separated from your aunt, my dear new sister. Would I not lose face if I were to deliver her up again after having once accepted her? No, no, she shall remain! And you may go on confidently trying to stop Chang Hua's mouth with money!"

To her secret satisfaction Chia Yung agreed to this.

"Very well, the most important thing is to get rid of this Chang Hua. And now let us go together and inform the old *Tai tai!*" she decided.

"But what am I to tell her?" asked Mother Yu, quite alarmed.

"Oh, if one is so helpless as that, one should not risk such daring undertakings," remarked Phoenix mockingly. "But since I am such a good-natured and sympathetic soul, I shall speak for you. Do not show yourself over there for the present! I shall present your daughter to the old *Tai tai* alone first. I shall tell her more or less that I intended in any case to buy my husband two secondary wives, as I could scarcely count on having any male descendant or on living much longer myself, and that recently I had become convinced of the sterling qualities of your second daughter and had given her the preference as a relation. In consideration of her rather straitened circumstances and to free her from anxiety about her livelihood, I had decided to depart a little from strict custom and take her into my house even before the end of the hundred days' mourning; and that as soon as the mourning period is over the official wedding ceremony will take place. There now, that is what I shall say! I shall thus take any eventual blame on myself. Are you satisfied?"

Mother Yu and Nephew Chia Yung enthusiastically praised her generosity and wisdom and gave her to understand that the Princess would pay her a special visit of thanks.

"That is all right; I do not want any thanks," said Phoenix coolly.

"I shall certainly know for the future what to think of you, young man," she said sharply, pointing her finger at Chia Yung.

"But, Aunt, this one little time you will surely forgive the wicked nephew!" begged Chia Yung, promptly falling on his knees again.

She threw back her head as if she wanted to overlook him, and turned towards the door.

CHAPTER 35

Phoenix, with cunning and malice, plays the young rival off against the older one. Driven to desperation, the second Yu kills herself by swallowing gold.

IMMEDIATELY AFTER HER TALK WITH MOTHER YU, PHOENIX VISITED the daughter Yu. First she frightened her with news of the sudden reappearance of her former betrothed, Chang Hua, and then calmed her by telling of the counter-measures which were being taken, not failing to extol her own services, and to spin a long yarn about how unselfishly she had sacrificed and harried herself and with what discretion she had arranged this and that, and how she had done everything to protect the two families from disgrace and blame. The second Yu was profuse with her expressions of gratitude and trustfully let herself be taken over to the old *Tai tai*. Mother Yu, who had not expected to be permitted to come, joyfully joined the two others. But she had had to promise to keep modestly in the background and leave the talking to Phoenix.

The old *Tai tai* was engaged in lively conversation with the young ladies from the Park of Delightful Vision when the three visitors appeared with their attendants.

"Whose child is this?" asked the Ancestress, pointing to the second Yu. "She seems to be a really pretty and pleasing person."

"Does she please you? Do look at her closely!" replied Phoenix, smiling; and taking the other by the hand, she drew her forward.

"This lady is our great Ancestress," she said, introducing her. "Quick, make a kowtow!"

The second Yu threw herself on the ground and duly performed the great ceremonial kowtow of salutation. Then followed the introduction of the young ladies present. In the meantime the Ancestress had leisure to inspect the newcomer from head to foot.

"What is your name and how old are you?" she asked the second Yu, who had stepped aside a little and shyly bowed her head.

"We have not got as far as that yet. You must first give your verdict. Is she prettier than I am?" interjected Phoenix, laughing.

The Ancestress put on her spectacles and ordered Mandarin Duck and Amber to lead the stranger nearer, so that she might inspect her more thoroughly. Amidst the suppressed giggles of the others, the waiting maid Amber had to take the stranger's hands and hold them close under the eyes of the Ancestress. After a thorough inspection she took off her glasses again and declared with a roguish smile to Phoenix: "Hm. She is a fine, well-formed child. She almost seems to me prettier than you."

Phoenix curtsied with a smile and delivered the long, carefully prepared speech the main points of which she had already told Mother Yu. The Ancestress was deeply touched by her noble-mindedness and willingly consented to the newcomer's taking up residence in the palace even before the expiration of the hundred days' mourning period. The official wedding ceremony would take place after the period of a year required by good form.

Phoenix thanked her, striking her forehead on the ground, then stood up and asked for two serving women to escort the newcomer to Princess Shieh and the *Tai tai* Cheng and introduce her to them on behalf of the Ancestress. The Ancestress gave her permission and so the second Yu was installed, in accordance with all the rules of good form, as an inmate of the western palace. And now she was allowed to move over from the park to Phoenix's residence and occupy the suite specially furnished for her in the west wing. It must be mentioned, moreover, that the good Lady Cheng welcomed and approved this change wholeheartedly; for now the position was clarified and the good name of the beautiful but poor girl, so long left unmarried, would no longer be in danger.

While Phoenix thus contrived to give the outward appearance of being selfless and noble-minded, she secretly continued coolly and tenaciously her game of intrigue against her absent husband and his new wife. She again sent to Chang Hua and stimulated him by substantial gifts of money to continue the legal proceedings and insist upon getting back his bride.

At the outset Chang Hua had only taken this action under pressure. Chia Yung, who had a meeting with him later on in the course of the negotiations, maintained that he had previously withdrawn from the engagement; besides, the second Yu was a near relation of the Chia family, and there was surely nothing against her finding a home and board with her own relatives. There was no question, he alleged, of her marrying into the clan. Chang Hua had been in debt to Prince Chen for a long time past and had only taken this action in order to force remission of his debt. The magistrate who had to judge the case was entangled and involved in friendly associations both with the Chias and with the Wangs, the relatives of Phoenix. He had received considerable gifts of money from both sides, from Prince Chen as well as from Phoenix. He therefore found himself in some embarrassment as to how he could act. Finally he gave his verdict against Chang Hua, reprimanded him as a slanderer and a quarreller, ordered that he should be given a few strokes, and drove him out of the Court. Now, just as he was leaving the Court a messenger from Phoenix came up to him, handed him a few silver pieces, and whispered to him that he must stand firm and fight on unflinchingly for his just cause; Phoenix would pay his debts and continue to stand by him. At the same time Phoenix sent word once more to the magistrate giving him this and that new instruction.

The result was a second action and new proceedings. This time the magistrate sentenced the plaintiff on the one part to pay back the old debt to Prince Chen, and on the other part he awarded him his legal bride and gave old Chang authority to fetch his daughter-in-law from the house of Chia and take her into his own home. Highly gratified with the double triumph of having found in Phoenix someone to pay his debts and at the same time being allowed to take possession of his daughter-in-law, old Chang set out for the western palace with the magisterial mandate in his pocket.

Phoenix, hiding her satisfaction and feigning pained surprise, hurried to the Ancestress and reported the new turn of events.

"Sister-in-law Chen is to blame for everything," she said, concluding her report. "In this matter she acted with an utter lack of discretion. She should have secured a valid document of relinquishment. How was I to guess that this Yu was already engaged to someone else? Naturally, the first bridegroom was justified in making a claim. Now we shall have the devil to pay!"

The Ancestress had Princess Chen brought before her and rebuked her angrily for her lack of wisdom and discretion.

"But the people did have an indemnity from us in return for which they made out a written document of relinquishment!" insisted the Princess, much astonished.

"Unfortunately, there is no mention of an indemnity and a deed of relinquishment in the legal protocol," interjected Phoenix quickly. "Moreover, old Chang declared in a legal statement that it had once been mentioned, without prejudice, that in the event of the death of her betrothed, the second Yu would marry into our family as a secondary wife. So there is nothing to be done about that. It is just lucky that my husband is away at present and that the marriage with Yu has not yet been formally celebrated. But the question is, how are we to get rid of old Chang? He is here. We cannot simply send the girl Yu away again just after we have accepted her ceremonially into the family. We would definitely lose face if we did that."

"But neither would we wish to violate the properly acquired legal rights of other people; that would not be becoming of us either. It is best, after all, for us to give her up," said the Ancestress.

"But my mother did pay old Chang an indemnity of twenty taels, in such a year, in such a month, and on such a day, and in return old Chang confirmed his relinquishment in writing," protested the second Yu. "My sister Chen is quite right. There is no question of a mistake. Old Chang has told lies to the Court and is only taking legal action in order to extort money!"

"A disgraceful, troublesome lot!" said the Ancestress indignantly. "Phoenix, go and get the matter put right somehow!"

Phoenix obeyed and first of all summoned Chia Yung for a confidential talk. Chia Yung then consulted with his father, Prince Chen. Prince Chen in his turn once more sent a secret message to Chang Hua, warning him not to go too far and challenge the princely anger. Otherwise he might one day die a miserable death and be left unburied. Let him be thankful for the money, and stop demanding the woman as well. Now was the time to vanish as quickly as possible; the Prince would give him money to get away.

Chang Hua considered the matter this way and that, and discussed it with his parents. The Prince's offer did not seem bad at all, and cash was not to be despised. They agreed among them to demand a further indemnity of a hundred ounces, and early the next morning the parents Chang and their son disappeared from the capital and returned to their native village.

Secretly full of malicious joy, Chia Yung told the Ancestress and Phoenix the news of their disappearance. The magistrate had recognized that the allegations brought forward by Chang Hua had been entirely without foundation. Fearing punishment, the whole rascally gang had disappeared. The magistrate had stopped the proceedings, and so the affair was at an end.

Phoenix received the news with very mixed feelings. On the one hand, she could not shut her eyes to the fact that if Chang Hua had taken Yu away with him, Chia Lien upon his return would probably do his best to get her back from him again, and she did not doubt but that Chang Hua would willingly deliver her up once more. Thus far, Chang Hua's disappearance did not change matters very much, and moreover it spared expenses. On the other hand, she had to fear that Chang Hua, being no longer within range of her influence, might gossip and expose her as the instigator of the whole intrigue. That would turn out unpleasantly for her and possibly even draw her into a lawsuit. She now had to protect herself against such an eventuality.

Having thought the matter over, she sent her confidant, the porter Little Wang, after the fugitives. His task was to render the troublesome Chang Hua harmless by hook or by crook. She left him free to do this either by means of legal accusation on account of alleged theft or some such offense committed on the road, or better still, to have him killed right away by hired assassins. Little Wang's conscience would not permit him to carry out such a dubious order; at the same time, however, he did not like to rebel openly against his mistress and put his position in jeopardy. He therefore pretended to obey her order, kept out of sight for some days, and upon his return dished up a fairy tale for Madame Phoenix. Chang Hua, on his journey home, had attracted the attention of highwaymen by thoughtlessly boasting of all the cash in his possession; on the third day of his flight he had been robbed and murdered and his father had died of a heart attack brought on by shock, in the next inn at which they stopped. Their bodies had been duly examined by a coroner, and they had been buried immediately, right on the spot. Phoenix received the news with some suspicion and threatened Little Wang that she would have his teeth knocked in if it should transpire afterwards that he had lied. But she left it at that; for she had no proof to the contrary, and no other confidant than Little Wang at her disposal. From now on her whole energy was directed, under the mask of friendliness, to making the life of the hated rival in the house as difficult as possible.

On his return from Ping an Chow, Chia Lien was greatly taken aback to find his house in the Lane of the Flowering Branch, which he visited immediately, shut up and empty. Only an old doorkeeper, who had remained as caretaker, was there. When he heard from the mouth of the doorkeeper how and why the place was deserted, he got such a shock that his foot slipped from the stirrup.

Then he went straight to his father, Prince Shieh, and gave him a report of his mission. Prince Shieh expressed his satisfaction and gave him as reward a hundred ounces of silver and a seventeen-year-old chambermaid named Chiu Tung. Chia Lien thanked him joyfully, striking his forehead on the ground, and went on to pay his respects to the old *Tai tai* and the other relatives.

Feeling somewhat guilty and embarrassed, he went to confront his wife Phoenix, but, contrary to expectation, Phoenix did not show the slightest trace of ill-humor. Smiling gaily, she came to meet him hand in hand with the second Yu and asked him casually about the journey, and the weather he had encountered, as if nothing had occurred between them. Chia Lien could not suppress a certain joyful satisfaction when he mentioned that his father had just given him a present of a seventeen-year-old concubine. This was really a new stab in Phoenix's heart before the first wound was quite healed, but she controlled herself as best she could, maintained a friendly appearance, and sent two serving women straight over to Prince Shieh's residence to bring back the new member of the household and introduce her properly to the assembled ladies. Chia Lien could not get over his astonishment at the unexpected amiability of his normally so jealous principal wife. How could he know that she was merely acting a part, hiding quite different thoughts.

At the next opportunity, when she was alone with the second Yu, she said to her, with ostensible concern: "Unfortunately, Sister, your reputation is not of the best. People are whispering about your doubtful past; you are said to have had an affair with your brother-in-law Chen, and that your former fiancé scorned and jilted you on that account—even the old *Tai tai* and the other ladies repeat such things. I am deeply sorry for you. I have been trying to find out who started all this talk, but up to the present without success. I have wanted to speak to you about it for quite some time, but as I did not wish to do so before the staff, I had to keep mute as a maggot. But the whole thing has so upset me that I have been quite ill and have not been able to enjoy a bite for days."

These and similar rumors she had sneeringly spread herself, and soon there was a general whispering throughout the whole house. There was not one among the female staff, with the sole exception of good Little Ping, who did not whisper and murmur within earshot of poor Yu, and who had not taken part in the game of spiteful remarks and hidden allusions and innuendoes by which one names the lime tree and really means the acacia.

The seventeen-year-old concubine, Chiu Tung, had a much better time. No one dared to censure or criticize her, for she had not come in by a back door but as an open gift from the family Senior, Prince Shieh. Accordingly, she considered herself to be far above the second Yu. Not even Phoenix or Little Ping impressed her greatly, much less that doubtful person who had been jilted and had wormed herself into her present position by way of a dubious and clandestine former association. Those were her actual words, and Phoenix heard them with satisfaction. She had found in her a suitable tool with which to work against the detested Yu.

Phoenix avoided Yu as much as she could. She constantly feigned illness and had Yu's meals served to her separately, and the food she had set before her was stale, unappetizing stuff. Good Little Ping was the only one to feel for the girl who was being so badly treated, and now and then she got better food for her out of her own pocket money. Through respect for Little Ping, no one in the house dared to object to this or to tell Phoenix. Only Chiu Tung was inconsiderate enough to backbite Little Ping.

"Your authority will go completely, *Nai nai,* if you continue to let your waiting maid do as she pleases," she said to Phoenix. "That exacting person, that Yu woman, leaves your good food untouched and secretly gets food from Little Ping in the park! What do you say to that?"

Thereupon Phoenix rebuked her maid soundly. "In other places the cats get mice to eat, as is proper. But you actually feed my cat with chicken!" she scolded. Little Ping did not dare to reply, but to live in such a heartless world revolted her; she wished she were elsewhere, and began to hate Chiu Tung.

Poor Yu also was greatly pitied by the young girls in the Park of Delightful Vision; but Phoenix was so feared and knew so well how to dissemble, that no one dared to speak. Only among themselves and secretly did they venture to bemoan and bewail the fate of the second Yu. And Chia Lien on his part also allowed himself to be deceived by the play-acting talent of his chief wife. When he was at home everything seemed smooth and in the best of order. Moreover, his interest in the second Yu had greatly abated since he had got the seventeen-year-old as a present. She was to him what dry wood is to a burning flame. Like glue and lacquer they clung together, and he did not stir from her side for whole days and nights together. Phoenix, of course, hated Chiu Tung no less than she hated the second Yu, but for the present the younger favorite was a valuable confederate and a weapon against the elder one. She wanted to sit up on a mountain height and look on as the two beasts tore one another to pieces below. Once the first one was finished, she intended to rush in herself upon the survivor for the kill.

"You are young and inexperienced and you do not know the danger you are in," she whispered to Chiu Tung. "She possesses his whole heart. Even I have to give way before her and submit to her. You will destroy yourself if you run into her so wildly."

In this way she incited and goaded her, and roused the fiery little one to defiance and rebellion.

"I would never dream of giving way before such a person!" retorted Chiu Tung indignantly. "One can see by your dwindling authority, *Nai nai,* what your weak-kneed tolerance leads to. Leave it to me! I will deal with this hussy. She shall get to know me!"

She had deliberately said this so loudly that the second Yu, who was in the next room, had to hear it. She was in despair at seeing herself surrounded by so much malice, wept the whole day long, and could not touch a bite of food, but the next day, when the Ancestress remarked her red and swollen eyelids and asked the reason, she was too timid to open her mouth. Instead, the cheeky Chiu Tung whispered to the Ancestress and the elder ladies that Yu only wanted to impress Chia Lien by her everlasting moaning and groaning and put him out of humor with his two other wives, whom she secretly wished dead.

The Ancestress, too, was completely taken in and said disapprovingly: "There, one sees again what baseness can be hidden beneath a beautiful exterior! Phoenix means so well by her, and now she shows her gratitude by intriguing against her benefactress! What a low creature!"

From that hour on, the favor which the second Yu had enjoyed up to now with the Ancestress dwindled away. And when the others saw that the Ancestress withdrew her affection, they gave up all consideration and trampled on the poor thing in such a way that all her desire to live vanished. Only good Little Ping remained true to her and secretly comforted her as often as she could.

For some time past the second Yu had been pregnant. It was inevitable that the ill-treatment which she had to put up with should have a harmful effect on her tender, lilylike body, which was so much in need of care. She began to ail and grow thin and lose her appetite. By day she felt tired and worn out, by night disturbing dreams robbed her of sleep.

Once her dead sister, the third Yu, appeared to her in her dreams. She held in her hand the bejewelled sword, engraved with the pair of ducks, and said to her: "Dear sister, all your life you have been too weak and good-natured. Now you are paying for it. Do not let yourself be deceived and fooled any longer by that false, jealous woman! Outwardly she feigns kindness and nobility of mind, but within she is full of malice and baseness, and she will not rest until she has harried you to death. If I were still alive I would not have let it come to this or permitted you to go and live with her. But, unfortunately, it is your unhappy destiny to have to suffer so much now. In your previous existence you indulged in sensual pleasures and destroyed other people's marriages. Now you have to do penance for it. Listen to my advice and take this sword and kill your enemy, that I may bring her before the judgment seat of the Fairy of Fearful Awakening! Otherwise you will suffer death yourself in vain and not a living being will regret you."

"Dear sister, my life is already ruined beyond all remedy; but as I have to do penance for former sins, I will submit to my fate and not add to my guilt," replied the second Yu, sorrowfully.

The third Yu sighed and disappeared. On the following day, when the second Yu was alone with Chia Lien she confided to him that she was pregnant, but that she felt ill and anxious about her own life and that of her child. Chia Lien sent for the doctor at once. He really wanted Doctor Wang, who was known to be good, but the latter was ill and could not come. In his stead, on the instructions of Phoenix, the servant fetched along the quack doctor, Hu, the one who had previously prescribed that "wolf and tiger cure" for Bright Cloud. The remedy which the quack doctor prescribed for poor Yu had the immediate effect of causing an abortion instead of curing her, and the stillborn child which she brought forth with great pain and loss of blood was a boy.

Chia Lien was beside himself. He sent for another doctor, and ordered his servants to seize the quack doctor Hu, and he wanted to take legal action against him. But Doctor Hu had got word in time and had already fled from the city. Chia Lien raged, and threatened to have the servant who had fetched the quack beaten to death. Phoenix, while secretly rejoicing, assumed the appearance of being if possible even more upset and indignant than her husband.

"Oh, what a misfortune!" she lamented. "Now, when we were so near to seeing our hopes of a legitimate heir fulfilled, this bungler of a doctor must come along and destroy our hopes! It seems to be our fate to remain without a son."

For the sake of effect she burnt incense and performed solemn prayers, imploring heaven and earth to strike her with illness, but to make the second Yu well again and to bless her body with new offspring. She vowed that until then she would fast and say daily prayers to Buddha. Of course everyone in the house was touched and ceaselessly praised her noble-mindedness and unselfishness. Phoenix went still further. With her own hands she made invalid soup for her rival and had a fortuneteller brought at her own expense to foretell the patient's fate. The fortuneteller, who had been appropriately worked upon beforehand by Phoenix, wanted to know if there was a woman born under the sign of the cock who might be bringing misfortune on the patient. Now, in the whole house there was only one person who was born under the sign of the cock, and that was the seventeen-year-old concubine, Chiu Tung.

Chiu Tung foamed at the mouth when Phoenix informed her of the soothsayer's verdict, at the same time advising her, in a friendly way, that if she valued her life and the peace of the house she should disappear for some time.

"Ah, what do I care about the foolish talk of a half-starved buffoon like that soothsayer!" she cried, indignantly. "I am just as much of a human being as Yu is. She was in contact with all kinds of people formerly; therefore, why should it be just I who should be said to bring her ill luck? And anyhow, why is there so much fuss about her child? Who knows where this everybody's darling got her bastard from? She may spin a yarn to our simple master, but she cannot hoodwink us! To have a child! What is wonderful about that, anyway? You wait just a bare year, and it comes of itself. Any woman can do that!"

Just as she was raging away like this, Princess Shieh happened to arrive to visit.

"I am to be scared away because a soothsayer asserts that I stand in the other one's way," she complained to her. "But I do not know where to go. Be so good as to stand by me, *Tai tai!*"

Princess Shieh then took her under her protection and reprimanded Chia Lien in her presence. How could he dare to cast aside, for the sake of a mere adventuress, the girl whom his own father had given him? To do so amounted to an affront to his father. And she angrily turned her back on him.

Chiu Tung now felt more on top than ever. Scarcely had the Princess left when she went out under the window of the neighboring pavilion and broke into loud abuse and execration of the second Yu, who was inside. The unhappy girl was completely crushed. That same night, while Chia Lien was enjoying himself with Chiu Tung, and Phoenix was asleep, she came to a sad decision after long brooding. Why should she continue this wretched, wrecked existence? She felt that she would never again be well and happy and that the beloved one was lost to her beyond recall. With the hope of a child shattered by the miscarriage, she had nothing more in the world to look forward to. Why, then, should she just drag on without a purpose? Death seemed to her to be the only decent way out of her misery. Merely to choose the kind of death was the one problem left. A violent kind of death such as hanging herself, or stabbing herself with a dagger, was repugnant to her. Then she remembered having often heard that one could kill oneself in a quick, painless way by swallowing crude gold; and her decision was made.

She rose with difficulty from her bed, opened her treasure trunk, and rummaged in it for a piece of loose gold suitable for her purpose. Just as the drum beat the fifth night watch outside, she gave herself a jerk and carried out her purpose. At first the deadly morsel would not go down her throat, but finally she swallowed it with a brave effort. Then she quickly put on a festive robe and her best jewelry, scrambled back onto her bed, and resignedly awaited her death.

It was already late in the morning, and only after being reprimanded by good Little Ping, that the lazy waiting maids felt obliged to look in at the sick mistress in the eastern wing, from whom not a call nor an order had come the whole morning. When they opened the door of the bedroom they found a dead woman before them. They ran out again terrified and shouted at Little Ping to come. Little Ping felt her heart torn with pity at the sight of the jewel-bedecked corpse, and paid respect to it with a loud lamentation. And the waiting maids and serving maids, who through fear of Phoenix had helped so zealously by their rudeness and disobedience to make poor Yu disgusted with life, now suddenly remembered that the deceased had always been a goodhearted, kind mistress who gave no one cause to complain, and overcome with remorse and pity they joined in Little Ping's lamentation, as long as Phoenix was not present.

Chia Lien was inconsolable, but Phoenix tried to outdo his grief, which was genuine, by her own hypocritical mourning. "Dear sister, why have you left me? Is that your gratitude for my love?" she lamented pathetically.

In accordance with Chia Lien's wish, the body remained laid out on a bier for a whole week in the Pear Garden, where he faithfully kept the death watch over it and had the customary funeral rites celebrated for the soul of the departed. But at the instigation of Phoenix, burial in the family temple, which he had desired, was refused him by the Ancestress. After a simple funeral, at which only the nearest relatives participated and from which Phoenix absented herself on the plea of not being well, the second Yu was laid to rest in a modest little grave outside the city walls, beside that of her sister.

CHAPTER 36

The bag with the springlike embroidery becomes a traitor in the hands of a simple girl. The girls in the Park of Delightful Vision fall into discredit and have to suffer the torture of a house search.

For months past Phoenix had been suffering from an obstinate female ailment which frequently confined her to her room and her sickbed. Without her constant supervision, discipline in the western palace had gradually become lax, and even in the Park of Delightful Vision irregularities had crept in, which were little in keeping with the strict order which should rule in this carefully sheltered domain of virtuous young ladies of the house. Recently Mandarin Duck, taking an evening walk through the park, had caught Greeting of Spring's chess maid on a secret rendezvous in the bushes with a young manservant, who had climbed in over the wall. It was an unheard-of happening, which would have meant a terrible flogging for both parties if it had become known. True, Mandarin Duck had very considerately kept silent about it, and of course the fellow had made off at once. Nevertheless, the culprit was to be detected later.

Late one evening, just as Pao Yu had gone to bed, the waiting maid Magpie, from the apartments of Aunt Chao, the secondary wife of Mr. Cheng, appeared in the Begonia Courtyard and, despite the late hour, asked to speak to Pao Yu. Her mistress had just been discussing something in a whisper with his father, and she had caught Pao Yu's name, so she wanted to give him advance warning for a talk with his father tomorrow. That was the only important thing she had to say. It was very little, to be sure, but it was enough to frighten Pao Yu very considerably.

He said to himself that it did not bode any good when the secondary wife, who was so ill-disposed towards him, made him the subject of a secret conversation with his father. Chia Cheng had recently returned from the provinces and at the time was enjoying a holiday which the Imperial government had granted him. Up to the present he had been spending this welcome leisure peacefully and meditatively at home, resting from the fatigues of service. Contrary to his usual habit, he had left Pao Yu alone this time and spared him the usual severe cross-examination about his studies and progress. Now Pao Yu was afraid that the secondary wife Chao might have suggested that a new examination of his offspring's work was overdue. Perhaps the dreaded examination might take place the very next day. And he felt completely unprepared! With one jump he leaped out of bed, dressed himself quickly, and took up the long-neglected classics. He was going to spend the whole night quickly preparing himself, in so far as he could, and brushing up his incomplete knowledge.

Of course the night's rest was also at an end for the waiting maids, who watched him poring over his books by the light of a candle and heard him groaning and moaning as he strenuously racked his brains.

"Such a beast! To surprise us in the middle of the night with her false alarms! A few good pricks of a needle would be the right thing for herself and her old mistress!" grumbled Bright Cloud angrily. Meantime the waiting maid Musk had poured out fresh tea and put a bowl of it in front of her worried master to refresh him. She was only lightly clothed in a short, thin petticoat.

"Will you not put on something warmer? The night is cool and you will catch cold," he said anxiously, looking up from his books.

"Oh, do not let us distract you from your work! You should only think of those now!" she warned him, smilingly pointing to his books.

At that moment two younger maids ran in frightened and shrieking. A man had got into the park over the wall, they reported breathlessly.

"It's terrible! Where has he run to? The park must be searched with lanterns for him!" they all said, chattering together excitedly. But the clever and compassionate Bright Cloud saw at once that here was a chance for her poor little master to escape the morning examination.

"This hard night work will not really help you very much," she whispered to Pao Yu. "Pretend you have become ill through fright, and just stay in bed in the morning! Then you will get over the trouble."

Pao Yu joyfully snatched at the suggestion, shut the detested books, and lay down quietly to sleep. But first of all he gave instructions for all the women and the male porters of the gate watch to search every corner of the park with lanterns for the intruder. The search was without result. Presumably the young girls had imagined things in their sleep and allowed themselves to be frightened by the wind rustling in the branches of the trees, the searchers said.

"Nonsense! The girls' report is probably quite correct; you have not searched well," Bright Cloud declared firmly to the servants of the gate watch. "The little master and we others have also heard the suspicious noise. Surely we cannot all have been deceived. The little master is ill from excitement; he has a fever and is sweating all over his body. I'm going to his mother to fetch pills to get down the fever. Would it be necessary for me to do that if the story was as harmless as you allege?"

Whereupon the gate watchers, mystified, renewed their search. Meantime Bright Cloud hurried over to the *Tai tai* Cheng and saw to it that the news of the nocturnal incident and of Pao Yu's illness was spread

394

everywhere throughout the palace. The frightened Madame Cheng brought the matter before the old *Tai tai* the next morning. The old *Tai tai* was beside herself and strongly criticized the carelessness of the staff in the park. "The worst of it is that our own people cannot be trusted. Perhaps they are hushing up the matter because the criminal is to be found in their own midst," she said.

While the older ladies present, Princess Shieh and Princess Chen, Madame Cheng, Phoenix, and the Widow Chu, maintained an embarrassed silence, Taste of Spring came forward and declared: "Since Cousin Phoenix has been ill and unable to attend to the park so much, the discipline among the servants has become more and more lax. Formerly the servants used to sneak away from their duties only for an occasional hour, for a little game of cards in private, three or four of them together. Recently the gambling has been going on quite openly and on a large scale, with a club committee and all the rest of it, and stakes of thirty to fifty thousand-piece strings of money. A short time ago there was actually a great fight."

"But that is an outrageous state of affairs! Why have you not reported it before?" asked the Ancestress indignantly.

"Mother always had so many other things to think about, and recently her health has been failing. I wanted to spare her annoyance; that is why I kept silent," said Taste of Spring.

"You take the matter far too lightly," said the Ancestress reproachfully. "If it stopped at a little game or a harmless dispute! But this gambling for money night after night leads in its turn to drinking and intemperance; wine and food are smuggled in by crooked means; then doors and gates are opened secretly; and the open doors and gates entice in thieves and vagabonds; and it goes on. You must bear in mind that among such a numerous staff there are bound to be many bad elements, and these, when encouraged by opportunity, give free scope to their wicked instincts and infect the others. And to think that such things are going on in the immediate neighborhood of you virtuous, well-protected young girls! The harm which you yourselves could come to in such corrupt surroundings is inconceivable!"

Taste of Spring returned silently to her place. But the energetic Phoenix forthwith summoned the four wives of the stewards who were directly responsible to her for the female staff, and reprimanded them severely in the presence of the Ancestress. The Ancestress then sent them into the park to find out the culprits who had been participating in the secret gambling and to bring them before her; and she offered a cash reward for each person informed upon and threatened punishment by flogging for any attempt at concealment.

The result of the investigation was that three chief gambling man-

ageresses, eight gambling submanageresses, and twenty other participants were indicted and brought before the Ancestress. The Ancestress
made them kneel down in the courtyard and subjected them to a thorough cross-examination. Dice, counters, and other gambling equipment were collected, stacked up in heaps, and burned. The gambling
funds were confiscated and divided among the other servants. The three
principal culprits received forty strokes twice over and were dismissed
from service. They were never to be allowed to enter the palace again.
The other persons implicated received twenty stripes and were punished besides by deduction of three months' wages, and reduced to the
lowest grade of service, that of lavatory attendants. Among the three
chief culprits was Greeting of Spring's nurse. Precious Clasp and Black
Jade and the other young girls appealed in vain for a pardon for the
nurse, to save their cousin's face; but the Ancestress remained unre-
lenting and, despite their intercession, chased her granddaughter's
nurse out of the house.

While the Ancestress, exhausted from the recent excitements, was
taking her midday rest, Princess Shieh set out on a tour of inspection
of the park. She was just about to enter the park gate when the maid
Numskull, chuckling gleefully to herself and swinging a green and red
embroidered bag in her hand, ran into her path.

The little fifteen-year-old had been in the household only a short time
and served the Ancestress doing rough work and running errands. The
Ancestress had taken a fancy to the hefty, uncouth creature, with the
broad face and the big strong feet, whose simplicity was a source of
constant amusement; it was she who had given her the name of Numskull. She treated the young girl with special indulgence, and even allowed her to play in the park now and then in her spare time. It was
on one of these frolics that she had just now picked up a brightly embroidered perfume bag, among some isolated rocks, off the roadway.
The embroidery was not of the usual patterns taken from the world of
flowers and birds, but showed on the front a couple in close embrace
and on the back a series of written characters. Our Numskull had no
inkling of the vernal significance of the picture. She innocently thought
that the two naked figures were either two demons fighting or a married couple brawling. Beaming with joy, she was about to take her find
to the Ancestress when she ran into Princess Shieh on the way.

"Oh, what beautiful thing has our Numskull picked up, that she's so
pleased about? Let me have a look," asked the Princess.

"Yes, it's something wonderfully beautiful! Here, look at it yourself,
Tai tai!" replied Numskull, as she held up the bag to the Princess. A
hurried glance sufficed to make the Princess recoil in horror.

"Where did you pick it up?" she inquired excitedly.

"I found it between the rocks when I was catching grasshoppers."

"It is something very wicked. You really deserve a sound thrashing for having touched it; but because you are our Numskull and don't know what it is all about, you shall be forgiven this time. In any case, keep your mouth shut and do not speak to anyone about what you have found. Do you understand?"

Numskull turned pale with fright, quickly made a kowtow of apology, and slipped away feeling thoroughly perplexed. The Princess hid the bag in the pocket of her sleeve and, shaking her head, set off for the pavilion of her stepdaughter, Greeting of Spring.

"That is a nice turn your nurse has played you! And to think that a big sensible girl like you could allow such a thing to happen and not open her mouth!" she said reproachfully to Greeting of Spring. "And that such a thing should happen to *my* daughter, of all people!"

Greeting of Spring sulkily bent her head for a moment and started lacing up her belt.

"I took her to task twice, but it was no use. What more could I do? After all, she as my nurse has more right to give me a talking to than I have to give her one," replied Greeting of Spring, ill-humoredly. She could not get over the hard sentence which her nurse had received.

"Nonsense! You are her mistress, and it was not only your right but also your duty to keep an eye on her, if she was not behaving properly. And if she did not obey you, you should have informed me. And what do these goings-on lead to? This person has probably been hiring out your jewelry and clothing to pay her gambling debts. But mind you: If you have been silly enough to grant her favors of this kind, you cannot count on any more pocket money from me. So, just look out where you are to get money from for the coming Mid-Autumn Festival!"

When Greeting of Spring remained defiantly silent, the Princess continued, appealing to her sense of honor: "Your own mother, the concubine Chou, is such a splendid woman! She is ten times better than the mother of your cousin Taste of Spring, the concubine Chao. You should make an effort to emulate your mother and also to be superior to your cousin. Unfortunately, you are not yet half as good as she is. Well, it is all the same to me. I have neither sons nor daughters of my own, and therefore I am fortunately not in danger of being shamed by my children. But . . ."

She was interrupted in her talk by a waiting maid who announced that the old *Tai tai* had finished her midday rest, whereupon the Princess hurriedly cut short her visit and took her leave in order to go back and keep the Ancestress company again.

"What about that jewelry of yours which was lost—the gold-braided phoenix clasp with the pearl insets?" asked the waiting maid Orange as soon as the Princess had left. "When I discovered the loss I at once suspected that your nurse might have taken the precious article and pawned it to pay her gambling debts. You thought at the time that the chess maid had put it away, but when I asked her she said she had last put it in the jewel case on the bookshelf, to have it ready for you for the fifteenth of the eighth month, the day of the Mid-Autumn Festival. But it has disappeared from the case. You ought to send for your nurse and ask her about it."

"Ah, what for!" replied Greeting of Spring indifferently. "Of course she has taken it. I myself gave her permission because she was in some difficulty at the time. I made her promise that she would return it soon and put it back in the box, but evidently she forgot all about it. Now that she has so many other troubles, I don't want to worry her with this matter."

"She remembers it well enough; she's just counting on your good nature and on your forgetfulness. Should we not inform Madame Phoenix and demand back your property through her? Or, if you do not want to make a fuss about it, perhaps we could induce your nurse to give it back for a few strings of money. What do you think?"

"Let it be! Why all this fuss? I do not miss the piece at all."

"How can one go to such lengths of good nature? You simply invite people to cheat you when you behave like that!" said Orange; and she thought, as she shook her head, that her mistress well deserved the nickname of "Blockhead" which she bore. The best thing is for me to try to get justice for her, she thought to herself, turning to go out the door.

Meantime a daughter-in-law of the dismissed nurse had arrived outside. She was the wife of the servant Yu Kwei, and had come to put in a good word with Greeting of Spring for her mother-in-law. While she was outside she had happened to hear the discussion between Greeting of Spring and Orange regarding the lost piece of jewelry. When she heard Orange's decision to go to Madame Phoenix and report the matter, she felt impelled to intervene, and she walked in with a smile. First of all she turned to Orange and asked her to refrain from going to Madame Phoenix, and thus avoid a new scandal. Naturally, it was a matter of honor for her family to redeem and return promptly the young lady's jewelry which her mother-in-law had borrowed and pawned on account of a temporary monetary embarrassment. Then she presented her further petition to Greeting of Spring, asking her to take up the cause of her old nurse and intercede for her with the Ancestress.

"It's completely useless! My cousins and I have already begged in vain for mercy for her," Greeting of Spring informed her curtly.

"Surely, Sister-in-law, you are not making the return of the jewelry

迎春

dependent upon my young lady's interceding for your mother-in-law? One matter has nothing to do with the other," said Orange sharply. "Kindly bring back the jewelry first, and then we will discuss matters further!"

"None of your impudence, Miss!" replied the other, annoyed at the double rebuff: "In other places people still have compassion for their old nurses. But here they are stingy, and if the account does not tally to the dot there is a hue and cry, and tales are told. Not even your own relative, Miss Wreath of Clouds, fared any better. All the time the poor young lady lived here she had to scrape a tael every month from her miserable bit of pocket money and hand it out to her mother. Was that noble or generous? No wonder that the poor young lady was always short of everything. And who was it who always helped her out? My mother-in-law. Up to thirty taels at the very least she paid out of her own pocket in this way up to today. And who repays her the loss, eh?"

Orange was going to reply angrily, but Greeting of Spring, touched to the quick by the all-too-well-merited reproach, stopped her from speaking.

"Enough of this quarrelling! I relinquish the jewelry," she decided. "If my mother asks about it, I will just say that I have lost it. And that settles the matter. And now go away! But you bring me tea!" she said, turning to Orange. Muttering and sulking, Orange went off to the kitchen, but Greeting of Spring lay down full length and casually took up a book.

It was a day full of exasperation for the worried Madame Phoenix. In the morning there was the bother about the happenings in the park, of which of course she had to bear the brunt. In the afternoon there was still another worry. The approaching Mid-Autumn Festival would have to be financed, but the funds were exhausted and the new rents had not yet come in. She had to send Mandarin Duck to a lumber-room in the dwelling of the Ancestress to get an ancient, dusty trunk full of old jewelry, and to pawn the contents, which brought in a thousand taels. And she heard from Chia Lien that the matter had got to the ears of her aunt through Numskull. How exasperating! So the Ancestress would also hear about it, and that would mean a reprimand.

While she was still discussing this latest mishap with Little Ping, her aunt, Madame Cheng, was suddenly announced. Without uttering a word, and showing every sign of the greatest agitation on her face, the *Tai tai* rushed into the room and sank down groaning on the divan. At a sign Little Ping and the other waiting maids had to leave the room. The *Tai tai* now pulled out of her sleeve pocket a brightly embroidered perfume bag, and with tears in her eyes silently held it up to Phoenix.

"Where on earth did you get such a thing?" asked Phoenix after she had noted with horror the indecent picture on the bag.

"Where did I get it?" replied the *Tai tai* in a tone of suppressed excitement. "It was lying about in broad daylight between the rocks in the park. Numskull found it and was already on her way to show it to the Ancestress. Luckily, Sister-in-law Shieh took it from her on the way; otherwise the Ancestress would have seen it, and then— Oh, I don't dare think of it! I am beside myself. I thought I could rely on you, and now you do this to me! How on earth could you be so thoughtless as to leave the thing lying about in the park?"

"But why do you assume that the thing belongs to me?" asked Phoenix, turning pale.

"Who else could it be but you? We others are middle-aged women, and long past such frivolities. Or could it possibly be one of the young girls in the park? No! There can be no question of that! No! It must have come originally from your husband. How like that incorrigibly frivolous fellow! You two are still young people, after all, and young people do find pleasure in silly trifles of the kind. Everyone knows that. You need not deny it. It is only lucky that it was not found by any of the park staff. That would have caused talk! Your cousins would have fallen into disrepute. And what if the innocent creatures themselves had caught sight of it? Oh, I dare not even think of that!"

Flushing and turning pale alternately, Phoenix had listened to the *Tai tai*. Now she threw herself at her feet.

"You are quite right, Aunt, but I assure you that I have never possessed such a bag, and I have no idea how it got into the park," she protested with tears. "Just look closely at this thing with its tassels. It is a cheap street-market article, a bad imitation of a palace pattern. I have never liked such tawdry stuff. But if I possessed anything of that kind I would have hidden it carefully and not have carried it around with me openly, or taken it into the park, where my cousins might possibly see it. How could you think me capable of such thoughtlessness? After all, I am not the only youngish woman in the palace. Over in the eastern palace there is Sister-in-law Chen, whom one can hardly regard yet as belonging to the older set, and there is her daughter-in-law Yung and her people, and there are various young women servants, and the park is just as open to all of them as it is to me. Or perhaps the owner is even one of the park staff herself. Among so many people it is impossible to keep a watch on the behavior of each individual. How can one know if this or that woman may be carrying on some secret love intrigue with some friend among the male staff? Why is it just I who am suspected?"

The *Tai tai* could not close her ears to the logic of Phoenix's words.

"Do get up!" she said, placated. "I know well that you are the best of all the young women of the family, and the one least capable of any impropriety. I have done you an injustice. But what shall we do now? I was almost frightened to death when your mother-in-law sent me this disgusting object just now."

"Do not worry. I know what to do. Above all, we must avoid any fuss, in order to spare the old *Tai tai* any new excitements. As it is, the dismissals of today have left some gaps among the older supervisory staff over there. Let us, for the time being, send some women supervisors over from this side—women whom we know thoroughly well and can rely upon, such as the wives of the stewards Chou Jui and Lai Wang, and have investigations made quietly, ostensibly in connection with the forbidden gambling. In this way, this and that offense will come to light and offer us an opportunity to weed out and dismiss any undesirable maids from among the older staff. We have far too many marriageable young women over there! Very well! Let them marry! A reduction in the staff is also very desirable for reasons of economy. What do you think?"

"You are quite right; I am in full agreement," replied the *Tai tai* with a sigh. "On the other hand, I would not like to be unfair to our young girls. After all, each of them has only got three useful waiting maids at her disposal. The remaining little devils hardly count, on the whole, though one would not like to deprive the girls of their service and their company completely. That would be neither in accordance with my ideas nor those of the old *Tai tai*. The best thing is for me to look into the matter myself as soon as I have time. Meanwhile the women supervisors whom you suggest can take up their posts over there and quietly make investigations."

Phoenix had the five reliable elderly ladies whom she had in mind brought in, and gave them the necessary instructions. The *Tai tai* Cheng added to these five the wife of the steward Wang Shan Pao, who had come in by chance to eavesdrop. She was one of Princess Shieh's serving women and enjoyed her special confidence, and it was she who had brought over the aforementioned perfume bag.

"Ask your mistress if she would send you for a time to the park as supervisor, as a special favor for me," Madame Cheng said to her. She was anxious to forestall any possible later reproaches regarding partiality. This sixth woman received the order with secret satisfaction. Here was a welcome opportunity to get her own back at last on the waiting maids in the park. She had never had a good word for that high-spirited, conceited lot, who showed her scant respect whenever she went into the park.

"There is no need to waste words on the subject; a strict investigation over in the park is long overdue," she growled. "You do not really go into the park much, *Tai tai,* so you could not know what goes on there. Those young things, the waiting maids, are as arrogant as if they themselves were real highborn 'Miss Thousand-Gold-Pieces' with Imperial titles of honor. The like of us dare not open our mouths or they at once put on airs of being offended and accuse us of persecuting them and intriguing against them. It's a nice state of affairs, indeed!"

"Well, they are no doubt our elite. No wonder that they think something of themselves," said Madame Cheng with a smile.

"That may be true of the others, but one of them, the maid Bright Cloud who serves our young master Pao Yu, is a really bad lot," continued the sixth vehemently. "She is certainly pretty, but does the conceited thing have to deck herself out on that account day after day, as if she was a Hsi Shih? And how brazenly and pertly she answers us back and rebels if one of us dares to make the slightest remark; you wouldn't believe it!"

Madame Cheng was astonished.

"Perhaps that is the one who struck me so unpleasantly by the loud, quarrelsome way she rebuked a maid in the Begonia Courtyard the last time we went for a walk in the park with the old *Tai tai?*" she said, turning to Phoenix. "I mean the one with the eel-like figure, and the narrow, sloping shoulders, and the undivided Hsi Shih eyebrows, which remind me of Black Jade's brows. I intended to rebuke her for her unseemly behavior, but I couldn't because I was tied to the old *Tai tai,* and later it slipped my mind."

"By your description it may have been she; but I cannot remember exactly," said Phoenix. "This Bright Cloud is no doubt pretty, but she is also an impudent, frivolous person."

"Just send for her, *Tai tai!* Then it can be seen if your surmise is correct," suggested the sixth. Madame Cheng followed her advice and ordered Bright Cloud to be sent for. Bright Cloud was not feeling well that day and had got up reluctantly from her bed when she was called. Now she appeared half dressed, flushed from sleep, and with dishevelled hair before the *Tai tai.* With a hasty glance of displeasure the *Tai tai* recognized her as the one she had recently encountered.

"So this is our lovely sick Hsi Shih," she remarked mockingly. "For whom do you put on all that vanity? You think, I suppose, that I do not see through you? Just wait, very soon I will have you skinned alive! How is my son Pao Yu?" she continued in an unfriendly tone.

Being quick-witted, Bright Cloud rapidly recovered from her first surprise and grasped the danger of her position, which demanded the utmost tact in her answers. She quickly fell on her knees.

"I really would not know, I so seldom come into the young gentleman's vicinity," she lied. "The *Tai tai* should inquire of his personal waiting maids, Pearl and Musk."

"You deserve a slap on your mouth! Simply pretending not to know anything! What are your duties?" asked the *Tai tai* sternly.

"I used to serve the old *Tai tai*, but because Master Pao Yu sometimes felt nervous and lonely in the big park I was later assigned to the Begonia Courtyard and I do night watch there in the outer chambers. Really I did not want to go, and I asked the old *Tai tai* to keep me with her, as I thought I was too unskillful to serve the young gentleman. But the old *Tai tai* scolded me and said that my work over there would not call for any special intelligence, and that I would have nothing to do with the personal affairs of the young gentleman. And so I gave in. I hardly ever meet the young gentleman, no more than once in a fortnight, when he calls me, and then I exchange a few words with him. His serving women and the waiting maids Pearl, Musk, and Autumn Wave do all the personal attendance. Besides, I frequently spend my hours of leisure with the old *Tai tai* doing needlework. So I scarcely ever have to look after the young gentleman. But if you wish, I can do so from now on."

"By Buddha, I am glad to hear that you have so little to do in his vicinity!" cried Madame Cheng, who took what the girl had said to be perfectly true. "I certainly don't intend to ask you to spend more time with your master in future. On the contrary, I shall ask the old *Tai tai* to take you away again. Until then, keep an eye on her! Do not allow her to be near him at night!" she said, turning to the six supervisors. And then to Bright Cloud: "Get out! What are you lingering here for? The sight of you gets on my nerves!" Bright Cloud slipped out quickly. The *Tai tai* angrily muttered something which sounded like "Witch" and "Seducer" as she went out, and ordered that a strict house-to-house search should take place in the park that same evening.

Early at night, after the Ancestress had retired, Phoenix set out on her tour of inspection with the overseers. All the park gates had to be locked after them when they had entered. The search started in the apartments of the night watch staff. There a slight excess over the prescribed stocks of lamps, candles, and oil was discovered.

"That counts as stolen property. It is not to be touched until I inform the *Tai tai* in the morning!" the wife of the steward Wang Shan Pao declared severely. Then they went on to the Begonia Courtyard.

"We are looking for a valuable object which has been lost. One of the waiting maids is suspected of being the thief," Phoenix explained to the astonished Pao Yu, as a reason for the late visit. While she sat down and took tea the supervisors proceeded with the search. All the staff, one after the other, had to open their boxes and trunks and turn out the contents. It came to a heated exchange of words between Wang and the indignant Bright Cloud, in which the former entrenched herself behind the order of her *Tai tai* and the latter used as her trump card her position of confidence with the old *Tai tai*. However, the search did not bring to light any forbidden, telltale things of masculine origin.

It was now the turn of the Bamboo Hermitage, the Jungle Courtyard having been passed over in consideration of the fact that its mistress did not belong to the inner circle of the family but only lived there as a guest. Black Jade had already gone to bed when the search commission arrived. She was about to dress hurriedly but Phoenix considerately stopped her, made her lie down again, and sat and chatted pleasantly with her while the delegation was at work. Here also the search was without result. There were only a few suspicious articles found among the maid Cuckoo's things, such as fans with writing on them, little bags, and belt buckles, but Phoenix at once confirmed these as being harmless birthday gifts from Pao Yu.

They went on to the pavilion of Taste of Spring, Pao Yu's half sister. She had already been informed of their coming and was awaiting the delegation in front of the door at the head of her waiting maids, a candle in her hand. She seemed really annoyed about the matter.

"If my waiting maids steal, then of course I am the head of the robber band. Will you not begin your search with me? My boxes and trunks are there open for you, you will certainly find the stolen articles in them," she replied irritably to the flowery apologies to which Phoenix treated her before beginning. She ordered the maids to spread out all her stock of clothing and linen and jewelry before the eyes of the high commission. Phoenix ordered the maids to clear them away again without looking at them.

"I am acting on higher authority; therefore you need not be angry with me," she said with an embarrassed smile, trying to pacify the angry girl.

"Oh, please, do not be deterred!" replied Taste of Spring, irritably. "What is fair to my maids is fair to me. Besides, I know up to the last needle what they have, and they certainly have nothing which is stolen, you may be sure of that! You would be more likely to find stolen goods with me. . . ."

She talked on in this way in the greatest agitation, even coming to tears. Phoenix, who knew Taste of Spring to be a difficult character, wanted to end the scene quickly and rose to go.

"Oh, do please search thoroughly! There may not be another opportunity immediately, and in any case I will not be here for it a second time," urged Taste of Spring.

"Oh, it's all right, I take your word that your waiting maids are not thieves," protested Phoenix with a smile.

"Have you searched thoroughly?" asked Taste of Spring, turning to the other members of the commission.

"Yes, thoroughly," replied the supervisors, smiling, as they followed Phoenix to the door. But one of them, namely, the wife of Wang Shan Pao, was not so easily satisfied. As confidential serving woman of Princess Shieh, and special delegate of the *Tai tai* Cheng, she felt conscious of her authority. Her pride would not allow her to be intimidated by this young girl, for whom in any case she had little respect. She went up to Taste of Spring, daringly seized the lapel of her gown, lifted it up, and inquisitively poked into every fold.

"Only a little personal search," she remarked, grinning maliciously.

"Come along, old woman! Stop this foolery!" Phoenix warned her angrily, and at the same moment she heard Taste of Spring give the old woman a resounding box on the ears.

"How dare you touch me!" cried Taste of Spring, enraged. "If the *Tai tai* wishes my person to be searched, very well, I will submit to it. But I will on no account permit myself to be touched by the like of you. You think, because you are old and have my aunt behind you, that you can bark at us and take all kinds of liberties. But this time your impudence has gone too far!"

While she fastened up the buttons of her gown with her left hand, she drew Phoenix back with her right.

"Will you search me, please? I have no objection, but spare me the ignominy of being searched by a slave!" she cried angrily.

Phoenix and Pearl together put her clothing right again.

"The old woman has drunk two mouthfuls too much wine; that explains her recklessness. She has just been with the *Tai tai*. Do not be angry with her!" said Phoenix, trying to pacify the excited girl. "And you get out of here!" she cried to old Wang.

"I will complain to the old *Tai tai* tomorrow," declared Taste of Spring, angrily.

"And I will complain to my mistress and to your mother," the scolding voice of the old woman, who had fled, called up from under the window. "Such a thing has never happened to me before in my life! To have my ears boxed in my old age! I demand satisfaction!"

"Do you hear her bawling? Apparently she has not yet had enough," said Taste of Spring scornfully, turning to her waiting maids. One of the waiting maids ran out in front of the window.

"Be reasonable and keep quiet at last!" she said to the old woman. "We won't mind if you go away, then we shall at last be rid of you, you old intriguer. But make haste! You are staying here too long for us!"

By their united efforts Phoenix and Pearl at last succeeded in calming the ruffled tempers on both sides, and the commission continued on its way. The next objective was the Rice Farm. In consideration of the fact that the Widow Chu was not well, they refrained from alarming her by waking her up, and confined themselves to a brief search of her servants' belongings, which yielded no result.

Then they went on to the near-by Little Castle of Warm Perfumes, the residence of Grief of Spring. Grief of Spring, the youngest of the cousins and still little more than a child, was naturally considerably frightened by the nocturnal search, which was quite incomprehensible to her, and Phoenix had all she could do to calm her. Who would have dreamed that the cause of all the trouble would be found in the house of this innocent, youngest girl, still half a child? Hidden in the painting maid's trunk they discovered a heavy parcel of thirty or forty silver bars, each weighing ten ounces. That was indeed a surprising discovery —that instead of the scandalous things they were looking for, stolen goods should be brought to light! But they did not have to wait long for the scandalous objects, too, for they rummaged out a jade belt tablet, and a whole pile of men's stockings and slippers. "Where did you get all this from?" Phoenix, her face quite yellow with shock, asked the painting maid.

"They are presents from Prince Chen to my brother," confessed the painting maid, falling on her knees in tears. "My brother gave me the things to keep for him, for my parents are on a journey to the southern provinces and my brother is living with Aunt and Uncle at present. And as Aunt and Uncle play cards and drink, my brother was afraid that they would take away his things and gamble them away or sell them for drink."

"That is outrageous! And I did not have the slightest suspicion of it! You must certainly punish her and take her away from here, Sister-in-law Phoenix. I do not like such a person to be near me," said Grief of Spring, indignantly.

"Did your brother bring the things here himself?" asked Phoenix severely.

"No, a serving woman brought them. I do not know her name."

"Well, that is a good thing," said Phoenix, relieved. "Now we must find out whether your information is correct. If you have told the truth then you may be forgiven. After all, it is not wrong of you to take care of other people's things. It is the woman who smuggled in the articles who deserves to be reprimanded. Certainly, if your brother had brought them here or if they were stolen goods, then it would go badly with you."

"Inquire of the serving woman and of Prince Chen! I have definitely told the truth," whimpered the painting maid. "Have me and my brother beaten to death if I have lied!"

"Now, calm yourself. Nothing will happen to you if the Prince confirms your information. But in future you must not take other people's belongings into your charge."

"Why are you so lenient, Sister-in-law Phoenix? I do not like her any more. At best she will corrupt the others," declared Grief of Spring.

"Let it be! After all, she is otherwise capable and useful. Everyone makes a little mistake sometime," said Phoenix with a placating smile. "If I only knew who it was who smuggled in the things."

"Probably old Chang at the back gate," said Grief of Spring. "She is always very friendly with our waiting maids, and the maids think an extraordinary lot of her."

"Take a note of her name! I shall question her later," said Phoenix, turning to her attendants and making ready to depart. The wife of the steward Chou Jui had to pack up the articles which had been found and take them with her.

It happened that the aforementioned Chang was a relative of old Wang but they had been on bad terms for some time past. Since old Wang had become the special confidante of Princess Shieh she had no time for her relatives, and when Chang reproached her with this one day they quarrelled fiercely and had not spoken to one another since. Now, hearing her enemy's name mentioned, it seemed to old Wang just the right moment to give full vent to the grudge she had been piling up since the abuse she had been given shortly before by Taste of Spring.

"Probably it was old Chang who smuggled the indecent perfume bag into the park," she whispered to Phoenix on the way. "You must certainly question her."

"No need for you to tell me that; I know it myself," replied Phoenix brusquely.

They had now arrived at Greeting of Spring's dwelling. Greeting of Spring was already asleep, her maids were going to bed, and it was quite a long while before the belated visitors' knocking was heard and they were admitted.

"The young lady need not be disturbed; let her sleep on," said Phoenix, and went straight into the waiting maids' room. When they had finished turning out and searching the belongings of all the other maids, they came at last to the chess maid's things.

Old Wang, elsewhere so thorough in her searching, was strikingly indulgent and superficial this time; for the chess maid was her own granddaughter. After she had looked hurriedly through her granddaughter's open trunk, she murmured "Nothing to be found" and was about to close the cover, when the steward's wife, Mrs. Chou Jui, stopped her.

408

司棋

"Now, now! I don't call that a thorough search! One must be just!" she said and began to root in the trunk herself. And lo and behold, she pulled out a pair of men's padded socks and of men's satin slippers. And that was not all. A *Jui* mascot dagger such as lovers present to each other was found, wrapped in a blue shawl; and a red greeting card, with writing on it. Chou handed the articles to Phoenix. Now, as manageress of the Yungkuo palace household, Phoenix came in touch every day with all sorts of accounts and written documents and so, in the course of time, she had acquired some knowledge of the written language. She was therefore able to decipher the writing on the card, and to her surprise she read the following: ". . . now our parents also know how we stand with each other, since your visit of last month, and they approve. Of course, as long as your young lady is still unmarried, we cannot think of getting married. If a meeting in the park is possible give me word again through Mother Chang. It is much easier to talk undisturbed in the park than at home. Today I duly received the prayer beads made of fragrantly perfumed wood which you sent me. I send you herewith a perfume bag, the decoration on which indicates my feelings for you. But put it away carefully! I wish you peace and bow my head,   "Your cousin Fan."

Phoenix was delighted with her discovery. Here in her hand she had the conclusive evidence which would clear and exonerate her completely in her aunt's eyes. She could not repress a self-satisfied smile.

"There must be blunders in the account to make the *Nai nai* laugh?" asked the illiterate old Wang, doubtfully and hesitantly.

"Oh, no, the 'account' is correct, only I had not added it up. But why does your granddaughter's cousin bear the name of Fan and not your family name of Wang?" asked Phoenix mischievously.

"You probably mean Fan Yo An, who ran away recently? Certainly he is my granddaughter's cousin; his mother is a Fan by marriage."

When she heard the contents of the supposed "account," which in reality was a love letter addressed to her granddaughter, and noticed the head-shaking around her, old Wang was so confounded and ashamed that she wished the ground could have swallowed her. She had been out to catch others sinning, and now she and her family were themselves exposed and disgraced.

"Now, what do you say to this piece of evidence, Mother Wang? It can't be quibbled or explained away," remarked her colleague Chou Jui, maliciously.

"They meant it well and wanted to spare their grandmother the trouble of negotiating. At night, when all the birds were silent, they met together," added Phoenix, derisively turning to Chou. She could not delight enough in old Wang's embarrassment. But the old woman who had been thus disgraced boxed her own ears and cried out in self-abasement that she must certainly have been an old whore in a previous existence, since she had to do such penance now. Meantime the guilty and convicted chess maid sat there silently with bowed head. Phoenix was disagreeably surprised to observe that her attitude betrayed neither fear nor shame. She looked on indifferently, sunk in her own thoughts, as if she had already finished with life and would like to kill herself. Phoenix therefore instructed two serving women to take charge of her and not let her out of their sight. And then, on account of the lateness of the hour, further searches were postponed.

CHAPTER 37

A sinister occurrence at the nocturnal banquet awakens dark forebodings. At the Mid-Autumn Festival a new stanza awakens happy promises for the future.

THE PURGE OF THE PARK STAFF WAS INTERRUPTED FOR SEVERAL DAYS because Phoenix was ill again, and also because of the Mid-Autumn Festival. As the period of mourning for the deceased Prince Hermit was not yet over, the festivities were on a smaller scale than usual this time. Prince Chen had never taken the mourning of his late father very seriously. As the Rites forbade him diversions outside the house during the months of mourning, he compensated himself by gathering round him every evening, under the pretext of practicing archery, a crowd of aristocratic young rakes with whom he indulged in disgusting orgies of eating and drinking; and the nights passed in dicing and card playing and other frivolous pastimes instead of in the practice of the noble art of archery.

On the fourteenth of the eighth month, the eve of the Mid-Autumn Festival, Prince Chen presided over a family banquet with all the wives and concubines in the Hall of the Green Thicket, which was situated in the Garden of Assembled Perfumes. To celebrate the day a boar and a ram had been roasted whole. After the meal the company turned to merry drinking and dice playing, at intervals sauntering out to enjoy the sight of the beautiful, clear, full moon. Then the concubine Wen Hua, who had a fine voice, treated the guests to a song, and the concubine Peh Fong accompanied her on a purple bamboo flute. The midnight hour, the third beat of the drum, had arrived. Everyone was in boisterous mood and the Prince was eight-tenths drunk, when suddenly a weird, long-drawn-out groaning was heard, from the direction of the

411

garden wall. Conversation ceased instantly. Everyone listened with hair standing on end to the sounds from outside.

"Who is there?" the Prince called out in a sharp voice. There was no answer.

"The sound must have come from behind the wall. Evidently one of the servants is loafing about there," whispered the Princess.

"Nonsense! The servants' quarters are much too far away. Who would have any business at that lonely place near the Hall of Glorification at such an hour?" said the Prince. He had not finished speaking when a short, howling gust of wind swept across from over the top of the wall. At the same time the side doors of the spirit porch in front of the Temple of Ancestors were distinctly heard to open and shut again with a bang. To the listening company this seemed more uncanny still. Moreover, the moon appeared to have become overcast and to shine less brightly than before. Everyone sat there for quite a while, paralyzed with fear, unable to stir. The Prince was the first to recover himself. Half his drunkenness and his desire to keep on drinking had disappeared. In silence he rose from the table and ended the party.

The following day, during the usual Mid-Moon ceremony in the Hall of Glorification he looked around carefully for any traces of the mysterious occurrences of the previous night. But he could not perceive the slightest change. On leaving the Hall of Glorification he personally made sure that the entrance was securely locked and bolted after him, but ordered his servants to keep the matter absolutely quiet.

In the evening he went with his wife to the home of the Ancestress to take part in a general family banquet. The seniors, Prince Shieh and Chia Cheng, had already arrived and were endeavoring to keep the Ancestress in a good humor with jokes. Beneath the platform of honor, at a respectful distance, the male juniors—Chia Lien, Pao Yu, Chia Huan, and Chia Lan—stood about, and were allowed to listen to the conversation of the elders.

"How has Pao Yu been progressing recently in archery?" the Ancestress asked Prince Chen, who had modestly sat down on the edge of a seat near the door.

"Splendidly," replied Prince Chen, politely jumping up. "He has not only improved his aim but is also becoming used to weapons of heavier caliber."

"That is good. But he should not overdo it and exert himself too much. And by the way, the moon cakes which you sent me taste wonderful; but the melons look better than they taste."

"The moon cakes were made by an expert confectioner whom I got recently for my kitchen. I, too, find that the melons do not taste so good this season as in past years; I do not know what is the reason."

"Probably it is because the summer was too wet," said Chia Cheng.

"Come, now! Let us go into the park! The beautiful, bright full moon is up long since," said the Ancestress; and leaning on Pao Yu's shoulder, she led the company to the park gate, hung all over with rams'-horn lanterns. On the moon terrace in front of the Hall of All Good Spirits a table had been set for an open-air banquet. The place was festively lighted up with candelabra, the air was scented with the fumes of incense, the ground was covered with carpets and cushions. First of all the whole company, led by the Ancestress, knelt down on the prayer carpet, washed their hands, bowed to the household deities, and burned incense sticks before their images. This done, the banquet could begin.

But the Ancestress thought it would be nicer to enjoy the view of the full moon from a more airy height, and she chose as a suitable place the Hall of Blossoms, which was the lookout pavilion situated on top of the near-by Emerald Cone. The pavilion was made ready in a great hurry. After resting for a short time, the Ancestress stood up to lead the ascent. Madame Cheng and the other ladies, afraid that she might miss her footing on the steep, stony, moss-covered pathway, appealed to her to allow herself to be carried up on a sedan chair; but the vigorous old lady, who had celebrated her eightieth birthday only a short time before, insisted on walking up. The pathways were well tended and in good order, and a little exercise and loosening up of her old bones and sinews could not harm her, she declared, laughing.

Led by Prince Shieh and Chia Cheng, the company moved off. Two serving women with rams'-horn lanterns lighted the way in front of the Ancestress, who walked along supported by Princess Chen and the waiting maids Mandarin Duck and Amber. At last they reached the summit without mishap, by a path of many windings.

There they sat down on round upholstered seats, which encircled two large round tables separated by a folding screen, which stood on the open terrace in front of the Hall of Blossoms. The round form had been chosen in honor of the round full moon. The Ancestress took her seat at one table with the male members of the family, while the ladies occupied the other table completely.

It worried the Ancestress to see a large vacant space at the lower part of the table. She therefore had the three Spring girls fetched from the ladies' table behind the folding screen, so that the space would be filled and the guests would form a complete round.

To raise the spirits of the company the Ancestress ordered a merry game with drinks as forfeits. A branch of cinnamon flowers was passed round the table from hand to hand, while a waiting maid beat a drum behind the folding screen. Once the drum stopped, the branch was to go no further, and whoever held it in his hand at that moment was sentenced to drink a goblet of wine and treat the company to an anecdote.

It happened that the first person in whose hand the branch remained was the stern Chia Cheng. A surreptitious ripple of giggles, accompanied by much secret tugging of sleeves and nudging of sides, ran around the table. What humor could be expected from this solemn-faced person? But today, for the sake of the Ancestress, Chia Cheng had no wish to be a spoilsport, and he declared himself ready to treat the company to the only anecdote he had in stock.

"But if it does not make us laugh there will be an additional fine," said the Ancestress.

"Agreed."

And Chia Cheng began: "There once lived a man who had a most terrible respect for his wife. . . ."

He had only got as far as this when the whole company burst out in loud laughter, forcing him to a brief rhetorical pause.

"Well?" he said, turning triumphantly to the Ancestress.

"I admit that the story must be splendid since everyone laughs in advance," said the Ancestress, herself shaking with laughter.

"Then it should be your own turn next to drink a glass by way of forfeit," joked Chia Cheng.

"Agreed."

And she tossed off the drink forfeit which Prince Shieh and Chia Cheng, ceremoniously standing side by side, presented to her after tasting it themselves. As soon as she had drunk it and the two seniors had resumed their seats, Mr. Cheng continued: "Moreover, the said man never dared to stay away from home for long, but once, on the day of the Mid-Autumn Festival, as he was shopping in the town, he chanced to meet a few old friends who induced him to join them in a merry carousal in the house of a mutual friend. In the end he became so tipsy that he quite forgot about going home, and spent the night with his friend. The next day, when he was sober again, he appeared before his wife repentant and conscience-stricken. His wife was just washing her feet. Having listened to his confession, she said: 'Just this once I will let you off the thrashing you deserve, but you are to lick my feet as a punishment!' This he did but immediately started to vomit. Now she became really angry and was about to thrash him. So he knelt down beside her and cried: 'Do not be angry with me, wife. It really was not your dirty feet but my sour stomach that made me vomit!' "

His story was greeted with general laughter, and the Ancestress consented to take another voluntary forfeit drink.

"Take this as a warning, you married men, and drink only warmed wine! It is more beneficial than cold wine," she said, amidst a renewed outburst of laughter. And she ordered punch to be served instead of the cold wine.

On its next round the wandering branch of cinnamon flowers remained in Pao Yu's hand. Because of his father's presence Pao Yu became terribly embarrassed. He knew plenty of jokes and anecdotes, but what would his father say? A bad joke would make his father mock him, but a good joke would make him angry and evoke the reproach that he had ability for jokes and mischief, but none for anything serious. It would therefore be better not to tell any funny story at all. So he stood up and declared: "I do not know any jokes or anecdotes. I therefore beg you to give me another task."

"Very well, then, compose a poem on the subject of autumn!" ordered Mr. Cheng. "If the poem is good you will get a reward. If it is bad, woe betide you! In that case you will have an examination tomorrow."

"But we only want to pass the time amusing ourselves. Do not torment him with such difficult tasks!" protested the Ancestress.

"Let it be! He will do it all right," replied Chia Cheng with a smile. So the Ancestress ordered paper, brush, and ink to be brought.

"And do not make use of threadbare phrases such as 'liquid crystal' and 'frozen jasper' and 'silver splendor,' and suchlike!" said Mr. Cheng severely and emphatically. "I beg you to be original! I wish to test your *own* ability."

Now, Pao Yu did not need to ponder long before he had composed his quatrain and put it on paper. Mr. Cheng read it and merely nodded in silence, which was interpreted by the Ancestress as a good sign. She eagerly asked his opinion.

"He has made an effort. But if only he would study history more diligently! Poetry writing alone does not get one anywhere," was the paternal verdict.

"Then it is all right!" cried the Ancestress, relieved. "But now you must give him a present to reward and encourage him!"

"Yes, I will do so."

Mr. Cheng turned round and ordered a serving woman to run and get his servants to give her two of the fans which he had brought back with him from his official tour in Hainan. Before the assembled family he presented them to his son as a mark of approval of his achievement. Pao Yu thanked him, striking his forehead on the ground, and returned to his place in better spirits.

A stanza improvised by Chia Lan, the offspring of Mr. Cheng's firstborn son Chu, who had died young, evoked even greater applause. The Ancestress and Mr. Cheng observed with satisfaction that the ancient

415

inherited fragrance of traditional culture, inherent in the house of Chia, was living on most auspiciously in the younger generation.

Prince Shieh, in whose hand the branch of cinnamon flowers now remained, contributed the following anecdote: "There once was a man who had a very good son. One day the mother fell ill. As no doctor could be found, an old woman quack healer was fetched. The old woman only knew how to give treatment with the puncturing needle, and she also knew a little about cauterization, but she had no idea of the higher arts of medicine. She diagnosed the illness as 'fire in the heart' and suggested treatment with the puncturing needle. 'But then, my mother will have to die all the same if her heart is pricked with a sharp needle,' the son objected in alarm. 'Do not worry, it will only be a matter of a little prick between the ribs,' the old woman assured him. 'Yes, but then the heart will not benefit from it. Heaven knows how far away from the ribs the heart is situated,' the son objected once more. 'That is all right. A true mother's heart is so big that it reaches right down to the ribs,' the quack doctor said, finally reassuring him."

Once more there was merry laughter. After the bastard Chia Huan had given a test of his ability, which in Mr. Cheng's opinion was a failure, the Ancestress ordered that the game should stop. The gentlemen might now take their leave and enjoy themselves with their personal friends at the other side. It was already the hour of the second night watch, and she wished to be alone with the young girls for a while, she said.

As soon as the gentlemen had gone the Ancestress had the folding screen removed and the two tables pushed together. The ladies then "changed their dresses," washed their hands, rinsed out their mouths with tea, and continued the feast by themselves. The Ancestress cast her eyes about her and remarked sadly that this year there were many gaps in the circle around the table. Phoenix and the Widow Chu were absent, owing to illness; Precious Clasp and Precious Harp had had to stay with Aunt Hsueh, who was also ill. She missed particularly the gaiety which Phoenix always contributed to these family gatherings.

"Last year it was more cheerful; true, the men were absent, but we women were all here and Phoenix provided enough entertainment for ten. This time the men were here, but we women are not in full number. It just shows how difficult it is to have everything one wants at the same time in this world," she sighed.

In order to raise the spirits of the company she had the little wine glasses replaced by big goblets, with the result that in a short time all present became drowsy from wine, with the exception of the Ancestress. For none of the ladies present could hold her own with the Ancestress in the matter of drink. Then she had carpets laid on the terrace steps in front of the Hall of Blossoms and ordered the serving women and maid-servants to sit comfortably on the steps and have a good time and enjoy the fruits and dainties which had been distributed to them, for the staff were also to have some part in the banquet. The moon was now fully risen and was shining if possible more magnificently than before.

"Flute music is just what we want in this glorious moonlight," proposed the Ancestress. The others wanted to send for a company of young girls with all the instruments necessary to make up a complete band.

"That would be too much of a good thing," objected the Ancestress. "Too much noise distracts the mind. I should like to hear only one single, simple flute playing very gently in the distance."

While the company was waiting for the flute-player whom they were expecting, one of Princess Shieh's serving women came and whispered something in her mistress's ear. The Prince had stumbled on a stone just now and sprained his foot, the Ancestress was told in reply to her inquiry. Thereupon the Ancestress gave the Princess permission to leave the company.

"Niece Chen may go with you at the same time; it is time for her to go home," the Ancestress added.

"Oh, no, I should like to keep our old Ancestress company all night," said Princess Chen.

"You are a nice wife indeed! Young married people should be in bed on this night! Do not neglect your wifely duty!" said the Ancestress with a smile.

"Oh, do not flatter me! I am already in the forties and have been married to my husband for over twenty years," said the Princess, blushing coyly. "Besides, we are still in the mourning period."

"You are quite right. I did not think of that. Yes, of course, it is only two years since your father-in-law died. How can one be so forgetful! That will cost me a good, big forfeit drink! But do stay and keep me company! Grandniece Yung may accompany my daughter-in-law."

Princess Shieh and young Mistress Chia Yung thereupon took their leave. The ladies who remained went on drinking and chatting, and at intervals strolled about a little in the moonlight and sniffed the flowering branches of the little cinnamon trees which had been planted around the Hall of the Blossoms, at the same time listening to the clear, gentle tones of a single flute which drifted through the quiet night from the other side of the cinnamon hedge. There was something so gentle, so liberating, and so refreshing about the music that they all fell into silent rapture and listened spellbound.

"Now, was it not beautiful?" asked the Ancestress, beaming pleasure, when the flute-playing ceased.

"Really, it was much more beautiful than we could have imagined," they all replied with enthusiasm.

"The old Ancestress has certainly shown us how to enjoy art properly."

"Oh, that was nothing very special. Our songbooks have many more beautiful airs. Above all, the notes should come over more gentle and more sustained."

The Ancestress had a full goblet of wine taken over to the flute-player, together with some requests regarding the program. Mandarin Duck appeared with a warm hood and a waterproof cloak, which she carefully wrapped around the Ancestress.

"It is late night. Soon the dew will be falling and the air will be getting cooler. The old *Tai tai* should go to bed in good time," the waiting maid warned her.

"Do not nag me!" growled the old lady. "I am in such good form today! You do not think, do you, that I can be bowled over by a little carousal at night? I will last out until morning."

She had her glass filled again and the feast continued. Now the single, thin strains of gentle flute music again penetrated through the darkness of the cinnamon hedge. This time the melody was so plaintive and so full of feeling that it touched the heart of the Ancestress and made her quite emotional.

"Now I should like to tell you an amusing story," suggested Princess Chen, to cheer her up, as soon as the flute-playing ceased.

"So much the better. Go right ahead!" urged the Ancestress, putting on a more cheerful face.

"There once was a man who had four sons," began the Princess. "The first had only one eye, the second only one ear, the third only one nostril; the fourth had all these parts complete, but he was dumb. . . ."

She stopped because she noticed that the Ancestress had apparently dozed off.

"We should take her to bed," she whispered to Madame Cheng.

"No, no, go on with the story!" said the Ancestress brightly, opening her eyes. "I only shut my eyes in order the better to concentrate on the story."

"Tomorrow is another day, and the moon will be shining again then; it is time to go to bed," they advised her gently.

"How late is it, then?"

"We are in the fourth night watch. It is already morning. The young girls were so tired they could not last it out, and have slipped off."

The Ancestress looked around the table. The young girls' places were indeed empty. Only Taste of Spring was still present.

"A flabby lot, they cannot stand anything!" she murmured. "Our

418

佩鳳

Taste of Spring deserves praise; she is a brave girl! But you are quite right; it is time to go to bed."

She took another drink of clear tea, and then she got into a sedan chair made of bamboo basketwork, borne by two strong maids.

But not all the young girls were by any means so soft as the Ancestress had believed them to be. Instead of remaining to enjoy the moonlit scene from the hilltop, Black Jade and Little Cloud had gone down below and were enjoying it by the Crystal Crevice—the belvedere built into the rocky wall at the foot of the Emerald Cone, by the brink of the fishpond. For here they had the additional delight of watching the silvery reflection of the moon playing on the rippling waters. On the way down the hill they had had a lively literary argument as to whether the two ideographs which had been applied by the experts to the hill and the lake belvedere when the park had been created—namely, the two characters *tu*, signifying "cone," and *wa*, signifying "crevice"—were admissible from the literary point of view or whether they were inappropriate and should be rejected.

Then they had sat down on two plaited bamboo stools on the open belvedere terrace, and, inspired by the sight of the two moons—the one in the sky and the other on the water—they had composed between them a long and wonderfully beautiful five-word stanza on the theme of this moonlit night. They intended next day to surprise and put to shame the other members of the Begonia Club with this nocturnal opus and so to spur the club on to renewed efforts, for unfortunately it had been very inactive for a long time now.

The two were joined later by the beautiful anchoress Miao Yu, who, like the rest, was unable to sleep that beautiful night of full moon, and had gone for a stroll through the park. She had helped the girls with their poetical composition and then taken them to her Kingfisher's Cage hermitage and regaled them with a bowl of her famous wonder tea. The first crows of the cock were already resounding from the Rice Farm when the two night revellers at last lay down to sleep on the same bed in the Bamboo Hermitage.

When the Mid-Autumn Festival was over and Phoenix had more or less recovered, thanks to the lavish use of the best ginseng root, the interrupted purge in the Park of Delightful Vision was resumed once more.

Madame Cheng, having received a report on the recent house-to-house search, took immediate action. Grief of Spring's painting maid was taken away from the park and transferred to the eastern palace at her mistress's request, and now Greeting of Spring's chess maid was chased out of the house. She was forbidden to take leave of her colleagues and the other inmates of the park with whom she had passed many happy years. When Pao Yu, whom she had met by chance as she was being chased away, and whom she had implored with tears to intercede for her, tried to get a reprieve, he was given a nasty reception from the grim supervisors of order. "Off to your books! This is none of your business!" they rebuked him, and ruthlessly pushed him aside. He could not refrain from shouting a few biting words after the troop of departing matrons. "It is a strange thing," he cried, "that as soon as you women marry you lose all your womanliness and adopt the bad ways of men. Indeed, you are even worse than men!"

"It seems that young girls are higher beings in your opinion and that men are a bad lot?" they scoffed back at him.

"Of course," said Pao Yu, nodding eagerly.

"Ha-ha! Better be off and prepare for a visit from your mother, for your Bright Cloud's turn is coming right away! Today at last we are making a clean sweep, and these witches will be chased away! Thanks be to Buddha! Ha-ha!"

Immediately after this Madame Cheng herself arrived at the Begonia Courtyard and turned Bright Cloud, whom she detested, out of the house. Though ill, Bright Cloud had to pack up a few belongings and leave the place with her relatives, who had been sent for to take her away. Pretty Little Fourth suffered the same fate for having been so imprudent as to boast that her birthday fell on the same day as that of her young master. Three members of the troupe of dancing girls from Suchow, who had stayed on in the park at their request when the troupe was dispersed last year, also met the same fate. The *Tai tai* would on no account allow such dangerous "vixens" and "professional seductresses" to remain any longer in the proximity of her son. The great purge terminated with a strict search of Pao Yu's own boxes and trunks, in the course of which every object which was considered in any way alluring or offensive, and all souvenirs coming from any suspicious source, were ruthlessly confiscated.

It may be mentioned that the chief supervisor of order, old Wang, who was the grandmother of the dismissed chess maid, had herself to put up with a few boxes on the ear from her mistress, Princess Shieh, and had remained invisible afterwards for many days on the plea of being ill.

CHAPTER 38

The charming maid cannot get over the wrong done her, and dies in the flower of her youth. The unhappy scion of princes dedicates a funeral hymn to the dead maid.

Pao Yu HAD BEEN PREPARED FOR THE ORDEAL OF A HOUSE SEARCH, BUT that Bright Cloud, the dearest and most lovable of his waiting maids, should be taken from him—this had hit him like a thunderbolt. After his mother had gone away in bad humor, he threw himself on his bed and gave himself up to his bewildered grief.

"Just be patient for a few days until the *Tai tai's* anger has cooled down, then go to the old *Tai tai* and beg her to take Bright Cloud back into the house, and then everything will be all right again," said Pearl, trying to comfort him.

"If I only knew what her great crime was," cried Pao Yu, passionately.

"She's too pretty; that's her only crime," replied Pearl, shrugging her shoulders. "The *Tai tai* considers so much charm a danger to the peace of the house. Only ugly, stupid creatures like me are pleasing in her eyes."

"That is quite ridiculous. There are lots of examples to the contrary in history. But there's something else bothering me. How did my mother know word for word certain intimate little things and jesting words that I had exchanged with Bright Cloud? Do you think there has been some spying going on here?"

"No need for that, since you yourself are usually heedless in what you say when you are among people and get warmed up. I have warned you again and again with words and looks; but it's no use."

"After all, I have often exchanged familiarities with you, and Musk, and Autumn Wave too; why was it Bright Cloud who was pounced upon?"

Pearl made no reply.

"I'm so terribly sorry for her!" continued Pao Yu, sobbing. "She has been used to such tender treatment here—and now this graceful, delicate orchid, barely opened into bloom, is roughly thrown into the hogs' furnace. And to make matters worse, she is sick and an orphan. The only relative she has to fall back upon is an elderly married cousin, an evil drunken creature. She won't survive a month in the house of that greasy reptile. I thought to myself that it was an evil omen when I saw this spring how the blooms of our golden begonia had suddenly died in some quite inexplicable way all over one half of the tree. Now it is clear to me that this bad omen referred to our poor Bright Cloud."

Pearl clapped her hands together in astonishment.

422

"How on earth can an enlightened, educated person like you pay heed to such old wives' superstitions as that?" she cried, much amused.

"People like you certainly cannot understand it," he said reprovingly. "It is not only mankind that has a soul; all nature is animate too, and at times nature proclaims her unity with man by strange and wondrous manifestations. To name a few examples, there is the juniper tree in front of the Temple of Confucius in Ku fu; there are the cypresses in front of the tomb of Chu Ko Liang, the wise counsellor of the time of the Three Kingdoms; the pines by the grave of Yo Fei, the great Marshal of the Sung dynasty. These age-old, indestructible, sacred trees have died down temporarily again and again in the course of the centuries in times of political corruption, only to burst forth in fresh verdure in times of prosperity and order. And it is probably exactly the same with our begonia."

Half unbelieving, half afraid, Pearl replied: "Those were great men, great figures in history, and your theory may very well apply to them. But what is Bright Cloud? A little, unimportant creature. The omen which you believe our golden begonia has shown might just as well, in fact with greater right, apply to me. Perhaps it really points to *my* early death?"

Horrified, Pao Yu put his hand over her mouth.

"Oh, be quiet. Don't mention a thing like that to me now! Let's drop the subject. There is something else that I want to talk to you about. I am very anxious to send our poor Bright Cloud secretly the things she had to leave behind here. I also want to send her some of the money we have put aside, so that she will be able to pay for a doctor and for some care. Will you undertake the sisterly service of love?"

"You must have a very poor opinion of me if you think that I had to be asked by you to do that. I had already thought of it myself and have put all her things away ready in a safe place. But I wanted to wait until evening. Now in the daytime there are too many prying eyes in the way. I will send old Sung; and she shall also take with her the thousand-piece rope of money that I have saved. For me, a little sacrifice like that is a matter of course, for I have always been a kind, unselfish soul, or haven't I?" remarked Pearl a trifle bitterly.

"Of course you are a kind soul," said Pao Yu, smiling, and gently stroking her cheeks. And he tried to drive the coldness from her heart with a few warm words.

So in the evening the serving woman Sung was sent off with the belongings and the money.

Before that Pao Yu himself set out to pay Bright Cloud a secret visit. None of his servants was allowed to accompany him, and no one was permitted to leave the Begonia Courtyard that evening. Having reached the back gate of the park, he prevailed upon the portress on guard there to show him the way to Bright Cloud's home, after much ado. The portress, who was afraid of losing her job and at first did not want to help him, gave in in the end when he promised her money.

When her parents had died Bright Cloud had been bought as a small child by the house steward, Lai Ta. Lai Ta's wife had later given her as a present to the Princess Ancestress, who had taken a fancy to the pretty little ten-year-old. Her cousin, Little Kwei, had been married off by Lai Ta to a sly little coquette, who deceived her blockhead husband in every conceivable way. The servants of her master Lai Ta were always after her like flies after a stink. From the time Bright Cloud had been serving Pao Yu this girl had been always pestering her to put in a word for her with Phoenix; she wanted a post as serving woman in the Yungkuo palace. At last she and her husband were allowed to live near the back gate of the park and were employed by Phoenix personally for all sorts of profitable errands and orders. They did not make much of a fuss over poor sick Bright Cloud. She was put out of the way in a back room and left to herself for the greater part of the day.

Having reached his destination, Pao Yu left the old woman at the house door to watch out, and went alone into Bright Cloud's room. He found her lying half asleep on a wretched bed of rush matting. Luckily, she had at least got a few cushions and a blanket from her former possessions to cover her. Pao Yu plucked her sleeve and called her softly by name. Half frightened, half pleased, she blinked at him with eyes that had grown dull.

"Oh, it's you! I thought I would never see you again," she gasped, convulsively drawing his hand up to her. When she had got over a fit of coughing, she continued: "By Buddha! You have come just at the right time. For hours I have been gasping for a drink of tea, but there was no one near. Do please pour me out half a bowl!"

"Where's the teakettle?" he asked, wiping his eyes.

"It's there on the edge of the stove."

Pao Yu looked around. So this filthy, rusty pot with the coal-black spout was the teapot? He picked up a dirty bowl, the only one he could find on the table. It had a nasty smell of rancid mutton fat. Shaking his head and with tears in his eyes, he washed it and then dried it with one of his silk handkerchiefs. Then he filled it half full from the black iron pot. So this cloudy, dark red brew was supposed to be tea? He tasted the bitter muck, and was overcome with nausea. It cut him to the heart to see how the sick girl greedily gulped down the contents of the bowl in one swallow, as if it were the sweetest dew from heaven.

"Have you anything else to say to me?" he urged. "If you have, make the best of this moment that we're alone."

"What else would I have to say to you?" she sighed. "I'm just dragging myself on from day to day. As things are going with me, I shall be over it all in three to five days. The only thing that is weighing on me is the thought that I am dying under a shadow. I may indeed have been prettier than the others, but to say that I was a seductress, a dangerous vixen—no, I didn't deserve that. I will not quarrel with the past, but perhaps it would have been better if I had never . . ."

Her breath failed her and she could speak no longer. Pao Yu perceived with a shock how cold her hands were. He felt as if his heart had been pierced with a thousand arrows. He anxiously rubbed her hands and patted her body lightly. How emaciated she had grown! It shook him to see how four silver bracelets rattled loosely around her skinny wrists.

"Take them off and wear them again when you're well once more and have filled out a bit!" he begged her in an agitated voice.

Bright Cloud suddenly raised her clenched left hand to her lips and with a great effort bit off two of her fingernails. She laid them in Pao Yu's hand. He hid them in his belt pocket. Now she slid her right hand under the blanket, drew off the short red silk petticoat which she still wore from better days, and handed it to Pao Yu as a further souvenir. Then, exhausted by the twofold exertion, she sank back, groaning. Guessing her thoughts, Pao Yu hurriedly removed his own shirt, spread it over her naked body, and put her garment on himself instead of it. In great haste, and without waiting to do up all the buttons, he dressed himself again.

"Lift me up so that I can sit!" she asked him in a dull voice, while he was still dressing.

Alas, Pao Yu had little trouble in lifting up her light, emaciated body. Now, sitting up, she pulled his shirt from under the bedclothes and put it on with great difficulty, with Pao Yu's assistance. Then he let her sink back gently on her pillows again.

"Now go!" she said. "It is horrible for you here in this filthy room. I am glad that you have come once more. Now I shall die happy."

She was about to say something more when the cloth curtain of the door was pushed aside, and Little Kwei's wife walked in with a lewd smile on her face.

"Ha-ha! This is a nice conversation you've been carrying on here! I've seen and heard everything!" she said. "Now, what brings the highborn young gentleman into my humble dwelling? No doubt he wants to have a look at me and to try out his arts on my youthful charms, eh?"

"Hush! Not so loud, good elder sister!" he pleaded, much embarrassed. "No one must know that I'm here. I just wanted to see Bright Cloud. She served me faithfully for a long time."

Smiling, she took him by the hand and drew him with her into her bedroom.

"You are surely a lady's man, all the world knows that! Very well, then, if you want me to keep my mouth shut you must show me a little favor."

And with this she sat down on the edge of the bed and drew him close against her, crushing him between her thighs. Nothing like this had ever happened to him before. He flushed a hot crimson.

"Don't do that!" he gasped in confusion.

"Pah! Don't pretend!" she said, with an ugly look. "You're crazy for women and girls, aren't you? So why so shy now?"

"Leave me alone! What if the old woman who brought me over here should see me? We can't do it now. We'll arrange for some other time."

"Oh, there's no fear we'll be seen. I have sent the old woman away already. She's waiting for you in front of the park gate. Now let me repeat: Either you do what I want or I'll raise a row and betray you, and then your *Tai tai* will hear what a crazy fellow you are. I was listening just now under the window of the room and I saw the familiar and intimate goings-on you had with Bright Cloud. I'm no fool!"

She began to open the waistband of his trousers and to lift up her own dress. Pao Yu resisted with all his strength and struggled to free himself from her embrace. In the middle of the fierce struggle, a voice was heard outside saying: "Does Sister Bright Cloud live here?"

Little Kwei's wife started up in alarm and let her prisoner free.

"She's here!" she cried, running up to the window. Out in the yard stood the servant Liu with her little daughter. She had been sent by the serving woman Sung to bring Bright Cloud the belongings she had left behind and Pearl's rope of a thousand coins. While she was stating her errand and being shown into Bright Cloud's room by the woman, through the window of the next room she caught a glimpse of a male form. As she was well aware of the character of Kwei's wife, she assumed she had one of her lovers in there, and thought no more of the matter. But her keen-eyed little girl had already recognized the shadowy form as Pao Yu.

"Wasn't Miss Pearl looking for the little master just now? He's in there," she whispered to her mother, as they went away. The woman Liu stopped and looked inquiringly at the wife of Little Kwei.

"Of course he's not. What would the little master want with me?" she lied. She was burning to resume and carry to victory the interrupted contest with Pao Yu, but Pao Yu frustrated her intention. Two things drove him out of his hiding place: the fear, on the one hand, that he would get back late and find the park gates closed, and, on the other, the dread of a renewed attack by the lusting woman.

"Hi, Godmother Liu, wait a minute and I will be with you!" he cried, suddenly emerging from under the door curtain, after Liu had already turned to go.

"Oh, so there's our little master! What brings you here?" asked the Liu woman, utterly astonished.

Pao Yu wasted no time in long explanations, but slipped past her out the door. Mother Liu and her daughter raced along after him, while Little Kwei's wife was left standing at the door with a long face, bewailing her beautiful, vanished dream.

Out of breath and with fast-beating heart, Pao Yu arrived back at the park in the nick of time before the gates were shut and reached the Begonia Courtyard without being seen by the evening patrols of park watchwomen. He had come from Aunt Hsueh, he told Pearl, and went straight to bed.

"Are you going to bed so early?" asked Pearl.

"That's my own business," he retorted brusquely.

Mindful of her dignity and of her responsibility to the Ancestress and to Madame Cheng, Pearl had become somewhat more reserved in her demeanor towards Pao Yu for the past few years, and she had also become somewhat estranged from him. The place in his heart which she had occupied previously she had lost in the course of time to her junior, Bright Cloud. Bright Cloud it was, too, who had the privilege of sleeping in his bedroom, for Pao Yu was afraid of being alone at night and had to have someone near him with whom he could exchange a few words now and then when he could not sleep. Since Bright Cloud had gone Pearl had resumed this nocturnal position of trust once more.

That night she heard him tossing about restlessly in his bed for a long time, and heaving sighs, short and long, before he fell asleep. Then, towards midnight, when she herself was just nodding off, she heard him calling loudly for Bright Cloud.

"What's wrong?" she asked.

He asked for tea.

"Ah, it's you, Pearl," he said, embarrassed, with an apologetic smile, when she brought him the tea. "I called for the other girl through absent-mindedness and habit."

"When she was new here you used to go on calling for me in your sleep; that's how times change," remarked Pearl with an air of resignation.

He went to sleep again only after two hours of tossing and turning. It was getting towards five in the morning when Bright Cloud appeared to him in a dream.

"I've come to bid you good-by," she said. "Farewell!" and disappeared once more. He leaped out of bed terrified and woke Pearl.

"Bright Cloud has just died," he told her dully. Pearl did not believe him and tried to talk him out of his "hallucination," but he held firmly to his belief and could hardly wait for the morning to send for news of Bright Cloud. And he had to hold his soul in patience until the afternoon before he got definite news. For he, his half-brother Chia Huan, and his nephew Chia Lan had to spend the whole day in the company of the stern father and various worthy seniors. There was an inspection of chrysanthemums, and on this occasion the juniors were required once more to show their literary ability. The test passed off to the satisfaction of Mr. Cheng, and after it Pao Yu was able to display proudly to his grandmother and mother the trophies with which the various worthy seniors had honored him—three fans, three prayer chaplets with sandalwood beads, three jade rings, and a little carved sandalwood Buddha as an amulet to wear on the breast. On his way back to the Begonia Courtyard he was accompanied by his two waiting maids Musk and Autumn Wave as well as two younger assistant waiting maids. On the pretext of making them go on ahead with his writing equipment, and his cap and festive outer garments which he had taken off on account of the heat, he had got rid of the two elder girls because he did not want to make them jealous by inquiring about Bright Cloud. He pretended he wanted to stroll for a while in the park, then, finding a somewhat secluded little place among the rocks, he took the two younger girls aside to cross-examine them.

"Did Pearl send over this morning to Bright Cloud?" he asked.

"Yes, she sent old Sung over," replied one of the girls.

"What news did she bring back?"

"Bright Cloud kept crying out the whole night, then towards morning she shut her eyes and lost consciousness."

"Whom was she calling for?"

"For her mother."

"For anyone else?"

"I don't know."

"Ah, you silly thing. I suppose you didn't listen attentively."

"That's right. She only half listened," the other chimed in eagerly. She was rather more intelligent than the other and guessed the reason for his urgent questioning. "I know a lot more, and I know it firsthand too."

"How is that?"

"I went over to her secretly at noon today. She was always so good to us younger ones, and I was sorry that she was treated so unjustly. I wanted to see her once more, for friendship's sake. I would have willingly taken the beating I'd have got if I'd been discovered. When I went in she opened her eyes and caught hold of my hand, and asked at once for you, young master. Where were you, was her first question. I said you had gone with your father to the display of chrysanthemums. At this she sighed and said: 'That's a pity; then I shall never see him again.' I said to her she should be patient for a bit, as you'd surely come to see her again. She shook her head and smiled and replied that today at exactly two quarters after the first half of the double hour of the sheep she would have to take up the vacant position of a flower spirit at the command of the Nephrite Emperor, but that you would come home a bit later than that, and therefore she could not see you again. She said she was not to be one of the damned whose souls the Prince of Hell, Wen Wang, sends his little devils to fetch, and who try to buy an hour's reprieve of their wretched existence by bribing the mercenary messengers of hell with sacrifices of food and paper money. No, she would be solemnly carried before the throne of the Emperor of Heaven by good spirits, and she did not wish to be late on any account in getting there. I did not believe her, but when she drew her last breath a little while afterwards I found her words confirmed by the clock in the next room. The hand pointed exactly to two quarters after the first half of the double hour of the sheep—just the time that she had foretold."

Pao Yu nodded earnest assent.

"If you were acquainted with our literature, you would know that there really is such a thing. Every single flower has its spirit, and over the spirits of each kind of flower there is set, again, a higher spirit. Only I would very much like to know to which species of flowers she is attached, and whether as an ordinary spirit or as a higher spirit."

The girl to whom his question was addressed was not long at a loss for an answer. It occurred to her that now, in the eighth month, the water lilies were just in bloom.

"I asked her about that too," she fibbed boldly and bravely. "I told her that we would like to know, so that we could give our special loving care to her species of flowers in future. Then she told me that she had been appointed upper guardian spirit of our water lilies in the park. But I would not like to betray that to anyone but you, young master."

Pao Yu let his gaze wander across to the water lilies in the near-by pond, and his sorrowful face brightened.

"She has been given a worthy and a beautiful office. To live on in that way, after having passed safely through the Sea of Bitterness, is indeed a happy fate," he murmured, comforted.

Feeling the urge to pay the dead girl the honor due to her, on her bier, he set out, unaccompanied, to go to the house of mourning by the usual secret way through the back gate of the park. He found the house empty and locked.

Little Kwei's wife, hoping for a small subscription towards the burial, had gone off to the Yungkuo palace immediately after Bright Cloud's death, and brought word of it to Madame Cheng. Madame Cheng had given her ten ounces of silver, but with the condition that, instead of keeping the dead girl for the usual period laid out on a bier in the house of mourning, they should take her outside the city walls and cremate her forthwith. For Bright Cloud had died of consumption of the lungs and Madame Cheng was afraid that some harmful influence might spread to the Yungkuo palace if the corpse were in its vicinity for a long time. So it happened that Little Kwei and his wife were already on their way to the city walls with the coffin when Pao Yu arrived; he had, therefore, to go home again without achieving his object.

He was deeply depressed and felt an urge to seek distraction in Black Jade's company, but when he arrived at the Bamboo Hermitage he was told that Black Jade had gone to Precious Clasp. He now set out for the Jungle Courtyard. He found it lonely and abandoned and Precious Clasp's rooms empty and dismantled. He then remembered having heard that Precious Clasp wished to leave the park and return to her mother. Recent events in the park had made an unpleasant impression on her and, moreover, she did not wish to expose herself to the painful possibility of another house search. Phoenix and Madame Cheng had both tried in vain to persuade her to stay, but she had remained firm and, on the excuse of being indispensable to her mother, who was in poor health, she had meantime carried out her intention.

A sorrowful feeling of utter desolation crept over Pao Yu. He saw the number of his intimate companions dwindling little by little. How would it be if Pearl or Black Jade were to die next? With a heavy heart he wandered back to the Bamboo Hermitage, but still Black Jade was not there. So desolate did he feel that he was almost glad now to be called away again to his father and the seniors. The session of poetic composition occasioned by the chrysanthemum show, which had been interrupted by the luncheon interval, was to be resumed now.

When he returned to the park in the hour of yellowish twilight and passed by the pond with its water lilies in bloom, his thoughts turned once more to the dead girl, Bright Cloud. He stopped at the edge of the pond, looking out at the water lilies and sighing. It had been denied him to offer sacrifice and intone a dirge at her bier, as would have been proper. Should he not make good his omission here, in the sight of the water lilies? This idea passed through his mind.

And as his muse had already been stirred by the literary activity of

430

the day, he asked the little maid who was carrying behind him "the four precious articles of the writing table" to hand him his writing brush and ink-stone. And there and then he composed a long hymn, which he named "Funeral Hymn to the Water-Lily Maiden," and wrote it down on a piece of that fine, wavy, ribbed silk which Bright Cloud had so loved. Meantime the little maid had to fetch eating bowls containing four of Bright Cloud's favorite dishes, and stand them one on top of the other by the edge of the pond, as an offering to the dead. Pao Yu, weeping, read his hymn aloud, then burned incense, and placed the sheet of silk with the hymn among the leaves of the nearest water lily within reach. Darkness was already falling when at last, at the entreaties of the little maid, he tore himself away from the scene of this strange act of homage to the departed.

CHAPTER 39

The Plaster Priest makes game of Pao Yu and invents a remedy for jealousy. Four beauties question fate with the fishing rod.

Pao Yu's tears for Bright Cloud were not yet dried when he met with another and yet more painful loss. Cousin Greeting of Spring had to leave the park and go to live with her stepmother, Princess Shieh. She was betrothed to a rich young man named Sun. The wedding was to take place very soon—indeed, in this same year. Until then the bride must live in strict seclusion, under protection of her mother, as the rules of etiquette required.

The ancient military family of Sun came from Ta tung fu, in the provinces, and since the grandfather's time had had friendly connections with the house of Chia. But the chief reason why Prince Shieh had sought young Sun, who lived in the capital and was a candidate for a small public appointment in the Ministry of War, as husband of Greeting of Spring, was that he had money. Chia Cheng had been against the match. For the great hulking thirty-year-old fellow, though certainly proficient in archery, and riding, and drinking, had not a trace of literary education or refinement, and did not seem to him a suitable partner for a daughter of the cultured Chia clan. But young Sun was able to pay a great deal of money for the match, and that was the determining factor for Prince Shieh, who was so greedy for money. The five thousand ounces of silver which he pocketed for Greeting of Spring were not to be despised.

Pao Yu found it hard to get over the loss of four playmates—Precious Clasp, Greeting of Spring, Bright Cloud, and the chess maid—which followed in such rapid succession. And to crown it all he heard that Grief of Spring would be taken away next, also to be married. Quite distraught, he wandered through the park, a prey to melancholy thoughts. Again and again he found himself drawn to the abandoned Jungle Courtyard and the desolate Damask Kiosk, where formerly the happy sound of girls' voices echoed, and now only dreary silence reigned. The falling autumn foliage harmonized well with his gloomy mood and made him think of the transient nature of earthly joys. His mental depression was intensified by the physical suffering of a cold. He fell ill and on doctor's orders had to keep to his room for a hundred days. The medical instructions were in fact based mainly on educational grounds. For once he was to spend the three winter months up to the New Year quietly at home. But now as in the past Pao Yu avoided his books and preferred to pass the time, in so far as he could, chatting and playfully trifling with his waiting maids. At the end of fifty days he was again bubbling over with the joy of life, and with every fiber of his being he craved to go out; but to his sorrow his mother and grandmother remained firm; he was not even allowed to attend the merry wedding feast of his cousin Hsueh Pan. For the Mad Robber Count, after much searching and choosing, had at last decided to marry. He believed he had found just the right bride in a former playmate. She was a proud, spoiled beauty whom he had met again during his recent business tour, the only daughter and heiress of one Hsia of Chang, a cinnamon planter and contractor to the Imperial Palace.

After his hundred days' confinement, Pao Yu had first of all, at his grandmother's wish, to pay a visit to the Temple of Heavenly Harmony outside the western city gate, to offer due thanks to the Nephrite Emperor for his recovery. What could he have desired more, after his long confinement, than this excursion into the open country? He could hardly close an eye the night before, so great was his joyful anticipation. Very early in the morning he drove out of the town in a carriage, accompanied by his two personal servants, Ming Yen and Li Kwei, as well as three serving women.

Pao Yu executed the ceremonial part of his visit to the temple as quickly as possible with the performance of a few kowtows and some kind of a burnt offering. He always felt somewhat timid and uncomfortable in the proximity of this idol, which wore such a majestic and severe expression.

Happy at escaping again from the oppressive semidarkness of the Hall of the Gods into the bright daylight, he set out with his suite on a tour of the extensive temple grounds, took breakfast, and then, tired after the early start and the long journey, lay down to rest in the guest cell. Lest he should nod off to sleep and miss the time for the return journey, his servants asked the High Priest to keep him awake by chatting with him a little.

High Priest Wang pursued the calling of miracle doctor as a side line, and carried on a lively trade throughout the whole neighborhood with his celebrated plasters and ointments and formulas of prayer for effecting cures, which had earned him the nickname of "the Quick Plaster Priest." He was well known, besides, as a joker and wit, and his merry jests were soon successful in dispelling his guest's midday tiredness.

"I have always heard so much praise of your famous ointments and medicines," remarked Pao Yu in the course of conversation. "For what ailments, then, are your prescriptions efficacious?"

"Oh, one cannot explain all that in just a few words. I have over a hundred prescriptions, for high and low, old and young, against physical and spiritual, external and internal infirmities; against pain in the chest, and stomach complaints, and indigestion, as well as against fevers and colds and blood poisoning and colic and everything you could think of. My remedies banish death and rejuvenate the aged, and simply work wonders."

"Now, now, you are surely exaggerating! I know, for instance, one ailment against which your skill would scarcely have any success."

"You may box my ears, pull my beard, and tear down my temple, if my remedies fail in one single case. Tell me what the ailment is!"

Pao Yu signed to the Plaster Priest to come nearer.

"Make one guess!" he whispered in his ear.

"Oh, I understand," said the priest, smiling slyly. "The little master no doubt wants a philter for use in the inner chambers, eh?"

"Do you want a few blows in the face?" asked Ming Yen, putting his hand over old Wang's mouth.

"What does he mean?" asked Pao Yu, naïvely.

"Ah, don't take his drivel seriously!"

"Do you know of anything which will cure young girls of jealousy?" asked Pao Yu, again turning to the priest.

The priest-doctor clapped his hands in astonishment.

"What ideas people take into their heads! This is the first case of the kind that I have come across in my practice. Nevertheless, I do know a remedy, though it doesn't work very quickly. You must have a little patience."

"Out with it! Speak! What is the remedy?" asked Pao Yu eagerly.

The priest-doctor put on a solemnly professional air.

"You dissolve one ounce of sugar candy in a cup of water, mix in half an ounce of dried orange peel, add a nice ripe, peeled pear, and let the sugary syrup soak into it. Every morning this preparation should be taken for breakfast, until the ailment in question has disappeared."

"Is that all? I do not think it very promising," objected Pao Yu, disappointed.

"Oh, but one has to persevere with the cure, even if it takes years! It will certainly have an effect in the end, if it is only on the death of the patient. But apart from all that, it's a tasty, wholesome food, good for the lungs and extraordinarily beneficial for the digestion."

Pao Yu had to laugh aloud. Only now did he realize that the old rascal was having his bit of fun and wanted to make him understand that no sugar cure in the world could have any effect on the bile of a jealous woman.

Upon his return Pao Yu found his recently married cousin, Greeting of Spring, visiting his mother. She complained that her marriage was unhappy and she did not want to leave when evening came and she was to be taken back to her husband's home. She implored Aunt Cheng with tears to keep her a few days as a guest, for her husband was an intolerable libertine, a drunkard and rowdy, she said.

"I must have been soaked in vinegar, he shouted at me when I ventured to take him to task for his unfaithful and inconsiderate behavior," she complained. "I have been legally sold to him for an honest five thousand ounces, and therefore I must submit and not say a word even if he beats me and locks me up in a servant's room. Oh, he's a beast!"

Moved with pity, all the cousins present and Madame Cheng broke into a chorus of sobbing and vied with one another in their efforts to comfort the unfortunate girl.

"Your Uncle Cheng was against this unhappy union from the beginning," lamented Madame Cheng, "but unfortunately your father was deaf to his well-meant objections. But what can be done now? You can only submit to your fate, my poor child."

"I cannot yet understand why I had to leave you all so suddenly and be torn from the dear places where I had spent such gay and happy years. Since then I have felt dazed and dreamy, as if I had been hit on the head. Ah, if only I could spend three days in my dear old home in the park just once more, I would gladly die," wailed Greeting of Spring.

"How can you talk of dying? Little misunderstandings between newly married couples are, after all, quite common. Very well, you shall have your way and stay with us for three days and live in your beloved park again," said the compassionate Aunt Cheng.

And she gave instructions for the Damask Kiosk, the former home of Greeting of Spring, to be comfortably fixed up at once.

"But take care not to blab and talk about it before the old *Tai tai!*

She must not know anything about it!" she earnestly enjoined Pao Yu.

And so Greeting of Spring returned that evening to the old familiar home in the park, and Pao Yu and her other cousins and the waiting maids faithfully kept her company for three whole days and vied with each other in enabling her to relive the good old days of the past. But the three days passed only too quickly, and then Greeting of Spring had to take her leave with a heavy heart and return to her unloved husband.

The tearful leave-taking touched the tenderhearted Pao Yu even more than it did Madame Cheng.

"I couldn't sleep the whole night thinking of her," he said to his mother the following morning. "I pity her, she is so kindhearted and pleasant. Why should it befall her to get such a bad, rough man for a husband?"

"It's her misfortune! What can any of us do about it?" said Madame Cheng. "Once a daughter marries outside the house she is lost to her relatives, and gone—thrown out like a pail of water, and that's all there is to it."

"Should we not try to talk the old *Tai tai* into taking Greeting of Spring home forever? She could stay in the Damask Kiosk and live happily in our company as before. And we wouldn't give her up even if that horrid fellow Sun sent for her a hundred times."

"In your simplicity you're just talking nonsense," said Madame Cheng, putting him off, half amused and half annoyed. "Grown-up daughters have to marry and leave the home; that is, after all, their destiny. How they get on with their husbands—that is always a matter of fate; once they are married, the family can do nothing about it. They cannot all strike such good luck as your elder sister, Beginning of Spring; one gets a cock of a fellow, the other a dog. They have to resign themselves to their fate and make the best of it. As the years go by they become used to each other, the conflicting characters and temperaments come to terms, and once a child is born, everything is all right in the end. So give up your silly idea, and do not dare to let out even half a word about the matter to the old *Tai tai!*"

Utterly perplexed, Pao Yu wandered back to the park. He called on Black Jade, who was just then at her morning toilet, and told her of his sorrow.

"Death would be the best thing for me, and the sooner the better. I've lost all joy in life," he said gloomily.

"Your mind seems to be confused!" she said, frightened.

"Indeed it is not; I feel quite normal. But does it not pain you too to think of poor Greeting of Spring's sad fate? What lovely, happy times those were when we founded our Begonia Club! How merry and cheerful and lighthearted we were when we held our meetings and feasts and poetry competitions! That is all over now, everything is breaking up. Precious Clasp is gone, Lotus is not allowed to come here any more, Greeting of Spring has been torn from us by her marriage. Why must unfortunate girls be handed over to any kind of strange man as soon as they are grown up, and exchange the happy freedom of their youth for the sad slavery of marriage? I simply cannot understand that. I wanted to ask the Ancestress to have Greeting of Spring brought back and to let her live here with us again, but my mother talked me out of the idea. She said I would be crazy if I did such a thing. I cannot get used to having everything here become so different now from what it used to be. What will it be like in a few years more?"

While he was speaking Black Jade had bowed her head lower and lower. A sigh was her only reply to him. Now she slipped down on the edge of the bed and silently buried her face in the pillows. Her sympathetic soul had been completely infected by his dejection. A little while later, when the maid Cuckoo came in with tea, she sat up and her eyelids were red with tears. While Pao Yu was trying to calm her and to persuade her that what he had just said was exaggerated, Pearl appeared to call him to the Ancestress.

Deeply dejected and sunk in melancholy thoughts, Pao Yu took a solitary stroll through the park that afternoon. Again he felt impelled towards the forsaken Jungle Courtyard and the Damask Kiosk. After he had gazed for a while at the closed-up windows and the lifeless gateways, he continued his way towards the Lotus-Root Kiosk by the edge of the lake. From a distance he perceived the heads of four young girls showing over the parapet by the lake. The girls were gazing intently over the surface of the water. He was seized with a desire to surprise the four, so he slipped quietly up behind them, under cover of the rocks.

"Do you think he will come along?" he heard one of them saying.

"Hush! There, he's gone away under there! I thought at once that he didn't want to come to you," he heard another say; it seemed to be the voice of Taste of Spring.

"Be quiet! He's coming along again," cried the third.

"There he is now!" the fourth, Cousin Wreath of Clouds, cried joyfully.

Pao Yu could not refrain from taking up a stone and throwing it into the water not far from the four girls.

"Who was that? Such impudence! Fie, how rude to frighten us like that!" they prattled excitedly all together. Pao Yu jumped out laughing from behind his rock and joined the group of girls. They were Taste of Spring, Wreath of Clouds, and the two cousins of Widow Chu.

436

"Look at that! Enjoying yourselves here and leaving me out of it!" he cried.

"I thought at once it was you, you rogue! You have meanly frightened away our beautiful fish. It's a pity, he was just going to bite," said Taste of Spring, pouting.

"Of course I had to punish you! Why did you not invite me, when you were amusing yourselves here?" retorted Pao Yu laughing. "And now let us five continue fishing, and combine with our fishing a game of questioning fate!" he suggested. "Whoever catches a fish will have some luck in this same year. Whoever gets no bite will have some unpleasant experience. And now to work! Let Taste of Spring begin!"

"Agreed. But heaven help you if you frighten away my fish again! That would ruin the game."

Taste of Spring was the first to dip her fishing line into the water, and in scarcely the time that it takes to say ten sentences a big goldfish had bitten, and was pulling the floater of the line under the water.

With a skillful swing she brought her struggling prisoner up on dry ground and got the waiting maid to drop it into the china pail of fresh water which was standing ready. The three other girls also succeeded in making a catch. Pao Yu's turn came last.

"I shall do as old Chiang Tzu Ya did," he said importantly. And he stepped over the stone balustrade and crouched down right at the water's edge. Legend relates that old Chiang, the celebrated wise counsellor of the Emperor Wen Wang of the Chou dynasty, was able to subdue even animals and spirits, and that the fishes came swarming forward of their own accord when he made a dart at them with a simple iron pole. Now, Pao Yu had very much overestimated his superhuman abilities. His shadow frightened the fishes away, none of them wanted to bite, and once when a rising bubble betrayed the proximity of a fish he swung his fishing rod towards the spot so hurriedly that the fish made off as quickly as possible.

"Dear fish, hurry up! I do not like waiting long. Come, come and make me happy!" he begged with such comic impatience that the four girls had to burst out laughing. At last something pulled at the hook. In his joyful exuberance Pao Yu swung the fishing rod around so hurriedly and awkwardly that the top became wedged firmly against a rock and the rod broke in the middle, and the upper half with the line and hook fell into the water and drifted away. There was a great burst of scoffing laughter from the onlookers.

"Did anyone ever see such awkwardness!" Taste of Spring burst out. She was going to say more when the waiting maid Musk came running along to call Pao Yu to the Ancestress. She had just had her midday sleep and wanted to question him about some very important matter, and she had also sent for Phoenix, reported Musk. She did not know any more details. Pao Yu got a great fright.

"Perhaps they want to take away another waiting maid on account of alleged danger of infection?" he let slip. But he was immediately reassured when he saw the Ancestress peacefully playing dominoes with his mother.

"Some years ago you had an attack of diabolical possession, from which you were eventually cured by those two strange fellows, the mangy-headed bonze and the lame Taoist priest. Do you still remember your condition at that time?" asked the Ancestress.

Pao Yu thought for a while.

"It seemed to me as if I had suddenly got a heavy blow with a stick on the back of the head. The pain was so great that everything went black as lacquer before my eyes. Then I thought I saw devils with hideous blue-black faces, showing their teeth, all over the room. They were waving knives and sticks, and they kicked me with their feet so that I fell out of bed. I felt as if my brain was pressed into an iron band. Afterwards I did not feel any more pain. As regards the moment of my recovery, I remember that a golden gleam of light suddenly appeared in my room, and the black devils dispersed in fright before its dazzling brilliance. From that moment on I felt well again, and clear in my mind."

"Exactly the same characteristics as in the case we have just been speaking of," said the Ancestress, turning to Madame Cheng. Meantime Phoenix had come in.

"The old Ancestress has sent for me. What is it that she wants to know?" she asked.

"Do you remember your condition a few years ago when you suddenly had an attack of possession?" asked the Ancestress once more.

"Not exactly. But I can more or less remember that I lost control of myself. It seemed to me as if I were being pulled about and seized by devils. I felt an urge to take hold of the first murderous weapon I could lay hands on and to kill the first living creature that came near me. In spite of the exhaustion which then overcame me I had to keep rushing on, flourishing the weapon in my hand."

"And how was it when you were cured later?"

"I thought I heard a voice in the air. But what it said I no longer remember."

"Your statement coincides with that of Pao Yu and confirms the observations made in the recent case," remarked the Ancestress. "There is no doubt about it—that accursed beast, old Ma, bewitched you and Pao Yu that time. And we were so simple as to choose that witch to be Pao Yu's godmother and adopted mother! Without the aid of the two strange monks you two would have been lost. And we have not yet been able to thank your rescuers!"

"What makes you go back to that old story just now?" Phoenix wanted to know.

"Your aunt can tell you that. I am too lazy to do so."

"As my husband has just now informed us, old Ma has recently been arrested on a charge of witchcraft and been shut up in prison. She is a very dangerous witch and is awaiting execution," reported Madame Cheng. "A few days ago her criminal activities were brought to light just by chance. A householder named Fan wanted to sell his house to a pawnbroker who lived opposite him. The latter had already offered him twice the value of the property, but he kept demanding more and more. Thereupon, the pawnbroker gave up the negotiations. Enraged at the deal's falling through, Fan hired old Ma to hunt down his opponent. Old Ma could do this without attracting particular attention, for she was frequently in and out of the women's quarters of the pawnbroker's house and was already well known there. She now applied her magic there and cast an evil spell on the pawnbroker's wives, causing them to become possessed. Then she came along again and offered her services to cure the possessed women. With the aid of incantations and of burning magic paper tinsel, she actually did drive out the evil spirits from the invalids. For these services she demanded a fee of some ten ounces. But old Buddha, who sees everything, exposed her evil doings this time.

"In her hurry to get away she once left her handbag behind. When examined, it was found to contain all kinds of paper figures of human forms and four very strong-smelling pills. This aroused suspicion, and when the old woman came back for her bag they took hold of her and searched her. Hidden under her clothing they found a box containing two carved ivory figures of naked demons, a male and a female, and seven vermilion embroidery needles. Thereupon the old woman was dragged off to the police. At the cross-examination it came out that she was mixed up in a great many secret love affairs of the wives and daughters of rich and respectable citizens, and had been making a thumping good profit out of her private knowledge.

"A search of her house brought to light a lot of figures of devils made of clay and earthenware and some boxes of magic powders for the possessed. Behind her bed, moreover, in a hidden closet, an oil lamp burning with seven little flames was found. Under the lamp was a pile of puppets in human form. Some had iron bands around their heads, others had nails stuck in their breasts, and there were some, again, with iron chains around their necks. A number of cardboard figures of men and women was found in a cupboard, together with bundles of accounts giving exact information as to the people for whom the old woman had worked her magic and the fees she had charged them. There were also found quantities of vouchers for oil used and incense burned on behalf of other people."

"Now I understand," cried Phoenix, astonished. "I got suspicious at once shortly after my recovery, when I saw the old woman frequently visiting the secondary wife Chao's apartments. I was told that the witch was trying to collect a debt from Chao. On one such occasion when she ran into me, her face showed visible embarrassment and she rolled the pupils of her eyes about timidly and restlessly like a startled clucking hen. Of course, with the position I hold in the house, it is not surprising that I should incur hate and ill will. But what crime has the innocent Pao Yu committed that the poison hand of this treacherous plot should clutch at him?"

"Who knows? Perhaps Chao bears a grudge against Pao Yu because I prefer him to her offspring, Huan," said the Ancestress.

"That is just it! The plot no doubt originated with Chao," interrupted Pao Yu's mother eagerly. "But how can she be convicted? The only possible witness for the prosecution, old Ma, is already condemned and may have already been executed. With this witness gone, Chao will simply deny everything. The reputation of our house would suffer if we let it come to a public scandal without having sufficient proof. The best thing is for us to observe Chao for the present and wait until she betrays herself."

"That is exactly my opinion," agreed the Ancestress. "We cannot proceed without proof. On no account must we open our mouths too soon! Let us leave the rest to our all-seeing Buddha! And so we will not do anything about the matter for the present!"

With this the consultation ended, and they went on to discuss catering and other everyday matters. Pao Yu's mother was called to Mr. Cheng, who wished to discuss some important matters with her. The result of this parental discussion was the decision that Pao Yu was to attend the family school once more after an interruption of several years. True, Master Tai Ju was only moderately learned, but he knew how to wield authority, and a little discipline could not harm Pao Yu, who was spoiled by having had too much freedom, said Mr. Cheng.

The following morning he himself took Pao Yu to the school, and earnestly requested old Tai Ju to form his son into a decent fellow, fit to face the world. There must be an end now to the playful dallying with verse and rhyme-making; from now on it must be a matter of learning history above all, and mastering the sound art of prose composition. As can well be imagined, Pao Yu was little pleased with the parental decision. The misfortune prophesied for him by the fishing rod had arrived sooner than expected.

CHAPTER 40

An evil dream frightens an unhappy lovesick maiden in the Bamboo Hermitage. Beginning of Spring is visited by her relatives on her sickbed in the Imperial Palace.

In the Begonia Courtyard, once so noisy and happy, a solemn silence reigned. Pao Yu was spending the greater part of the day in the family school, and when he was at home, the homework which Schoolmaster Tai Ju thoughtfully gave him made it, alas, impossible for him to romp about and waste his time with waiting maids and maidservants. "Early to bed and early to rise" was the watchword now. Moreover, Madame Cheng had given his waiting maids to understand that if they dared to distract Pao Yu from his studies they would fare as Bright Cloud had done. So, whether they liked it or not, they had to take to their needlework in real earnest now.

One day Pearl was crocheting her new betel-nut bag and letting her thoughts wander in the meanwhile. What would become of her later? No doubt Pao Yu would take her for his "side-chamber" when he married, and of course he would treat her well, but how would she get on with his "first"? Would she have the same tragic fate as the second Yu, who had been tortured to death by her rival, Phoenix? Or would she fare like poor Lotus, who had been frightened away from the common home by Hsueh Pan's domineering and quarrelsome wife shortly after he had married, and was now a servant of Precious Clasp? If she could only find out who was to be Pao Yu's future wife! According to everything she had heard, Black Jade had the best chance. She decided to take a walk over to the Bamboo Hermitage and to sound out the feelings of her future mistress a little.

Black Jade laid her book aside, amiably invited her guest to sit down, and got the waiting maid Cuckoo to serve her with tea. After a few polite nothings, Pearl began with a smile, turning to Cuckoo: "I hear from Autumn Wave that you've been saying recently how terribly our life in the park has been changed?"

"Yes, indeed, it's become terribly dull—unbearably dull. That's what I said," admitted Cuckoo fervently. "Pao Yu at school, Precious Clasp gone away, Greeting of Spring gone away, and Lotus not allowed to come over here any more. Isn't that so?"

"Indeed it is. And speaking of Lotus, the poor girl seems to have had very tough luck with her 'First'; that woman is even more ruthless and difficult to get on with than a certain other one. . . ."

Pearl stopped and significantly lifted two fingers, by which she meant Phoenix. She did not dare to mention the name. It struck Black

Jade that this was the first time she had heard Pearl, who ordinarily was most discreet, speaking unfavorably of someone absent. But she had to admit that she was right.

"Incidents of that kind are inevitable in a big household where there are several wives; there will no doubt always be rivalry between the east wind and the west wind," she remarked philosophically; and she thought to herself of her own rivalry with Precious Clasp. As if summoned by telepathy, a serving woman sent by Precious Clasp appeared at this moment with a dish of litchi plums preserved in honey, for Black Jade. The old woman stared fixedly at Black Jade for a moment, then with a grin she remarked point-blank to Pearl: "I don't wonder now that our *Tai tai* Hsueh always says that your young lady is just the right bride for young Pao Yu. She is indeed a real angel."

This familiar and downright assertion naturally embarrassed Pearl and still more Black Jade. Pearl tried hard to put her off the subject and pressed her to take a cup of tea, but the old woman seemed to feel ill at ease. With a show of being busy and important she took her leave immediately. She had no time, she said, they all had their hands full over there getting ready for the wedding of Miss Precious Harp.

"Give Miss Precious Clasp my greetings and thanks," Black Jade told her as she went off, and she could hear the old woman muttering to herself something which sounded like: "Those are nice manners indeed! No man except Pao Yu could put up with that one!" But she pretended that she had not heard her.

"Did anyone ever hear such impudent babbling! One hardly knows whether to be angry with her or to laugh at her," Pearl blurted out when the old woman was gone; and she too went off after a short time. The chance information which the garrulous old woman had betrayed was all she wanted to hear and made it unnecessary for her to remain longer with Black Jade.

But the old woman's words went on revolving in Black Jade's mind and released an endless stream of dreamy thoughts, as if from an inexhaustible spool. Was her marriage to Pao Yu really a settled affair? True, she felt she could be sure of him and his feelings; but his mother and his grandmother would also have a say in the matter. Why had her parents not betrothed her while they were still alive? If they had done so, she would be relieved of all this torturing uncertainty. On the other hand, if her parents had already chosen for her, would the person of their choice be as desirable and as compatible with her as Pao Yu definitely was? Exhausted by all this brooding and conjecturing, she lay down on her bed, still dressed, as darkness fell.

As she lay there half asleep, it suddenly seemed to her that little Snowgoose was standing before her and telling her that Mr. Yu Tsun

was outside and wished to speak to her. She sent him word that she thanked him for his visit, but excused herself on the plea of not being well. For although he had been her tutor, it would nevertheless be unseemly for a young girl like her to receive the visit of a gentleman, as she gave Snowgoose to understand.

"I believe he only came to congratulate you," replied Snowgoose, "and various other people have come to visit you too."

And immediately in came Phoenix and Princess Shieh and Madame Cheng and Precious Clasp, all smiling, to her room.

"We come in the first place to congratulate you and in the second place to escort you away," they said.

"What does that mean? I do not understand you," she replied, perplexed.

"Do not pretend to be so dull-witted! Surely you must know!" said Phoenix. "Don't you know that your father has been promoted Corn Treasurer of the Province of Hu Pei, and has contracted a most happy second marriage? He does not wish to leave you here any longer in your isolation, so he has appointed Mr. Yu Tsun as negotiator to arrange your betrothal to a nephew of your stepmother. You are to go home now and get married. Chia Lien has been appointed your escort and protector."

While Phoenix was speaking Black Jade felt a cold sweat breaking out all over her body.

"That is all nonsense! It's a bad joke thought up by Phoenix," she cried excitedly, whereupon Princess Shieh threw the others a significant look and said: "She doesn't believe us. Come! Let us go away!"

Black Jade was about to beg them, with tears, to remain, but the four visitors walked silently and stiffly to the door, with a cold smile on their faces. Black Jade was left alone, a prey to her grief. Then all of a sudden she seemed to be standing opposite the Princess Ancestress. She knelt down before her, clasped her around the thighs, and implored her with tears not to send her away, as it would be her death. Her stepmother was a stranger to her; she wanted only to remain with the old *Tai tai*. But the Ancestress looked at her coldly and replied that this matter did not concern her.

"What does that mean?" asked Black Jade, astounded.

"After all, it is also very nice to get married. You will have lots of wonderful dresses and loads of jewelry," was the answer.

"I don't care in the least about all those things. I only want to stay here. Help me, old *Tai tai!* Don't let me leave you!" implored Black Jade.

"Stupid child! You cannot remain here all your life. A time comes when young girls have to leave home and marry!"

"No, no; I would rather go on living here, even as a servant, as the lowest maidservant, and earn my own bread! Have pity on me, for the sake of my mother, your own daughter; have pity on me, old *Tai tai*, and do not turn me out!" cried Black Jade passionately.

But the Ancestress remained pitiless.

"Take her out!" she ordered her waiting maid, Mandarin Duck, brusquely. "I am tired and weary of her!"

In desperation she rushed out. Had all the love shown her up to this by grandmother, aunts, and cousins been only wretched hypocrisy? She felt that the world was too much for her, and thought of suicide. Then Pao Yu came into her mind. Perhaps she would find help from him? And then she found herself opposite him.

"I congratulate you on your great good fortune, *Mei mei!*" he said quite cheerfully.

Enraged at hearing such a thing and in such a tone from his lips, she forgot all her accustomed timidity and reserve, drew him close up to her, and said to him furiously: "Now you are betraying yourself, dearest! Do you call that love and fidelity?"

"What are you saying about love and fidelity? You have got another, haven't you? Our ways have parted," he replied calmly.

"No, it is not decided yet whom I shall follow. It lies with you! I am waiting for your word!" she burst out vehemently.

"And I have been waiting the whole time for your word. Originally we two wished to belong to each other, didn't we? So if you wish, stay."

His words changed her sorrow into joy.

"In life and in death I am yours!" she said solemnly. "But you—you must declare yourself once more: Shall I go or shall I remain?"

"Remain!" he cried, equally solemnly. "But if you doubt that this is my sincere will, just look at my heart!"

With these words he took a sharp dagger and drove it right into his breast. Horrified at the sight of the crimson stream which gushed out, she pressed her hand over the open wound and cried plaintively: "Why did you do that? Kill me first!"

"Don't be afraid!" said Pao Yu, quite calmly. "I only want to take out my heart and show it to you."

And he stuck his hand into the gaping wound and fumbled about in it as if looking for something. Suddenly he cried out in dismay: "Oh, woe! I have lost my heart! Now I must die!"

He turned up his eyes and slumped to the ground with a heavy thud. At this Black Jade uttered a stifled cry of agony. Suddenly she recognized the voice of her maid Cuckoo. "Miss! Miss!" cried the maid. "What kind of horrible nightmare are you having? Wake up! Undress and go to bed properly!" She realized then that she had been deluded by a dream. Her throat was still as if tied up, her heart was bounding wildly, her undergarment and her pillow were drenched with cold sweat. Limp and exhausted, she allowed Cuckoo to undress her and put her to bed properly.

But the whole night through she could not sleep. She tossed restlessly from side to side and listened full of fear to the noises of the night which reached her ear from outside. At one moment she would hear the babbling of the near-by brook, then it was the plaintive moaning of the wind, or the monotonous dripping of the autumn rain, or, again, some confused human sound from somewhere in the distance.

She listened with something like envy to the regular snoring tones of sound sleep which came over from Cuckoo's bed near by. Tired of lying down, she hurriedly assumed a sitting position, until the icy draft, which she felt cutting through the slits in the window parchment, obliged her to lie down again and wrap herself like a mummy in the protecting blankets. When at last she fell into an uneasy half sleep the many-voiced twitter of birds was already audible from the bamboo plantation in the front garden, and the pale light of dawn was creeping in the window.

Suddenly she was shaken by a severe fit of coughing, and this awoke Cuckoo, who rushed to her bedside.

"Awake so early?" she asked, looking with anxiety at the fatigued, suffering face of her mistress.

"I couldn't sleep. Please take out the spitting bowl and fetch me a clean one."

Cuckoo put a clean bowl by her bed and took the other one out to the courtyard. As she was emptying it she noticed many spots of blood mingled with the sputum.

"Oh, how terrible!" she gasped involuntarily. Black Jade heard her exclamation distinctly from inside.

"What frightened you just now?" she asked the maid afterwards.

"Oh, it was really nothing. The bowl nearly slipped out of my hand," lied Cuckoo, but her looks, her hesitant tone, and her tear-stained eyes betrayed her. Black Jade had in fact perceived the sweetish taste of blood in her mouth when she was coughing shortly before. She had long since ceased to deceive herself regarding her condition.

"I know well that my spittle has frightened you," she said calmly.

"You should take more care of your health and confide in the old *Tai tai* and the other ladies. They all really do mean so well by you, dear young lady!" Cuckoo admonished her tenderly.

But her reference to the ladies recalled to Black Jewel's mind her terrible dream of the night before, which belied the words of the waiting maid. She felt a stab through her stomach, her eyesight grew suddenly

446

dim, she became dizzy and had to bend over the bowl which Cuckoo held up to her just in the nick of time. While Snowgoose clapped her back she looked into the bowl. Yes indeed, there was a thin coil of purplish red bloody mucus. She sank back unconscious on her pillows.

Cuckoo sent Snowgoose out to fetch someone from the family to help. After a short while Snowgoose came back with the cousins Taste of Spring, Grief of Spring, and Little Cloud. The three had just been together at Grief of Spring's pavilion inspecting her great painting of the park and had been about to send for Black Jade to come and join them. Black Jade was not pleased at all to see them. Still under the influence of her dreadful dream, and anyway suspicious by nature, she said to herself that, if she could not trust the Ancestress, still less could she rely upon her cousins.

She invited the three rather frostily to sit down, but conversation was exceedingly labored. In consideration of her wretched state the visitors, on their part, did not wish to remain long, and they soon rose to leave. They were just going away when a loud, screeching woman's voice was heard outside, crying: "What do you think you're doing here, you brazen hussy! You have no business here in the park! Get out at once!"

As was soon to be seen, the outcry came from an old garden woman and was addressed to her granddaughter, a dirty, wild little tomboy who, urged by curiosity, had sneaked into the forbidden park behind her back as she came in. But alas, Black Jade, in her morbidly excited condition, took the outcry to refer to herself and interpreted it as a confirmation of her evil dream.

"Do you hear her? I am not to be allowed to remain here any longer! And I have to be told that by an old maidservant!" she cried in a shrill voice to her astounded cousins, pointing towards the window with a trembling hand. They reassured her as best they could, and then withdrew, shaking their heads. "She's delirious," they said to each other. Of course they knew nothing about her dream.

Soon afterwards Pearl appeared. She had been sent by Pao Yu, who was consumed with anxiety, and before she went up to the sickbed she got a detailed report from Cuckoo outside the door.

"We had a bit of excitement in the Begonia Courtyard last night too," her colleague whispered to her. "About midnight Pao Yu suddenly jumped up with a stifled cry and began raving something about a dagger which he had stuck in his breast. He didn't get to sleep again until nearly morning, and he has had to stay home from school today."

Black Jade got a new fit of coughing, and this made an end to their whispered conversation and obliged Cuckoo to hurry back to her mistress's bedside.

"To whom have you been talking just now?" Black Jade wanted to know.

"To Pearl."

"Tell her to come in!"

Pearl had to sit down on the edge of the bed.

"Who did you say just now had a bad dream last night?"

"Pao Yu. It was a bit of a nightmare, no doubt."

"Do you know what he said in his dream?"

"No," lied Pearl.

She's keeping it from me to spare my feelings, thought Black Jade to herself. She had heard quite well the whispered words about the dagger stuck in the breast. How strangely Pao Yu's dream corresponded with her own!

While two patients, the one in the Begonia Courtyard and the other in the Bamboo Hermitage, were still being treated in accordance with the prescriptions of the family doctor, Wang, whom the old *Tai tai* had sent for, news came of the illness of the Imperial wife, Beginning of Spring.

One day two chief eunuchs arrived at the Yungkuo palace and delivered an Imperial order to Prince Shieh and Chia Cheng. The *Niang niang,* the high lady, had been suffering some disquiet for a short time past. Four ladies of her family would be permitted to enter the inner precincts of the Imperial Palace and visit the great lady. Each lady would be permitted to take one female servant to accompany her. Male relatives might join the party, but would only be permitted access to the entrance of the Inner Palace; there they would have to send in their visiting cards, offer their salutations, and await news. The next day had been fixed for the visit, and the period of time allowed, moreover, was between the double hour of the dragon and that of the cock, namely between eight in the morning and six in the evening.

Standing respectfully, the two seniors of the Chia clan had listened to the Imperial message. They served the chief eunuchs a bowl of tea and accompanied them personally to the doors of their sedan chairs in front of the inner gateway. A family council followed. The Ancestress decided that for the four female relatives permitted to visit, there could only be a question of herself, Princess Shieh, Madame Cheng, and Phoenix; while it was agreed that Prince Shieh and Chia Cheng should represent the male relatives.

Accordingly, the next morning, at the hour of the dragon, four ladies' sedan chairs covered with green damask, and ten carriages, set out from the Yungkuo palace for the Forbidden City. The personal servants Li Kwei and Ming Yen rode at the head of the procession, and a numerous retinue of servants brought up the rear. All had to dismount at the western gateway of the Inner Palace. Young eunuchs conducted the ladies to the residence of Beginning of Spring. The gentlemen had to wait in front of the gateway with the servants.

Two ladies-in-waiting instructed the ladies that they were only permitted to wish the patient a good recovery and were forbidden any discussion of the illness itself. Beginning of Spring, lying in a magnificent bed, welcomed her visitors, received their *tsing an,* and graciously invited them to be seated.

"How is your health?" she asked the Ancestress.

"Thanks to the overwhelming graciousness of the *Niang niang,* I am still fairly sound," replied the Ancestress, standing and trembling with awe in all her members in the manner prescribed by Court etiquette. After a few more friendly questions to the three other ladies, each of whom replied standing, Beginning of Spring glanced down the list of names of the male and other relatives, which a lady-in-waiting laid before her on behalf of the two family seniors who were waiting outside. As she did so she was overcome with emotion and another lady-in-waiting had to wipe her tearful eyes.

"How fortunate ordinary mortals are compared with us," sighed Beginning of Spring. "They can cherish their family associations to their hearts' content, and see each other as often as they wish.

"And how is Pao Yu?" she continued.

"At the earnest wish of his father he has been devoting himself seriously to his studies of late, and has already made excellent progress," declared the Ancestress.

"I am glad to hear that."

Beginning of Spring signed to her attendants to conduct the guests to the table which was laid for them in another pavilion. After the meal they talked a little longer with the illustrious lady, and then took their leave. After a few days the reassuring news reached the western palace that the Imperial wife was quite well again. At the same time eunuchs brought rich gifts on her behalf for every single one of her relatives.

"She is still deeply devoted to Pao Yu," remarked the Ancestress to Chia Cheng during the distribution of the gifts. "She inquired particularly graciously for him the other day."

"He does not deserve that in the least, the ungrateful, lazy rascal," interjected Mr. Cheng.

"On the contrary, I praised him to the skies for his recent progress."

"Come! Come! He does not quite deserve that yet."

"Indeed? I thought he did. He's been going to school long enough and you have been calling him up for interviews often enough. Surely some wisdom must stick in his mind at last!"

"Naturally. The old *Tai tai* is right again there."

"And by the way, while we are talking about Pao Yu, I just remember something I have been wishing to discuss with you for a long time past. He is almost grown up already, and would it not be well to look out for a suitable wife for him in time? That is a matter which will affect his whole life. In my opinion we should not ask whether the girl in question is rich or poor, of our own clan or of another, but only set store on a good character and a pleasing exterior."

"You are quite right. Only I would add as a counter-stipulation that he himself should have something to offer in the way of character and achievement. I would not wish that he should prove a weed which would spoil the noble plant from some other family."

His objection annoyed the Ancestress somewhat.

"It may be that I have spoiled him from childhood and hindered the development of his character. Nevertheless, he is a good, well-behaved boy. I cannot imagine him ill-treating his young wife. At any rate, he is a much better fellow than your other scion, Chia Huan."

"The old *Tai tai* has a great knowledge of human nature; no doubt she is able to judge correctly, and Pao Yu must certainly be congratulated on the fact that she has such a good opinion of him," admitted Mr. Cheng. "Only I am anxious to see him develop at last into a mature, balanced character. That is what is on my mind."

"But after all, he is hardly more than a child. He has no experience of life or years of public office behind him, as people like you have. Therefore one must not expect too much of him," growled the Ancestress, and turning to Princess Shieh and Madame Cheng, she continued in a lighter tone: "This fellow was a very much more odd and eccentric boy than Pao Yu in his youth. It was only when he got married that he became somewhat more sensible."

"Splendid! Our old *Tai tai* always knows how to have the last laugh on her side," cried the two ladies, laughing heartily.

The conversation was interrupted by a maid coming to announce that supper was ready, and the company went to table in the best of humor. This was the first time that Pao Yu's marriage had been seriously discussed in family council.

That same evening Chia Cheng called Pao Yu up for an interview. He made him produce the three essays which he had presented during the two months' term to Master Tai Ju, and discussed them thoroughly with him, altering this and improving that, and finally sent him off, not ungraciously, to the Ancestress.

Pao Yu found Aunt Hsueh there; she had come to unburden herself on the subject of her ill-behaved daughter-in-law who had made a violent scene with herself and Precious Clasp only that very day. She met with general sympathy, and Precious Clasp's gentle, wise character was much praised: how different she was from the insufferable Hsia; she would undoubtedly rejoice the heart of any mother-in-law.

Pao Yu, who had no liking for family discussions, had already been watching for his chance to steal away on the first excuse, but the mention of Precious Clasp's name held him back.

"Yes, she may indeed be quite a good, capable girl," sighed Aunt Hsueh, "but what good is that to me? After all, she is only a girl, and my son is all the more worry to me for that reason. I live in constant fear that he will get into some serious trouble again with his constant carousing outside the home."

Pao Yu felt obliged to put in a good word for Cousin Hsueh Pan and to assure the ladies that the company he kept consisted entirely of absolutely unimpeachable, honorable big businessmen. Then, disappointed at the uninteresting turn which the conversation had taken, he left the company and went back to his books.

Meantime Chia Cheng had gone into the guest hall and revealed to the friends and colleagues assembled there that, having just put his son, Pao Yu, through his paces, he now considered him worthy to take a wife. With this intimation he gave the company to understand that he would have his ear open for suitable proposals.

Thereupon one of the guests proposed the only child of the rich former *Taotai* Chang of Nanchow, and offered his services as intermediary. The family in question was related, moreover, to Princess Shieh. Chia Cheng, who did not know the Changs personally, decided to consult his wife first before instructing the would-be middleman to proceed.

The next morning, when breakfasting with the Ancestress, Madame Cheng spoke of the latest marriage project. When Princess Shieh mentioned that, to her knowledge, old Chang was a selfish, miserly person who would not let his only child out of his house under any circumstances or risk exposing her to the rod of some mother-in-law, but would wish his son-in-law to marry into his own house, the Ancestress declared at once that the proposal was out of the question, as she would not dream of letting Pao Yu leave the house.

"But why go hunting round among strangers?" remarked Phoenix, smiling. "After all, a kindly Providence has arranged things wonderfully conveniently for us."

"How is that?" asked the Ancestress.

"Has the old *Tai tai* forgotten the corresponding inscriptions on the stone amulet and the golden amulet? Nephrite and gold, Pao Yu and Pao Chai—Precious Stone and Precious Clasp—belong together by the will of Providence."

"Why, of course! My eyes have certainly grown dull with age!" exclaimed the Ancestress, nodding agreement. Princess Shieh and Madame Cheng eagerly nodded agreement too. And from that hour it was a settled matter, within the inner council of the ladies of the Yungkuo palace, that Pao Yu and Precious Clasp should become man and wife.

CHAPTER 41

The beautiful saint is caught up in the fire of sin as she sits on her prayer cushion, and is carried away into ecstasy by demoniacal forces. Black Jade is frightened by the shadow of the snake in the beaker, and rejects all nourishment with sublime resolution.

JUST AS THE LADIES OF THE YUNGKUO PALACE WERE ENGAGED IN EAGER discussion of the latest marriage plan, Pao Yu appeared on the scene. He came from the palace of the Prince of the Northern Quietness, who was celebrating his birthday today. The three seniors, Prince Shieh, Mr. Cheng, and Prince Chen, and the two juniors, Chia Lien and Pao Yu, had together conveyed their congratulations to him. The Prince had conversed almost exclusively with Pao Yu, had informed him before anyone else of the coming promotion of his father to the office of State Councillor in the Ministry of Works, and graciously honored him on parting with the gift of a beautiful jewel. Full of pride, Pao Yu showed the Prince's gift to the Ancestress and the other ladies. The Ancestress decided that it would be wise to put the precious souvenir away in the treasure chamber lest it should be lost.

"And are you wearing your own stone as you should be? Do keep it safe!" she said.

Pao Yu pulled out from under his tunic the stone which hung on its five-colored cord.

"Yes, I do mind it well, for it's no ordinary stone," he assured her. "And by the way, that reminds me of something very strange. One night recently, when I was going to sleep and had hung it on the bed-curtain near my pillow, it suddenly shone so brightly that a whole patch of the curtain behind it glowed red."

"Don't talk nonsense! It must have been the reflection from the lamp or from the fire in the brazier; for the curtain is of red material, of course."

"No, the brazier had already burned out and the lamp was quenched. It was as dark as lacquer in the room."

The ladies looked at each other with significant smiles.

"The phenomenon doubtless points to a happy event soon to come," interjected Phoenix.

"I don't know what it would be," he said guilelessly.

"And you do not need to know, either! Now, don't stay talking twaddle any longer. You have been out the whole day. Go back to the park and rest now!" said the Ancestress, putting a stop to further conversation.

"Have any of you informed Aunt Hsueh of our plan meantime?" she asked, when her grandson had gone out.

"Yes, I have," replied Madame Cheng. "She is ten-tenths in agreement, but she would like to discuss the matter with her son Hsueh Pan before giving her final consent. So we must wait until Hsueh Pan is back from his business journey."

"Good. Then we will keep the matter between ourselves," decided the Ancestress.

Meanwhile, over in the Begonia Courtyard, Pao Yu was telling his Pearl about the conversation he had just taken part in and asking her how she would interpret Phoenix's mysterious pronouncement. Pearl pretended that she also could not make head or tail of it.

"Was Miss Black Jade over there?" she wanted to know.

"No. You know that she's been ill for days, and isn't going out yet."

They were distracted from the matter by a little quarrel between Musk and Autumn Wave. But Pearl had in fact put two and two together. She was firmly convinced that Pao Yu's marriage was the coming event hinted at, which it was intended to keep secret from him for the present. The fact that Black Jade had been absent strengthened her firm conviction that she was the chosen bride.

Two events, one of them happy, the other unhappy, pushed the marriage question into the background for a time. The appointment of Chia Cheng as State Councillor in the Ministry of Works brought swarms of guests to the house, to offer their congratulations, and for days on end there was the usual bustle of festivities. The festive mood was forthwith damped by an unfortunate affair of Cousin Hsueh Pan. The terrible disgrace which his mother had long been dreading in secret had come to pass at last. In order to get some respite from his quarrelsome wife, née Hsia, Hsueh Pan had set out on another business tour of the South. At an inn on the way in a sudden fit of rage he had thrown a wine goblet at a waiter who, he considered, had not treated him with adequate respect. The goblet had hit the poor devil so hard on the back of his head that he had died of his injuries. Hsueh Pan had been sent to prison and charged with murder. And now there was an excited running hither and thither between the capital and the provincial town in which Hsueh Pan was imprisoned. His cousin Hsueh Kuo was sent off posthaste to his aid. Messengers came and went; Aunt Hsueh had to dip into her pocket and produce thousands of taels for bribing purposes, and Uncle Cheng had to throw into the scale all the weight of his position and influence in an effort to get the unlucky nephew out of his painful dilemma. Naturally, such a happy event as a wedding could not be thought of while such urgent matters as these remained unresolved.

One day when he was free from school Pao Yu set out on a stroll through the park after the midday meal. His first impulse was to turn towards the Bamboo Hermitage, but as Black Jade was just having her midday nap, he did not want to disturb her, and decided to visit Grief of Spring instead. He found her dwelling place, the Little Castle of Warm Perfumes, sunk in deepest silence. There was not a sound to be heard, nor even the shadow of a human being to be seen. She's probably asleep, he said to himself, and had already turned to go on when a soft clapping sound from within made him halt his footsteps once more. He listened. Again came the soft clapping sound, and then a voice: "It's your turn. Why don't you move a piece?"

That sounds like chess, conjectured Pao Yu. If only he knew with whom Grief of Spring was playing. The voice that he had just heard sounded strange to him. Now he identified the voice of Grief of Spring, and disconnected words such as: "Come on! Move for move! First you, then me. Quietly! Quietly! We're getting on!" Then after a while, another voice, groaning: "I'm just finished!"

And then again, Grief of Spring, hoarse and dejected: "I'm not yet! Go on! Now, now there's the revolt from within! I give up!"

Seized with breathless curiosity, Pao Yu slipped cautiously under the curtain and peered into the room. Thereupon, to his astonishment, he recognized Grief of Spring's chess partner. She was the young saint of the Kingfisher's Cage, the beautiful anchoress, Miao Yu. The two were still so engrossed and absorbed in their game that they did not notice him coming up behind them.

I'd call that a strange game of sleight of hand that's being played here! thought the eavesdropper, amused, remaining motionless where he was, to continue listening.

"Surely your unicorn has had enough?" he heard Miao Yu whispering with bent head to Grief of Spring.

"Indeed he hasn't. If you cannot make a move, I can!" said Grief of Spring, eagerly.

"Pssh! It's just a matter of trying!" said Miao Yu, smiling; and continuing the game, she succeeded, in a few clever moves, in checkmating and eliminating Grief of Spring's unicorn, which was the vanguard of her field of play.

"That is what is called the 'Chess Game of Pulling Off Boots,'" she declared, smiling.

Now the eavesdropper could keep quiet no longer.

"That was certainly an exciting fight for the unicorn!" he suddenly blurted out, laughing loudly. The two players jumped to their feet, very much startled.

"What on earth do you mean? To force your way in without a word and simply take us by surprise! Have you been here long?" asked Grief of Spring, half angrily and half nervously.

"Oh, no! I've only just come in. And you, reverend sister, you do not leave your holy cloister very willingly. What, then, leads you into our impious, worldly regions today?" he asked, bowing with an ironical smile to the beautiful anchoress.

Miao Yu blushed, and silently bent her head still lower over the chessboard. She had cast only a hurried glance at him.

"It's your turn. Won't you make a move?" she said to Grief of Spring as casually as possible; stood up, smoothed her crushed gown, and sat down again. Then, turning to Pao Yu: "Where have you come from?" she asked.

The one hurried glance which she threw him so confused him that he, in his turn, flushed up and failed to hear her embarrassed question. He felt caught and at the same time encouraged by this one glance.

"Come, speak up! Surely the question is not so difficult to answer that it should make you blush?" said Grief of Spring.

"It's time for me to go. I have already stayed too long," said Miao Yu, anticipating him; she rose and turned towards the door.

"I only hope I shall not lose my way, I'm so unfamiliar with this labyrinth of winding paths," she remarked with a smile as she reached the door, glancing aside at Pao Yu. He read a silent invitation in her glance.

"I will guide you," he offered promptly.

"Oh, how very kind of you. Then please walk ahead!"

And the beautiful and saintly lady gladly allowed the scion of princes, the child from the world of red dust, to guide her back to her hermitage by winding paths.

That night she had to go through a bitter fight with the demons of temptation. After she had taken her frugal evening meal, burned incense, prayed through her daily Sutra breviary, and had sat down with her legs tucked crosswise under her on her round prayer cushion, she sought in vain, for several hours of strenuous meditation, to banish all frivolous, worldly thoughts and to achieve the prescribed inner peace pleasing to God. In the middle of the night the noise of a tile falling from the roof caused her to start up from her prayer cushion and hurry out to the veranda. How mild the night was! How beautifully the moon shone! Like a little waterfall, its beams rippled through a thin layer of cloud which stretched before it. The racket which had just startled her had come from a pair of cats which were frisking about on the roof, alternately caterwauling amorous airs to each other. How she envied the little creatures! How forsaken and lonely she felt! Again and again the honeyed words which Pao Yu, the child of the red dust, had lavished on her today, came into her mind. For a long while she stood leaning on the parapet, gazing dreamily into the moonlit night, before she turned back with a sigh to her cushion of meditation. All her peace of mind was at an end. In the latter half of the night her spirit broke loose from its holy bonds and swept her into forbidden regions of worldly actions. The demons of temptation entered into her body and dangled fleshly visions before her. At first these took the form of high-born and high-spirited youths who wooed her and whom she proudly scorned; female marriage brokers scrambled for possession of her and tried to drag her into a bridal litter; and finally she saw herself as the booty of robbers, who dragged her away and were about to violate her. Bathed in sweat, foaming at the mouth, with outspread hands and staring eyes, she awoke from her ecstasy. For days she lay in a semi-conscious state until, by dint of swallowing quantities of medicines which the doctor prescribed "for the cooling of the fire in the blood," she finally recovered.

For a long while her illness was the subject of conversation among the young bloods of the town, who declared with many a significant sigh that a beautiful young girl like her was born for marriage and not for self-chastisement and renunciation of the world. Who knows into what unholy hands the beautiful saint might one day fall!

She has not yet been able to free herself completely from the red dust of this world, thought Grief of Spring to herself when she heard of the collapse of her chess companion. What a pity that it is not my good fortune to dedicate my life to the service of Buddha, as she has done, and to live together with her. I would chase away the demons of temptation with the power of my prayer if they ever again should take it into their heads to torture and plague her."

And once more she became zealously immersed in the study of her "Manual of the Art of Chess Playing," in order to be well prepared for the next game with her beloved playmate.

His studies and his attendance at school had occupied Pao Yu so intensively recently that his visits to Black Jade had become gradually less and less frequent. Moreover, Black Jade found him altered in his nature too, for he had become very grave, reserved, and silent with her of late. She thought sorrowfully of the old days, the first happy years of their life together. The things that were a flimsy pretext for blame in those days, a harmless source of annoyance and tiffs—his boyish vehemence, his exuberant, thoughtless chatter—these were just the things that she missed most in him now. When her maid Cuckoo had laid out her warm winter clothing for her a little time ago, and she had found packed away among them in a little bundle three souvenirs of those days—the unfinished perfume bag, the tassel from his amulet which she had once defiantly cut with scissors, and the two handkerchiefs which had come from him and which she had covered with verses, the blotted writing of which still bore traces of the tears she had shed then—she was overcome with intense emotion. For a long time she could not tear her eyes away from those dear memories, and new tears were added to the traces of the old ones. The somber atmosphere of melancholy which the park breathed in those gray days of falling autumn leaves matched her own somber mood exactly. The one thing which upheld her was the belief which she, like her maids, still firmly held: that she was Pao Yu's destined bride.

One day, after one of the usual brief and conventional visits of the beloved, she had lain down on her bed and sent the maid Cuckoo away, so that she might be alone with her thoughts. When Cuckoo went into the maids' room she found little Snowgoose there, looking obviously upset, hunched up on a chair, brooding by herself.

"Is there something worrying you?" she asked. The little one nodded sadly and, putting her finger significantly to her lips, drew the elder girl out of the door with her on to the terrace facing the front garden.

"I've sad news. Pao Yu is betrothed to someone else!" she whispered.

"Oh, but that can't be true!" cried Cuckoo, horrified.

"Hush! Don't talk so loud! It is true! Everyone except ourselves knew it long ago."

"How did you find out?"

Snowgoose drew Cuckoo two steps farther away, for coughing and a creaking of the bed had become audible inside. With her head turned back she listened intently until all was quiet again in Black Jade's room. Then she continued in a lower voice: "I heard it yesterday in the Hermitage of Clear Autumn Weather. Miss Taste of Spring was not there. We maids were talking together about the latest news of the house, and the conversation turned on Pao Yu. He was so immature and childish and full of naughtiness, not a bit a gentleman yet, the writing maid remarked quite casually; it was unbelievable that he was already engaged and would marry soon. When I asked, very much astonished, to whom he was betrothed, I was told to the only daughter of a certain rich retired prefect named Chang, a distant relative of Princess Shieh. Because of the relationship, so it was said, there was no need for lengthy negotiations. Mr. Cheng had accepted straight away the proposal which was made by the go-between, a young colleague in the Ministry, named Wang. In short, the engagement was an accomplished fact. Of course, I was simply knocked over by this news. Our poor little mistress!"

"But why were we told nothing?" asked Cuckoo after a pause.

"At the express wish of the old *Tai tai* the engagement was to be kept secret for the time being for the sake of Pao Yu. She's afraid that if he hears of it too soon he'll get out of hand and become quite hopeless at his studies. And the writing maid told the secret to me under the seal of silence. Our young lady must not get to know anything about it on any account!"

A screeching voice behind their backs:

> "Go to the young lady!
> Take her a cup of tea!"

caused the two waiting maids to wheel around in alarm, but it was only the parrot, saying the little piece he had learned. They gave the gaily colored disturber a few words of scolding, then darted back to their mistress.

"Where were you two hiding? One can call and call, and no one comes," said Black Jade in a weak voice; then she asked listlessly for a few things, and immediately dismissed the maids again. When Cuckoo brought her food in the evening she found her mistress lying apathetically on her bed, almost uncovered. She carefully drew the disarranged bedclothes up over her and crept softly out, as she did not seem to be wanted. When she came back later to clear away the dishes, she found the food untouched. The bedclothes were again pushed down to the foot of the bed as if it were hot summer and not cool autumn. Once more Cuckoo drew up the bedclothes, let down the curtains, and carried out the untouched meal.

"Do you think she could have heard us? Such an extraordinary change has come over her!" she remarked anxiously to Snowgoose when she got outside.

As a matter of fact, Black Jade had understood only about seven- to eight-tenths of the whispered conversation out on the terrace steps, but what she had heard had broken over her head like a tidal wave of despair. How uncannily her terrible dream was being fulfilled. Life seemed to be without a purpose henceforth. Was she to look on and see her beloved bringing home another bride? The thought was intolerable to her. She resolved to quench the flame of her own life slowly and deliberately, instead. She would not touch another bite of food or

鶯兒

take any more medicine, and in this way would artificially undermine her already frail health, so as to bring about an early end. A great and joyful sense of peace pervaded her. Was it not a beautiful and worthy task gradually to free oneself from the red dust of worldly strivings, and to float upwards, as it were, into the spiritual region of great illumination and negation? She carried out her grim resolution with such determination that by the end of two weeks she no longer had the physical strength to eat as much as a single grain of rice, even if she had had the will to do so. No one in the house except her two maids guessed the reason of her fading, and for fear of being blamed by the Ancestress the maids did not dare to open their mouths. And now matters had gone so far that Black Jade's life seemed on the point of coming to an end.

"I must run over and tell the ladies that our little mistress is near her end; sit by her while I am away!" said Cuckoo to Snowgoose, and left her alone with the sick girl. In her childish ignorance of nature the little maid thought that her mistress must be already dead, so still and motionless was she. While she was watching alone by her, in fear and trembling, the writing maid from the Hermitage of Clear Autumn Weather appeared outside. She had been sent by Taste of Spring to ask how Black Jade was. Snowgoose was immensely relieved to have company at last, and she took the visitor into the sickroom.

"Where's Cuckoo?" asked the writing maid.

Snowgoose pointed to Black Jade.

"She has just run over to tell them that our little mistress is dying."

Believing that there was no need to restrain her tongue since her mistress was after all no longer conscious, she continued: "Was what you told me some time ago really true about the news of the betrothal of Pao Yu to the daughter of one Prefect Chang?"

"Of course it was true. I had it from the maid Siao Hung, and she had heard of it from her mistress, Madame Phoenix, but there's been a change since. When Miss Taste of Spring sent me over to Madame Phoenix the next day to find out more about it, Madame Phoenix told me that the old *Tai tai* had not approved this betrothal, and had said that it was the rash plan of a young ministerial colleague and guest of our Mr. Cheng. The gentleman had put forward his proposal to curry favor with Mr. Cheng and secure future advantages from him in his career. When examined more closely, the plan proved to be quite unfeasible. The Ancestress declared that she already had another bride in mind for Pao Yu, one who lived with us in the park. Moreover, she declared that she wished him to marry within the clan."

This was certainly an undreamed-of revelation to Snowgoose.

"What? Then my poor little mistress has thrown away her life for no reason at all, and it is all my fault!" she cried, astonished and dismayed.

"What do you mean by that?"

"When I was telling Cuckoo the news of the alleged engagement to the daughter of Prefect Chang, she overheard us, and she took it so terribly to heart that it has finished her."

"Do be careful! Do be quiet! She might hear us!"

"Oh, it's not necessary, alas, to be careful any more. She lost consciousness long ago. In another few hours . . ."

A faint "hem" from Black Jade caused Snowgoose suddenly to stop talking. Cuckoo, who had just come back, rushed in and bent over the patient.

"Water!" came the voice, faint as a breath yet audible, from the mouth of the girl they had thought was all but dead. Snowgoose dashed into the kitchen and brought back half a bowl of boiled water. By a scarcely perceptible movement of her head the patient indicated that she wished to sit up. Cuckoo pushed one hand gently under her neck and raised her head while with the other hand she lifted the bowl of water carefully to her lips. With breathless expectation the three maids followed every movement. And in fact the bloodless lips did draw in the vivifying liquid. Once, twice, thrice, she swallowed, then shook her head. Cuckoo set down the bowl. Taking a deep breath, Black Jade let her head fall back on the pillows. Then, after quite a long while, she opened her eyes.

"Wasn't Taste of Spring's writing maid here just now? I thought I heard her voice," she said, faintly.

"Yes, here I am!" replied the writing maid, coming up close to her.

"Greet your young lady from me!" the words came faintly but distinctly after another pause. The writing maid nodded and quietly withdrew. She was hardly out the door when a swarm of ladies of the Yungkuo palace—the Ancestress, Madame Cheng, Widow Chu, and Phoenix with their attendants—came in breathless with excitement and haste. After Cuckoo's alarming report they had come expecting to find a dead girl before them, and were not a little surprised now to find a patient who, though physically weak, was nevertheless already well on the way to recovery, to judge by the bright expression of her face. Quite dumfounded, Phoenix took Cuckoo aside: "What were you telling us just now, and why did you frighten us unnecessarily? Why, she's not so bad at all!"

"I cannot understand it! She was really very bad a little while ago, and now this sudden improvement . . ." stammered Cuckoo, embarrassed.

"Come now! Do not scold her for being too careful! Better a visit for nothing than to arrive too late," said the Ancestress, turning with a smile to Phoenix. And fully reassured, she withdrew with her retinue.

Shortly before, when the writing maid had come in, Black Jade was in fact lying seemingly lifeless physically, but she still had sufficiently clear consciousness left to be able to catch the main gist of the maids' loud conversation. The joyful news that the first marriage plan had been given up meantime and that according to the will of the Ancestress a girl of the clan, who lived in the park—who could surely be only herself—was the bride destined for Pao Yu, had acted on her condition like a magic drug. New joy in living instantly flooded her body. Her austere resolve to enter as a spirit into the great void was forgotten. Her life was worth living once more, and she wanted to live.

Black Jade recovered quickly. Her two maids breathed sighs of relief and recited many fervent prayers of thanksgiving to Buddha. They recalled the similar instance when Cuckoo had let drop a hint about Black Jade's return to her native place and Pao Yu had immediately become mortally ill, and they concluded from this that the two must definitely be destined by Providence for each other. Snowgoose felt relieved of a heavy weight on her conscience and swore she would never blab again, even if she were to see with her own eyes Pao Yu leading home another bride. The truth about Black Jade's sudden illness and sudden recovery naturally could not remain hidden indefinitely, and it went from mouth to mouth and was gossiped about thoroughly among the servants. And so it finally reached the ears of Phoenix and the other ladies of the Yungkuo palace. As it was, they had already silently put two and two together, and now saw their assumptions verified.

"As long as the two were children I let them live and play freely together," said the Ancestress, "but now that they are grown up, it seems to me more wise and proper to separate them. What do you think?" she asked the other ladies.

"Of course Pao Yu is still only a very silly boy, but Black Jade is already a mature, fully developed young lady," remarked Madame Cheng after an embarrassed pause. "It might be wrongly interpreted if they were to be suddenly separated now. It would be better if we made them man and wife without delay."

The Ancestress knit her brows.

"Black Jade may have her good points, but she also has her peculiarities and whims. Besides, her health is very poor. I am afraid that she will not live long. I do not want her as wife for Pao Yu; Precious Clasp is the right girl for him," she decided.

That was exactly what Madame Cheng wanted, but because Precious Clasp was more closely related to her than Black Jade was, she had refrained out of discretion from saying so at first.

"The old *Tai tai* is perfectly right," she now agreed fervently. "But let us also plan for Black Jade's future at the same time. A big girl like her certainly needs an object for her affections. If she is really fond of Pao Yu it will come hard on her to see another girl getting him."

"Pao Yu is nearer to us than Black Jade; besides, she is younger than he is. Therefore, we must first settle Pao Yu; that is the right order in which to proceed, not the other way. But we will keep his betrothal secret from Black Jade, so as not to hurt her," declared the Ancestress.

"Did you hear that?" said Phoenix emphatically, turning to the serving women and waiting maids. "Not a word about Pao Yu's betrothal! Anyone who chatters will have to look out for her skin!"

If the ladies had had their way, the marriage decided upon would have been an accomplished fact without further delay, now that Aunt Hsueh too had given her consent in principle. But Mr. Cheng considered that as long as the wretched business of the nephew Hsueh Pan, who was still in prison, remained hanging over the family, the festive spirit fitting a wedding would be wanting. Besides, the New Year Festival, with all its bustle, was close at hand. It was therefore decided, at his suggestion, to postpone the customary exchange of betrothal gifts until after the New Year Festival, and to celebrate the wedding itself in the early spring, after the birthday of the Ancestress.

All this was decided behind Pao Yu's back, while at the same time Black Jade, victim of a beautiful delusion, was setting her feet once more in the red dust of earthly desires.

CHAPTER 42

The Ancestress puts a reverse interpretation upon the evil omen of the begonia blossoming in winter and tries to drown anxious doubts in the joyous tumult of a banquet. Pao Yu loses the spirit stone and forfeits his reason as a consequence.

PAO YU LIVED ON UNAWARE, AS BEFORE, OF WHAT HAD BEEN DECIDED behind his back. To be sure, it seemed peculiar to him that he had not seen his cousin Precious Clasp for such a long time, and that she no longer appeared at any of the family gatherings. But when he asked her mother, Aunt Hsueh, why that was, he always received such plausible and specious answers, as reasons for her absence—such as that she was not very well or was kept away by domestic duties—that his anxiety was immediately dissipated.

The same ignorance pervaded the Bamboo Hermitage, and under its protective veil Black Jade improved perceptibly from day to day. Once this veil was very near to being cruelly torn down. One morning in the eleventh month Cuckoo had visited Mandarin Duck, and had to hear from her, at great length, how the Ancestress had been overwhelmed of late by female marriage-brokers who tried to persuade her now to this and now to that splendid match for Pao Yu, and how heartily sick and tired the Ancestress was of these futile importunings. Cuckoo was naturally very eager to know why the Ancestress so resolutely turned down all these tempting proposals. Mandarin Duck was in the very act of opening her mouth to come out with the truth when she was called away to the Ancestress, who had just waked up. No wiser than before, but filled with secret misgivings, Cuckoo had returned to the Bamboo Hermitage. Black Jade was still in bed, and was busily engaged in putting literary manuscripts in order.

"Well, where have you been?" she asked Cuckoo.

"I was visiting another maid."

"I bet it was Pearl," cried Black Jade merrily.

"I don't know what I'd want to be visiting her for."

Black Jade, whose thoughts were centered only in Pao Yu and the Begonia Courtyard, was immediately peeved. She had been hoping for a message from the beloved one.

"It's really all the same to me whom you visit; bring me my breakfast!" she snapped. She was just drinking her first bowl of tea when she heard an excited buzz of voices coming over from the park path, not far from the front garden. Several garden women were standing there, chattering eagerly together, instead of sweeping the paths. Black Jade sent out to ask what the important cause of discussion was.

"A miracle of nature has happened in the park," they said. "The withered side of the golden begonia in the Begonia Courtyard has suddenly come into bud in the middle of the winter, and today it has broken into flower. Our little master spoke of it yesterday, when he noticed that it had buds in several places, but no one took him seriously. Today the buds have opened and everyone is rushing to the Begonia Courtyard to view the miracle. The Ancestress is expected to arrive with her ladies at any moment. We have been sent by Madame Phoenix to sweep the park paths clear of fallen leaves and branches before her."

"Oh, I must go there too and be ready to receive the old *Tai tai*," cried Black Jade; and she jumped quickly out of bed and slipped on her clothes. She had barely time to glance at the mirror and tidy her hair before Snowgoose announced that the old *Tai tai* had arrived, and that she, Black Jade, was expected in the Begonia Courtyard. Accompanied by Cuckoo, she set out and saluted the Ancestress and her company—Princess Shieh and Madame Cheng, and Widow Chu, and the cousins Taste of Spring, Grief of Spring, and Wreath of Clouds. Phoenix was absent, owing to indisposition. They all stood chatting merrily around the Ancestress, who had sat down on Pao Yu's favorite bench in front of the golden begonia, and were gazing with astonishment at the strange phenomenon of nature and indulging in a host of excited comments and varying interpretations.

"The normal time for the begonia to bloom is certainly the third month," said the Ancestress. "To be sure, we are now well into the eleventh month, but the weather is so exceptionally mild that it might be the tenth or the third month. I find nothing disturbingly strange about this late blooming."

"The old *Tai tai* has more experience and judgment than the rest of us, and doubtless sees the matter in the right light. The phenomenon is certainly not an evil omen," agreed Madame Cheng fervently.

"But the part which is now in bloom has been withered for the past year. Why does it come into bloom now, at such an unusual time? This must certainly have some meaning!" objected Princess Shieh.

"It surely has a meaning, and a favorable one. In my simple view this blossoming points to a joyful event soon to happen in Pao Yu's life," said the Widow Chu, laughing.

Every freak of nature is of evil omen. This untimely blossoming is contrary to nature and certainly forebodes evil, thought Taste of Spring to herself. But she did not dare to express her opinion lest she should annoy the Ancestress.

Black Jade, on the other hand, eagerly and joyfully accepted the Widow Chu's assertion about the approaching happy event, and related it as a matter of course to her own wedding with Pao Yu.

"Trees and shrubs are creatures with souls, and there are many examples to prove that they react in sympathy with the weal or woe of the human beings who live beside them," she declared. "It would seem that by this blossoming the begonia is showing its joy at the fact that Cousin Pao Yu has been studying so well of late and is pleasing his father so much."

Her interpretation met with the lively approval of the Ancestress. Meanwhile the seniors, Prince Shieh and Mr. Cheng, had arrived together with the juniors, Chia Huan and Chia Lan, to view the phenomenon of nature.

"The thing bodes no good. The tree of ill omen should be simply cut down," demanded the superstitious Prince Shieh.

"Why cut it down? For those who do not fear ghosts, no ghosts exist," said the calm and rational Confucian, Mr. Cheng.

"Who is muttering about evil omens and ghosts? We are not going to let any kill-joys depress our spirits! Any misfortune that may befall I take upon myself alone!" snapped the Ancestress.

The two seniors bore their mother's rebuke in meek silence and disappeared immediately on some excuse. But the optimistic Ancestress sent a message to the kitchen, having decided to celebrate what she pleased to consider the joyful event of the miraculous winter blossoming by having a large and merry banquet with the rest of the clan. At the desire of the Ancestress the three juniors, Pao Yu, Chia Huan, and Chia Lan, had to help to enhance the enjoyment of the feast by composing and reciting poetical quatrains in honor of the blossoming begonia.

"We have to thank you for all this jollity," said the Widow Chu jestingly to Taste of Spring.

"What do you mean?"

"Well, it was you, after all, who founded our Begonia Club long ago. And now the begonia itself is making its presence felt; perhaps it wants to become an honorary member of our club."

While everyone was still laughing at her jest and trying to keep the Ancestress in good humor, Pao Yu was secretly torn by two conflicting emotions. On the one hand, he could not help thinking of the dead girl, Bright Cloud, and regretting that she could not blossom into new life again like the half of the begonia tree which had died away. This thought made him sorrowful. On the other hand, he recalled that he had heard shortly before that Phoenix intended soon to let him have a pretty little new maid in place of Bright Cloud. Possibly the sudden blossoming of the begonia pointed to this pleasant change, and this thought cheered him up again. A little while later the maid Little Ping arrived and handed to Pearl on behalf of her mistress Madame Phoenix, who excused herself on the plea of not being well, two strips of satin of the lucky color red, which Pao Yu was to spread over the blossoms, ostensibly as ornamentation but at the same time as a protection against the night frosts, as she explained to the company.

"My goodness! Phoenix thinks of everything! Such consideration for others in spite of all her illness!" said the Ancestress appreciatively.

But when the company had gone Little Ping took her colleague Pearl aside and said to her, looking very solemn: "My mistress puts a bad interpretation on this phenomenon of nature. She wants Pao Yu to cut the red satin into strips and hang the little strips over the ill-omened blossoms so that the lucky red may counteract their unlucky influence."

Pearl followed her advice, but apparently the counter-magic was not strong enough, as was to be seen at once.

Pao Yu had changed his clothes for the visit of the Ancestress, and put on a festive garment. Because the visit came as such a surprise, he had to change very hurriedly. In short, in his haste, he had quite forgotten to put on again the necklet with the spirit stone, which he had taken off. Now, when he was changing again after the visitors had gone, Pearl suddenly missed the amulet from his neck.

"Where's the stone?" she asked, alarmed.

"The stone? You're right. I believe that in my hurry I left it on the little divan table a while ago."

Pearl dashed out to the divan table, but there was no stone there. She looked under the covers and cushions, rummaged through boxes and drawers, ransacked every corner of the room, but she found not a trace of the stone. Pearl began to perspire with excitement.

"Don't worry. It will turn up all right!" he assured her. "Some one of the servants will surely have found it."

But the servants were questioned in vain. None of them knew anything about the whereabouts of the stone.

"There were so many people in the house just now. Perhaps one of your cousins took it for fun, to play a trick on you. It would be a bad joke, but you must take it in good part all the same. Even if you have to beg her for its return on your knees, even if you have to pay a forfeit or a reward to get it back, the main thing is to get it back, for it is a part of yourself, your very life," said Pearl, trembling.

So Musk and Autumn Wave were sent off to the neighboring pavilions in the park, but they soon came back empty-handed. A general state of perplexity and confusion reigned in the Begonia Courtyard; the inmates looked at each other with bleak, listless faces, like wooden statues or plaster idols. Pao Yu's cousins came in one after another. At the suggestion of Taste of Spring the park gates were locked and reliable serving women and trusted waiting maids were sent out to conduct house-to-house searches throughout the park. At the same time a big reward was offered for finding the stone. But although all the buildings, even the most secluded nooks, were thoroughly searched, the stone remained lost.

Widow Chu suggested that a search of the persons of all the female park personnel should be carried out. The young ladies should search their personal maids, and the personal maids should search all the other personnel. This measure, which entailed complete undressing and stripping in the presence of others, was not, to be sure, quite in accordance with the strict rules of decency, but in view of the importance of the missing object it was deemed unavoidable, and the usual considerations were set aside. The proposal was approved by all with the exception of Taste of Spring, who withheld her consent. And so a great hubbub of undressing and washing and cleaning arose immediately.

But this procedure of stripping naked had hardly started when it was stopped again at the instance of Taste of Spring. Taste of Spring had still got the painful memory of the house search and the search of her person which she had suffered at the hands of Wang, the wife of the majordomo, and she scolded the Widow Chu for adopting the methods of that repellent woman.

"This bodily inspection is quite superfluous," she continued. "Who would be so simple as to keep stolen property for a long time on her person and so betray herself? Moreover, I doubt very much whether the stone has been stolen for the sake of gain. After all, it is only of sentimental value to our family, and has no market value for strangers. What would anyone pay for it? I believe that someone who wanted to play a nasty trick on Pao Yu has taken the stone."

Her view met with general agreement, and suspicion was immediately centered on Chia Huan, whose hatred of his more favored half brother was known to all. Chia Huan had, of course, been present earlier at the viewing of the begonia flowers. The maid Little Ping was accordingly sent to fetch the bastard under some innocent pretext. He was invited to a cup of tea and left alone for a while first with Little Ping, who had been assigned the task of coaxing an admission out of him.

"Have you seen Pao Yu's stone, by any chance? It has been missing since this morning," she said in the course of conversation.

Despite her smiling face, the boy felt the pointed allusion to himself. He got red and stared at her, full of hatred.

"What have I got to do with other people's lost belongings? So it seems I'm suspected as the thief, eh?" he muttered angrily.

"No offense meant. We merely thought that you might have wanted to play a little joke; that's why I asked," said Little Ping, intimidated.

"Please ask him yourself! When there are gifts to be distributed I am not present, but when something is missing, people come running to me and suddenly remember me," growled Chia Huan, and went off in a huff. And no one tried to hold him back. Pao Yu was heartily glad to be rid of the repellent fellow.

"You shouldn't have brought him over here," he said. "Now he'll probably kick up a row over there, and everyone will get to know of what has happened. The stone is not so important to me as all that! Let it remain lost and gone for all I care! To look for it any more would be a waste of time. We might as well try to find a needle in a bundle of straw."

"You take the loss too lightly, little ancestor!" wailed Pearl. "The old *Tai tai* will be beside herself when the story gets to her ears, and we maids will be beaten till our bones are broken. It would be better to tell her the truth quite openly at once."

"Nonsense! Tell her that I smashed the stone in pieces!"

468

"That's impossible. She will ask how and why, and will punish us for it. And if she asks to see the pieces, what then?"

"Very well. Then it's better to say that I lost the stone when I went into the town recently."

"But you have been neither to school nor in the town for the last two days."

"No, but I was at a theatrical performance in the palace of the Prince of the Southern Peace the day before yesterday. I could have lost it on that occasion."

"That won't do either," objected Taste of Spring. "Grandmother will ask why you did not announce the loss to her at once, two days ago."

While they were discussing the matter this way and that, and trying to think up a white lie, the excited voice of the secondary wife Chao, the mother of Chia Huan, was heard in the distance. "What does this mean? Accusing my son of theft behind my back! How can my son help it if other people are careless with their belongings and lose them? I won't stand for this underhand treatment. Here, I'm bringing you the thief, and now cross-examine him openly before my eyes, and if he is really guilty you may cut his throat for all I care, or do what you like with him!"

And pushing the howling and bucking boy in front of her, she entered the Begonia Courtyard panting and out of breath. While Widow Chu was trying to calm her, who should be announced—to make matters worse—but Pao Yu's mother! Pearl was so frightened that she would have liked the ground to swallow her. Madame Cheng's arrival had at least the good effect of instantly silencing the screeching of the secondary wife Chao and her son.

The consternation on the faces of those present proved to Madame Cheng that there must be some truth in the rumor that had reached her ears.

"Has the stone really been lost?" she asked. No one had the courage to answer. Pearl felt so guilty that she was about to throw herself at her feet and confess what had happened, but Madame Cheng ordered her to set out on the search forthwith instead of wasting time with useless explanations.

"Pearl could not help it," said Pao Yu, gallantly taking the part of his maid. "I lost the stone the day before yesterday on my way back from the Palace of the Prince of the Southern Peace."

"Why, then, did you not have it searched for earlier? Moreover, it was Pearl's duty to inform me at once. She has the task of helping you to dress and undress. She must surely have noticed the loss of the stone the day before yesterday," replied Madame Cheng, sternly and distrustfully. The secondary wife Chao now chimed in shrilly: "That is even better! He lost it on the road, and he falsely accuses my innocent son . . ."

"Please refrain from those irrelevant interruptions, which have nothing to do with the matter!" said Madame Cheng, harshly cutting her short. At this Widow Chu and Taste of Spring blurted out the truth with one voice. Madame Cheng was utterly dumfounded. There was no use thinking of hushing it up. She would have to shoulder the painful task of taking the Ancestress the news of the misfortune. As she was rising to leave, Phoenix too came in.

"Have you heard it yet?" asked Madame Cheng, turning to her niece with a groan. "Pao Yu's stone is lost and can't be found anywhere. It's terrible. You must do something about it! The stone will have to be found! Pao Yu's life depends on it!"

Phoenix replied: "It will be difficult to find the guilty person if the stone has been stolen. Our servants are too numerous; we can at most know their faces, but how can one see into the heart of each one? In my opinion we must above all avoid allowing any fuss or excitement about it to be known outside. Otherwise the guilty person will be forewarned, and as he has to expect death without burial if convicted, he will be doubly cautious. No, let us instead represent the matter as being of no importance, and spread the rumor that Pao Yu never thought anything of the stone and threw it away deliberately, as he was tired of it. Among ourselves, we must agree and make the servants also understand that, in order to avoid unnecessary disturbance, neither the old *Tai tai* nor Pao Yu's father is to hear anything of the loss. Of course we shall continue to search for the stone, but unobtrusively and secretly, and try to coax it out of its hiding place by cunning. What does the *Tai tai* say to this suggestion?"

"That is all very well, but how shall I hide the loss from my husband?" asked Madame Cheng, after a moment's reflection. She had Chia Huan brought before her.

"You have just been making a row because you were questioned tentatively about the loss of Pao Yu's stone," she said to him harshly. "Do not take it into your head to make any fuss again, and thereby endanger the inquiries which are being made. If you do, woe betide you! Do you understand?"

Mother and son promised to hold their tongues, and withdrew, disconcerted. Madame Cheng then called the most important waiting maids and serving women, and said to them: "The stone cannot have flown away. It must be somewhere in the house. So search for it, but in doing so avoid all gossip and excitement. I give you three days. I cannot conceal the loss from my husband longer than that. If the stone is not found within three days, it will be a serious matter for you all!"

470

After she and Phoenix had gone, there were further earnest discussions in the Begonia Courtyard as to what measures were to be adopted. The wife of the majordomo Ling was called to the council and initiated into the matter. It was arranged with her that none of the servants should be allowed out of the park for three days. If the reason for this measure was asked, only a vague answer should be given about an object which had been lost and must be found, but on no account should it be divulged that the object was Pao Yu's stone.

The wife of the majordomo Ling mentioned in this connection that her husband had recently recovered a lost article with the help of a street soothsayer named Liu, who bore the nickname of "Iron-Jaw." Pearl besought the Ling woman to send her husband at once to find the man and question him about Pao Yu's stone. The woman went straight off to her husband. When she had gone Wreath of Clouds said: "Why need we send out for some wandering soothsayer? Surely, we have all that here much nearer, and much better too; for as far as I know, our saint in the Kingfisher's Cage also understands the art of soothsaying."

This was something new to the others, and at the urgent entreaty of Pao Yu's maids, Wreath of Clouds went off to the Kingfisher's Cage to visit the anchoress Miao Yu. After a while the woman Ling came back and reported that her husband had already questioned the soothsayer Liu. Iron-Jaw had predicted favorably, the stone would quite definitely be found again. At present it was in a certain pawnshop. Her message gave general satisfaction and relief. Now it would surely not be hard to get hold of the stone. It would only be necessary to search in all the pawnshops of the town one after another. And once the stone had been located the name of the thief could be found out with the aid of the shop account books. The woman Ling had to set out once more, this time to inform Madame Cheng and Phoenix of the latest development. Meantime everyone waited eagerly for the answer which Wreath of Clouds would bring back from the Kingfisher's Cage.

The beautiful anchoress refused at first when Wreath of Clouds laid her request before her. Her intercourse with the young ladies was of a purely spiritual, selfless nature and did not serve any utilitarian, prosaic ends, she said; and besides, she was not yet deeply versed in the art of soothsaying. Only when Wreath of Clouds had represented to her in truly moving words and with many humble bows that Pao Yu's life was at stake did she allow herself to be persuaded. "I have not renounced the world to be bothered again and again with worldly matters," she sighed, "but that has been the case ever since I came to live among you. If I do what you ask of me now, no doubt others will come in the future and disturb me in my holy peace."

On her house altar, before the statue of Buddha, she laid a flat soothsayer's dish covered with a layer of sand, set some incense alight, and wrote down a formula of incantation. After she and Wreath of Clouds had performed a kowtow before the image of Buddha and recited the magic formula aloud as the incense burned, the two together, with blindfolded eyes, took hold of the magic stylus and allowed it to trace its magic writing on the layer of sand in the dish. And the stylus wrote:

"Whence came I,
Whither go I,
　　No sign betrays.
Under a green crag,
Near an old pine tree—
　　Those are my ways!

"You would seek me?
You'd come to me?
　　Not so, not so!
Tall hills divide us—
Loud laughter only
　　Will greet you. Go!"

That certainly sounded very mysterious. Neither Wreath of Clouds nor Miao Yu was able to interpret the verses. But there were such clever people among the inmates of the park, they would surely be able to make it out, said the anchoress ironically, and sent her visitor away.

"Well, what news?" Wreath of Clouds was received with cries of tense expectation when she came back to the Begonia Courtyard. She silently showed them a copy of the magic rhyme. They all craned their necks over the bit of paper and tried to interpret the verse, but in vain. Where were they to find the old pine tree by the green rock? Was this to be understood literally, or was it only an ambiguous paraphrase of the magic language? Pearl took it literally and began searching feverishly all about the park wherever there were rocks and pine trees, naturally without success.

All this time Pao Yu had sat there extraordinarily listless and apparently absent-minded and let the others do the talking. He did not even ask Pearl about the result of her searching when she came back hot and exhausted. At a late hour—it was already nearly midnight—they broke off the long council and went to bed.

As they parted, in depressed spirits, there was one among them who could conceal only with difficulty her secret pleasure at the loss of the stone, and that was Black Jade. Now there would be an end at last to the talk of the union between nephrite and gold desired by fate, which had been occasioned by the corresponding inscriptions on Pao Yu's stone and Precious Clasp's golden amulet, and which to her annoyance had been interpreted as referring to the future marriage of the two.

岫煙

That obscure monk from whom Precious Clasp had received her magic rhyme long ago had been proved a liar and no longer stood between Black Jade and her desires. She now saw the way free for her own union with Pao Yu. This comforting thought caused her to forget her past trials and all her present tiredness, and when she returned at a late hour to her Bamboo Hermitage she actually still felt in a mood for reading.

This time it was not anxiety but joyful excitement which kept her awake until dawn.

The energetic inquiries which Madame Cheng and Phoenix had carried out from the next morning onwards, both in the pawnshops of the town and among the servants, were without success. The stone did not turn up. The three days' limit was long past, but Madame Cheng still did not dare to tell her husband or the Ancestress and preferred to keep the matter dark for a while longer.

It was regarded almost as a piece of good luck that in those very days the Ancestress and Mr. Cheng were distracted by an outside event and thereby hindered from paying the usual attention to Pao Yu. Beginning of Spring, the Imperial wife, had suddenly fallen ill with pneumonia and had died on the eighteenth of the twelfth month, at the age of nineteen. The Court mourning ceremonial now occupied the senior ladies and gentlemen of the Yungkuo palace for many weeks, and Pao Yu, who moreover had been excused from school on account of his bereavement, was left almost entirely to his own devices. One might have expected, perhaps, that he would have used his freedom to play and fool about to his heart's content with his cousins and the maids in the park in his usual way. But since he had lost the stone, the most extraordinary change had come over him. He was sunk in dull apathy and listlessness which increased from day to day and gradually degenerated into actual imbecility. He acted, spoke, ate, and drank only when told to do so. When he was not told explicitly what to do, he simply did nothing, and did not stir from the spot. He could be moved only by definite orders to pay even his accustomed duty visits to his mother and his grandmother.

Pearl, who felt responsible alike for his person and for the loss of the stone, was practically in despair. In her perplexity she turned repeatedly to Black Jade through Cuckoo, and tried to move her to pay a visit to the Begonia Courtyard, for she felt confident that her presence would have a revitalizing effect upon Pao Yu's mind. But Black Jade privately regarded herself as Pao Yu's bride and considered that it would be unseemly to go to visit the betrothed. She would have received him in her own dwelling if he had come to her, but he was unable to rouse himself to this effort.

Precious Clasp was in exactly the same position. She had been informed by her mother meanwhile of her secret betrothal, and since then would trust herself less than ever in Pao Yu's vicinity; she did not even venture to speak his name any more, for this was the correct demeanor of a virtuous bride. Even Taste of Spring no longer put in an appearance; the Begonia Courtyard had become a sinister place, to her mind. Her secret suspicion that the winter blossoming of the begonia was an evil omen had indeed been doubly confirmed by the loss of the stone and the death of Beginning of Spring, which had followed immediately afterwards. And so it became more and more lonely around Pao Yu and Pearl became more desperately uneasy every day.

One day, after the mourning solemnities for the late Beginning of Spring had come to an end, the Ancestress remembered the long-neglected grandson and set out to visit the Begonia Courtyard together with his mother. She was amazed to perceive the change which had taken place in Pao Yu. She had imagined to find him physically sick. But now, when she heard him stammering his *tsing an* with effort and difficulty at Pearl's prompting, and saw his expressionless eyes and his stupid grimaces at all her questions, she realized to her horror that it was his mind that was affected.

"What is the meaning of this? This is a totally different kind of illness from what I have been led to expect," she said, turning sternly to his mother. Madame Cheng realized that the tactic of concealment practiced up to now would no longer serve, and that she would have to confess the truth. She told the Ancestress in a low voice how Pao Yu had recently lost his stone on the way back from a theatrical performance at the palace of the Prince of the Southern Peace—for this was what he had told her at the time—and how he had become manifestly feebleminded since, and how they had searched the park and the pawnshops of the town in vain for the stone.

The Ancestress started up, utterly dismayed. "But this is terrible!" she cried. "The stone is an essential part of his person, his living self. No wonder that he has lost his reason since the stone has been gone! But how on earth could that happen? You are responsible for it. His father will be beside himself when he hears it. We must send word to him at once and ask him to come over here."

Pearl and the other maids had fallen to their knees, terrified. Madame Cheng hung her head guiltily.

"Please do not do that!" she begged. "My husband will get excited and vent his anger on the poor, sick boy. It will make matters worse instead of better."

"Do not be uneasy. If that happens, I am still here," insisted the Ancestress; and she sent Musk to fetch Mr. Cheng. But Musk came back without Mr. Cheng. He had gone out to pay a visit, she reported.

"Very well, we will do without him," decided the Ancestress. "For the time being I will leave the question of blame aside. Chia Lien shall forthwith write a notice announcing the loss of the stone. Whoever brings back the stone shall receive a reward of ten thousand ounces. Whoever gives the first reliable information regarding the whereabouts of the stone shall receive half that sum. Several copies of the notice shall be hung out in the streets through which Pao Yu passed recently on his way home from the Prince's palace. There is no other way of dealing with the matter. If I were to wait for you and your people I might wait a long time before the stone would turn up."

In the same hour Chia Lien had to write the notice and have it publicly displayed in the streets of the town. Furthermore, the Ancestress took her sick grandson out of the park and brought him to live in her quarters over in the western palace. With him she took two of his staff, Pearl and Autumn Wave.

"That winter blossoming of the begonia plant now seems to me to have been rather sinister," she said to Madame Cheng by way of explanation. "There would have been nothing to be uneasy about as long as the stone was there, but now Pao Yu will be defenseless and at the mercy of any evil spirits which may be about. I do not want this; that is why I have brought him over here with me."

"Oh, he will surely be safe from all harm in the auspicious presence of the old *Tai tai*," said Madame Cheng ingratiatingly.

"What do you mean by 'auspicious presence'? The main thing is that order and cleanliness reign in my home, and I shall make him read sutras diligently; that will restore the balance of his mind. Go and ask him whether he is pleased with the change."

But Pao Yu's sole reply to his mother's question was a silly grin. Pearl had to repeat the question for him before he got out a halting *hao*, "good." Madame Cheng was moved to tears at this and came back to the Ancestress in such an agitated state that the old lady dismissed her at once.

"I do not need your help any more here," she said. "I shall be able to manage Pao Yu quite well alone. Mandarin Duck will prepare a soul-strengthening cordial for him, but you must conscientiously tell your husband the truth when he comes home this evening. He need not come to visit me today, however, as I do not wish to have any discussions before I go to bed."

When Chia Cheng was returning home that evening he came upon a crowd which had gathered around a poster displayed at a street crossing, and as the traffic was blocked his carriage had to stop for a time so that he was able to hear snatches of talk from the surrounding crowd, such as "A fellow could be a rich man in a twinkling that way!" and

"Just look at that poster! It's there in black and white! Some son of the house in the Yungkuo palace has lost some kind of stone. The exact description of the stone is given on the poster, and underneath the reward: Ten thousand ounces for the finder; five thousand for the first person who reports the whereabouts of the stone."

Mr. Cheng felt he could not believe his ears, and he urged his coachman to drive faster. He could not bring himself to wait to get confirmation inside, so on entering the gateway he straight away asked the porter what the story was. The porter confirmed that at midday today, at the order of Mr. Chia Lien, posters had been put up in the streets. That was all he knew. Mr. Cheng muttered something about the "child of misfortune" and "curse of the family" and dashed off to his wife, from whom he learned the rest. He disapproved of the public announcement of the ridiculously high reward, yet out of consideration for the old *Tai tai* he did not dare to offer any outspoken opposition but confined himself to raging alone with his wife. Furthermore, behind the back of the Ancestress he ordered his servants to have the notices taken down at once. It was repugnant to him to have his name bandied about in public in this way and to see the private events in his house made the talk of the town.

When his servants went out to carry out his orders, it transpired that several of the posters had already been torn down by some unauthorized hand. Several days had passed when a stranger of humble class appeared at the main gateway of the Yungkuo palace and asserted that he had brought back the lost stone.

"Hand it over!" cried the gatekeeper brusquely but at the same time joyfully.

The stranger smilingly produced a roll of paper from under his coat.

"Quietly now! Do you recognize this poster? It was put up by your bosses. And it's written here in black and white: Ten thousand ounces for the finder! Now look at me. I come in here to you a poor devil, right enough, but I'll come out a rich man straight away. So you'd better show me more respect, if you please."

"But you might at least let us see it, then we will go in and give your message and announce you," said the doorkeepers, already perceptibly more polite.

After some resistance the stranger produced a precious stone and held it before their eyes on the palm of his hand.

"Well, isn't that the right one?" he asked with an air of assurance. The doorkeepers looked at the stone for a few moments; then they rushed into the palace to announce the stranger in the inner rooms. Although, being engaged outside, they had only a vague idea of Pao Yu's stone, they did not doubt that they had just seen the real one.

"But is it the real one?" asked Chia Lien, who was deputizing for the two absent seniors.

"We have convinced ourselves of it with our own eyes!" the door-keepers assured him eagerly. "But the man will only give up the stone when he gets the reward into his hand."

Chia Lien hurried off at once with the joyful news to Madame Cheng, and she in turn informed the Ancestress. The news put the whole house in a joyful uproar. Pearl clapped her hands with joy and sent up a fervent prayer of thanksgiving to Buddha. The Ancestress had the stranger brought into the library as an honored guest, and the promised sum laid ready there. But she insisted that before paying it out she must have the stone to examine quietly herself, and she succeeded in having her way.

The ladies who were assembled with the Ancestress watched and waited with feverish impatience for the moment when they would see the stone. At last Chia Lien appeared with a little packet of red cloth in his hand. Before he had time to open it, Phoenix had snatched it and laid it unopened in the hand of the Ancestress.

"She must always get ahead of me! Not the smallest tribute will she allow me to lay personally at the feet of the old *Tai tai!*" said Chia Lien in jest.

The Ancestress made Mandarin Duck put her glasses on her nose, then she slowly opened up the red wrapping, rubbed and felt the glittering thing in the middle of the cloth, and eyed it attentively from every angle. In size and shape it was absolutely identical with Pao Yu's spirit stone, nor was the well-known inscription on the front and back lacking. Yet it seemed to the Ancestress that the tone was somewhat darker and the sparkle somewhat more subdued than she remembered from before. Undecided, she invited Madame Cheng to examine it. Madame Cheng was also unable to give a definite verdict and asked Phoenix what she thought.

"The similarity is deceptive, but there is a perceptible difference in the brilliance and the color," said Phoenix. "The best thing is to let Pao Yu himself examine the stone."

The Ancestress agreed and entrusted the stone to her to show to Pao Yu. Pao Yu happened to be half asleep when Phoenix came in to him with Pearl and Madame Cheng.

"Your stone is found!" said Phoenix, pressing the stone into his hand. Without even troubling to glance at it, Pao Yu listlessly let it fall to the ground.

"Leave me alone! You're only making fun of me!" he jabbered. Phoenix bent down and picked up the stone.

478

"Do at least look at it and say whether it is your stone!" she urged. But Pao Yu's only answer was an imbecile bleat.

"The stone has not got the slightest effect on his mental condition," said Madame Cheng. "That proves that it is not the real one. It is obviously a clever counterfeit which has been made from the description on the poster."

The others had to agree that she was right, and the general rejoicing gave place to indignation and disappointment.

"The impudent faker must be well punished! It is outrageous to carry on such hocus-pocus against strangers!" raged Chia Lien.

"Here! Give him back his stone and send him about his business!" ordered the Ancestress. "Apparently it's some poor devil who was tempted by the high reward. There is nothing new under the sun. Well, this time he's tried it on the wrong people and spent his money and trouble for nothing. And for that reason let us not be too hard on him; if we are, we shall frighten away the real honest finder. Give him a few silver pieces and let him off!"

Chia Lien rushed off angrily with the stone to the library, where the stranger was sitting calmly waiting for his hoped-for windfall. Chia Lien had him bound with ropes by the servants and would have liked to give him a good flogging, but out of consideration for the wishes of the Ancestress he had to control himself. So he confined himself to frightening the man with angry words and threats of legal action, and in this way induced him to confess. The assumption of the Ancestress proved correct. With the help of borrowed money he had got the stone made in accordance with the picture and description on the poster, in order to earn the wonderful reward and to rise above poverty at last— so the poor rogue admitted, with many kowtows of apology. And not with head held high as a rich man, as he had boasted shortly before to the gatekeepers, but timidly and in pathetic hurry, like a fugitive rat, he passed out the gates of the Yungkuo palace, just as poor as he had come in.

But the story of Pao Yu's false stone went the round of the streets and squares, and provided a topic for amused gossip and laughter for a long time.

CHAPTER 43

Black Jade consigns her poetical works to the flames and finally re-
nounces her unhappy love. Precious Clasp crosses the threshold of her
maidenly bower for the last time, and goes through the great ceremony
of her life.

Round about the New Year two outside events, one happy and
the other sad, once more disturbed the accustomed equilibrium of life
in the Yungkuo palace. Chia Cheng was received in gracious audience
by the Son of Heaven and appointed Corn Treasurer of the rich province of Chiang hsi at the suggestion of the Minister of the Interior in
recognition of his incorrupt and disinterested official record. While the
congratulatory banquets and the preparations for his journey were in
full swing the sad news arrived that the Imperial Marshal, Wang Tzu
Teng, Madame Cheng's brother, had fallen ill on his journey from the
provinces to the capital, and had died on the way home owing to lack
of proper medical attention. Thus joy and sorrow were mingled in
equal parts.

One day after his audience of thanks and farewell, Mr. Cheng was
summoned to the Ancestress. She desired, she said, to settle an important matter with him before his departure.

"I am now an old woman of eighty-one years," she began. "You
are about to leave us to take up your new post in the provinces; your
brother-in-law Wang Tzu Teng is dead, alas, so the only supporter and
adviser who will be left to me now is your unpractical brother Shieh.
The problem nearest my heart at present is the welfare and future of
my grandson Pao Yu. His condition causes me grave anxiety, and for
this reason I have sent the wife of our majordomo Lai Sheng into the
town to have his horoscope cast by a renowned soothsayer. The soothsayer considers that only an exciting event of a joyful nature, such as
a marriage, can cure Pao Yu and that otherwise we have to fear the
worst for him. He declared, moreover, that the element gold is of decisive importance for his happiness, thereby confirming that Precious
Clasp is destined for him by Providence. I know that you do not think
much of soothsaying of this kind; therefore I have sent for you and
also for your wife, so that we may discuss the matter together and
come to a decision. Shall we act, or shall we just sit back and let things
take their course? That is the question."

"The old *Tai tai* has always had a motherly care for the welfare of
her son, therefore it is obviously the duty of the son to show himself
worthy of her example by his paternal care for the well-being of his own
child," replied Mr. Cheng. "If I have often been angry with Pao Yu, it

was not through lack of fatherly affection, but solely because it grieves me to see him making so little progress, and to observe that the iron is not turning into steel. I also am troubled about his condition; I also would like to see him happy, and I have nothing against a marriage if it makes him happy and healthy. But I should only like first to assure myself with my own eyes what his present condition is, provided the old *Tai tai* approves. I promise her that I will refrain from any expression of displeasure in his presence."

From the tone of his voice and the redness of his eyelids Madame Cheng could see that he meant this sincerely. At a sign from her, Pearl disappeared, only to reappear immediately with Pao Yu. Pearl led him up to his father as if he were a child, and whispered something in his ear, whereupon he obediently said his *tsing an*. With horror Chia Cheng perceived his wasted appearance and the lackluster of his eyes. After he had observed him for a few moments in silence he signed to Pearl to lead him away. He was moved to the depths of his being by the pitiable sight of his son, and his wife was no less so, as the shine of tears in her eyes betrayed. He stood up and turning to the Ancestress said: "To judge by appearances, the old *Tai tai* is right. We must definitely act, but there is one point still in doubt: Has Aunt Hsueh actually given her consent?"

"She approves, but she would not care to announce her formal consent until the charge against her son Hsueh Pan is settled," replied his wife.

"Hm, as long as Hsueh Pan is in prison his sister cannot very well gaily celebrate her wedding. That would be tactless. And there is another doubtful point too. Pao Yu on his part is still restricted by the mourning for his sister, Beginning of Spring. He would naturally like to let the prescribed mourning period of nine months elapse before thinking of marriage. Reverence for the dead demands this. And there is yet a third matter for doubt. I have to take up my new appointment shortly. I must not render myself guilty of neglect of duty because of a domestic matter. Even if the two other obstacles did not exist, how could we prepare a wedding in the few days at our disposal?"

"Your doubts are fully justified; but, alas, Pao Yu's condition does not allow of any postponement," replied the Ancestress. "I know, however, what we can do. Leave the question of Aunt Hsueh's consent to me. I will go to her together with your wife and put the matter before her. She must send Hsueh Kuo once more to Hsueh Pan's prison and bring back the brother's consent. When he hears that Pao Yu's life depends upon it, Hsueh Pan will surely agree, and then Aunt Hsueh too will no longer withhold her official consent.

"As regards the second point in question, we must for once bow to necessity and set aside the normal rules of etiquette. We will celebrate the wedding extremely simply and quietly. A bridal litter carried by eight men, with twelve pairs of lantern bearers following, should be sufficient. All noisy pomp such as festive music and a wedding banquet will be eliminated. We can make up for this later after the nine months' mourning is over. We shall confine ourselves to selecting an auspicious date for the quiet taking home of the bride; she shall make her kowtows to us and to the ancestors; we will set her on the bridal bed and open the bed-curtain for her; this much ceremony will be sufficient. Precious Clasp is a sensible girl and will not take it amiss if we cut the proceedings short. Further, she will find in Pearl a pleasant and reliable adviser and support. All that remains, then, to be settled is the preparation of a suitable home for the young couple. That is your task, and I am sure that it will not offer any further difficulties. This disposes of the third point in question. And you will embark upon your journey twice as tranquil and contented if you have put this domestic matter in order first and seen the two happily united."

All the same, Chia Cheng was not completely convinced, but out of deference to the Ancestress he expressed no opposition.

"The *Tai tai*'s suggestion is splendid," he said with a somewhat forced smile. "I agree to it, but we must impose the strictest silence on the staff, if we are to escape unnecessary censure and gossip. We shall avoid this only if the wedding is celebrated absolutely quietly."

"Good. Then I do not wish to detain you any longer," said the Ancestress; and much relieved, she dismissed him.

Mr. Cheng chose an imposing, self-contained suite of twenty rooms, situated near his wife's suite, for the future home of the young couple. The furnishing of the rooms and all the other preparations for the wedding he left to the ladies.

Although Pao Yu's rooms in the residence of the Ancestress immediately adjoined the room in which the decisive family council took place, owing to his state of apathy not one word of the loudly conducted discussion had penetrated his consciousness; but Pearl had listened to it all the more attentively. Her own name had struck her ear; the Ancestress had mentioned her with approval and called her the reliable support of Pao Yu's future wife. This made her secretly rejoice; for she saw her future assured and her path in life as smooth and as straight in its course as the waters of the Imperial Canal. It would be easy to get on with a mistress as reasonable as Precious Clasp, who would take off her shoulders at least half the burden of responsibility for Pao Yu. On the other hand, the thought of poor Black Jade saddened her profoundly. Fortunately, she knew nothing of all this as yet; but how would it be when she would awake from her cruel illusion? When that happened one would have to be prepared for the worst. And would Pao Yu be willing to give her up? The two had mutually vowed that they would love each other unto death. She recalled that summer day when, completely carried away by the intoxication of his feelings, he had accidentally addressed to the ears of her, Pearl, the confession of love which was meant for Black Jade. She thought of how he had almost died of grief when Cuckoo, by way of testing his feelings, had hinted at an alleged future parting threatening him and Black Jade.

Should he learn now that he was to marry Precious Clasp and sacrifice Black Jade, catastrophe would be inevitable if he had even one spark of clear consciousness left. Was it not her duty to prevent this catastrophe? Could she reconcile it with her conscience to remain silent, and so allow three people to be made unhappy?

Her mind was soon made up. Leaving Pao Yu in the care of the maid Autumn Wave, she entered the adjoining room where the ladies were still assembled. Bending down to Madame Cheng's ear, she asked her to come out as she wished to speak to her. Madame Cheng rose, and together they sought out a quiet, secluded room some distance away. The Ancestress took no particular notice of their departure; she thought that Pao Yu probably wished to speak to his mother, and she went on discussing this and that detail of the wedding ceremonial eagerly with Phoenix.

When Pearl found herself alone with Madame Cheng, she threw herself on her knees before her, sobbing. Madame Cheng raised her to her feet.

"Has someone done you a wrong? Please tell me everything," she said kindly.

"It's not about myself that I wish to speak to you, and actually, it's none of my business, but I can't help saying it," began Pearl. "The old *Tai tai* has chosen Miss Precious Clasp as bride for Pao Yu. The choice is of course splendid, but does the old *Tai tai* not really think that his heart is closer to Miss Black Jade than to Miss Precious Clasp?"

"That may be so. Black Jade also was his companion and playmate from childhood."

"Not only his companion," said Pearl. And in moving words she described the deep and intimate relationship which had developed between the two in the course of the years. And she mentioned too—a thing which she had never mentioned before to anyone—the open declaration of love which, overcome by his feelings, Pao Yu had addressed in error to her instead of to Black Jade that summer evening. Then she recalled how later one little hint from Cuckoo of an alleged future parting had instantly made him mortally ill.

Madame Cheng pressed Pearl's hand with emotion.

"What you tell me only confirms my own private conjecture," she assured her. "How, then, has he taken his father's decision? For he must have been listening to our conversation just now."

"I do not think it is likely. In his present numbed and listless state he is not aware of everything that goes on around him."

"Well, what should we do now?"

"You cannot do otherwise than put the matter to the old *Tai tai* and think up some clever way of preventing disaster."

"Very well. I will speak to the old *Tai tai*," decided Madame Cheng; and she went back to the others.

"What has Pearl been whispering to you so mysteriously just now?" the Ancestress asked her when she came in. Madame Cheng told her everything which she had just heard from Pearl. When she had finished the three ladies remained thoughtfully silent for quite a long while. At last the Ancestress sighed and said: "There is really no need to bother about the girl; but if the boy has also set his heart upon the girl, the situation is certainly difficult."

"I have a plan," exclaimed Phoenix.

"And what might it be?"

"We shall have to carry through a little deception."

"What do you mean by that?"

"At first we must pretend to Pao Yu that Black Jade is finally destined for him, and wait to see how he takes the news. If it leaves him indifferent, no deception will be necessary. If he shows joy, then we simply must use deception."

"And how do you think to carry it through?" Madame Cheng wanted to know. Phoenix bent down and whispered something in her ear, to which Madame Cheng nodded eager agreement.

"Let me into your secret too!" said the Ancestress eagerly. Phoenix unfolded her plan to her, but because of the presence of the servants she whispered once more. This time she had to explain her plan in more detail, for the Ancestress did not understand at once, but finally a smile of enlightenment and secret satisfaction spread over her face.

"Splendid!" she exclaimed. "But certainly somewhat bitter for Precious Clasp. And what about Black Jade?"

"We will leave her out of the game completely. The whole comedy will be enacted only before Pao Yu, and besides it will remain strictly between ourselves."

One day Black Jade set out after breakfast to say good morning to the Ancestress. On the way she found that she had forgotten her handkerchief, and sent her companion, Cuckoo, back to fetch it. Meantime she continued her way alone at a leisurely pace. As she sauntered along, and was getting near that little nook hidden behind rocks where she used once to bury withered blossoms with Pao Yu, a pitiable whimpering sound reached her ear from the bushes by the wayside. She went towards the place from which the voice sounded, and soon came upon a crude and ungainly-looking young girl with big eyes overshadowed by heavy eyebrows, who was sitting on a moss-grown rock, weeping bitterly, all alone. Back Jade guessed that the strange young creature must be a maid employed for rough work somewhere in the palace, and she asked herself with amused surprise how such a rough, uncouth creature as this could feel anything so deeply that she must come here to weep in this heart-rending fashion. The strange girl had suddenly stopped crying and stood up politely at Black Jade's approach, and was now busily drying her eyes.

"Come, what has someone done to hurt you so?" asked Black Jade kindly.

"Judge for yourself, Miss! Was it fair to beat me because I disobeyed an order to keep things dark which I knew nothing about, and because I said a word too much?"

"Who are you, and what order to keep silent are you talking about?"

"I'm Numskull and I'm the old *Tai tai's* kitchen maid. The ban on talking, which I didn't know of, was about the marriage of Master Pao Yu and Miss Precious Clasp."

Black Jade felt as if a thunderbolt had fallen beside her. The ground seemed to quake under her feet, and it was quite a while before she could pull herself together.

"Follow me!" she gasped, and walked on in front of Numskull to the little, quiet nook where the flower grave was. Here they would be quite undisturbed and safe from eavesdroppers.

"So Master Pao Yu is to marry Miss Precious Clasp? And why did they beat you?"

"Mr. Cheng is to go off in a few days to his new position in the province of Chiang hsi. Before he goes Master Pao Yu and Miss Precious Clasp are to be married in a great hurry. That is why there was a big long conference recently between Madame Cheng, the old *Tai tai*, and Madame Phoenix. They were saying that Master Pao Yu needs a strong sensation of a happy kind or something like that, and that the consent of Miss Precious Clasp's mother must be got as quickly as possible. After that . . ."

Here Numskull stopped short and stared grinning at Black Jade. Then, though Black Jade was hardly listening, she continued: "Later, when the two have become man and wife, a man is to be found for you too, Miss. But for this and that reason none of all this was to be talked about out loud. I knew nothing about that order. And when I said to Pearl just now, never thinking, that I was longing for the wedding and that there'd be great goings-on in the house, my big sister, who also works for the old *Tai tai,* came up and boxed my ears. I had disobeyed the order of the old *Tai tai* and I'd be chased from the house in punishment, she said. But what do you think, Miss? Did I deserve to be treated like that, when I knew nothing about that order not to talk?"

"That's what comes of your silly chattering. And now go!" murmured Black Jade in a distracted, absent-minded manner, and slowly turned away. She felt horribly sick. Her stomach heaved and hurt as if it were full of one solid mass of some indigestible, burning mixture of vinegar, and oil, and pepper, and salt, and sugar.

Lost in her thoughts, she moved painfully step by step, and at each step it seemed to her as if her legs were made of cotton-wool instead of bones and sinews and had to bear a load of a hundredweight, so limply and flabbily did they do their work. Without goal or direction she dragged herself along, turning aimlessly and senselessly, now this way, now that, and so moving in a circle, with the result that she found herself back again and again in the vicinity of the footbridge near the blossom grave. At last she stumbled into the maid Cuckoo, who had been searching for her in vain for a long time, to bring her the forgotten handkerchief. With horror Cuckoo observed the faltering gait of her mistress, the fixed expression of her eyes, the deadly pallor of her face. In the distance she saw the retreating figure of a maid, disappearing behind a bend of the path.

"Where are you going? This is the way we get back to the Bamboo Hermitage," she said tactfully, turning to her distraught mistress.

"I want to go to Pao Yu to ask him a question," said Black Jade as if in a trance. Though she did not quite understand her answer, Cuckoo took her gently by the arm and led her out of the park to the residence of the Ancestress. At the entrance to the rooms of the Ancestress Black Jade slackened her pace. She seemed only now to become conscious of the presence of Cuckoo.

"What are you doing here?" she asked in a tone of surprise.

"Don't you remember, I was to come after you with your handkerchief, and I have accompanied you over here from the footbridge."

"Ah, yes. Then you also want to see Pao Yu?"

Cuckoo nodded very slightly. It was clear to her that her mistress must be in a state of temporary mental derangement, and she guessed that her condition somehow had something to do with her encounter with the maid whom she had just caught a glimpse of disappearing around a bend of the path. There may be a nice spot of trouble now when these two poor irresponsible creatures, one of them mad and the other imbecile, meet and talk together, she thought to herself, full of uneasiness. Nevertheless she did not dare to hold her mistress back.

Black Jade seemed suddenly to overcome her former weakness in the most extraordinary way. She no longer needed the supporting arm of the maid, but strode along with a firm and assured gait right up to the entrance of the Ancestress's rooms, and pushed the door-curtain aside with her own hands. Inside, the deepest silence reigned. The Ancestress was just having her midday nap. Nearly all her maids had retired too, some to have a little nap to themselves, others to play a game of dominoes. Startled by the tinkling of the bead curtain, Pearl, who was near the door, stuck out her head.

"Is Pao Yu at home?" asked Black Jade, apparently quite sanely, and without waiting for an answer she walked across to the adjoining room, while Cuckoo tried behind her back by looks and signs to make the unsuspecting Pearl understand that the visitor was in an irresponsible mood. Pao Yu, who was squatting on the divan, dull and listless, did not stir from the spot when Black Jade entered, and did not greet her, but just sat grinning vacantly to himself. Black Jade sat down in an armchair not far from him. He turned his head towards her and for a long while the two sat staring at each other, smiling inanely.

"What do you want?" asked Black Jade at last.

"I want Black Jade," came the answer.

Another long pause followed, during which the two continued to stare at each other. It now became clear to Pearl that the visitor was no less mentally deranged than Pao Yu himself. She could not bear any longer to watch this weird conversation between the imbecile boy and the crazy girl and signed to Cuckoo and Autumn Wave to take Black Jade away. The two took hold of her, one at each side, and gently raised her to her feet. Black Jade allowed them to do so, but then stood for a while staring fixedly back at Pao Yu, smiling and nodding.

"It's time to go back, Miss," Cuckoo insisted gently.

"You are right; it's time for me to go back," repeated Black Jade mechanically, and smilingly turned to go. As soon as they were outside she disengaged herself from her two companions who had been supporting her, and ran so quickly into the park and across to the Bamboo Hermitage that Cuckoo and Autumn Wave were hardly able to keep pace with her.

"*Amida Buddha!* We're safe home at last!" cried Cuckoo, with relief, just as they reached the gate of the Bamboo Hermitage. At the same moment she saw Black Jade stagger forward, and a stream of blood pour from her mouth. The two maids were just able to catch hold of her in time to prevent her from falling. They gently carried her, half unconscious, into the room and laid her on her bed. Snowgoose relieved

Autumn Wave, who had to go back, and she and Cuckoo sat watching by the bedside, weeping.

"Why are you crying?" asked Black Jade quite calmly, when she opened her eyes after a while.

"You have just had a little attack of faintness on the way back here, and it made us a bit uneasy."

"Oh, I'm not in such a hurry to die as all that," replied Black Jade, cheerfully.

After the hemorrhage she felt freed from the inner pressure of sudden excitement which had clouded her mind, and was now quite clear in her head.

On the other hand, she had only a vague memory of what had happened between her meeting with Numskull and the hemorrhage.

With calm resignation she went over in her mind once more the frightful fact which the maid in her simplicity had divulged to her. Now that the beautiful illusion had been shattered, nothing remained for her but to die quickly. That was clear to her. Cuckoo and Snowgoose were actually thinking of running to the old *Tai tai* and reporting what had happened, but then they gave up the idea again, because they did not wish to be reproached for giving false alarms, as had happened once before. Meantime, however, the matter had come to the knowledge of the old *Tai tai* through Autumn Wave, whose agitated manner had attracted attention when she got back. The Ancestress thereupon hurriedly summoned Madame Cheng and Phoenix to a discussion, for they all guessed that Black Jade had somehow or other learned about the decisions reached at the family council.

"I should like to know who has been tittle-tattling. I emphatically ordered the strictest secrecy. Naturally, this makes it more difficult for us to carry through our plan," said Phoenix crossly.

"We can discuss that later, but first let us see how Black Jade is," suggested the Ancestress, and the three of them set out for the Bamboo Hermitage. They found Black Jade in bed, and her deathly pallor horrified them. There seemed to be not another drop of blood left in her cheeks, and her breathing was very weak. Before she could utter a word she had to get over a bad fit of coughing, and her sputum, which she spat into a bowl held by Snowgoose, was profusely mingled with blood.

"The old *Tai tai* lavishes her kindness in vain on me," she said at last, in faltering gasps. The Ancestress was deeply moved. "Do not be uneasy, dear child! If you just take good care of yourself all will be well again," she said consolingly. Then the doctor came, and the ladies had to cut short their visit.

"I certainly would not wish her ill, but I greatly fear she will never get up again," said the Ancestress to Phoenix as they went away. "You must make all the necessary preparations in good time, in case anything should happen to her."

Then she questioned Cuckoo in an effort to find out who had chattered to Black Jade, but Cuckoo could not give her any information.

"It is true that they grew up together as children, and so have become fond of each other," she continued rather dejectedly, turning to her ladies, "but now they are grown up and sensible enough to realize that this kind of intercourse must have its limits. It is necessary to demand that a young girl should be particularly reserved. If Black Jade has been imagining something which she had no right to imagine, then she has shown herself unworthy of all my love and kindness. I have never before spared money where her health was concerned, but if her condition is due to such unseemly thoughts, I have no desire to go to any great expense for her."

"The old *Tai tai* should not worry herself too much about the girl! At the moment Pao Yu's welfare is of more importance," whispered Phoenix. "Above all, we need Aunt Hsueh's final consent as soon as possible. The old *Tai tai* should summon her for a consultation this evening. We can talk things over more peacefully here than over there, with Precious Clasp about."

Her suggestion was acted upon and Aunt Hsueh was summoned to a family council that evening. Before it took place Phoenix visited the sick Pao Yu. She wished to put him to the test.

"Congratulations, Cousin Pao Yu!" she greeted him gaily. "The lucky day for your marriage has been fixed. Well, are you glad?" Pao Yu stared at her and nodded silently.

"Black Jade will be your wife. Are you glad?"

Now Pao Yu beamed all over his face.

"But first you must get quite well and sensible. As long as you behave foolishly, there will be no marriage, your father says," continued Phoenix. She was still not quite clear about his mental state.

Suddenly Pao Yu assumed a completely serious, sensible expression. "I am not foolish at all. It is all of you who are foolish!" he said. Then he stood up and went towards the door.

"I want to go to Black Jade and reassure her," were his words. Phoenix jumped up and pulled him back.

"Black Jade has already been informed. As a virtuous bride she cannot, of course, receive you."

"Shall I at least see her later, at the wedding?"

"Naturally. But only if you are perfectly sensible."

"I have given her my heart. Only she can put it back in my breast," he declared solemnly.

That again sounded very odd. Phoenix, who had just been thinking

489

that he was already cured, felt dubious once more. She visited the Ancestress and informed her of her observations and her doubts. The Ancestress did not know whether she should be happy or saddened by her report; but being in the habit of always looking on the bright side of things, she decided that there was no reason to be too worried about him for the time being, and with Pearl he was in the best of hands.

And so, that evening, the great consultation with Aunt Hsueh took place. She could not shut her eyes to the soundness of the reasons brought forward, and accordingly gave her consent to the hasty and abbreviated procedure. It was decided that Phoenix and her husband Chia Lien should act the part of go-between and that Hsueh Kuo should be sent posthaste to Cousin Hsueh Pan, who was still in prison, to obtain his consent as male head of the family. After everything had been discussed backwards and forwards to the accompaniment of numerous bowls of tea, the consultation ended late that night to the satisfaction of all parties.

Four days later Hsueh Kuo came back from Hsueh Pan's prison bringing the latter's consent. Moreover, he was able to announce that Hsueh Pan would soon be freed. The charge of murder had been dropped, the judge had approved a verdict of accidental manslaughter, and pronounced a judgment which involved only payment of a fine. Aunt Hsueh was greatly relieved. Now the marriage could be celebrated with a good conscience.

The execution of the prescribed formalities was put in hand at once. Hsueh Kuo had to design a beautiful gilded card with the four cyclical double signs of the year, the month, the day, and the hour of Precious Clasp's birth, and hand it over ceremonially to Chia Lien. Chia Lien, on his part, presented the eight-sign card of Pao Yu. The betrothal gifts for Precious Clasp followed two days later. Before they were sent the Ancestress held a great review of them together with her ladies. Pao Yu was also brought to this review. Under the delusion that the presents were for Black Jade, he remarked thoughtfully: "Why all this fuss and bother? First the things are brought into the park at great trouble, then they are taken out of the park again and brought back here. Surely this dragging to and fro twice over is quite unnecessary."

Everyone laughed and exchanged significant glances.

"That does not sound imbecile by any means—on the contrary, it's devilishly clever," remarked the Ancestress contentedly to Pao Yu's mother. And then she proceeded to count and examine the gifts one by one, from a list. This was no small task, for the list contained no less than eighty items of jewelry made of gold and pearls—necklaces, hair ornaments, bracelets, and rings; some forty articles for the toilet; one hundred and twenty bales of silk materials, both fine and coarse, as well as one hundred and twenty ready-made garments for all four seasons. The money which was economized by the omission of the usual wedding feasts was sent in cash together with the gifts.

Under the supervision of Chia Lien and two majordomos, the long column of bearers carrying the bridal gifts set out for Aunt Hsueh's residence in the eastern palace. In order to avoid arousing attention the procession was not allowed to pass through the main gateway, but had to go through the park instead, and out through a back gate. Moreover, Phoenix had given instructions that when passing through the park they were to make as big a detour as possible to avoid going near the Bamboo Hermitage; and none of the park servants was to breathe a word about it in the Bamboo Hermitage. And thus the delivery of the bridal gifts was effected so quietly that the outside world noticed nothing and Black Jade and her maids heard not a word about it.

During the last few days Black Jade had been sinking steadily. She had finished with life and was facing her last hour with calm resignation. In vain her maids tried to raise her spirits and persuade her that her grief was unfounded; had she not seen with her own eyes how mentally sick Pao Yu was, and that a marriage for him in that condition would be utterly out of the question? But all their well-meant efforts only evoked a wan, ethereal smile.

In her anxiety Cuckoo ran at least three or four times a day to the residence of the Ancestress and reported the disquieting state of things, but Mandarin Duck, who no doubt had noticed that Black Jade had lost favor in the eyes of the Ancestress of late, suppressed the messages more often than not. And even when something did trickle through to the ears of the Ancestress, she did not take much notice, for recently her head had been full of other things. Her whole attention was now occupied with the young couple and their approaching marriage. She had the doctor sent for, but that was all the trouble she took for Black Jade. The many visits which Black Jade used to receive when ill in the past, from cousins and aunts, waiting maids and serving women, had also ceased completely. Not a soul bothered about her any more. It had become very quiet and lonely in the Bamboo Hermitage. Black Jade said to herself that it was now time for her to take her leave.

"You have always understood me best of anyone, Cuckoo," she said one day to her first waiting maid, when they were alone together. "Through all these years you have been more to me than a mere servant —you have been a real sister."

Her breath failed her, and she had to pause, while Cuckoo broke into sobs.

"Sister Cuckoo, do be so kind as to raise me in a sitting position; I can speak better then," she continued, with a groan. With the help of Snowgoose, Cuckoo tenderly raised the sick girl in her bed and carefully propped her up behind and at both sides with pillows, so that she could lean back comfortably.

"Bring me my copybook of poems," said Black Jade, turning to Snowgoose. Snowgoose jumped up and brought her what she demanded. Black Jade nodded and indicated with her eyes a chest by the wall but was unable to make her further wish understood, as a fit of coughing stifled her voice. The maids tried to help her, one giving her a drink of water, the other wiping her mouth with a handkerchief. Black Jade took hold of the handkerchief and with it pointed once more in the direction of the chest.

"The one with the writing . . ." she gasped with difficulty.

Now at last the maids guessed her thoughts. Apparently she wanted the two little white silk handkerchiefs, stained with ink and tears, which she had kept in the chest as souvenirs of Pao Yu. Snowgoose opened the chest and took out the two handkerchiefs. Black Jade nodded and had them dropped into her hands.

"Don't bother yourself reading that now, dear young lady! Wait until you're well again!" pleaded Cuckoo gently. But Black Jade, without casting a single glance at the tear-blotted writing, was only occupied in convulsive efforts to tear the handkerchiefs to pieces. She was too weak to do so, however; her trembling hands refused to serve her. Cuckoo guessed that frustrated love moved her to this act.

"It's not worth the trouble," she remarked soothingly. Black Jade nodded and pushed the two little handkerchiefs up her sleeve.

"Light the lamp!" she ordered now, and while Snowgoose was lighting the lamp she continued, after a pause for breath: "Make a fire in the brazier!"

Cuckoo thought that she was cold and wanted to warm herself at the brazier.

"It will be better if you lie down, Miss; I'll put another blanket over you. The fumes of the fire might do you harm," she said. But Black Jade shook her head petulantly. So Snowgoose obeyed her; she went into the kitchen and shovelled glowing charcoal into the bronze brazier, then set it down on its pedestal a little way from the bed.

Black Jade indicated by a movement of her head that she wanted it closer to the bed, so Snowgoose moved it right up to the bed, then ran out to fetch the tablelike brazier pedestal specially meant for bedside use. Hardly had she turned her back when Black Jade pulled the two written-on silk handkerchiefs out of her sleeve. Bending down to the brazier, she gazed into the red glow for a few moments lost in thought, then let the handkerchiefs flutter down on the fire. In a trice the light stuff was burned to ashes. Cuckoo could not prevent it, as she was supporting her mistress and did not have a hand free.

"What are you doing, Miss?" she cried in alarm. Black Jade did not heed her, grabbed the copybook containing her poems, looked into it dreamily, then let it slip out of her hands onto the coverlet again. Cuckoo, fearing she would consign it to the flames too, pushed her shoulder against Black Jade's back, and was about to make a grab for the copybook with her freed hand, when Black Jade with a sudden movement forestalled her and dropped the copybook onto the fire. Just at that moment Snowgoose returned with the wooden bedside pedestal. When she saw the copybook already catching fire in the brazier, she hurriedly set down her load and, heedless of the flames, pulled the burning book out of the fire, threw it on the floor, and trampled it with her feet until the flames were out. But, alas, only a sorry, charred remnant of Black Jade's poetic compositions had survived. Black Jade now closed her eyes contentedly, and sank back exhausted on her pillows.

The next morning when she awoke she seemed to feel somewhat better, but immediately after breakfast alarming attacks of coughing and shortness of breath began again. Cuckoo, fearing the worst, left her in charge of Snowgoose, and dashed off to the Ancestress. She found the place extraordinarily quiet and empty. Neither the Ancestress nor her attendants were there; only three serving women and a few kitchen maids were left behind in the deserted rooms. When she asked where the Ancestress was she got only vague, evasive answers. There was no trace of Pao Yu, Pearl, or Autumn Wave either.

Cuckoo thought she could guess up to eight- or nine-tenths what it all meant and, overcome with bitter feelings, slipped out again. She meant to visit Pao Yu and in her distraught state went to the Begonia Courtyard by mistake. She found the front door ajar and the rooms inside likewise desolate and deserted. Suddenly it occurred to her that Pao Yu had not been living in the Begonia Courtyard for quite a long while past, and certainly would not return there with his young wife, since the place was exposed to the evil influences of the abnormally blooming begonia, but would go to live in a new home somewhere else. If she only knew where! As she walked irresolutely up and down in front of the entrance, she saw a maid who belonged to the household of the Ancestress rushing along in a great hurry. She stopped her and asked her where the new home of the young couple was going to be.

"I really shouldn't tell you," said the maid, lowering her voice, "but if you promise you won't tell Snowgoose . . ."

"Of course I won't."

"Well, the new home which the old master has assigned to the young couple is situated beside Madame Cheng's suite behind the Hall of Fame and Benediction, and they will be entering into occupation today. For the wedding is taking place this evening."

Saying this, she dashed off. Cuckoo stood for a while, overcome by her painful thoughts. Poor forsaken Black Jade, lying wrestling with death on her bed of suffering, and Pao Yu gaily celebrating his wedding behind her back! Was it not enough to draw tears from a stone? How would he face her tomorrow when she went to take him the news of Black Jade's passing? Was he not a detestable creature? Dejected and infuriated, gnashing her teeth and with angry tears in her eyes, she returned to the Bamboo Hermitage.

At the entrance she saw two young maids hanging about, craning their necks watching for her. Their worried, frightened faces boded no good. With a gesture of her hand she signed to them to be quiet as she flew past them. Inside, she found Black Jade lying in a fever, with burning red cheeks, and in her perplexity she sent for old Wang, Black Jade's nurse. But instead of advising her what to do, the old woman exhausted herself in useless lamentations. Suddenly she thought of Widow Chu. She was experienced and prudent, and would be a real help to her. Her assumption that she would absent herself from the wedding ceremony because of her widowhood proved to be correct, and she came over immediately, eager to help, accompanied by two waiting maids. Cuckoo received her at the door and, weeping and sobbing, escorted her in. Unable to speak a word, she just pointed silently to Black Jade's bed. The sight made words superfluous. Widow Chu was deeply moved. She called Black Jade softly by name. To be sure, Black Jade opened her eyelids a little bit and her expression too betrayed understanding, but her bloodless lips remained silent. Her breathing was very weak.

Widow Chu turned to speak to Cuckoo, but Cuckoo had disappeared. Snowgoose pointed to the next room. There she found Cuckoo lying on a divan, sobbing loudly. The colored silk cushion under her head had a wet spot the size of a plate.

"You silly creature! This is no time for crying!" exclaimed Widow Chu, shaking her. "Quick! Get your mistress's shroud ready! Is the poor girl to set out naked on the great journey?"

But Cuckoo sobbed more violently than ever and could not be persuaded to get up. Widow Chu, too, was infected with her tearfulness.

"Come on, my good girl! Get to work! Pull yourself together! You make me as distracted as yourself with your howling!" she continued, wiping her tears and slapping the other on the shoulder.

Hurried footsteps were heard outside, and immediately afterwards

494

the waiting maid Little Ping came rushing in. Taken aback, she stopped on the threshold.

"What do you want? Why are you not over with the others?" asked the Widow Chu.

"My mistress Phoenix sent me over to see how Miss Black Jade was doing, but as you are here my mistress need not worry any more. I would like just to have a look at her."

As she disappeared into the death chamber, the wife of the major-domo Ling Chih Hsiao appeared.

"You have come just at the right time. You must go to your husband at once and tell him to send over the young lady's coffin as quickly as possible," said the Widow Chu. The majordomo's wife nodded, but made no move to go.

"What are you standing there for? Is there something else?" continued Widow Chu impatiently.

"The old *Tai tai* and Madame Phoenix have just had a consultation. I'm to fetch Cuckoo. She's wanted urgently over there."

Before Widow Chu had time to answer, Cuckoo stood up and interposed angrily: "Please go away! Let them kindly wait until my young lady is dead! Then I will go over of my own accord."

She checked herself, suddenly realizing that such bad-tempered speech might perhaps be taken amiss. Then, in a more restrained tone she went on: "Besides, I might take some harmful influences over there, if I am called straight from a deathbed!"

"Leave her alone! She is obviously destined by heaven to be the inseparable companion of her mistress. Won't Snowgoose do instead of her? For though she has belonged to Black Jade from childhood and came with her from her southern home, she is much less devoted to her than the other," said Widow Chu, coming tactfully to the rescue. The majordomo's wife, who was just about to attack Cuckoo angrily, was placated to some extent.

"Very well. I will regard what Miss Cuckoo has said as unsaid. But what shall I say to the old *Tai tai* and Madame Phoenix?"

"Yes, do take Snowgoose over! It will be all the same whichever you take!" interjected Little Ping, who had just come out of the death chamber, wiping her eyes.

"But will she be suitable for the same purpose?" asked the Widow Chu dubiously. Little Ping whispered something in her ear. Widow Chu nodded, satisfied.

"Very well, then. Snowgoose may go!" she decided.

"Yes, if you take the responsibility," declared the majordomo's wife.

"Very well, if you're afraid to; but you are surely old enough to bear some responsibility yourself," said the Widow Chu derisively.

"It is not that I'm afraid, but I want to act correctly and not be responsible for botching the plan which has been decided upon in higher places and which I myself do not know exactly," said the majordomo's wife in embarrassed self-defense. Snowgoose offered no objection, and at Little Ping's instructions quickly put on her best clothes and followed Little Ping to the new home of the young couple, where the wedding party was assembled. She had no inkling of what she was needed for, or why she had had to put on her best clothes. Old Ling was ordered meantime to inform her husband that Black Jade's death was to be expected at any moment and that he should make the necessary arrangements without delay.

From the moment that he had heard from the lips of Phoenix the joyful news that he was to marry Black Jade, Pao Yu had revived visibly. True, he had not yet recovered his mental powers sufficiently to be able to see through the deceit which was being practiced on him, but in the last few days he had been transformed physically and mentally, so to speak, and so great was his joyful impatience that he could hardly wait to see the beloved again as bride. He was now sitting, dressed in his wedding finery, in the midst of the assembled ladies of both palaces, feverishly awaiting the arrival of Black Jade.

"Why is she not coming? After all, the way from the Bamboo Hermitage to here is not so far," he asked, turning anxiously to Pearl.

"Be patient! She will arrive punctually at the lucky hour which has been fixed," said Pearl, trying to calm him. Then he heard Phoenix saying to his mother: "Even if noisy wedding music with beating of drums must be dispensed with in view of the Court mourning, a wedding quite without music seems to the old *Tai tai* to be really too dull and colorless. Therefore, at her wish I have ordered our troupe of house musicians to play a little accompaniment of flute music at the arrival of the bride and during the ceremony."

The lucky hour which had been sought out in the calendar had come at last, and, preceded by twelve pairs of palace lantern bearers, the gay red bridal litter arrived.

The troupe of girl musicians, who had taken up their position in front of the Hall of Fame and Benediction, began playing a gentle melody on their flutes. Now the procession halted and the litter was set down. The master of ceremonies came up to the door and invited the "New Lady" to dismount. With strained attention Pao Yu watched from his hidden vantage point inside as the heavily veiled "New Lady" allowed herself to be helped out of the litter and, leaning on the arm of a red-robed "Maid of Joy," slowly mounted the steps leading up to the hall. And who do you think, esteemed reader, that red-robed "Maid of Joy" was? No other than Snowgoose!

Why is Snowgoose and not Cuckoo escorting her? thought Pao Yu to himself, surprised. Why yes, of course, she brought Snowgoose with her years ago from her southern homeland, so Snowgoose is nearer to her than Cuckoo, who only began her service with her here, he concluded after further reflection, and was reassured once more.

Inside the hall the bride now performed, one after another, on the instructions of the master of ceremonies, the prescribed kowtows before heaven and earth, before the Ancestress, and before the father-in-law and mother-in-law. Then she was led into the bridal chamber, where the ceremonies of "climbing onto the bed" and "raising the bed-curtain" were performed in accordance with old Chin ling[1] custom.

In fact Chia Cheng had not given any credence to the verdict of the soothsayer that Pao Yu required some strong impression of a joyful nature for his cure. Only respect for the Ancestress had restrained him from expressing his doubts aloud. His satisfaction was all the greater now when he perceived that Pao Yu had become a perfectly reasonable being once more under the influence of this wedding.

The new bride had taken her place in the prescribed manner on the edge of the bed. Now the time had come for the ceremony of the lifting of the veil, which, according to correct form, was to be carried out by the bridegroom. This was the great moment to which the Ancestress and her ladies were looking forward with tense expectation and secret trembling. Pao Yu walked up to the new bride, but a chance access of foolish shyness at first paralyzed his hand and caused him to put his mouth in motion instead. "Are you quite well again, now, *Mei mei?* It's so long since I've seen you! But why do you keep going about with that silly thing on your head?"

He was about to make a grab at the veil, and the movement of his hand was already causing the Ancestress to perspire with fear from every pore. But then he let his hand drop again irresolutely, for it suddenly passed through his mind that Black Jade was easily offended and did not like any hasty action. He must be very careful in his behavior with her. So he paused quite a while before at last taking hold of the veil and drawing it gently off the head of the "New One." Snowgoose took the veil from him and carried it out, but the vacancy caused by her disappearance was immediately filled by Precious Clasp's waiting maid Oriole.

Pao Yu blinked hard. Was not that Precious Clasp who was sitting

[1] The scene of the story is usually described merely as "the capital" but sometimes as Chin ling or Golden Tombs, a name believed to be derived from the Tombs of the Emperors in the vicinity of Peking.—*Translators' Note.*

before him on the edge of the bed? He shone the lamp on her face; he rubbed his eyes. There was no doubt about it; it was she. And there was her maid Oriole suddenly standing by her side. Where, then, was Snow-goose gone to? Pao Yu did not know whether he was awake or asleep. Listlessly and without will, he let them take the lamp out of his hand and press him down onto a chair. And he just sat there, unable to get out even half a word.

The Ancestress became desperately uneasy. She feared that he would relapse into his former condition. While Phoenix and Princess Chen brought Precious Clasp into the next room, she herself took charge of Pao Yu, led him personally to the bed, and told him to sit down comfortably on it.

"Where am I? But it's all only a dream, isn't it?" he said, turning to Pearl, after thinking for a long time.

"It's not a bit of a dream! It's absolute reality! Today is the happy day of your wedding! How can you talk about dreaming? Please don't let the old master hear you; he's in the next room!" replied Pearl.

Pao Yu looked into the next room. He saw Precious Clasp sitting there.

"Who is that beautiful girl there?" he whispered to Pearl, pointing with his finger.

"Your new bride, of course!" replied Pearl, restraining herself with difficulty; and all those present turned their heads away to hide their laughter.

"And who is my new bride?" asked Pao Yu, continuing his questions undeterred.

"Miss Precious Clasp."

"And what about Black Jade?"

"The old master has given you Precious Clasp for a wife. Why do you keep on speaking Black Jade's name?" said Pearl impatiently.

"But she was here just now! I saw her Snowgoose with my own eyes. It seems to me that you have all joined in a plot against me and are making game of me."

Phoenix came up to him and exhorted him gently: "Do have consideration for Precious Clasp! She is sitting there listening to everything you are saying. You must not offend her or the old *Tai tai* will be angry with you."

But her warning had no effect. He lost the last remnant of his self-control.

"I want to go to Black Jade!" he shouted, suddenly becoming violent. The ladies pressed anxiously around him and tried in vain to calm him, while Precious Clasp sat in the next room, looking on and listening, deeply pained, to the whole scene. It is certainly a relapse into his former condition, she said to herself, and continued in her attitude of bridal reserve. At last, with the help of lavish clouds of narcotic incense, they succeeded in causing him to fall asleep and in this way reduced him to silence. Sometime later Precious Clasp, apathetically obedient, allowed herself to be led away by Phoenix, not to the bridal bed, but to a partitioned-off sleeping place, where she was put to bed fully dressed. The ladies now retired, relieved, to their places in the adjoining room. There all of them, with the exception of the Ancestress, had to sit up, remaining awake, until the next morning, as custom prescribed.

It happened that the next day was the lucky day which had been picked out in the calendar for Chia Cheng to set out on his journey to the South. Mr. Cheng had no knowledge of what had happened in the bridal chamber the evening before. He was under the delusion that everything was as it should be, and he was consequently in excellent spirits. Actually, the ladies were deliberately keeping him in ignorance, for they did not wish to depress his spirits before the journey. At the great farewell the Ancestress was able to arrange matters in such a way that he only saw his son face to face during the few brief moments required for receiving his farewell kowtow.

"Strictly speaking, he should go with you the prescribed ten miles of the parting escort," she said, "but he has only partially recovered his health. He was so exhausted by the excitements and exertions of yesterday that we could not even allow him to sleep in the bridal bed with his bride last night. I consider that it would be unwise to expose him to great physical exertion again today in his poor health. But if you insist, of course, I shall have him got ready for the journey at once. Yet perhaps you will be satisfied if he comes to you for a few moments and performs his farewell kowtow once more?"

"I set no store on his parting escort," replied Chia Cheng. "The principal thing is that he should devote himself zealously to his studies from now on. That is much more important to me than the fulfillment of an empty formality."

The Ancestress, well satisfied, beckoned to Mandarin Duck, and whispered an order to her. Mandarin Duck ran off, and after a little time Pao Yu appeared, escorted by Pearl. His father addressed a few words of exhortation to him. Pao Yu replied with an obedient *Shih*, performed his farewell kowtow, and was dismissed. Finally, Chia Cheng once more enjoined his wife very earnestly to watch sharply over Pao Yu and to see that he was well prepared, and sat for next year's State examination. Then Precious Clasp also appeared and dutifully accompanied Chia Cheng as far as the steps leading to the main hall. The rules of etiquette required no more than this of a newly married daughter-in-law who was a member of the household. The other female members of the family went a bit farther with him—up to the second gateway. But the male relatives who were Chia Cheng's juniors, having drunk a parting goblet with him, gave him the prescribed farewell escort as far as the first ten-mile resting station.

CHAPTER 44

The plant Purple Pearl returns to the Sphere of Banished Suffering. The spirit stone drenches with tears the place of dear memories.

FROM THE HOUR WHEN PAO YU HAD BIDDEN HIS FATHER FAREWELL and gone back to his room, he had sunk more and more into the former state of apathetic semiconsciousness out of which the delusive thought of a union with Black Jade had drawn him for a short time. Once more he was treated by the doctors with every possible medicine, but without success. Veil upon veil wound itself round his spirit and darkened his mind; his body refused nourishment and failed in its functions more and more. More dreaming than waking, he just dragged on from day to day.

The ninth day since the wedding night had now come—the day upon which custom requires that the son-in-law should pay his parents-in-law a visit. Could one permit Pao Yu to be seen by Aunt Hsueh in this condition? On the other hand, would not Aunt Hsueh be offended if he omitted this visit? These questions were hotly argued by the ladies of the western palace.

"True, his mind is somewhat unhinged, but physically he would certainly be able to make a short visit. I should like to keep to the correct formality and not cause Aunt Hsueh to feel offended," said the Ancestress. Her view met with general agreement, and so Pao Yu was sent through the park in a sedan chair accompanied by Pearl, to visit Aunt Hsueh.

Aunt Hsueh had not been prepared to see her son-in-law in such a wretched plight and reproached herself bitterly for having given her consent to this overhasty marriage. At her instance, every known doctor was called once more, but to no purpose, until at last an obscure healer, who lived in the ruins of an old temple outside the town, came along and was the first to perceive that the origin of the boy's illness was not of a physical but of a spiritual nature. And actually the medicine prescribed by him proved successful after only a few hours. Pao Yu began to awaken from the apathy in which he had been sunk for many days, and suddenly asked for food and drink. This happened at the hour of the second night watch. Despite the lateness of the hour, the Ancestress sent Aunt Hsueh word to come as quickly as possible, so that she also might witness the gratifying change and look on with the other ladies while the patient partook of a hearty meal.

When the ladies had gone and Pao Yu was once more alone with Pearl, he took her by the hand and, as if awakening from a dream, asked her about the recent sequence of events.

"How is it that Precious Clasp is here? I distinctly remember being told that I was to marry Black Jade. How on earth can Precious Clasp have forced herself forward in her place? I should not care to ask Precious Clasp myself lest I should offend her, but I must find out the truth. How terrible it must be for poor Black Jade! She will certainly fret herself to death over it."

Pearl did not dare to tell him the whole truth, and merely stated briefly that Black Jade was very ill.

"Then I must go at once to see her," he declared passionately, and tried there and then to get up from his bed, but, alas, he was unable to do so. After so many days without nourishment of any kind, his body was so weak that it failed him utterly. Only now did he become really aware of his wretched state.

"Very well! Then I shall at least die with her!" he cried in his grief. "That is the only wish I still have left, and you must do me the kindness of asking my grandmother to let me be carried over to Black Jade immediately. Separated from her, I have no wish either to live or to die. A simple, bare room is enough for us both, if we can only be together. If it is granted us to remain alive, very well, then I will gladly be nursed back to health side by side with her. If fate ordains otherwise, I will at least die together with her and be laid on my bier side by side with her. For the sake of our long years of friendship, I entreat you to heed my request!"

While Pearl strove in vain to overcome the emotion which choked her voice, Precious Clasp suddenly walked into the room with the maid Oriole. She had been listening to Pao Yu's words from the next room.

"Enough of this futile and morbid prating!" she said to him calmly and firmly. "The old *Tai tai* has just become somewhat reassured about you, and now you want to cause her more agitation. Do have a little consideration for her years! Has she not been touchingly devoted to you all your life? Do you feel no gratitude for that? Show her that you are not only the descendant of your illustrious ancestors, but also a good fellow yourself! Then she will be happy and will see that she has not squandered her love in vain on you. And think of your mother, too, who has sacrificed her heart's blood for you. Do you want to do her the wrong of cravenly throwing away the life that you owe to her, before it is half through? Follow my example! Surely I would have more reason than any of you to quarrel with my fate, yet I do not despair. So pull yourself together and do not quarrel with the higher decrees of heaven, which demand that you live! Have patience, and in four or five days your mind will be freed from the black demons of confusion and will have recovered its former clarity and harmony."

The only response which her sensible words evoked in him was a silly, inane, uncomprehending grin.

"For heaven knows how long past we two have had nothing more to say to each other. What is it that suddenly gives you the right to preach to me?" he remarked at last. At this she lost patience.

"Very well, then! You shall hear the whole truth! Days ago, while your mind was enveloped in darkness, your Black Jade died!"

With a shriek, Pao Yu leaped up in his bed.

"Is that true?"

"Of course it is true! How would I dream of brazenly saying that someone was dead if it were not true? It was solely to spare your feelings that your mother and grandmother kept the truth from you until now."

Utterly broken, Pao Yu sank back on his pillows. It became black as lacquer before his eyes, and his spirit became lost in the semidarkness of a distant dreamland. Someone crossed his path.

"Where am I?" he asked the Someone.

"On the road to the Springs of the Realm of Shades. But your destiny is not yet fulfilled. What are you looking for here?" replied the Someone.

"I am looking for a person who is dear to me, and who died a short time ago. I have lost my way on the road."

"Who is that person?"

"She is a girl named Black Jade of the family of Ling, from the town of Ku su."

The Someone uttered a dry laugh.

"Oh, that girl? She is a special case. In life she was different from other people; in death she is different from other spirits. You would be looking a long time for her! To find even ordinary spirits is hard enough, let alone a spirit such as Black Jade. So turn back at once, and be off!"

Pao Yu remained standing there irresolutely.

"Where is she?" he asked again.

"She has returned to the Phantom Realm of the Great Void. It will be granted you to see her again, but only after your time has been fulfilled. If, however, you incur the guilt of departing from life before your time and of your own free will in order to seek her, the Judge of the

Realm of Shades will punish you by preventing you from ever meeting her, and you will make atonement for your crime with untold suffering in the dungeons of the underworld."

Saying this, the mysterious Someone took a stone out of his sleeve and aimed it at Pao Yu's heart; then he disappeared. Pao Yu distinctly felt a hard blow in the region of the heart. Terrified, he turned to go, when suddenly he heard his name called. He could distinguish several women's voices. He started up and then he recognized his grandmother, and his mother, and Precious Clasp, and Pearl, who were all crowded around his bed, weeping. A red glow of lamplight fell on him from the table; the silvery disk of the moon, peering from behind bushes, could be seen through the window. There was no doubt about it: this was the familiar world of reality. He had only been dreaming. He breathed a deep sigh of relief, and sank back on his pillows.

His whole body was covered with cold sweat, but the strange thing was that he felt completely reposed and clear in his head. He had recovered his reason. What doctors and medicines had been unable to do, Precious Clasp had achieved by her ruthless frankness. The sudden violent emotion which her announcement caused had jolted his deranged mind back into its proper track. Pearl, who had fully intended to reprove Precious Clasp afterwards for her ruthless candor, took good care not to say a word in view of this astounding success, for his physical condition also now improved rapidly. In the course of a few days, to everyone's joy, he was completely restored to health.

In a quiet hour Pearl had to describe to him once more the exact sequence of events at the wedding, and explain to him why Precious Clasp had been chosen for him rather than Black Jade, why Black Jade's waiting maid Snowgoose had been substituted for Precious Clasp's maid as bridesmaid, and why he had been kept in the dark until right up to the ceremony of the lifting of the veil. Now he had to recognize the good and just motives for the deceit which had been practiced on him. And even though the thought of Black Jade still evoked sorrowful tears from him, nevertheless he realized that the old prophecy of the union of gold and nephrite willed by Providence had proved true. He was resigned to his fate and, under the influence of his recent dream, banished the last remnant of the thought of death into the farthest corner of his mind.

Precious Clasp was able to win his confidence more and more by her mild and gentle ways, and so it came to pass that the affection which he had previously had for Black Jade became gradually and imperceptibly transferred to Precious Clasp. But we shall return to this later.

As already reported, the day that Pao Yu celebrated his wedding,

Black Jade's life was hanging by a thread. On the evening of that day she seemed to revive again for a short time. Soon after Snowgoose had been called for, she half opened her eyes and asked for water in a weak voice. Cuckoo actually succeeded in giving her three little spoonfuls of a sweet cold fruit preparation. The last reflection of the setting sun, thought Widow Chu to herself, and she dashed off to see her own household in the Rice Farm. She estimated that Black Jade would live about half a day longer.

Shortly after she had gone Black Jade opened her eyes again, clutched Cuckoo's right hand, and, mustering the last remnants of her strength, uttered a few words of farewell.

"I'm no good for life," she gasped. "Thank you for your faithful service. I had hoped that we would be together for a long time more. I did not think . . ."

Exhausted, she stopped and closed her eyes, but did not relax the grip of her hand. Nor did Cuckoo venture to free it, but waited on in silence for anything more she might have to say.

"I'm a stranger here, Sister," gasped Black Jade after a long pause. "Do me the kindness of seeing that they bury my body, my chaste body, in the earth of my southern homeland. . . ."

Again she had to pause and close her eyes. Cuckoo felt her hand being grasped more and more tightly and convulsively. With an anxious heart she listened to the irregular breathing. The dying girl seemed to be exhaling more than inhaling breath. In her uneasiness Cuckoo sent word for Widow Chu to come back at once. Shortly before she returned Taste of Spring came in. Weeping silently, she bent over the dying girl and bade her farewell with a last pressure of the hand. Black Jade's hand already felt ice-cold.

The three of them were just beginning to rub Black Jade with damp towels, when she suddenly cried out: "Pao Yu! Pao Yu! How . . ."

Those were her last words. Her limbs became covered with cold sweat, and then grew rigid. She died in the very same hour in which Pao Yu and Precious Clasp were completing the ceremony of their wedding.

In the midst of the dirges of the women delicate and exquisite music suddenly sounded from somewhere in the far distance. Everyone fell silent and listened. It could not be the wedding music in the western palace—the distance between the Bamboo Hermitage and the home of the young couple was too great for that. Taste of Spring and Widow Chu ran into the park, to hear more distinctly, but there was no longer any music to be heard—nothing but the gentle rustling of the bamboo branches, which, swaying in the night wind, cast fleeting shadows along the moonlit garden wall. It all seemed so uncanny to the two that they turned away from the place of death and fled on winged feet back to their respective dwellings.

The following morning, after all the commotion of Mr. Cheng's departure had died down, the ladies of the western palace were informed of Black Jade's death.

"I have her death on my conscience!" wailed the Ancestress in belated self-accusation. "But it was her own fault, too. She was a far too peculiar, difficult creature."

"The old *Tai tai* has no grounds for self-reproach. She was unsparing of her love and kindness. It was the will of the higher powers that Black Jade should die young," said Madame Cheng, comfortingly. "But we will do still more for her; we will pay her the tribute of a really beautiful and worthy funeral."

It was decided to keep the sad news from Pao Yu until his condition had improved. The Ancestress visited Precious Clasp personally and told her of what had happened.

"She died of a broken heart, and that is the explanation of Pao Yu's condition too. I know you lived long enough in the park to understand what I mean. So not a word to Pao Yu!" said the Ancestress emphatically.

Yet Precious Clasp, normally so docile, went her own way this time. If his malady is of a mental nature, then it can only be healed through the mind, she said to herself, and contrary to the orders of the Ancestress she decided to tell him the exact truth at the first good opportunity. How her success proved her right has already been told; and her disobedience was duly praised and admired later as a particularly intelligent action.

When Pao Yu had recovered to some extent he was permitted to visit the Bamboo Hermitage accompanied by his mother, and grandmother, and Phoenix, and to give free rein to his grief in a loud dirge beside the coffin of his beloved. After he had wept his fill he took Cuckoo aside and made her tell him the entire story of the death of her mistress. Cuckoo had actually taken a deep dislike to him, and only the proximity of the ladies had prevented her from giving him a good piece of her mind for what she believed to be his breach of faith and plighted troth. But now, when she witnessed his sincere grief and deep feeling, she felt somewhat reconciled to him again, and she faithfully reported to him in the fullest detail how Black Jade had met her end; how, almost at death's door, she had consigned to the flames all the written testimony of her feelings—the two ink- and tear-stained silk handkerchiefs and the copybook of her poems—and what her last words had been.

Again Pao Yu broke into violent lamentations, and continued until his hoarse throat could not utter another sound and his eyes could not shed another tear. Then he allowed Phoenix to take him by the hand and draw him reluctantly away from the place of dear memories.

The important final act necessary to make a perfect circle of the series of separate, solemn acts was still lacking to the wedding ceremonial, namely, the entering of the nuptial bed. One day the Ancestress asked Aunt Hsueh to come over again for a family council, and said to her: "We have now come to the point when we need no longer worry about Pao Yu's health. A hundred days have passed since the beginning of his critical illness; now he is well and his old self again. The Court mourning for Beginning of Spring is also at an end now. Therefore it seems to me that it is time to make good the injustice which Precious Clasp has been suffering, and at long last to perform the ceremony which alone can make the bridal chamber really 'round,' a true nuptial chamber. I should like to give you the precedence in choosing a suitable lucky day."

"Oh, there can be no question at all of injustice," protested Aunt Hsueh meekly. "My daughter may be a bit slow and clumsy physically, nevertheless she possesses sufficient intelligence to realize that we simply could not have acted otherwise. Naturally, it would do much to reassure us all if the young people found an opportunity of realizing their desire for harmonious consummation, not only spiritually but also otherwise. But the honor of fixing a suitable lucky day for this should not be mine but the old *Tai tai's*. Besides, she will no doubt wish the event to be celebrated only in the very simplest way, within the inner circle of the family."

"Quite the contrary!" protested the Ancestress energetically. "In the first place, for the children it is a question of the most important event of their lives. And secondly, we have gone through so much worry and excitement recently that it is time we were merry again at long last, and could celebrate to our hearts' content. The whole clan shall be present at the festivities, and the banquet will be a really magnificent and lavish affair. My harassed old heart is craving to see some jollity again at long last."

Aunt Hsueh was very much pleased to hear this, and so, a hundred days after the formal wedding, there was a magnificent after-celebration in the form of a great family banquet, and the bridal chamber was at last made "round," as Pao Yu and Precious Clasp became in truth husband and wife.

CHAPTER 45

*Taste of Spring marries far from home, and Pao Yu weeps bitter tears
after her. Ghosts disport themselves at night in the deserted park.*

Pao Yu had recovered, to be sure, but mentally he was no
longer his old self. This became plain when Precious Clasp took it
into her head to read old books and discuss literary matters with him.
She found on these occasions that he was inclined to adhere too literally
to the actual words which he had before his eyes. She missed the vital
spark, the sprightliness of mind, the soaring flights of thought, which
were formerly his. He himself was quite unable to explain the change,
but she said that doubtless he had lately expended somewhat too much
"penetrating spiritual power." The alteration in him did not escape
Pearl either.

"He has lost his former wit but kept his former humors and troublesome ways; it would have been better the other way round," said Pearl,
shaking her head. Otherwise she was contented with her lot and very
glad that the prudent Precious Clasp now relieved her of the difficult
task of superintending him and bringing him to reason now and then.
The new mistress was well liked by the rest of the servants too for her
peaceful, gentle, steady character. For Pao Yu's taste, however, she
was a bit too calm and steady, for he hated monotony and loved
change, and he often fled from her competent presence to go strolling
about the park in the old way, looking for adventures. But the Ancestress did not like these outings in the park one bit; she feared that
he might become beset with memories in his old haunts and fall into
his melancholy condition again. True, the coffin containing Black
Jade's body had already been taken away and brought to the family
temple outside the town, but the Bamboo Hermitage was still there.

Apart from this, it had become terribly silent and empty in the
park. Precious Harp had gone to live with Aunt Hsueh in the eastern
palace, to fill the place of Precious Clasp. Little Cloud had gone back
to the parental home once more, for her father had returned to the
capital. She also was soon to be married, and therefore she came very
seldom to visit, and when she did so she stayed with the Ancestress
and barely had a word for Pao Yu. Since he had married and she herself was betrothed, her attitude towards him had altered completely.
Her exuberant gaiety, her high-spirited banter, was a thing of the past.
Wreath of Clouds, Princess Shieh's niece, had gone to live with her
aunt, to take the place of Greeting of Spring. Widow Chu's two cousins
no longer lived in the Rice Farm either, and only turned up for a
hurried visit now and then. Of all the inmates of the park, once such a

507

gay company, only three now remained there—Widow Chu, Grief of Spring, and Taste of Spring.

And now Pao Yu was to lose his half sister, Taste of Spring, too. Mr. Cheng had written a letter to the family from his official residence in the province of Chiang hsi saying that a former fellow student of his named Chou Chiung, now High Commissioner of the coastal districts, had just asked for the hand of Taste of Spring for his son. The match had been arranged privately between the fathers long since, and as it was perfectly suitable, the Ancestress could not refuse the desired consent, though she was sorry to have to let this granddaughter go so far away from her, since she was unlikely ever to see her again. The one comforting circumstance was that the official residences of the two fathers-in-law were not too far apart, and so Taste of Spring would at least have her father near her. Thus the calendar was once more consulted to find a lucky day on which Taste of Spring should set out on her bridal journey to the South.

Taste of Spring herself did not know whether to laugh or to cry. She felt the need of a heart to heart talk with Pao Yu, the intimate comrade of her beautiful childhood days, now gone. But Pao Yu, who knew nothing as yet about her betrothal, did not give her a chance to say a word, but talked the whole time only of Black Jade.

"You were present, I know, when Black Jade died. Did you also hear sounds of mysterious, distant music?" he asked.

"Yes, it could be heard distinctly through the stillness of the night. It sounded very strange, quite different from ordinary, earthly music."

Pao Yu thought of the dream in which that unknown Someone said to him that Black Jade was a special case, in life different from other people, in death different from other spirits. Perhaps those sounds came from the blessed spirits who had come down to the profane world to meet Black Jade's soul and escort it to their kingdom. He was so lost in thought that Taste of Spring left again without having mentioned her own affairs.

Only after Taste of Spring had gone did he catch by chance some fragments of a conversation between Precious Clasp and Pearl and learn in this way of the betrothal and impending departure of his half sister. With a loud cry he threw himself on his bed. Precious Clasp and Pearl rushed up to him greatly alarmed and asked him what was the matter.

"One after the other they go and leave me!" he lamented. "First Beginning of Spring died; that was not so terrible, since she was not with me constantly like the others. But Black Jade! She has joined the blessed. Then Greeting of Spring. She was given to an intolerable fellow and is pining away in the fetters of a hateful marriage. Little Cloud and

Precious Harp are gone, and will be married very soon too. And now Taste of Spring! Everybody is leaving! What shall I do alone here?"

Pearl wanted to calm him, but Precious Clasp signed to her to go away.

"Let me deal with him!" she said, and then, turning to Pao Yu, went on: "So if you had your way, all your sisters and cousins should remain here and be around you to the end of your life? In your opinion, it seems, they are there only for you and for no one else? To be logical, I should not have been allowed to marry either. To think that a person of your education should have such senseless thoughts! Very well, if your cousins are so indispensable to you as that, Pearl and I will go and make way for them!"

"No! No! Not yet! Wait at least until I have turned to ashes!" he cried passionately, grasping them with both hands as if he did not want to let them go. Pearl put her hand over his mouth.

"Be quiet! One does not say things like that! Control yourself somewhat, or else you will lose us too!"

"I understand, and I will control myself, but I cannot yet accept that Taste of Spring is going away."

Precious Clasp took no more notice of his talk but proceeded calmly to prepare a heart-strengthening potion, and after he had drunk it he calmed down gradually. Pearl suggested that they should arrange with Taste of Spring that she would not come to say good-by to Pao Yu before leaving, lest the wound should be torn open afresh.

"Ah, why not? By then he will surely have become reasonable again," objected Precious Clasp. "They are welcome to talk to each other to their hearts' content. Taste of Spring is a sensible girl, not like a certain other person, with her tragic pose."

Late that evening Phoenix set out to walk across the park to the Hermitage of Clear Autumn Weather in order to discuss with Taste of Spring some matters concerning her trousseau. As it was already getting dark, she had taken a maid to walk in front of her with a lantern on a post, as well as the two waiting maids who accompanied her. But when she stepped out into the open, the harvest moon was rising so clear that the lantern seemed to be an unnecessary nuisance and she sent the maid back.

As she was passing by the teahouse she heard a lively conversation in women's voices going on inside. It sounded at one moment like quarrelling and weeping and the next like merry chatter and laughter. Her suspicions were awakened at once. She scented new irregularities among the personnel and sent the waiting maid Siao Hung in to do a little spying on some harmless pretext. Thus she had only the waiting maid Little Fong still with her as she passed through the park gate, which was standing ajar.

Inside the park the moon was shining more clearly and magnificently, if possible, than outside. The shadows of the trees were sharply silhouetted on the ground. Unlike former days, when the park was still inhabited, a depressing silence now reigned. Not a human sound was to be heard. Only now and again a brief gust of wind blew through the summits of the trees, and then the soft rustle of falling autumn leaves, the creaking and cracking of swaying branches, and the flapping of birds startled from sleep became audible from every direction, like an echo. When she set out Phoenix had been somewhat heated by the wine which she had drunk at supper, and she had not put on a warm outer garment. Now in the park she felt the cool night air perceptibly, and she shivered slightly.

"Run back quickly and bring me my ermine cape!" she ordered Little Fong. "Meantime, I shall be going on to the Hermitage of Clear Autumn Weather. Call for me there!"

Little Fong disappeared, and Phoenix continued on her way alone. She had not gone far when suddenly she heard close behind her a sound of heavy breathing and snuffling. She was so terrified that her hair stood up on end. Involuntarily she looked back and she saw a black, shaggy beast trotting along behind her with its muzzle to the ground. Its two eyes glowed like lamps in the darkness. Phoenix uttered a hoarse cry of terror, whereupon the animal, which seemed to be a big dog, dropped back and, with its tail between its legs, sprang up on a sloping hillside by the pathway, only to turn back again immediately and once more approach her threateningly.

Goaded by fear, Phoenix ran as quickly as her legs would carry her on and on in the direction of the Hermitage of Clear Autumn Weather. She was already near her goal and just about to skirt a projecting rock, when her feet suddenly failed her. From behind the rock the shadow of a human form was distinctly silhouetted across the path. She did not dare to go on, and called out twice, terrified: "Who is there?"

But no one appeared, and the shadow continued to bar her way. Almost fainting with paralyzing fear, she had to lean against the wall of rock to prevent herself from sinking to the ground. Suddenly she seemed to hear someone calling to her from behind: "Do you not know me any longer, Aunt?"

She turned her head, and saw a graceful female figure before her. The charming features seemed familiar to her, but she could not recollect who it was.

"Why do you only think of the pleasures of the hour, Aunt? Why did you disregard my well-meant advice, which took the future into account, and throw it to the bottom of the Eastern Sea?" continued the specter.

Phoenix bent her head and tried hard to remember. Still she could not recall who it was.

"Ah, yes! You were most wonderfully loving and sweet to me then, but today the memory of me seems to have flown away into the ninth sphere of the heavens," continued the stranger, with a derisive laugh. Now at last it dawned on Phoenix who she was. Before her stood Ko Ching, Chia Yung's first wife, who had died young.

"Oh, are you the ghost of Ko Ching? How is it that you are here?" she cried in horror, and started running again, her one thought being to get away from the haunted spot. But just where the shadow barred her path, she tripped and fell. Covered with perspiration, she awoke from her terrifying dream. She found herself lying on the ground, and saw her maids Little Fong and Siao Hung rushing up to her. Not wishing her menials to see her humiliating plight, she picked herself up quickly.

"Why have you been so long?" she asked with affected casualness. "Quick, put my fur cape around my shoulders. And now, we can go back at once; they are all asleep already in the Hermitage of Clear Autumn Weather," she lied. And she strode along as quickly as she could towards the park exit, accompanied by the two waiting maids. The girls thought they noticed a strange, haunted expression on her face which they had never seen on it before, but respect forbade them to ask any questions.

After Taste of Spring had set out on her bridal journey to the southern seacoast, the last remaining inhabitants, Grief of Spring and Widow Chu, could no longer bear to go on living in the desolate, autumnal park. Now all the pavilions, formerly echoing with merry girlish laughter, stood silent and forsaken. Only a few park guardians, elderly women and younger ones, had remained behind. The day after her nocturnal visit to the park Phoenix had fallen ill and, contrary to her normal habits, had the oracle consulted in a temple outside the town. Her experience of that night had profoundly shaken the self-assurance of her practical nature, which had hitherto made her ignore the supernatural completely. Even though she had kept her experience of that night to herself, enough had trickled out to give rise to the belief that the park was haunted. There were rumors of an uncanny black animal with a gleaming, shaggy coat and glowing eyes as big as lamps, which was said to roam at night among the hills in the park. The monster was said, moreover, to have a human voice. It had followed Phoenix that evening and frightened her so much that she got ill.

And now, some days later, Princess Chen had suddenly fallen ill; it was, moreover, immediately after an evening walk through the park. She had raved in delirium about a "woman in red" and a "woman in green" who had followed her, and she said that she simply had to go into the park. The woman in green and the woman in red could only mean her two unfortunate sisters, the late Yu Number Two and Yu Number Three, who used to dress in green and red respectively. Prince Chen and his son Chia Yung both agreed that the park must be haunted.

"I know from Pao Yu's servant, Ming Yen, that Bright Cloud's ghost also haunts the park, and moreover, around the pond where the water lilies are," said Chia Yung. "And then there was that strange music when Black Jade lay dying. There is no doubt about it. The park is haunted."

And so it went from mouth to mouth: the park is haunted! The park guardians and garden women who had remained behind were likewise seized with the general panic, and as soon as the yellow twilight began to fall they took to throwing aside their brooms and rakes and watering cans and hedge clippers, and fleeing from the park in a body, only to venture in again in broad daylight, all together, and well armed.

When, to crown it all, Prince Chen and his son and daughter-in-law became slightly ill too, and Bright Cloud's cousin-in-law, the wife of Wu Kwei, who, as already mentioned, lived with her husband in a cottage just outside the back gate of the park, died suddenly one evening after taking a wrong dose of medicine, everyone took it as certain that the spook-ridden park exhaled a fatal influence which was to blame for all these misfortunes.

As the woman Wu Kwei was notorious for her marital infidelities, it was said that she had had secret intercourse with the park ghosts, and that this led to her destruction. In cases of illness Prince Chen no longer called doctors; instead, he had incense and gold leaf burned in the park, or called down the protection of benignly disposed celestial bodies, so convinced was he that the only way to avert evil was to placate the angry spirits which frequented the park.

Things went so far that the mere rustling of the night wind in the treetops or the distant cry of the cranes which frequented the park sufficed to make the inmates of both palaces tremble and imagine they heard the voices of ghosts in the air. In the end the members of the park staff no longer ventured in there even in the daytime and one after another left their uncomfortable jobs on one excuse or another. Finally, the park gates were bolted fast and barricaded and no longer opened at all. All the beautiful kiosks and graceful pavilions were now allowed to fall into ruin and desolation, and to become the dwelling places of rats and bats and other creatures which shun the daylight.

The Ancestress was concerned above all else with protecting her beloved Pao Yu from possible nocturnal attacks by the park spirits, and to this end she had his dwelling surrounded at night by a big staff of watchmen. And morning after morning the watchmen, anxious to make their jobs seem important, told blood-curdling stories of ghosts—one time they were awful monsters with red, grimacing faces, another time beautiful girls full of seductive charm—whom they had seen in the night. Thus they contributed considerably to the growth of the general panic.

Only one person remained untouched by all this, and could not be aroused from his peaceful ways, and that was the phlegmatic Prince Shieh. He simply refused to believe that ghosts could have made such a beautiful place as the park their playground. In order to prove how unafraid he was he decided to take a walk through the park with a few other people one fine clear day. In order to be prepared for any eventuality he provided himself and his reluctant companions with weapons.

There was no denying that a certain sinister and oppressive atmosphere, which even Prince Shieh could not ignore, pervaded the forsaken and neglected park. But he did not wish to show any weakness and strode bravely ahead, while his companions, timidly peering this way and that, followed him at some distance. Little Kuan, the youngest of the party, was the most frightened of them all. Now, hearing a suspicious rustling, and immediately afterwards seeing a brilliant opalescent something flashing through the bushes, he lost his last shred of courage and plopped to the ground uttering a loud cry of terror.

"What's wrong?" asked the Prince, stopping.

"A ghost!" gasped the terrified boy, picking himself up with difficulty. "I saw it with my own eyes. It had a frightful yellow face, a red beard, and a bluish green coat. It crept into that hole in the rock over there, behind the trunks of the trees!"

Now even Prince Shieh became a bit nervous. "Did you see it too?" he asked, turning to the rest of his train of followers. Among these men there were some who deemed it wise to exploit the favorable trend of events in order to get out of the ill-omened place as quickly as possible.

"Of course we saw it!" they replied readily. "The old master was too far ahead; otherwise he too would have seen it. We did not want to worry him; that is why we did not say anything; but our knees are still quaking with fright."

In these circumstances Prince Shieh decided to turn back as quickly as possible, but he instructed his people not to mention one word about the occurrence, but on the contrary to assert that the park had been thoroughly examined and that nothing of a suspicious nature had been observed. He did not realize that his people, encouraged by his own weakening, would chatter more than ever now. And they did it so thoroughly, and exaggerated so excessively, that they made their listeners' flesh creep and their tongues hang out with terror.

Prince Shieh could see no other way out now than to send for a well-known master of magic, who would drive the haunting ghosts out of the park by his magic spells. A suitable day was looked up in the calendar, on which the great act of exorcism was to take place. An altar was erected on the entrance terrace before the great hall, which had previously served as the reception place for the Imperial spouse. Above it, on a terrace, stood the images of the three greatest Taoist saints, the divine Nephrite Emperor, the first man Pan Ku, and the wise Lao Tzu, and on both sides there were pictures of the twenty-eight most important heavenly constellations. Statues of the four heavenly field marshals, Ma, Chao, Wen, and Chou, stood at either side of the terrace steps. Below the terrace, ranged in rows, stood the images of the thirty-six heavenly generals.

Amid rolling clouds of incense, in a glow of flaming torches and burning candles, to the roll of drums and the ringing of bells, the great act of magic began. The grand master wizard and his forty-nine assistant wizards came up and grouped themselves around five banners, representing the five directions of the heavens, which were planted in front of the altar. The magicians wore high seven-starred tiaras and long magicians' mantles, embroidered with eight diagrams and with portrayals of the nine heavenly spheres. Their feet were encased in high "cloud" cothurni, and they held in their hands ivory writing tablets. After three master magicians had walked around the altar with burning incense sticks and sprinkled it with holy water, the grand master wizard stepped forward as the drums of exorcism rolled, bowed before the three saints, and recited a prayer invoking their assistance against the evil spirits of the park. An inscribed tablet had been set up on the altar, solemnly inviting all the good spirits of the neighborhood to hasten along and take part in the meritorious work of driving away the devils.

The male members of the Chia clan, all of whom, both young and old, had come as spectators, followed the sequence of events with devout expectation.

"If so many mighty spirits join in the good work, these wretched spooks will have to clear out pretty quickly," people said cheerfully.

Meanwhile three magicians had detached themselves from the circle of their forty-nine colleagues and taken up their position apart, in front of the altar. One of them held in his right hand a jewel-studded magic sword, in his left a jug of holy water; the second carried a black, seven-starred magic banner; the third held gripped in his hand the carved peachwood handle of a magic whip. Suddenly the music ceased. From

514

his dais on the terrace the grand master wizard ordered three bows to the "Three Spirits of Holy Clarity" and addressed another formula of exorcism to the air. Then he stepped down from the terrace and took his place at the head of his corps of magicians, who were lined up in processional order.

With the members of the Chia clan leading, the procession now wound its way in turn to each one of the buildings and dwellings, pavilions and kiosks, hills and gorges, fishponds and streams of the park. Every single place was sprinkled with holy water and freed from the ban of enchantment by application of the great exorcism. The magic sword drew its magical circles in the air, the banners were waved in conformity with the rules of the art, the magic whip swished thrice through the air, to chase away the invisible haunting demons; the drums rolled and the lips of the magicians spoke magic incantations.

Despite all the outward pomp and the beating of the tom-toms, some juniors of the Chia clan could not suppress a certain feeling of disappointment. They had come in the pleasantly creepy expectation of seeing one or other of the spooks caught and actually wriggling in the claws of its pursuers. But nothing of the kind had happened. There were no exciting apparitions to be seen, no suspicious noises to be heard. The mysterious manipulation of empty bottles and earthenware pitchers, in which the grand master magician was alleged to have imprisoned the captured demons, seemed to them a very poor substitute for the sensational things which did not happen. The chief magician had the bottles and pitchers carefully stoppered and sealed, and with his own hand he wrote with red ink on the closures decrees forbidding anyone to open them. Then the sealed bottles and pitchers were immured for perpetual imprisonment at his direction in the cellar under the Look-Out Pagoda.

The great act of exorcism concluded with a solemn prayer of thanksgiving which the grand master, standing before the altar, addressed to the heavenly armies which had given their powerful assistance at the hunting down and extirpation of the evil park demons. Then the altar, with all its trappings, was dismantled. While Prince Shieh was thanking the grand magician on his knees for the service which he had rendered, the juniors could not resist from airing their disappointment behind his back by contemptuous witticisms and mockery.

"Why all this hocus-pocus?" they whispered. "After hoping to have a sight of some real live spooks, we see nothing but empty bottles and jugs. That is all the success there is to show for all the expense. What proof have we got that the spooks have really been done away with?"

Prince Chen felt that it was due to his position as senior of second rank to reprimand the frivolous juniors.

"Don't talk nonsense, you silly boys!" he cried. "Ghosts can make themselves visible or invisible at will. In the presence of so many powerful spirits, they naturally take care not to show themselves visibly. Nevertheless, the magician, with the help of his magic, has captured them in their invisible form and shut them up in the bottles and pitchers. Now they are caught and they cannot haunt the place any more."

The juniors held their peace but decided to wait and see whether the park would be haunted in future by spooks and queer noises. If it was, they were determined to make themselves heard. But the servants believed in the great act of exorcism, and the thought that the whole spookish company was now safely locked up in bottles and pitchers made them feel very much reassured and calmed. And their faith was strengthened still more by the fact that the various illnesses in the two princely families disappeared remarkably quickly very soon afterwards, which of course could only be ascribed to the mighty spells of the magicians.

But among the servants there was one man who did not share the general faith. He had been present at Prince Shieh's unlucky reconnoitering expedition into the park.

"I also saw the suspicious apparition which terrified our little Kuan so much that time," he laughingly declared in the servants' hall. "What was it? Just a harmless golden pheasant! We simply fooled the old master when he asked us whether we had seen the ghost. And he has got up this whole rumpus of magicians and their spells all on account of an innocent pheasant! Isn't it ridiculous?"

But his sober and realistic statement of the situation found no sympathetic echo from the others. Surely it was much nicer to think of the imprisoned spooks as being securely bottled up and immured in their prison under the Look-Out Pagoda, and they were certainly not going to let themselves be done out of their pleasant fantasy by anyone.

CHAPTER 46

Yu Tsun recognizes in the mysterious hermit his old friend and benefactor. The moneylender Ni, known as the Drunken Diamond, becomes the pike in the carp pond.

FOUR SINISTER WARNING SIGNS, FOLLOWING IN QUICK SUCCESSION, HAD alarmed the inmates of the eastern and western palaces—the nocturnal groans in the Hall of Ancestors on the eve of the Mid-Autumn Festival, Prince Shieh's stumble on the day of the Mid-Autumn Festival, the sudden glowing of Pao Yu's stone, and the winter blossoming of the

516

begonia. From that time the blows of fate which rained down on the Chia clan increased to an alarming degree. First there was the loss of Pao Yu's stone followed by Pao Yu's serious illness; then the death of Beginning of Spring; then the death of Black Jade; then lightning struck Aunt Hsueh's home. The Minister of Justice had revoked the mild sentence passed upon Hsueh Pan and referred the charge of man-slaughter to a higher court for a second hearing and verdict. This meant renewed anxiety and more enormous sacrifices of money for Aunt Hsueh. Furthermore, Hsueh Pan's name was struck off the list of official Imperial buyers upon his arrest, and with this his income from the State ceased. In addition, his license to operate his three pawnshops in the capital was withdrawn and the current cash of two of them was con-fiscated. The manager of the third pawnshop had absconded sometime previously with several thousand taels, and this involved Hsueh Pan in new trouble with the Treasury. In order to compensate itself the Treas-ury withdrew the license of a fourth pawnshop which Hsueh Pan carried on in Ying tien fu, and confiscated the cash balance as well as a piece of land which belonged to the Hsueh family in Ying tien fu. All at once the Hsueh family was reduced to poverty. Aunt Hsueh was in bleak despair. She did not know which way to turn.

Chia Cheng was no less perturbed when one day, sitting in his office in the provinces, he looked through the newspaper from the capital and saw a detailed account of the bad turn which the legal proceedings against his nephew Hsueh Pan had taken. For the sake of Aunt Hsueh he had bribed the judge of the first court, the district mandarin of Tai ping hsien, where Hsueh Pan was imprisoned. Now he feared that his maneuver would be discovered and brought to light by the higher court. Since then he had not had an hour's peace of mind and was in fear and trembling lest he should lose his position and rank. And sure enough, the thunderbolt was to come down on his own head soon afterwards, though in fact it came from another direction than the one from which he had expected it.

In his earlier official service Mr. Cheng had had very little contact with everyday practical life. His position at the Ministry of Public Works had entailed only office work; his activity as Imperial Examiner had brought him into contact only with the higher levels of noble-minded intellectuals. As Corn Treasurer of the province of Chiang hsi he found himself faced for the first time with practical administrative work. He had to supervise the many public granaries in the prefecture and in the chief towns of his province; to examine the corn as it came in and went out; and to superintend the dispatch of the tribute corn destined for the palace and the capital. What did he know of the sharp practices which were applied in collecting the public corn deliveries;

517

of the percentages and commissions which the individual courts were accustomed to levying, and which the higher courts passed on to the lower courts, and the lower courts in their turn passed on to the poor stupid peasants?

He had heard of all this, to be sure, and it had been explained to him in theory by friends and colleagues. And as he took his duties seriously and wished to prove himself in every respect a strict and honorable official worthy of his illustrious ancestors, immediately on taking up his appointment he issued explicit instructions to the prefects and district mandarins and corn bailiffs that the dubious practices hitherto customary were to cease at once and that he would not tolerate any irregularities or levying of percentages or commissions. And in order to prove how seriously he meant what he said, he sent out assessors and overseers all over his administrative district to keep a sharp eye on the officials and bailiffs and underbailiffs through whose hands the deliveries of corn passed. Such procedure was quite new and unheard of and caused consternation on all sides. Further, he put a stop to the practice of gifts of money among the civil servants themselves. On taking up office he had contemptuously rejected the gifts offered him on all sides by subordinates eager to win his favor; he likewise scorned to offer the customary monetary tribute to his own superior officer, the Governor of the province, on the latter's birthday.

His own office and domestic staff were affected particularly painfully by the rigorously correct and austere regime of the new Corn Treasurer. The staffs banded together, went to him boldly in a body, and, hoping to make an impression upon him by this step, demanded general leave of absence; but Mr. Cheng refused to be intimidated and put it to them quite coolly that anyone who was dissatisfied was at liberty to leave the service. His attitude caused a split in the ranks. The local people, whom Mr. Cheng had taken over from his predecessor, left the service murmuring and sulking. They had been accustomed to better times, and as they had their family homes, they were able to afford to take holidays for a time and quietly look around for new positions.

But his own servants, whom Mr. Cheng had taken with him from the capital, were in a very different position. If they went off defiantly they would find themselves on the street, as they were strangers in the place. Besides, they were up to their necks in debt. In the expectation that they would quickly enrich themselves in their fat provincial positions, they had plunged into all kinds of expenses before their departure, and borrowed money to fit themselves out. After all, they were city men, from the capital, and they wished to live up to their position in the provinces. Moreover, they had promised money and jewelry to the wives and relatives whom they had left behind. They would certainly lose face if they were to return home suddenly in poverty. So they remained.

They held out for a while by pawning one article after another of the outfits they had bought dearly in the capital. When nothing was left to pawn they tried new tactics with the old Governor. They simply absented themselves from duty on the occasion of official gatherings, festivities, excursions, and receptions, where the utmost splendor was called for. On being taken to task for this by Mr. Cheng, they excused themselves on the plea that they had nothing to wear—everything was pawned. The head chef sent up bad food on the excuse that the housekeeping money allowed him was inadequate. In short, they carried on a campaign of passive resistance.

It was suggested to Mr. Cheng that he should consider the lot of his acquaintances; those mandarins whom he had always praised for being just and strictly correct had not made progress in their careers; those whom he had reprimanded had quickly been promoted to higher positions. Without presents and bribes there was no getting on—that was all there was to it. He must not antagonize his colleagues by imposing an overstrict standard of honor; that might injure his career, it was hinted. Mr. Cheng realized that something must be done, but he still obstinately refused to choose the usual easy way of gaining riches through his office; rather than this, he compromised by agreeing to pay certain supplementary allowances out of his own pocket. For this purpose he was about to send to the capital to have some cash made available; but that was too slow for his subordinates' liking, and besides, some of his people knew better than he did that the finances of the western palace had been in a bad state for a long time, and they doubted whether sufficient money could be obtained from this source.

And so for good or ill Mr. Cheng reluctantly consented to allow his subordinates a free hand, but he, personally, intended to keep clear of it all and to continue to keep face outwardly as a completely blameless, incorruptible official. The personnel of the official residence now joined forces with the office staffs; documents and signatures were forged, and each man tried as hard as he could, behind the old master's back, to make up for lost time. The success of these efforts appeared very soon in the beautiful new jewelry shown off by the wives who had been left behind in the western palace.

A few days after the singular ceremony of exorcism had taken place in the park, Prince Shieh was busy in his library making out a list of the people who were to resume guard duty in the park, now purged and cleansed of evil. He was troubled lest the many dwellings should ultimately become the hiding places of vagabonds and criminals if permanently left unguarded. While he was absorbed in his list, his son Chia Lien came rushing in.

"I've just heard the most astonishing news over at Cousin Chen's," he reported excitedly. "Uncle Cheng is said to have been denounced to the Throne by his provincial Governor. He is alleged to have been guilty of carelessness in supervising his subordinates, who are said to have extorted exorbitant deliveries of corn from the population behind his back. The Governor has proposed his dismissal from office, they say."

"That must certainly be only an unfounded rumor," said the Prince, astounded. "I cannot think at all why the Governor should suddenly show a hostile attitude towards him. In his last letter, telling us of Taste of Spring's safe arrival, he explicitly mentioned that a relationship had been found to exist between Taste of Spring's father-in-law and the Governor, and that the Governor had congratulated him most heartily on the connection and had given a great banquet in his honor, and had shown other signs of friendliness towards him too. Surely the Governor will not denounce his own cousin-in-law! You must go immediately to the Ministry of Home Affairs and make inquiries."

Chia Lien hurried off and learned at the Ministry that a petition had in fact been laid before the Imperial Court in which the Governor of Chiang hsi proposed that Chia Cheng should be relieved of office. But the Son of Heaven had shown mercy and, in view of the fact that Chia Cheng was inexperienced in provincial administration and had been a victim of the machinations of his subordinates owing to his lack of practical experience, he had merely reduced his rank by three degrees and had been gracious enough to reinstate him in his old position in the Ministry of Works.

"At the Ministry I chanced to meet a prefect from Chiang hsi who is here on official business," Chia Lien reported to Prince Shieh on his return. "He assured me that all his colleagues and also the Governor himself were full of praise of Uncle Cheng. Not the slightest reproach can be attached to him personally. His only fault is his failure to supervise his subordinates sufficiently. The Governor was in fact well-intentioned when he proposed that he should be recalled. He wanted to forestall more serious developments."

That sounded somewhat reassuring, and the step the Governor had taken was actually welcomed and approved by the ladies of the Yung-kuo palace, as the Chia clan, which felt the lack of its natural leader, would get him back again.

"The goings-on of his subordinates might actually cost him his head if he were to remain longer in the province," said Madame Cheng to her nephew Chia Lien, when he brought her, in confidence, the news of the change of office.

"How does it come that the *Tai tai* knows about the goings-on?" asked Chia Lien.

"After all, I have got eyes in my head. The servants left here loaded with debts, and they had hardly arrived at their posts in the province when they were able to heap on their wives here quantities of gold and silver jewelry; and soon the women were going about wearing the newest and most beautiful clothes. Where did the wealth come from all at once? If that had continued, not only would my husband have lost office and position, but our illustrious ancestors would probably have been deprived posthumously of all their titles and honors. One dare not even think of such a disgrace."

"That is quite true. We may actually regard it as a lucky thing that the Governor interfered in good time."

Hardly had the excitement over Mr. Cheng's recall from office died down when a new piece of horrifying news arrived. Golden Cinnamon, Hsueh Pan's young wife, died suddenly of arsenic poisoning. There was a stormy domestic scene at Aunt Hsueh's. The mother of the deceased, who had quickly arrived at news of her death, alternately accused Aunt Hsueh, Precious Clasp, and Lotus of poisoning her daughter, and wanted to strangle them. Her boor of an adopted son, who accompanied her, forced his way into the women's apartments of the house, smashed a chair, and was about to wreck everything, big and small, but Chia Lien came to the rescue just in time and got his servants to overpower the raging fellow. Precious Clasp, in her prudent, tactful way, succeeded in restoring order out of chaos, and by clever questioning drove Toad, the deceased woman's waiting maid, into a corner, so that she eventually made a full confession.

It transpired that Golden Cinnamon, disappointed in her marriage and thirsting for love, was secretly infatuated with Hsueh Pan's cousin, Hsueh Kuo. Hsueh Kuo, who was a gentle young fellow, did not wish to break faith with his betrothed, Wreath of Clouds; with great difficulty he had tried to evade the pursuit of the lustful fellow inmate of the house. Nevertheless, Golden Cinnamon had once been very near attaining her aim. She had caught Hsueh Kuo in front of her door and was just drawing the hesitant young man into her bedroom when Lotus had come between them and thwarted her intentions. From that time on she had conceived a deadly hatred of Lotus and had sworn vengeance on her.

Under a hypocritical pretense of friendship she had asked Lotus, who had been living with Precious Clasp since her rejection by Hsueh Pan, to come and live in the house again as her companion. Through friendly treatment she had made Lotus unsuspecting. Then there had been talk of a troublesome plague of rats in the kitchen and larder, and it was said that in order to exterminate them arsenic must be brought into the house. She had procured the arsenic through her boor of a foster brother, whom she had recently taken as a lover in place of the inaccessible Hsueh Kuo. He had been the attraction behind the remarkably frequent visits which she had been paying recently to her mother, who had come to live in the capital a short time before. During these meetings it was planned that Golden Cinnamon should flee from her mother-in-law's house, where she had only experienced grief and disappointment. But before doing this she wanted to get the hated Lotus out of the way by poisoning her with arsenic.

Twice she had tried to poison her, but each time Providence had preserved Lotus from the fate prepared for her. The first time Lotus had tipped over, by an awkward movement of the hand, the glass of poisoned medicine which Golden Cinnamon had prepared with her own hand and brought to her sickbed. At the time it had struck Lotus as strange that the proud, spoiled Golden Cinnamon should have deigned to gather up the fragments and the traces of liquid from the broken medicine glass with her own hand instead of ordering a maid to do this inferior work.

Having failed this first time, Golden Cinnamon now decided to carry through her purpose by means of poisoned soup. She had ordered the waiting maid Toad to prepare a good soup for herself and Lotus. It annoyed Toad that Lotus, whom she disliked, should share with her mistress the benefit of her culinary art. She decided that she would at least thoroughly oversalt her soup. Therefore she put a handful more salt than necessary in the soup bowl meant for Lotus, and in order not to mix up the two bowls when serving, she had made a slight scratch on the bowl intended for Lotus, to serve her as a secret identification mark. Just as she had placed the two bowls on the tray Golden Cinnamon came into the kitchen, and sent her out for a hired carriage, as she wanted to visit her mother.

When Toad came back Golden Cinnamon had already taken the two bowls into the bedroom, where Lotus lay ill. Toad noticed to her horror that her mistress, who of course knew nothing about the oversalting trick, had actually got the marked bowl with the oversalted soup in front of her. Fearing a scolding for oversalting the soup, Toad, who knew nothing of the poisoning plan, took advantage of a brief absence of her mistress from the room and quickly exchanged the two bowls. Lotus, being sick and exhausted, had not yet touched the first bowl which Golden Cinnamon had set before her, and was lying with her eyes shut, and so did not notice the changing of the bowls.

When Golden Cinnamon came in again she sat down by the edge of the bed with the bowl which Toad had secretly exchanged, and she and Lotus ate their soup together. Shortly afterwards Golden Cinnamon died of agonizing stomach pains. By a remarkable chain of circumstances she had fallen a victim to her own poisoning hand.

Precious Clasp brought all these details to light through her clever cross-examination, and Lotus, who had already been bound with ropes as a suspected murderess, was now cleared of all suspicion and regained her freedom. The mother of the dead girl, who before had been raging, and threatening Aunt Hsueh, Precious Clasp, and Lotus with a charge of murder, now became quite subdued and suddenly lost interest in a legal prosecution. It was mutually agreed to hush up the occurrence and inform the authorities that it was a case of suicide, and so, through Precious Clasp's prudence, it was found possible to prevent a family scandal from becoming a public scandal.

Chia Yu Tsun, the poor starving scholar of former days, in the course of his brilliant career had become, thanks to ability and patronage, a prefect in the capital. One day he went on an official round outside the city gates to inspect certain new rural settlements within his jurisdiction. On the way through the district of Chi ki hsien he had to cross a rushing river. As he had a large retinue with him, there was a rather long delay at the ford. Yu Tsun availed of this delay to go for a little walk and look around the neighborhood. Not far from the nearest village he discovered an old forsaken temple, the red-washed walls of which made a picturesque sight among a group of old pine trees. Yu Tsun dismounted from his sedan chair and directed his steps towards the temple gate.

Inside he found dilapidated halls with cracked pillars, crooked walls and ramshackle roofs, faded idols from which the golden paint had peeled off almost completely. The stump of a broken memorial pillar with a half-obliterated inscription stood out amidst the ruins. In the grounds behind the temple Yu Tsun came upon a hut made of reeds and bulrushes, which nestled against the trunk of a blue-green cypress tree. In the open hut he saw an old hermit sitting on the prayer-mat, his legs crossed under him, his eyes shut, in a state of holy contemplation. It seemed to Yu Tsun that he had seen the face of the old man somewhere and sometime before.

"Hi, holy old man!" he cried, going up to him.

"What is it, Your Grace?" asked the old man in reply, opening his eyes a little and modifying his fixed expression with a faint smile.

"I am engaged on an official tour, and have just come this way by chance. I perceive that you have penetrated very deeply into the secrets of the higher life, and I should like to profit a little by your wise instruction."

"Our coming and our going—each has its time and its place," was the mysterious answer of the hermit.

Yu Tsun bowed politely and continued his questions: How was it that he had come to set up his hut in this abandoned place, of which one did not even know the name; why had he not chosen in preference some renowned mountain temple in which to practice holiness, and so on.

"One can also live in a simple hut made of gourd stalks. Why should one need a famous mountain? Why the foolish striving to rise higher? I am not one of those who cannot wait for 'the excellence of the precious stone to enchant the world' and 'the clasp to take wings to fly to the bride.' "

Yu Tsun became suddenly enlightened. Who but Shih Ying could quote the very words which he had once put into verse when he was a poor student in his lonely cell in the Temple of the Gourd? There was no doubt about it, the man before him was Shih Ying, the benefactor of his youth. He looked at him attentively once more. It was strange how little his features had changed since those days.

"Are you not Master Shih Ying?" he asked, after he had discreetly signed to his servants to withdraw, for he did not wish them to learn of his obscure past.

"To seem is to be and to be is to seem," was the smiling reply of the old man.

Yu Tsun bowed still more deeply. The word *chia*, "seem," sounded exactly like his family name, Chia. Obviously the old man wished to give him to understand that he had also recognized him. Now at last had come the chance to pay his benefactor a long-standing debt!

"Your kindness long ago made it possible for me to continue on my journey to the capital. Through your help I got a seat in the coach of State, and I was able to attain to office and dignity. Only later did I hear of your awakening. I learned that you had soared up from the dusty lowliness of daily life to the lofty regions of the spirit. After having long sought for you in vain I count myself fortunate to have at last met you again today. May the simple scholar hope that the worthy holy man will grant him the favor of his esteemed company? I live in the capital not far from here and would deem myself fortunate if I might have you as my honored guest for the rest of my life, and be permitted to listen to your exalted instructions by day and by night."

The hermit had risen, and now thanked him with a polite bow.

"My desire does not extend beyond the circumference of this simple round prayer-mat," he said. "Beyond it I know of nothing else between heaven and earth. Therefore the meaning of your words remains closed to me."

He sat down to immerse himself once more in holy contemplation.

Yu Tsun was undecided. Was it really Shih Ying or was it not? To judge from his face and from the words he had quoted, it was he. Between that time and today there lay nineteen long years. How wonderfully unchanged his features had remained! This was no doubt due to the life-lengthening power of his holy exercises. But how detached from the world he was! The prospect of a good, carefree life seemed not to make the slightest impression on him. Was there any use, then, in speaking to him about personal, family affairs, or telling him what had become of his wife and his daughter Lotus? At any rate, he would make another effort.

"The holy master would like to let the past rest, but the lowly scholar has still so many things on his mind which he would like to discuss. . . ."

He was about to continue when the members of his retinue approached and warned him that it was time to cross the ford, as otherwise night would overtake them before they could reach their intended rest station.

"Your Grace should not delay!" the hermit also warned the hesitant Yu Tsun. "It is certain that we shall meet again. I shall wait for you one day by the ford."

When he had finished speaking he shut his eyes to continue his mystic contemplation. Yu Tsun bade him farewell and returned to his retinue by the river-bank.

He was just about to cross over when one of his retinue, who had been with him in the temple and had stayed behind on account of stomach pains, came running along and told him that the old temple which he had just inspected was in flames. Yu Tsun looked behind him and, true enough, saw in the direction of the temple a red glow of fire and a mighty cloud of smoke which darkened the setting sun. He was surprised that the fire could have arisen so suddenly in the short time since he had left the temple, and he wondered anxiously whether his old friend Shih Ying had perished in the fire or was still alive. He was about to turn back to search for him himself. But if he did so, he would not be able to cross the river today and reach the town before nightfall.

"Did you see an old hermit coming out of the temple?" he asked the messenger. The man said he had not.

"Then stay behind, and when the fire is burned out search in the ruins for any trace of him! You can spend the night in the nearest village inn and follow on tomorrow!"

The following morning when Yu Tsun was going through the city gate in his sedan chair he heard a sound of loud quarrelling coming from the head of the procession. The heralds had come into collision with somebody on the way. Upon inquiry he was told that a quarrelsome drunkard had run into the procession and would not get out of the way, but instead had lain down in the middle of the street in order to give trouble. The disrespectful culprit was immediately dragged to the door of the sedan chair.

"Do you not know that you are obliged to make way for the prefect of your town when he passes by? How dare you bar the road to him?" Yu Tsun asked the man, haughtily.

"Come, now! Am I not to be allowed to get drunk with my own good money, and when I'm drunk, to lie down for a bit in the street? Besides, the street does not belong to you, but to the Emperor; so the great gentleman had nothing at all to complain about," came the impudent answer.

"What an insolent boor! Ask him his name!" said Yu Tsun, enraged.

"My name is Ni, otherwise known as 'the Drunken Diamond,' because I like a good drink and can be hard as a diamond when there are debts to be recovered," babbled the drunkard.

"Indeed? Well, we shall see straight away whether he's as hard as a diamond! Beat him!" ordered the enraged Yu Tsun. Thereupon the servants threw the drunken man to the ground and gave him a few heavy blows with a whip. Thanks to this painful cure, he very quickly became sober again and humbly begged for mercy.

"A fellow like that calls himself a diamond, and he gives way after only a few gentle blows!" scoffed Yu Tsun from his sedan chair. "That was no real beating at all. He will get a proper flogging after the hearing at the yamen. Bind him and take him away!" he ordered his servants. And so, despite his struggling and shouting the well-known moneylender was seized and fettered and dragged off with the procession to the house of the Prefect amidst the malicious glances and comments of the crowd.

The rumor of his arrest spread from the street to his home and to the ears of his wife and daughter. When he did not come home that evening his wife sent her daughter out to look for him in all the well-known gambling inns which he was in the habit of frequenting. But the daughter looked for him in vain, and the rumor of his arrest was confirmed to her wherever she went. When at last, in her perplexity, she began to weep, people comforted her, saying:

"You need not despair. After all, the Prefect belongs to the Chia clan, and there is a young Chia who is a neighbor and good friend of your father. You and your mother must visit him as quickly as possible

526

and ask him to put in a good word for your father with his relatives, and procure his release."

The daughter Ni then remembered that a young man named Chia Yun, who was on friendly terms with her father, lived right beside them. She hurried home and that same evening mother and daughter together visited their neighbor. They found him at home. Chia Yun politely invited them to be seated, got his mother to give them tea, and listened to their story. When they had finished he said, with a boastful and important air, that he was quite willing to help them. He only needed to say the word in the western palace and the arrested man would be released; for Mr. Cheng, the senior of the western palace, had served the Prefect well in days gone by.

Highly delighted, mother and daughter went to the prefecture next day and secretly informed the imprisoned head of the family that he need not worry, for his friend and neighbor, young Mr. Chia Yun, had promised to see about his release. The moneylender Ni was delighted with the news and looked forward with confidence to being soon released.

It must be remarked here that since the time that Chia Yun had tried to buy the favor of the influential Madame Phoenix by gifts, he had only seldom and unwillingly ventured to go near the Yungkuo palace. He had the uncomfortable feeling that, as a poor begging cousin, he did not count for much with the rich clan, and was barely tolerated by them. The porters at the Yungkuo palace were in the habit of treating callers exactly in accordance with how they stood in the eyes of their masters. When it was a matter of respected visitors, who were gladly received, they were very quick in admitting and announcing them. But when it was a question of less important people, they were extraordinarily slow to do anything, whether the visitors belonged to the clan or not.

So it happened that when Chia Yun called that day at the main gate of the Yungkuo palace on behalf of his protégé, and asked admission on the pretext that he wished to say good day to his uncle, Chia Lien, he was informed gruffly that young Mr. Chia Lien was not at home, but that if he wished to do so and had time, he could wait until he returned. Chia Yun knew what this evasive answer meant. He might have to wait a very long time indeed.

It seemed to him utterly useless to ask for Phoenix or Pao Yu, who were less kindly disposed to him than Chia Lien was, so he returned home with his task unfulfilled, but the mother and daughter importuned him so continuously that he decided to try a second time. This time he intended to use the back entrance, going through the park, but to his surprise he found the back gateway locked and barred.

With bowed head, utterly discouraged, he set out for home. He remembered how nobly neighbor Ni had helped him out that time with money for the spices by means of which he had luckily wangled that gardening job from Phoenix. How he would love to do him a service in return now! How would he face the mother and daughter Ni, who had been counting on him? Could he tell them the truth? Dare he let them know that the hardhearted Madame Phoenix avoided him as a poor nephew and shut the doors of the western palace against him? That she preferred to lend out the family fortune, inherited from their common ancestors, to complete strangers at exorbitant interest rates rather than use it to help poor members of the clan? He dare not speak about these things, or he would not only damage his own name and credit in the neighborhood, but also endanger the reputation of the Chia clan.

"My efforts have been in vain. True, at my pressing request the western palace people did take steps with the Prefect, but alas, the Prefect is relentless," he said on his return. "But perhaps you might try your luck with the curio dealer, Long Tzu Hsing. He is related to the majordomo Chou Jui of the western palace, and has known the Prefect for a long time."

"If the masters can do nothing for us, the servants will not fare better," replied mother and daughter, disappointed.

"You are mistaken there. Nowadays the servants sometimes have more influence than the masters," remarked Chia Yun, as he turned away, annoyed. So the two women had to wait several days more before they got back their breadwinner. He had got off with nothing more than a light flogging. On his return his disgruntled wife and daughter told him about Chia Yun's futile visits to the Yungkuo palace, and twisted the matter in such a way as to give the impression that, for lack of good will, Chia Yun had not exerted himself sufficiently on his behalf.

"What? Just wait! I'll give the ungrateful scoundrel a good piece of my mind!" roared the usurer Ni, who had immediately got drunk again to celebrate his release. "That time when he was starving, did I not help him, with my money, to get a fat job in the western palace? And now, when I was in a fix myself, he left me in the lurch! Just wait! If Ni, the Drunken Diamond, once opens his mouth and raises a rumpus, the grand people in the eastern and western palaces will have reason to rue it!"

"Be quiet! Was the last flogging not enough for you? Do you want to get into trouble again with your drunken chattering?" said his wife, trying to quiet him.

"Pah! I'm not afraid! While I was sitting in the cooler I palled up with a few decent fellow sufferers, and lots of things came to my ears about the fine Chia clan: what extortioners they are, how they fleece the poor peasants in the provinces, how they cheat their fellow beings of their property and their women, and harry them to death! Several of their scoundrelly people have already been laid by the heels and will be brought to trial very soon here in the capital for their infamous deeds. But the fine lords themselves should be brought before the judgment seat. Just you wait! They shall get to know me, Ni, the Drunken Diamond, in time!"

"Ah, shut up and come to bed!" his wife interrupted. "You're so drunk that you don't know what you're saying. Cheating other people of their women? That is surely only silly gossip!"

"You women do not leave your own four walls. What do you know of what goes on outside? Two years ago I became acquainted with a young man named Chang at a gaming table. He told me everything, and it is he whom the noble gentlemen in the eastern and western palaces cheated of his betrothed, one Yu girl. If I only knew where young Chang is now! I'll explain to him how he must take action against the noble clan. The gang will have to go down on their knees to me yet! But you women need not trouble about it. Leave it to me!"

He lay down in bed, muttered for a while to himself, then dozed off.

CHAPTER 47

The unhappy lover, Pao Yu, stirs up past feelings. The bailiffs of the Minister of Finance take possession of the western palace.

DIRECTLY AFTER HIS RETURN FROM THE PROVINCES CHIA CHENG HAD been summoned, straight from his travel litter, to an Imperial audience to receive the reprimand of the Most High and perform his kowtow of repentance. He emerged covered with perspiration, and with his tongue hanging out with shock and dismay.

"Confound it all! Confound it!" he gasped, as he came out, to the crowd of friendly dignitaries and colleagues who had surged around him expectantly in the vestibule and besieged him with questions as to how the audience had passed off. Now, as far as his own person was concerned, the much-dreaded audience of reconciliation had fortunately passed off fairly well. But the Most High had asked the most extraordinary questions concerning his relationship to certain other bearers of the name of Chia, who held various offices in distant provinces and had recently been feathering their own nests very assiduously. Mr. Cheng got the uncomfortable feeling that a thunderstorm was brewing and threatening to break over the entire Chia clan.

His friends and colleagues tried to dissipate his fears, and congratulated him on still having his quiet, pleasant position in the Ministry of Works, in which he would not be exposed to vexations such as he had had to contend with in his former post of Corn Treasurer in the provinces. His elder brother Prince Shieh was also, they admitted, a man of honor and above all reproach. But at the same time they discreetly gave him to understand that perhaps it would be advisable for him to keep an eye on his various nephews, especially the nephew in the eastern palace, Prince Chen. All kinds of unfavorable things were being whispered about this nephew, and it appeared that he was regarded with some displeasure in certain high ministerial and eunuch circles. So it was that Chia Cheng's feelings were not entirely happy when he entered the western palace after the audience and was solemnly received by the clan.

For all that, the joy of seeing his family again, and especially the outward well-being of his son Pao Yu, the flourishing appearance of the latter's young wife Precious Clasp, whom he found more plump and resplendent than ever, and the favorable development of his grandson Chia Lan, enabled him to forget his secret anxieties for a few hours.

"But there is one person still missing!" he suddenly exclaimed when he had finished greeting all the female relatives. His wife understood that he meant Black Jade; no one had yet told him by letter of her sad end.

"Cousin Ling is ill," lied Madame Cheng, not wishing to damp the joys of reunion with mournful news. Pao Yu, who was present, felt as if his heart had been pierced with a dagger, but filial respect bade him hide his pain. Only later, after the communal feast of welcome, when husband and wife were alone together and were discussing the various events which had taken place in the family in the interval, did Madame Cheng venture to mention Black Jade's death. Chia Cheng was extremely shocked, and fell into a deep, mournful meditation. Madame Cheng too became quite emotional, and a waiting maid had to pluck at her skirt to remind her to pull herself together and change the conversation to a subject more calculated to cheer her husband up again.

The following morning, in accordance with custom, Mr. Cheng visited the Temple of the Ancestors together with the male members of the family, to announce his safe return home to the spirits of the ancestors and to thank them by a ceremonial offering for the protection accorded him. After the ceremony he took his two nephews, Prince Chen and Chia Lien, aside and appealed to their consciences in earnest and impressive words. Unfavorable things were being said about them in the town, he told them; they were no longer children, and were kindly to keep a better watch on themselves in the future. From their embarrassed air, and the dejected *shih* with which they promised to mend their ways, it was obvious that their consciences were not quite clear. The reunion celebrations closed with a grand procession of all the male and female servants of the western palace, who performed their kowtow of welcome.

Pao Yu was deeply shocked when he heard his mother say that Black Jade was ill, rather than admitting her death. Painful memories had reawakened in him and left him no peace the whole day. He felt an urgent desire to have a quiet talk with Cuckoo, Black Jade's trusted companion. True, Cuckoo had meantime been taken into the service of Precious Clasp, who greatly esteemed her, but he seldom saw her and she seemed to shun him deliberately. When he returned home that evening he did not visit Precious Clasp, as was his custom, but remained in his study, alone and depressed. Precious Clasp sent Pearl over to him with tea, and herself came to cheer him up. She thought he was depressed by the prospect of being examined by his father soon, and besides, it was time to go to bed, she told him. He pretended to agree with her assumption.

"Yes, you're right, but will you please go to bed? I should like to stay up alone for a while and collect my thoughts," he said to her. "My memory is not what it used to be; I do not want to disgrace myself before my father. Pearl will keep me company for a while. You others can go to bed now!"

Precious Clasp did as he asked her and went to her bedroom alone.

"Send Cuckoo over to me!" he asked Pearl in a low voice. "I very much want to speak to her."

"Oh, we thought you wanted to collect your thoughts for the forthcoming examination. So you only want to chat! Could you not do that in the daytime?"

"Who knows when I shall get a chance to do so, now that my father is back? This evening is just the right time for it. Please do me the kindness and bring her along quickly!"

"She only obeys your wife."

"I cannot possibly have her called by Precious Clasp."

"Why not?"

"Precious Clasp would ask the reason, and it is just about the other, Black Jade, that I want to talk to Cuckoo. I know that Cuckoo wrongly thinks that I am faithless, and turns away from me on that account. I must at last convince her of my true sentiments."

He pointed towards Precious Clasp's bedroom.

"Cuckoo must at last learn that I did not want to marry that girl in there at all. She has become my wife through subterfuge. It is not my fault, it is the fault of the old *Tai tai* and the others that Black Jade had to die of grief. I want to explain all this to Cuckoo so that she may not also, like Black Jade, pass to the next life with an unjustified grudge against me. For I know from Taste of Spring that that is what happened with Black Jade. Do you also consider me unloving and faithless? You may not know it, but I am telling you today: When Bright Cloud died I ceremonially made an offering to her at the water lily pond and dedicated a dirge to her. And Bright Cloud was only a servant! Is not Black Jade more deserving of a worthy funeral offering?"

"That is your affair. What have we others to do with it?" replied Pearl coolly.

"I have intended for a long time past to compose a dirge for her, but since I recovered from my last illness my mind has been so extraordinarily dull. I might have been able to write something straight away for any other person. But to write a hymn in honor of Black Jade I would need to consider every word carefully. I wanted to ask Cuckoo to help me with it. Her memory of the last incidents and the last phase of Black Jade's life is more complete than mine. Why did she die so suddenly after she had been so well and cheerful all the time before? Why were we not allowed to see each other during those days? Why did she burn the copies of her poems shortly before her death, and leave me no keepsake, although she thought of me up to the last? Those are puzzles which I cannot solve. And why did Precious Clasp take away from me the souvenirs which I managed to get from Black Jade through tricks in past years?"

"She did not wish the sight of them to open up old wounds in you. Do you want to know anything else?"

"What did the mysterious music at her death mean? Perhaps she did not die as a human being at all, but soared up to heaven as a spirit? I did see her coffin, it is true, but it was closed. Perhaps it was empty?"

"What crazy ideas you have! Do you really believe that an empty coffin was set up and that it was given out that someone died, who did not die? That is just nonsense!"

"I do not know why it should be nonsense. A spirit can make itself invisible. Be good enough to bring Cuckoo along to me!"

"It's too late tonight. I must first prepare her for it. Who knows whether she will be ready to render you an account straight away? The best thing is for us to choose a time when your wife is with the old *Tai tai*, perhaps tomorrow or the day after."

"Very well, but do not forget about it. You have no idea how much I want to talk to Cuckoo."

The waiting maid Musk appeared, sent by Precious Clasp, and reminded Pao Yu that it was already long past midnight. He should come to bed at last, she said.

"The conversation must have been wonderfully exciting to make one forget the time completely," she remarked sarcastically to Pearl.

"Yes, indeed it was, but tomorrow is another day," replied Pearl coolly.

"Very well, and do not forget tomorrow!" Pao Yu again whispered in her ear.

"Why! What important secrets have you got between you? Should I not suggest to the *Nai nai* that she had better let you sleep with Pearl? Then you could talk to each other to your hearts' content."

"Stop your chatter!" said Pearl to Musk, then, turning to Pao Yu: "See how you cause us to be gossiped about," she said reproachfully, pushing him before her into Precious Clasp's bedroom.

Though in no mood for festivities himself, Chia Cheng gave way to the importunings of his friends and acquaintances and held a great banquet two days after his return home. But he declined with thanks the festival music and theatrical performances with which they wished to honor him.

In the midst of the merry feasting the Yungkuo palace suddenly received a strange, uninvited visitor. "Mr. Chao, the Minister of Finance, is outside with a number of his officials, and wishes to pay his respects," the majordomo Lai Wang announced excitedly. "He came straight in the gate without ceremony and without having first presented his visiting card, and he is already on the way to the banqueting hall."

While Mr. Cheng, utterly dumfounded, was wondering what on earth could have moved the Minister of Finance, whom he knew only slightly, to pay this sudden visit, and whether he would be obliged to invite him to the banquet, a second report was brought to him to the effect that the Minister had already passed through the second gateway and would arrive in the hall immediately.

Mr. Cheng dutifully hurried to welcome him. He saw him already, accompanied by six attendants, walking straight up to the main hall without ceremony or greeting, with an ironical smile on his lips. That certainly did not look like a private visit, but rather, an official one. As he appeared a sudden hush fell on the merry banqueting table. Everyone rose and bowed stiffly and respectfully, and then half the people slipped away, one after another, out of the hall. Mr. Cheng pressed Mr. Chao, who still remained silent, smiling disdainfully, to take a seat, and was just beginning a conventional conversation about the weather when another surprising announcement was heard: "The Prince of the Eastern Covenant is entering!"

Mr. Cheng hurried out of the hall to meet the second illustrious visitor, and respectfully greeted him, falling on his knees. The Prince helped him to his feet in a friendly manner.

"Naturally, I would not have intruded here in this unceremonious fashion without special reason," he said seriously but courteously. "It is my duty to announce an Imperial decree to Prince Shieh. Will the honored friends and guests please withdraw first? The decree is only meant for the people of the western palace."

"Your Highness no doubt means well, but in order not to render more difficult the task of the Prince who is officiating in the western palace as executor of the Imperial wishes, I have already had all the exits closed by my officers," objected Mr. Chao.

"Very well. Send some of your men with the gentlemen so that they can get out without difficulty," said the Prince with a smile.

The frightened friends and guests dispersed like smoke. Only Prince Shieh, Chia Cheng, and a few male relatives remained in the hall, trembling and livid. Meantime uniformed men suddenly swarmed all over the palace. All the buildings were occupied; all the gates were locked. No one was allowed to move from where he was. As soon as Mr. Chao announced that the task of locking up and occupying the palace premises had been completed, the Prince of the Eastern Covenant stepped forward to make his ceremonial proclamation of the Imperial decree. Lying submissively on their stomachs in the courtyard, at the foot of the steps leading to the hall, Prince Shieh and the members of his clan listened while the Prince, standing on a dais above, read the decree in the name of the Most High One. Prince Shieh had been carrying on unlawful intrigues with officials in the provinces, and had misused the power of the State to oppress the weak. He had thereby forfeited the Imperial favor which had been lavished upon him for the sake of his illustrious ancestors, and as punishment he would lose the princely title and the privileges which went with it. The Prince had been instructed, with agreement of the Minister of Finance, to take him into custody and to confiscate his property. So the decree ran.

"Arrest Chia Shieh!" thundered the Minister of Finance to his officers, when the Prince had finished reading the decree.

The search of the premises and the confiscation of property could now start in real earnest. Divided into groups, the constables and sheriff's officers, who were burning with eagerness for the hunt and rubbing their hands with joy in anticipation of the rich booty, were let loose on the individual dwellings. There was a slight difference of opinion between the Prince, who was trying to mitigate the measures to be taken and chose to interpret them as referring only to the dwelling of Prince Shieh, and the Minister, who insisted that they should extend

534

to the whole palace without discrimination. He had special designs on the residence of Madame Phoenix, for he knew that most of all would be found there.

"But do not let your men act too violently and roughly, and at least give the ladies time to withdraw!" the Prince warned him. After a little time it was announced to him that a number of dresses and objects had been found which had come from the Imperial Palace and which, as such, ordinary mortals were forbidden to use. And then, again, he was informed that in the home of Madame Phoenix two chests had been confiscated which were found to be full of promissory notes and mortgage documents, from which it transpired that Madame Phoenix had been lending out money at illegally exorbitant rates of interest.

"So they have been carrying on usury too! The gang deserve no mercy! Go on boldly confiscating everything!" urged the Minister of Finance. And he asked the Prince for authority to use still stronger and more ruthless measures. He was jubilant when his secret opponent was just then called outside to receive the Prince of the Northern Quietness, who had come over from the eastern palace with a new Imperial decree in his pocket. Now that he was rid of the troublesome princely watcher, he would at last be able to do as he liked and show his full power, thought the overofficious Minister Chao. But his triumph was short-lived. The new decree, which the Prince of the Northern Quietness proclaimed immediately afterwards in the reception hall, stated emphatically that the authority of the Minister of Finance was to be limited solely to procedure against Prince Shieh, while only the Prince of the Eastern Covenant was authorized to determine the measures to be taken against the other householders of the western palace. The Prince, who had secretly procured the issue of this decree in great haste, listened to it with satisfaction, and was very happy to be in a position to stop the raging Mr. Chao from further activity. He made it clear to him that his task was now completed, and sent him off with instructions to hand Prince Shieh over to the Prefect of Police.

The two Princes kept back only a dozen elderly, steady sergeants from the police force; the remaining men had to clear off as quickly as possible.

"You have arrived just in time," the Prince of the Eastern Covenant said with a smile to the Prince of the Northern Quietness. "Who knows what mischief the energetic Minister of Finance would have done here if the new decree had not fortunately rendered him harmless."

The Prince of the Northern Quietness was concerned above all for Mr. Cheng and Pao Yu. At his request Mr. Cheng was brought to him from the servants' hall, into which the overzealous Mr. Chao had had him locked. Mr. Cheng threw himself on his knees before the Prince and with tears implored mercy. The Prince kindly raised him to his feet and informed him of the comforting terms of the new decree, whereupon Mr. Cheng, greatly relieved, turned towards the north and performed a kowtow of thanksgiving.

"The matter of the forbidden articles from the Imperial Palace and the usurious money business is, of course, a delicate one," the Prince hinted to him. "It can be maintained, however, that the former objects were presents from your eldest daughter, the late Imperial wife, Beginning of Spring, and this would excuse their presence here. On the other hand, how can this money business be excused? That will be more difficult. As regards the confiscations, I have to request you to compile a complete and truthful list of the movable goods belonging to your brother Shieh."

While the male members of the clan had been banqueting with their friends and acquaintances in the great hall on that unfortunate afternoon, the female members of the family had assembled in the home of the Ancestors, likewise to celebrate Chia Cheng's return with a feast. In the midst of the merry banquet one of Princess Shieh's serving women came running in crying excitedly: "Woe! Woe! Thieves and robbers are breaking up the cupboards and boxes, and turning everything upside down, and dragging our things away!"

The ladies had not yet recovered from the first shock when the waiting maid Little Ping came rushing in, uttering shrill cries of distress, with her hair hanging loose, dragging the little daughter of Phoenix after her.

"I was just taking a meal with the little girl," she reported breathlessly, "when suddenly our Lai Wang was brought in laden with chains by a troop of men in uniform. 'I want to inform the ladies that they should withdraw at once,' was all that he said, for a squad of police was on his heels to make a search and to seize things. I wanted to gather up a few valuable things quickly, but the strange men pushed me out the door. The ladies must take the most necessary things with them quickly and hide themselves!"

The utmost confusion ensued. All the ladies jumped up from their seats and hurriedly grabbed at this and that. Everyone shouted at the same time, and not a sensible word could be heard. Phoenix, normally so efficient in dealing with difficult circumstances, had not moved a limb and listened with strangely terrified, wide-open eyes to the maid's report; now she suddenly fell down in a faint. In the general confusion, while some were attending to the fainting woman and others were grabbing hold of useless articles without knowing where to take them, Chia Lien came rushing in, panting.

536

"Good news!" he cried to the frightened women. "Thanks to the intervention of the Princes, the worst danger has been averted!"

He was stormed with questions from all sides. He waited until some kind of order had been restored and until the maid Little Ping had helped the distraught Phoenix to her feet and Mandarin Duck had put the Ancestress, who was gasping for breath, down on a couch. Then he related in the fullest detail how the two Princes had kindly intervened and fortunately put a stop just in time to the havoc which was being wrought by the ruthless Minister of Finance. But in order not to cause the ladies renewed consternation he did not mention for the present the fact that Prince Shieh had been arrested. As soon as he had fulfilled his mission of calming the ladies he left them and hurried off to his own dwelling to see what was going on there.

He found his home in a state of wild disorder. Cupboards and boxes and chests had been broken open and half the contents plundered. While he was observing the damage, petrified with shock and rage, he heard a murmur of voices which came from a group of men outside in the forecourt. He went out and found Chia Cheng, in the presence of the two Princes and several officers of the Minister of Finance, making out a list of Prince Shieh's possessions, which were being confiscated. Prince Shieh's majordomo was assisting him. Finally the list was completed and read aloud, and Chia Lien heard:

Gold head ornaments, one hundred and twenty pieces; twelve pearl necklaces; two flat gold dishes; four gold cups; forty gold spoons; eighty silver eating bowls; twenty silver plates; three sets of gilded ivory chopsticks; four gilded pitchers; six gilded goblets; seventy silver plates; thirty-six silver wine tankards; fifty ounces of gold ingots; five thousand two hundred ounces of silver ingots; seven thousand thousand-piece strings of copper money; thirty-six sable skins; so and so many skins of all kinds of animals; hundreds of furs and state robes, hundreds of bales of all kinds of material, hundreds of bronze and jade ornaments . . . and so it went on and on in a seemingly endless list. The promissory notes of Phoenix's money transactions were also mentioned.

"Who has actually been carrying on this usurious business?" Chia Lien heard the two Princes asking severely. Mr. Cheng threw himself on the ground, made a kowtow, and replied: "I, the laggard official, have not concerned myself about the business of the household. I know nothing about it. But perhaps my nephew Chia Lien can give you some information."

When Chia Lien heard his name he promptly came forward, threw himself at the feet of the Princes, and admitted: "Since the confiscated mortgage deeds and promissory notes were found in my home, I naturally take the blame for them. I beg of you graciously to free my uncle of any responsibility in the matter. He knew nothing about it."

"Very well. Your admission does you credit. Since your father has been found guilty in any case, we shall let him atone for this offense also. You yourself must remain for the present under police supervision. The other members of the family are free and may return to their respective dwellings," the Princes decided.

"But you ought to supervise your family more closely in the future, old Cheng! And now may it please you to await further instructions. We must return to the Imperial Palace at once and place our report before the Throne."

And so Chia Lien, acting on a noble impulse, saved Madame Phoenix from disgrace and in doing so made amends for much of the injustice which he had done her in the past.

The Princes got into their sedan chairs and were borne away. Mr. Cheng, at the head of those male members of the clan who were still free, escorted them to the gates. At the inner gate the Prince of the Northern Quietness had his sedan chair stopped once more. Mr. Cheng and his companions immediately genuflected at the door. The Prince stretched out his hand to Mr. Cheng.

"Do not worry! Everything will be all right," he said kindly. Friendly sympathy was distinctly written on his face. Mr. Cheng turned back greatly reassured, and directed his steps towards the inner chambers. Passing through groups of excited serving women and maids, who were all chattering at the same time, he arrived at the home of the Ancestress. He found her lying on a couch, weeping quietly, surrounded by her ladies, and also Mandarin Duck, and Pao Yu, and Precious Clasp. Princess Shieh sat a little apart, crying loudly. She was the only one who had not yet pulled herself together. His arrival inspired the ladies with new courage.

"I did not think that I would see you again," said the Ancestress, opening her eyes and breaking into loud sobbing, in which the rest of the company immediately joined. His reassuring account of the Princes' protection, which had averted the worst and which could be counted upon for the future, caused the chorus of sobbing to ease off, only to rise again at the news of the arrest of Prince Shieh. Princess Shieh felt oppressed by the company of the others, and slipped away to weep alone in her own home. But she found the gates locked against her and none of her staff was to be seen; they were all shut up behind bolted doors.

Crying loudly, she ran to the home of Phoenix to find comfort with her. She found the entrance to a side building, in which Phoenix kept her account books and treasure chests, locked and sealed up with red official tape. As she entered the living room the sound of subdued weeping met her ears. It came from the waiting maid Little Ping, who was busily and anxiously tending her mistress. Phoenix was lying as if dead on a divan, her face pale as ashes and her eyes closed. Princess Shieh thought she was already dead, and was about to raise a loud dirge, but Little Ping warned her to keep still and not to disturb her poor mistress, who had only just awakened from a fainting fit and urgently needed quiet. The same misery everywhere, thought Princess Shieh to herself, and returned sadly to the Ancestress. On the way she began to realize the utter wretchedness of her own state—the sudden fall from a brilliant, high position, her husband arrested, her son under police surveillance, her daughter unhappily married, she herself locked out of her own house, without a roof, without servants, and without means, the former Princess become a beggar! She was full of self-pity.

Fortunately, however, her lot was not quite so unhappy as she, the pampered lady of fashion, imagined it to be. The relatives befriended her kindly. Widow Chu willingly made room for her in her own home, and Madame Cheng placed a waiting maid and a serving woman from her own staff at her disposal, and so she was safe and well cared for.

Meantime Chia Cheng was walking up and down in a state of acute agitation and palpitation, nervously rubbing his hands, awaiting the new decree, which the Prince of the Northern Quietness had promised as consolation. While he was impatiently pacing up and down his study, he heard the guards who were keeping watch outside the door sharply challenging somebody. "Hi, there!" they cried. "Where have you come from? What are you loafing around here?"

Mr. Cheng stepped outside the door, and there he saw, standing in the courtyard, the bad-tempered old grumbler, Chiao Ta, the oldest inmate of the eastern palace and former companion-in-arms of the Ancestor Prince of the Ningkuo line.

"What brings you over here?" he asked him.

"Have I not admonished and warned my dissolute and incorrigible masters day after day?" stormed the old man. "They took my well-meant advice ill, they looked upon me not as a good friend but as an enemy, and they quite forgot what I had gone through and suffered for our old Ancestor! And now there's the devil to pay! Prince Chen and his son Chia Yung arrested and dragged away on the order of a Prince So-and-So! The Princess and her women shut up in empty rooms by police officers! Ha! Ha! The whole fine company locked up like dogs and pigs! The furniture and fittings looted or smashed! Ha! Ha! They wanted to get hold of old Chiao Ta too, but they came to the wrong man! Old Chiao Ta did not fight side by side with our Ancestor Prince, and battle his way through a hundred dangers, to let himself be locked up in his old age! I belonged to the western palace, I told them, and made off. They stopped me on the way and brought me here. And who would have thought I'd find things just as bad here as over in the eastern palace? But to be locked up? No! I'd rather die a free man!"

And lunging forward defiantly as in his fighting days of long ago, the old champion made to attack his guards. But out of respect for his gray hairs, and remembering the Prince's instructions to treat the servants with the greatest consideration, the guards avoided an actual fight and talked persuasively and appeasingly to the old hothead. They were here on higher orders and were only doing their duty, they told him. Since he was here now they had no objection to his staying here quietly. He should just make himself comfortable and wait patiently until new instructions arrived. At this the old man calmed down.

And so Chia Cheng learned by chance from the mouth of the faithful but tough old man of the ruin which had befallen the eastern palace. And he had to admit with shame that the scorned and resented old admonisher and grumbler had been right in his well-intentioned warnings all those years.

"This is the end! We're finished! Who would have thought that our proud race should one day sink in mud and filth like this?" muttered Mr. Cheng as he turned back to his study, deeply dejected. He had been pacing up and down for some time, sunk in thought, and tense with expectation, when Hsueh Kuo came rushing in, panting and gasping.

"It's good that you have come," said Mr. Cheng to the welcome messenger from the outside world. "But how did you get them to let you in?"

"With money and friendly words."

"Well done! I shall need you as a messenger. One may have a host of good friends and acquaintances, but when there is a fire, they all leave one in the lurch," muttered Chia Cheng. "What, actually, is the charge against our people over in the eastern palace?"

"I was at the Ministry of Justice this morning inquiring about Hsueh Pan," reported Hsueh Kuo. "There I found out some details regarding the reason for the proceedings against Cousin Chen. The action had its origin in two bills of indictment lodged by two public Censors. He is accused of holding gambling orgies in his palace and seducing and leading astray young sons of noble families. But that is the lesser charge. The other accusation is more serious, and it is that he forced young girls of good family into concubinage and then harried them to death by bad treatment. By this they mean our cousins, the second Yu and the third Yu. The Censors base their accusation on the evidence of the gambler and waster, Chang Hua, who was formerly betrothed to the second Yu, and of your former servant, Little Pao, who later, with his wife, kept house for the second Yu when she lived behind the palace in the Lane of the Flowering Branch. Further . . ."

Chia Cheng did not let him finish speaking. "Terrible! Terrible! This is the end!" he raged, angrily stamping his foot.

"Moreover, the Censor Li has handed in a bill of indictment against the Prefect of Ping an Chow," continued Hsueh Kuo. "He is charged with having accepted bribes and defeated the ends of justice in collusion with a corrupt clique of influential people in the capital, and caused innocent citizens . . ."

"Stop!" interrupted Chia Cheng impatiently. "We have enough troubles of our own. Why should other people's affairs concern us?"

"Why shouldn't they, indeed? The person who bribed the Prefect is your own elder brother, Prince Shieh, and the clique are your good friends and acquaintances! That is just why they are remaining invisible, and even today they did not dare to appear at the morning audience at the Court. They have fled from the capital and will stay at a safe distance until the storm has blown over. The matter is the talk of the town, of course, and people are wondering to whom the princely titles, honorably acquired by the Ancestors of the Chia family, will pass when the present holders, Cousin Chen and Uncle Shieh, have been deprived of them."

Mr. Cheng would not listen to Hsueh Kuo any longer.

"They have both acted most irresponsibly," he said angrily, "but this is no time for lengthy recrimination. I must go to the old *Tai tai* at once and see if she is still alive. You keep your ears open and try to find out what is going on, and if there is anything new to report, do not fail to come over at once."

CHAPTER 48

The Princess Ancestress, prostrate before heaven, nobly takes upon her own head the guilt of the whole clan, and generously distributes her treasures. The Imperial grace is showered upon Chia Cheng, and the princely title, restored once more, is passed on to him.

CHIA CHENG FOUND THE ANCESTRESS IN A SERIOUS CONDITION. SHE had just had a severe attack of asthma, and was still struggling laboriously for breath. He implored her not to excite herself too much and to take care of her precious life, so that her undutiful sons would not have even more cause for self-reproach.

"What is there left for me to live for?" she gasped. "I am over eighty years of age. Thanks to the blessings which have come from our ancestors I was able to enjoy a happy youth and married life. And now to come to such disgrace in my old age! It would have been better had I closed my eyes long ago!"

While Mr. Cheng was still anxiously trying to cheer her with kind words, the longed-for news came at last that a messenger had arrived from the Imperial Palace. With a palpitating heart Mr. Cheng rushed off to the front reception hall. There the palace superintendent of the Prince of the Northern Quietness was awaiting him. His expression promised good news.

"Good tidings!" he began with a smile. "My master the Prince has represented your case very earnestly before the Throne, and he and the Prince of the Eastern Covenant have succeeded between them in touching the heart of the Son of Heaven. Moreover, the memory of his virtuous wife, your eldest daughter, only recently deceased, has inclined the Imperial Lord to clemency and moved him to permit you to retain your position at the Ministry of Works. The confiscation of property is to be confined solely to the personal property of your brother Shieh. Whatever else has been confiscated from the western palace will be restored. Of course, the loan documents taken from your nephew Chia Lien will be examined again by my princely master. If it is proved that usurious business of an illegal nature has been carried on, the documents must remain under confiscation. Your nephew Lien will lose his official rank, but otherwise he will be free and he need not expect any further punishment."

Mr. Cheng joyfully performed two kowtows of thanks, one for the Son of Heaven and one for the Prince. He would appear at the early morning audience tomorrow without fail, to pay his respects to the Prince, he said. Shortly after the superintendent had gone the promised Imperial decree arrived and was put into force immediately. Unfortunately, Chia Lien's pleasure at being let off so easily was clouded by the fact that the treasure chests belonging to himself and his wife had already been plundered by the constables and bailiffs of the Minister of Finance before the Prince had intervened, and the goods could not be reclaimed for want of an inventory and receipts. A hoard amounting to seventy or eighty thousand ounces of gold, which Phoenix had busily accumulated throughout the years, was thus irretrievably lost. From one day to the next Phoenix saw herself cheated of the fruits of her longstanding, efficiently operated private business; she was never to recover from the blow.

Of course, within the family circle there was no lack of mutual reproach and bad-tempered recrimination. Mr. Cheng, who had never concerned himself previously with the accounts and the practical management of the great household, was now horrified to discover that for many years past they had been living above their means in the western palace; that the treasure chamber was empty; that the farm rents from the property in Manchuria were always already spent a year in advance. He reproached himself for his foolishness and incompetence in allowing this irresponsible management to go on for so long, and bitterly deplored the fact that there was not a single one among his sons and nephews upon whom he could rely, as he could have done on his first-born son, Chia Chu, who, alas, had died all too soon.

Meantime, on hearing of the recent favorable turn of events, the good friends and colleagues rallied around Mr. Cheng to congratulate him and seek his favor once more. There was a great spate of conjecturing and belated wise talk.

"For a long time past we had our doubts about your somewhat negligent elder brother Shieh and your frivolous nephew Chen," it was now said.

"Other families have their scandals without a Censor's coming and denouncing them at once to the Imperial Court. The worthy gentlemen appear not to have been sufficiently astute in the matter of cultivating profitable connections," others said.

"The Censors are said to have taken this step on the information of aggrieved servants who had been dismissed and humble citizens who had been offended. A drunken moneylender named Ni, well known in the town, has been mentioned in particular," said others. "Perhaps it would be wise to treat such subordinates and small people less roughly, and not to annoy them unnecessarily."

"On the contrary, you would be wise to supervise your servants more rigorously and to punish them more severely than hitherto when they are at fault. When you were Corn Treasurer you learned what too good-natured and easy treatment leads to. On no account should you allow your good name to be brought into discredit again through your subordinates. You could scarcely count on receiving mercy from the Imperial Court a second time," was the view of a fourth group.

While these different opinions, alternated with good advice, were being aired, a messenger arrived from young Hsia, the tyrannical husband of poor Greeting of Spring. His master, he said, was unable to come himself owing to another engagement. He was still willing to divorce his wife, Greeting of Spring, but must first insist on being returned the five thousand ounces which he had given for her. Since his father-in-law, Prince Shieh, had been arrested and dispossessed, he now claimed this sum from Mr. Cheng.

"This is the last straw!" groaned Mr. Cheng. Under the present circumstances where could he find five thousand ounces immediately?

"Such a scoundrel of a son-in-law! Instead of assisting his father-in-law in his need, or at least showing him sympathy, he comes along with such unfilial and unreasonable demands!" said Mr. Cheng's friends indignantly.

"I warned against this match from the beginning, but no one would listen to me. My poor, unfortunate niece," sighed Mr. Cheng. Sorry as he was, he had to let the messenger depart shrugging his shoulders and with empty hands, and Greeting of Spring had to continue languishing in the power of an unworthy husband.

The next day, at the early audience, Mr. Cheng performed his kowtow of thanks, and then he paid his respects to the Princes of the Eastern Covenant and of the Northern Quietness and also to the Chancellor, and begged their kindly intercession for Brother Shieh and Cousin Chen.

Phoenix was completely broken by all that had happened, and tortured by frightful qualms of conscience. Now she bitterly regretted that she had not taken the late Ko Ching's advice and invested the surplus money in a family trust property which would be safe from confiscation by the State. Instead of that, she had been foolish enough to pile up bars of gold and silver and to fill treasure trunks, which could be plundered at any time. How cruelly the wise prediction which her niece Ko Ching had made years ago on her deathbed had come true!

In addition, she felt painfully aware that the charge which the Censors had hurled at Cousin Chen—that daughters of good families had been forced to be concubines and then harried to death by ill-treatment—actually applied to her. The unhappy second Yu, whose death was on her conscience, rose before her eyes like a ghostly presence. In the Censors' bill of indictment the name of young Chang, her secret tool and the second Yu's former betrothed, was explicitly named. If the Court went to the root of the matter, her own guilt would have to come to light. She did not dare consider the consequences. A quick death was the only thing she desired. She, who up to now had been one of the most valued and respected persons in the Yungkuo palace, had lost face forever. She realized this from the gruff answer with which her husband Chia Lien had brushed off Little Ping when she had urged him to send for a doctor for her. He had no money to spare for that now, he had to think of himself, he had rebuffed her, brusquely.

"How can you even think of getting a doctor?" she said reproachfully to Little Ping afterwards. "What does my wrecked life matter to me now? I can hardly wait for the end, and I am only hesitating because I can't decide whether to swallow gold or take poison."

From that time on the faithful, anxious Little Ping did not move from her side.

The Ancestress had recovered with surprising rapidity, thanks to the comforting knowledge that at least her second son Cheng still enjoyed the Imperial favor and that she had her two favorite grandchildren, Pao Yu and Precious Clasp, always with her; in the midst of the general confusion she was all activity and motherly care. She opened her strongboxes and her cupboards and provided the impoverished ladies, Phoenix and Princess Shieh and Princess Chen, with money and clothing. She sent a carriage to the eastern palace and had Princess Chen and her daughter-in-law and two of the secondary wives who had stayed on brought over to the western palace. The other secondary wives had fled. None of the numerous staff was there any longer. Like Prince Shieh's servants, they had come under the official confiscation and had been dragged away by the bailiffs to be publicly auctioned. The Ancestress allowed the ladies from the eastern palace to occupy several rooms in her residence, placed two waiting maids and four serving women at their disposal, had them provided with food from the great kitchen, and allotted them a fixed monthly sum as pocket money, on the same lines as that normally allowed the members of the Yungkuo clan.

Cash had also to be made available for the imprisoned members of the clan—Prince Shieh, Prince Chen, and Chia Yung—to ease their captivity. Faced with an embarrassing lack of funds, Chia Lien knew no way out except to sell secretly part of the family property in the country. True, he did procure a few thousand ounces in this way and had ready cash for the moment, but the doubtful wisdom of this measure, which again was contrary to the wise advice of the deceased Ko Ching, will be seen later on. The farm stewards, who saw their masters' splendor disappearing and were anxious about their own future, sought to save what could be saved before the gates were closed and, in secret agreement with the tenants, stuffed as much as they could of the profits of the Manchurian property into their own pockets.

The Ancestress was depressed by Phoenix's perpetually downcast face and the ceaseless laments of the Ladies Shieh and Chen. As head of the Chia clan, she felt herself to be primarily responsible for the suffering which had come over the clan. One evening Mandarin Duck and Amber had to build an incense altar out in the open courtyard and spread a red prayer-carpet in front of it. Then the Ancestress hobbled out on her stick, supported by her waiting maids, went down on her old knees on the carpet, set alight the sticks of incense, touched the ground with her forehead several times, and, weeping, sent up a solemn, fervent prayer to heaven:

"O Mighty Heaven up above us! I, of the family of Shih, the unworthy head of the Chia clan, humbly lay myself at Thy feet and implore mercy of Thy divine majesty. Throughout many generations my race has striven to keep to the path of virtue and not to turn to the ways of evil. As far as lay in my power I have endeavored to be a devoted wife, mother, and grandmother to my husband, children, and grandchildren respectively. Even if I cannot claim to have done any outstandingly meritorious work, neither can I accuse myself of any outstandingly wicked deeds. In consequence of the arrogant, dissolute, and sinful mode of life of some of the younger descendants of our illustrious ancestors, the race of Chia has fallen into disgrace and ruin. A son, a grandson, and a great-grandson have to expiate their crimes in prison. I take the blame for all the evil, because I failed to give them the proper training. Now, O Mighty Heaven, I implore Thy gracious protection and support. Have pity on my children and grandchildren! Let me atone for them by a speedy death! Punish me and spare them! Turn their sorrow into happiness, their mourning into joy! . . ."

Her prayer ended in violent sobbing. Mandarin Duck and Amber raised her to her feet and, speaking comforting words to her, escorted her in again.

A few days later Chia Cheng was ordered by an express messenger to go to the Imperial Secretariat. At last the new Imperial decree had been issued which was to free him of uncertainty regarding the ultimate fate of the imprisoned members of the clan. Thanks to the benevolent representations put forward by the Imperial Secretariat to the Imperial Court through the mouth of the Prince of the Northern Quietness, the new decree viewed the offenses of the princely prisoners much more indulgently than hitherto, excused as legitimate family relations the connivance between Prince Shieh and the Prefect of Ping an Chou, acknowledged that the eccentric fan-collector had met his death through his own foolishness and not as a consequence of improper pressure on the part of Prince Shieh, and allowed, moreover, that Prince Chen had only meant well when he preferred to see his sister-in-law, the second Yu, lawfully provided for as secondary wife to his cousin Lien, in view of the complete poverty of her betrothed, Chang Hua, especially since her mother too had agreed to this. In the case of the third Yu, also, who had committed suicide in consequence of a tragic error, there could be no question of compulsion. To be sure, the accused had been guilty of numerous offenses against the law, among them the suppression of a legal action, the arrangement of a marriage during the period of Court mourning, and the secret burial of a member of the family.

However, in consideration of the fact that they were descendants of two men who had rendered great service to the Throne, they would be given a mild punishment: they would forfeit their princely titles and would be banished to the frontiers of the Empire, there to atone for their guilt by devoted service to the State—Prince Shieh in one of the lonely stations of the Great Wall in the Far West, Prince Chen in a remote coast-guard station on the eastern seaboard. In view of his youth, Chia Yung was absolved from all punishment.

Chia Cheng shed tears of joy and thanked the Prince of the Northern Quietness, who had informed him of the contents of the decree, by falling at his feet and touching his forehead to the ground.

He obtained permission for his brother Shieh and his nephew Chen to return home for one day to take leave of their families before going into banishment.

The message which Chia Cheng brought home from the Imperial Secretariat aroused mixed feelings, partly joyful and partly sad, among the clan. Princess Shieh and Princess Chen were inconsolable at losing their husbands and wept at the thought of their own uncertain future. The Ancestress was not particularly touched by the fate of her elder son and her grandnephew, who were not very near to her heart, but she had sufficient sympathy to wish to relieve the lot of the two exiles with monetary help.

"We should give them a couple of thousand ounces from our treasury to take with them," she remarked lightly to Chia Cheng.

She was utterly dumfounded when he informed her that the treasury was now empty, that the clan had been living beyond its means for years past, and that the farm rents from the Manchurian landed property had already been spent a year in advance. Probably the only thing they could do would be to sell the family jewels, he thought.

"So this is what we have come to! Then, it seems, we have been putting on false splendor for years and years past. I thought we had been laying by wonderful reserves!" exclaimed the Ancestress, bursting into tears.

"We have considerable sums of money invested in distant parts of the country, but on account of the confiscation we cannot draw upon that money now. Yes, we are indeed impoverished and we will have to reduce our expenditures drastically in future, and also reduce our staff. Nephew Chia Lien has been managing badly," explained Chia Cheng gloomily. He considerately kept silent that Phoenix, the favorite of the Ancestress, had in such large measure contributed to the downfall of the family, owing to her secret moneylending.

While the Ancestress was still debating with her second son this and that plan for scraping up money in great haste, the three delinquents,

Shieh, Chen, and Chia Yung, appeared. They fell penitently at the feet of the Ancestress and, covered with shame, begged for forgiveness. There was a touching family scene; the Ancestress was moved to tears, and soon had forgotten all her anger.

"Now go to your wives and make the best of the few short hours you have together!" With these words she dismissed her elder son and her grandnephew. Then, following the impulse of her generous heart, she beckoned to her side the Ladies Shieh and Cheng and the waiting maid Mandarin Duck, and bade them open her treasure chests and take out all the treasure which she had saved and accumulated in her married years. Magnanimously, she made a just distribution of her belongings.

Her elder son, Chia Shieh, received three thousand ounces of silver. He was to give one thousand to his wife and take the other two with him into banishment. Grandnephew Chen likewise received three thousand ounces, but he was allowed to keep only one thousand for his own use; the other two thousand he had to leave with his wife. She sent another three thousand ounces to Phoenix on her sickbed, but in her guileless ignorance of the facts she added a message that Phoenix was to manage the money herself and not allow her frivolous husband to spend it foolishly. Chia Lien received five hundred ounces with the condition that he should himself take Black Jade's coffin to her native town of Yangchow the following year and provide for a worthy burial there. Furthermore she set apart a certain sum for Grief of Spring, to provide the trousseau for her future wedding. A number of articles of jewelry and ceremonial attire were divided among the various male and female members of the family. Chia Cheng received a large sum of money in gold ingots, with which to bridge the existing shortage of cash and defray the household expenses for the immediate future. Pao Yu was given gold and silver jewelry to the value of several thousand ounces. Madame Cheng, Widow Chu, and her son Chia Lan, the great-grandson of the Ancestress, were also given proportionate shares of the treasure.

Finally, the Ancestress gave Chia Cheng additional instructions regarding reduction of staff and disposal of all unnecessary landed property. The Park of Delightful Vision was also a superfluous luxury in the present circumstances, she said. An end must be made, once and for all, to the former easygoing ways—to this life of pretense and false splendor. She had given away everything now, and they could not count upon her for any more help. Whatever residue she would leave at her death was to go to her maids and maids-in-waiting. So the family had better repent and mend their ways.

They all knelt down, contrite and deeply moved, promised reform, and devoutly wished that the Ancestress would live to be a hundred.

But the Ancestress declared that she would be glad to be united soon with the departed souls of her illustrious ancestors. A visit of consolation to Phoenix on her sickbed formed the last gentle rumble of the storm, now finally abated, which had swept over the family. Phoenix held her breath in terror and, covered with shame, hid her head under the bedclothes when she saw the Ancestress entering her room, accompanied by Aunt Cheng, Pao Yu, and Precious Clasp. Conscious that she was the chief cause of the financial ruin of the family, she had been prepared for a merciless storm of abuse. She believed the favor of the Ancestress forfeited forever, and was wishing for nothing but a speedy death. Instead of the reproaches which she expected, however, she not only received comforting words but was loaded with all kinds of useful presents as well as three thousand ounces of money; all this thanks to the fact that her secret money manipulations had been so considerately kept from the knowledge of the Ancestress. As her mind was set only on worldly possessions and prosperity, the improvement in her position immediately renewed her spirits. She performed her kowtow of thanks with astounding cheerfulness and agility in her bed and promised that in future she would work and strive for the Ancestress and the family with all the industry of a kitchen maid.

The next day Chia Shieh and Chia Chen had to take their leave and set out on their journey into banishment. Several of Mr. Cheng's own servants were obliged, very much against their will, to accompany them. There was the usual farewell drink and the prescribed escort of honor to the ten-mile halting place outside the city walls. Finally, Mr. Cheng spoke a few more words of admonition to the departing members of the clan, exhorting them to expiation and atonement for their wrongdoing by zealous service to their country. Then he turned back and rode home with Pao Yu and the other juniors.

On his return he found the gateway to the western palace besieged by a crowd of reporters and news hunters, who were violently remonstrating with the gatekeepers and noisily demanding their "good news bounty." They had arrived in haste in order to be first to bring news of a further Imperial decree whereby the princely title of the Yungkuo line, which had been forfeited by Prince Shieh, was restored and conferred on Chia Cheng. The gatekeepers had refused to pay the "good news bounty," saying that the news was no surprise, and had been expected as a matter of course.

"Not in the least," the reporters had protested. "A princely title is in itself an exceedingly rare gift. But to have it given to your old master, despite the recent scandal, is a piece of good fortune such as does not occur once in a thousand years. Most certainly we deserve our 'good news bounty'!"

549

Chia Cheng smilingly gave orders for their hungry mouths to be stopped; then he visited the Ancestress and told her the latest happy news. His joy and pride were somewhat damped by the thought that his good fortune was the consequence of his elder brother's disgrace. The news of the latest favorable turn of events had quickly spread in the town and in a trice all the good friends and acquaintances, the flatterers and spongers, so conspicuously absent during the time of urgent need, now turned up in force.

After he had rendered thanks at the Imperial audience the next day, Chia Cheng's strict sense of duty moved him to propose to the Emperor that as he did not deem himself worthy to remain any longer in enjoyment of the western palace and the Park of Delightful Vision, he placed both at the disposal of the State. But on the recommendation of the Grand Secretariat, the Son of Heaven graciously refused to accept his act of renunciation.

CHAPTER 49

Robbers loot the property left by the Ancestress and abduct the beautiful anchoress. Pao Yu gets back his stone and is awakened.

THE EXCITEMENTS OF THESE DAYS HAD GIVEN A SHOCK TO THE OLD heart of the Ancestress from which it was destined not to recover. Once more she tried to animate and lighten the dreary everyday life and to bring back the gaiety of happy days now past by a family feast. The newly married granddaughter Little Cloud had just by chance arrived shortly before Precious Clasp's birthday. At her suggestion, the Ancestress secretly invited all the female relatives within reach, and gave them a sumptuous banquet in honor of Precious Clasp's birthday, as a surprise for the latter. To all outward appearances everything was as of old, but the lightheartedness which used to animate such family gatherings was missing. Phoenix's pleasantries sounded forced and awoke no echo. The dismal faces of the impoverished Ladies Shieh, Chen, and Hsueh, the absent-mindedness of Pao Yu, who was thinking sorrowfully of Black Jade, the look of suffering on the face of Greeting of Spring, who was tearfully telling of the miseries of her married life —all these things effectively prevented a festive mood.

"It will probably be the last time I shall see you," said Greeting of Spring, full of sorrowful forebodings, as she was fetched away on the order of her tyrannical husband in the midst of the birthday celebrations. A few days later the Ancestress fell ill and died. The news that poor Greeting of Spring, like a crushed flower, had died of a broken heart shortly after returning home from the birthday party had been considerately kept from her.

The Ancestress had attained the ripe old age of eighty-two years and died a beautiful, gentle death surrounded by her children and grandchildren. She still had a kind word for each one in her last hour. A peaceful smile illumined her features as she closed her eyes. Her passing was mourned far and wide. As she had been the grandmother of an Imperial wife, the Most High contributed the sum of a thousand ounces towards the expenses of her burial and by special decree ordered the Minister of Public Worship to have a solemn State sacrifice offered in her honor.

The role of organizer and hostess during the arduous weeks of mourning until the funeral was once more laid upon Phoenix. With a heavy heart she undertook the onerous task. She could not hide from herself the contrast with that other occasion when, on the death of her niece Ko Ching, she had superintended the mourning pomp in the eastern palace as deputy of Princess Chen. At that time she had been at the height of her power, had more than a hundred servants under her, and could draw on lavish funds. Today she was a sick woman, she had only twenty-one male and nineteen female servants, and very limited means at her disposal. That meant economizing, and pinching, and saving on all sides. Besides, she had lost face and had never regained her former standing. Her measures of economy, dictated by sheer necessity, were interpreted by the clan and the other mourners as lack of filial devotion to the Ancestress, who certainly deserved more splendor and pomp, while the servants abused her as a miserly slave-driver.

On the eve of the funeral procession to the family temple, when the house was filled with guests and Phoenix was wanted everywhere at the same time, she was pained to hear from a waiting maid that her mother-in-law Shieh had run her down in front of the guests, alleging that she was shirking her duties. Mental excitement over this, coupled with physical exhaustion, brought on a collapse. She had a violent hemorrhage and had to be put to bed in a fainting condition. She was unable to take part in the chief ceremonies the next day when the coffin was taken to the Temple of the Iron Railings. The ladies of the eastern palace drove in hired carriages in the funeral procession. How the proud Princess Chen used to smile compassionately in the past when this or that poor relation had come to visit in a hired carriage! Times had changed indeed!

The night before the funeral procession the good Mandarin Duck gave magnificent proof of her fidelity and devotion by strangling herself and thus voluntarily remaining in attendance on her mistress of so many years in her journey to the Yellow Springs. Her action was praised by all. Mr. Cheng made her family a gift of a hundred ounces of silver and gave orders that the excellent girl was to be buried with the honors due to an actual granddaughter of the Ancestress. Her coffin was to be carried in procession the next day behind the coffin of the Ancestress and placed beside it in the family temple.

Very early the next morning the long funeral procession of more than a hundred carriages and sedan chairs set out for the Temple of the Iron Railings. Mr. Cheng had entrusted the care of the western palace, which was almost denuded of servants, to Grief of Spring and Chia Yun, Grief of Spring being responsible for the women's apartments in the place of Phoenix, who was ill, and Chia Yun taking responsibility for the rest of the palace together with the steward Ling. That afternoon Grief of Spring received a visit from her beloved chess companion, the beautiful anchoress, Miao Yu, who still lived in her Kingfisher's Cage in the farthest corner of the park. In her loneliness she kept the welcome comforter for the night and passed the time eagerly playing chess with her until dawn. In the fourth morning hour the beautiful anchoress was about to withdraw for her holy "session of contemplation," which it was her custom to make at this hour, when suddenly there were loud cries outside of "Help! Thieves! Robbers!" The cries, which first came from the female members of the night watch who were patrolling the women's quarters, were immediately taken up and passed on by the male watchers who were at the other side of the locked inner gate.

The timid Grief of Spring was so frightened that she could hardly breathe, but her brave companion extinguished the lamp and, leaning over the window sill, peered into the courtyard, but immediately drew back and locked the window again as quickly as she could.

"There are strange men in the courtyard," she whispered to Grief of Spring. Now the uproar outside increased, the inner gate creaked, and the sound of numerous voices and cries came nearer. The booming voice of one man rose above the tumult crying: "Where are the fellows hiding? Hold them! Fight them!" At the head of a few brave watchmen, armed with a strong cudgel, the sturdy Pao Yung came rushing along. He was the new park watchman, only recently taken into service, a fearless and sturdy fellow, who up till now had been somewhat disliked because of his rough manner, but who was to have an opportunity of proving his worth now. The strange intruders fled onto the roofs at the approach of his squad, and tried to ward off their pursuers from above with a shower of wooden roof tiles. But the brave Pao Yung pursued them up onto the roofs and dealt such ferocious blows with his cudgel that they took to their heels and quickly disappeared over the wall again.

When the servants inspected the field of battle by torch and lantern light they discovered doors and cupboards forced open and chests looted in the deserted residence of the Ancestress; in the courtyard they found the body of a man who had been killed by Pao Yung's cudgel. They recognized him as a former servant named Hou San, an adopted son of the majordomo Chou Jui, of the eastern palace.

This Hou San had been flogged and driven from the house in the previous year by his master, Prince Chen, on account of a trifling offense. Since then he had taken to gambling and fallen into doubtful company. At the news of the death of the Ancestress he had hung around for days on end at the gate of the western palace, in the hope of being taken into service as an extra help during the mourning period, but he had been overlooked. He had returned to his habitual gambling den and in the midst of his friends had given free expression to his anger against his former masters. He had casually remarked that he had heard from his foster mother that the Ancestress was not by any means without property when she died; that when she had generously distributed her treasures, this had by no means been everything; in reality she had left behind her whole chests and boxes full of gold and silver. Thereupon Hou San's companions urged and persuaded him not to be a fool but grasp his chance. Since he had been prevented from sharing the crumbs from the masters' table in a decent, honorable manner, he should take his share himself. His friends introduced Hou San to some daring fellows, members of a powerful band of pirates who were at present in the capital. Hou San was to give them the benefit of his knowledge of the place and lead them over the walls and roofs to the home of the Ancestress. The day of the funeral was chosen as most suitable for the robbery. The western palace would be almost completely deserted of male inmates. They would have an easy job with the few women. When the work was done they would leave the capital and seek safety in the hidden haunts of the pirate band on the shores of the Eastern Sea.

The attack was made under cover of night. The plundered gold and silver treasures of the Ancestress had already been taken over the wall and piled onto the carts kept in waiting, when some of the bandits noticed light in a room of the near-by west wing. There Grief of Spring was at her chess game with her companion. The sight of the two girls, especially of the one who, though she wore a nun's habit, still displayed the full glory of her head of hair, inflamed the lustful desires of the robbers. They crept along towards the lamplit room thinking to drag off the two young girls as unforeseen booty, but the sturdy Pao Yung foiled their intentions in good time and frightened them off over the roofs.

But the robbers' desires were now thoroughly roused; the leader of the band in particular could not get the alluring picture of the beautiful girl in the nun's habit out of his mind.

"If I only knew which convent she belongs to!" he said to his companions the following day when they were dividing the booty and discussing their further plans for flight.

"She is probably the nun from the Kingfisher's Cage at the bottom of the park," one of the band was able to inform him. "There was a lot of talk about her two years ago when she suddenly became possessed by demons while sitting on her pillow of contemplation. A chance meeting with some youth from the palace—Pao Yu or something like that was the name of the boy—was said to have caused the devil of temptation to take possession of her virgin body in the night."

"Aha, so that's the one!" said the ringleader, smacking his lips in anticipation of the tasty fruit. "I will carry her off tonight! I will need a coach and two men. You others go on in advance! We will meet tomorrow morning on the Twenty-Mile Hill outside the city walls."

It was about the hour of the fourth night watch. The park lay in complete darkness. From only one window of the Kingfisher's Cage shone the dull reddish glow of a single altar lamp. The beautiful Miao Yu was sitting on her round prayer-pillow, her legs crossed under her, endeavoring to compose her mind, which was still distracted by yesterday's events, and to dispose her soul to holy contemplation. Tonight, as always, she did not allow any of her servants to be near her during her prayer session. Her three maids had gone to bed long ago. She had already been about three hours persevering in her holy meditation when she perceived a slight chill from the coolness of the early morning. She was just about to call out for a bowl of hot tea when she heard a suspicious sound of footsteps outside the window.

Terrified, she called her maids, but no answer came from the next room. Suddenly she perceived a strong, stupefying smell. She was overcome by a strange heavy numbness which made her feel rigid and stiff, as if she were a jointed doll made of wood and hemp. She was unable to move, no sound would come from her lips; a veil, as it were, floated before her eyes. But even through the veil she could see a man entering through the window. In the reflection from the altar lamp she saw the dagger shining in his right hand. Now he pushed the blade into his belt, then came up and stretched his hands out towards her. In her semiconscious state, incapable of defending herself, she had to let him have his way. Now she felt herself being lifted through the window and carried through the courtyard to the wall of the park. They got her over the wall by a rope ladder. Then she was pushed into a carriage.

The carriage was driven to the eastern gate of the city at a head-long speed. It was the hour of the morning drum roll, and the city gates had only just been opened. The gatekeepers were surprised at first to see the carriage with curtained windows flying along in such haste at this early hour. But when they saw the words "Open the gates! Open the stables!" written in large letters on the two yamen lanterns set up beside the driver's seat, they were reassured. An express courier, they thought, and let the vehicle pass through without question.

The three maids in the Kingfisher's Cage awoke later than usual that morning. They felt a strange numbness in their heads, and there was a strong smell of coal gas in their room. The youngest of them, who was sleeping beside her mistress's oratory, distinctly remembered hearing her mistress call about the fifth hour of the morning, and later the sound of a man's voice. She was about to get up and go over but her limbs refused to move and she dozed off again immediately. Filled with anxious forebodings, they went into the oratory. It was empty. The window stood wide open. There was no trace of the beautiful Miao Yu to be found in the other rooms either. In a corner of the courtyard by the wall of the park they found a rope ladder, and below, not far from the ladder, a dagger sheath and a burned-out brazier. They still cherished a faint hope of finding the missing girl with her friend, Grief of Spring. But in the western palace they knew nothing of her where-abouts either. Now there was no further doubt about it: robbers had come at dawn, rendered the inmates of the Kingfisher's Cage insensible with noxious fumes, and abducted the beautiful saint!

Poor Miao Yu! She had dedicated herself to a life of chastity and purity and now had to suffer this iniquity. And still worse, the foul slander that she had connived with the robbers and, urged by fleshly desires, willingly allowed them to abduct her was noised abroad. What happened to her later—whether she became reconciled to her fate or preferred a voluntary death to shame—remained unrevealed.

Pao Yu and Grief of Spring wept bitter tears for their lost friend. How they had admired and even envied Miao Yu, who was able to live her own independent life beyond the tedious limitations and conven-tions of society! Grief of Spring was inconsolable at the loss of the only human being who was near to her heart. She had always looked up to her as a leader and a model, and had long ago made up her mind to do as she had done and renounce the world. She considered the circle of her relatives. Was there one among them who had been happy in love and marriage? Phoenix, the Yu sisters, Black Jade, Greeting of Spring—they had all been sacrificed to convention, to the obligations of society. Little Cloud had got a kindhearted husband, it was true, but he was a consumptive, doomed to early death. Taste of Spring, too, seemed to have been fortunate, but she had had to go far away from her family, to distant parts, and was consumed with homesickness. Wherever Grief of Spring looked, she saw only instances which discouraged and frightened her. She dreaded being the unhappy victim of a conventional marriage. No, she wanted to remain free like her friend Miao Yu, who was her own mistress and could rise at will above the clouds like the wild geese.

Now it was the day before yesterday, the day of the funeral, that this disaster had befallen the house. The very first time that she had been entrusted with a responsible task this deplorable misfortune had to befall her! She had lost face; she had shown herself incapable of carrying out household duties. This sad experience strengthened her in her idea of forsaking the world. Suddenly resolved, she seized a pair of scissors while nobody was with her, and had already cut off half of her hair when her waiting maid came in and forcibly stopped her. The maid was accompanied by a maid from the Kingfisher's Cage, who brought news of the disappearance of the beautiful anchoress. In her consternation, Grief of Spring submitted to having the scissors wrested from her and allowing the remaining half of her hair to be dressed up as well as could be managed in the normal worldly fashion. But even the sad fate of the friend whom she admired did not induce her to falter in her resolution. She was resolved to cut off the remainder of her hair at the next opportunity and enter a convent. But at the persuasion of her maid she agreed to wait a while before carrying out her decision, until some degree of calm had returned to the house after the recent excitements.

But the Ancestress and Mandarin Duck had only just been taken to the family temple, and the excitement over the night burglary and the abduction of Miao Yu had hardly died down, when the house was again thrown into a tumult by yet another death. Phoenix, who for a long time past had been physically sick and mentally worn out by pangs of conscience and the depressing feeling of having irretrievably lost face and forfeited her former position, died a few days after the funeral procession of the Ancestress. She died embittered at the early age of thirty years. She, who had formerly been the heart and soul of the house, the powerful mistress of the household, had felt more and more isolated and shunned since the collapse for which she had been to blame. Only good Little Ping remained true to her to the end. When the relatives came home after their three days in the Temple of the Iron Railings, they did not even deem it necessary to pay a personal

惜春

visit to her sickbed, but confined themselves merely to inquiring for her health through their maids. This heartlessness was the final blow which had killed her.

In her last hours she was tortured by terrible dreams. One time it was the second Yu who frightened her; another time the shades of Chin Yo and her betrothed emerged reproachfully and warningly out of the past—those two young people whom she had defrauded of their life's happiness through avarice and driven to suicide at the instigation of the Abbess of the Temple of the Watery Moon. She breathed her last in a state of confused raving. On account of the precarious financial situation, Chia Lien was only able to give her a lamentably wretched funeral, and if the faithful Little Ping had not helpfully intervened and placed her personal savings at his disposal it would have been even more wretched.

Grief of Spring confided in Pao Yu and found in him a kindred soul. She did not feel that she was made to be a housewife, and he did not feel that he was made to be an official; they both felt unfit for a practical life. Two nuns from the Convent of Earthly Seclusion, who had taken part in the mourning services for the Ancestress, and in their tour of the women's apartments of the western palace had also visited Grief of Spring, helped to confirm her in her holy decision. The pious soul-catchers had an easy task with the fourth young lady of the house and did not need to waste many words. Grief of Spring loosened her coiffure and smilingly showed them the shorn half of her head as a visible proof of her decision. From now on she started to fast and chastise herself secretly.

When she was told a few days later that she was intended to be given in marriage to the son of the family of Chen from Kiang nan, who had long been friends of the Chia family and had recently moved to the capital, she declared forthrightly that she did not wish to marry. She dreaded sharing the fate of Greeting of Spring, she said, and was firmly resolved to remain single and dedicate her life to holiness. There was a violent family discussion. Mr. Cheng stamped his feet in rage and said that this was the last straw. The clan was burdened enough in having a degenerate son, and did not need to have a degenerate daughter also. And if Grief of Spring persisted in her defiance, he could no longer regard her as belonging to the family. They importuned her from all sides and tried to talk her out of her strange ideas. But Grief of Spring stood her ground and threatened suicide if they did not let her have her way. Besides, she did not request to enter a convent right away, she said; all she wanted was to live peacefully in the King-fisher's Cage and emulate her model, Miao Yu. Then she would not be completely out of the world, and they could see each other from time to time and she could keep in touch with the family. At least they should allow her to live in the Kingfisher's Cage for the present and leave the ultimate decision to her brother Chen when he returned from his banishment. Otherwise, they might offend the head of her family and lay themselves open to the accusation of having driven her to suicide—an argument that did not sound so very unreasonable.

Grief of Spring's problem had not yet been solved when the attention of all was directed to another domestic crisis. Pao Yu suffered a recurrence of his old trouble. The thought of Black Jade was still gnawing at him, and the accumulated blows of fate which had befallen the family had made him more and more conscious of the futility and vanity of this transitory life. His supply of tears was exhausted; he was tired; his heart longed for rest, for liberation from the torture of these hundred conflicting human feelings. If only he did not have to feel! He wished he were made of wood or stone. He buried himself more and more in the negative, ascetic world of ideas of a Chuang Tzu.

To crown it all, his father had recently announced that he would soon again give him an opportunity of showing the progress he had made in the art of prose composition. If his attainment should prove inferior to that of his half brother Chia Huan or of his nephew Chia Lan, a sound punishment was threatened. Let him study and prepare diligently meantime! Mr. Cheng had obtained a long leave of absence on account of the mourning for the Ancestress, and during his leisure at home he was seriously concerning himself once more, after a very long time, with the education of the three juniors.

With horror, Pao Yu saw the approaching examination by his father like a specter before him, and in the further distance the still more frightening bogey of the approaching State examination. So his youthful dream would soon be at an end! Was this detested male world of harsh clashes of opinion, tedious place-hunting, contemptible office-seeking—this utterly loathsome world of humdrum commonsense and conventional morality—really to become his world? His whole nature recoiled from it. Still exhausted by the mental shocks of recent weeks, he was unable to pick up enough strength this time to comply with his father's order. His will failed him, he broke down and fell into a state of complete lethargy. And soon the alarming news ran from room to room throughout the western palace: Pao Yu has got his old bad turn again! After he had eaten nothing for several days the family doctor was called. The doctor shook his head doubtfully. Medicine would do him no good this time, he said; he was obviously approaching his end, and they should prepare in time for his last hour.

With a sigh of resignation and perhaps also of relief, Mr. Cheng ordered his nephew Chia Lien to get the coffin delivered for his ill-fated son. Chia Lien was just about to go in search of the servants who were to fetch the coffin-maker when one of the gatekeepers came rushing in gasping.

"That old starveling and vagabond is outside again, wanting to sell a jewel for good money!" he reported breathlessly.

"What does the fellow want?" asked Chia Lien rudely.

"He wants to sell a precious stone," repeated the gatekeeper. "He looks like a wandering monk. He has a precious stone in his hand and asserts that it is young Master Pao Yu's lost stone. He wants ten thousand silver batzes for it."

"Don't bother me with this nonsense!" snorted Chia Lien at the gatekeeper. "Once before we were taken in by a swindler like that, who wanted to talk us into buying a false stone. In any case, it's already too late. Cousin Pao Yu is at his last gasp."

"I told him that too. But the fellow won't take no for an answer. We have only to pay the money and our young master would recover immediately, he asserts."

While they were speaking a tumult of voices and calls was heard in the distance, drawing quickly nearer. Chia Lien heard words like "Impudent bonze!," "Intruder!," and "Stop the fellow!" He was about to give an angry order to chase the stranger away when he heard him in close proximity shouting through the window of the study in which Mr. Cheng was sitting:

"Come, pay up! Pay up! Ten thousand batzes for a human life!"

Mr. Cheng too had become aware of the noise and the shouting of the strange monk. He remembered that once, years ago, when Pao Yu was very ill, two strange mendicant monks like that one had appeared and cured him. Was it possible that the stranger was really bringing him back the genuine stone? If he only knew where he could at once obtain the large sum of money which the monk was demanding! He thought he would like to chance it. In case of success ways and means would have to be found.

Mr. Cheng had the stranger politely invited to come to his study. But without taking any notice of the invitation, the odd fellow ran straight to the inner chambers, to the room in which Pao Yu was lying ill. Chia Lien and the servants tried in vain to bar his way.

"Say, where are you going, you wild creature? That is the way to the women's apartments!" Chia Lien called after him.

"Do not stop me! If you do, my help will be too late!" replied the stranger, and as if by magic he dispersed the throng of people who were resisting him. The crowd ran after him shouting; but now the stranger reached the sickroom. The women who were gathered around Pao Yu's bed weeping—Madame Cheng, Precious Clasp, Pearl, and the others —did not even have time to hide themselves, so suddenly did the unannounced visitor enter. Startled, they only moved aside a step and stared as if bewitched at the strange apparition of the big bald-headed fellow in the dirty monk's hood.

Without any formality or greeting he walked up to Pao Yu's bed.

"Esteemed patrons and believers in Buddha, I bring you back the lost stone!"

With these words he produced a glistening jade stone. He held it up in the air for all eyes to see, and continued: "And now, quick! Out with the money, so that the work of saving his life may be consummated!"

"First let us see him saved, and then the money will be found," they shouted back at him.

"No, the money first!" he insisted.

Did he wish to put their faith and self-sacrifice to the test?

"Do not worry! Whatever happens, you will get your money even if we have to sell or pawn all our possessions!" said Madame Cheng, thereby showing her true mother's heart.

The monk laughed aloud and bent down close to the ear of the sick boy: "Pao Yu! Pao Yu! Your stone is back again!" he whispered to him. In tense expectation the bystanders watched for his words to take effect; and in fact Pao Yu slowly opened his eyes.

"He's cured!" gasped Pearl, joyfully.

"Where is the stone?" they heard Pao Yu asking. The monk pushed the stone into his hand. Pao Yu held it tight for a while, as if he were afraid it would escape from him again. Carefully and gradually he then loosened his grip, and held the stone up in the air before his eyes in order to look at it attentively.

"Ah, how long we have been separated!" he sighed. "Thanks be to Buddha!" All of them, even Precious Clasp, forgot the proximity of the stranger and pressed close around Pao Yu's bed. There was no doubt about it; he was cured. Chia Lien ran to take the good news to Mr. Cheng. The monk went with him. Mr. Cheng thanked him on his knees, politely pressed him to take a seat, and asked him various formal questions—in what place the master had set up his precious prayer-mat, what his worthy name was, and so on. He also wanted to know where he had found the precious stone, and how it had happened that his loathsome little cur of a son had got well almost as soon as he had caught sight of the stone.

"That I do not know either," the strange guest answered with a smile. "I should like to have my ten thousand batzes, and that is all!"

What rude, low behavior! thought Mr. Cheng to himself, but he did not want to offend the unknown benefactor by an ungracious reply.

"The money will be produced," was all he said in reply.

"Then out with it quickly! I must be on my way at once!" urged the man. Mr. Cheng requested him to stay a while. He would go and see about collecting the money.

"Hurry up and do not forget to come back!" the stranger called derisively after him. Mr. Cheng hastened off to the inner chambers where the women were still gathered around Pao Yu. With the words "Here it is!" Pao Yu, beaming, handed him the stone. Mr. Cheng did not give himself time to look at it for long.

"The boy does seem to be cured. But how can we collect the money?" he said, turning to his wife, embarrassed.

"I will give all my possessions. The proceeds will cover the amount," declared Pao Yu's mother generously once more.

"I do not think he wants any money," said Pao Yu.

"But he demanded it loudly, again and again. Strange, very strange indeed!" said Mr. Cheng, shaking his head. And he returned to the front part of the palace to discuss the money question openly with the stranger.

Meantime Pao Yu had asked for food and drink. His appetite was so good that his mother had to order him to stop, as she feared that he might eat too much.

"No fear! I am quite well again!" he said joyfully, and reached out for another helping. After the meal he felt strong enough to get up. While the waiting maid Musk was helping him to get up, in her joy at his recovery she let fall the remark: "Now at last you believe in the miraculous power of your stone. What a good thing it was that you did not succeed in breaking and destroying it!"

She had uttered the remark rather thoughtlessly. Her words had an unexpected effect. He suddenly changed color, let the stone fall, and sank back as if lifeless. There was great consternation. Musk reproached herself bitterly and silently vowed to follow Mandarin Duck's example and commit suicide if he did not recover consciousness this time. When calling and shaking him proved useless Madame Cheng in her despair sent for the monk, who, she supposed, was still with her husband. But Mr. Cheng came without him. When he had returned to the reception hall just now, the strange fellow had already disappeared.

Mr. Cheng found his son lying there as if dead. His eyes and mouth were firmly closed, his breathing and his pulse had stopped, but his body was still warm. They sent for the doctor in a great hurry.

Pao Yu was not dead. His spirit had only temporarily freed itself from his body and departed on a long journey. First he returned to the guest hall. There the strange monk was awaiting him. He took him by the hand and silently led him away. Pao Yu felt that all the weight of his body had left him; he seemed to float and soar through the air light as a leaf. Some way or other, but certainly not by the usual route through the gateway, he went out of the palace into the outside world. A wild, desert country loomed up. In the distance a vaulted stone arch stood out. It seemed to Pao Yu that he had passed through a similar archway once before. He was just about to question his companion about it when his attention was caught by the beautiful form of a woman which suddenly rose before him not far from the gateway. The beautiful one exchanged a greeting with his companion, and then disappeared again. Pao Yu thought he recognized her as the third Yu. Was that beautiful, heroic maiden assigned to them as guide? While Pao Yu was pondering this they arrived at the stone archway. Above it, written in four characters, was the inscription: "Blessed Realm of Purified Semblance" and on the pillars to right and left, the lines:

"Being in place of Seeming is more than Seeming.
Something in place of nothing is no longer nothing."

A little way behind the stone arch a palace gate opened before them. Inside he saw once more a woman beckoning to him from a distance. He thought he recognized her as Mandarin Duck. We have already been a long time on our journey—who knows how long—and have we still not come out of our park? But how strangely altered it is, thought Pao Yu to himself, perplexed. He was about to hurry up to Mandarin Duck and speak to her, but she had suddenly vanished. When he came to the spot where she had just been standing, he saw opposite him a stately building with a forecourt. The entrance door stood half open. Pao Yu turned inquiringly towards his companion, but he also had disappeared in the meantime. He raised his eyes and read on the façade of the building, written in slanting writing, the words: "For Awakening from the Folly of Love." To the right and left he read the inscriptions:

Joy, grief, gladness, pain—
All is illusion. Why the care?
Longing, striving, desire, yearning—
All is vanity. Why the effort?

Pao Yu heaved a sigh and thoughtfully nodded agreement. Where on earth had Mandarin Duck gone to? Perhaps she was inside. He picked up courage and pushed in the half-open door. Inside pitch darkness surrounded him. He felt frightened and very nearly fled again, but curiosity held him back. In the meantime his eyes had become accustomed to the darkness and he could distinguish a suite of rooms with half-open latticed doors. He suddenly remembered his dream of years ago in the bedroom of his niece Ko Ching. At that time he had come in his dream to a similar place, but the Fairy of Fearful Awakening had not allowed him to remain long in the vicinity of the rooms. Happy at being alone and undisturbed this time, he forgot that he wanted to look for Mandarin Duck and, urged by curiosity, forced his way into the first room.

The room contained a bookshelf which was filled with volumes of files. He picked out a volume at random. On the cover of the volume he saw the inscription "History of the Twelve Beauties of Chin ling" and next to it several blurred pictures. He did not spend much time on the pictures but began to turn over the pages and plunge into the contents. That must have been the story of Beginning of Spring, he said to himself after he had read the first chapter from beginning to end. And he eagerly set about the second chapter and did not stop until he had read through all the twelve chapters, which were written in a highly elaborate literary style. Much of what he read was not clear to him, but much of it impressed itself on his mind so easily that he knew it by heart afterwards. What a precious discovery! He actually had before him the life stories of all his sisters and cousins, though they were not identified by their ordinary names, but by secret, symbolic titles, each of which, however, he found no difficulty in attributing to the right individual. How exciting to learn in this way the different girls' secrets, the knowledge of which I had been endeavoring to obtain for so long in vain! If only I had ink and brush and paper at hand to write down everything and take it home with me! Of course I would not be indiscreet, but it would be fun to play the prophet and fortune teller a bit in the family. Such were the ideas which ran through his mind. It was a pity that no writing materials were to be found in the room.

He had just opened a supplementary volume to the "History of the Twelve Beauties of Chin ling," and had been moved to tears at a specially touching passage, when he heard a voice behind him saying: "Have you got your foolish impulses again? Miss Ling is asking for you!"

It sounded like Mandarin Duck's voice. And really, when he turned round he saw Mandarin Duck outside the open door, beckoning him. Happy to see her near again, he hurried up to her, but she slipped away from him back through the dark passage and out into the open, farther and farther away, like a light shadow which cannot be caught. In vain he called to her to stop; she floated away farther and farther, and he could not catch up with her.

All at once he was standing in front of the towering hall of a palace, with high curved pinnacles of richly carved woodwork. Urged by the desire to observe the beauty of the construction more closely, he calmly walked through the outer porch into the inner precincts. He had forgotten all about Mandarin Duck. He found himself in a front garden. In the midst of the flower beds of exotic, strangely scented flowers he noticed a single green foliage plant. It was fenced around with a decorative curb of white marble. He noticed that the leaves had red tips. The leaves were moving to and fro and rustling in a gentle breeze. They seemed to be nodding and bowing in greeting.

Though only a simple plant, and without blossoms, it had a rare and noble gracefulness which could not fail to delight and charm the eye and the heart of the beholder. And so Pao Yu too became wrapt in devout contemplation. A scolding voice suddenly tore him from his meditation: "How dare you sniff around our spirit plant, impertinent trespasser!" Frightened, he turned his head. An elf was standing beside him.

"I strayed in here looking for Sister Mandarin Duck," he stammered in confusion. "Forgive me my criminal curiosity! But may I ask, where am I? And how does Sister Mandarin Duck happen to be here? She appeared to me just now and told me that little Sister Ling wanted me."

"Your sister and your little sister are all one to me!" came the unfriendly reply. "I am the appointed guardian of our spirit plant here and it is my duty to keep at a distance profane creatures such as you."

"It must be a rare and exquisite plant, since you are appointed to protect it?" he asked, tearing himself away reluctantly from the vicinity of the spirit plant.

"Certainly; for it is the plant Purple Pearl. Its place was once on the banks of the River of the Spirits. At that time the Guardian of the Radiance of the Stone of the Gods, who served in the Palace of the Red Clouds, often visited it and secretly sprinkled it with sweet dew, thus preserving its tender body from withering too soon. Later it was allowed to come down to the profane world and thank with tears the Guardian of the Radiance of the Stone of the Gods for the loving service which he had rendered. Now it has returned to the Realm of the Blessed. The Fairy of Fearful Awakening has appointed me its guardian. I dare not allow even bees or butterflies to go near it, let alone your kind."

"Then there is, no doubt, a guardian elf of the water lily here also?" he asked, thinking of Bright Cloud.

"My mistress can best give you information about that."

"Who is your mistress, Sister Elf?"

"The Princess of the Weeping Bamboo Hermitage!"

"Oh, that is surely my cousin Black Jade!"

"Nonsense! Between the Realm of the Blessed and your profane world there is no kinship. And if you continue to make yourself a nuisance with foolish chatter, I shall have you thrown out by the guards."

Abashed, Pao Yu turned to go. Suddenly a second elf came running up.

"Where on earth is the Guardian of the Radiance of the Stone of the Gods? He is being asked for inside," she said to the first elf.

"I have been looking for him in vain all over the world," replied the first.

"But there he is running away," said the second, laughing, and hurried after Pao Yu.

"Come back, Guardian of the Radiance of the Stone of the Gods!" she called after him. But Pao Yu, still under the impression of the rude reception which had been given him, did not venture to connect this summons with himself and, thinking that he was being pursued, ran more and more quickly towards the exit from the palace. Suddenly somebody stepped into his path. It was a beautiful young girl with a stern face. In her right hand she held a precious sword.

"Stop! Where are you going?" she asked him severely.

He looked up at her timidly. It was the third Yu. Now he picked up courage again.

"Why have I been treated so rudely, Cousin? Won't you at least be a little kind to me?" he said reproachfully.

"On account of your infamous cousins I cannot," came the blunt reply. "They wantonly destroyed the honor and happiness of myself and my sister. Now you have to atone with them!"

Pao Yu, much embarrassed, was about to protest his innocence when he heard the elf who was pursuing him call out to the third Yu: "Stop him! Do not let him get away!"

"Do not worry! I know our Princess's instructions. I have been waiting for him a long time. Today the hour has come to cut with this sword his connection with the red dust of the world."

Pao Yu turned from the grim maiden with the sword dumfounded, trying to escape in the other direction. Now he saw the elf who had run after him. It was Bright Cloud.

"It is you, Bright Cloud! How good that you are here!" he cried, joyfully surprised. "I have lost my way and have run up into this wicked enemy. You must help me and take me home quickly!"

"Do not call me Bright Cloud! I have got instructions to take you to the Princess! Now do not hesitate, but follow me!" replied the elf.

"Who, then, is your Princess?"

"You will see that for yourself, when you meet her. Come along!"

She walked on in front and he followed behind. There was no doubt about it: to judge by her walk and her deportment, her face and her voice, she was Bright Cloud. But why did she deny who she was? Soon, after the visit to the Princess, he would challenge her again. If she bore him a grudge on account of any wrong, and therefore treated him like a stranger, he would beg her pardon very politely. Girls' hearts were soft and easily touched, as he well knew.

They had arrived at the glittering hall of a palace. It was set in the midst of a splendid bright green bamboo grove. Before the entrance the somber dark green of some cypress trees met his gaze. Several maids, all dressed in the uniform of palace waiting maids, received the stranger.

"So this is the Guardian of the Radiance of the Stone of the Gods?" they asked Pao Yu's guide in a whisper. The elf nodded in the affirmative. Smilingly, they beckoned him in. They went through various vestibules before they arrived at the principal chamber. They stopped in silence in front of a high, glistening bead curtain. A waiting maid disappeared through the curtain. After a while she returned.

"The Princess asks the Guardian of the Radiance of the Stone of the Gods please to come in."

At the same moment the curtain was raised. Pao Yu took a step nearer. He saw opposite him a regal-looking woman sitting on a throne. She wore a crown of fresh flowers on her head. Her face had the unmistakable features of Black Jade.

"So I have found you here again, *Mei mei!* How I have longed for you!" he could not keep from crying out.

"What ill-bred behavior! Quick! Take him away again!" the waiting maids whispered outside. And then the curtain dropped again right in front of his nose. He stared stupefied, undecided as to whether he should stay or go. He turned around to look for help; he wanted to ask Bright Cloud's advice, but he could not find her again. The other waiting maids were strangers to him; he did not venture to ask them questions. They showed him out sullenly, and he slipped off in dejection.

This time no one accompanied him. He searched for the road by which he had come, but he could not find it again. Suddenly he saw Cousin Phoenix standing under the projecting eaves of a house and beckoning to him. Oh, then I am at home again! How could I have lost my way so! he thought to himself and in delight he hurried up to the cousin who was beckoning him.

"It's good that I have found you!" he called to her from a distance. "The others drove me away. Even Black Jade would not receive me, I really do not know why."

He had got nearer to the spot where the beckoning cousin was standing. Suddenly she was no longer Phoenix but her friend, his beautiful niece, Ko Ching. He stood there dumfounded.

"Where is Phoenix gone to?" he asked the other one. But Ko Ching kept silent and disappeared inside.

567

"What crime have I committed that everyone avoids me today?" he sighed, perplexed, and burst into tears. He did not dare to follow Ko Ching, so he wandered sadly off. Suddenly a group of watchmen appeared dressed in yellow smocks and holding long whips in their hands.

"Hi, fellow! Who are you that you dare to trespass so boldly into these blessed places? Off with you, quickly!" they shouted at him, roughly. Frightened, he started to walk more quickly. If he could only find the exit! As he gazed around him he saw in the distance a group of women coming towards him, chatting merrily. He thought he recognized Greeting of Spring, and Gold Ring, and the second Yu among them. "I have lost my way, come and help me!" he cried out to them and ran as fast as he could, for the watchmen were close at his heels. He thought he was already safe with the women, but alas, they suddenly turned into ugly devils with horrible red faces and white hair, and they made straight for him. In his danger he suddenly became aware of the presence of the monk, who had accompanied him there. He held a glistening mirror in his hand.

"My divine mistress, the former Imperial wife, has sent me to save you."

While he was saying this he turned the glittering face of the mirror towards the crowd of Pao Yu's pursuers, and in a trice all the ghostly devils had disappeared. The magnificent dwellings and palaces had also vanished. Pao Yu found himself again in a wild and deserted wilderness. He pressed his rescuer's hand with gratitude and confidence and said to him: "Master, you accompanied me here, as I well remember. Why did you disappear all of a sudden? I met various women and girls of our clan, but each and all of them would have nothing to do with me. Some of them turned into ugly devils and threatened me. What does that mean? Was all that a dream or was it reality?"

The monk looked at him searchingly.

"Did you look at anything secretly?"

Pao Yu said to himself that anyone who was able to lead him into this spirit region must certainly be a spirit himself, and that he could not well deceive a spirit. And so he admitted frankly: "I was in a room and I secretly rummaged through files."

"Indeed, and then you ask that question? You are not yet free from worldly desires. On that account the blessed spirits do not want you, and on that account those devils frightened you. The devils are nothing but the worldly desires which exclude the profane creatures from admittance to the Realm of the Blessed. And now go! But take good note of what you have seen and experienced! I shall come to you later and explain everything to you. Go!"

He gave Pao Yu such a hefty push that he tumbled over and fell down. A suppressed cry escaped his lips. After its long wandering his spirit had returned to his body.

"He has come to himself again!" he heard his mother's voice saying. He opened his eyes and saw his mother, his wife, and the waiting maids standing around his bed, their eyes red from weeping, a half-anxious, half-joyful expression on their faces. He quickly recapitulated his dream in his mind. Luckily, most of it was firmly fixed in his memory.

"Yes, that is it!" he said laughing, with an air of happy relief.

The bystanders looked at one another surprised, not knowing how to interpret his exclamation.

CHAPTER 50

Pao Yu passes the examination with honors and renounces the red dust of the world. Shih Ying and Yu Tsun meet once more and conclude the story of the stone.

Pao Yu had recovered rapidly after his long spell of unconsciousness and to everyone's joy was fully restored to health. The coffin-maker did not need to exert himself now, and Musk was able for the time being to give up with an easy mind her sublime resolve to follow Mandarin Duck's example. Happily, in view of the favorable turn of events, nobody thought of reproaching her afterwards.

As Mr. Cheng was now relieved of worry about Pao Yu and saw peace and order gradually restored to the house, he resolved to avail himself of the remainder of his mourning leave to take the coffin of the Ancestress from the Temple of the Iron Railings at long last, and to lay it to rest, as was proper, in the ancestral vault of the Shih family in her southern homeland. After having arranged various domestic matters with Chia Lien, and once more seriously appealed to Pao Yu's conscience regarding the approaching State examination, he took leave of the family and the ancestors, and set out to journey south on board ship with some of the servants and the coffins of the Ancestress and her faithful Mandarin Duck. The coffin of Ko Ching, Chia Yung's first wife, who had died young, and that of Black Jade were also taken at the same time, to be likewise laid in their native southern earth. Cuckoo was given the honor of escorting her dead mistress, Black Jade, back to her native town of Yangchow, while Chia Yung had charge of the coffin of his first wife.

After his recovery Pao Yu showed himself extraordinarily changed in character as compared with his former self. He was silent and wrapt in meditation; he buried himself in his books, mostly of Taoist literature, avoided conversation and company, and—a fact which was particularly remarked with much shaking of heads—paid no more attention to his feminine environment. Cuckoo simply could not get over the cool and indifferent reception he gave her when she came back from Yangchow, where she had laid Black Jade's remains in their last resting place. There she was, sitting lonely and forsaken in her room, mourning her dead mistress, and he did not think it necessary to pay her a visit, to speak a word of comfort to her, and shed a tear together in silent memory of her who had once been his beloved.

"One can see now how foolish we girls were to have taken his flowery talk so seriously and to have lavished our affections on him. That's how he thanks us, the heartless fellow!" she complained to Musk. And Musk and Pearl and the others confirmed her verdict. What did they know of the change which had taken place within him in the interval? He was waiting and preparing himself for the promised visit of his mysterious friend from the other world.

And one day he came.

"That crazy fellow who brought the stone is back again! He is asking for his ten thousand batzes!" So the message ran, and it set the whole house in an uproar. Pao Yu rushed to the gate in joyful haste.

"Where is my dear master?" he was heard calling out as he went to meet him, to everyone's surprise. Yes indeed, there the fellow was standing in the gateway, and Pao Yu recognized him as his recent travelling companion. The servant Li Kwei was barring the monk's way. At a sign from Pao Yu he had to let him go. Pao Yu conducted him into the reception hall as an honored guest.

"Please make no fuss about me. I have only come to fetch my money!" declared the visitor, brusquely. Pao Yu thought that this was not the language of holy instruction which he had expected. But when he saw him, with his scabious bald head, in his dirty, torn monk's habit, outwardly a picture of the utmost neglect, he remembered the old saying that the wise man does not care for outward display, and that those who do care for it are usually not wise men. He was therefore at pains not to think the less of his visitor because of his appearance.

"Do not worry about the money, Master! My mother is collecting it right now. But please take a seat meantime. The unworthy disciple has a few questions that preoccupy him. Do you not come from the Phantom Realm of the Great Void?" he asked politely.

"What do I know of Phantom Realm and Great Void? I come from somewhere and I am going somewhere; that is all," was the cryptic answer. "By the way, do you know the origin of the stone that I brought back to you?"

Pao Yu was unable to reply straight away.

"Then you do not know your own origin, yet you ask me about mine?" continued the bonze, laughing.

True, Pao Yu had been already awakened by his recent dream vision, but not yet completely. Now, so sudden was his awakening that the bonze's last remark felt like the blow of a cudgel on his head.

"I understand. It is not the money but the stone which the master demands. I will go and fetch it."

"Yes, you must do so," nodded the bonze, smiling.

Pao Yu hurried into his bedroom and fetched the stone out of its hiding place in the treasure chest near the bed, where the careful Precious Clasp had recently been keeping it. She and the maids happened not to be present, so he could do this unhindered. He was hurrying back with the stone in his hand, and in his haste heeded so little where he was going, that he unexpectedly bumped into Pearl turning a corner. She shrank back, startled.

"So you're here?" she asked, astonished. "Your mother imagines that you're in the front reception hall with the stranger. At the moment she is conferring with your wife as to how the large sum of money which he is demanding for the stone can be got together straight away."

"Run and tell her that she need not worry about the money. I'm giving him back the stone itself, instead," he told her, and began to move on.

"That's impossible!" cried Pearl, horrified, and tried to stop him. "The stone is your life! Without it you're lost!"

"Don't you worry! I have my soul back, so I do not need the stone any more."

After a short struggle he shook her off and ran away. She ran after him shouting, and overtook him again. She clung to his belt desperately and allowed herself to slip to the ground so that he could not stir from the spot.

Her frantic cries of "Help! He wants to give up his stone!" attracted other waiting maids and maids, and later his mother and Precious Clasp, to the spot. Cuckoo helped Pearl, and by exerting their united strength they held him fast.

"Don't make such a fuss about a stone! Would it grieve you as much as that if I had to go away myself next?" he asked, laughing between gasps. A cry of horror from the two was the answer. Meantime Madame Cheng and Precious Clasp had joined the others.

"Are you up to mischief again?" asked his mother sternly. He saw that he had no chance of escaping now, so he gave up the struggle.

"It's of no importance," he said reassuringly to his mother; then, pointing with a smile at Pearl and Cuckoo, he said: "They are too easily scared. The stiff-necked monk would not hear of any bargaining. He would not reduce his demand by even a copper piece. That annoyed me, and I just left him standing there. I will offer to return the stone to him, and tell him that it's not the real one after all and that we do not set any great store by it. Then he will surely modify his ridiculous demand and be glad to get whatever we give him. That's all."

His cleverly calculated words sounded very reasonable to a thrifty housewife, and in fact Madame Cheng was instantly reassured.

"Oh, that's all right!" she said. "I thought that you wanted actually to hand him over the stone. Why didn't you tell that to the two girls at once, and spare them this altercation?"

But Precious Clasp, full of anxious forebodings, was of another opinion.

"That sinister monk fellow is not to be trusted! Who knows? If he is allowed to have the stone even for a moment, he may suddenly disappear with it. Better safe than sorry! I would prefer to sacrifice my jewelry."

And before Pao Yu could stop her, she had wrested the stone from his hand in a trice.

"So that is settled," she continued. "Now you need not go back to him at all. Your mother and I will raise the money between us."

"Very well. But I want at least to say good-by to him properly, for decency's sake," he remarked with affected indifference. That also sounded reasonable. Pearl let go of him at last.

"It seems to me that you women set more store on the stone itself than on my own person. What if I ran off with the monk now? What good would the stone be to you then?" he jested. He wished to prepare them with such jokes for things to come. Pearl's suspicions were immediately reawakened. She caught hold of him again, then, remembering that two ladies of the house were present, withdrew her hand quickly and forced herself to a more restrained demeanor. And now the way was free for Pao Yu.

But Pearl was so frightened that she sent word to his personal servant, Ming Yen, behind his back, urgently asking him and his subordinates at the third gateway to keep a sharp eye on the little master, lest he might possibly be enticed away without ado by the strange monk.

Madame Cheng and Precious Clasp had retired to their rooms again, and there in privacy they got Pearl to tell them the whole story of the noisy incident which had just taken place. When Pearl repeated word for word the mysterious utterances which Pao Yu had let drop during the struggle, the two ladies became extremely perturbed again, and gave orders that the front hall, where Pao Yu was with his guest, should be surrounded by watchers, who were also to watch unobtrusively through the window what was going on inside. Waiting maids were sent to run back and forth and report what the watchers were able to catch of the conversation which was taking place.

"The little master does not seem to be quite right in the head," one messenger reported mysteriously. "The people listening under the window heard him saying to the strange monk that he could not deliver him the stone—his inner self prevented him from doing so—but that he offered him his person instead. He was ready to go away with him."

"Why, that's quite mad!" exclaimed the horrified *Tai tai.* "And what did the monk say to that?"

"He said he demanded the stone and not the person."

"The one is the same as the other," interjected Precious Clasp excitedly. "The stone and Pao Yu are one! The fellow is just being funny! Did he say nothing about money, then?"

"I don't know. After that the conversation became very lively, in fact merry, but the men under the window were not able to understand much of it."

"What nonsense! They don't have to be so very learned to be able to understand a simple conversation. That's the last straw!" cried Madame Cheng, flying into a passion. And she sent for one of the listeners. Naturally, he could not show himself before the ladies but had to give his report through the window from the veranda.

"We were unable to follow the conversation completely," he said, "as it was above our heads. We could only catch something about 'mountain wilderness' and 'green crags' and 'Realm of the Great Void' and 'red dust' and 'severing from earthly destiny,' and the like."

Madame Cheng did not know, either, what these expressions meant, but Precious Clasp did understand, and became extremely perturbed. She was so frightened that she was just giving orders for Pao Yu to be fetched back at once when he arrived himself. He seemed to be in very high spirits.

"Everything went off splendidly!" he announced gaily.

"Drop the foolery and pull yourself together!" said his mother sternly.

"Foolery? Oh, I feel perfectly clearheaded. The monk is a good old friend of mine. He only came to say hello to me. What he said about the money he didn't mean seriously. All he asked in return for his services was that I should change my ways and remember my original higher destiny. He made that quite clear to me. Then he suddenly floated away. So we still have the stone, and we did not have to pay the money. Isn't that splendid?"

The others exchanged incredulous glances. Madame Cheng gave orders through the window to the listener who was still waiting outside to run to the front of the palace and find out if this was true. After a while the man came back and reported: "Yes, that is true. The gate watchmen saw the strange monk going away. He said to tell the *Tai tai* that she need not worry; he asked no money as recompense; he only wished that the little master should visit him now and then. And he said, moreover, that whatever happens is predestined by the higher powers."

Madame Cheng breathed a sigh of relief. She was now freed from a great financial worry.

"He seems to be quite a nice, reasonable fellow after all," she said contentedly. "But where is my son to visit him? Did the gate watchmen ask that?"

"He lives far away and near, according to how you look at it," interposed Pao Yu with a smile. How puzzling this remark sounded, too!

"Come back to your senses at last and take your head out of the clouds!" said Precious Clasp impatiently. "Have you no feeling for your parents, who are suffering so much on your account? Pull yourself together and reward their love by achieving something noble."

"Oh, is what I intimated not a noble achievement? Do you not know the saying:

"A son who to the Buddha vows his life
Opens heaven's gate to seven ancestors."

Madame Cheng felt her heart torn when she heard him.

"How frightful! What curse has come over our house?" she cried, beside herself. "These perverse notions of fleeing the world! First Grief of Spring, and now Pao Yu . . . I'll never survive it!"

And she broke into violent sobbing.

"I was only joking," said Pao Yu, smilingly trying to reassure her.

But he was not joking. It was observed that he shut himself off more and more from his friends and the people of the house and withdrew to the silence of his study, ostensibly to prepare for the approaching State examination but in reality to bury himself more and more in his beloved philosophy. The only person in the house with whom he still indulged in an exchange of thoughts now and again was his cousin and kindred spirit, Grief of Spring. A mysterious utterance which he made on the occasion of Grief of Spring's removal to the Kingfisher's Cage aroused a great deal of comment.

After a quarrel with her sister-in-law Chen, for whom she had little love, Grief of Spring had suddenly decided to cut off the remaining

574

half of her hair, and once more she gave her relatives the choice: either the Kingfisher's Cage or voluntary death. There was an agitated family council which lasted far into the night. Finally Grief of Spring had got her way. She was allowed to withdraw to the Kingfisher's Cage. The waiting maid Cuckoo willingly offered to follow her there. She was wont to reproach herself in secret for not having followed her mistress Black Jade to the grave after their long years together. And now she thought she would atone for this wrong done to Black Jade by leading a life of penance and chastity in the self-chosen solitude of the Kingfisher's Cave.

When Grief of Spring bade farewell to the family everyone expected that Pao Yu would get another of his bad turns and raise a passionate lament over the new loss of a little sister, but to everyone's surprise he remained quite calm this time.

"*A-mi-to-fo!* You have done it! What a pity that I am not ready yet!" These were all the words of farewell that he said.

Now he was completely alone, with no one to turn to, only the intellectual intercourse with his philosophers. Precious Clasp noted with growing uneasiness how he was shutting himself up and neglecting her and his family. At last she could no longer look on in silence. So one day she gave him a good lecture, urgently entreating him to finish at last with his useless philosophizing and turn instead to the practical philosophy of a Confucius and of the old idealistic rulers such as Yao, Shun, Yu, and Cheng Tang; and to remember the highest commandment of human morals, namely, filial duty and childlike reverence, and fulfill the just expectations of his father by doing well at the coming State examination. And she kept at him until finally he took her words to heart and did as she wished.

He had all the works of his favorite philosophers—Lao Tzu, Chuang Tzu, and other apostles of the Tao—simply packed into an empty lumber-room, and from that time on zealously dedicated himself solely to the study of the Six Classical Books and similar writings, Confucian in spirit, the knowledge of which would stand him in good stead at the State examination.

With a sigh of relief Precious Clasp noted the change in him, but then she became tortured once more with fresh doubts. "His encounter with the crazy monk had one good result—since then he has given up his everlasting fooling and flirting with the girls. Who knows whether this latest change may not cause him to fall back into his old bad ways again?" she confided to Pearl.

And at Pearl's suggestion she took the precaution of arranging that the innocuous Oriole, whom he did not like particularly and who, besides, was her own confidential maid, should take over the duty of bringing him his tea and similar services of a personal nature, instead of pretty little Wu, the youngest of the waiting maids, who had been given to him in replacement of the late Bright Cloud. So now he would probably not get silly ideas and be distracted from his books.

Her apprehension was unfounded, however. He had resolved of himself not to look at any girl again, and up to the day of the examination be subjected himself to a life of strict voluntary seclusion. During those days of preparation he did not even pay the accustomed morning and evening duty visit to his mother, but got waiting maids to convey to her his daily *tsing an*.

The time for the great examination, which was awaited with tremulous anxiety by the ladies of the western palace, had come at last. On the morning of the opening day Pao Yu, accompanied by his nephew Chia Lan, came to take leave of his mother. It was the first time that Madame Cheng had had to allow her son to pass the night away from home. For during the three days of the examination the candidates were kept in strict confinement, and were not permitted to leave their bare examination cells even at night. And so, though Pao Yu, at nineteen, was pretty well grown up by now, his mother gave him plenty of practical, maternal advice, and also wept some motherly tears of farewell. Pao Yu himself took the parting very solemnly too. He knelt down before his mother and saluted her with a ceremonial kowtow, touching his forehead to the ground three times.

"Up till now I have had no opportunity of repaying my mother for all the love that she has shown me since I came into the world," he said earnestly. "I will exert myself to pass the examination as well as I can and thereby make good my former negligence. If it is granted me to give my parents joy by a notable success, I shall regard my filial duty as fulfilled and the injustice which I have been doing my parents all my life as atoned for."

How solemn that sounded! Like a parting for ever!

"My good, good boy! If only your old grandmother had lived to see this hour!" sobbed the *Tai tai*, deeply moved, as she raised him to his feet.

"Even though she is no longer bodily among us, her spirit will be our witness and will rejoice with us," he declared simply.

"Do not weep, *Tai tai*," the others said comfortingly to Madame Cheng. "You have every reason to be joyful, seeing that he has matured at last into a sensible and conscientious son and adult."

And with many fond wishes the two youths, the future hope of the whole clan, were seen off on their way to the arena.

When the three days of the examination were over, Chia Lan came back—without Pao Yu. It was already late in the evening.

"But where is your Uncle Pao Yu?" asked the ladies, dismayed.

"I have lost him," replied Chia Lan unhappily.

"What nonsense! How can a grown-up man, with whom you have been together the whole time, simply get lost?" said his mother, Widow Chu, sharply.

"I shared the same cell with him and ate at the same table, and in the examination hall, too, he was always within my sight. This morning we handed in our examination papers together, and then left the examination hall together. On our way home—it was at the Dragon Gate—I suddenly lost sight of him in the crowd. Li Kwei, who had come to meet us at the Dragon Gate with his people, had seen him a moment before, walking a few steps behind me. Then he had suddenly disappeared. I have been searching and inquiring for him with Li Kwei and the other servants all day, but he could not be found."

This news put the whole house into a turmoil of excitement and grief. The male servants, who were already looking forward to the customary feast, instead of sitting down to a banquet had to go out, despite the lateness of the hour, to search the city once more for the lost youth. The only person in the palace who did not seem particularly touched by Pao Yu's disappearance was Grief of Spring.

"Did he have his stone with him when he went away?" she asked Precious Clasp, and this was her only inquiry. Precious Clasp nodded, whereupon she made no further remark. But Pearl remembered the oath which Pao You had sworn years before to Black Jade, and Precious Clasp also put two and two together, with a sigh.

It was already long past midnight when the searchers who had been sent out returned. They had no result to report. All the inquiries made in the days that followed likewise proved in vain. And then, early one morning, while the ladies were still asleep, the great and joyful news arrived that the results of the State examination had just been made known at the early morning audience. Pao Yu had won seventh place on the list of successful candidates. His nephew Chia Lan had also passed. His name was the hundred-and-thirtieth on the list. Both had thereby won the second doctor's degree, and henceforth might proudly count themselves one of the elect company of *ku yen,* or "Exalted Ones." Jubilation filled the halls of the western palace, but Pao Yu still remained missing. Yet there was some little comfort in the thought that a new *ku yen,* whose name would be carried on the wings of fame throughout all the provinces of the Empire, could hardly remain undetected for long.

Chia Cheng had laid the body of the Ancestress to rest in her southern homeland, and was on his way back. One day he received a letter from the family telling him of the latest important events at home. The news that his ill-fated child, Pao Yu, had passed the examination so brilliantly filled his parental heart with proud joy, which was dimmed, alas, by his anxiety over the boy's sudden mysterious disappearance. He learned, further, that the Imperial master had particularly mentioned the magnificent achievement of the seventh candidate on the list, and had asked the examination commission to furnish him with a detailed report regarding the personal circumstances of the highly promising and talented young man. When he learned from the report of the Chairman of the examination commission, the Prince of the Northern Quietness, that the seventh on the list was a full brother of the former Imperial wife, Beginning of Spring, and that the Chia family had produced two *ku yen* on this occasion, he felt moved to pour out his Imperial favor over the Chia clan once more. Being gratified, moreover, by the success of the recent offensive against the pirate pest, and the generally contented and peaceable state to which the realm of the ten thousand families had now been happily restored, he graciously ordered a great general amnesty throughout the Empire. Thanks to this amnesty, the two exiled members of the clan, Shieh and Chen, were to be permitted to return from banishment; their confiscated property would be restored to them. Chia Chen, as Lord of the eastern palace, was, moreover, raised again to the nobility, though to be sure only to the third rank, namely, that of a count. Chia Cheng remained the only possessor of the title of prince, and, furthermore, was restored to his office of State Councillor in the Ministry of Works. In addition, the Imperial Lord gave orders that an official search was to be made for the seventh successful candidate on the list.

Chia Cheng heard all this cheerful news with tears of mingled joy and shame. How unjust he had been in the past to his despised, degenerate son. The Chia clan had now to thank this despised and degenerate son for the fact that the roof of the Hall of Ancestors was being adorned with new luster!

Torn by a multitude of conflicting emotions, Chia Cheng urged the crew of his ship to greater speed, for he himself was unable to rest either day or night. He was burning with longing to see his family again, and also to throw himself upon his knees before the steps of the Throne, there to render heartfelt thanks.

He arrived one day at the post station Kun ling. Here he made a brief halt in order hurriedly to complete a letter in reply to the one from his wife. A sudden spell of cold had brought a light fall of snow that day, which enveloped the landscape in a mantle of white. Chia Cheng had sent all his staff onto land with the exception of one young fellow. They had to present his visiting card to the various people of distinction and rank and acquaintances in the neighborhood, explaining that unfortunately their master did not have time to interrupt his journey long enough to visit them personally.

He himself was sitting all alone in the ship's cabin, writing to his family. He was just about to speak of Pao Yu; he laid down his writing brush and looked up to reflect for a moment. In that same moment he seemed to see a figure emerging from the midst of the falling snow on the bank of the river, opposite the bow of the ship. Suddenly there stood someone, bareheaded and barefooted, dressed in a long monk's habit made of coarse reddish brown monkey-hair wool. Now he went to his knees to Chia Cheng in a solemn kowtow, striking his forehead on the ground. Four times he pressed his forehead deep into the snow. Mr. Cheng jumped up and hurried over the gangway onto the bank. He stepped up to the peculiar stranger, who was still standing there, and was about to ask him who he was and whence he came. He had just raised his crossed hands to his breast to return the salutation when, looking more closely, he recognized the stranger. It was Pao Yu.

"It's you, Pao Yu!" he cried, astounded.

The other remained silent. His face expressed joy and sorrow at the same time.

"If you are Pao Yu, how is it that you are here, in that attire?" continued Mr. Cheng.

The other seemed to want to reply, but did not get around to it. Suddenly two other monkish figures came and stood beside him, one to the right and the other to the left. The one was a servant of Buddha, the other a disciple of the Tao.

"Your earthly destiny is fulfilled! Do not delay now, but follow us!" Mr. Cheng heard them say to Pao Yu, then he saw the three of them floating lightly upwards together over the sloping river-bank. Heedless of the slippery ground, Mr. Cheng rushed after them, but he was unable to catch up with them. Ever more quickly they sped away from him, and their outlines became more and more indistinct. He could still hear, out of the distance, the sound of singing, and could just catch some disjointed words about "green crag" and "great void" and "wandering into the far unknown"; then they disappeared behind a hill.

Mr. Cheng had run until he was completely breathless. He could not take another step, and had to stop to recover his breath. When he turned round he saw his servant tramping towards him through the snow.

"Did you just see the three fellows in monks' habits?" he called out to him.

"Yes, I saw them," replied the boy, "and I ran after you, and then all of a sudden I could see only you."

Mr. Cheng ran on a bit farther with the boy, but it was no use. Far and wide there was nothing to be seen but the white, snowy, empty landscape. Shaking his head, he turned back. Meantime his other servants had returned to the ship. Mr. Cheng told them of his strange encounter. They said he should interrupt the journey and have the whole district searched thoroughly for his son Pao Yu.

Mr. Cheng shook his head and sighed. He was lost in thought.

"It is strange, very strange!" he murmured to himself. "I saw him and his companions with my own eyes. I also distinctly heard their singing. It was definitely not imagination, or some empty phantom vision. Many things are now becoming clear to me. He came into the world with a precious stone in his mouth. That was uncanny enough; I always felt uneasy about it from the very beginning. But . . . well, for the sake of his grandmother we reared and fostered the spirit child. Then these two peculiar fellows appeared on the scene. Three times they have intervened in his life. Once, when the boy lay ill, they restored the power of the stone with their incantations and made him well again. Then one of the fellows, the one in the bonze's cowl, brought back the lost stone and saved the boy from death for the second time. That time I saw him with my own eyes sitting in the reception hall, then all of a sudden he disappeared. And now today they have spirited away the boy himself. In the past I was filled with wonder over the fortunate fellow who had exalted spirits from the other world for his friends and helpers. But who would have thought that one day he himself would join the world of spirits? For nineteen long years, clothed in the form of a human being, he fooled his grandmother. Now he has become once more what he was before—a spirit. No! It is quite useless to go searching for spirits!"

And with a sigh Chia Cheng picked up his writing brush to finish the letter home which he had begun. He reported his amazing encounter with Pao Yu, and added the remark that they should not mourn the lost son any more. In any case he had no aptitude whatever for the career of an official. Who knows what mischief he would have got into in an official position, and what disaster he might have brought on the clan? To have produced a bodhisattva was quite an honor for the family, and certainly no disgrace.

The various members of the clan who had been away arrived home in rapid succession—Chia Cheng from his journey to the South; Chia Shieh and Chia Chen from their exile; Hsueh Pan, pardoned and ransomed from his imprisonment. The latter was completely repentant, and on returning home swore a solemn oath that he would take his life if he ever again fell back into his old vices. At his mother's wish, he raised his concubine Lotus to the position of principal wife in place of Hsia, who had met her end by poisoning. And so the former slave girl eventually reached the position in society which was proper to her birth and education.

On the very next day after his return home Chia Cheng called at the Grand Secretariat and, through the good offices of the Grand Secretaries, who were kindly disposed towards him, obtained an audience of thanks with the Lord of the Thousand Years. The Emperor inquired sympathetically for the lost son, Pao Yu, and was deeply moved when he heard of Mr. Cheng's strange encounter in the snow. Once more he recalled appreciatively the magnificent achievement of the seventh candidate on the examination list. It had been his intention to call the young man up for service in the Imperial Palace near his own person. By his Imperial grace he awarded him by decree the exalted title of "The Immortal of Marvellous Literary Achievement." The conferring of this honor consoled the clan to some extent for the physical loss of the son of the family. Another consolation was the fact that Precious Clasp was expecting a child. Thus Pao Yu would still, after all, live on physically too, in a certain sense, in the clan.

Yu Tsun was also among those affected by the great amnesty. In one day he had slipped from a great height, being dragged straight from his prefect's seat to prison, in chains. Corruptibility, self-enrichment through office, and defeating the ends of the law were the abuses of office laid to his charge by the Censors before the Imperial Throne. These offenses were enough to call for a severe punishment, for the ruling Son of Heaven was an enlightened ruler with a keen social conscience, ready to fly into a rage at the mere words "self-enrichment through office," "oppression of the people," and "exploitation." Thanks to the great amnesty, however, Yu Tsun got off quite lightly. He merely lost office and rank, was reduced once more to the status of a commoner, and had to return to his native town of Suchow as an ordinary subject. And so the proud career of the ambitious place-hunter ended just where it had begun in a small and humble way many years ago.

Yu Tsun had sent his family on ahead and was following with his baggage-cart and one servant, and so he had lots of time on the way to meditate on the futility of earthly ambition and the transitory nature of fame and splendor.

His way chanced to lead him over the ford in the vicinity of which he had had that remarkable encounter in a temple a year before. This time he noticed not far from the ford a hut made of reeds and bulrushes. At his arrival a hermit came out of the hut and raised his hands in greeting to him. It was Shih Ying. He bowed quickly, returning the greeting.

"Greetings, worthy Mr. Chia! How have you been since . . .?" began the old hermit.

"Are you not Master Shih Ying?" asked Yu Tsun. "Why did you hide your identity at our last meeting? I was greatly troubled about you after your temple was burned down and count myself lucky to see you again today. Only now do I realize how well you have done for yourself, thanks to your exalted and wise insight. I, wretched fool, on the contrary, was obdurate and deluded. Now I have received the deserved reward of my folly."

"The last time, you were resplendent in office and dignities. How could the miserable-looking hermit take the liberty of knowing you?" replied Shih Ying with the shadow of a smile. "It was only because of our old relations that I ventured to open my mouth at all. I feel deeply honored by your loyalty. Good fortune and misfortune, wealth and poverty, are predestined things. Our meeting today is no mere chance either."

"How did the master come to free himself from the red dust of the world that time long ago?" Yu Tsun wanted to know.

"Quite unexpectedly, with the speed of thought," replied the old man, smiling evasively, and countering the question with another: "In the great world, in the circles of soft, luxurious living, riches, and distinction, did you not meet a certain Pao Yu?"

"Indeed I do know him. I have been in and out of his home frequently. It is rumored that he also has passed through the gateway of the Great Void recently. I would never have imagined that worldly, effeminate fellow taking such a resolution."

"But I would have. I knew his whole story long in advance. Do you remember that summer evening many years ago, when you saw me standing in front of the door of my old home near the Temple of the Gourd? Shortly before that I had met him."

"Impossible! Your Suchow is many miles distant from the capital."

"In the intercourse between spirits there are no boundaries of space and time."

"Then you know, no doubt, where he is now?"

"His place is now again, as it was before, in the Blessed Realm of Purified Semblance, under the green crag, by the old pine tree. For Pao Yu is a precious stone. What? You do not understand me? Come with me into my hermitage, which is near by. There I will explain to you the Story of the Stone."

2812-15
22-70

582